BESTSELLING AUTHOR COLLECTION

In our Bestselling Author Collection, Harlequin Books is proud to offer classic novels from today's superstars of women's fiction. These authors have captured the hearts of millions of readers around the world, and earned their place on the *New York Times, USA TODAY* and other bestseller lists with every release.

As a bonus, each volume also includes a full-length novel from a rising star of series romance. Bestselling authors in their own right, thcsc talcntcd writers have captured the qualities Harlequin is famous for—heart-racing passion, edge-of-your-seat entertainment and a satisfying happily-ever-after.

Don't miss any of the books in the collection!

BESTSELLING AUTHOR COLLECTION

New York Times and *USA TODAY* Bestselling Author

LAVYRLE SPENCER

Sweet Memories

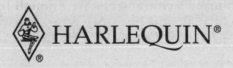

HARLEQUIN®

TORONTO • NEW YORK • LONDON
AMSTERDAM • PARIS • SYDNEY • HAMBURG
STOCKHOLM • ATHENS • TOKYO • MILAN • MADRID
PRAGUE • WARSAW • BUDAPEST • AUCKLAND

Recycling programs
for this product may
not exist in your area.

ISBN-13: 978-0-373-38990-2

SWEET MEMORIES

Copyright © 2010 by Harlequin Books S.A.

The publisher acknowledges the copyright holders
of the individual works as follows:

SWEET MEMORIES
Copyright © 1984 by LaVyrle Spencer

HER SISTER'S BABY
Copyright © 1995 by Janice Kay Johnson

This edition published by arrangement with Harlequin Books S.A.

For questions and comments about the quality of this book
please contact us at Customer_eCare@Harlequin.ca.

® and TM are trademarks of the publisher. Trademarks indicated with
® are registered in the United States Patent and Trademark Office, the
Canadian Trade Marks Office and in other countries.

www.eHarlequin.com

Printed in U.S.A.

CONTENTS

SWEET MEMORIES   9
LaVyrle Spencer

HER SISTER'S BABY   289
Janice Kay Johnson

With love to the Huebners:
Jeannie
George
Jason
Tracy
and
Duke

SWEET MEMORIES

New York Times and **USA TODAY** Bestselling Author

LaVyrle Spencer

LaVYRLE SPENCER

New York Times and *USA TODAY* bestselling author LaVyrle Spencer is an accomplished author known for her witty earthiness, sensitivity and innovative plots. Twelve of her books have been *New York Times* bestsellers, and several of them have been made into movies. In 1988 she was inducted into the Romance Writers of America Hall of Fame. She retired from writing in 1997, and now devotes her time to her passions of traveling and music. LaVyrle Spencer lives in Minnesota.

Chapter 1

At last, Jeff was coming home, but he wasn't alone. Watching the big-bellied jet taxiing to a stop, Theresa Brubaker felt two conflicting emotions—excitement that her "baby brother" would be here for two whole weeks, and annoyance that he'd dragged along some stranger to interfere with their family holiday. Theresa never liked meeting strangers, and at the thought of meeting one now, especially a *man,* a nervous ache grabbed her between the shoulder blades. She worked her head in a circle, flexed her shoulders and tried to shrug away the annoyance.

Through the soles of her knee-high snow boots she felt the shudder and rumble of the engines as they wheezed a last inflated breath, then whistled through a dying decrescendo and sighed into silence. The accordion pleats of the jetway eased forward, its mouth molded against the curve of the plane, and Theresa riveted her eyes on the doorway set in the wall of glass. As the first footsteps of disembarking passengers thudded down the tunnel, she self-consciously glanced down and made sure her heavy gray wool coat was buttoned up completely. She clutched a small black leather purse against her left side in a way that partially concealed her breast and gave her reason to cross her arms.

Her heart tripped out a staccato beat of anticipation—*Jeff. My crazy clown of a brother, the life of the family, coming home to make Christmas what all the songs said it should be. Oh, there's no place like home for the holidays.* Jeff—how she'd missed him. She bit her lower lip and trained her eyes on the door as the first passengers debarked: a young mother carrying a squalling baby, a businessman with a topcoat and briefcase, a bearded, blue-jeaned ski bum hefting a blue satchel boasting the word *vail,* two long-legged military men clad in dress blues and garrison caps with visors set squarely across their eyebrows. *Two long-legged military men!*

"Jeff!" Her arm flew up joyously.

He caught sight of Theresa at the same moment she saw his lips form her name. But sister and brother were separated by a fifteen-foot-long ramp and handrail, and what seemed to be one-quarter of the population of Minneapolis greeting incoming arrivals. Jeff pointed her out while she read his lips again—"There she is"—and shouldered through the crowd toward the crown of the ramp.

She was scarcely conscious of her brother's companion as she flew into Jeff's arms, lifting her own around his neck while he scooped her off the floor and whirled her in a circle. His shoulders were broad and hard, his neck smelled of lime, and her eyes were suddenly swimming with tears while he laughed against her temple.

He plopped her onto her feet, smiled down into her joyous face and said gruffly, "Hiya, Treat."

"Hiya, snot-nose," she choked, then tried to laugh, but it came out a chugging gulp before she abashedly buried her face against him again, suddenly conscious of the other man looking on. Beside her ear, she heard the smile in Jeff's voice as he spoke to his friend.

"Didn't I tell you?"

"Yup, you did," came the stranger's voice, rich and deep.

She backed up. "Tell him what?"

Jeff grinned down teasingly. "That you're a sentimental fool. Look at you, tears flooding everything, and all over my dress blues." He examined his crisp lapel where a dark blotch showed.

"Oh, I'm sorry," she wailed, "I'm just so glad to see you." She dabbed at the tear spot on his jacket while he touched her just beneath an eye.

"You'd be sorrier if you could see how those tears make the freckles you hate so much stand out like new pennies."

She slapped his finger away and dabbed at her eyes self-consciously.

"Don't worry about it, Theresa. Come on, meet Brian." Jeff clapped an arm around her shoulders and turned her to face his friend. "This is the light o' my life, who never let me chase women, smoke pot or drive when I drank." At this last, Jeff winked broadly. "So let's not tell her what we did last night, okay, Scanlon?" He squeezed her shoulder, grinned down fondly while his teasing did absolutely nothing to disguise the deeper note of pride in his voice. "My big sister, Theresa. Theresa, this is Brian Scanlon."

She saw his hand first, with long, tapered fingers, extended in greeting. But she was afraid to look up and see where his eyes rested. Thankfully, the way Jeff had commandeered her shoulders, she was able to half hide behind him with one arm about his waist while extending her own hand.

"Hello, Theresa."

She could no longer avoid it. She raised her eyes to his face, but he looked straight into her eyes, smiling. And what a smile!

"Hello, Brian."

"I've heard a lot about you."

I've heard a lot about you, too, she thought, but answered gaily, "I'll just bet you have. My brother could never keep anything to himself."

Brian Scanlon laughed—a pleasant baritone rumble like a soft roll on a timpani—and held her hand in a hard grip, smiling at her from beneath the horizontal visor of his military hat that made her suddenly understand why some women shamelessly chase soldiers.

"Don't worry, he only told me the nice stuff."

Her glance fluttered away from his translucent green eyes that were far more attractive than in the photographs Jeff had sent, then Brian released her hand and moved to flank her other side as they headed away from the gate area toward the green concourse, still talking.

"All except for a couple of stories about our nasty childhood pranks, like the time you stole a handful of Grandpa Deering's pipe tobacco and taught me how to roll it up in those white papers that come with home permanents, and we both got sick from the chemicals in the paper when it got in our lungs, and the time—"

"Jeffrey Brubaker, I did not steal that tobacco. You did!"

"Well, who found the leftover papers in the bathroom vanity?"

"But who put the idea in my head?"

"I was four years younger. You should have tried to talk me out of it."

"I did!"

"But that was after we got sick and learned our lesson."

All three of them dissolved into laughter. Jeff squeezed her shoulder once more, looked across the top of her head at Brian and set things straight. "I'll be honest. After we got greener than a pair of garter snakes she'd never let me smoke again. I tried it more than once when I was in junior high, but she squealed on me every time and managed to get me grounded more than once. But in the end, she saved me from myself."

To Theresa's left, Brian's laugh rolled like faraway thunder. She noted its full, mellow tone, and now, when he spoke, that tone became even fuller, richer.

"He did tell me about another incident with home permanents when you gave him one against your mother's orders and forgot to set the timer." While he teased, he studied her hair. Jeff had said it was red, but Brian hadn't expected it to be the hue of a poppy!

"Oh, that," she wailed, hiding a cheek behind a palm. "Jeff, did you have to blab that to him? I could have died when I took those curlers out and saw what I'd done to you."

"*You* could have died? Mother was the one who could have died. That time it was *you* who should've gotten grounded, and I think you would have if you hadn't been eighteen already and going to college."

"Let's finish the story, little brother. In spite of the fact that you looked like an explosion in a silo, it got you that spot in the band, didn't it? They took one look at that ball of frizz and decided you'd fit right in."

"Which also put you beyond mother's good graces for the remainder of the summer, until I could prove I wasn't going to start sniffing cocaine and popping uppers every night before we played a gig."

They had reached the escalator to the lower level where the luggage return was located, so were forced to break rank while riding down.

Studying the backs of the two heads below him, Brian Scanlon couldn't help envying the easy camaraderie between sister and brother. They hadn't seen each other for twelve months, yet they fell into a familiar groove of affectionate bantering as if they were good friends who saw each other daily. *They don't know how lucky they are,* he thought.

The revolving luggage carousels were surrounded, for holiday travel was at its heaviest with only a couple days left till Christmas. As they waited, Brian stood back and listened while the two of them filled in each other on family news.

"Mom and Dad wanted to come and pick you up, but I got nominated instead because today was the last day of school before vacation. I got out at two, right after the Christmas program was over, but they both have to work till five, as usual."

"How are they?"

"Do you have to ask? Absolutely giddy. Mom's been baking pies and putting them in the freezer, and worrying about whether pumpkin is still your favorite and Dad kept asking her, 'Margaret, did you buy some of those poppy-seed rolls Jeff always liked?' And Mom would lose patience and say, 'Willard, that's the third time you've asked me that, and this is the third time I'm answering. Yes, of course I bought poppy-seed rolls.' Yesterday she baked a German chocolate cake, and after all that fussing, came out and found Dad had taken a slice from it. Boy, did the fur fly then. When she scolded him and

informed him she'd baked the cake for dessert tonight, Dad
slunk off and took the car to the car wash and filled it up with
gas for you. I don't think either one of them slept a wink last
night. Mother was absolutely grumpy this morning, but you
know how she gets when she's excited—the minute she sees
you it'll dissolve like magic. Mostly she was upset because she
had to work today when she'd rather have stayed home and
gotten things ready, then come to the airport herself."

It was plain to Brian that this homecoming had taken on
premiere proportions in this family's hearts, even before
Theresa went on.

"And just guess what Dad did?"

Jeff only smiled a query. Theresa tipped him a smile with
hidden meaning. "Get ready for this one, Jeff. He took your
old Stella up to Viking Music and had new strings put on it and
polished it all up and brought it out to the corner of the living
room where you always used to leave it."

"You're kidding!"

"God's truth."

"Do you know how many times he threatened to turn both
me and my fifteen-dollar Stella out of the house if the two of
us didn't quit bruising his eardrums with all our racket?"

Just then a duffel bag came circling toward them, and Jeff
shouldered forward to grab it. No sooner had he set it behind
him than a guitar case followed. As he leaned to snag it,
Theresa exclaimed, "Your guitar! You brought your guitar?"

"Guitars. Both of ours."

She glanced up at Brian Scanlon, remembering he, too,
played. She caught him studying her instead of the luggage
return, his eyes the hue of rich summer moss, and Theresa
quickly dropped her gaze.

"Can't let those calluses get soft," Jeff explained, "and
anyway, two weeks without pickin' would be more than we
could stand, right, Scan?"

"Right."

"But I promise I'll pick a few on the old Stella, just for dad."

A second guitar came bumping down the conveyor belt,

followed by another duffel bag, and Theresa watched Brian's shoulders stretch his blue uniform jacket taut as he leaned to retrieve them. A young woman just behind Brian was giving him the once-over as he straightened and turned. The end of the guitar case caught her on the hip, and Brian immediately apologized.

The blonde flashed him a smile, and said, "Anytime, soldier boy."

For a moment he paused, then politely murmured, "Excuse me," and shouldered his duffel, glancing up to meet Theresa's eyes, which slid away shyly.

"All set?" She directed her question at her brother, because Brian made her uncomfortably aware of how inordinately pretty his eyes were for a man, and ever aware that they never dropped lower than her coat collar.

"Yup."

"Homeward bound. Let's go."

They stepped beyond the sliding doors of Minneapolis–St. Paul International into the crisp bite of December cold. Theresa walked between them again as they entered the cavernous concrete parking lot. But when they approached the correct row, she announced, "Dad and I traded cars for the day. I have his wagon, he has my Toyota."

"Hand me the keys. I'm dying to get behind a wheel again," her brother declared.

They loaded guitars and duffel bags into the rear and clambered inside. Through the fifteen-minute ride to the nearby suburb of Apple Valley, while Jeff and Theresa exchanged pleasantries, she tried to overcome her resentment of Brian Scanlon. She had nothing against him personally. How could she? She'd never met him before today. It was strangers in general—more particularly *male* strangers—she tried to avoid. Somehow she'd always thought Jeff guessed and understood. But apparently she was wrong, for when he'd called and enthusiastically asked if he could bring his buddy home to spend the Christmas holidays, then explained that Brian Scanlon had no family, there'd been no hesitation from Margaret Brubaker.

"Why, of course. Bring him. It would be just plain unchristian to make a man spend Christmas in some miserable barracks in North Dakota when there are beds to spare and enough food for an army."

Listening on the extension phone, Theresa had felt her heart fall. She'd wanted to interrupt her mother and say, Just a minute! Don't the rest of us have any say about it? It's *our* Christmas, too.

There were frustrations involved with living at home at age twenty-five, and though sometimes Theresa longed to live elsewhere, the certain loneliness she'd suffer if she made the move always gave her second thoughts. Yes, the house belonged to her mother and father. They could invite whom they chose. And even while Brian Scanlon's intrusion rankled, she realized how selfish her thoughts were. What kind of woman would deny the sharing of Christmas bounty with someone who had no home and family?

But as they drove through the late-afternoon traffic, Theresa's apprehension grew.

They'd be home in less than five minutes, and she'd have to take her coat off, and once she did, it would happen again, as it always did. And she'd want to slink off to her room and cry…as she often did.

Even as the thoughts flashed through her mind, Brian said in his well-modulated voice, "I certainly want to thank you for letting me come along with Jeff and horn in on your holidays."

Theresa felt a flush of guilt working its way past her high gray coat collar, and hoped he wasn't looking at her as she politely lied. "Don't be silly. There's an extra bed in the basement and never a shortage of food. We're all very happy that Jeff thought of inviting you. Since you two started up the band together you're all we hear about when he calls or writes. Brian this and Brian that. Mother's been dying to get an eye on you and make sure her *little boy* has been traveling in good company. But don't pay any attention to her. She used to practically make his girlfriends fill out an application form with three references."

Just then they drew into the driveway of a very run-of-the-mill L-shaped rambler on a tree-lined street where the houses were enough alike as to be almost indistinguishable from one another.

"Looks like Mom and Dad haven't gotten home yet," Theresa noted. A fresh film of snow dusted the driveway. Only one set of tire tracks led from the garage, but a single pair of footprints led up to the back door. "But Amy must be here."

The doors of the station wagon swung open, and Jeff Brubaker stood motionless beside the car for a moment, scanning the house in the way of a man seeking reassurance that none of the familiar things had altered. "God, it's good to be home," he breathed, sucking in a great gulp of the cold, pure Minnesota air. Then he became suddenly effervescent, almost jogging around to the tailgate of the wagon. "Come on you two, let's get this junk unloaded."

Thinking ahead to the next five minutes, Theresa appropriated a guitar case to carry inside. She didn't know how she'd manage it, but if worse came to worst, she might be able to hide behind it.

At the sound of the tailgate slamming, a gangly fourteen-year-old girl came flying out the back door. "Jeffy, you're home!" Smiling with a flash of tooth braces, Amy Brubaker threw her arms wide with an open gesture Theresa envied. Not a day went by that Theresa didn't pray her sister be granted the blessing of growing normally.

"Hey, dumpling, how are ya?"

"I'm too big for you to call me dumpling anymore."

They embraced with sibling exuberance before Jeff plopped a direct kiss on Amy's mouth.

"Ouch!" She jerked back and made a face, then bared her teeth for inspection. "Look out when you do that. It hurts!"

"Oh, I forgot about the new hardware. Let's see." He tipped her chin up while she continued curling her lips back as if not in the least daunted by her unattractive braces. Looking on, Theresa wondered how it was her little sister had managed to remain so uninhibited and charmingly self-assured.

"I tell everybody I got 'em decorated just in time for

Christmas," Amy declared. "After all, they do look a little like tinsel."

Jeff leaned back from the waist and laughed, then quirked a smile at his friend. "Brian, it's time you met the rambunctious part of the Brubaker family. This is Amy. Amy, here he is at last—Brian Scanlon. And as you can see, I've talked him into bringing his guitar so we can play a couple hot ones for you and your friends, just as ordered."

For the first time, Amy lost her loquaciousness. She jammed her hands as far as they'd go into the tight front pockets of her blue jeans and carefully kept her lips covering the new braces as she smiled and said almost shyly, "Hi."

"Hi, Amy. Whaddya say?" He extended his hand and smiled at Amy with as charming a grin as any of the rock stars beaming from the postered walls of her bedroom. Amy glanced at Brian's hand, made an embarrassed half shrug and finally dragged one hand from the blue denim and let Brian shake it. When he released it, the hand hung in the air between them for a full fifteen seconds while her smile grew and grew, until a reflection flashed from the bars of metal spanning her teeth.

Watching, Theresa thought, *oh, to be fourteen again, with a shape like Amy's, and the total lack of guile that allows her to gaze point-blank in unconcealed admiration, just as she's doing now!*

"Hey, it's cold out here!" Jeff gave an exaggerated shiver. "Let's go in and dig into mom's cake."

They carried duffel bags and guitar cases into the cheery front-facing kitchen of the simple house. The room was papered in a flowered pattern that was repeated in the fabric inserts of the shutters on the windows flanking the eating area, which looked out on the front yard. An ordinary house on a street with others just like it, the Brubaker home had nothing exceptional to set it apart, except a sense of familial love that Brian Scanlon sensed even before the mother and father arrived to complete the circle.

On the kitchen table was a crocheted doily of white, and in the center sat a pedestal plate bearing a mouthwatering German chocolate cake under a domed lid. When Jeff lifted the lid, the

gaping hole came into view. In the hollow wedge was a slip of
folded paper. He took it out to reveal a recipe card from which
he read aloud: "'Jeff, it looked too good for me to resist. See
you soon. Dad.'"

The four of them shared a laugh, but all the while Theresa
stood with the broad end of Jeff's guitar case resting on the
floor at her toes, and the narrow end shielding the front of her
coat. She was the delegate hostess. She should ask for Brian's
jacket and hat and make a move toward the hall closet.

"Come on, Brian," Jeff invited, "see the rest of the place."
They moved to the living room and immediately four raucous,
jarring chords sounded from the piano. Theresa grimaced and
glanced at Amy who rolled her eyeballs. It was "Jeff's Outer
Space Concerto."

They drew deep breaths in unison, signaled with nods and
bellowed simultaneously, "Je-e-e-eff, knock it off!" While the
sisters giggled, Jeff explained to Brian, "I composed that when
I was thirteen...before I became an impresario."

Theresa quickly hung up her coat in the front-hall closet and
hustled down the hall to her bedroom. She found a pale blue
cardigan sweater and whisked it across her shoulders without
slipping her arms into the sleeves, then buttoned the top button
at her throat. She glanced critically in the mirror, realigned the
button-and-buttonhole panels so the sweater covered as much
of her as possible, but found to her dismay it did little to
disguise her problem. *Oh God, will I ever learn to live with it?*

Her usual, end-of-the-day backache plagued again, and she
sighed, straightening her shoulders, but to no avail.

The house tour had stopped in the living room where Jeff
had found his Stella. He was twanging out some metallic
chords and singing an offbeat melody while Theresa tried to
bolster her courage and walk out there. Undoubtedly it would
be the same as it always was when she met a man. Brian
Scanlon would scarcely glance at her face before his eyes
would drop to her breasts and he would become transfixed by
them. Since puberty she had relived those awful moments too
many times to count, but Theresa had never become inured.

That horrifying instant when a man's eyebrows twitched up in surprise, and his lips dropped open while he stared at the outsized mammary glands that had, through some unfortunate freak of nature, grown to proportions resembling volleyballs. They rode out before Theresa like a flagship before a fleet, their double-D circumference made the more pronounced by her delicately boned size-nine frame.

The last time she'd been introduced to a strange man he was the father of one of her second-grade pupils. Even as a parent, the poor man hadn't been able to remember protocol in his shock at glimpsing her enormous breasts. His eyes had riveted on them even while he was shaking Theresa's hand, and after that there'd been such awful tension between them the conference had been a disaster.

If she had carved a notch on her bedroom dresser every time that had happened down through the years, there'd be nothing before her now but a pile of wood chips. Now meeting the apprehensive eyes of the woman reflected in the mirror, Theresa quailed with all the familiar misgivings. Red hair and freckles! As if it wasn't enough that she'd been cursed with these mountainous breasts, she'd landed hair the color of paprika and skin that refused to tan. Instead it broke out in brilliant orange heat spots, as if she had an incurable rash, each time the sun grazed her skin. And this hair—oh, how she hated it! Coarse, springy ringlets that clung to her scalp like a Brillo pad if cut short, or if allowed to grow long, developed untamable waves reminiscent of those disastrous messes fried onto women's heads in the early days of the century before hot permanents had been perfected. Detesting it either way, she'd chosen a middle-of-the-road length and as innocuous a style as she could manage, brushing it straight back from her face and clasping it at her nape with a wide barrette, below which the "tail" erupted like a ball of fire from a volcano.

And what about eyelashes? Didn't every woman deserve to have eyelashes that could at least be seen? Theresa's were the same hue as her hair—pale threads that made the rims of her eyelids look pink and sickly while framing eyes that were almost the identical color of her freckles, a pale tea-brown. She thought of the dark spiky lashes and the stunning green of Brian Scanlon's eyes, and her own drooped to check her sweater once again, and tug it close together, as Theresa realized she could no longer avoid confronting him. She must return to the living room. And if he stared at her breasts with lascivious speculation she'd think of the strains of her favorite Chopin Nocturne, which always had a calming effect upon her.

Amy and Jeff were sitting on the davenport while Brian faced them from the seat of the piano bench. When Jeff caught sight of her, he thwacked the guitar strings dramatically, and let the chord reverberate in fanfare. "There she is!"

So much for slipping quietly into their midst.

Brian was no more than five feet away, still wearing his formal garrison cap. She was conscious of a wink of silver on the large eagle medallion centered above the black leather visor as his eyes swerved her way, directly on a level with the objects of Theresa's despair. Her pale brown eyes met his of sea green. The certainty of what would happen next seemed to lodge in her throat like a pill taken without water. *Now!* she thought. *Now it will happen!* She steeled herself for the sickening embarrassment that was certain to follow.

But Brian Scanlon relaxedly stretched six feet of blue-clad anatomy to its feet and smiled into Theresa's eyes, his own never wavering downward for even a fraction of a second or giving the impression that it even crossed his mind.

"Jeff's been demonstrating the old Stella. She doesn't sound too bad."

Aren't you going to gawk like everybody else? She felt the blush begin to tint her face because he *hadn't* looked, and to cover her fluster grabbed onto the first words that entered her mind.

"As usual, my brother thinks of nothing but music." Theresa strove to keep her voice steady, for her heart was knocking crazily. "And here you sit with your hat and jacket still on. I'll show you where you'll sleep, since neither one of these two had the courtesy to do it."

"I hope I'm not putting anybody out of their bed."

"Not at all. We're putting you on a hideaway bed in the family room downstairs. I just hope nobody puts you out of yours, because it'll be in front of the TV and fireplace, and Dad likes to stay up at least until after the ten-o'clock news."

He didn't look! He didn't look! The exaltation pounded through her brain as Theresa led the way back through the kitchen to the basement door that opened into the room just behind the stove wall. Oddly enough, she seemed more aware of Brian Scanlon because of the fact that he'd assiduously remained polite and refrained from dropping his eyes. She took his guitar and he his duffel bag, and she led him downstairs into a large basement area with a set of sliding glass doors facing the rear yard. The room was paneled in warm pecan and carpeted in burnt orange that burst into a glow as Theresa switched on a table lamp.

Brian watched her hair light up as she paused above the lamp, then scanned the room, which contained a country pine coffee table, a cushioned davenport and pillowed rockers in the Colonial style. A fireplace was flanked by a television set, and at the end of the room where Brian stood, a thick-legged kitchen set of glossy pine was centered before the sliding glass door.

"Mmm...I like this room. Very homey." His eyes came back to settle upon Theresa as he spoke.

He seemed the type who'd prefer art deco or chrome and glass, but an appreciative reaction riffled through Theresa, for her mother had largely let her choose the colors and textures of the furnishings when they'd redecorated two years ago. It wasn't her own house, but it gave Theresa a taste of home planning, making her eager for the day when she could exercise her own tastes through an entire house.

Brian noted her tightly crossed arms beneath the baby-blue sweater and the nervousness that was absent only while her sister and brother were close by.

"I'm sorry it has no closet, but you can hang your things up here." She opened a door leading to an unfinished portion of the basement where the laundry facilities were housed.

He crossed toward her, and she stepped well back as he popped his head around the laundry-room doorway, one foot off the floor behind him. There was a rolling laundry rack with empty hangers tinging in the air currents from the opening of the door. "There's no bath down here, but feel free to use the upstairs tub or shower any time you want."

When he turned to her, his eyes again rested directly on hers as he noted, "It sure beats the BOQ on base, especially at Christmas time." She was conscious of how crisp and correctly knotted his formal navy blue tie was, how smoothly the dark blue military "blouse" contoured his chest and shoulders over the paler blue of his shirt, of how flattering the square-set cap was to the equally square-cut lines of his jaw.

"BOQ?" she questioned.

"Bachelor Officers' Quarters."

"Oh." She waited for his eyes to rove downward, but they didn't. Instead, he began freeing the four silver buttons bearing the eagle-and-shield U.S. Air Force insignia, turning his back on her and taking a stroll around the room while freeing the "blouse" and shrugging out of it. He slipped his hat off the back of his head with a slow, relaxed movement, and she saw his hair for the first time. It was a rich chestnut color, trimmed— according to military regulations—far too short for her taste, and bearing a ridge across the back from the band of his cap. He turned toward Theresa again, and she noted that around his face the chestnut hair held the suggestion of waves, but was cut too short to allow them free rein. It would be much more attractive an inch and a half longer, she decided.

"It feels good to get out of these things."

"Oh, here! Let me hang them up."

"Just the blouse—I mean the jacket. We get in trouble if we hang up our caps."

As she came forward to take his jacket, he extended his cap, too, and its inner band was still warm from his head. As she scuttled away around the laundry-room doorway again, that warmth seemed to singe her palm. When she tipped the cap upside down to lay it on the rack above the clothes bar, a spicy scent of some hair preparation found its way to her nostrils. It seemed to cling to the jacket, too, as she threaded its shoulders over a hanger and hooked it on the rack.

When she returned to the family room, Brian was standing in front of the sliding glass doors with his hands in his trousers pockets, feet widespread, gazing out at the snowy yard where twilight was falling. For a long moment Theresa studied the back of his sky-blue shirt where three crisp laundry creases gave him that clean-cut appearance of a model on a recruiting poster. The creases rose up out of the belted waistline of his trousers but disappeared across his shoulders where the blue fabric stretched taut as the head of a drum.

She crossed the room silently and flipped on an outside spotlight that flooded her father's bird feeder. Brian started at the snap of the light, glancing aside at her as she crossed her arms beneath the sweater and joined him at the wide window, studying the scene beyond.

"Every winter Dad tries to entice cardinals, but so far this year we haven't had any. This is his favorite spot in the house. He brings his coffee down here in the mornings and sits at the table with his binoculars close at hand. He spends hours here."

"I can see why." Scanlon's eyes moved once more to the view outside where sparrows, caught in the beam of light that lit the snow to glimmering crystals, twittered and searched for fallen seed at the base of the feeder pole. The far edge of the property was delineated by a line of evergreens that appeared almost black in the waning light. Their limbs were laden with white. Suddenly a blue jay darted from them, squawking in the crass, impertinent note of superiority only a blue jay can muster, scattering the sparrows as he landed among them, then cocking his head and disdaining the seeds he jealously guarded.

"I wasn't sure if I should come with Jeff. I felt a little like I was horning in, you know?"

His hands were still buried in his trousers pockets, but she felt his eyes turn her way and hoped she wouldn't blush while attempting to lie convincingly. "Don't be silly, you're not horning in."

"Any stranger in the house at this time of the year is like a fifth wheel. I know that, but I couldn't resist Jeff's invitation when I thought about spending two weeks with nothing to do but stare at the bare walls of the quarters and talk to myself."

"I'm glad you didn't. Why, Mother didn't hesitate a minute when Jeff called and suggested bringing you home. Besides, we've all heard so much about you in Jeff's letters, you hardly seem like a stranger. As a matter of fact, I believe *one* of us had a tiny bit of a crush on you even before you stepped out of the car in the driveway."

He laughed good-naturedly and shook his head at the floor as if slightly embarrassed, then rocked back on his heels. "It's a good thing she isn't six years older. She's going to be a real knockout at twenty."

"Yes, I know. Everybody says so."

Brian heard no note of rancor in Theresa's words, only a warm, sisterly pride. And he need not lower his eyes to her chest to see that as she spoke, her forearms unconsciously guarded her breasts more closely.

Thanks for warning me, Brubaker, he thought, recalling all that Jeff had told him about his sister. *But apparently Jeff told his family as much about my background as he told me about them,* he thought, as Theresa went on in a sympathetic note.

"Jeff told us about your mother. I'm sorry. It must have been terrible to get the news about the plane crash."

He studied the snow again and shrugged. "In a way it was, in a way it wasn't. We were never close after my dad died, and once she'd remarried, we didn't get along at all. Her second husband thought I was a drug addict because I played rock music, and he didn't waste any more time on me than was absolutely necessary."

She evaluated her own family, so warm, supporting, so full of love, and resisted the urge to lay a comforting hand on Brian's arm. She felt guilty for the many times she'd wished Jeff wouldn't bring him home. It had been thoroughly selfish, she chided herself, guarding her family's Christmas from outsiders just as the jay guarded the seeds he didn't want to eat.

This time when she said the words, Theresa found they were utterly sincere. "We're glad to have you here, Brian."

Chapter 2

"They're home!" shouted Jeff overhead, then he stuck his head around the basement doorway and ordered, "Hey, you two, get up here!"

As an outside observer, Brian couldn't help envying Jeff Brubaker his family, for the greeting his friend received in the arms of his mother and father was an emotional display of honest love. Margaret Brubaker was hiking her rotund body out of the deep bucket seat of the low-slung Celica when Jeff swooped down on her. The grocery bag in her arms was unceremoniously dropped onto the snowy driveway in favor of hugs and kisses interspersed with tears, hellos and general exuberance while Willard Brubaker came around the car and took his turn—albeit with far fewer tears than his wife, but there was an undeniable glitter in his eye as he backed off and assessed Jeff.

"Good to have you home, son."

"I'll say it is," put in his mother, then the trio shared an enormous three way hug. Margaret stepped back, crushing a loaf of bread. "Land! Would you look at what I've done with these groceries. Willard, help me pick 'em up."

Jeff waylaid them both. "Forget the groceries for now. I'll come back and get 'em in a minute. Come and meet Brian." With an arm around each of his parents' shoulders, Jeff shepherded them into the kitchen where Brian waited with the two girls. "These are the two who had the courage to have a kid like me—my mom and dad. And this is Brian Scanlon."

Willard Brubaker pumped Brian's hand. "Glad to have you with us, Brian."

Margaret's greeting was, "So this is Jeff's Brian."

"I'm afraid so, for all of two weeks. I really appreciate your invitation, Mrs. Brubaker."

"There are two things we have to get settled right now," Margaret stated without prelude, pointing an accusatory finger. "The first is that you don't call me Mrs. Brubaker, like I'm some commanding officer. Call me Margaret. And the other is…you don't smoke pot, do you?"

Amy rolled her eyeballs in undisguised chagrin, but the rest of them shared a good-natured laugh that managed to break the ice even before Brian answered frankly, "No, ma'am. Not anymore." There was a moment of surprised silence, then everyone burst into laughter again. And Theresa looked at Brian in a new light.

To Brian it seemed the Brubaker house was never quiet. Immediately after the introductions, Margaret was flinging orders for "you two boys" to pick up the groceries she'd dropped in the driveway. Supper preparations set up the next clatter as fried potatoes started splattering in a frying pan, and dishes were clinked against silverware at the table. In the living room, Jeff picked up his old guitar, but after a few minutes, shouted, "Amy, will you go shut off your damn music! It's thumping through the wall loud enough to drive a man crazy!" The only quiet one of the group appeared to be Willard, who calmly settled himself into a living-room chair and read the evening newspaper as if the chaos around him didn't even register. Within ten minutes it was evident to Brian who ruled the Brubaker roost. Margaret issued orders like a drill sergeant whether she wanted to be called Margaret or not. But she controlled her brood with a sharp tongue that wielded as much humor as hauteur.

"Theresa, now don't fry those potatoes till they're tougher than horsehide the way you like 'em. Don't forget your father's false teeth. Jeff, would you play something else in there? You know how I've always hated that song! Whatever happened to the good old standards like 'Moonlight Bay'? Amy, get two folding chairs out of the front closet and keep your fingers off that coconut frosting till dessert time. Willard, keep that dirty newsprint off the arms of the chair!"

To Brian's surprise, Willard Brubaker peered over the top of his glasses, muttered too softly for his wife to hear, "Yes, my little turtledove," then caught Jeff's eye, and the two exchanged grins of amused male tolerance. Willard's gaze caught Brian's next, and the older man gave a quick wink, then buried himself behind his paper again, resting it on the arms of the chair.

Supper was plentiful and plain: Polish sausage, fried potatoes, baked beans and toast—Jeff's favorite meal. Willard sat at the head of the table, Margaret at the foot, the two "girls" on one side and the two "boys" across from them.

While they ate, Brian observed Margaret's buxom proportions and realized from whom Theresa had inherited her shape. Throughout the pleasant meal Theresa kept her blue sweater over her shoulders, though there were times when it plainly got in her way. Occasionally, Brian glanced up to find Amy gazing at him with an expression warning of imminent puppy love, though Theresa never seemed to look at him at all.

Midway through the meal the phone rang, and Amy popped up to get it.

"Hello," she said, then covered the mouthpiece and looked disgusted. "It's for you, Jeffy. It sounds like dumb old Glue Eyes."

"Watch your mouth, little sister, or I'll wire your top braces to your bottom ones." Jeff took the phone and Amy returned to the table.

"Glue Eyes?" Brian glanced at Theresa.

"Patricia Gluek," she answered, "his old girlfriend. Amy never liked the way Patricia used to put on her makeup back in high school, so she started calling her Glue Eyes."

Amy plopped into her chair with a grunt of exasperation.

"Well, she plastered it on so thick it looked like her eyelashes were glued together, not to mention how thick she used to plaster Jeff with all those purrs and coos. She makes me sick."

"Amy!" snapped Margaret, and Amy had the grace to desist.

Brian curled an eyebrow at Theresa, and again she enlightened him. "Amy worships Jeff. She'd like to keep him all to herself for two solid weeks."

Just then Jeff dropped the receiver against his thigh and asked, "Hey, you two, want to pick up Patricia after supper and go to a movie or something?"

Brian craned around to look over his shoulder at Jeff.

Theresa gulped. "Who, me?"

Jeff flashed an indulgent smile. "Yeah, you and Bry."

Already Theresa could feel the color creeping up her neck. She never went on dates, and most certainly not with her brother's friends, who were all younger than herself.

Brian turned back to Theresa. "It sounds fine with me, if it's all right with Theresa."

"Whaddya say, Treat?" Jeff was jiggling the phone impatiently, and the eyes of everyone at the table turned to the blushing redhead. A bevy of excuses flashed through her mind, all of them as phony as those she'd dreamed up on the rare occasions when single male teachers from school asked her out. At her elbow she sensed Amy gaping in undisguised envy.

Brian realized the house was totally silent for the first time since he'd entered it and wished the rock music was still throbbing from Amy's room. It was obvious Theresa was caught in a sticky situation where refusal would be rude, yet he could tell she didn't want to say yes.

"Sure, that sounds fun."

She avoided Brian's eyes, but felt them hesitate on her for a minute while Jeff finalized the plans, and she withdrew from center stage by going to get dessert plates for the German chocolate cake.

When the meal was finished and Theresa was helping with dishes, she cornered Jeff for a moment as he passed through the kitchen.

"Jeffrey Brubaker, what on earth you were thinking of, to suggest such a thing?" she whispered angrily. "I'll pick my own dates, thank you."

"Lighten up, sis. Brian's not a date."

"You bet he's not. Why, he must be four years younger than I am!"

"Two."

"Two! That's even worse! Why, it makes it look like—"

"All right, all right! What are you so upset about?"

"I'm not upset. You just put me on the spot, that's all."

"Did you have other plans for tonight?"

"On your first night home?" she asked pointedly. "Of course not."

"Great. Then the least you'll get out of the deal is a free movie."

Oh no! the peeved Theresa vowed. *I'll pay my own way!*

Getting ready to go, Theresa couldn't help but admire how carefully Brian had concealed his reluctance. After all, who'd want to be saddled with a *big* sister? And worse yet, a freckle-head like her? She scowled at the copper dots in the mirror and despised each one with renewed intensity. She tried to yank a brush through her disgusting hair, but it was like a frayed sisal rope, only not nearly as pleasing in color. *Damn you, Jeffrey Brubaker, don't you ever do this to me again.* She drew the hair to the nape of her neck, tied it with a navy blue ribbon and considered makeup. But she owned none except lipstick, which she slashed onto her surly lips as if scrawling graffiti on a restroom wall. *I'll get you for this, Jeff.* Little thought was given to the clothing she chose, beyond the certainty that she'd put on her gray coat and leave it buttoned until they got back home.

She wasn't, however, planning on running into Brian in the front hall by the coat closet. When she did, she came up short, caught without a sweater or guitar or table to hide behind. Instinctively, one hand went up to finger her blouse collar—it was the best she could do.

"Jeff went out to start the car," Brian announced.

"Oh." The word was barely out of her mouth before Theresa realized Brian had shed military attire in favor of brown tennis shoes, bone-colored corduroys and a polo-style shirt of wide horizontal stripes in red and beige. He'd been carrying a brown leather waist-length jacket, and shrugged it on while she watched, transfixed. If Brian had subjected Theresa to the blatant inspection she gave him, she'd have ended up in her room in tears. She hadn't even realized how pointedly she'd been staring until her eyes traveled back up to his. She felt utterly foolish.

But if he noticed, he gave not the slightest clue beyond the hint of a smile that disappeared as quickly as it had come. "All ready?"

"Yes." She reached for her gray coat, but he took it from her hands without asking and held it for her. Even as Theresa felt the flush coloring her cheek at the unfamiliar gesture of good manners, she could do nothing but slip her arms into the coat, exposing the front of her so there was no hiding her proportions.

They called good-night to her parents and Amy and stepped out into the biting winter night. Theresa had gone on few enough dates in her life that it was difficult not to feel seduced into believing this was one, for he held the door of the station wagon while she slid in next to Jeff, then slipped his arm across the back of the seat as he settled in, too. She caught the drift of the same scent she'd detected when he handed her his cap earlier, and since Theresa wasn't a woman given to using perfumes herself, his faint hint of...sandalwood, that was it, came through all the clearer.

Jeff had the radio on—there was always a radio on—and he turned it louder as the gravelly voice of Bob Seger came on. Jeff's own voice had the grating earthiness of Seger's, and he picked up the refrain and sang along.

"We've got to learn this one, Bry."

"Mmm...it's smooth. Nice harmony on the chorus."

When the chorus came around again, the three sang along with it, their harmony resonant and true. "Ooo, shame on the moon..." Beside her, Theresa heard Brian's voice for the first time—straightforward, mellow, the antithesis of Jeff's. It sent shivers up her arms.

When they reached Patricia Gluek's house, Jeff went inside while Theresa and Brian transferred to the back seat, leaving a respectable distance between them. The radio was still playing and the lights from the dashboard lent an ethereal glow to the space beyond the front seat.

"How long have you and Jeff been playing and singing together?"

"Over three years now. We met when we were stationed together in Germany and started up a band there, and luckily we both landed at Minot Air Force Base, so we decided to look for a new drummer and bass player and keep a good thing rolling."

"I'd love to hear the band sometime."

"Maybe you will."

"I doubt it. I don't have many chances to swing by Minot, North Dakota."

"We'd like to get a new group started when we get out next summer, and hire an agent and make it a regular thing. Hasn't Jeff mentioned it?"

"Why, no, but I think it's a great idea, at least for Jeff. He's wanted to be a musician since he spent that first fifteen dollars on his Stella and started picking up chords from anybody who'd teach him."

"Same with me. I've been playing since I was twelve, but I want to do more than just play."

"What else?"

"I'd like to try writing, arranging. And I've always had the urge to be a DJ."

"You have the voice for it." He certainly did. She remembered her first appreciative surprise upon hearing it earlier. But it went on now, turning attention away from himself.

"Enough about me. I hear you're into music, too."

"Grades one through six, Sky Oaks Elementary."

"Do you like it?"

"I love it, with the rare exceptions like yesterday during the Christmas program when Keri Helling and Dawn Gafkjen got into a fight over who was going to be the pink ornament and who was going to be the blue one and ended up crying and getting the crepe-paper costumes all soggy." She chuckled. "No, seriously, I love teaching the younger kids. They're guileless, and open, and..." *And they don't gawk.* "And accepting," she finished.

Just then Jeff returned with Patricia, and introductions were made as Brian and Patricia shook hands over the front seat. Theresa had known the girl for years. She was a vivacious brunette, now in her second year at Normandale Community College. She was waiting to step into her former status as Jeff's girlfriend the moment he got out of the service, though they'd agreed to date others during their four years apart. So far, though, the attraction had not faded, for each of the three times Jeff had been home, he and Patricia had been inseparable.

When the pretty brunette turned toward the front, Theresa was chagrined to see her and Jeff share a more intimate hello than they'd apparently exchanged inside the house. Jeff's arms went around Patricia, and her head drifted to his shoulder while they kissed in a way that sent the blood filling up the space between Theresa's freckles. Beside her, Brian sat unmoving, watching the kiss that was taking place in such a forthright manner it was hard to ignore.

Goodness, would they never stop? The seconds ticked away while the music from the radio didn't quite conceal the soft murmurs from the front seat. Theresa wanted to crawl into a hole and pull the earth over her head.

Brian laced his fingers over his belly, slumped low in the seat, dropped his head back lazily and politely turned to gaze out his side window.

I am twenty-five years old, thought Theresa, *and I've never known before exactly what was implied by "double date."* She, too, gazed out her dark window.

There was a faint rustle, and, thankfully, it was Jeff's arm lifting from around Patricia's shoulders. The wagon chunked into gear, and they were moving at last.

At the theater, Theresa made a move toward her purse, but Brian stepped between her and the counter, announcing unceremoniously, "I'll get it." So, rather than make an issue of the expenditure, she politely backed off.

When he turned, she said, "Thank you."

But he made no reply, only tipped his shoulders aslant while slipping his billfold into a back pocket where the beige wales of the corduroy were slightly worn in a matching square that captured Theresa's eyes and made her mouth go dry. He turned around, caught her gaze, and she wished she'd never come.

Things got worse when they'd settled into their seats and the movie began, for it had an "R" rating, and exposed enough skin to create sympathetic sexual reactions in a sworn celibate! Halfway through the film the camera zoomed in on a bare spine, curved hips and a naked feminine back over which two masculine hands played, their long, blunt fingers feathered with traces of dark hair. A naked hirsute chest rolled into view, and the side of an apple-sized breast, then—horror of horrors!—an upthrust nipple, controlled by the broad, dark hand. A bearded jaw eased into the frame, and a mouth closed over the distended nipple.

In her seat beside Brian, Theresa wanted more than ever to simply, blessedly, *die*. His elbows rested on the armrests, and his fingers were laced together, the outer edges of his index fingers absently stroking his lips as he slumped rather low in the seat.

Why didn't I consider something like this happening? Why didn't I ask what was playing? Why didn't I wisely stay home in the first place?

Theresa tolerated the remainder of the love scene, and as it progressed a queer reaction threaded through her body. Saliva pooled beneath her tongue. She could feel her pulse throbbing in the place where her purse was pressed tightly against her lap. And a quicksilver liquid sensation trickled through her innards, setting her alive with sensations she'd never experienced before. But outwardly, she sat as if a sorcerer had cast a spell upon her. Not so much as a pale eyelash blinked. Not a muscle twitched. She stared spellbound as the climax was enacted, reflected in the facial expressions of the man and woman on the screen and the animal sounds of fulfillment.

And not until those climaxes ended did Theresa realize Brian's elbow had been skewering hers with pressure that grew, and grew, and grew....

The scene changed, and he wilted, pulling his elbow against his side as if only now realizing what he'd been doing. Her elbow actually hurt from the pressure he'd been applying. He shifted uncomfortably in his seat, crossed an ankle over a knee and negligently dropped his laced fingers over the zipper of his corduroy pants.

Considering what had happened within her own body, Theresa had little doubt the same had happened to Brian. The remainder of the film was lost on her. She was too aware of the man on her right, and she found herself wondering who he'd been thinking of while the pressure on her elbow increased. She found herself wondering things about the male anatomy that the screen had carefully hidden. She recalled pictures she'd seen in the bolder magazines, but they seemed as flat, cold and lifeless as the paper upon which they'd been printed. For the first time in her life, she ached to know what the real thing was like.

When the film ended, she took refuge in chattering with Patricia, making certain she walked far enough ahead of Brian that their elbows didn't touch or their eyes meet.

"Anybody hungry?" Jeff inquired when they were back in the station wagon.

Theresa felt slightly queasy, sitting once again with Brian only a foot away. If she tried eating anything, she wasn't sure it would stay down.

"No!" she exclaimed, before anybody else could agree.

"Yeah, I—" Brian spoke at the same time, then politely changed course. "I've been thinking about a piece of your mother's German chocolate cake all through the movie."

In a pig's eye, thought Theresa.

Oddly enough, nobody talked about the film as they drove back to Patricia's house. Nobody said much of anything. Patricia was snuggled up with her shoulder behind Jeff's. Now and then he'd turn and smile down at her with the dash lights clearly outlining the ardent expression on his face. Patricia's shoulder moved slightly, and Theresa conjured up the possibility of where her hand might be. Theresa gazed out her window and blushed for perhaps the tenth time that day.

When they pulled up in Patricia's driveway, Jeff turned off all the lights and gathered Patricia into his arms without a moment's hesitation. Behind the couple, another man and woman sat like two bumps on a log.

Kisses, Theresa discovered, have more sound than you'd think. From the front seat came the distinct rush of hastened breathing, the faint suggestive sounds of lips parting, positions changing, the rustle of hands moving softly. The rasp of a zipper sizzled through the dark confines of the car, and Theresa jumped, but immediately wished she hadn't, for it was only Jeff's jacket.

"Come on, Theresa, what do you say we go for a little walk?" Brian suggested. The overhead light flashed on, and she hustled out his door, so relieved she wanted to throw her arms around him and kiss him out of sheer gratitude.

When the door slammed behind them, Theresa surprised herself by releasing a pent-up breath and bursting out with the last words she expected to say. *"Thank you."*

He stuck his hands into his jacket pockets and chuckled. "No need to thank me. I was getting a little uncomfortable myself."

His admission surprised her, but the frankness definitely relieved some of the tension.

"I can see I'll have to talk with my little brother about decorum. I wasn't exactly sure what to do!"

"What did you used to do when that happened on double dates?"

She was embarrassed to have to admit, "I've never been on a double date bef—" She stopped herself just in time and amended, "I've never been on one."

"Aw, think nothing of it. They're both adults. He loves her—he's told me so more than once—and he intends to marry her soon after his hitch is done."

"You amaze me. I mean, you take it all in stride." *Heavens,* thought Theresa, *do couples do things like that in the same car with as little compunction as her brother showed and think nothing of it?* She realized suddenly how very, very naive she must seem to Brian Scanlon.

"He's my friend. I don't judge my friends."

"Well, he's my brother, and I'm afraid I do."

"Why? He's twenty-one years old."

"I know, I know." Theresa threw up her hands, exasperated with herself and uncomfortable with the subject.

"How old are you, Theresa? Twenty-five, right?"

"Yes."

"And I take it you haven't done a lot of that sort of thing."

"No." *Because every time I got in a car with a boy, he went after only the most obvious two things, never caring about the person behind them.* "I was busy studying when I was in high school and college, and since then...well, I don't go out much."

They were ambling down a snowy street, feet lifting lazily as the streetlights made the surface snow glitter. Her coat was still buttoned high, and her hands were buried in its pockets. Their breaths created white clouds, and their soles pressed brittle ice that crunched with each step.

"So, what did you think of the movie?" Brian asked.

"It embarrassed me," she admitted.

"I'm sorry."

"It's not your fault, it's Jeff's. He's the one who picked it."

"Next time we'll be sure to ask before we blindly follow him, okay?"

Next time? Theresa glanced up to find Brian smiling down at her with an easy laziness that was meant to put her at ease, but that lifted her heart in a strange, weightless way. She should have answered, "There won't be a next time," but instead smiled in return and concurred. "Agreed."

They turned around and were heading toward the Gluek driveway when Jeff backed the station wagon onto the street and its lights arced around, caught them in the glare, and he pulled up beside them.

"Would you two mind if we took you home?" Jeff asked when Theresa and Brian were settled in the backseat again.

"Not at all," Brian answered for both of them.

"Thanks for understanding, Bry. And Treat, you'll take good care of him, won't you?"

She wanted to smack her brother on the side of the head. Jeffrey Brubaker certainly took a lot for granted!

"Sure." What else could she have answered?

When they pulled up at home, Brian opened his door and the light flashed on. Patricia Gluek turned around and hooked an elbow over the back of the seat.

"Listen, a group of us are getting together at the Rusty Scupper on New Year's Eve, and you're both invited to join us. We plan to have dinner there and stay for the dancing afterward. It'll be a lot of the old gang—you've met them all before, Theresa—so what do you say?"

Damn it, does the whole world think it has to line up escorts for the wimpy little Theresa Brubaker who never gets asked out on dates? But she knew in her heart that Patricia was only being cordial and thinking about Brian, too, who was Jeff's houseguest and couldn't very well be excluded. He had one foot on the driveway, but this time instead of putting Theresa on the spot, he answered, "We'll talk it over and let you know, okay?"

"Some people from school are having a party in their home, and I told them I might go." The manufactured tale came glibly to Theresa's lips while she was still puzzling out where it had come from.

"Oh." Patricia sounded genuinely disappointed. "Well, in that case, you'll come, won't you, Brian? We have to make dinner reservations in advance."

"I'll think it over."

"Fine."

Brian swiveled toward the open door, but Jeff reached out and caught his arm. "Listen, Scan, thanks. I mean, I guess I ought to come in with you and play the host, but I'll see you in the morning at breakfast."

"Go on. Have a good time and don't worry about me."

When the car pulled away, Theresa and Brian stood on the back step while she dug in her purse for the house keys. When she found them and opened the door, they stepped into a dim kitchen where only a single bulb shone down on top of the white stove. It was silent—no music, no guitar, no voices.

They were both excruciatingly aware of what Jeff and Patricia were probably going off to do, and it created a corresponding sexual tension between them.

Seeking a diversion, Theresa whispered, "You said you were hungry for cake. There's plenty of it left."

He wasn't, really, but Brian wasn't at all averse to spending a little more time with Theresa, and the cake offered an excuse.

"I will if you will."

"It sounds good."

She moved toward the front hall, which was in total shadow, and made no move to turn on the light while removing her coat. Again, Brian was behind her to help her out of the garment, then hang it up. She left him there with a murmured thanks and returned to the kitchen to find two plates, forks and glasses of milk, taking them to the table where the cake still sat.

He joined her, choosing a chair at a right angle to hers, and they sat for a long time eating, saying nothing. The rafters of the house creaked in the December cold, and though it was very dark with only the small hood light illuminating the blotch of stove beneath it, she sensed Brian Scanlon studying her while he downed gulps of milk that sounded clearly in the silence.

"So, you're going to a party with someone from school on New Year's Eve?"

"No, I made that up."

His chin came up in surprise. "Oh?"

"Yes. I don't like people arranging dates for me, and furthermore, you don't need to be saddled with *me* on New Year's Eve. You go with Jeff and meet his friends. He's got some really nice—"

"*Saddled* with you?" he interrupted in that smooth, deep, unnerving voice that sent shivers up her nape.

"Yes."

"Did I give you the impression tonight that I resented being with you?"

"You know what I mean. You didn't come home with Jeff to have to haul me around every place you go."

"How do you know?"

She was stunned, she could only stammer. "You... I..."

"Would it surprise you to know that you're a big part of why I wanted to meet Jeff's family?"

"I..." But once again, she was struck dumb.

"He's told me a lot about you, Theresa. A lot."

Oh, Lord, how much? How much? Jeff, who knows my innermost fears. Jeff, who understands. Jeff, who can't keep anything to himself.

"What has he told you?" She tried to control the panic, but it crept into her voice, creating a vibrato that could not be disguised.

He made himself more comfortable, stretching his long legs somewhere beneath the table to find the seat of a chair as he leaned back to study her shadowed face speculatively. His eyes held points of light as he caught an elbow on the table edge and braced one jaw on his knuckles, tipping his head.

"About how you looked out for him when he was a kid. About your music. The violin and piano. How you used to sing duets for your family reunions and pass the hat for change afterward, then, as soon as you had enough, go to the store to buy your favorite singles." His lips lifted in a slow half smile, and his free hand moved the milk glass in circles against the tabletop.

"Oh, is that all?" Her shoulders wilted with relief, but in the dimness she had crossed her elbows on the tabletop and took refuge behind them as best she could.

"You always sounded as if you'd be someone I could get along with. And maybe I liked you even before I met you because he likes you so much, and you're his sister and I also like him very much."

Theresa was unused to being told she was liked. In her lifetime a few of the opposite sex had overtly tried to demonstrate what they "liked" about her, in the groping, insulting way she'd come to despise. But Brian seemed to have come to admire something deeper, her little-exposed self, her musicality, her familial relations. All this before he had ever laid eyes on her.

But those eyes were on her now, and though she could not make out their color in the veiling shadows, she caught the sparkle as he continued perusing her freely, the tip of his little finger now resting in the hollow beneath his full lower lip. She seemed unable to draw her eyes away from it as he went on quietly.

"I'd love to go to that party with you on New Year's Eve."

Their eyes met, hers wide with surprise, his carefully un-flirtatious.

"But you're…you're two years younger than I am." Once she'd said it, she wanted to eat the words.

But he asked undauntedly, "Does that bother you?"

"Yes, I…" She blew out a huge breath of air and leaned her forehead on the heel of one hand. "I can't believe this conversation."

"It doesn't bother me in the least. And I sure as hell don't want to go to that kind of a thing alone. Everybody'll be paired off, and I won't have anybody to dance with."

"I don't dance." *That* was the understatement of the night. Dancing was a pleasure she'd abandoned when her breasts grew too large to make fast dancing comfortable, their sway and bob not only hurting, but making Theresa feel sure they must appear obscene from the sidelines. And chest-to-chest dancing was even worse—being that close to men, she'd found, only gave them ideas.

"A musical woman like you?"

"Music and dancing are two different things. I've just never cared for—"

"There's time before New Year's Eve to learn. Maybe we can change your mind."

"Let me think about it, okay?"

"Sure." He got to his feet, and the chair scraped back, then he carried their two plates across the room and set them in the sink with a soft chink.

She opened the basement door and snapped on the light above the steps. "Well, I'm not sure if Mother made your bed down here or not."

She heard his steps following her down the carpeted incline, and prayed she'd find his bed all decked out, ready for him, so she could simply wish him good-night and escape to her own room upstairs.

Unfortunately, the davenport wasn't either opened or made up, so Theresa had little choice but to cross the room and begin the chore. She tossed the cushions aside, conscious now that Brian had snapped on the lamp, and it flooded the area with mellow light that revealed her clearly while she tugged on the folded mattress and brought it springing out into the room.

"I'll get the bedding," she explained, and hustled into the laundry room to find clean sheets and blankets on a shelf there. He had turned on the television set when she came back out to the family room, and a late movie was glimmering on the screen in black and white. The volume was only a murmur as she shook out a mattress pad, concentrating fully on it when Brian stepped to the opposite side of the davenport to help her.

His long fingers smoothed the quilted surface with the expertise of a soldier who's been trained to keep his bunk in inspection-ready order. A sheet snapped and billowed in the air between them, and above it their glances met, then dropped. Images of the movie's love scene came back to titillate Theresa, while they tucked the corners of the sheets in, and Brian's hands pulled it far more expertly than hers, for hers were shaking and seemed nearly inept.

"Tight enough to bounce a coin," he approved.

She glanced up to find him looking at her instead of the sheet, and wondering what this man was doing to her. She had never in her life been as sexually aware of a male as she was of him. Men had brought her nothing but shame and intimidation, and she'd avoided them. Yet here she stood, gazing into the green eyes of Brian Scanlon over his half-prepared bed, wondering what it would be like to do with him the things she'd seen on a movie screen.

Redheads look ugly when they blush, she thought.

"The other sheet," he reminded her, and abashed, she turned to find it.

When the bed was finally done, she found her pulses leaping like Mexican jumping beans. But there still remained one duty she, as hostess, must perform.

"If you'll come upstairs, I'll give you clean towels and washcloths, and show you where the bathroom is."

"Jeff showed me after supper."

"Oh. Oh…good. Well, feel free to shower or…or whatever, anytime. You can hang your wet towels over the sink in the laundry room."

"Thank you."

They stood one on either side of the bed, and she suddenly realized she was facing him fully for the first time without shielding her breasts. Not once since she'd met him had she noticed him looking at them. His eyes were fastened on the freckled cheeks, then they moved up to her detestable red hair, and she realized she'd been standing without moving for a full thirty seconds.

"Well…good night then." Her voice was soft and shaky.

"Good night, Theresa." His was deep and quiet.

She scuttled away, racing up the stairs as if he were chasing her with ill intent. When she was settled into bed with the lights out, she heard him come upstairs and use the bathroom.

Put a pillow over your ears, Theresa Brubaker! But she listened to all the sounds coming from beyond her bedroom wall, and two closed doors, and envisioned Brian Scanlon performing his bedtime rituals and wondered for the first time in her life how a husband and wife ever made it through the intimacies of the first week of marriage.

Chapter 3

The following morning, Theresa was awakened by the thump-thump-thump of Amy's music reverberating through the floor. Rolling over, she squinted at the alarm clock, then shot out of bed as if it was on fire. Ten o'clock! She should have been up two hours ago to fix breakfast for Brian and Jeff!

Within minutes she was washed, combed, dressed in blue jeans and a loose white blouse with a black cardigan slung across her shoulders and buttoned beneath the blouse collar.

Her parents had gone to work long ago. Jeff's door was closed, and the sound of his snoring came from beyond. It appeared Amy was still in her room, torturing her hair with a curling iron while Theresa tried to tame her springing curls by smoothing a hand over the infamous tail that bounced on her shoulders.

She crept down the hall to the kitchen but found it empty. The basement door was open—it appeared Brian was up. She was filling the coffeepot when he slipped silently to the doorway leading directly to the kitchen from one side of the living room.

"Good morning."

She spun around, sending water flying everywhere, pressing a hand to her heart.

"Oh! I didn't know you were there! I thought you were still downstairs."

"I've been awake for a long time. Routine is hard to break."

"Have you been sitting in there all by yourself?"

"No." He grinned engagingly. "With Stella."

She grinned back. "And how did you two get along?" She put coffee in the percolator basket and set the pot on the stove burner.

"She's a brassy old girl, but I talked sweet to her and she responded like a lady."

It wasn't what he said, but how he said it that made Theresa's cheeks pink. There was an undertone of teasing, though the words were totally polite. She wasn't used to such a tone of voice when speaking with men, but it, combined with his lazy half smile while he leaned one shoulder against the doorway, gave her the feeling she imagined a cat must have when its fur was slowly stroked the wrong way.

"I didn't hear you playing."

"We were whispering to each other."

Again, she couldn't resist smiling.

"I…I'm sorry nobody was up to fix breakfast for you. It's my first day of Christmas vacation, and I guess my body decided to take advantage of it. I never even wiggled at the usual wake-up time. I heard Jeff still snoring. He must have come in late."

"It was around three."

So—he hadn't been able to sleep. Neither had she.

"Three!"

He shrugged, his shoulder still braced on the doorway. He was wearing tight, faded blue jeans and a white football jersey that hugged his ribs just enough to make them tantalizing.

She recalled how long it had taken her to get to sleep after the curious way he'd managed to stir her senses last night, and wondered what had really kept him awake. Had he lain in the dark thinking of the movie as she had? Thinking of Jeff and Patricia in the car? Himself and her having cake and milk in the dusky kitchen?

His slow perusal was beginning to make Theresa's nerves jump, so she shrugged. "Why don't you sit down, and I'll pour you a glass of juice?"

He obliged, though she still wasn't rid of his gaze, even after she gave him a glass of orange juice. His eyes followed her lazily as she turned the bacon, scrambled eggs and dropped bread into the toaster.

"What do you and Jeff have planned for today?"

"I don't know, but whatever it is, I was hoping you could come along."

Her heart skipped, and she was disappointed at what she had to reply. "Oh, no, I have too much to do to help Mother for tomorrow night, and I have to get ready for the concert I'm playing in tonight."

"Oh, that's right. Jeff told me. Civic orchestra, isn't it?"

"Uh-huh. I've been in it for three years and I really enjoy—"

"Well, good morning, you two." It was Amy, barely giving her sister a glance, aiming her greeting primarily at Brian. To his credit, he didn't flinch even slightly at the sight of Amy, decked out in crisp blue jeans that fit her like a shadow, a skinny little sweater that fit nearly as close, craftily styled hair with its shoulder-length auburn feather-cut blown and curled back from her face in that dewy-fresh style so stunningly right for teenage girls. Her makeup application could have taught "Glue Eyes" a thing or two several years ago.

"I thought teenagers spent their vacations flopping around in baggy sweats these days," Brian noted, managing to compliment Amy without encouraging any excess hope.

"Mmm…" Amy simpered. "That just goes to show what you know."

But Theresa was fully aware that had Brian not been under the roof, that's exactly how Amy would have spent her day, only she wouldn't have poked her nose out of her burrow until one o'clock in the afternoon.

Amy stepped delicately to the stove and lifted a piece of cooling bacon, nibbled it with a provocative daintiness that quite surprised her sister. Where in the world had Amy learned to act this way? When? Just since Brian Scanlon had walked into the house?

"Amy, if you want bacon and eggs, get yourself a plate," Theresa scolded, suddenly annoyed by her sister's flirtatiousness. Even though she realized how small it was to feel a twinge of irritation at this new side Amy was displaying, Theresa was undeniably piqued. Perhaps because the fourteen-year-old had the remarkably freckle-free skin, hair the color of most Kentucky Derby winners and a trim, tiny shape that must be the envy of half the girls in her freshman class at school. Theresa suddenly felt like a gaudy neon sign beside an engraved invitation, in spite of the fact that it was Amy who wore the makeup. Theresa held her sweater over her elbow as she reached to turn off a burner.

From the table, Brian observed it all—the quick flash of irritation the older sister hadn't quite been able to hide, the guarded movements behind the camouflaging sweater and even the guilt that flashed across her face for the twinge of envy she could not quite control in moments such as these.

He rose, moved to her side and smiled down into her startled eyes. "Here, let me pour the coffee, at least. I feel like a parasite sitting there and doing nothing while you slave over a hot stove." He reached for the pot while she shifted her eyes to the eggs she was removing from the pan.

"The cups are…" She half turned to find Amy watching them from just behind their shoulders. "Amy will show you where the cups are."

They had just begun eating when Jeff came slogging out of his room in bare feet and faded Levi's, scratching his chest and head simultaneously.

"I thought I smelled bacon."

"And I thought I smelled a rat," returned Theresa. "Jeff Brubaker, you should be ashamed of yourself. Bringing Brian here as your houseguest, then abandoning him that way."

Jeff shambled to a chair and strung himself upon it, more lying then sitting. "Aw hell, Brian didn't mind, did you, Bry?"

"Nope. Theresa and I had a nice long talk, and I got to bed early."

"What did you think of old Glue Eyes?" put in Amy.

"She's just as cute as I expected from Jeff's descriptions and the pictures I've seen," replied Brian.

"Humph!"

Jeff leaned his elbows on the table and closely scrutinized his younger sister. "Well, lookee here now," he singsonged. "If the twerp hasn't taken a few lessons from old Glue Eyes herself."

Amy's mouth puckered up as if it was full of alum. She glared at her brother and snapped, "I'm fourteen years old, Jeffrey, in case you hadn't noticed! And I've been wearing makeup for over a year now."

"Oh." Jeff lounged back in his chair once again. "I beg your pardon, Ms. Teen U.S.A."

She lurched to her feet and would have stormed out of the room, but Jeff caught her by the elbow and swung her around till she landed on his lap, where she sat stiffly with her arms crossed obstinately over her ribs, an expression of strained tolerance on her face.

"Wanna come along with Brian and me to shop for Mom and Dad today? I'm gonna need some help deciding what to get for them."

Her irritation dissolved like a mist before a wind. "*Reeeally?* You mean it, Jeff?"

"Sure I mean it." He pushed her off his lap, swatted her on the backside and sent her on her way again. "Get your room cleaned up, and we'll go right after we eat." When she was gone he looked at the spot from which she'd disappeared around the hallway wall. "Her jeans are too tight. Mother ought to talk to her about that."

Left behind, Theresa recalled the breakfast conversation with something less than good humor. Why was it so irritating that Jeff had noticed Amy's burgeoning maturity? Why did she herself feel lonely and left out and—*oh, admit it, Brubaker!*—jealous, because her sister of fourteen was accompanying Brian Scanlon, age twenty-three, on an innocent Christmas-shopping spree?

With the house to herself, Theresa put on her classical favorites, and spent the remainder of the morning boiling potatoes and eggs for the enormous pot of potato salad they'd take to the family gathering scheduled for the following night, Christmas Eve. In the afternoon she washed her hair, took a bath, filed her nails and rummaged in Amy's room for some polish with a little more pizzazz than the colorless stuff she usually wore. She came up with something called "Mocha Magic" and grimaced as she painted the first stripe down a nail. *I'm simply not a "Mocha Magic" girl,* she thought, but completed the single nail, held it aloft and assessed it stringently. She fluttered her fingers and watched the light dance across the pearlescent surface and decided—thinking in Amy's current teenage vernacular—what the heck, go for it!

When all ten nails were finished she wasn't sure she'd done the right thing. She imagined them glistening, catching the lights while she fingered the neck of her violin. *I'm a conservative person trapped inside the body of a Kewpie doll,* she decided, and left the polish on.

She put on a beef roast for supper and pressed her long, black gabardine skirt and the collar of the basic long-sleeved white blouse that completed the orchestra "uniform" worn by its female members. The blouse was made of a slick knit jersey, and there'd be no sweaters to hide behind, no bulkiness to disguise the way the slippery fabric conformed to her frame.

She was at the piano, limbering up her fingers with chromatic scales, when the shopping trio returned.

Jeff was bellowing her name as he opened the door and followed his ears to the living room. He reached over her shoulder and tapped out the melody line to "Jingle Bells," then sashayed on through the living room with two crackling sacks on his arm, followed by Amy, also bearing packages. By the time the pair exited to hide their booty, Brian stood in the opposite doorway, his cheeks slightly brightened by the winter air outside, jacket unzipped and pulling open as he paused with one hand in his back pocket, the other surrounding a brown paper sack. His eyes were startlingly attractive as the dark lashes dropped, and he glanced at Theresa's hands on the keyboard.

"Play something," he requested.

Immediately she folded her palms between her knees. "Oh, I was only limbering up for tonight."

He moved a step closer. "Limber up some more, then."

"I'm limbered enough."

He crossed behind her toward the davenport, and her eyes followed over her shoulder. "Good, then play a song."

"I don't know rock."

"I know. You're a classy person." He grinned, set his package down on the davenport and drew off his jacket, all the while keeping his eyes on her. She pinched her knees tighter against her palms. "I meant to say, you're a classical person," he amended with a lazy grin. "So play me a classic."

She played without sheet music, at times allowing her eyelids to drift closed while her head tipped back, and he caught glimpses of her enraptured eloquent face. When her eyelids opened she focused on nothing, letting her gaze drift with seeming unawareness. He had little doubt that while she played, Theresa forgot he stood behind her. He dropped his eyes again to her hands—fragile, long-fingered, with delicate bones at wrist and knuckle. How supplely they moved, those wrists arching gracefully, then dropping as she weaved backward, then forward. Once she smiled, and her head tipped to one side as the pianissimo chords tinkled from her fingertips while she inhabited that captivating world he knew and understood so well.

Watching the language of her hands, her body, was like having the song not only put into words but illustrated as well. He sensed that within Theresa the music acted as bellows to embers and saw what passions lay hidden within the woman whose normally shy demeanor never hinted at such smoldering fires.

By the time the song ended and Theresa's hands poised motionless above the keys, he was certain her heart must be pounding as heavily as his own.

He laid a hand on her shoulder and she jerked, as if waking up.

"That's very nice," he praised softly, and she became conscious of that warm hand resting where the strap of her bra cut a deep, painful groove into her flesh. "I seem to remember an old movie that used that as its theme song."

"The Eddy Duchin Story."

The hand slipped away, making her wish it had stayed. "Yes, that was it. Tyrone Power and…" She heard his fingers fillip beside her ear and swung around on the bench to face him, again tucking her palms between her knees.

"Kim Novak."

"That's it. Kim Novak." He noted her pose, the way she rounded her shoulders to minimize the prominence of her breasts, and it took an effort for him to keep his eyes on her face.

"It's Chopin. One of my favorites."

"I'll remember that. Chopin. Do you play Chopin tonight, too?"

He stood very close to her, and Theresa raised her eyes to meet his gaze. From this angle, the shoulder-to-shoulder seam across his white jersey made his torso appear inordinately broad and tapered. His voice was honey smooth and soft. Most of the time he spoke that way, which was a balm to her ears after the affectionate grate of Jeff's clamorousness and her mother's usual bawling forte.

"No, tonight we do all Christmas music. I believe we're starting with 'Joy to the World' and then a little-known French carol. We follow that with…" She realized he probably couldn't care less what they were playing tonight, and buttoned her lip.

"With?"

"Nothing. Just the usual Christmas stuff."

She was becoming rattled by his nearness and the studied way he seemed to be itemizing her features, as if listing them selectively in credit and debit columns within his head. She suddenly wished she knew how to apply makeup as cleverly as Amy, picturing her colorless eyelashes, and her too-colorful cheeks, knowing Brian could detect her many shortcomings altogether too clearly at such close range.

"I have to peel potatoes for supper." Having dredged up

that excuse, she slid off the bench and escaped to the kitchen, where she donned a cobbler's apron to protect her white blouse as she worked.

A short time later her mother and father returned from work, and in the suppertime confusion, the quiet moment with Brian slipped to the back of Theresa's mind. But as she prepared to flee the house with her violin case under the arm of her gray coat, she came to a halt in the middle of the kitchen. There stood Brian with a dish towel in his hands, and Amy, with her arms buried in suds, having uttered not a word of her usual complaints at having the job foisted on her.

"I'm sorry I had to eat and run, but we have to be in our chairs ready to tune up by six forty-five."

Jeff was on the phone, talking with Patricia. "Just a minute—" He broke off, and lowered the receiver. "Hey, sis, do good, okay?"

She gave him a thumbs-up sign with one fat, red mitten as she headed toward the door, found it held open by Brian, his other hand buried inside a dish towel and glass he'd been wiping.

"Good luck," he said softly, his green eyes lingering upon her in a way that resurrected the closeness she'd shared at the piano earlier. The cold air rushed about their ankles, but neither seemed to notice as they gazed at each other, and Theresa felt as if Chopin's music was playing within her heart.

"Thanks," she said at last. "And thanks for taking over for me with the dishes."

"Anytime." He smiled, grazed her chin with a touch so light she wondered if she'd imagined it as she turned into the brisk night that cooled her heated cheeks.

The annual Christmas concert of the Burnsville Civic Orchestra was held each year at the Burnsville Senior High School auditorium. The risers were set up and the curtains left open and the musicians made their way to their places amid the metallic premusic of clanking stands and metal folding chairs. The conductor arrived and tuning began. The incessant drone of the A-note filled the vaulted space of the auditorium, and gradually, the room hummed with voices as the seats slowly filled. The footlights were still off, and from her position at first chair Theresa had a clear view of the aisles.

She was running her bow over the honey-colored chunk of resin when her hand stopped sawing, and her lips fell open in surprise. There, filing in, came her whole family, plus Patricia Gluek, and of course, Brian Scanlon. They shuffled into the fourth row center and began removing jackets and gloves while Theresa's palms went damp. She had played the violin since sixth grade and had stopped having stage fright years ago, but her stomach drew up now into an unexpected coil of apprehension. Amy waggled two fingers in a clandestine hello, and Theresa answered with a barely discernible waggle of her own. Then her eyes scanned the seat next to Amy and found Brian waggling two fingers back at her. *Oh, Lord, did he think I waved at him?* Twenty-five years old and waving like her giggling first graders did when they spotted their mommies and daddies in the audience.

But before she could become any further unnerved by the thought, the footlights came up, and the conductor tapped his baton on the edge of the music stand. She stiffened her spine and pulled away from the backrest of the chair, snapped her violin into place at the lift of the black-clad arms and hit the opening note of "Joy to the World."

Midway through the song Theresa realized she had never played the violin so well in her life, not that she could remember. She attacked the powerful notes of "Joy to the World" with robust precision. She nursed the stunning disso-nants of "The Christmas Song" with loving care until the tension eased from the chords with their familiar resolutions. As lead violinist, she performed a solo on the compelling "I Wonder As I Wander," and the instrument seemed to come alive beneath her mocha-colored fingernails.

She began by playing for him. But she ended playing for herself, which is the true essence of the real musician. She forgot Brian sat in the audience and lost the inhibitions that claimed her whenever there was no instrument beneath her fingers or no children to direct.

From the darkened house, he watched her—nobody but her. The red hair and freckles that had been so distracting in their brilliance when he'd first met her took on an appropriateness lent by her fiery zeal as she dissolved into the music. Again, there were times when her eyelids drifted shut. Other times she smiled against the chin rest, and he was somehow certain she had no idea she was smiling. Her sleeves draped as she bowed the instrument, her wrist arched daintily as she occasionally plucked it, and the hem of her black skirt lifted and fell as she tapped her toe to the sprightlier songs.

The concert ended with a reprise of "Joy to the World," and the final thunder of applause brought the orchestra members to their feet for a mass bow.

When the house lights came up, Theresa's eyes scanned the line of familiar faces in row four, but returned to settle and stay on Brian, who had lifted his hands to praise her in the traditional way, and was wearing a smile as proud as any on the other faces. She braved a wide smile in return and hoped he knew it was not for the others but just for him. He stopped clapping and gave her the thumbs-up signal, and she felt a holiday glow such as she'd never known as she sat to tuck her instrument back into its case.

They were waiting in the hall when she came from the music room with her coat and mitts on, her case beneath an arm.

Everybody babbled at once, but Theresa finally had a chance to croon appreciatively, "Why didn't you *tell* me you were coming?"

"We wanted to surprise you. Besides, we thought it might make you nervous."

"Well, it did! No, it didn't! Oh, I don't know what I'm saying, except it really made the concert special, knowing you were all out there listening. Thanks, all of you, for coming."

Jeff looped an elbow around Theresa's neck, faked a headlock and a punch to the jaw and grunted, "You did good, sis."

Margaret took command then. "We have a tree to decorate yet tonight, and you know how your father always has trouble with those lights. Let's get this party moving home!"

They headed toward the parking lot, and Theresa invited, "Does anybody want to ride with me?" She could sense Amy reserving her reply until she heard what Brian answered.

"I will," he said, moving to Theresa's side and taking the violin case from her hands.

"I will, too—" Amy began, but Margaret cut her off in mid-sentence.

"Amy, you come with us. I want you to run into the store for a carton of milk on our way home."

"Jeff? Patricia?" Theresa appealed, suddenly feeling as if she'd coerced Brian into saying yes, since nobody else had.

"Patricia left her purse in the station wagon, so we might as well ride with them."

The two groups parted, and as she walked toward her little gray Toyota, Theresa suddenly suspected that Patricia had had her purse with her all along.

In the car she and Brian settled into the low bucket seats and Theresa turned on the radio. Rachmaninoff seemed to envelope them. "Sorry," she offered, and immediately pushed the button for another station. Without hesitation, he reset it to the original station and the dynamic Concerto in C-sharp Minor returned.

"I get the idea you think I'm some hard-rock freak. Music is music. If it's good, I like it."

They drove through the moonlit night with the power and might of Rachmaninoff ushering them home, followed by the much mellower poignance of Listz's "Liebestraum." As its flowing sweetness touched her ears, Theresa thought of its English translation, "Dream of Love." But she kept her eyes squarely on the road, thinking herself fanciful because of the residual ebullience of the performance and the occasional scarlet, blue and gold lights that glittered from housefronts as they passed. In living-room windows Christmas trees winked cheerfully, but it wasn't just the trees, it wasn't just the lights, it wasn't just the concert and not even Jeff's being home that made this Christmas more special than most. It was Brian Scanlon.

"I saw your foot tapping," he teased now.

"Oh?"

"Sure sign of a dancer."

"I'm still thinking about it."

"Good. Because I never get to dance much anymore. I'm always providing the music."

"Never fear. If I don't go, there'll be plenty of others."

"That's what I'm afraid of. Rhythmless clods who'll abuse my toes and talk, talk, talk in my ear."

"You don't like to talk when you dance?" Somehow she'd always imagined dancers using the close proximity to exchange intimacies.

"Not particularly."

"I've been led to believe that's when men and women whisper...well, what's known as *sweet nothings*."

Brian turned to study her face, smiling at the old-fashioned phrase, wondering if he knew another woman who'd use it. *"Sweet nothings?"*

She heard the grin in his voice, but kept her eyes on the street. "I have no personal knowledge of them myself, you understand." She gave him a quarter glance and lifted one eyebrow.

"I understand. Neither do I."

"But I'll give it some thought."

"I already have. Sounds like not a half-bad idea."

She felt as if her face would light up the interior of the car, for it struck Theresa that while she had no knowledge of sweet nothings, she and Brian were exchanging them at that very moment.

They made it home before the others, and Theresa excused herself to go to her room and change into jeans, blouse and loose-thrown sweater again. From the living room she heard the soft, exploratory notes of the piano as a melody line from a current rock hit was picked out with one finger. She came down the hall and paused in the living-room doorway. Brian stood before the piano, one thumb hooked in the back pocket of his pants while he lackadaisically pressed the keys with a single forefinger. He looked up. She crossed her arms. The piano strings vibrated into silence. She noticed things about him that she liked—the shape of his eyebrows, the way his expression said *smile* when there really was none there, his easy unhurried way of speaking, moving, shifting his eyes, that put her much more at ease the longer she was with him.

"I enjoyed the concert."

"I'm glad."

"My first live orchestra."

"It's nothing compared to the Minneapolis Orchestra. You should hear them."

"Maybe I will sometime. Do they play Chopin?"

"Oh, they play everything! And Orchestra Hall is positively sensational. The acoustics are world acclaimed. The ceiling is made of big white cubes of all sizes that look like they've been thrown up there and stuck at odd angles. The notes come bouncing off the cubes and—" She had looked up, as if expecting the living-room ceiling to be composed of the same cubes she described, not realizing that she looked very girlish and appealing in her animation, or that she had thrown her arms wide.

When her eyes drifted down, she found Brian grinning in amusement.

The kitchen door burst open and the noise began again.

When the Brubaker family decorated their Christmas tree, the scene was like a three-ring circus, with Margaret its ringmaster. She doled out commands about everything: which side of the tree should face front, who should pick up the trail of needles left scattered across the carpet, who should fill the tree stand with water. Poor Willard had trouble with the tree lights, all right, but his biggest trouble was his wife. "Willard, I want you to move that red light so it's underneath that branch instead of on top of it. There's a big hole here."

Jeff caught his mother by the waist, swung her around playfully and circled her arms so she couldn't move, then plopped a silencing kiss on her mouth. "Yes, his little turtledove. Shut up, his little turtledove," Margaret's tall son teased, gaining a smile in return.

"You're not too big to spank yet, Jeffrey. Talking to your mother like that." But her grin was as wide as a watermelon slice. "Patricia, get this boy off my back." Patricia made a lunge at Jeff and the two ended up in a heap on the sofa, teasing and tickling.

Margaret had turned on the music in the living room, but while she played Christmas music, Amy's bedroom was thumping with rock, and though the door was closed, the sound came through to confuse the issue. Jeff sang with one or the other in his deep, gravelly voice, and before they got to the tinsel, the phone had rung no less than four times—all for Amy.

Brian might have felt out of place but for Patricia's being an outsider, too. When it was time to distribute the tinsel, she was given a handful, just as he was, and protesting that it was *their* tree would have sounded ungracious, so he found himself beside Theresa, hanging shimmering silver icicles on the high branches while she worked on the lower ones. Jeff and Patricia had taken over the other half of the tree while the two elder Brubakers sat back and watched this part of the decorations, and Amy talked on the phone, interrupting herself to offer some sage bit of direction now and then.

They ended the evening with hot apple cider and cinnamon rolls around the kitchen table. By the time they finished, it was nearing eleven o'clock. Margaret stood up and began stacking the dirty cups and saucers.

"Well, I guess it's time I get Patricia back home," Jeff announced. "Do you two want to ride along?"

Brian and Theresa both looked up and spoke simultaneously.

"No, I'll stay here and clean up the mess."

"I don't feel like going out in the cold again."

Theresa took over the task her mother had begun. "You're tired, Mom. I'll do that."

Margaret desisted thankfully and went off to bed with

Willard, ordering Amy to retire also. When the door closed behind Jeff and Patricia, the kitchen was left to Theresa and Brian. She carried the dishes to the counter and filled the sink with sudsy water and began washing them.

"I'll dry them for you."

"You don't have to. There are just a few."

Overruling her protest, he found the dish towel and stood beside her at the sink. She was conscious that he was comfortable with silence, unlike most people. He could go through long stretches of it without searching for ways to fill it. The music was off. Jeff's teasing was gone, and Margaret's incessant orders. Only the swish of water and the clink of glassware could be heard. It took them less than five minutes to wash and dry the cups and saucers and put the room in order. But while five minutes of silence beside the wrong person can be devastating, that same five beside the right man can be totally wonderful.

When she'd hung up the wet cloths and switched out all the lights except the small one over the stove, she found a bottle of lotion beneath the sink and squirted a dollop in her palm, aware of Brian watching silently as she worked the cherry-scented cream into her hands.

"Let's sit in the living room for a while," he suggested.

She led the way and sat down on one end of the davenport while he sat at the other, leaning back and draping his palms across his abdomen, much as he had in the theater. Again silence fell. Again it was sustaining rather than draining. The tree lights made Theresa feel as if she was on the inside of a rainbow looking out.

"You have a wonderful family," he said at last.

"I know."

"But I begin to see why your dad needs to spend some quiet time with the birds."

Theresa chuckled softly. "It gets a little raucous at times. Mostly when Jeff's around."

"I like it, though. I don't ever remember any happy noise around my house."

"Don't you have any brothers and sisters?"

"Yeah, one sister, but she's eight years older than me, and she lives in Jamaica. Her husband's in exporting. We were never very close."

"And what about your mom and dad? I mean, your real dad. Were you close to them?"

He stared at the tree lights and ruminated at length. She liked that. No impulsive answers to a question that was important. "A little with my dad, but never with my mother."

"Why?"

He rolled his head and studied her. "I don't know. Why are some families like yours and some like mine? If I knew the answer and could bottle it, I could stop wars."

His answer made her turn to meet his eyes directly—such stunning, spiky-lashed beauties. She was struck again by the fact that such pretty eyes somehow managed to make him even more handsome. In them the tree lights were reflected—dots of red and gold and green and blue shining from beneath chestnut eyebrows and lashes, studying her without a smile.

His steady gaze made Theresa short of breath.

There were things inside this man that spoke of a depth of character she was growing surely to admire. Though he was really Jeff's senior by only two years, he seemed much older than Jeff—much older than her, too, she thought. Perhaps losing one's family does that to a person. It suddenly struck Theresa how awesome it must be to have no place to call home. She herself had clung to home far longer than was advisable. But she was a different matter. Brian would leave the Air Force next summer, and there would be no mother waiting with pumpkin pies in the freezer. No familiar bedroom where he could lie on his back and consider what lay ahead, while the familiar lair secured him to the past. No siblings to tease or go Christmas shopping with. No old girlfriend waiting with open arms....

But how did she know? The thought was sobering. She suddenly wanted to ask if there was a woman somewhere who was special to him, but didn't want to sound forward, so she veiled the question somewhat.

"Isn't there anyone left behind in Chicago?"

The smile was absent, but why did it feel as if he was charming her with the twinkle in his eye? "Since we've already eliminated parents and sisters and brothers, you must mean girlfriends." She dropped her eyes and hoped the red tree lights camouflaged the heat she felt creeping up her neck. "No, there are no girlfriends waiting in Chicago."

"I didn't mean—"

"Whether you did or not doesn't matter. Maybe I just wanted you to know."

The silence that followed was scarcely comfortable, quite unlike that which had passed earlier. It was filled with a new, tingling two-way awareness and a thousand other unasked questions.

"I think I'll say good-night now," he announced quietly, surprising Theresa. She wasn't *totally* naive. She'd sat on living-room davenports with those of the opposite sex before, and after a lead-in like Brian's, the groping always followed.

But he rose, stretched and stood with his fingers in his hip pockets while he studied the tree a minute longer. Then he studied her an equal length of time before raising a palm and murmuring softly, "Good night, Theresa."

Chapter 4

Brian Scanlon lay in bed, thinking about Theresa Brubaker, considering what it was that attracted him to her. He'd never cared much for redheads. Yet her hair was as orange as that of a Raggedy Ann doll, and her freckles were the color of overripe fruit. When she blushed—and she blushed often—she tended to glow like the Christmas tree.

Brian had been playing in a band since high school. In every dance crowd there were women who couldn't resist a guitar man when he stepped down from the stage at break time. They flocked around like chickens to scattered corn. He'd had his share. But he'd always gone for the blondes and brunettes, the prettiest ones with artful makeup and hair down to the middle of their backs, swinging like silk—women who knew their way around men.

But Theresa Brubaker was totally different from them. Not only did she look different, she acted different. She was honest and interesting, intelligent and loving. And totally naive, Brian was sure.

Yet so much heart lay beneath that naivety. It surfaced whenever she was around her family, particularly Jeff, and whenever she was around music. Brian recalled her voice, when the three of them had been harmonizing in the car, and the verve she radiated when playing the violin and the piano. Why, she even had him listening to classical music with a new, tolerant ear. The poignant strains of the Chopin Nocturne came back to him as he crossed his wrists behind his head in the dark and thought of how she'd looked in the long black skirt and white blouse. The blouse had, for once, been covered by no sweater.

He wondered how a man ever got up the nerve to touch breasts like hers. When they were that big, they weren't really…sexy. Just intimidating. He'd been scared to death the first time he'd felt a girl's breasts, but since then he'd touched countless others, and still the idea of caressing Theresa's breasts gave him serious qualms. There'd been times when he'd managed to study them covertly, but Theresa allowed few such opportunities, covered as she usually was with her cardigans. But when she'd been playing the piano, he'd stood behind her and looked down at the mountainous orbs beneath her blouse, and his mouth had gone dry instead of watering.

Forget it, Scanlon. She's not your type.

The next morning, when Brian arose at his usual wake-up hour and crept barefoot upstairs to the bathroom, he came face-to-face with Theresa in the hall.

They both stopped short and stared at each other. He wore a pair of blue denim jeans, nothing else. She wore a mint-green bathrobe, nothing else. There wasn't a sound in the house. Everyone else was still asleep, for it was Christmas Eve day so neither of her parents had to go to work.

"Good morning," she whispered. The bathroom door was right beside them.

"Good morning," he whispered back. Her feet were bare, and it was obvious even without a glance that her breasts were untethered beneath the velour robe, for they drooped nearly to her waist while she lifted her arms and pretended the zipper needed closing at her throat.

"You can go first," she offered, gesturing toward the doorway.

"No, no, you go ahead. I'll wait."

"No, I…really, I was just going to put on a pot of coffee first."

He was about to raise another objection when she swept past him toward the kitchen, so he hurried into the bathroom, taking care of necessities without wasting time, then heading for the kitchen to tell her the room was free. She was standing before the stove waiting for the coffee to start perking when he padded up silently beside her.

The sun wasn't up yet, but it had lightened the sky to an opalescent gray that lifted over the east windowsills of the kitchen, providing enough light for Theresa to see very clearly the dark hair springing from Brian's bare chest and diving into his waistline like an arrow. His nipples were like twin raspberries, shriveled up in the centers of squarely defined muscles. The only bare chests she'd ever seen in this house had been Jeff's and her father's. But this one was nothing like either of theirs, and the sight of him brought to mind vivid scenes from the movie they'd seen two nights ago. She dropped her eyes after the briefest glance, but down below she encountered more hair—dark wisps on his big toes. And suddenly she couldn't stand there beside him a moment longer, with him only half dressed and her coming totally unstrung inside her mint-green robe.

"Would you mind watching the coffee till it starts perking, then turn it down to low?"

In the bathroom she switched on the light above the vanity and checked her reflection in the mirror. Sure enough, beet red! That horribly unflattering red that made her look as if she was going to go off like a Fourth of July rocket. She pressed her palms to her cheeks, closed her eyes and wondered how it felt to be *normal* and come up against a half-naked man like Brian Scanlon in your kitchen.

Lordy, he flustered her so.

What do other women do? How do they handle the first attraction they feel? It must be so much easier when you're fourteen, like Amy, and you go at the natural pace: a first exchange of glances, a first touch of hands, a first kiss, then nubility taking over as boy and girl together begin exploring their awakening sexuality.

But I was thwarted at square one, Theresa thought miserably, looking at her awful freckles and hair, which by themselves would have been enough to overcome without the other even greater obstacles. *I was cheated by nature out of those first kittenish glances that might have led to all the rest, because all the first glances I ever received contained no more than shock or lasciviousness. And now here I am, midway through my twenties, and I don't know how to handle my very first sexual attraction to a man.*

She took a bath, washed her hair and didn't reenter the kitchen until she was properly dressed in a color she wore defiantly—cranberry. She loved it, but when it got anywhere near her hair, the two hues went to war and made her look like beets and carrots mixed in the same bowl. She had to keep the cranberry corduroy slacks separated from her flaming hair by a band of neutral color across her torso. When she explored her closet, she came upon a wonderful white sweatshirt Amy had given her for Christmas last year, which Theresa had never worn, no matter how many times she'd been tempted. To the average woman the sweatshirt would have been absolutely dishwater plain. It had hand-warmer pockets on the belly, zipper up the front and two sport stripes running down the sleeves: one of navy, the other of cranberry.

She took it from the hanger, slipped her arms into it and stepped before her mirror while she zipped it up. But the reflection that met her eyes made her want to cry. It looked like two dirigibles had been inflated beneath the garment. There was no power on earth that could make her wear this thing out to the kitchen and face Brian.

Angrily, she jerked it off and tossed it aside, replacing it with a prim oxford-cloth shirt in off-white with long sleeves and a button-down collar, over which she draped the everlasting, hated cardigan.

She was saved from encountering Brian's bare chest again, when she heard him take over the bathroom while she was arranging her hair in a round mound just above her collar. When it was confined, at least it didn't look as if it was going to carry her away into the wild blue yonder if a stiff wind came up.

In the bathroom, Brian, too, assessed himself in the mirror. *She's scared of you, Scanlon, so the issue is settled. You don't have to think about the possibilities of falling for her.*

But the room was scented with feminine things—the flowery essence of soap left behind in the damp air. There was a wet washcloth over the shower-curtain rod, and when he grabbed it down to close the curtains, he found himself staring at it for a long moment while he rubbed a thumb across the cold, damp terry cloth. With an effort, he put her from his mind and folded the cloth very carefully, then laid it on a corner of the tub. But while he stood beneath the hot spray, soaping his body, he thought of her again, and of the movie, and couldn't help wondering what it would be like in bed with that freckled body, the generous breasts and red hair.

Scanlon, it's Christmas, you pervert! What the hell are you doing standing here thinking about your best friend's sister like some practiced lecher?

But that's not the only reason I can't get her off my mind, his other self argued honestly. *She's a beautiful* person. *Inside, where it counts.*

He intentionally kept things light and breezy when he met Theresa in the kitchen again. But it was easier, for the rest of her family was beginning to rouse, and one by one they padded out to have coffee or juice. By the time they all sat down to breakfast together, the day had changed mood.

It was set aside for preparations. There was a family gathering planned at Grandma and Grandpa Deering's house, and everybody would take something for the supper buffet. Then tomorrow, the pack would descend upon the Brubaker house for Christmas dinner, so Margaret, Theresa and Amy were busy all day in the kitchen.

Margaret was at her dictatorial best, issuing orders like a drill-team sergeant again while her daughters carried them out. Willard spent part of the day watching for cardinals, while Jeff and Brian broke out their guitars at last, and from the kitchen Theresa heard her first of Brian's guitar playing. She dropped what she was doing and moved to the living-room doorway, pausing there to observe him tuning, then fingering an augmented chord of quietly vibrating quality, bending his head low over the instrument, listening intently as the six notes shimmered into silence. He sat at the piano bench, but had swung to face the davenport where Jeff sat, and didn't know Theresa stood behind him.

Jeff, too, strummed random chords, the two guitars quietly clashing in that presong dissonance that can be as musical in its own off-harmonic way as cleanly arranged songs.

Jeff played lead, Brian rhythm, and from the moment the discordant warm-up crystalized into the intro to a song, Theresa recognized a marvelous communion of kindred musicians. No signal had been spoken, none exchanged by eye, hand or tongue. The inharmonious gibberish of tuning had simply resolved into the concord of one single silently agreed-upon song.

Between musicians there can be a connection, just as between friends who somehow single each other out, recognizing empathy from the moment of introduction, just as a man and woman sometimes attract each other at first glimpse. It's something that cannot be prompted or dictated. Among members of a band this connection makes the difference between simply playing notes at the same time and creating an affinity of sound.

They had it, these two. There was almost a mystical quality about it, and as Theresa looked on and listened from the kitchen doorway, shivers ran up her arms and down her legs. They had picked up on "Georgia on My Mind." Where was the clashing rock? Where were the occasional sour chords she used to hear from Jeff's guitar? When had he gotten so *good?*

Neither Brian nor Jeff looked at each other while they played. Their heads were cocked lazily, eyes blankly turned to the waists of their guitars in that indolent, concentrative pose Theresa recognized well. How many times had she stood before Jeff and asked him a question when he was in such a trance, only to be separated from him by the wall of music until the song finished and he looked startled to find her standing there?

Jeff began to sing, his softly grating voice evocative of Ray Charles's immortal rendition of this song. A lump formed in Theresa's throat. Amy had come up silently behind her, and they stood as motionless as the hands of a sundial. Jeff "took a ride" at the break, and Theresa stared at his supple fingers running along the frets with an agility she'd never seen before. Pride blossomed in her heart. *Oh, Jeff, Jeff, my little brother, who started on that fifteen-dollar Stella in the corner, just listen to you now.* He vocalized the last verse, then together he and Brian "rode it home," and as the last poignant notes ebbed to fade-out, Theresa looked back over her shoulder into Amy's wide, amazed eyes. The room was silent.

Jeff's eyes met Brian's, and they exchanged smiles before they concurred, in their two deep voices, "All ri-i-ight."

"Jeffrey," Theresa said softly at last.

He glanced up in surprise. "Hey, Treat, how long have you been standing there?"

Brian swung around on the piano seat, and she gave him a passing smile of approval but moved to her brother, bending across his guitar to give him a hug. "When did you get so good?"

"You haven't heard me for over a year, closer to a year and a half. Brian and I have been hittin' it hard."

"Obviously."

She turned back to Brian. "Don't take me wrong, but I think you two were made for each other."

They all laughed, then Brian agreed, "Yeah, we kind of thought so the first time we picked a song together. It just happened, you know?"

"I know. And it shows."

Amy, with her hands jammed in her jeans pockets, inched closer to Brian's shoulders. "Gol, wait'll the kids hear this!"

Theresa couldn't resist the temptation to tease. "Is this Amy Brubaker speaking? The same Amy Brubaker who inundates us with AC/DC and scorns anything mellower?"

Amy shrugged, showed a flash of braces behind a half-sheepish grin, and returned, "Yeah, but these guys are really *excellent,* I mean, *wow.* And anyway, Jeff promised they'd do some rock, too. Didn't you, Jeffy?"

Instead of answering, Jeff struck a straight D chord, hard and heavy, with a dramatic flourish, and after letting it sizzle for a prolonged moment he met Brian's eye, and the next chord bit the air with the brashness of unvarnished rock. How they both knew the chosen song was a mystery. But one minute only Jeff's chord hung in the air, and the next they were hammering away at the song as if by divine design. Amy stood between them, getting into the beat with her hips. "Yeah…" she half growled, and Brian gave her a nonchalant quasi smile, then turned that same smile on Theresa, who shrugged in reply, a proud smile on her face while she enjoyed every note, rock or not, and each sideward thrust of Amy's hips.

When the song ended, Margaret and Willard were standing in the doorway, applauding. Amy rushed for the telephone, undoubtedly to rave on about the good tidings to as many friends as possible, and Theresa reluctantly returned to the kitchen to listen from there while she worked.

In the late afternoon, they all went to their respective rooms to change and get ready for the trip across town to Grandpa and Grandma Deerings'. When they rendezvoused in the kitchen to load the car, it was Margaret who suggested, "Why don't you bring your guitars? We'll do some caroling. You know how your grandparents enjoy it."

So the station wagon was packed with potato salad and cranberry jello, a vintage Gibson hollow-body 335 and a classic Epiphone Riviera, a rented amp, a stack of Christmas presents and six bodies.

Willard drove. Theresa found herself in the back seat sandwiched between Jeff and Brian. His hip was warm, even through her bulky coat, and when he and Jeff exchanged comments, she was served up tantalizing whiffs of his sandalwoody aftershave, for he'd slung an arm across the back of the seat and repeatedly leaned forward to peer around her.

If Brian thought he'd feel out of place at the family gathering, the delusion was put to rout within minutes of arriving.

The tiny house of mid-forties' vintage was popping at the seams with relatives of all ages and sizes. Grandpa Deering was deaf, and when Jeff took Brian over to introduce him to the shriveled little man, he shouted for his grandfather's benefit. "Grandpa, this is my friend, Brian, the one who's in the Air Force with me."

The old man nodded.

"I brought him home to spend Christmas with us," Jeff bawled at the top of his lungs.

Mr. Deering nodded again.

"We play in a band together, and we brought our guitars along tonight to do a few carols."

The bald head nodded still once more. Grandpa Deering raised a crooked forefinger in the air as if in approval, but said not a word until the two were turning away. Then he questioned in his reedy old quake, "This y'r friend who fiddles with you?"

It was all Brian could do to keep a straight face. Jeff turned back to his grandfather, leaning closer. "Guitar, grandpa, guitar."

The old man nodded and said no more, replaced his arthritic palms one on top of the other atop a black, rubber-tipped cane and seemed to drift into a reverie.

When Brian and Jeff turned away, Brian whispered in his friend's ear. "Doesn't his hearing aid work?"

"He turns it down whenever it's convenient. When the music starts he'll hear every note."

The thirty-odd aunts, uncles and cousins ate from a table containing more food than Brian had ever seen in one place, and after the buffet supper, opened gifts, having exchanged names at Thanksgiving. When it was time for the music, everyone found a spot as best he could on the floor, the kitchen cabinets, end tables, arms of furniture, and the entire group sang the old standard carols while Theresa was cajoled into playing along with the guitars on an ancient oak organ whose bellows were filled by foot pedals. She complied good-naturedly and pulled out the old stops from whose faces the mother-of-pearl inserts had long ago fallen. For the benefit of the small children in the group, Brian and Jeff were enticed into doing a run-through of "Here Comes Santa Claus," which evolved into a jazz rendition that would have shocked its composer, Gene Autry. Jeff took an impromptu ride, taking outrageous liberties with the melody line, ad-libbing arpeggios while Brian modified the chords to smooth, fluid jazz. When it was over, the house burst into whistles and clapping, and the youngsters called for "Jingle Bells." When that was finished, someone called, "Where's Margaret? Margaret, it's your turn. Get up there."

To Brian's surprise, the hefty-chested dictatorial Margaret stepped center front, and while her daughter played an accompaniment on the wheezy organ, she belted out a stunning "Oh Holy Night." When the song ended, and Theresa spun around on the seat of the claw-foot organ stool to face Brian's eyebrows raised in surprise, she leaned near his ear and whispered, "Mother was a mezzo-soprano with a touring opera company before she married Daddy."

"That leaves only Amy. What about her?"

From his far side, Amy spoke up. "I only got the beat, I didn't get the voice, so I play drums in the school band."

Brian smiled. "And dance, I'll bet."

"Yeah. Just wait and see."

Theresa knew a kind of keen envy. Amy could dance the socks off any three partners who tried to keep up with her. The sample she'd given earlier today in the living room had been only a hint of the rhythm contained in her svelte, teenage limbs. Theresa had always been extremely proud of Amy's dancing ability, and more so, her sister's lack of inhibition whenever any music started. While Theresa herself had felt a lifelong urge to dance, she'd never yielded to it.

She should have grown inured to giving up enjoyments such as dancing. By now, she shouldn't miss them, but she did. She transferred all her emotions into her music and took from it the satisfaction she was denied in other modes of self-expression, as she did now on this Christmas Eve.

She shunned the petty envy that she'd come to hate in

herself and lauded, "Amy is the best dancer I know. It's too bad she isn't old enough to go with you on New Year's Eve."

Brian only smiled from one sister to the other, hoping the older of the two would agree to go with him, after all.

On the way home they dropped Jeff off at Patricia's house, where another family celebration was winding down. Jeff would get in on the end of it. When the remainder of the group reached the Brubaker house, the two older ones toddled off to bed while the remaining three turned on the tree lights and sat in the cozy living room exchanging anecdotes about past Christmases, music, the Air Force, school dances, Grandpa Deering and a myriad of subjects that kept them up well past midnight. Jeff joined them then, announcing that he'd just flown in on his jet-propelled sleigh and was looking for a plate of cookies and glass of milk before he filled any stockings.

When Theresa went to sleep that night, it was not to visions of sugar plums dancing in her head, but to visions of Brian Scanlon's long, dexterous fingers moving along the fingerboard of an Epiphone Riviera, picking out the chords to a love song whose words she strove to catch.

On Christmas morning Theresa was awakened by Amy, pouncing on her bed, giggling. "Hey, come on! Let's make it to those prezzies!"

"Amy, it's blacker than the ace of spades outside."

"It's seven o'clock already!"

"Ohh!" Theresa groaned and rolled over.

"Come on, get your buns out of here and let's go get the boys and Mom and Dad."

From down the hall came a hoarse call. "Who's doin' all that giggling out there?" Jeff. "Come in here and try that!"

Amy sprang off Theresa's bed and went to wage an attack on her brother, and the squealing that followed told clearly of a bout of tickling which soon awakened Margaret and Willard. The thumping on the floor aroused their houseguest downstairs, and within ten minutes they had all gathered in the living room and snuggled around the Christmas tree, dressed in hastily thrown-on robes, jeans, half-buttoned shirts, bare feet and bedroom slippers, sipping juice and coffee while gifts were distributed.

Brian was sharing a Christmas unlike any he'd ever experienced. This boisterous, loving family was showing him depths he'd never known. The gifts exchanged among them underscored that love again, for they were not many but well chosen.

For Willard, his children had decided on a telescope that would take its place before the sliding glass door downstairs; for Margaret, a mother's ring that would take its place proudly on her right hand, and which prompted a listing of the three birthdays. Brian carefully marked in his memory the date of Theresa's. To Margaret and Willard together the children gave a gift certificate for a weekend at the quiet, quaint Schumaker's Country Inn in the tiny town of New Prague, an hour's ride from the Twin Cities.

From their parents, Jeff, Amy and Theresa received, respectively, a plane ticket home for Easter, a pair of tickets to an upcoming rock concert and a season ticket to Orchestra Hall.

To Brian's surprise, each of the Brubakers had bought a gift for him. From Margaret and Willard, a billfold; from Amy, guitar picks; from Jeff, a Hohner harmonica—they'd been fooling around on one at a music store, and Brian had said he'd always wanted to play one—and from Theresa, a recording of classical music, including Chopin's Nocturne in E-flat.

When he opened the last gift, he looked up in surprise. "How did you have time to find it on such short notice?"

"Secret." But her eyes danced to her father's, and Brian remembered Willard's leaving the house for "last-minute items" yesterday.

To Brian's relief, he, too, had brought gifts. For Mr. and Mrs. Brubaker, a selection of cheese and bottle of Chianti wine; for Amy, a pair of headphones, which brought a round of good-natured applause from the rest of the group; for Jeff, a wide leather guitar strap tooled with his name; and for Theresa, a tiny pewter figurine—a smiling frog on a lily pad, playing the violin.

She smiled, placed it on her palm and met Brian's irresistible green eyes across the living room.

"How did you know I collect pewter instruments?"

"Secret."

"My darling brother, who can't keep anything to himself. And for once, I'm happy he can't. Thank you, Brian."

"Thank you, too. You'll make a silk purse of this sow's ear yet." Which was ironic, for Brian was far, far from a sow's ear.

She studied the frog with its bulging pewter eyes and self-satisfied smile and lifted a similar smile to Brian. "I'll call him 'The Maestro.'"

The fiddling frog became one of Theresa's most cherished possessions, and took his place at the forefront of the collection shelved on a wall in her bedroom. It was the first gift she'd ever received from any male other than a family member.

That Christmas Day, filled with noise, food and family, passed in a blur for both Brian and Theresa. They were more conscious of each other than of any of the others in the house. The family ate and got lazy, ate again, and eventually their numbers began thinning. That lazy wind-down prompted dozing and eventually, an evening revival of energy. As most days did in this house where music reigned supreme, this one would have seemed incomplete without it. It was eight o'clock in the evening, and the crowd had dwindled to a mere dozen or so when out came the instruments, and it became apparent the family had their favorites, which they asked Jeff and Theresa to play. Margaret and Willard were nestled like a pair of teenagers on the davenport, and applauded and chose another and another song. Eventually, Brian and Jeff branched off into a rousing medley of rock songs, during which Theresa joined in on the piano. Then Jeff had the sudden inspiration, "Hey, Theresa, go get your fiddle!"

"Fiddle!" she spouted. "Jeffrey Brubaker, how dare you call great-grandmother's expensive Storioni a *fiddle*. Why, it's probably cringing in its case!"

Jeff explained to Brian. "She inherited her fiddle from one

of our more talented progenitors, who bought it in 1906. It's modeled after a Faratti, so Theresa is rather overzealous about the piece."

"Fiddle!" Theresa teased with a saucy twitch of the hip as she left the room. "I'll show you *fiddle,* Brian Scanlon!"

When the beautiful classic violin came back with Theresa, Brian was amazed to hear the sister and brother strike into an engaging, foot-stomping rendition of "Lou'siana Saturday Night," along with which he himself provided background rhythm, while he wondered in bewilderment how Theresa happened to know the song, so different from her classics. After that, the hayseed in all of them seemed to have stuck to their overalls, and Jeff tried a little flat picking on "Wildwood Flower," and by that time, the entire group had gotten rather punchy. The usually reserved Willard captured Margaret and executed an impromptu hoe-down step in the middle of the room, which brought laughter and applause, to say nothing of the sweat to Margaret's brow as she plopped into a chair, breathless and fanning her red face but totally exhilarated.

"Give us 'Turkey In The Straw'!" someone shouted.

Again Brian was shown a new facet of Theresa Brubaker, a first-chair violinist of the Burnsville Civic Orchestra, as she sawed away on her 1906 classic Storioni, scraping out a raucous version of the old barn-dance tune, in the middle of which she lowered the violin and tapped the air with the bow, the carpet with her toe and watched her mother and father circling and clapping in the small space provided, while in a voice as clear as daybreak, Theresa sang out:

Oh, I had a little chicken
And it wouldn't lay an egg
So I poured hot water up and down her leg
Then the little chicken hollered
And the little chicken begged
And the damn little chicken
Laid a hard-boiled egg.

She was joined by the entire entourage as they finished by bellowing in unison, "Boom-tee-dee-a-da…*slick chick!*"

Brian joined in the rousing round of applause and shrill whistles that followed. As he laughed with the others, he saw again the hidden Theresa who seemed able to escape only when wooed by music and those she loved most. She covered her pink-tinged cheeks with both hands, while the "fiddle" and bow still hung from her fingers and her laughter flowed, sweet and fresh as spring water.

She was unique. She was untainted. She was as refreshing as the unexpected burst of hayseed music that had just erupted from her grandmother's invaluable 1906 Storioni.

He watched Theresa bestowing hugs of goodbye on her aunts and uncles. She had forgotten herself and impulsively lifted her arms in farewell embraces. Already Brian knew how rare these moments of forgetfulness were with Theresa. Music made the difference. It took her to a plane of unselfconsciousness nothing else could quite achieve.

He turned away, wandered back to the deserted living room, wondering what it would take to make her feel such ease with him. He sat down on the piano bench and picked out a haunting melody, one of his favorites, with a single finger, then softly began adding harmony notes. Soon he was engrossed in the quiet melody as his hands moved over the keyboard.

The house quieted. Amy was in her room with the new headphones glued to her ears. Willard was downstairs setting up his new telescope. Margaret had gone to bed, exhausted.

There were only three left in the room where the tree lights glowed.

"What are you playing?" Theresa asked, pausing behind Brian's shoulder, watching his long fingers on the piano.

"An old favorite, 'Sweet Memories.'"

"I don't think I know it."

Jeff wandered in. "Play it for her." He swung the old Stella up by its neck, extending it toward Brian, who looked back over his shoulder, with a noncommittal smile. "Do old Stella a favor," Jeff requested whimsically.

Brian seemed to consider for a long moment, then nodded once, turned on the bench to face the room and reached for the scarred, old guitar. The first soft note sent a shudder up Theresa's spine.

Jeff sat on the edge of the davenport, leaning forward, elbows to knees, for one of those rare times when he didn't have a guitar in his hands. He simply sat and paid homage. To the song. His friend. And a voice that turned Theresa's nerve endings to satin.

She realized she had not heard Brian sing before. Not alone. Not…not…

It was a song whose eloquent simplicity brought tears to her eyes and a knot to her throat, tremors to her stomach and goose bumps to the undersides of her thighs as she sat on the floor before him.

My world is like a river
As dark as it is deep.
Night after night the past slips in
And gathers all my sleep.
My days are just an endless string
Of emptiness to me.
Filled only by the fleeting moments
Of her memory.
Sweet memories…
Sweet memories…

He hummed a compelling melody line at the end of the verse, and she watched his beautiful fingers, the tendons of his left thumb grown powerful from years of barring chords, the square-cut nails of his right hand plucking or strumming the steel strings.

She watched his eyes, which had somehow come to rest on her own as the words of the last verse came somberly from his sensitive lips.

She slipped into the darkness
Of my dreams last night.
Wandering from room to room
She's turning on each light.
Her laughter spills like water
From the river to the sea
Lord, I'm swept away from sadness
Clinging to her memory.

The haunting notes of the chorus came again, and Theresa
softly hummed in harmony.

Sweet memories...
Sweet memories...

She had crossed her calves, hooked them with her forearms
and drawn her knees up, raising her eyes to his. And as he
looked deeply into the brown depths, grown limpid with
emotion, Brian realized she was not some soulful groupie,
gazing up in adulation. She was something more, much more.
And as the song quietly ended, he realized he'd found the way
to break down Theresa's barriers.

The room rang with silence.

There were tears on Theresa's face.

Neither she nor Brian seemed to remember her brother was
there beside them.

"Who wrote it?" she asked in a reverent whisper.

"Mickey Newbury."

She was stricken to think there existed a man named Mickey
Newbury whose poignant music she had missed, whose words
and melodies spoke to the soul and whispered to the heart.

Since she could not thank the composer, she thanked the performer who had gifted her with an offering superseding any that
could be found wrapped in gay ribbons beneath a Christmas
tree.

"Thank you, Brian."

He nodded and handed the Stella back to Jeff. But Jeff had

quietly slipped from the room. Brian's gaze returned to Theresa, still curled up at his feet. Her hair picked up the holiday colors from the lights behind her, and only the rim of her lips and nose was visible in the semidarkened room.

He slipped from the piano bench onto one knee, bracing the guitar on the carpet, his hand sliding down to curl around its neck. He could not make out the expression in her eyes, though he sensed the time was right...for both of them. Her breathing was fast and shallow, and the scent he'd detected in the steamy bathroom seemed to drift from her skin and hair—a clean, fresh essence so different from the girls in smoky night spots. Bracing elbow to knee, he bent to touch her soft, unspoiled lips with his own. Her face was uplifted as their breaths mingled, then he heard her catch her own and hold it. The kiss was as innocent and uncomplicated as the Chopin Prelude, but the instant Brian withdrew, Theresa shyly inclined her head. He wanted a fuller kiss, yet this one of green, untutored innocence was oddly satisfying. And she wasn't the kind of woman a man rushed. She seemed scarcely woman at all, but girl, far less accomplished at the art of kissing than at the art of playing the violin and the piano. Her unpracticed kiss was suddenly more refreshing than any he'd ever shared.

He pushed back, straightened and intoned quietly, "Merry Christmas, Theresa."

Her eyes lifted to his face. Her voice trembled. "Merry Christmas, Brian."

Chapter 5

The week that followed was one of the happiest of Theresa's life. They had few scheduled duties, the city at their feet and money with which to enjoy it. She and Brian enjoyed being together, though they were rarely alone. Everywhere they went the group numbered four, with Jeff and Patricia along, or five, if Amy came, too, which she often did.

They spent an entire day at the new zoo, which was practically at their doorstep, located less than two miles away, on the east side of Burnsville. There they enjoyed the animals in their natural winter habitat, rode the monorail part of the time, then walked, ate hot dogs and drank hot coffee.

It was a sunless day, but bright, glittery with hoarfrost upon the surface of the snow. The world was a study in black and white. The oak branches startled the eye, so onyx-black against the backdrop of pristine landscape. The animals were sluggish, posed against the winter setting, their breaths rising in nebulous vapors, white on white. But the polar bears were up and about, looking like great shaggy pears with legs. Before their den, Theresa and Brian paused, arms on the rail, side by side. The bears lumbered about, coats pure and as colorless as the day. A giant male lifted his nose to the air, a single black blot against all that white.

"Look at him," Brian said, pointing. "The only things that are black are his eyes, lips, nose and toenails. On an arctic ice floe he becomes practically invisible. But he's smart enough to know how that nose shows. I once saw a film of a polar bear sneaking up on an unsuspecting seal with one paw over his nose and mouth."

It was a new side of Brian Scanlon: nature lover. She was intrigued and turned to study his profile. "Did it work?"

His eyes left the bears and settled on her. "Of course it worked. The poor seal never knew what hit her." Their eyes clung. Theresa grew conscious of the contact of Brian's elbow on the rail beside hers—warm, even through their jackets. His eyes made a quick check across her shoulder where the others stood, then returned to her lips before he began to close the space between them. But Theresa was too shy to kiss in public and quickly turned to study the bears. Her cheeks felt hot against the crisp air as Brian's gaze lingered for a moment before he straightened and said softly, "Another time."

It happened before the habitat of another animal whose coat had turned winter white. They were watching the ermine coats of the minks when Theresa turned toward Brian saying, "I don't think I could wear—"

He was only three inches away, encroaching, with a hand covering his nose and mouth, eyes gleaming with amused intent.

She smiled and pulled back. "What in the world are you doing?"

From underneath his glove came a muffled voice. "I'm trying the polar bear's sneaky tactics."

She was laughing when his glove slipped aside and swept around her, his two hands now holding her captive against a black railing. The quick kiss fell on her open lips. It was a failure of a kiss, as far as contact goes, for two cold noses bumped, and laughter mingled between their mouths. After the brief contact, he remained as he was, arms and body forming a welcome prison while she leaned backward from the waist, the rail pressed against her back and her hands resting on the front of his jacket.

"There, you see," she claimed breathily, "it didn't work. I saw you coming anyway."

"Next time you won't," he promised.

And she hoped he was right.

Patricia took them on a guided tour of Normandale College campus, beaming with pride at its rolling, wooded acres. They were walking along a curving sidewalk between two buildings with Patricia and Jeff in the lead, when Jeff's elbow hooked Patricia's neck and he hauled her close, kissing her as they continued ambling. Brian's eyes swerved to Theresa's, questioning. But Amy walked with them, and the moment went unfulfilled.

The following night they went to St. Paul's famed Science Omnitheater and lay back in steeply tilted seats, surrounded by an entire hemisphere of projected images that took them soaring through outer space, whizzing past stars and planets with tummy-tickling reality. But the dizzying sense of vertigo caused by the 180-degree curved screen seemed nothing compared to that created by Brian when he found Theresa's hand in the dark, eased close and reached his free hand to the far side of her jaw, turning her face toward his. The angle of the seats was severe, as if they were at a carnival, riding the bullet on its ascent before the spinning downward plunge. For a moment he didn't move, but lay back against his seat with the lights from the screen lining his face in flickering silver. His eyes appeared deep black, like those of the polar bear, and Theresa was conscious of the vast force of gravity pressing her into her chair and of the fact that Brian could not lift his head without extreme effort.

His forehead touched hers. Again their noses met. But their eyes remained open as warm lips touched, brushed, then gently explored this newfound anxiety within them both. There was a queer elation to the sense of helplessness caused by their positions. She wished they were upright so she could turn fully into his arms. But instead she settled for the straining of their bodies toward each other, and again, the unfulfilled wishes that grew stronger with each foray he initiated.

The elementary kiss ended with three teasing nibbles that caught, caught, caught her mouth and tugged sensuously before he lay back in his seat again, watching her face for a reaction.

"No fair making me dizzy," she whispered.

They were still holding hands. His thumb made forceful circles against her palm. "You sure it's not the movie?"

"I thought it was at first, but I'm much dizzier now."

He smiled, kept his eyes locked with hers as he lifted her hand and placed its palm against his mouth, wetting it with his tongue as he kissed it.

"Me, too," he breathed, then carried the hand to his lap and held it against his stomach, folded between his palms before he began stroking its soft skin with the tips of his callused fingers while he turned his attention back to the broad screen. She tried to do likewise, but with little success. For the interstellar space flight happening on the screen was vapid when compared to the nova created by Brian Scanlon's simplest kiss.

One evening Brian and Jeff provided the music for the promised rock session, to which Amy invited a mob of her friends. The house was inundated with noisy teenagers who gave their approval by way of prompt, rapt silence the moment the music began.

Theresa was cajoled into joining the two on piano, and before ten minutes were up, the boys and girls were dancing on the hard kitchen floor, after Margaret came through the living room decreeing, "No dancing on my carpet!" She seemed to forget she and her husband had danced a hoedown on it within the past week.

Still, the evening was an unqualified success, and at its end, Amy was basking in the reflected glow of "stardom," for all her friends went away assured that Jeff and Brian would be cutting a record soon.

The day following the party there were no plans made. All five of them were together in the living room, lounging and visiting. The stereo was tuned to a radio station, and when a familiar song come on, Brian unexpectedly lunged to his feet, announcing, "The perfect song to learn to dance to!" He exaggerated a courtly bow before Theresa and extended his hand. "We've got to teach this woman before Saturday night."

"What's Saturday night?" Amy asked.

"New Year's Eve," answered Patricia. "I've invited these two to join Jeff and me and a group of our friends."

Jeff added, "But your sister claims ignorance and has declined to go."

Theresa dropped her eyes from the hand Brian still held out in invitation. "Oh no, please. I can't..." She felt utterly foolish, not knowing how to dance at age twenty-five.

"No excuses. It's time you learned."

She replied with the most convenient red herring she could dream up on short noticc. "No dancing on thc carpct!"

"Oh, go ahead," Amy said, then admitted, "the girls and I dance on the carpet all the time when Mother's at work. I won't tell."

"There!" Theresa looked up at Brian, feeling her face had grown red. "Dance with Amy."

To Theresa's relief, Brian willingly complied. "All right." He directed his courtly gesture to the younger girl. "Amy, may I have this dance? We'll demonstrate for your reluctant sibling."

Amy's braces caught a flash of afternoon sun from the window as she beamed in unabashed delight. "I thought you'd never ask," she replied cheekily.

Looking on, Theresa felt years younger than Amy, who, at fourteen, could bound to her feet, come back with a coquettish response, then present her slim body for leading. Theresa wished she could be as uninhibited and self-confident as her younger sister. Jeff and Patricia joined in the demonstration, Jeff holding his partner stiffly and frowning. "Watch carefully now...a-one...a-two..."

As he always could, Jeff made Theresa laugh with his proficient clowning, for he held Patricia in a prim, stiff-backed, wide-apart mime of the traditional dance position, until the girl threw up her hands and declared laughingly, "You're a hopeless case, Brubaker. Find yourself another partner."

Jeff didn't ask, he commandeered. One minute Theresa was watching from the piano bench, the next she was on her feet, being sashayed around in Jeff's arms. Askance, she saw Brian watching her progress. In all honesty, Theresa had no delusions about being able to dance and dance gracefully. Now, with her brother, her natural rhythm couldn't be denied. Theresa's feet took over where her self-consciousness left off. Within a dozen bars, she was moving smoothly to the music.

She'd been hoodwinked—she realized it later—by Jeff and Brian, who'd probably been in cahoots the entire time; for she'd been following Jeff's lead no more than a minute when her hand was captured by Brian's. "I'm cutting in, Brubaker. Snowball time."

After that there seemed no question about New Year's Eve. And when Theresa surreptitiously took Patricia aside to ask what she was wearing, the issue seemed settled.

On Friday, Theresa knocked on Amy's door, but when she got no answer, she peeped inside to find her sister lying in a trancelike state, arms thrown wide, ankle draped over updrawn knee, eyes shut, with the black vinyl headset clamped around her skull.

Theresa went in, closed the door behind herself and touched Amy's knee.

Amy's eyes came open, and she lifted one earpiece from her head. "Hmm?"

"Would you take that thing off for a minute?"

"Sure." Amy flung it aside, braced up on both elbows. "What's up?"

"Hon, I have a really big favor to ask you."

"Anything—name it."

"I need you to come shopping with me."

Amy mused for a minute, then rolled to one hip, reaching for the controls to stop the music that was still filtering through the headphones. Then she sat up. "Shopping for what?"

Even before she asked, Theresa realized how ironic it was that she, the older, should be seeking the advice of a sister eleven years her junior. "Something to wear tomorrow night."

"You goin' to the dance?"

For a moment Theresa feared Amy might display an adolescent jealousy and wasn't sure how she'd deal with it. But when Theresa nodded, Amy bounded off the bed exuberantly. "Great! It's about time! When we goin'?"

An hour later the sisters found themselves in the Burnsville Shopping Center, scouring three levels of stores. In the first dressing room, Theresa slipped on a black crepe evening dress that gave her shivers of longing. But it was scarcely over her head before her perennial problem became all too evident: her bottom half was a size nine, but her top half would have required a size sixteen to girth her circumference.

Theresa looked up and met Amy's eyes in the mirror. They'd never before exchanged a single word about Theresa's problem. But, distraught, the older sister suddenly became glum and depressed. Her gaiety evaporated, and her expression wilted. "Oh, Amy, I'll never find a dress. Not with these damn, disgusting...*dirigibles* of mine!"

Amy's expression became sympathetic. "They make it tough, huh?"

Theresa's shoulders slumped. "Tough isn't the word. Do you know that I haven't been able to buy one single dress without altering it since I was the age you are now?"

"Yeah, I know. I...well, I asked Mom about it one time...I mean, if it's hard for you and stuff, and if...well, if I might get as big as you."

Theresa turned and placed her hands on Amy's shoulders. "Oh, Amy, I hope you never do. I worry about it, too. I wouldn't wish a shape like mine on a pregnant elephant. It's horrible—not being able to buy clothes and being scared to dance with a man and—"

"You mean, *that's* why you wouldn't dance with Brian?"

"That's the only reason. I just..." Theresa considered a

moment, then went on. "You're old enough to understand, Amy. You're fourteen. You've been growing. You know how the boys look at you funny as soon as you have a pair of goose bumps on your chest. Only when mine started growing they just kept right on until they got to the size of watermelons, and the boys were merciless. And when the boys were no longer boys, but men, well…" Theresa shrugged.

"I figured that was why you wear those ugly sweaters all the time."

"Oh, Amy, are they ugly?"

Amy looked penitent. "Gol, Theresa, I didn't mean it that way, I just meant…well, I know you never wore that neat sweatshirt I gave you last Christmas. It was way more *in* than anything you had—that's why I bought it for you."

"I've tried it on at least a dozen times, but I'm always scared to step out of my bedroom in it."

"Gol…" The word was a breathy lament as Amy stood pondering the everyday dilemmas her sister had to face. "Well, we could pick out something nice for tomorrow night if we got separate pieces, like a skirt and sweater or something."

"Not a sweater, Amy. I wouldn't be comfortable."

"Well, you can't go out for New Year's Eve in corduroy slacks and a white blouse with an old granny cardigan over your shoulders!"

"Do you think I *want* to?"

"Well…" Amy threw up her palms in the air. "*Horse poop,* there's got to be something in this entire shopping center that's better than *that*." She cast a scathing look at the fashionless shirt Theresa had discarded.

Theresa found her sense of humor again. "Horse *poop?* I suppose Mother doesn't know you say things like that, just like she doesn't suspect you dance on the living-room carpet?" Theresa knew perfectly well that at fourteen, Amy experimented with a gamut of profanity much worse than what she'd just uttered—she was at the age where such experiments were to be expected.

Suddenly the gleam in Amy's eyes duplicated the one from

her dental hardware. "Listen, what about the sweater? Don't say no until you try, okay?" She splayed her fingers in the air and gazed toward heaven, theatrically. "I have *theee* perfect one. *Theee* most *excellent* sweater ever created by sheep or test tube! I've had my eye on it since before Christmas, but I was outa bucks, so I couldn't get it for myself. But if they have one left in large, you're gonna love it!"

A quarter hour later, Theresa stood before a different mirror, in a different shop, in a different garment that solved all her problems while remaining perfectly in vogue.

It was a lightweight bulky acrylic of rich, deep plum. The neckline sported a generous cowl collar that seemed to become one with wide dolman sleeves. Because it draped rather than clung, it seemed to partially conceal Theresa's overly generous silhouette.

"Oh, Amy, it's perfect!"

"I told you!"

"But what about pants?"

Amy nabbed a pair of finely tailored gabardine trousers of indefinable color: soft, subtle, as if tinted by the smoke from burning violets. She stood back to assess her older sister and proclaimed in the most overused word of her teenage vernacular, *"Excellent."*

Theresa whirled around and grabbed her sister in a compulsive hug. "It is! It is excellent."

Amy beamed with pride, then took command again. "Shoes next. He's got a good six inches on you, so you could stand a little extra height. Some classy heels. Whaddya say?"

"Shoes...right!"

Theresa was pulling her head from beneath the sweater when she thought of the one last thing she'd need help with. "Amy, do you think I'd look too conspicuous if I tried a little bit of makeup?"

Amy's lips were covering her braces as Theresa asked, but her smile grew crooked, and wide, then winked in the glow of the dressing-room's overhead light fixture. "Well, it's about time!" she declared.

"Now, just a minute, Amy," Theresa said as she noted the gleam in her sister's eye. "I haven't decided for sure…."

But that evening, something happened that crystallized the decision. She was in her room, the door open as she was examining the new sweater, when she felt someone's eyes on her. She looked up to find Brian in the doorway, studying her. It was the first time he'd seen her bedroom, and his eyes made a lazy circle, pausing on the shelf holding her pewter figurine collection, then dropping to the bed, neatly made, and finally returning to Theresa, who had quickly replaced the sweater in the closet.

"Have I managed to change your mind about the dance yet?" He crossed his arms and nonchalantly leaned one shoulder against the door frame.

Theresa had never been honorably pursued before; it took some getting used to. It was disconcerting, having him peruse her bedroom, which seemed an intimate place to come face-to-face with a man. She'd turned toward him, and he remained very still, one hip cocked as he lounged comfortably and kept his eye on her. *Do I look him in the eye? Or in the middle of his chest? Or at some spot beyond his shoulder? Twenty-five years old and acting less self-confident than I'm sure Amy would act in this situation.* She chose the middle of his chest.

"Yes, you have, but don't expect me to dance as well as Amy."

"All I'll expect is that at some point during the evening, you'll at least look me in the eye."

Her unsettled gaze flew up to his, caught a teasing grin there and dropped again, flustered.

"So this is where you hide away." As he moved farther into the room, he nodded toward the shelf. "I see The Maestro has joined the others. I envy him his spot, looking down on your pillow." He stopped close before her.

She searched but could find not a single reply and swallowed hard, feeling the blush creep up.

"Jeff was right, you know?" Brian teased softly.

She raised questioning eyes to his teasing green ones.

"R...right? About what?"

"The blush camouflages the freckles. But don't ever stop."
With a gentle fingertip he brushed her right cheek. "It's completely irresistible." Then he turned and sauntered off down the
hall, leaving Theresa with her fingertips grazing the spot of
skin he'd so lightly touched. It seemed to tingle yet. The touch
had been petal light, but she'd felt the calluses on his fingertips. Both the sensation and his teasing had left her with a light
head and a fluttering heart.

That night, late, Theresa tapped softly at Amy's door, then
went in to announce, "I'm going to need your help learning
how to put on makeup, and I'll have to borrow some of yours,
if you don't mind."

Amy's only answer was a beam of approval as she
dragged Theresa farther into the room and shut the door with
a decisive click.

They did a trial run that lasted till the wee hours. Sitting
before a lighted makeup mirror in Amy's room, Theresa experienced the full range of giddy adolescent give-and-take
she'd missed out on when she'd been at the age of puberty. The
makeup session brought a twofold benefit: not only did it free
the butterfly from the chrysalis, it also brought the two sisters
closer. Given the disparity in their ages, they'd had little chance
to share experiences of this kind.

Amy began by experimenting with foundation colors, trying
a rainbow of skin tones on various sections of Theresa's face until
the redhead declared, "I look like a Grandma Moses painting!"

Assessing, Amy corrected, "No, more like her palette, I
think." They shared a laugh, then went to work finding the right
hue that skillfully camouflaged the freckles and gave Theresa
a new, subdued radiance.

Next came the eyes, but as Amy bent over Theresa's shoulder
and peered critically in the mirror at the blue grease they'd
smeared on one freckled eyelid, they burst out laughing once
more.

"Yukk! Get it off! It feels like lard and looks like I took
a beating."

"Agreed!"

Next they tried a green powder-base eyeshadow, but it made Theresa look like a stop-and-go light, so off it went, too. They settled on an almost translucent mauve that had so little color it couldn't clash with the skin and hair tones that needed to be catered to.

The first time Theresa tried to use the eyelash curler, she pinched her eyelid and yelped in pain.

"This is like trying to curl the hair on a caterpillar's back!" she despaired. "There's nothing there. I hate my eyelashes anyway. They have as much color as a glass of water."

"We'll fix that."

But the tears rolled from beneath her abused lids, and it took several long, painful minutes before Theresa got the hang of the curler, then learned how to brush her lashes with a mascara wand. The results, however, surprised even herself.

"Why, I never knew my lashes were so long!"

"That's 'cause you never saw the ends of 'em before."

They were a total wonder—quite spiky and alluring and made her whole face look bright and...and sexy!

The powdered blush proved an absolute disaster. They swabbed it off faster than they'd brushed it on, deciding Theresa's natural coloring couldn't compete with added high-lighting, and decided to stick with the foundation hue only.

Theresa had always worn lip gloss, but now they tried several new shades, and Amy demonstrated how to skillfully blend two colors and accent the pretty bowed shape of her sister's upper lip with a highlighter stick.

With the makeup complete, Theresa appeared transformed. It was a drastic change but one that made her smile at Amy in the mirror.

Yet, Amy wasn't totally pleased. "That hair," Amy grunted in disgust.

"Well, I can't change the color, and I can't keep it from pinging all over like it was shot out of a frosting decorator."

"No, but you could go to the beauty shop and let somebody else figure out what to do with it."

"The beauty shop?"

"Why not?"

"But I'm going to look conspicuous enough with all this makeup on. What would he think if I showed up with a different hairdo, too?"

"Oh, horse poop!" Amy pronounced belligerently, jamming her hands onto her trim hips. "He'll think it's super."

"But I don't want to look like…well, it's a date."

"But it *is* a date!"

"No, it's not. He's two years younger than I am. I'm just filling in, that's all."

But in spite of her protests, Theresa recalled Brian's teasing earlier this evening and admitted he'd seemed fully amenable to being her escort.

Several minutes later, standing before the wide mirror at the bathroom vanity, she caught her glistening lower lip between her teeth in an effort to contain the smile of approval that wanted to wing across her features. Then her lip escaped her teeth, and she smiled widely at what she saw. She liked her face! For the first time in her life she genuinely liked it. It seemed a desecration to have to cleanse the skin and remove the radiance from the creature who looked so happy and pleased with herself.

As she forced herself to turn on the water and pick up the bar of soap, it seemed as if tomorrow night would never get there.

But New Year's Eve day arrived at last, and Theresa managed to get an eleventh-hour appointment on this busiest day of the year in the beauty shops. In the late afternoon, she returned home the proud possessor of a new haircut and of the simple tool required to achieve the natural bounce of ringlets on her own: a hair pick.

The beautician's suggestion had been to simply shape the hair and stop trying to subdue it but to soften it with a cream rinse and let it bounce free, with just a few flicks of the wrist and pick to guide it into a halo of color about her head. Even the redness seemed less offensive, for with the light filtering through it, it looked less brash.

While she hung up her coat in the entry closet, Brian called from the living room, "Hi."

But she avoided a direct confrontation with him and hurried down the hall to her room with no more than a "Hi" in return.

And now everyone was scuttling around, getting ready. The bathroom had a steady stream of traffic. Theresa took a quick shower, then went to her room and was applying a new after-bath talc she'd ventured to buy. It had a light, petally fragrance reminiscent of the potpourri used by women in days of old. Subtle, feminine.

She paused with the puff in her hand and cocked her head. On the other side of her bedroom wall was the bathroom, so sounds carried through. She heard a masculine cough and recognized it as Brian's. The shower ran for several minutes during which there were two thumps, like an elbow hitting the wall, while images went skittering through her mind. There followed the whine of a blow-dryer, then a long silence— shaving—after which he started humming "Sweet Memories." Theresa smiled and realized she'd been standing naked for some time, dwelling on what was going on in the bathroom.

Crossing to the mirror, she assessed her devastatingly enormous breasts and wished for the thousandth time in as many days that she'd been in the other line when mammary glands were handed out. She turned away in disgust and found a clean brassiere. Donning it, she had to lean forward to let the pendulous weights drop into the cups before straightening to hook the back clasp of the hideous garment. It had all the feminine allure of a hernia truss! The wide straps had shoulder guards, meant to keep the weight from cutting into her flesh, but the deep grooves dented her shoulders just the same. The bra's utilitarian white fabric was styled for "extra support." How she hated the words! And how she hated the lingerie industry.

Just once—oh, just once!—how she'd love to browse along the counters of feminine underthings with tiny bikini panties and bras to match and consider buying a foolishly extravagant teddy, only to see what it felt like to have such a piece of feminine frippery against her skin.

LaVyrle Spencer   95

But she wasn't given the chance, for a teddy with size double-D cups would look as if it were two lace circus tents.

White undergarments in place, Theresa covered the full-figure white cotton bra with the new sweater and immediately felt more benevolent toward both herself and the clothing industry. The sweater was stylish and attractive and helped restore her excitement. The smoke-hued trousers fit smoothly, flatteringly, over her small hips, and the strappy high-heeled sandals she'd chosen added just the right touch of frivolity. Theresa had never been fond of jewelry, particularly earrings, for they only drew attention to a woman's face. But as she slipped a wristwatch beneath the cuff of the sweater, she decided her new mocha nail treatment deserved setting off, so clipped a delicate gold chain bracelet around her left wrist. Finally, into the draped cowl neck of the sweater, she inserted a tiny gold stick pin shaped like a treble clef.

Then she went across the hall to Amy's room to reproduce the makeup magic created in last night's secret session. But Theresa's hands were so shaky she couldn't seem to manage the applicators and wands.

Amy noticed and couldn't help teasing. "Considering this is *not* a date, you're in a pretty twittery state."

Theresa's brown eyes widened in dismay. "Oh, does it show?"

"You might want to stop wiping your palms on your thighs every thirty seconds. Pretty soon your new pants are going to look like a plumber's coveralls."

"It's silly, I know. I wish I could be more like you, Amy. You're always bright and witty, and even around boys you always seem to know the right things to say and how to act. Oh, this must sound ridiculous coming from a woman my age."

Somehow Amy's next comment was again just the perfect choice to calm Theresa's nerves somewhat. "He's going to love your new hairdo and your makeup and your outfit, too, so quit worrying. Here, give me that eyeshadow and shut your eyes."

But as Theresa tipped her head back and did as ordered, her sister was given the difficult job of applying makeup to trembling lids. Yet, she managed to produce the same magical effect as the night before, and when Theresa looked into Amy's lighted makeup mirror, all complete, dewy and lashy, she unconsciously pressed a palm to her chest in astonishment.

Smiling, Amy encouraged, "See? I told you."

And for that precious moment, Theresa believed it. She swung around to give Amy an impulsive hug, thinking how happy she suddenly was that none of this had ever happened before. It was wonderful experiencing these first Cinderella feelings at age twenty-five.

"Good luck, huh?" Amy's smile was sincere as she stood back and stuck her hands in the pockets of her jeans.

In answer, Theresa blew an affectionate kiss from the doorway. As she turned to leave, Amy added, "Oh, and put on some perfume, huh?"

"Oh, perfume. But I haven't got any. I got some new bath powder, but you must not be able to smell it."

"Here, try this."

They chose a subtle, understated fragrance from the bottles cluttering Amy's dresser top, leaving nothing more for Theresa to do but face Brian Scanlon. That, however, was going to be the most difficult moment of all.

Back in her room, Theresa puttered around, putting away stray pieces of clothing, checking her watch several times. She heard the voices of Jeff and Brian from the other end of the house, joined by Amy's and her parents'. Everyone was waiting for her, and she suddenly wished she'd been ready first so she wouldn't have had to make a grand entrance. But it was too late now. She didn't care if she soiled her new trousers or not, she gave one last swipe of her palms along the gabardine, took a deep breath and went out to face the music.

They were all in the kitchen. Her mother and father were sitting at the table over cups of coffee. Amy stood with her hands in her front pockets telling Jeff she was going babysitting tonight. Brian was at the sink, running himself a glass of water.

Theresa stepped into the room with her heart tripping out sixteenth notes. Jeff caught sight of her, and his smiling response was instantaneous. "Well, would you lookit here…I think I asked the wrong girl to go out with me tonight." He swooped Theresa into his arms and took her on a Ginger Rogers–Fred Astaire swirl while grinning wickedly into her eyes, then affecting a convincing Bogart drawl, "Hiya, doll, whaddya say we get it on tonight?"

Brian looked back over his shoulder, and the water glass stopped half way to his lips.

As Jeff brought his sister to a breathless halt, she was laughing, aware that Brian had spilled out the water without drinking any. He turned away from the sink and crossed to clap a hand on Jeff's shoulder.

"Just your tough luck, Brubaker. I asked her first." His approving gaze settled on Theresa, creating a glow about her heart.

"Isn't her new hairdo great?" piped up Amy. "And she bought the outfit especially for tonight."

Amy Brubaker, I could strangle you. Jeff lightened his hold and settled Theresa against his hip. "She did, huh?"

Brian's eyes made a quick trip down to her knees, then back up to her makeup and hair. To the best of Theresa's recollection, it was the first time his eyes had ever scanned anything below her neck.

Margaret spoke up then. "Jeffrey, turn your sister around. I haven't had a look at what that beauty operator did to her yet."

Does everybody in the house have to blurt out everything? Beneath her fresh, translucent makeup Theresa could feel the pink ruining the entire effect and hoped that for once it didn't show. Jeff swung her around for her mother and father's approval, but at her shoulder she felt Brian's eyes following.

To Theresa's further chagrin, her mother's verdict was, "You should have done that years ago."

"You look pretty as a picture, dear," added Willard.

Unaccustomed to being the center of attention like this, Theresa could think only of escape.

"It's time to leave."

Jeff released her to check his watch. "Yup. You can head out. Patricia should be here any minute. She's picking me up in her car."

Theresa whirled around in surprise. "Aren't we all going together?"

"No, she's afraid I might overindulge tonight, and since she claims she's always levelheaded, she thought it would be best if she drove her car and dropped me off at home instead of the other way around."

"Oh." Once she grunted the monosyllable, Theresa felt conspicuous, for nobody said anything more. She realized she sounded rather dubious and ill at ease about being left alone with Brian. But he went to get her coat from the front-hall closet, and Jeff nudged her in the back. She followed and let Brian ease the coat over her shoulders, then she found herself doing something she'd never done before: helping Brian with his. He was dressed in formfitting designer blue jeans, and a corduroy sport coat of cocoa brown under which showed a neutral tweed rag-knit sweater with the collar of a white shirt peeking from under its crew neck. As he struggled to thread his arms into a hip-length wool coat, she reacted as politeness dictated, reaching to assist him when the shoulder of his jacket caught. Theresa experienced an unexpected thrill of pleasure, performing the insignificant service.

"Thanks." He lifted the outer garment and shrugged his shoulders in a peculiarly masculine adjustment that made her knees feel weak. He smelled good, too. And suddenly all she could think of was getting out of the house and into the car where darkness would mask the feelings she was certain were alternately making her blush and blanch.

She kissed her mother and father good-night. "Happy New Year, both of you." They were spending it at home, watching the celebration in Times Square on television. "Amy…" Theresa turned to find her sister's eyes following her wistfully. "Thanks, honey."

"Sure." Amy leaned her hips back against the edge of the kitchen counter and followed their progress as Brian opened

the door for Theresa and saw her out. "Hey, you're both knock-
outs!" she called just before the door closed.

They smiled goodbye, and a moment later were engulfed
by the cold silence outside. Theresa's car waited in the
driveway where she'd left it as she'd rushed in from the hair
appointment. Brian found her elbow while they crossed the icy
blacktop, but she suddenly didn't want to drive. It would take
some of the magic away. "Would you mind driving, Brian?"

He stopped. They were at the front of the car, heading
around toward the driver's side. "Not at all." Instead of leaving
her there, he guided her to the passenger side, opened her door
and waited while she settled herself inside.

When his door slammed, they found themselves laughing
at his knees digging into the dashboard.

"Sorry," Theresa offered, "my legs are shorter than yours."

He fumbled in the dark, found the proper lever, and the seat
went sliding back while he let out a whoof of breath. "Whoo!
Are they ever!"

She handed him the keys and he fumbled again, groping for
the ignition. "Here." In the blackness, their knuckles brushed
as she reached to point out the right spot. The brief touch set
off a tingle in her hand, then the key clicked home and the
engine came to life.

"Thanks for letting me drive. A person misses it." He
adjusted the mirror, shifted into Reverse, and they were rolling.

The quiet was disarming. The scent she remembered emanated
from his hair and clothing and mingled with her own borrowed
perfume. The dash lights lit his face from below, and she wanted
to turn and study him, but faced front, resisting the urge.

"So that's where you went this afternoon—to the beauty
shop. I wondered."

"Amy and her big mouth." But Theresa grinned in the dark.

He laughed indulgently. "I like it. It looks good on you."

She glanced left and found his eyes on her dimly lit hair and
quickly looked away.

"Thank you." *What is a woman expected to reply at a time
like this?* Theresa wanted to say she loved his hair, too, but she

really preferred a man's hair longer than the Air Force allowed, though she loved the smell of his, and the color of it. She heartily approved of the clothing he'd chosen tonight, but before she could decide whether or not to say so, Brian suggested, "Why don't you put on something classical? We'll have our fill of rock before the night is over."

The music filled the uncomfortable transition period while they rode, with Theresa giving occasional directions. Within fifteen minutes they reached the Rusty Scupper, a nightspot frequented by a young adult crowd, many of them singles. They helped each other with coats, left them at the coat check and were shown to a long table set up for a large group. Theresa recognized some of Jeff's friends and performed introductions, watching as Brian shook hands with the men and was ogled by some of the women, whose eyes lingered on him with that inquisitive approval of the single female presented with an attractive male novelty. She watched their eyes drop down his torso and realized with a start that some women checked out men in much the same way men checked out women. She was totally abashed when an attractive sable-haired beauty named Felice returned her eyes to Brian's and smiled with a blatant glint of sexual approval. "Keep a dance free for me later, okay, Brian? And make sure it's a slow one."

"I'll do that," he replied politely, withdrawing his hand from the one that had retained his longer than was usual. He returned to Theresa's side, pulled out her chair and settled himself beside her.

In a voice low enough for only her ears, he questioned, "Who's she?"

Theresa felt dreadfully deflated that he should ask. "Felice Durand is one of the crowd. She's hung around with Jeff and his bunch since high school."

"Remind me to be monopolized by you during the slow dances," he returned wryly, filling Theresa with a soaring sense of relief. She herself had little experience on the boy-girl social scene, and Felice's bold assessment of Brian's body, followed by her forward invitation, was unnerving. But apparently not all men were hooked by bait as obvious as that dangled by Felice Durand. Theresa's respect for Brian slid up another notch.

Jeff and Patricia arrived then, and the table filled with lively chatter, laughter and orders for cocktails. Soon thereafter menus arrived, and Theresa was astounded at the inflated New Year's prices that had been substituted but told herself an evening with Brian would be worth it.

Carafes of wine were delivered, glasses filled and toasts proposed. Touching his glass to Jeff's, Brian intoned, "To old friends…" And with a touch of the rim upon Patricia's glass, and finally upon Theresa's, he added, "and to new."

His eyes held a steady green spark of approval as they sought hers and lingered after she self-consciously dropped her gaze to the ruby liquid, then drank.

Dinner was noisy and exuberant, and for the most part Theresa and Brian listened to the banter without taking part. She felt relieved that he, like her, was rather an outsider. She felt drawn to him, in a welcome semiexclusion.

Over tiny stem glasses of crème de menthe, they relaxed, sat back in their chairs and waited for the dancing to begin.

The dancing. Just the thought of it filled Theresa with a mixture of apprehension and eagerness. It hadn't been so difficult turning into Brian's arms that day in the living room. Here, the dance floor would be crowded; nobody would notice them among all the others. It should be easy to submit to the embrace of an attractive man like Brian, yet at the thought, Theresa felt a tremor tumble through her lower belly. *He's been stuck with me.*

Just then the waitress approached and spoke to the group at their general end of the table. "As soon as the dancing starts, it's a cash bar only, so if you wouldn't mind, we'd like to get the dinner bill settled up now."

Automatically, Theresa reached for her purse, just as Brian lifted one hip from the chair, pushed back his sport coat and sought his hip pocket. As he came up with a billfold, she produced the purse and was reaching to unzip it when his fingers closed over hers.

"You're with me," he ordered simply. Her eyes flew to his. They were steady, insistent. His cool fingers still rested upon her tense ones while her heart sent out a crazy stutter step.

Yes, I am, she thought. *I'm really with you.*

"Thank you, Brian."

He squeezed her fingers, then his slipped away, and for the first time she truly felt like his date.

Chapter 6

The band had a lot of talent wrapped up in five members, plus a female singer. They played a mix of mid-to-easy rock, but all their music had a hard, sure beat to encourage dancers onto the floor, then once they were warmed up, back to the tables to cool down with another round of drinks. When half the group deserted their table in favor of the dance floor, Brian and Theresa remained behind in companionable silence, watching the dancers.

The band slammed into the driving beat of a recent hit, and Theresa found herself mesmerized by the back view of Felice Durand's gyrating hips. She was wearing a fire-engine red dress that slithered on her derriere with so much resistance that Theresa was certain the friction would soon send up a trail of smoke. But she was good. She moved with feline seductiveness, never missing a beat, incorporating hands, arms, shoulders and pelvis in a provocative invitation to naughtiness. Watching, Theresa felt a twinge of jealousy.

Suddenly Felice spun in a half circle, her back now to her partner as she sent an openmouthed look of innuendo over her shoulder at him. Two more shakes and her eyes spied Brian. His chair was half turned toward the dance floor while one elbow hung on the table edge. A quick glance told Theresa he'd been watching Felice for some time.

Without missing a beat, the woman somehow managed to

shift all her attention to Brian. Her hips traced corkscrews, her mouth puckered in a glistening pout, and her hands with their glossy bloodred nails conveyed come-hither messages. Theresa's eyes moved back to Brian, and she saw his gaze drop from Felice's face to her breasts to her hips and stay there.

A moment later, Felice spun adroitly to face her partner, then maneuvered herself into the crowd where she couldn't be seen, as if to say, you want more, boy, come and get it.

Brian glanced at Theresa and caught her watching him. She quickly dropped her eyes to a plastic stir stick she'd been playing with. She felt herself coloring and felt suddenly very much out of place. This young, brash crowd wasn't for her. Jeff fit in here, maybe even Brian, but she didn't.

Just then the music changed. The keyboard player chimed the distinctive intro to "The Rose"—slow, moody, romantic.

From the corner of her eye, Theresa caught a flash of fire-engine red zeroing in on Brian, but before it quite registered, he'd lunged to his feet, captured Theresa's hand and was towing her toward the dance floor. They'd barely left their chairs when they were intercepted by Felice and her partner returning to the table.

The sable-haired beauty looked attractively flushed and sheeny from her exertions as she stopped Brian's progress with a hand on his chest. "I thought this one might be mine."

"Sorry, Felice. This is our song, isn't it, Theresa?" Too astounded to answer, she let herself be pulled through the crowd onto the dance floor, where she was swung loosely into Brian's arms.

"Is it?" She peered up at him with a gamine grin.

"It is now." His own conspiratorial grin eased the discomfiture Theresa had been feeling while watching him observe Felice.

"It occurs to me that in less than two short weeks we've gathered enough of *our songs* to fill a concert program."

"Imagine what a mixed-up concert it would be. Chopin's Nocturne and Newbury's 'Sweet Memories.'"

"And 'The Rose,'" Theresa added.

"And don't forget 'Oh, I had a little chicken and he wouldn't lay an egg....'"

"*She* wouldn't lay an egg."

"What's the dif—"

"*He* chickens don't lay eggs, not even when you pour hot water up and down their legs."

Brian laughed, a melodic tenor sound that sent ripples of response through his dance partner. Something wonderful had happened. During their foolishness their feet had been unconsciously moving to the music. Theresa's natural musicality had taken over of its own accord. With her guard down, and distracted by both Felice and their conversation, she'd forgotten to bring her shy reservations along with her onto the dance floor. She was following Brian's graceful, expert lead with a joyous freedom. He was a superb dancer. Moving with him was effortless and fluid, though he kept a respectable distance between their bodies.

When had their laughter died? Brian's green eyes hadn't left Theresa's but gazed down into her uplifted face, while both of them fell silent.

"Brian," she said softly. "I don't care if you dance with Felice."

"I don't want to dance with Felice."

"I saw you watching her."

"It was rather unavoidable." His dark eyebrows drew together with a brief flicker of annoyance. "Listen, Felice is like the countless groupies who hang around at the foot of the stage and shake it for the guitar man, whichever one is playing that night, hoping to score after the dance. They're a dime a dozen, but that's not what I want tonight, okay? Not when I have something so much better."

At his last words his arms tightened and hauled her against him, that place she'd so often wondered about with half dread, half fascination. Her breasts were gently flattened against the corduroy panels of his sport coat, and her thighs felt the soft nudges of his steps. Upon her waist pressed a firm, secure palm, while hers found his solid shoulder muscle, his cool, extended palm. Against her temple his jaw rested.

I'm dancing. Breast to breast and thigh to thigh with a man. And it's wonderful. Theresa felt released and loose and altogether unselfconscious. Perhaps it was because, in spite of the fact that their bodies brushed, Brian retained a hold only possessive enough to guide her. His hips remained a discreet space apart while the other spots where Theresa's body touched his seemed alive and warmed.

He hummed quietly, the notes sure and true. The gentle vibrations of his voice trembled through his chest, and she felt it vaguely through her breasts. He smelled clean and slightly spicy, and she thought, *Look at me, world. I'm falling in love with Brian Scanlon, and it's absolutely heavenly.*

The song ended, and he retreated but still held her lightly. His smile was as miraculous as the revelation she'd just experienced. Her own smile was timorous.

"You're a good dancer, Theresa."

"So are you."

The band eased into another song without a pause, and as the notes began, it became understood Brian and Theresa would dance again. He took her against his body, dipping his head down a little lower this time, while she raised hers a fraction higher. And somehow it seemed portentous that the first word of the song was, *"Love..."*

"Theresa, you look as pretty tonight as I imagined you when Jeff first told me about you."

"Oh, Brian..." she began to protest.

"When I turned around and saw you standing in the kitchen I couldn't believe it."

"Amy helped me. I...well, I'm not too experienced at getting ready for dances."

He lifted his head, gazed into her eyes, folded her right palm against his heart and whispered, "I'm glad."

And the next thing she knew, her eyes and nose and forehead were riding within the warm, fragrant curve of his neck. Her cheek felt the textures of corduroy, wool and cotton and freshly shaved masculine skin. She drifted in his spicy scent that grew more pronounced as the heat of their joined skins released it

from his jaw and neck. Somehow—some magical somehow—
their hips had nestled together, and she felt for the first time
the contour of his stomach against hers, of his warm flesh
within the tight blue jeans, seeking to find hers as his forearm
held her securely about her waist, pressing her and keeping her
close.

She tried closing her eyes but found she was already dizzy
from the emotions his nearness stirred in her, and the slow turns
he executed increased her vertigo. She opened her eyes and saw
through her own lacy lashes the outline of his Adam's apple
only an inch away. She watched his thumb as it rubbed the
backs of her knuckles in rhythm with the music. He had
captured her hand by cupping its backside, and her palm lay
flat, pressed against his chest. She felt the steady thump of his
heart, then became aware of how callused his fingers were as
they stroked her hand. She recalled that long-fingered left hand
upon the neck of the guitar as he'd been singing to her. Her eyes
drifted closed again as she basked in the new feeling of wonder
at where she was, who she was with and what kind of man he
was.

This time when the song ended, neither of them moved immediately. He squeezed the back of her hand harder and tightened his right arm until his elbow dug into the hollow of her
spine.

Brian, she thought. *Brian.*

He eased back, never releasing her hand as he led the way
to their table, and the band announced a break.

At their places, Theresa sat in a private cloud with nobody
but him. Their chairs were side by side, turned slightly outward
from the table, and when Brian sat, he crossed an ankle over
a knee in such a way that the knee brushed the side of her thigh.
He left it there intentionally, she thought, a thread of contact
still bonding them together while they had to forgo dancing.

"So, tell me about what it's like to teach music to elementary-school kids."

She told him. More than she'd ever shared with any other man.
And while she talked, Brian studied her face, with its

shifting expressions of laughter, thoughtfulness and something utterly pure and wholesome. *Yes, wholesome,* he thought. *This woman is wholesome in a way I've never encountered in another woman. Certainly in none of the Felices whose offers I've taken up whenever the mood struck me.*

Women like Felice, in their siren-red dresses, with their sleek hair and slithery hips—women like that are one-nighters. This woman is a lifetimer. What would she be like in bed? Naive and unsure and very likely a virgin, he thought. *Totally opposite to the practiced felines who could purr deep in their throats and press themselves against a man with skilled teasing, which somehow always managed to repel even as it allured. No, Theresa Brubaker would be as honest and fresh as...as the Chopin Nocturne,* he thought.

"So, tell me what it's like to be on a Strategic Air Command base during the day and playing at the officer's club in the evenings."

He told her.

And while he talked, Theresa pictured the Felices, the "townies" who gazed up at the guitar man from the foot of the stage, for his and Jeff's band also played gigs in the canteens where enlisted men were allowed to bring civilian dates. Theresa thought about what he'd said—something about countless groupies hanging around the stage and *shaking it* for the guitar man, hoping to score after the dance. But he'd added, that's not what he wanted tonight. *Tonight?* The implication was clear. Back at their air base there would doubtless be others who'd capture Brian's attention, others in fire-engine red dresses with faces and bodies like Felice Durand's. A man like him wouldn't be content for long with a wallflower like herself.

She imagined Brian stepping off the stage, taking up the offer of some groupie, tumbling into bed with her for the night.

And if Brian had ample opportunity, she supposed her brother did, too. The thought was sobering.

She came from her musing to find Brian's eyes steady on her face as he spoke in a sober voice. "Theresa, next June, when

Jeff and I get out, I'm thinking about settling around Minneapolis someplace so he and I can get another band going here."

"You are?" Crazy commotion started in the vicinity of her
heart. Brian, returning here to live permanently? "But what
about Chicago?"

"I've got no ties there anymore. None that matter. The
people I knew will practically be strangers after four years."

"Jeff has mentioned that you two talked about staying
together, but what about the rest of the band?"

"We'll audition a drummer and a bass player here, and
maybe a female singer, too. We'd like to get into private parties,
but it'll take a couple of years of playing night spots and bars
before we can manage that."

He seemed to be waiting for her approval, but she was
speechless. "Well…" She gestured vaguely, smiled brightly
into his eyes and tried to comprehend what this could mean to
her future relationship with him.

"That's not exactly the reaction I'd hoped for." She dropped
her eyes to her lap and needlessly smoothed the gabardine
over her left knee as he went on. "I told you before, what I
really want to be—ultimately—is a DJ. I want to enter Brown
Institute and go to school days and play gigs nights. Jeff is all
for it. What about you?"

"Me?" She lifted startled brown eyes and felt her heartbeat
tripping in gay expectation. "Why do you need my approval?"

Not a muscle moved on Brian for a full fifteen seconds. He
skewered Theresa with his dazzling green eyes, but they were
filled with unsaid things.

"I think you know why," he told her at last, his voice coming
from low in his throat.

A resounding chord announced the beginning of the next
set, and Theresa was saved from replying by the booming
sound that filled the house. She and Brian were still staring into
each other's eyes when the undauntable Felice appeared out
of nowhere and commandeered Brian's left arm, hauling him
out of his chair while his eyes still lingered on Theresa.

"Come on, Brian, let's see what you've got, honey!"

He seemed to shake himself back to the present. "All right, just one."

But Theresa was subjected to the prolonged torture of watching Felice appropriate her date for three throbbing, upbeat songs. It took no more than sixty seconds of observation for Theresa's mouth to go dry. And in another sixty, wet.

Brian moved his body with the understated liquidity of a professional stage dancer. But he did it with a seemingly total lack of guile. When he rotated his hips, the movement was so subtle, so sexy, Theresa's lips unconsciously dropped open. The supple twisting of his pelvis appeared to come as naturally to Brian as walking. His face wore a pleasant expression of enjoyment as he occasionally maintained eye contact with Felice. She circumnavigated him in a sultry trip that ended when she almost touched him with her breasts, shimmying her shoulders while the suspended offerings swayed, unfettered, within the folds of her halter-style dress. Felice said something, and Brian laughed.

The song ended and he placed a hand at the small of her back as if to guide her off the floor, but she swung to face him, pressing both hands on his chest, looking up into his face. He glanced briefly toward the table, and Theresa looked quickly away. The music gushed out in another jungle rhythm, and when Theresa's eyes returned to the dance floor she was stung with jealousy. Watching the lurch and roll, the toss and pitch of Brian's lean, oscillating body set up queer yearnings in her own, and it occurred to Theresa that she was as human as some of the men who ogled her when she walked into a room.

Felice managed to link her arm with Brian's at the end of the song and introduce him to somebody on the floor, thereby commandeering him for a third dance. But as Theresa looked on, she saw him put up no resistance.

When the pair arrived at the table, Felice cooed to Theresa. "Ooo, if I were you, I'd hang on to this one. He's a live one." Then, to Brian, "Thanks for the dance, honey."

Jealousy was something new for Theresa. So was the feeling of sexual attraction. Although Theresa no longer spoke in the teenager vernacular, a phrase of Amy's came to her now: *strung out*. She suddenly knew what it meant to be strung out on a man. It had to be this hollow, gutless, wonderful awareness of his masculinity and her own femininity; this sensation that your pulses had somehow found their way to the surface of your skin and hovered there just beneath the outermost layer, as if ready to explode; this supersensitivity to each shift of muscle, each facial expression, even each movement of his clothing upon his body. She watched in a new acute fascination as Brian shrugged out of his corduroy jacket and hung it on the back of his chair. It seemed each of his motions was peculiar to him alone, as if no other man had ever performed this incidental task in as attractive a way. Was this common? Did others who found themselves falling in love feel such out-of-proportion pride and possessiveness? Did they all find their chosen one flawless, superlative and sexy while performing the most mundane movements, such as sitting on a chair and crossing his ankle over a knee?

"I'm sorry," Brian muttered, taking his full attention back to Theresa.

"You didn't look very sorry. You looked like you were enjoying every minute of it."

"She's a good dancer."

Theresa's lips thinned in disapproval.

"Listen, I said I was sorry I left you sitting here for three dances."

She glanced away, finding it difficult to deal with her newfound feelings. Brian wiped his brow on the sleeve of his sweater, reached for a glass with some partially melted ice cubes and slipped one into his mouth. Theresa watched his lips purse around it as he turned to study the dance floor. The ice cube made his cheek pop out, then she watched his attractive jaw as he chewed and swallowed it.

When his eyes roved back to hers, she quickly glanced away. Her forearm rested on the table, and his warm palm fell across the sleeve of her sweater.

Their eyes met. He squeezed her arm once, gently. Her

heart lifted. Though not another word was said about Felice, the issue was set aside.

A powerful force, this jealousy, thought Theresa, loving the feel of his hand on her arm.

When the tempo of the music slowed, Brian rose without asking her and reached for her hand. On the dance floor, wrapped close to his rag-knit sweater, she could feel how the exertion had released both heat and scent from his skin. The moist warmth radiated onto her breasts. His palm, too, was warmer than before. The keen scent of his aftershave and deodorant was stronger than ever since he'd danced with Felice, and with a secret smile against his shoulder, Theresa thanked the bold temptress for warming Brian up.

Jeff and Patricia danced past, and Jeff leaned toward Brian to ask, "Hey, man, wanna change partners on the next dance?"

"No offense, Patricia, but not a chance."

He resumed his intimate hold on Theresa, who peered over Brian's shoulder at her brother to receive a lopsided smile and a broad wink.

Several times during the remainder of the evening Felice tried to snare Brian for a slow dance, but he refused to be appropriated again. He and Theresa sat out the up-tempo songs together and danced only the slow ones. She was growing increasingly aware of the approach of midnight. When they were at their table she surreptitiously checked her watch as Brian slipped his jacket back on. The discreet time check proved that she'd been consulting her watch at the rate of once every two minutes or less. ·

They were on the dance floor when a song ended, and Theresa turned toward their table to be waylaid by Brian's hand on her forearm. "Not so fast there, young lady." When she turned back to him, he lifted a wrist, tugged his corduroy sleeve up over his watch. "Only five minutes to go. Let's stay out here until the big moment, okay?"

A flush of sexual awareness radiated through Theresa. Without realizing where her eyes were headed, they centered on Brian's lips. His mouth was very beautiful, very sensual, the lower lip slightly fuller than the upper, those lips slightly parted now, glistening enticingly as if he'd just passed his tongue along them. She remembered the brief times they'd touched her own, and the maelstrom of emotions his fleeting kisses had created within her heart. The same reaction began again, just from her gazing at his lips.

Her eyes raised to find his upon her own mouth. The lingering gaze held sensual promise she'd never dreamed of finding in a man. She had kissed relatively few men in her life, and all of them in private. The idea of doing so in public heightened Theresa's inhibitions. She glanced around the dance floor: there was a certain amount of anonymity when so many people were pressed almost shoulder to shoulder in a throng of this size and density.

Just then someone nudged Theresa from behind. She turned to find a waitress elbowing through the dancers, passing out hats and noisemakers, confetti and streamers. Brian got a green foil top hat that would have done Fred Astaire proud. He perched it on his head, then adjusted its brim to a rakish angle and pulled it low over the left side of his forehead. He touched the brim, looking as though he wished his hands were encased in formal white gloves, and cocked an eyebrow at Theresa. "How do I look?"

"Like Abraham Lincoln gone Irish."

He laughed. "A little respectable and a little roguish?"

"Exactly." The green hat set off his dark, handsome face and hair in a way that made it difficult for Theresa to draw her eyes away.

"Aren't you going to put yours on?"

"Oh!" She lifted the tiara and turned up her nose in disgust. It was covered with horrible, shocking pink glitter that would clash abominably with her red hair. But she lifted her hands and gamely settled the circlet atop her head. As she felt with her fingertips to determine if it was on straight, Brian took over.

"Here, let me."

He brushed her fingertips aside, then adjusted the gaudy headpiece on Theresa's bouncy curls. His touch seemed to send fire straight down each hair follicle into her scalp. Just being near the man did the most devilish things to her senses.

"How do *I* look?" she asked, trying to get command of herself, keeping spirits light.

"Like the angels sprinkled you with stardust." He touched a fingertip to her left eyebrow. It felt as if she'd received a 110-volt shock. "But there's nothing wrong with a little stardust. Guess I'll put it back." Again he touched her, replacing the flake of pink glitter, this time on the crest of her left cheek, then running the finger slowly down to her chin before dropping his hand between them and capturing both of her hands without looking away from her astounded eyes. His own were penetrating, admiring and seemed to be radiating messages much like those she was unable to hide.

"You'd better close your eyes, Brian, or all this color will give you a headache," Theresa warned, realizing how garish she must look in the gaudy vermilion tiara, with hot-pink glitter highlighting her freckle-splattered cheeks.

The drummer began a drum roll. It seemed to both Brian and Theresa the sound came from the opposite side of the universe, so wrapped up in each other had they become.

"Gladly," Brian agreed, "but not because anything gives me a headache." He was clutching her hands so tightly she completely forgot about everything except his eyes, reaching toward hers with a deep, probing knowledge of something she'd yearned to see in the eyes of one special man, a man just like the one before her now. Around them the crowd bellowed the countdown to midnight. "Five…four…three…two…one!" The band hit the opening chord of "Auld Lang Syne," and neither Theresa nor Brian moved for the duration of several heartbeats.

Then she was being enfolded in strong, warm arms and dragged against his hard chest, against his belly, against his hips and his warm, seeking mouth.

A coil of pink paper came flying through the air and drifted across the brim of Brian's green top hat, trailing down over his ear and jaw, but he was totally unaware of it. A shower of

confetti settled onto Theresa's hair and shoulders and drifted
down the bridge of Brian's nose, but they were lost in each
other, aware only of the closeness they'd at last achieved. Their
eyes were closed as they kissed with a full, lush introduction
of tongues that sent shock waves skittering down Theresa's
spine. Her arms were threaded beneath his, and her palms
rested on the center of his back while one of his pressed
between her shoulder blades, and the other slipped up into the
warm secret place at her nape, under the cloud of soft hair.

The interior of his mouth was warm, wet and compelling.
The shifting exploration of his tongue brought hers against it
in answer, as a river of longing coursed through Theresa's
body.

Brian started moving as if unable to be drawn from a deep
spell—slowly, seductively—carrying her with him to the nostalgic rhythm and words of the song. Their hips joined, pressed
and swayed together, but their feet scarcely shuffled on the
crowded floor. He moved his head in a sensuous invitation to
deepen the kiss and opened his mouth wider over hers. Her
response was as natural as the evocative dance movements
they shared: her own mouth opened more fully. She felt the
sensuous drawing of his lips and tongue, and the moist heat of
his mouth seemed to burn its way down the length of her body.

In her entire life, nothing like this had ever happened to
Theresa. The kisses of her past had been accompanied either
by timidity or groping, and sometimes by both in rapid succession. She let Brian rub her hips with his own, lightly at first,
then with growing pressure until the side-to-side motion
evoked images of further intimacies. Finally, he drew her
against him with a possessiveness that made her ribs ache
sweetly. And still the kiss continued....

He began humming into her open mouth, and auld acquain-
tances were indeed forgotten by both of them while she
answered by humming, too. Before the song was half through,
before the new year had been completely ushered in, before
she could quite capture the realization that it was really happening to her, Theresa felt Brian's body go hard within the blue

jeans. But she remained against him, marveling that someone at last had unlocked her to the wondrous side of physical contact.

"Auld Lang Syne" drifted to an end, and somewhere in the reaches of her consciousness Theresa knew the song had changed into another as Brian lifted his head but not his hands. He held her in a warm embrace while they rocked, remaining hip to hip, breast to chest, gazing into each other's eyes.

"Theresa." He lifted his eyes to her hair, let them skim back to her enraptured face, which reflected amazement, arousal and perhaps a touch of apprehension. "This started before I ever met you. You know that, don't you?" His voice was rich with passion. Her lips dropped open, and she found it very difficult to breathe.

"B...before you met me?"

"Jeff told me things that used to make me lie in bed at night and wonder what you'd be like when I met you. I would have been the most disappointed man in the world if you hadn't turned out to be exactly as you are."

She dropped her eyes to the dusting of confetti on his shoulders. "But, I'm—"

"You're perfect," he murmured, lowering his head until his mouth cut off further words. Then, to her astonishment, he did something utterly provocative, and distractingly sexy. He loosened his hold momentarily and opened his corduroy jacket so that its bulk no longer disguised the state of his body—not in the least. Then he took her back where she belonged, inside the open jacket, with her hands between it and her sweater while they danced the remainder of the song.

When it ended, he backed away, but kept his arms looped behind her waist as their hips rested tightly together.

"Let's get out of here," he suggested in a low, throaty voice.

"B...but it's only midnight," she stammered, awed by the suddenness of the sexual urgings she felt. He lifted his eyes to her hair. It was peppered with confetti. The glittered crown had tipped awry, and he plucked it from her hair, then smiled down at her open lips.

"Let's go home."

"What about Jeff and—"

"Are you scared, Theresa?"

She felt the press of blood staining her neck and pushing upward, but he lifted her chin and forced her to meet his eyes. "Theresa, are you scared of me? Don't be. I want to be alone with you, just once before I leave."

But, Brian, I don't do things like that. I'm not like your groupies. The words crossed her mind, but not her lips. She'd look like a complete idiot if she said them and his intentions were honorable all along. Yet he'd opened his jacket and made his sexual state unquestionably clear! And she was a twenty-five-year-old virgin who was both tormented and compelled by the traumatic first that might very well happen if she agreed to leave early with him.

Instead of waiting for her answer, he turned her toward the edge of the dance floor, his palm riding the hollow of her spine while she led the way to the table, found her purse and couldn't quite meet Jeff's eyes as she and Brian said good-night.

He drove again, by tacit agreement. Inside her warm woolen coat, Theresa was shuddering throughout most of the ride home, even after the heater was blowing warm air. In the familiar driveway, he pulled the car to a stop, killed the engine and handed her the keys in the dark. She began pivoting toward her door when his strong grip on her wrist brought her up short.

"Come here." His command was soft-spoken, but tinged with gruff emotion. "It's been a long time since I kissed a girl in a car. I'd like to take the memory back to Minot Air Force Base with me."

It had been easier on the crowded dance floor when proximity took care of logistics. Now Theresa had to willingly lean her half of the way across the console that separated them. She hesitated, wondering how women ever learned to perform their part in these rites that seemed to inhibit her at every turn.

He exerted a light pressure on her wrist, pulling her slowly toward him, and tipped his head aside to meet her lips with a new kind of kiss that, though lacking in demand, was no less sensitizing. It was a tease of a kiss, a falling rose petal of a kiss. And it made her long for more.

"Your nose is cold. Let's go in and warm it up."

Chapter 7

Inside, the house was quiet. The light above the stove was on again, and she hurried past its cone of brightness to the shadows of the hallway, knowing that if Brian got a look at her face, he'd see how uncertain and scared she'd suddenly become. She felt his hands taking the coat from her shoulders, though she hadn't known he'd followed her so closely. A myriad of conversational subjects jumped into her mind, but scattered into pieces like the colors in a kaleidoscope. Unable to believe she'd sound anything less than petrified if she introduced any of them, she was preparing to wish him a fast goodnight and skitter off to bed, when he turned from the closet and lazily took her hand in one of his.

"It sounds like your mom and dad are in bed already."

"Yes...yes, it's awfully quiet."

"Come downstairs with me."

Trepidation stiffened her spine. She tried to dredge up a reply, but both yes and no stuck in her throat. He threaded his fingers through hers as if they were setting out to stroll hand in hand through a meadow and turned them both toward the basement stairs.

She allowed herself to be led, for it was the only way she could approach the seduction she knew was in the offing.

At the top of the basement stairs she snapped on the light, but once downstairs, he released her hand, crossed to the

ruffled lamp and substituted its mellower glow, then unconcernedly switched off the garish overhead beacon.

Theresa hovered by the sliding glass door, staring out at the
black rectangle of night, while she chafed her upper arms.

Behind her, Brian noted, "It looks like your folks had a fire.
The coals are still hot."

"Oh," she squeaked, knowing what he wanted, but unwilling to abet it.

"Do you mind if I add a log?"

"No."

She heard the glass doors of the fireplace being opened, then
the metallic tinkle of the wire-mesh curtains being pushed
aside. The charcoal broke with a crunching sound as he settled
a new log, and the metal fire screen slid closed again. And still
Theresa cowered by the door, hugging herself while her knees
trembled.

She was staring out so intently that she jumped and spun to
face Brian when he reappeared beside her and began closing
the draperies. He was watching her instead of the drapery pulls
while he worked the cord, hand over hand. She licked her lips
and swallowed. Behind him, the fresh log flared with a *whoosh*
and she jumped again as if the puff had announced the leaping
arrival of Lucifer.

The draperies drew to a close. Silence bore down. Brian kept
his disconcerting gaze riveted on Theresa as he came two steps
closer, then extended his hand in invitation.

She stared at it but only hugged herself tighter.

The hand remained, palm up, steady. "Why are you so
scared of me?" His deep, flawlessly modulated voice delivered
the question in the softest of tones.

"I…I…" She felt her jaw working but seemed unable to
close it, to answer, or to go to him.

He leaned forward, balancing on one foot while capturing
one of her hands and tugging her along after him toward the
far side of the room where the sofa faced the hearth. The fire
glowed brightly now; passing the lamp he switched it off,
leaving the room dressed in soft, flickering orange. He sat,

gently towed her down beside him, and resolutely kept his right arm around her shoulders while he himself slunk rather low, catching the nape of her neck on the cushion, and crossing his calves on the shiny maple coffee table before them.

Beneath his arms, Brian could feel Theresa's shoulders tensed and curled. Everything had changed during their ride home. She'd had time to consider what she was getting into. Her withdrawal gave him a corresponding sense of hesitation, which he hoped he was hiding well. One skittish partner in such a situation was enough. He had misgivings about kissing her again in an effort to break down her reserve. She was pinched up as tightly as a newly wound watch, and he knew she hadn't done anything like this very often in her life. Jeff had told him she was spooked by men, that she turned down most invitations or advances that came her way. And Jeff had told Brian, too, the reason why. That knowledge hovered above him like a wall of water about to curl in upon his head. He felt as if he was savoring his last lungful of air in anticipation of being sucked under when the tidal wave hit.

Brian Scanlon was scared.

But Theresa Brubaker didn't know it.

She rested against the side of his ribs, with her head cradled on his shoulder and the crown of her hair against his cheek. But her arms remained crossed as tightly as if she wore a straitjacket.

With the hand that circled her shoulders, he gently rubbed her resilient upper arm. Her hair smelled flowery and created a warm patch of closeness where it pressed beneath his cheek. He pinched the knit sleeve of her sweater between thumb and forefinger and drew it away from her flesh.

"Is it true that you bought this whole new outfit just for tonight?"

"Amy's worse than Jeff. She can't keep *any* secrets."

His hand fell lightly upon her arm again. "I like the new clothes. The color goes great with your hair."

"Don't mention the color of my hair, please." She clasped an open hand over the top of her head, burying her face against his chest.

He smiled. "Why? What's the matter with it?"

"I hate it. I've always hated it."

The arm that had been circling her shoulders lifted, and what he'd done with the sweater, he did with her hair, lifting a single strand, rubbing, testing it between his fingers while studying it lazily. "It's the color of sunrise."

"It's the color of vegetables."

"It's the color of flowers—lots of different kinds of flowers."

"It's the color of a chicken's eye."

Beneath her cheek she felt his chest heave as he laughed silently, but when he spoke, it was seriously. "It's the color of the Grand Canyon as the sun slips down beyond the purple side of the mountains."

"It's the color of my freckles. You can hardly tell where one stops and the others start."

His index finger curled beneath her chin and forced her to lift her face. "I can." The way he lounged, his chin was tucked against his chest, and she gazed up across his corduroy lapel, feeling its raised wales digging into her cheek as she met his slumberous green eyes. "And anyway, what's wrong with freckles?" he teased, running the callused tip of his left index finger across the bridge of her nose and the crest of one cheek. "Angel kisses," he whispered, while the finger moved down the tip-tilted nose and the rim of her lips, over the pointed chin and on to her soft throat where a pulse thrummed in rapid tempo.

She tried to say, "Heat spots," but nothing came out except shaky breath and a tiny croak.

His nape came away from the back of the sofa in slow motion while his sea-green eyes locked with hers. "Angel kisses," he whispered, closing her eyes with his warm lips— first touching the left, then the right eyelid. "Have you been kissed by angels, Theresa?" he murmured. The tip of his tongue touched and wet the high curve of her left cheek, and the end of her nose, then her right cheek.

"Nobody but you, Brian."

"I know," came his final murmur before his soft mouth possessed hers. His kiss plucked at her reserve, encouraging a foray into the unknowns of sensuality, but her crossed arms still maintained a barrier between them. His tongue sought nooks and crannies of her mouth that it seemed her own tongue had never discovered before. It swept across warm, moist valleys from where tiny explosions of sensation burst upon her senses. He eased the pressure, catching her upper lip between his teeth, sucking it, releasing it, sensitizing the lower one next in the same seductive way.

Framing the contours of her open lips with his, he eased her back firmly against the sofa, twisting at the waist until his chest pressed her crossed wrists.

"Put your arms around me like you did when you were dancing."

He waited with his lips near her ear, measuring her hesitation by the number of thundering heartbeats that issued the pounding blood through her body and raised a delicate pulse-point at her temple, just beside her hairline. Just when he thought it was hopeless, she at last moved the first hesitant hand, and he lingered above her until finally her arms curved about his shoulders.

"Theresa, don't be afraid. I'd never hurt you."

She began to say, "Brian, don't!" just as his mouth stopped the words from forming, and she felt herself flipping sideways beneath the force of his chest and hands. He shifted and adjusted her without moving his mouth from hers, until she lay beneath him, stretched out on the long sofa, with one foot clinging to the floor for security. Panic and sexuality seemed to be pulling her in opposite directions. *Let him kiss me, let him lie on me, but please, please, don't let him touch my breasts.*

His body was warm and hard, and when he'd tucked her beneath him, Brian opened his knees wide, lifting one to press it over her left thigh, while the other flanked the outside of her right leg all the way to the floor. His belt buckle and zipper pressed hard into her thigh, biting through the thin gabardine of her slacks and bringing to mind images from the movie that was her chief frame of reference to a man's physique. This was more than she had ever willingly let a man do with her. She remembered watching Brian on the dance floor, and his hips took up the same rhythmic tempo that had stirred her earlier. It worked an identical magic on her now, releasing a flood of inner enticement that answered the dance of his body on hers.

"Theresa, I've thought of you for months and months, long before I ever met you." His eyes, as he pulled away only far enough to look into hers, held neither smile nor twinkle. To Theresa's awestruck wonder, they held what seemed to be a look of near reverence.

"But why?" she whispered.

His left hand contoured her neck underneath her hair, while his right meandered across her brow as he traced her bone structure with two fingertips. "I knew more about you than any man has a right to know about a woman he's never met. Sometimes I felt almost guilty about it, but at the same time it drew me to you as if I'd been hypnotized."

"So Jeff told you more than you let on before."

His parted lips pressed against the side of her nose, then he looked into her eyes again. "Jeff loves you as much as any brother could love a sister. He understands what makes you tick…and what doesn't. I had a picture of you as a sweet-natured little music teacher, directing freckle-faced kids for their mommies and daddies, but until I met you, I had no idea you'd look quite so much like one of them yourself."

She tried to turn aside.

"No." He captured her chin, rubbed his index finger along her jawbone. "Don't turn away from me. I told you, I like your freckles, and your hair, and…and everything about you, just because they're you."

She stiffened involuntarily as his hand left her nape and slid between her shoulder blade and the cushion of the sofa. He felt her rigidity, so instead of slipping the hand around to the front of her ribs, he moved it to her shoulder, then down the length of her arm to entwine Theresa's fingers with his. He forced their joined hands up between his chest and her breasts, his forearm now pressing against one of the warm, generous orbs.

Brian thought of the hours he and Jeff had lain in their bunks and talked about this woman. He knew about the times she'd come home in tears over the teasing of some boy, as long ago as when she was only fourteen years old. He knew about the time Jeff had beaten one of her persecutors and been kicked out of school on probation. He knew about the time she'd gone to the high-school prom but came home in tears after her date had proved he was only after two handfuls of the most obvious thing. He knew why she hid in an elementary school where she had to deal mostly with children who were too young and innocent to care about her accursed size; and why she hid inside dark, unattractive clothes; and behind sweaters; and beneath the chin rest of a violin. He knew he was in a spot where, to the best of Jeff's knowledge, no man had ever been allowed before. And he understood that by making the wrong move, he could cause her interminable hurt, and himself as well.

He sought to relax her with soothing endearments, all of them genuinely from the heart. "You smell better than any girl I've ever danced with." He nuzzled her neck, stringing kisses along her jaw like pearls upon a waxed thread. "And you dance just the way I like a girl to dance." He dropped a kiss on the corner of her mouth. "I love your music…" On her nose. "And your innocence…" On her eye. "Your Nocturnes…" On her temple. "And your long, beautiful fingers on the piano keys…" He kissed five knuckles in turn. "And being with you at midnight on New Year's Eve." At last he kissed her mouth, lingering there to dip his tongue between her soft, innocent lips, to join her in a celebration of a new year, a new discovery, a new awareness of how right they seemed for each other.

Theresa felt lifted, transported above herself, as if this must certainly be someone other than herself in Brian Scanlon's arms, hearing his murmured words of admiration. Perhaps she was an understudy having stepped in at curtain time when the star performer fell ill. Perhaps these words were meant for that other woman, the one with the silhouette of a sylph, with mink-brown hair and golden, flawless skin. That other woman had performed this part so many times she knew instinctively how to react to this man's voice and movements.

But Theresa was not that practiced artiste. She was a hesitant ingenue to whom the part did not come naturally. She wanted to lift her arms around Brian's shoulders and return the string of kisses he'd just bestowed upon her, but relinquishing the guard she'd maintained for years was no easy thing. Experience had taught her only too clearly that to believe she could attract someone because of her hidden attributes was a pipe dream. Each time she had done so, the man upon whom she'd pinned her hopes had proved himself no more honorable than the boy who'd made one blossom-kissed May prom night eight years earlier not a memorable celebration of the end of a school year but an ugly memory of shame and disgust she'd made sure had never been repeated since.

Brian's forearm rested across her right breast, depressing it in an almost lackadaisical fashion that felt natural and acceptable to Theresa, until he began moving his wrist back and forth as if something had tickled it and he was relieving the itch by rubbing the skin across her sweater. His fingers were still interlaced with Theresa, and he carried her own hand atop his, turning it now so that the back of only his hand came into contact with her breasts.

Don't panic. Don't resist. Let him. Let him touch you and see if it makes you react like the woman reacted in the movie. Theresa swallowed, and Brian's tongue did sensuous things to the inside of her mouth.

He pulled back, teased the rim of her mouth with a butterfly's touch of his lips. "Theresa, don't be scared." She tried not to be, telling her muscles to relax as he released her tense fingers and rested his warm palm upon the ribbed waist of her sweater. *No. Don't let him be like all the others. Don't let him want me for only that. Not Brian, who's been so careful not to even look at me there during all these wonderful days while he grew dearer.*

Beside them the fire danced, sending warmth radiating against the sides of their faces and bodies. But she pinched her eyelids shut, unaware of the troubled expression on Brian's face as he gazed down at her. She lay beneath him with the stillness of fallen snow, pale and motionless, and breathing with great difficulty. But her breath was not drawn through lips fallen open in passion, rather through nostrils distended in apprehension.

Her flesh was warm beneath the sweater, and her ribs surprisingly fine-boned, the skin over them taut and toned. Her frame, Brian now realized, was built for bearing much smaller breasts than those with which she'd been endowed. *Trust me, Theresa. It's you, your heart, your uncomplicated simple soul that I'm learning to love. But loving the soul of you means loving the body of you as well. And we must start with that. Sometime, we must start.*

He moved his hand up her ribs, his warm palm molding itself to the arch of her rib cage, finally placing four fingertips in the warm hollow just beneath one breast. Gently he brushed back and forth, giving her time to accept the idea of his imminent intrusion. Beneath the heel of his hand he felt an unnatural tremor, as if she were holding her breath to keep from crying. Against his belly her midsection was arched up off the cushions, not in enthusiastic acquiescence, but in fortification as if steeling herself to defend at a second's notice.

He covered her lips with his in forewarning, then rolled aside just enough to allow freedom of access to the warm, soft globe of flesh that brushed his fingernails and moved toward it with as much gentleness as he could muster. Seeking not to violate or to trespass, he breached the remaining space, playing her the first time with as fluttering a touch as he might have used to chime the strings of a guitar instead of strumming them. Beneath his mouth, hers quivered. *Easy, love, easy,* he thought.

His first touch brushed scarcely more than the seam of the stiff cotton garment that covered her, as he ran his fingertips along its deep curve, from the center of her chest across her breast to the warm, secret place beneath her arm.

She shuddered and tensed further.

He lightened his hold on her lips until their kiss became

more of a commingling of breath than of flesh, a foretoken of the gentleness he was preparing for her. *Trust me, Theresa.* Once more he nudged her lips with a blandishment so weightless it might have been the gossamer approach of nothing more than the shadow cast by his head bending over hers.

But caution cracked through Theresa's nerves and kept her from mellowing and melting beneath him. She waited, instead, like a martyr at the stake, until at last he enfolded her breast, firmly, fully, running his thumb along the horizontal seam of her bra. She acquiesced for the moment, allowing him to discover the breadth, resilience and warmth of her breast.

As his hand caressed and explored, Theresa waited in agony, wanting so much more than what she was able to allow herself to feel in the way of response. She wanted to stretch and loll, to utter some thick sound in her throat as the woman had in the movie. She wanted to know the pleasure other women seemed to derive from having their breasts caressed and petted. But her breasts had never been objects of pleasure, only of pain, and she found herself recalling the hurt of countless callous insults, feeling diminished by those recollections, even while Brian bestowed a touch of utmost honor and respect. But as he pushed her sweater up to her breastbone, she was like a hummingbird poised for flight.

He sensed it, yet steeled himself and moved the next step further along the road toward mutuality, inching down until his hips rested on the sofa between her open legs, and his head dipped down, his open mouth replacing his hand, kissing her through the cotton fabric that separated her flesh from his.

Brian's breath was warm, then hot, and it sent waves of sensation shimmying up her ribs and along the outer perimeter of her breasts, cresting in a tightening sensation that drew her nipples up into a pair of hard knots, shriveling them like rosebuds that refuse to open. Through her bra he gently bit, and the sweet ache it caused made her hands fly into the air behind him, palms pushing at nothing.

He lifted his head. She heard him whisper, "Shh…" but she could not open her eyes and meet his gaze, for behind her lids was the vivid image of her nipples. She saw again the tiny, demure nipples of other girls in shower scenes from years ago, envying them their delicacy, their femininity, and her terror grew. If she could be assured he'd go no further, she might have relaxed and enjoyed the shivering sensation his kiss sent through her. But she knew, as surely as she knew the shape of her own bovine proportions, that the next step was one she could not suffer. She could not bare herself to the eyes of any man. Her breasts were freckled, unattractive and when released fell aside like two obscene mounds of dough.

Oh, please, Brian, I don't want you to see me that way. You'll never want to look at me again.

The fireplay illuminated their bodies, and she knew if she opened her eyes she would see too clearly how visible she was by its light. His mouth bestowed a breath-stealing warmth to her opposite breast, and, as with the first, it was a seductive nip through stiff cotton whose very scratch seemed to beguile her flesh to succumb.

But when Brian braced himself above her and slipped his hands behind her back to free the catch of her brassiere, no power on earth could allow Theresa to let him see her naked.

"Don't!" she whispered fiercely.

"Theresa, I—"

"Don't!" She pushed against the hollows of his elbows, her eyes wide with trepidation. "I…please…"

"All I'm going to do—"

"No! You're not going to do anything!" She flattened her shoulder blades to prevent his captured hands from doing what they'd been reaching behind her to do. "Please, just get off."

"You haven't given me a ch—"

"I'm not that kind of woman, Brian!"

"What kind?" Relentlessly he held her where she was.

"Loose, and…and easy." She struggled, unable to free her writhing limbs from the weight of his.

"Do you really believe I could ever think of you that way?"

Tears of mortification stung her eyes. "Isn't that what all men think?"

She saw the hurt flash across his green eyes; the line of his jaw harden momentarily. "I'm not *all men*. I thought maybe you'd come to realize that since I've been here. I didn't start this to see how much I could get out of you."

"Oh, no? Considering where your hands are right now, I'd say I have cause to doubt that."

He closed his eyes, let his head droop forward and shook it in a slow gesture of exasperation while emitting an annoyed puff of breath. He withdrew his hands and dragged himself away, rolling to sit on the edge of the sofa. But their limbs were still half tangled, and she was caught in a vulnerable, splayed pose, with one knee hooked beneath his, the other updrawn behind his back.

She arched up and tugged her sweater down to her waist while he heaved a frustrated sigh and ran a hand through his hair, then slouched forward, elbows to knees, letting his hands dangle limply while he stared absently into the fire, a deep frown upon his face.

"Let me up," she whispered.

He moved as if only now realizing he had her pinned in a less than modest sprawl. She disentangled herself and curled into the corner of the sofa, not quite cowering, but withdrawn behind her familiar shield of crossed arms.

"You really are an uptight woman, you know?" he said angrily. "Just what the hell did you think I was going to do?"

"Exactly what you tried!"

"So what does that make me?" He flung up both palms. "A pervert? Theresa, for God's sake, we're adults. It's hardly considered perverted to do a little petting."

She found the word distasteful. Her expression soured. "I don't want to be gawked at like some freak in a sideshow."

"Oh, come on, aren't you being a little dramatic?"

"To you it's dramatic, to me it's…it's traumatic."

"Are you saying you've never let a guy take off your bra before?"

She only puckered her mouth and refused to look at him.

He pondered her silently for several seconds before asking,

"Had you considered that's not exactly normal—or healthy—for a twenty-five-year-old woman?"

Now her eyes met his, but they shot sparks. "Oh, and I suppose you're volunteering to break me in for my own good, is that it?"

"You'll have to admit, it might be good for you."

She snorted quietly and cast her eyes aside while he grew increasingly upset with her. "You know, I'm getting awfully damn tired of you crossing your arms like I'm Jack the Ripper...*and* of having my motives questioned when the way I look at it, I'm the one with the normal impulses here."

"Well, I've had plenty of lessons on the *normal impulses* of the American male!" she shot back.

They sat stonily for several long, strained minutes, staring straight ahead, disappointed that this night that had started so magically was ending this way.

Finally Brian sighed and turned to study her. "Theresa, I'm sorry, all right? But I feel something for you, and I thought you felt the same about me. Everything between us was right tonight, and I thought it led to this quite naturally."

"Not every woman in the world agrees with you!" she shot back.

"Would you look at me...please?" His voice was low, caring, hurt. She pulled her gaze away from the fire, feeling as if its hue had been drawn to the skin of her face, which was flooded with a heat of a very different kind. Theresa confronted his eyes to find a wounded expression there that disconcerted her. He rested an elbow along the back of the davenport, his fingertips very near her shoulder. "I don't have much time, Theresa. Two more days and I'll be gone. If I had weeks, or months to woo you, things would be different, but I don't have. So I used the accepted approach, because I didn't want to go back to Minot and wonder for the next six months about your feelings." His fingertips brushed the shoulder of her sweater very lightly, sending a shudder down her spine.

"I like you, Theresa, do you believe that?" She bit the soft inside of her lip and stared at him, becoming undone by his words, his sincerity. "*You.* You, the person. The sister of my friend, the musician who shares a love of music with me, the girl who kept her brother straight, and who laughs while she fiddles a hayseed hoedown on her classic 1906 Storioni and understands what I feel when I play Newbury's songs. I like the you that never knew how to put on makeup before tonight and had to learn how from her fourteen-year-old sister, and the you that walked into the kitchen with the refreshing shyness of a fawn. I like the fact that you wouldn't know the first thing about dancing the way Felice does. As a matter of fact, there's not much about you I don't like. I thought you understood all that. I thought you understood the reason why I tried to express my feelings the way I just did."

Her heart felt swollen, her throat thick, and her eyes and nose stung. Words like these, she'd always thought, were always spoken only in love stories, to the other girls, the pretty ones with miniature figures and silken hair.

"I do." She wanted very much to reach out and touch his cheek, but her inhibitions were long nurtured and would take time to crumble. So she attempted to tell Brian with the wistful, downturned corners of her lips, with the aching expression in her tear-bright eyes how remorseful she was at that moment. "Oh, Brian, I'm sorry I said that. And it wasn't true. I said it because I was scared, and I…I just got panicky at the last minute. I said the first thing I could think of to stop you, but I didn't mean it. Not about you."

His fingertips still brushed her shoulder. "Did you think I didn't know you were scared?"

"I…" She swallowed and dropped her eyes.

"I've known it since before I met you. I've watched you hiding behind sweaters and purses and even your violin ever since I first got here, but I thought if I took it slow, if I showed you that other things came first with me, you'd…" He made a gesture with his palms, then his hands went limp. She felt her face heating up again, radiating with the embarrassment she felt at confronting this issue. It seemed impossible that she was actually talking about it…and with a *man.*

"Theresa, don't look away from me, damn it. I'm not some pervert who took a bead on you and came here to see if he could make another score, and you know it."

Her tears grew plump and then spilled over, and at the moment of her discomposure, she drew her knees up tightly, circled them with her arms, dropped her forehead and emitted a single sob.

"B-but you don't know wh-what's it's like."

"I understand that when you feel something as strong as I feel for you, it's natural to express it like I tried to."

"Maybe for you its n-natural, but for me it's awful."

"*Awful?* You find being touched by me *awful?*"

"No, not by *you*, just...*there*. On my breasts, I...kn-knew you were going to and I was so...so..." She couldn't finish but kept her face hidden from him.

"My God, Theresa, do you think I don't know that? The village idiot couldn't miss seeing how you hide them. So what should I have done? Bypassed them and touched you someplace else? What would you have thought of me then? I told you, I wanted—" he stopped abruptly, glowered at the fire, ran his hands down the length of his face and grunted, almost as if to himself. "Oh, damn." He seemed to gather his thoughts for a minute, then faced her again and gripped her shoulder to force her to meet his eyes. Her own were still streaming, and his were angry. Or perhaps frustrated. "Listen, I knew about your hang-up before I stepped off that plane. I've been trying to come to grips with it myself ever since I've been here, but I like you, damn it! And part of it is physical, but that's how it is. Your breasts are part of you, and you like me, too, but if you're going to shy away every time I try to touch you, we've got a real problem."

She was surprised with his directness in stating the issue. Even the word *breasts* had inhibited her all her life. Now here he was, pronouncing it with the candor of a health teacher. But she could see he didn't understand how difficult it was for her to cast off her mantle of self-consciousness. It was seated in too many painful memories from her teenage years. And he,

Brian Scanlon, long, lean, perfect, the target of admiration of countless enamored females, could hardly be expected to fathom what it was like to be shaped the way she was.

"You just don't understand," she said expressionlessly.

"You keep saying that. Give me a chance, will you?"

"Well, it's true. You're…you're one of the lucky ones. Look at you, all lean and trim and handsome and…well, you take for granted being…being *normal* and shaped like everyone else."

"Normal?" he frowned. "You don't think you're normal, just because you're built like you are?"

"No!" She glared at him defiantly, then dashed away a tear with an angry lash of her hand. "You couldn't possibly understand what it's like to be…to be gawked at like a…a freak in a sideshow. They started growing when I was thirteen, and at first the girls were jealous that I was the first one to need a bra. But by the time I was fourteen the girls stopped being jealous and were only…amazed."

Oddly Brian had never considered how girls had treated her. This was a secret hurt even Jeff hadn't known. He felt Theresa's remembered pain keenly as she went on.

"In school when we had to take showers the girls gaped at me as if I was the ninth wonder of the world. Gym class was one of the greatest horrors of my life." A faraway look stole over her face, and her eyes closed wearily. "Running." She laughed ruefully, the sound seeming to stick in her throat as her lids lifted again. "Running wasn't only embarrassing, it hurt. So I…I gave up running at an age when it's a natural part of a teenager's life." She blinked once, slowly, staring at a distant point while wrapping her arms around her knees. Brian gently closed a hand over her forearm, urging her to meet his gaze.

"And you resent it? You feel cheated?"

He understood! He understood! The knowledge freed her to admit it at last. "Yes! I couldn't…." She choked and tears came to her eyes. "I gave up so many th-things I wanted. Trading clothes w-with my friends. B-bathing suits. Sports. Dancing." She took a deeper gulp. "Boys," she finished softly.

He rubbed her arm. "Tell me," he encouraged.

Her gaze shifted to his face. "Boys," she repeated, and again stared at the patterns in the fire. "Boys came in two categories then. The gawkers and the gropers. The gawkers were the ones who went into a near catatonic state just being in the same room with me. The gropers were…well…" Her voice trailed away and she looked aside.

Brian understood how difficult this was for her. But it had to be said to clear the air between them. He touched her jaw. "The gropers were…"

She turned and met his eyes, then hers dropped as she went on. "The gropers were the ones who ogled and leered and liked to talk dirty."

A shaft of heat and anger speared through Brian, and he wondered guiltily if there were times in his youth when he might have tormented a girl like Theresa. Again she continued.

"I went on a couple of dates, but that was enough. Their side of the front seat hardly got warm before they were over on my side to see if they could get a feel of the…the notorious Theresa Brubaker." She turned and asked sadly, "Do you know what they called me, Brian?"

He did, but he let her admit it so the catharsis might be complete.

"Theresa Boob-Acres. Acres of boobs, that's what they said I had." She laughed ruefully, but tears like sad diamonds shot with orange from the fire glow dropped down her cheeks. She seemed unaware they had fallen. "Or sometimes they called me Tits Boobaker. Jugs. Udders—oh, there are a hundred insulting words for them and I know every one."

Brian's heart hurt for her. So much of this he'd learned from Jeff, but it was far more wrenching, hearing it from Theresa herself.

"The gropers…" she repeated, as if steeling herself to face one memory worse than the rest. Brian sat without moving, one hand along the back of the sofa, the other still lightly resting on her arm. Her voice was thick and uneven. "When I was in the ninth grade a bunch of boys caught me in the hall after school one day. I can remember exactly what I was wearing b-because I came home and b-buried it in the bottom of the g-garbage can." Her eyelids slid closed, and he watched her throat working. He'd heard it before and wished he could prevent her from going on, but if she shared it all it meant she trusted him, and this he wanted very badly. "It was a white blouse with little pearl buttons down the front and a tiny round collar edged with pink lace. I'd always l-loved it because it was a C-Christmas present from Grandma Deering." A tear plunged over her eyelid and she dashed it away, then gripped her own sleeves again. "Anyway, I had an armful of books when they—they caught me. I re-remember the books skittering along the floor when they…p-pushed me back against the lockers, and how… c-cold the lockers were." She shivered and rubbed her arms. "Two of the boys held my arms straight out while the other two f-felt me up." Her eyes closed, lips and chin quivered. Brian's hand squeezed the back of her neck, but she was lost to all but the memory and the hurt it revived. She drew a deep, shaking breath and her lips dropped open. "I was too sc-scared to tell Mother, but they'd torn the b-buttonholes of my blouse, and I d—" She shrugged helplessly. "I didn't know how I'd answer questions about it, so I…I threw the blouse away where I was sure she wouldn't find it." A sob erupted at last, but she immediately firmed her lips and lifted her chin.

He could bear it no longer and gently forced her close, circling her neck with one arm, urging her into the curve of his body until her updrawn knees pressed his chest and her feet slipped beneath his thigh. She was trembling terribly. He rested his cheek against her hair and felt a devastating sting at the back of his eyes. He closed them and uttered, "Theresa, I'm sorry," and kissed her hair and made futile wishes that he could change her memories to happier ones. She remained tightly curled in the circle of his arms. Again her voice went on tremulously, and she unconsciously plucked at the fibres of his sweater.

"In eleventh grade there was a boy I liked a lot. He was nothing like those other boys. He was quiet and musical and he…he liked me a lot, too. I could tell. Prom time came, and

I'd catch him staring at me across the orchestra room—not at my breasts, but at my face. I knew he wanted to ask me to the prom, but in the end he chickened out. I knew he was scared of my…my enormous proportions.

"But s somebody else asked me. A boy named Greg Palovich. He seemed nice enough, and he was handsome and really polite…until…until the end of the evening when we were in the c-car." All was silent for a long, tense moment. Her voice was sorrowful as she finished. "He didn't t-tear my dress. He was very careful not to." She turned her face sharply against Brian's chest. "Oh, B-Brian, it was so humiliating, s-so degrading. I still cringe every t-time I hear the word prom."

Brian's hand found her head and smoothed her hair, holding her face protectively against the aching thud of his heart. Again he experienced the deep wish to be sixteen, to be able to invite her to the prom himself and give her a glowing memory to carry away with her. He tipped her face up and ran a thumb beneath her eye, wiping the wetness aside. "If we were in school now, I'd see to it you had some happy memories."

Her heart swelled with gratitude. She watched the fire light the planes and curves of his face. "Oh, Brian," she said softly, "I believe you would." She sat up regretfully and resumed her former pose, feeling his eyes on the side of her face as she again stared at the fire and hugged her knees. "But nobody can change what's past. And neither can you change the nature of man."

"It's still happening?" he questioned quietly. When she only gazed ahead absently without answering, he caught her chin with a finger and forced her to look at him. "Look at me, Theresa. Tell me the rest so we can put it behind us. It's still happening?"

She shifted her chin aside and dropped her eyes to her crossed arms. "It happens each time I walk into a room where there's a strange man I've never met before. I tell myself this time it won't happen. This time it'll be different. When we're introduced, his eyes will stay on my face." Theresa's voice was nearly a whisper now, filled with chagrin and an edge of shame. "But no man ever meets my eyes when he meets me. Their eyes always drop straight down to my chest." She fell silent, sensing his frowning scrutiny. His hand was gone from the back of her neck. Only his gaze touched her. When he spoke, his voice was firm.

"Mine didn't."

No, his didn't. And that was why she'd begun liking him almost immediately. But she knew why.

"You were forewarned."

He couldn't deny it, or the fact that if he hadn't been, his eyes very likely would have widened and dropped. "Yes, I'll admit it. I was."

She stared at a spurting blue flame that gathered a sudden surge of life, even as the fire dwindled. The shadows in the room were deep fingers of gray.

"I've never talked about this with anyone else before in my life."

"What about your mother?"

She turned her troubled eyes to his, and each of them saw the glint of the dying flames reflected beneath unsmiling eyebrows. "My mother?" Theresa gave a soft, rueful chuckle deep in her throat, closed her eyes and dropped her head back against the sofa cushion. Brian watched the curved line of her throat as she spoke. "My mother's answer to the problem was to tell me all I needed was a heavy-duty bra. Oh God, how I hate them. They aren't pretty, and when you tried to…" She lifted her head but wouldn't meet his eyes. "Well, *before,* I couldn't bear the thought of you seeing me either with my bra or without it. I'm not a very pretty sight either way."

"Theresa, don't say that." He eased closer and laid a hand on the top of her head and stroked her hair, then let his palm lie lightly on her bright, airy curls.

"Well, it's true. But it was never anything I could talk about with my mother. She's generously endowed herself, and once when I was around fourteen and came to her crying over how big I was getting, she treated the problem like it was something I'd get over when I got older. After all, she said, *she did.* When

I asked if I could talk to somebody else about it, like our doctor or a counselor, she said, 'Don't be foolish, Theresa. There's nothing you can do about it but accept it.' I don't think she ever realized she's got a totally different personality than mine. She's…well, brazen and domineering. A person like that *can* overcome their hang-ups more easily than someone like me."

They sat in silence for several long minutes. She heard Brian draw a deep breath and let it out slowly. "So how do you feel about it now, now that you've talked about it with me?"

"I…" She glanced up to find him watching her closely. His hand had fallen from her head, but those knowing eyes held her prisoner. "Surprised that I really managed to tell you everything like I did."

"I'm glad you confided in me, Theresa. Somehow I think it'll help you in more ways than just…well, letting go."

She studied him now as carefully as he studied her. "Brian, tell me something." Her forearms were crossed atop her updrawn knees, and she picked at a thread of her knit sleeve, thoughtful for a moment, before turning to catch his eyes again. "Tonight at the dance you said that Felice reminded you of the groupies who hang around the stage and hope to…to score with the guitar man after the dance. You said…" She swallowed, amazed at her own temerity, but somehow finding herself unleashed in a new way. "Well, you said they were a dime a dozen, but that wasn't what you wanted…*tonight.*" Again she swallowed, but he refused to help her along. He was going to make her voice her question if she wanted an answer. "Does that mean you've…indulged with lots of girls like this…on other nights?"

"Some." The word was quiet, truthful.

"Then why…I mean, I'm not…experienced like those girls. Why would you want to be with me instead of them?"

He moved closer, his right elbow hooked on the back of the sofa, his hand gently stroking her arm. "Because bodies are not what love is about. Souls are."

"Love?" Her eyes widened and met his in surprise.

"You don't have to look so threatened by the word."

"I'm not threatened by it."

"Yes, you are."

"No, I'm not."

"If you fell in love, you'd have to face the inevitable sooner or later."

"But I haven't fallen in love, so I'm not threatened." She'd had to deny it—after all, he hadn't actually said he loved her.

"Fair enough. I answered your question, now you answer one of mine. And I want an honest answer."

But she refused to agree until she knew what he was going to ask.

"Why did you go through all the trouble of buying new clothes, learning how to put on makeup and fingernail polish and going to the beauty shop before our date tonight?"

"I...I thought it was time I learned."

He smiled, a slow grin that appeared briefly, then was gone, replaced by his too-intense study. He moved nearer, until she had to lift her face to meet his eyes above her. "You're a liar, Theresa Brubaker," he stated in a disarmingly quiet tone. "And if you didn't feel threatened, we wouldn't have had the discussion we just had. But you've got nothing to fear from me."

"Brian..." Her breath caught in her throat as he moved unhesitatingly to encircle her in his arms.

"Put your damn knees down and quit hiding from me. I'm not Greg Palovich, all right?"

But she was too stunned to move. He wouldn't! He wouldn't! Not again. Her muscles were tensing tighter, and she'd just begun to tighten her hold around her knees when with one swift sweep of his hand, Brian knocked her feet off the edge of the davenport. His strong hands closed around her shoulders, and he jerked her forward with deadly accuracy, pulling her up against his chest with their arms around each other. "I'm getting damn sick of seeing you with your arms crossed over your chest. And I'm starting back at the beginning, where you should have started when you were fourteen. Let's pretend that's how old you are, and all I want is a goodnight kiss from the girl I took to the dance."

Before Theresa's astonishment could find voice, she was neatly enfolded against the strong, hard chest of the guitar man who'd had plenty of experience at seduction. His warm, moist, open mouth slanted across hers while one warm hand slipped up her neck and got lost in her hair. His tongue tutored hers in the ways of one far beyond fourteen years of age, slipping erotically to points of secrecy that started sensual urges coursing through her limbs and spearing down her belly. He lifted the pressure of his lips only enough to be heard while their tongues still touched. "I'm going to be so damn good for you, Theresa Brubaker. You'll see. Now touch me the way you've been wanting to since we left the dance floor." His tongue returned fully to her mouth, teasing, stroking hers with promises of delight. But he kept one arm around her ribs, the other hooked over the side of her neck, and his hands played only over her back, caressing it slowly but thoroughly while she let hers do the same upon him. Her hand wandered up his neck, to the soft, short hair that still retained the vestige of masculine toiletries she'd first smelled when she'd taken his cap. She thought of a line from the Newbury song: "Wandering from room to room, he's turning on each light…." And it felt as if Brian was showing her the light, one small room at a time. Their kiss grew more intimate as he murmured wordless sounds of approval, and she wanted to respond in kind, to give voice to the new explosive feelings she was experiencing. But just at that moment, he pushed her back gently.

"I'll see you tomorrow, okay, sweets? I can only be honorable up to a point."

He got to his feet and tugged her along behind him. Looping a lazy arm around her shoulders, he sauntered with her to the stairway. There he stopped her just as she'd gained the first step. He stood on the floor so their eyes were now on the same level. In the deep shadows, his palms held her hips and he turned her to face him before he enclosed her in a warm embrace once again, found her lips for a last, lingering kiss, then turned her away with a soft, "Good night."

Chapter 8

Theresa and Brian were not alone long enough during that day to speak of anything that had happened the night before, or to exchange touches or insight as to what the other was thinking of all that had passed between them. It was a lazy day. They'd all been up late and took turns napping, sprawled in chairs and on floors before the New Year's Day football games that flickered on the television screen or tucked into their own rooms. It seemed to take until nearly suppertime for everyone to come fully alive, and even then, it was a subdued group, for with only one more day before Brian and Jeff would be gone, they all felt an impending sense of loss.

The following morning, Theresa awakened shortly after dawn and lay staring at the pewter frog Brian had given her. She recalled everything that had happened between them since the first night when they'd sat side by side with his elbow pressing hers throughout that extremely sensuous love scene.

Who was she trying to fool? It had almost been predestined, this feeling she had for Brian Scanlon. She was falling in love with him, with a man two years her junior who admitted he'd had sexual encounters with any number of admiring fans. The idea that he was fully experienced and worldly made her feel inadequate and puerile. Again she wondered why he'd want an introverted, frightened virgin like her. She was daunted by his physical beauty, for it seemed to dazzle when compared to her ordinary-to-homely features, making her believe he couldn't possibly be attracted to her, as he'd said he was. How could he possibly be? With women like Felice fawning over him, pursuing him, eager to share more than just a bump-and-grind dance with him, why would Brian Scanlon possibly pursue Theresa Brubaker?

She sighed, closed her eyes and tried to imagine lying naked with him but found it impossible to picture herself in that context. She was too inhibited, too freckled, too redheaded to fit the part. She wished she were shaped like a pencil and had russet skin and sleek, auburn hair. She wished she'd found at least one boy or man sometime during her life who'd have been able to break through the barriers of self-consciousness to give her some sense of what to expect if she allowed Brian more sexual liberties.

The pewter frog sat on the shelf, caught in a still life, fiddling his silent note and smiling. *I'm like that frog. My life is like a silent note; I play, but I haven't felt the music of the heart.*

It was seven-thirty. She heard her parents leave for work, but the rest of the house was silent. She dragged herself from bed, dressed and made coffee, and still nobody else roused. Tomorrow Brian and Jeff would leave, and the house would seem abandoned. The mere thought of it filled her with loneliness. How would she make it from day to day when Brian was gone? How unfair that he should be snatched away just when they discovered their attraction for each other. She wandered to the bathroom, collected the dirty towels from the rack, hung up fresh ones, went to her room and added her own soiled laundry to the pile. She wondered how long she should wait before starting the washing machine to launder Jeff's clothes so he could take them back clean and save a laundry bill.

They had been running free all week, the whole bunch of them, and nobody had bothered much with homemaking chores. The pile of dirty clothes at the bottom of the laundry chute would be mountainous.

She waited until ten o'clock before creeping down the basement stairs like a burglar, sneaking onto each tread, afraid the step would creak and awaken Brian, who lay on his belly with both arms flung up, his ear pressed to one bicep. She halted in her tracks, gazing across the dim room at his bare back, at the outline of his hips and legs beneath the green blanket. His right leg was extended, his left bent with the tip of its knee peeking from under the covers. The only men she'd ever seen in bed were her father and Jeff. But seeing Brian there, listening to the light snuffle of his regular breathing, had a decidedly sensual effect upon Theresa.

She clutched her armload of dirty laundry and tiptoed to the laundry-room door, turned the knob soundlessly and latched it behind her with equally little noise.

She sorted out six piles of colors, dropped the first stack into the machine and grimaced at how loud the selector dial sounded when she spun it to its starting position—the clicks erupted through the silence like a tommy gun. When she pushed the knob to start the water flowing, it sounded like Niagara Falls had just rerouted through the basement. Soap, softener, then she picked her way across the floor between hills of fabric and opened the door to the family room.

She had just managed to get it closed silently again when Brian—still on his belly—lifted his head, emitted a snort and scratched his nose with the back of one hand. She stood transfixed, watching the light from the sliding glass door find its way across the ridges of his shoulder blades and the individual ones of his spinal column to the spot where the sheet divided his body in half. He cleared his throat, lifted his head again and intuitively glanced back over his shoulder.

Theresa stood rooted to the spot, holding onto the doorknob behind her, feeling the blood raddle her cheeks at being discovered there, watching him awaken.

His hair was standing up at odd angles. His cheek and jaw wore the shadow of a night's growth. His eyes were still swollen from sleep. "Good morning," he managed in a voice raspy from disuse. The greeting was accompanied by a slow over-the-shoulder smile that drew up one side of his mouth engagingly. Lazily, he rolled over, crooking one arm behind his head, presenting an armpit shadowed by dark hair and a chest sprinkled with a liberal portion of the same.

"Good morning." Her voice came out a whisper.

"What time is it?"

"After ten." She flapped an apologetic palm at the laundry-room door. "I'm sorry I woke you up with the washer, but I wanted to get the laundry started. Jeff's clothes…are…he…" To Theresa's dismay the words chugged away into silence, and she stood staring at half of a naked man, one who made everything inside her body go as watery as the sounds emanating from the other side of the wall.

"Come here." He didn't move; nothing more than the beguiling lips formed the invitation. His right arm cradled the back of his head. His left lay flat on his belly, the thumb resting in his navel, which was exposed above the blanket. One knee was straight, the other one bent so that its outline formed a triangle beneath the blankets. "Come here, Theresa," he repeated, more softly than before, lifting a hand toward her.

Her startled expression warned him she'd dreamed up an excuse, even before she began to voice it. "I have to—"

"Come." He rolled to one hip, and for a horrifying moment she thought he was going to get up and come to get her. But he only braced up one elbow and extended a hand, palm up.

She wiped her own palms on her thighs and advanced slowly across the room but stopped two feet from the edge of his mattress. His hand remained open, waiting. Upon it she could see the calluses on each of its four fingertips from playing the guitar. He had very, very long fingers. And he slept with his watch on.

It was so still just then she thought she could hear its electronic hum.

He moved himself up just high enough and strained forward across the remaining two feet to capture her hand and drag her toward him. Her kneecaps struck the frame of the bed, and she toppled down, twisting at the last minute to land half on one hip but coming to rest at an awkward angle, half across his bare chest.

"Good morning." His smile was thorough, teasing and warming places inside Theresa that she'd never realized hadn't known complete warmth before. He slipped one arm between her and the mattress and rolled to his hip facing her, managing to maneuver her stomach flush against his. She recalled in bemused fascination that she'd read that men often wake up fully aroused, but she was too ignorant to know if it was true of Brian this morning. He brushed her cheek with the backs of his knuckles, and his voice was charmingly gruff. "I find it hard to believe there's one woman left in this world who still blushes at age twenty-five." He dipped his head to touch her lips with a nibbling kiss. "And you know what?" He ran the tip of an exploring index finger across the juncture of her lips, causing them to fall open as she caught a breath in her throat. "Some day I'm going to see you wearing only that." He dipped his head again, but when their mouths joined, he rolled her over on her back and lay half across her body. His back was warm, firm, and beneath her palm she felt each taut muscle across his shoulders, then explored his ribs, like a warm, living vibraphone upon which her fingers played.

His naked chest was pressed against her breasts, flattening them in a way that felt wholly wonderful. She was wearing a thick wool hunter's shirt of gold and black squares, buttoned up the front, its deep tails flapping loose about her hips, which were squeezed tightly into a pair of washed-out denim Levi's. The shirt left her totally accessible—she realized that just as his weight bore down on her, and he lifted one knee across her thighs, rubbing up and down repeatedly, slowly inching higher until the inner bend of knee softly chafed the feminine mound at the juncture of her legs. Still kissing her, he found the arm with which she was protecting her breast and forced it up over his shoulder. Then his hand skimmed down the scratchy wool shirt, up under its tails and onto the bare band of skin between her jeans and bra. He drew a valentine on her ribs, then cupped her breast with unyielding authority, pushing on it so hard it caused a queer but welcome ache in the hollow of her throat. She felt the nerves begin to jump deep in her stomach, but controlled the urge to fight him off. The caress was brief, almost as if he was testing her, telling her, get used to it, try it, just this much, a little at a time. But, to Theresa's surprise, when his fingers left her breast, they skimmed straight down the center of her belly, along the hard zipper of her jeans and cupped the very warm, throbbing spot at the base of the zipper. Within the constricting blue denim her flesh immediately responded with a heat so awesome it caught her by surprise. She sucked in a quick, delighted breath, and her eyelids slammed closed. Her back arched up off the mattress and fire shot from the spot he caressed down to her toes. He clutched her with a hard, forceful palm, pushing upward until she was certain he could feel the pulse beat throbbing through the hard, flat-felled seams of the Levi's. He stroked her through the tight, binding denim—once, twice, almost as if marking her with his stamp of possession.

Before she could decide whether to fight or yield, his hand was gone. She lay looking up at his stormy green eyes while he braced on both elbows, and their labored breathing pounded out the message of mutual arousal.

"Theresa, I'm going to miss you. But six months and I'll be back. Okay?" His voice had gone even huskier with desire. What was he asking? The answer to the ambiguous question stuck in her throat.

"Brian, I…I'm not sure." She didn't think she could make such a promise, if he meant what she thought he did.

"Just think about it then, will you? And when June comes, we'll see."

"A lot can happen between now and June."

"I know. Just don't…." His troubled eyes traveled up to her hair. He soothed it back almost roughly, then returned his gaze to her amazed brown eyes, sending a message of fierce possession as absolute as that he'd delivered in his startling caress of a moment ago. "Don't find somebody else. I want to be first, Theresa, because I understand you, and I'll be good for you. That's a promise."

Just then Jeff's voice boomed from above; the washing

machine had brought the house to life at last: "Hey, where is everybody? Brian, you awake?"

"Yeah, just dressing. I'll be right up."

Theresa nudged Brian aside and leaped off the bed. But before she could scamper away he captured her wrist and pulled her back down. She landed with a soft plop, sitting on the edge of the bed. He braced on one elbow, half curling his body around her to look up into her face.

"Theresa, will you kiss me just once, without looking like you're scared to death?"

"I'm not very good at any of this, Brian. I think you'd be a lot happier if you gave up on me," she whispered.

He frowned, released the hand she'd been tugging in an effort to regain her freedom. But when it was released, it lay on the mattress beside her hip with the fingers curled tightly underneath. He studied it, then with a single finger stroked the backs of the freckled knuckles. Looking up into her uncertain eyes, he said, "Never. I'll never give up on you. I'll be back in June, and we'll see if we can't get you past age fifteen."

How does a person grow to be so self-assured at twenty-three, she wondered, meeting his unsmiling gaze with her own somber eyes.

His weight shifted. He kissed her fleetingly and ordered, "You go on up first. I'll make my bed and wait a few minutes before I follow."

That night they spent quietly at home. Patricia came over to be with Jeff. Margaret and Willard sat side by side on the sofa while Jeff sat cross-legged on the floor and Brian took the piano bench, and the two played their guitars and sang. Theresa was curled up in one armchair, Amy in another, and Patricia sat just behind Jeff, sometimes resting her forehead on his upper arm, sometimes stroking his shoulder blade, sometimes humming along. But Theresa sat wrapped up with feet beneath her, and palms tucked between her thighs, watching Brian only when his eyes dropped to the fingerboard of his guitar or veered away to some other spot in the room.

She waited for the song she was certain would come sooner

or later, and when Jeff suggested it, her heartbeat quickened, and she felt hollow and hot and sad.

Brian was playing his own guitar this time, a classic Epiphone Riviera, with a smooth, mellow sound and a thin body. She stared at the guitar cradled against Brian's belly, and imagined how warm the mahogany must be from his skin.

> My world is like a river
> As dark as it is deep.
> Night after night the past slips in
> And gathers all my sleep....

The poignant words affirmed the melody, speaking directly to Theresa's heart. Long before the song reached its second verse, her eyes had locked with Brian's.

> She slipped into the silence
> Of my dreams last night.
> Wandering from room to room
> She's turning on each light.
> Her laughter spills like water
> From the river to the sea
> I'm swept away from sadness
> Clinging to her memory.

Theresa's eyes dropped to Brian's lips. They seemed to tremble slightly as they formed the next words.

> Sweet memories...
> Sweet memories...

His lips closed as he softly hummed the last eight notes of the song, and Theresa didn't realize Jeff's voice had fallen silent, leaving her to hum the harmony notes with Brian.

When the final chord diminished into silence, she became aware that everyone in the room was watching the two of them, adding up what seemed to be passing between them.

Jeff broke the spell. "Well, I've got packing to do." He began settling his guitar into its velvet-lined case. "I'd better get Patricia home. We'll have to get up and rolling by eight-thirty in the morning."

The guitar cases were snapped shut. Jeff and Patricia left, and within twenty minutes the rest of the household had all retired to their respective beds.

Theresa lay in the dark, not at all sleepy. The words of the song came back to beguile with their poignant message.... "Night after night the past slips in and gathers all my sleep." She knew now what true desire felt like. It was tingling through each cell of her body, made all the more tempting by the fact that he lay in the room directly below hers, probably just as wide-awake as she was, and for the same reason. But desire and abandon were two different things, and Theresa Brubaker would no more have gone down those stairs and lain with Brian Scanlon beneath her parents' roof than she would have at age fourteen. Along with desire came an awareness of immorality, and she was a very moral woman who retained the age-old precepts taught her throughout her growing years. Knowing she would be disdained as "Victorian" in this age of promiscuity, she nevertheless had deeply ingrained feelings about right and wrong and realized she would never be able to have a sexual relationship with a man unless there was a full commitment between them first.

But the tingling, pulsing sensations still coursed through her virgin body when she thought of lying on the bed with Brian that morning, of his intimate touches. She groaned, rolled onto her belly and hugged a pillow. But it was hours before sleep overcame her.

They had a last breakfast together the next morning, then there were goodbye kisses for Margaret and Willard, who went to work with tears in their eyes, waving even as the car moved off up the street.

Theresa was driving to the airport again, but this time Amy was coming along. All the way, the car had a curious, sad feeling of loneliness, as if the plane had already departed. By unspoken agreement, Brian had taken the front seat with Theresa, and she occasionally felt his eyes resting on her. It was a sunny, snowy morning, its brightness revealing every colorful freckle, every strand of carroty hair she possessed. There was no place to hide, and she wished he wouldn't study her so carefully.

At the airport, they each carried a duffel bag or a guitar case to the baggage check, then entered the green concourse through the security check and walked four abreast down the long, slanting floor that echoed their footsteps. Their gate number loomed ahead, but just before they reached it, Brian grabbed Theresa's hand, tugged her to a halt and told the others, "You two go on ahead. We'll be right there." Without hesitation, he dragged her after him into a deserted gate area where rows of empty blue chairs faced the walls of windows. He took the guitar case from her hand and set it on the floor beside his own duffel bag, then backed her into the only private corner available: wedged beside a tall vending machine. His hands gripped her shoulders and his face looked pained. He studied her eyes as if to memorize every detail.

"I'm going to miss you, Theresa. God, you don't know how much."

"I'll miss you, too. I've loved…I…" To her chagrin, she began to cry.

The next instant she was bound against his hard chest, Brian's arms holding her with a fierce, possessive hug. "Say it, Theresa, say it, so I can remember it for six months." His voice was rough beside her ear.

"I've l-loved being w-with you…."

She clung to him. Tears were streaming everywhere, and she had started to sob. His mouth found hers. Theresa's lips were soft, parted and pliant. She lifted her face to be kissed, knowing a willingness and wonder as fresh and billowing as only first love can be—no matter at what age. She tasted salt from her own eyes and smelled again the masculine scent she'd come to recognize so well during the past two weeks. She clung harder. He rocked her, and their mouths could not end the bittersweet goodbye.

When at last he lifted his head, he circled her neck with both hands, rubbing his thumbs along the bone structure of her chin and jaws, searching her eyes. "Will you write to me?"

"Yes." She grasped one of his hands and held it fast against her face, his fingertips resting upon her closed eyelid before she pulled them down and kissed them, feeling beneath her sensitive lips the tough calluses caused by the music that bound Brian to her, made him someone so very, very right for her.

She raised her eyes at last, to find his etched with as much dread of parting as she herself felt. Oddly she had never thought men to be as affected by sentiment as women, yet Brian looked as if his very soul ached at having to leave her.

"All right. No promises. No commitments. But when June comes…" He let his eyes say the rest, then scooped her close for one last long kiss, during which their bodies knew a renewed craving such as neither had experienced before.

"Brian, I'm twenty-five years old, and I've never felt like this before in my life."

"You can stop reminding me you're two years older, because it doesn't matter in the least. And if I've made you happy, I'm happy. Keep thinking it, and don't change one thing about yourself until June. I want to come back and find you just like you are now."

She raised up on tiptoe, taking a last heart-sweeping kiss she couldn't resist. It was the first time in her life she had ever kissed a man instead of the other way around. She laid a hand on his cheek then, backing away to study him and imprint the memory of his beloved face into her mind.

"Send me your picture."

He nodded. "And you send me yours."

She nodded. "You have to go. They must be boarding by now."

They were. As Brian and Theresa rounded the wall toward their gate area, Jeff was nervously waiting by the ramp. He noted Theresa's tearstained face and exchanged a knowing glance with Amy, but neither said anything.

Jeff hugged Theresa. And Brian hugged Amy. Then they were gone, swallowed up by the jetway. And Theresa didn't know whether to cry or rejoice. He was gone. But, oh, she had found him. At last!

At home the house seemed as haunted as an empty theater. He was there in each room. Downstairs she found the hideaway bed converted back to a davenport, and his sheets neatly folded atop a stack of blankets and pillows. She picked up the folded, wrinkled white cotton and stared at it disconsolately. She lifted it to her nose, seeking the remembered scent of him, pressing her face against the sheet while she dropped to the sofa and indulged in another bout of tears. *Brian, Brian. You're so good for me. How will I bear six months without you?* She dried her eyes on his sheet, brought his pillow into her arms and hugged it to her belly, burying her face against it, wondering how she would fill 176 days. She experienced the profound feeling that seemed to be the true measure of love—the belief that no one had ever loved so before her, and that no one would ever love in the same way after her.

So this was how it felt.

And it felt the same during the days that followed. School began and she was happy to get out of the house with its memories of him, happy to be back with the children, schedules, the familiar faces of the other faculty members she worked with. It took her mind off Brian.

But never for long. The moment she was idle, he returned. The moment she got into her car or walked into the house, he was there, beckoning. The way in which she missed him was more intense than she'd ever imagined loneliness could be. She cried in her bed that first night he was gone. She found smiling difficult during the first days back at school. Brooding came easily, and dreaminess, once so foreign to her, became constant.

On the first day after he'd left, Theresa returned home from school to find a note pinned to the back door: "Bachman's Florist delivered something to my house when they couldn't find anyone here at home. Ruth."

Ruth Reed, the next-door neighbor, answered Theresa's knock with a cheery greeting and wide smile. "Somebody loves somebody at your house. It's a huge package."

It was encased in orchid-colored paper to which was stapled a small rectangle of paper bearing the terse delivery order: "Brubaker...3234 Johnnycake Lane."

"Thank you, Ruth."

"No need for thanks. This is the kind of delivery I'm happy to take part in."

Carrying the flowers home, Theresa's heart skipped in gay anticipation. *It's from him. It's from him.* She jogged the last ten feet up the driveway and catapulted into the kitchen, not even stopping to take off her coat before ripping aside the crackling lavender paper to find a sumptuous arrangement of multicolored carnations, daisies, baby's breath and statice, interlaced with fresh ivy, all billowing from a footed green goblet. Theresa's hand shook as she reached for the tiny envelope attached to a heart-shaped card holder among the greenery.

Her smile grew, along with the giddy impatience to see his name on the gift card.

His name was there all right, but hers wasn't. The card read, "To Margaret and Willard. With many thanks for your hospitality. Brian."

Instead of being disappointed, Theresa was more delighted than ever. *So he's thoughtful, too.* She studied the handwriting, realizing it was written not by Brian but by some stranger in a florist shop someplace across town. But it didn't matter; the sentiment was his.

Brian's first letter came on the third day after he'd left. She found it in the mailbox herself, for she was always the first one home. When she flipped through the envelopes and found the one with the blue wings in the upper left-hand corner and the red and blue jets on the lower right, her heart skittered and leaped. She took the letter to her room, got the fiddling frog from his perch on the shelf and held him in her hand while she sat cross-legged on the bed, reading Brian's words.

But his picture was the first thing that fell out of the envelope, and she dropped the pewter frog the moment Brian's face appeared. He was clothed in his dress blues, his tie crisply knotted, the visor of his garrison cap pulled to the proper horizontal level over his brow. He was unsmiling, but the green eyes looked directly into hers from beneath their familiar, sculptured brows. Dear face. Dear man. She turned the picture over. "Love, Brian," he'd written on the back. Theresa's heartbeat accelerated, and warmth stole over her body. She closed her eyes, took a deep breath and pressed the picture against her breast, against the crazy upbeat rhythm his image had invoked, then laid the picture face up on her knee and began reading.

Dear Theresa,
I miss you, I miss you, I miss you. Everything has suddenly changed. I used to be pretty happy here, but now it feels like prison. I used to be able to pick up my guitar and unwind at the end of a day, but now when I touch it I think of you and it makes me blue, so I haven't been playing much. What have you done to me? At night I lie awake, thinking of New Year's Eve and how you looked when you came out into the kitchen dressed in your new sweater and makeup and hairdo, all for me, and then I wish I could get the picture out of my head because it just makes me miserable. God, this is hell. Theresa, I want to apologize for what happened that morning on my bed. I shouldn't have, but I couldn't help it, and now I can't stop thinking about it. Listen, sweets, when I come home I'm not going to put the pressure on for that kind of stuff. After everything we talked about, I shouldn't have done it that day, okay? But I can't stop thinking about it, and that's mostly what makes me miserable. I wish I'd been more patient with you, but on the other hand, I wish I'd gone further. Man, do I sound mixed up. This place is driving me crazy. All I can think about is your house, and you sitting on the piano bench. Last night I put the Chopin

on but I couldn't stand it, so I shut it off. When I can handle it again I'll make a recording of "Sweet Memories," and send it to you, okay, sweets? It says it all. Just how I'm feeling every minute. You, slipping into the darkness of my dreams at night, and wandering from room to room, turnin' on each light. I don't think I can make it till June without seeing you. I'll probably go AWOL and show up at your door. Do you get Easter vacation? Could you come up here then? Listen, sweets, I gotta go. Jeff and I play a gig this Saturday night, but no girls afterward. That's a promise.

                                                    I miss you,
                                                    Brian

She read the letter nonstop for half an hour. Though each line thrilled her, Theresa returned time and again to his offhand question about Easter vacation. What would her parents say if she went? The thought rankled and made her chafe against having to tell them at all, at her age. The house seemed restrictive after that, and she felt increasingly hemmed in.

She had put off writing to Brian, feeling that to write too soon would seem…what? Brazen? Overstimulated? Yet his words were thrillingly emotional. His impatience and glumness were a surprise. She'd never dreamed men wrote such letters, holding back nothing of their feelings.

She didn't want to send her picture. But now that she knew what heart's ease there was to be found in having Brian's picture to bring him near, she realized he'd probably feel the same. She got out one of her annual elementary-school pictures, but for a moment wavered. It was a full-color shot: black and white would have pleased her more. The camera had recorded each copper-colored freckle, each terrible red uncontrollable hair and the breadth of her breasts. Yet this was just how she'd looked when he first met her, and still he'd found something that pleased him. Along with the photograph, Theresa sent the first love letter of her life.

Dear Brian,

The house is so lonely since you've been gone. School
helps, but as soon as I step into the kitchen, everything
sweeps back and I suddenly wish I lived somewhere else
so I wouldn't have to see you in every room. The flowers
you sent are just beautiful. I wish you could've seen the
look on Mom's face when she first saw them (and on
mine when I opened the package and found they weren't
for me). Naturally, Mom got on the phone right away and
called everyone in the family to tell them what "that
thoughtful boy" had sent.

I really wasn't disappointed to find the flowers
weren't for me, because what I got two days later was
dearer to me than any of nature's beauties.

Thank you for your picture. It's sitting on the shelf in
my room beside The Maestro, who's guarding it carefully. When your letter came I was really surprised to
read how you were feeling, because everything you said
was just what's happened to me. Playing the piano is just
awful. My fingers want to find the notes of the Nocturne,
but once I start it, I can't seem to finish. Songs on the
radio we listened to together do the same thing to me. I
seem to have withdrawn from Mom and Dad and Amy,
even though I'm miserable when I sit in my room alone
in the evenings. But if I can't be with you, somehow I
just don't want to be with anyone.

It's really hard for me to talk about this subject, but I
want to set the record straight. I know I'm really naive
and inexperienced, and when I think of how uptight I get
about the really quite innocent things we did together, I
realize I'm paranoid about…well, you know. I really
want to be different for you, so I've decided to talk to the
school counselor about my "problem."

Did you really mean it about Easter? I've read that
part of your letter a hundred times, and each time my
heart goes all sideways and thumpy. If I came I'm afraid
you'd expect things I'm not sure I'm prepared for yet. I

know I sound mixed up, saying in one breath I'm going to see the counselor and in the next I'm still old-fashioned. I'm sure Mother and Dad would have a fit if their little Theresa announced she was going up to spend Easter with Brian. Some days Mother drives me crazy as it is.

Here's my awful picture, taken in October with the rest of the Sky Oaks Elementary student body and faculty. You say it's the color of flowers. I still say vegetables, but here I am anyway. I miss you so much.

Affectionately,
Theresa

P.S. Hi to Jeff
P.P.S. I like the name "sweets."

Dear Sweets,
I can't believe you didn't say no, flat out. Now I'm living on dreams of Easter. If you come, I promise you'll set the rules. Just being with you would be enough to tide me over. You'll probably think I'm speaking out of turn, but I think somebody twenty-five years old shouldn't even be living with their parents anymore, much less having to get their okay to go off for a weekend. Maybe you're still hiding behind your mother's skirts so you won't have to face the world. God, you'll probably think I'm an opinionated sex maniac now, and that all I want is to get you up here so I can act like Greg What's-His-Name. Don't be mad, sweets, okay? Ask the counselor about it and see what she says. Your picture is getting curled at the edges from too much handling. I've been thinking, I wouldn't mind getting away from this place for a while. Instead of coming up here, maybe we could meet halfway in Fargo. Let me know what you think. Please decide to come. I miss you.

Love,
Brian

* * *

The counselor's name was Catherine McDonald. She was in her mid-thirties, always dressed in casual yet extremely up-to-date clothes and always wore a smile. Although they hadn't had many occasions to work together, Theresa and Catherine had shared many friendly visits in the teachers' lunch room, and Theresa had come to respect the woman's inherent poise, objectivity and deep understanding of the human psyche. There were school counselors whom Theresa thought more qualified to be truck drivers. But Catherine McDonald suited her role and was immensely respected by those with whom she worked.

Rather than meet in school, Theresa requested that they get together over cups of tea at the Good Earth Restaurant at four o'clock one Thursday afternoon. Potted greenery and bright carpeting gave the place a cheerful atmosphere. Theresa was led past the Danish tables and chairs on the main floor to a raised tier of booths overlooking it. Each booth was situated beside a tall window, and it was in one of these where Catherine was already waiting. The older woman immediately stood and extended a hand with a firm grip. Perhaps the thing Theresa had first admired about Catherine was the way the woman's eyes met those of the person to whom she spoke, giving an undivided attention that prompted one to confide in her and believe she cared deeply about the problems others unloaded upon her. Catherine's intelligent, wide-set blue eyes remained unwaveringly on Theresa's as the two greeted each other, settled down and ordered herbal tea and pita-bread sandwiches, then got down to the crux of the meeting.

"Catherine, thank you for taking time to meet me," Theresa opened, as soon as their waitress left them alone. Catherine waved a hand dismissively.

"I'm happy to do it. Anytime. I only hope I can help with whatever it is."

"It's personal. Nothing to do with school. That's why I asked you to meet me here instead of in the office."

"Herbal tea has a mellowing influence anyway. This is much much nicer than school. I'm glad you chose it."

Catherine stirred unrefined sugar into her tea, laid down the spoon and looked up with a laserlike attention in her blue eyes. "Shoot," she ordered tersely.

"My problem, Catherine, is sexual." Theresa had rehearsed that opening line for two weeks, thinking once the last word fell from her mouth the barriers might be broken, and it would be easier to talk about the subject that so easily made her blush and feel adolescent.

"Go ahead, tell me." Again the blue eyes held, while Catherine leaned her head with prematurely silver hair against the tall back of the booth in a relaxed attitude that somehow encouraged Theresa to relax, too.

"It has to do mostly with my breasts."

Amazingly, this woman still kept her eyes on Theresa's. "Am I correct in assuming it's because of their size?"

"Yes, they're…I've…" Theresa swallowed and was suddenly overcome by embarrassment. She braced her forehead on the heel of a hand. Catherine McDonald reached across the table and circled Theresa's wrist with cool, competent fingers, letting her thumb stroke the soft skin in reassurance before gently lowering the hand and continuing to hold it for a full thirty seconds. The contact was something strange and new to Theresa. She had not held a woman's hand before. But the firm squeeze of the counselor's fingers again inspired confidence, and soon Theresa went on speaking.

"I've been this size since I was fifteen years or so. I suffered all the usual persecution, the kind you might expect during adolescent years…the teasing from the boys, the awed stares from the girls, the labels males somehow can't help putting on that part of a woman's anatomy, and even the misplaced jealousy of certain other girls. I asked my mother at the time if I could talk to a doctor or counselor about it, but she's almost as big as I am, and her answer was that there was nothing that could be done about it, so I'd better learn to live with it…and start buying heavy-duty bras—"

Here Catherine interrupted with a single brief question. "You still live with your mother and father, don't you, Theresa?"

"Yes."

"I'm sorry. Go on."

"My normal sexual growth was…impaired by my abnormal size. Every time I found a boy I liked, he was scared by the size of them. And every time I settled for a date with somebody else, he was out for nothing but a groping session. I heard rumors at one time in high school that there was a bet among the boys that anybody who could produce my bra would win a pot worth twenty-five dollars." Theresa looked into her teacup, reliving the painful memory. Then she swept it from her mind and squared herself in her booth. "Well, you don't want to hear all the sordid details, and they're not really as important anymore as they once were." Theresa's eyes grew softly expressive, and she tipped her head slightly to one side. "You see, I've met a man who…who seems to…to look beyond the exterior and find something else that attracts him to me." Theresa sipped her almond tea.

"And?" Catherine encouraged quietly. This was the hard part.

"And…and…" Theresa looked up pleadingly. "And I'm a virgin at twenty-five, and scared to death to do anything with him!"

To Theresa's amazement, Catherine's response was a softly exclaimed, "Wonderful!"

"Wonderful?"

"That you've come right out and unloaded it at last. It was hard to say, I could tell."

"Yes, it was." But already Theresa found herself smiling, loosening up and feeling more and more eager to talk.

"All right, now let's get down to specifics. Tell me why."

"Oh, Catherine, I've been living with this oversize pair of pumpkins for so many years, and they've caused me so much pain, I hate them. The last thing on earth I want to do is let a man I think I love see them naked. To me they're ugly. I thought when he, if he saw them, he'd never want to look at me without my clothes on again. So I…I…"

"You held him off?" Catherine's eyes were steady as Theresa nodded. "And you denied your own sexuality."

"I...I hadn't thought about it that way."

"Well, start."

"Start?" Theresa was astounded by the advice.

"Exactly. Work up a good healthy anger at what you've been robbed of. It's the best way to realize what you deserve. But first, let me back up a square and ask about this man."

"Brian."

"Brian. Did his reaction to your size offend you?"

"Oh, no! Just the opposite! Brian was the first man I've ever met who *didn't* stare at my breasts when we were introduced. He looked me straight in the eye, and if you knew how rare that was, you'd understand what it meant to me."

"And when he tried to make sexual contact and you put him off, was he angry?"

"No, not really. He told me he'd come to like other things about me that went deeper than superficialities."

"He sounds like a wonderful man."

"I think he is, but I have such an odd feeling about...well, he's two years younger than I am—"

"Maturity has nothing to do with chronological age."

"I know. It's silly of me to bring it up."

"Not at all. If it's a concern, you're right to introduce it. Now go on, because I interrupted again."

For the next hour and fifteen minutes Theresa expounded on all her secret hurts gathered up, stored through the years. She expressed her dismay over the things she'd had to forgo because of her problem, and the reluctance she'd always felt to discuss it with her mother, once Margaret had expressed her opinion on the subject all those years ago. She admitted she'd gone into elementary music because it allowed her to work with children who were less discerning than adults. She confessed that Brian had accused her of hiding in various ways. It all came out, and when Theresa had spilled every thought she'd harbored for so many years, Catherine pushed her teacup away, crossed her forearms on the table edge and studied Theresa intently.

"I'm going to suggest something, Theresa, but I want you

to remember it's only a suggestion, and one you should think about for a while and mull over. There *is* an answer for you that you may never have considered before. I believe in time you and Brian will come to work out your self-consciousness, because he sounds like a man willing to go slowly at building your self-confidence. But even when you achieve sexual ease with this man, the other problems will not go away. You'll still feel angry about the clothes you're forced to wear, about your Rubenesque proportions, about the stares of strange men. What I'm suggesting you inquire about is a surgical procedure called mammoplasty—commonly called breast-reduction surgery."

Theresa's eyes widened unblinkingly. Her lips fell open in surprise.

"I can see it never entered your mind."

"No, it…breast-reduction surgery?" The words came out on a breathy note of suspicion. "But that's *vanity* surgery."

"Not anymore. The surgery is becoming an accepted treatment for more than just bruised egos, and the idea that it's prompted only by self-indulgence is antiquated. It's my guess that you have more physical discomfort than you even attribute to breast size, and the surgery is being used to eliminate many physical ailments."

"I don't know. I'd have to think about it."

"Of course you would. It's not the kind of thing you jump into on a night's consideration. And it may not be the answer for you, but dammit, Theresa! Why should you live your life with backaches and rashes and without the amenities of a woman of more modest proportions comes to take as her due? Don't you deserve them, too?"

Yes, came the immediate, silent answer. *Yes, I do. But what would people think? Mother, Dad, the people I work with.*

Brian.

"The yellow pages still list the surgeons under Surgeons— Cosmetic. The term has come to have negative connotations in some circles, but don't let it deter you if you decide to look into the possibility. Better yet, I know a woman who's had the surgery, and I know she'd give you the name of her surgeon and be willing to share her feelings with you. She spent her life suffering all the same ignominies as you, and the surgery has made a profound change not only in her self-image but in her general health. Let me give you her name." Catherine extracted a note pad and pencil from her purse and wrote down the name, then reached out to touch the back of Theresa's hand. "For now, just consider it, let the idea settle in, with all its constituent possibilities. And if you're worried about facing people, don't be. It's your life, not theirs. Not your mother's or your father's or those you work with." The sharp blue eyes brightened further. "Aha! I can see I've struck a nerve already. People be damned, Theresa. This decision is one you make for yourself, not for anyone else."

As they left the restaurant, the silver-haired woman turned toward the redhead. "Whenever you want to talk again, let me know. I'm always available."

That night in bed, Theresa considered the rather stupendous possibilities of "Life After Surgery." She thought of what it would be like to walk proudly, with shoulders back, wearing a slim size-nine sundress. She considered how it would feel to lift her arms and direct the children without the drogueish weights pulling at her shoulders. She dreamed of having no more painful shoulder grooves from the slicing bra straps that marred her flesh. She thought of summer without rashes beneath her breasts where the two surfaces rubbed together constantly now. She imagined the sheer joy of buying the sexiest underwear on the rack, and of having Brian see her in it, then without it.

Brian. What would he think if she did such a thing?

In the dark, beneath the covers, Theresa ran her hands over her breasts, feeling their enormity, hating them afresh, but suddenly smitten by a hundred unasked questions about what it would entail to have them reduced in size. It was heady simply knowing she had the option!

She tried to imagine the freedom of having only half as much where all this flesh was now, and it seemed almost unbelievable that it could happen for her. But it was too important a decision to make on one night's consideration, and without all the facts, as Catherine had pointed out.

And there was her mother to consider. Somehow, she knew her mother would disapprove—her fatalistic attitudes already having been voiced. And the people at work—what would they think? How many times in her life had women—ignorant of the attendant miseries of having massive breasts—told her she should be happy she was endowed as she was? Their attitude was programmed by a cultural bias toward large breast size, so she shouldn't blame them for their uninformed opinions.

But with the new seed of suggestion planted, those countless comments and hurts from the past had already ceased to hurt as much.

But what if Brian objected? Always her thoughts went back to Brian, Brian, Brian. What would it feel like to have him see her naked if she was proud of her body instead of ashamed of it?

Chapter 9

Theresa didn't mention it in any of her letters to Brian, though their correspondence continued weekly, and more often semi-weekly. He sent the recording of "Sweet Memories," and the first time she played it Theresa knew an aching loneliness. She closed her eyes and pictured Brian playing his guitar and singing the poignant song, felt again his kisses, yearned to see him, touch him. She still hadn't given him her answer about meeting him in Fargo. She wanted to—oh, how she wanted to—but she trembled to think of telling her parents about her plan. And no matter what Brian had said in his letters, she was sure if she went he'd expect a sexual commitment before the weekend was over.

In early March, Theresa was crossing the parking lot at school, picking her way across the ice-encrusted blacktop when one of her two-inch heels went skittering sideways and dumped her flat onto her back. Books flew, scattering across the pitted ice while she lay looking at the leaden sky with the wind knocked out of her.

Joanne Kerny, a fellow teacher, saw Theresa go down and hurried to help her sit up, a worried frown on her pretty face. "Theresa, what happened? Are you hurt? Should I get help?"

"N...no." But Theresa felt shaky. "No, I think I'm all right. My heel slipped, and I went down so fast I didn't realize I was falling until my head hit the ice."

"Listen, stay right here and I'll go get somebody to help you inside, right away."

The fall had made Theresa's head hurt, but she managed to stay on the job through the remainder of the day. She worked the following day, also, but by the third day she was forced to call for a substitute teacher: her back was in spasm. She went to the doctor, and his examination turned up no broken bones, but some very painfully bruised muscles, for which he prescribed a relaxant. But in the course of his examination and questioning, Dr. Delancy asked some questions he'd never asked before.

"Tell me, Theresa, do you have back pain regularly?"

"Not exactly regularly. Rather *ir*regularly and more so in my shoulders than my back."

He probed further. How often? Where? What seems to bring it on? Does it bother you to wear high heels? Are you on your feet all day? At what age did the back irritation start? And when he stopped at the door on his way out, his next order sounded dire enough to strike a bolt of fear through Theresa: "When you're dressed I'd like to talk to you in my office."

Five minutes later Dr. Delancy informed her without preamble, "I believe, young lady, that you're in for increasing back problems unless something is done about the cause of these aches, which, if I diagnose them correctly, are happening with increasing frequency the older you get. They can only be expected to get worse if untreated." At her startled expression he rushed on. "Oh no, this fall is only a temporary inconvenience. It'll heal and cause nothing permanent. What I'm speaking of is the strain on your back, knees and chest by the extreme weight of your breasts. The back and shoulder aches you've had, which started in your teen years, are undoubtedly being caused by a bone structure too small to support all that weight. I'm going to recommend a good specialist for you to talk to about it, because there is a solution to the problem, one that's far less critical, less risky, and less painful than the back surgery you may eventually have to undergo if you ignore the problem."

She knew what Dr. Delancy was talking about even before she put the question to him. "Are you talking about breast-reduction surgery?"

"Oh, so someone's suggested it to you before?"

She left the doctor's office with an odd feeling of predestination, as if the fall in the parking lot had happened to lend her a further and more valid reason for considering the surgery. Certainly if she were to bring up the subject to her mother and tell Margaret what Dr. Delancy's prognosis was, her mother would accept the idea of breast reduction far more readily than if Theresa suggested having it only to relieve herself of sexual hang-ups, and so she could wear the clothing of her choice.

> Dear Brian,
> I've done the most foolish thing. I slipped and fell down in the parking lot at school. We'd had rain on top of ice and I was wearing shoes with little heels, and down I went. I'm staying home for a couple of days, on doctor's orders, but he says it's just bruised muscles and they'll fix themselves. But meanwhile, I have another vacation (sort of), but I wish you were here to spend it with me.

The pen fell still. Theresa's gaze wandered off to the dismal gray day beyond the window. The clouds scuttled low while sleet pelted down to run in rivulets along the pane.

What would he think if she wrote, I've been thinking about having my breasts made smaller?

She hadn't realized, up to that point, she *was* considering it. But there were many questions yet to be answered before she could make her decision. And somehow, it seemed too intimate a revelation to make to Brian yet.

She pulled herself from her musing and touched the pen to the paper again.

> I've been thinking a lot about Easter. I want to come, but you're right. I'm afraid to tell my folks....

* * *

Two days later the phone rang at four in the afternoon.

"Hello?"

"Hello, sweets."

It seemed the winds and rain of March dissolved, and the world erupted in flowers of spring. Theresa's free hand clutched the receiver and joy spiraled up through her limbs.

"B...Brian?"

"Do any other men call you sweets?"

"Oh, Brian," she wailed, and the tears suddenly burned her eyes. Her back still hurt. She was depressed. She missed him. Hearing his voice was the sweetest medicine of all. "Oh, Brian, it's really you."

He laughed, a brief dissatisfied sound ending with a gulp. His voice sounded shaky. "How are you? How's your back?"

"Suddenly it's much better." Through her tears she smiled at the phone cord, picturing his face. "Much, much better."

"Your letter just came."

"And yours just came."

"But I didn't know about your accident when I wrote. Oh, babe, I got so worried, I—"

"I'm fine, Brian, really. All except..." All except her life was none of the things she wanted it to be. She was afraid to have the surgery. Afraid not to have it. Afraid to tell her parents about it. Afraid to meet Brian in Fargo. Afraid her parents would disapprove. Angry that she had to seek their approval at all.

"Except what?"

"Oh, I d-don't know. It's s-silly. I...I just..."

"Theresa, are you crying?"

"N-no. Yes!" She placed a hand over both eyes, squeezing. "Oh, Brian, I don't know why. What's wrong with me?" She tried to hold back the sobs so he couldn't hear.

"Sweetheart, don't cry," he pleaded. His voice sounded muffled, as if his lips were touching the phone. But his plea brought the tears on in force.

"No one's ever c-called me sweetheart bef-before."

"You'd better get used to it."

The tender note in his voice reverberated through her pounding heart. She dashed the tears from beneath her eyes with the back of a hand and clung to the phone. So much to say, yet neither of them spoke. Their trembling feelings seemed to sing along the wire. She was unused to having emotions of this magnitude. Voicing them the first time was terrifying. Essential. She could not live with the sweet pain in her chest.

"I've m-missed you more than I ever th-thought human beings missed one another."

A throaty sound, much like a groan, touched her ear. Then his breath was indrawn with a half hiss and expelled in a way that made her picture him with eyelids clenched tightly. Silence swam between them again, rife with unsaid things. Her body was warm and liquid with sudden need of him.

When he spoke again his words sounded tortured, almost guttural. "You're all I think of." Tears were trailing freely over her cheeks, and she felt weighted and sick. Scintillating, silent moments slipped by, while the unspoken took on greater meaning than the spoken. If the house had not been totally silent she might have missed his next throaty words. "You and Easter."

Still he did not ask. Still she did not answer. Her heart trembled. "Brian, nothing like this…" She stopped to swallow a sob that threatened.

"What? I can't hear you, Theresa." In her entire life of painful shyness, no teasing, no taunts had ever hurt like this shattering longing.

"N-nothing like this has ever hap-happened to me before."

"To me either," he said thickly. "It's awful, isn't it?"

At last she released a sniffly laugh that was much sadder than tears, meant to allay the tension, but failing miserably. "Yes, it's awful. I don't know what to do with myself anymore. I walk around unaware."

"I forget what I'm supposed to be doing."

"I h-hate this house."

"I think about going AWOL."

"Oh, no, Brian, you mustn't."

"I know...I know." She listened to the sound of his labored breathing. Was he running a hand through his hair? Again stillness fell. "Theresa?" he said very, very softly. Her eyes slid closed. She touched the phone with parted lips. "I think I'm falling."

Her soul soared. Her body was outreaching, yearning, denied.

Again came his ragged breath, seeking control. "Listen, kiddo, I've got to go, all right?" The gaiety was decidedly forced. "Now you go rest and take care of your back for me, okay? There'll be a letter from me day after tomorrow or so. And I promise I won't go AWOL. Tell everybody there hello." At last he fell quiet. His voice dropped to a husky timbre. "I can't take this anymore. I have to go. But I won't say goodbye. Only...sweet memories."

Don't go! Don't hang up! Brian...wait! I love you! I want to meet you at Easter. We'll...

The phone clicked dead in her ear. She wilted against the wall, sobbing. *Why didn't you tell him you'd come? What are you afraid of? A man as gentle and caring as Brian? Do all who love suffer this way?*

Perhaps it was the bleakness and unhappiness that finally prompted Theresa to call the woman whose name had been given her by Catherine McDonald. She desperately needed to talk to somebody who understood what she was going through.

As she dialed the number several days later, her stomach went taut, and she wasn't sure she could voice the questions she'd rehearsed so often during the days she'd lain in bed under doctor's orders.

But from the moment Diane DeFreize answered the phone and greeted warmly, "Oh yes, Catherine told me you might call," the outlook in Theresa's life began to change. Their conversation was encouraging. Diane DeFreize radiated praise for the change wrought upon her life by the surgery she'd had. In little time at all she'd made Theresa eager to take the first step.

It was a day in the third week of March when she met Dr. Armand Schaum. He was a lean, lanky surgeon, one of the growing number of people she'd met lately who maintained eye contact on introduction. Dr. Schaum had the blackest hair she'd ever seen and a piercing look of intelligence in his nut-brown eyes. She liked him immediately. Obviously, Dr. Schaum was used to skittish women coming in with diffident attitudes and uncertain body language, as well as with the slumped shoulders caused by their condition. Theresa, like most, huddled in her chair at first, as if she'd come to his pleasant office asking him to perform some perverted act upon her.

Within five minutes, her attitude changed drastically, and she was struck by a sense of how very ignorant and misinformed she'd been all these years. She'd maintained the same outdated viewpoint as the rest of society: that plastic surgery was vain and unnecessary.

Dr. Schaum explained the probable physical ailments Theresa could expect in the future if her breasts remained as they were now: not only backaches but also a bent spine; leg and knee troubles as well as varicose veins; breathing problems later in life when the chest wall responded to the excessive weight; recurrent rashes on the undersides of her breasts; an increase in breast size and its related discomforts if and when she chose the pill, pregnancy or nursing.

Vanity surgery? How few people understood.

But there were two negative factors Dr. Schaum was careful to point out. His long, angular face took on an expression of somber, businesslike concern.

"It's important that you understand there's a chance of losing sensitivity in the breast and altered erogenous function."

Dr. Schaum leaned forward in his chair. "The other consideration you have to make is whether or not you ever want to breast-feed a baby. There is a possibility that you will no longer be able to breast-feed after the procedure.

"So having the surgery means accepting the fact that two

important things are at stake: the breast's ability to produce milk and to respond to sexual stimulation."

So that was the risk. Theresa was devastated. She lay in bed that night wide-eyed, more uncertain than ever. The idea of having all sensation irreversibly numbed was terribly frightening and very disheartening. Suppose the feeling never returned? She recalled those tingles, the feminine prickles of sexuality brought to her breasts by Brian's briefest touch, by nothing more than dancing close enough to lightly rub the front of his corduroy jacket, and she wondered what he'd think if she robbed *him* of the ability to arouse her in that particular way and herself of the ability to respond.

She cupped her breasts in her palms. They remained unstimulated. She moved her pajamas flutteringly across the nipples. Little happened. She thought of Brian's mouth…and it began.

Sweet yearning filled her, made her curl, wanting, wondering. What if this powerful feminine reaction was severed before she'd ever known the sweet evocative tug of a man's lips here? He had said, "You'll set the rules." Would he think her a tease if she asked for that much and then pulled back? Could she ask for that, then pull back herself?

She only knew that once…just once she must know the wonder before she wagered it.

He answered the phone in a crisp, military fashion. "Lieutenant Scanlon here."

"Brian, it's Theresa."

All was silent while she sensed his great surprise. She wasn't sure she should have called him in the middle of the day.

"Yes, can I help you?"

His brusqueness was a dash of cold water. Then she understood—there was someone nearby.

"Yes, you can help me by telling me you haven't given up on me yet, and that it's not too late for me to say yes to your invitation."

"I…" He cleared his throat roughly. "We can proceed with those plans, as discussed."

Her heart was going wild. She imagined how difficult it was for him to remain stern and unemotional-sounding. "Good Friday?"

"Right."

"The Doublewood Inn in Fargo?"

"Affirmative. At 1200 hours."

"D-does that mean noon, Brian?"

"Yessir. Have the proper people been notified?"

"I plan to tell them tonight. Wish me luck, Brian."

"You have it."

"Whoever's with you, turn your face away from him because I think you're going to smile." She paused, taking a deep breath, picturing him as he'd been that first day, with his back to her while he looked out the sliding glass door at the snowy yard, wearing dress blues, his too-short hair showing only slightly beneath the stern visor of his garrison cap. She clearly recalled the warmth and scent lingering in that cap when he'd handed it to her. "Lieutenant Scanlon, I think I'm falling in love with you." Silence. Shocked silence. "And I think it's time I did something about it."

After a short pause, he cleared his throat. "Affirmative. Leave it all to me."

"Not quite all. It's time I took my life into my own hands. Thank you for being so patient while I grew up."

"If there's anything we can do at this end to implement matters—"

"I'll see you in two and a half weeks."

"Agreed."

"Goodbye, dear Lieutenant Scanlon."

Again he cleared his throat. But still the last word came out brokenly. "Good…goodbye."

Theresa tackled her mother and father that night, before she could lose her nerve. As it happened, Margaret provided the perfect lead-in.

"Easter dinner will be at Aunt Nora's this year," Margaret

informed them at the supper table. The meal was over. Amy had zipped off to do homework with a friend. "Arthur and his family will be coming from California on vacation. Land sakes, it must be seven years since we've all been together. Grandpa Deering will be celebrating his sixty-ninth birthday that Saturday, too, so I promised I'd make the cake and you'd play the organ, Theresa, while we—"

"I won't be here at Easter," Theresa interrupted quietly.

Margaret's expression said, don't be ridiculous, dear, where else could you possibly be. "Won't be here? Why, of course you'll—"

"I'm spending Easter in Fargo...with Brian."

Margaret's mouth dropped open. Then it pursed as a chalky line appeared around it. Her eyes darted to Willard's, then snapped back to her daughter. "With Brian?" she repeated tartly. "What do you mean, *with* Brian."

"I mean exactly that. We've agreed to meet in Fargo and spend three days together."

"Oh, you have, have you?" Margaret bit out. "Just like that. Off to Fargo without benefit of a wedding license!"

Theresa felt herself blushing, and along with it rose indignation. "Mother, I'm twenty-five years old."

"And unmarried!"

"Had you stopped to think you might be assuming things?" Theresa accused angrily.

But Margaret had ruled her roost too long to be deterred by any one of them when *she knew she was right!* Her face was pink as a peony by this time, the double chin quivering as she claimed distastefully, "When a man and woman go off, *overnight,* alone, what else is to be done but *assume?"*

Theresa glanced to her father, but his face, too, was slightly red, and he was studying his knuckles. Suddenly she was angered by his spinelessness. She wished he'd say something one way or the other instead of being bulldozed by his outspoken wife all the time. Theresa faced her mother again. Though her stomach was churning, her voice remained relatively calm. "You might have asked, mother."

Margaret snorted and looked aside disdainfully.

"If you're going to assume, there's nothing I can do about it. And at my age I don't feel I have to justify myself to you. I'm going and that's all—"

"Over my dead body, you're going!" Margaret lurched from her chair, but at that moment, unbelievably, Willard intervened.

"Sit down, Margaret," he ordered, gripping her arm. Margaret turned her fury on him.

"If she lives in our house, she lives by rules of decency!"

Tears stung Theresa's eyes. It was as she'd known it would be. With her mother there was no discussing things. There hadn't been when Theresa was fourteen and sought consolation over her changing body, and there wasn't now.

"Margaret, she's twenty-five years old," Willard reasoned, "closer to twenty-six."

Margaret pushed his hand off her arm. "And some sterling example for Amy to follow."

The words sliced deeply in their unfairness. "I've always been—"

But again, Willard interceded. "Amy's values are pretty much in place, don't you think, Margaret? Just like Theresa's were when she was that age."

Margaret's eyes were rapiers as she glared at her husband. It was the first time in Theresa's life she'd ever seen him stand up to her. And certainly, she'd never seen or heard them fight.

"Willard, how can you say such a thing? Why, when you and I were—"

"When you and I were her age, we'd already been married for a couple of years and had a house of our own without your mother telling you or me what to do."

Theresa could have kissed her father's flushed cheeks. It was like discovering some hidden person, much like herself, who'd been hiding inside Willard Brubaker all these years. What a revelation to see that person assert himself at last.

"Willard, how in the world can you as much as give permission to your own daughter to go off—"

"That's enough, Margaret!" He rose to his feet and turned

her quite forcefully toward the doorway. "I've let you steam-roll me for a lot of years, but now I think it's time we discussed this in the bedroom!"

"Willard, if you...she can't..."

He led her, sputtering, down the hall until the sound of his voice drifted back. "I think it's time you rememb—" Then the closing bedroom door cut off his words.

Theresa didn't know they were in the kitchen later that night when she roamed restlessly from her room thinking, she'd get something to drink, then maybe she'd be able to fall asleep.

They were standing in the shadows of the sparsely lit room when Theresa came up short in the dark entry, realizing she was intruding. She could see little of her mother, who stood in front of Willard. Their backs were to Theresa, their feet bare, and they wore tired old robes she'd seen around the house for years. But from the movement of her father's elbows, she suspected his hands were pleasantly occupied. A soft moan came from the throat of the woman who was so glib at issuing orders. "Will...oh, Will..." she whispered.

As Theresa unobtrusively dissolved into the shadow of the hall and crept back to her room, she heard the murmur of her father's very young-sounding chuckle.

In the morning the word *Fargo* didn't come up, nor did the name Brian Scanlon. Margaret was as mellow as a softly plucked harp, wishing Theresa good morning before humming her way toward the bathroom with a cup of coffee. The sound of Willard's shaver buzzed louder as the door opened. Then, from far way, she heard laughter.

It was Willard who sought out Theresa in her bedroom at the end of that day and questioned quietly from the doorway, "Are you planning to drive up to Fargo?"

Theresa looked up in surprise. "Yes, I am."

He scratched his chin contemplatively. "Well, then I'd better take a look at that car of yours, in case anything needs tunin' up." He began to turn away.

"Daddy?"

He stopped and turned. Her arms opened as she came across the soft pink carpet on bare feet. "Oh, Daddy, I love you," she said against his less-than-firm jowl as his arms tightened around her. A hand came up to pet her head with heavy, loving strokes. Rough, then gentling a bit. "But I think I love him, too."

"I know, pet. I know."

And so it was, from Willard, the quiet one, the unassertive one, Theresa learned a lesson about the power of love.

Chapter 10

The five-hour drive from Minneapolis to Fargo was the longest Theresa had ever made alone. She'd worried about getting drowsy while driving but found her mind too active to get sleepy behind the wheel. Pictures of Brian, memories of last Christmas and anticipation of the next three days filled her thoughts. At times she'd find herself smiling widely, realizing a rich appreciation for the rolling farmland through which she drove, as if her newly expanded emotions had opened her senses to things she'd never noticed before: how truly beautiful tilled black soil can be, how vibrant the green of new grass. She passed a pasture where newborn calves suckled their mothers, and for a moment her thoughts turned dour, but she wouldn't allow herself to think of anything except the thrill of seeing Brian again.

The sapphire lakes of the Alexandria area gave way to the undulating farmland of Fergus Falls, then the earth gradually flattened as the vast deltaland of the Red River of the North spread as far as the eye could see: wheat and potato fields stretching endlessly on either side of the highway. Moorhead, Minnesota, appeared on the horizon, and as Theresa crossed the Red River that divided it from its sister city, Fargo, on the Dakota side, her hands were clammy, clutching the wheel.

She pulled the car into the parking space before the Doublewood Inn, then sat staring at the place for a full minute. It was the first time in her life that Theresa was checking in to a motel by herself.

You're only having last-minute jitters, Theresa. Just because the sign says motel doesn't mean you're doing anything prurient by checking in to the place.

The lobby was beautiful, carpeted in deep, rich colors, and decorated with comfortable-looking furniture and a plethora of live green plants that seemed to bring the golden spring day inside.

"Good morning," greeted the desk clerk.

"Good morning. I have a reservation." She felt conspicuous and suddenly wished the clerk were a woman instead of a man—a woman would sense her honorable intentions, she thought irrationally. "My name is Theresa Brubaker."

"Brubaker," he repeated checking his records. In no time at all she had a key in her hand, and to her surprise the clerk told her brightly, "Oh, Miss Brubaker, your other party has already arrived. Mr. Scanlon is in Room 108, right next to yours." She glanced at her key: 106. Suddenly it was all real. She felt her face coloring and thanked the clerk, then turned away before he could see her discomposure.

She drove around to the back of the motel, wondering if their rooms faced this side, if Brian was watching her from one of the windows above. She found herself unable to glance up and peruse the spaces on which the draperies were drawn back. If he was watching her, she didn't want to know it. Inside, she stopped before room 108. Staring at the number on his door, her heart thudded. The suitcases grew heavy and threatened to slip from her sweating palms. *He's in there. I'm standing no more than twenty feet from him right now.* It was odd, but now that she was here she was suddenly reluctant to face him. What if either of them had changed in some way since Christmas? What if the attraction had somehow faded? *What will I say to him? What if it's awkward? What if…what if…*

Her own door was only one foot away from his. She opened it and stepped into a room with a queen-size bed, a dresser, console, mirror and television. Nothing extraordinary, but to Theresa, experiencing independence for the first time, the room seemed sumptuous. She set her luggage down, sat on the end of the bed, bounced once, walked into the tiled bathroom, turned on the light, switched it off, crossed the long main room to open the draperies, switched on the TV, then switched it off again at the first hint of sound and color, unzipped her suitcase, hung up some garments near the door, then looked around uncertainly.

You're only delaying the inevitable, Theresa Brubaker. She stared at the wall, wondering what he was doing on the other side of it. *Just a minute more and my nerves will calm. I'd better check my makeup.* The mirror revealed everything fresh and unsmudged except her lips, which needed color. She dug out her lipstick and applied it with a shaking hand. It tasted faintly peachy and contained flecks of gold that glistened beneath the light when she moved. *You don't put on fresh lipstick when you want a man to kiss you, Brubaker, you dolt.* She jerked a white tissue from the dispenser on the wall and swiped it swiftly across her lips, removing all but a faint smudge of remaining color. The tissue was rough and left her lips looking faintly red and chapped around the edge. Nervously she uncapped the silver tube and reapplied the peachy gloss. She met her own eyes in the mirror. They were wide and bright with anticipation. But they were not smiling. She glanced at her breasts beneath the baby-blue blouse she'd bought new for this occasion. She wore no sweater today, but felt naked without it, though the tiny blue heart-shaped buttons went from the waist of her white skirt up to the tight mandarin collar that was edged with a blue ruffle. The short gathered sleeves of the blouse had a matching miniature ruffle around their cuffs. Suddenly the puffy sleeves seemed to accentuate the size of her breasts but she forced herself to look instead at her very tiny waistband into which the blouse was securely tucked.

All it takes is a knock on his door, and this uncertainty will be over.

A minute later she rapped on 108 twice, but at the third flick of her wrist her knuckles struck air, for the door was already being flung open.

He stood motionless for a long moment, one hand on the doorknob. She, with her knuckles in the air, stared at him wordlessly. Theresa saw nothing but Brian's face, the searching green eyes with their dark spiky lashes, the lips open slightly, the familiar nose, short hair, cheeks shaven so recently they still shone. Then she became aware of how accentuated his breathing was. The formfitting baby-blue knit shirt fit his chest like liquid, hiding no trace of the swiftly rising and falling muscle beneath it.

Her body felt warm, thrumming, yet uncertain. She wanted to smile but stood immobile, staring at the face before her as if he were an apparition.

"Theresa," was all he said, then he reached out a hand and caught hers, drawing her into the room with firm certainty. And still he didn't smile, but only found her free hand, gripping both palms with viselike tenacity while gazing unwaveringly into her eyes. He swung her around, then turned his back to the door and closed it with his hips. "You're really here," he said hoarsely.

"I'm really here." What had happened to all the charming greetings she'd rehearsed for days? What had happened to the smooth entrance with all its urbane chic, meant to put them both on a strictly friendly basis from the first moment? Why wouldn't her lips smile? Her voice work? Her knees stop trembling?

Suddenly she was catapulted into his arms as he thrust forward, hugging her body full against his and taking her mouth with a slanting, wide, possessive kiss. Nothing gentle. Nothing hinting at easing into old familiarities, but the familiarity arising magically between them with all its stomach-lifting force. She found her arms around his trunk, hands pressed against his warm back. And, wonder of wonders, his heart was slamming against her so vibrantly she could feel the very difference between its beats. Her own heart seemed to lift each cell of her skin, sealing off her throat with its solid hammering. His hands at first forced her close, as if he couldn't get close enough, but then as their tongues joined in sleek reunion,

Brian's palms roved in wide circles on her back, and as if it were the most natural thing in the world, he drew them up both her sides simultaneously, pressing her breasts, reaching inward with two long thumbs to seek her nipples briefly. His left arm returned to her back and he angled away from her slightly, cupping one breast fully, then exploring it through her blouse and brassiere while his tongue gentled within her mouth. Shudders climbed her vertebrae and raised the hairs along the back of her thighs while the pressure on her nipples continued in faint, sensuous, circular movements. It was so natural. So right. Theresa had no thoughts of stopping his explorations. They seemed as much a valid part of this reunion as the looks of reaffirmation they'd exchanged when she first stood before him.

The kiss went on unbrokenly as his hands clasped her narrow hipbones and pulled her pelvis securely against his. He rocked against her, undulating, weaving from side to side, pressing his most masculine muscles against her acquiescent stomach. Without realizing it, she found herself meeting each stroke of his hips, pressing against him, lifting up on tiptoe because he was so much taller and she yearned to feel his hardness closer to her point of desire.

Still clasping her hips, Brian ended the kiss. His warm palms pushed downward until her heels again touched the floor, then he held her firmly, so she couldn't move. He rested his forehead against hers while their strident breaths mingled, and their moist lips hovered close, swollen and still open.

Her hands were still on his back. She felt the muscles grow taut with resolution as he pressed firmly on her hipbones. It suddenly struck her how easily these things happen, how readily she had lifted against him, how opportune was the hand of Nature in making a body thrust and ebb when the circumstances called for it.

She was chagrined to think that now he might believe she'd come here with sex in mind. She hadn't, not at all. But how fast her body had dictated its wishes.

"I was so scared to knock on that door," she admitted. He

lifted his forehead from hers, bracketed her cheeks with his palms and studied her at close range.

"Why?"

"Because I thought…" His eyes were as stunning as she remembered. They wore an expression of ardency that surprised her. "I thought, what if things aren't the same between us? What if we imagined…this?"

His thumbs brushed the corners of her mouth. His lips were parted and glittered with fragments of gloss from her lipstick. "Silly girl," he whispered, before pulling her face upward to meet his descending one. Again she raised on tiptoe, but this time their bodies barely brushed. The peach-flavored kiss was bestowed by his tongue and lips in a testing circle around her mouth, tugging, wetting once again while his hands drew upon her jaws, first lifting her, then letting her recede as if she were drifting in the surf, mastered by its rush and release. "Oh, Theresa," he murmured while her eyes fell closed. "Nothing's changed for me. Nothing at all." He pressed her away only far enough to gaze into her eyes. "Has it for you?"

How incredible that he should ask. He, who emerged so flawless in her loving eyes. When she studied him again, reality seemed to buckle her lungs and knees. The expression in his eyes said he'd been as uncertain as she had. Theresa ran her hands from his elbows along his hard arms to the wrists. "Nothing," she whispered, allowing her eyelids to close once more while pulling first his left hand from her jaw to kiss its palm, then doing likewise with his right. "Nothing." She looked into his somber eyes and watched them change, grow light, relieved. Her gaze dropped to his mouth. "You have more of my lipstick on than I do."

He smiled and hauled her close, speaking against her mouth so that she could scarcely discern the words. "So clean me up." Her tongue seemed drawn to his by some magical attraction, and she learned a new delight in taking command during a kiss.

"Mmm…you taste good," she ventured, backing away only slightly. She ran her nose along his jaw. "And you smell good, just like I remember, only stronger." She backed away and ran a fingertip over his jaw. "You just shaved."

He grinned, his hands now on her back, holding her against him, but undemandingly. "Just like a teenager getting ready for his first date."

"How long have you been here?"

"Twenty minutes or so. How long have you?"

"About ten minutes. I was in my room, putting on fresh lipstick, then wiping it off, then putting it on again and wondering which was the right thing to do. I was so nervous."

Suddenly it struck them how funny it was that they'd been so apprehensive. They laughed together, then gazed into each other's eyes, and without warning simultaneously answered the compulsion to hug. Their arms went about each other—tight, tight—reaffirming. His hands roved her back. Hers touched his hair. When he backed away, he looped his hands around her hips until she rested against his again.

"What do you want to do first?" he asked.

"I don't know. Just…" Her heart pulsed crazily. "Just look at you some more." She shrugged shyly. "I don't know."

He moved not a muscle for a long, silent moment. Then he nudged her backward with his thighs, directing her shoulders with his hands. "Come here then. Let's indulge ourselves for a while." He lifted a knee to the bed, then fell, tugging her along till they lay on their sides, each with an elbow folded beneath an ear. He rested a hand on her hip. Their eyes locked, their feet trailed off the end of the mattress.

Incredible. She had been in his room less than five minutes and already she was lying on the bed with him. But she had no desire to get up or to protest at his taking her there. His head lifted slowly. His mouth covered hers, urging her lips open once again, his tongue delving into the soft recesses, tickling the skin of her inner cheeks then threading its tip along her teeth, as if counting each. Her body came alive with desire, and her breathing grew fast and harsh, as did his. But when he'd explored to his satisfaction, he lay as before, head upon elbow, his hand still resting on her hip, but undemandingly.

It seemed best to set things straight immediately. Timidity brought color rushing to Theresa's face and made her voice unnatural. "Brian, I…" His eyes were so close, so intense, burning into hers. "I didn't come here because I was ready to go all the way with you."

His hand left her hip and fell to the hollow of her waist. "I know. And I didn't come here to force you to. But I want to. You know that, don't you?"

"I'm not ready for that, Brian, no matter what I…well, I might have led you to believe something else when we first kissed."

"I think we're both in for a hell of a weekend then. It's not going to be easy. Obviously your conscience and your libido are at odds." His hand left her waist, squeezed her upper arm gently, then caressed its length until his hand rested on the back of hers. "And my libido…well, there's no hiding it, is there?" Then, unceremoniously, he carried her hand to the zipper placket of his white brushed cotton slacks. It happened so unexpectedly she had neither the time nor inclination to pull away. One moment her hand rested on his hip, the next it was flattened along his zipper, and he'd raised his upper knee as he gently forced her fingers to conform to the ridge of hot, hard flesh within. His hand disappeared from atop hers and he rolled closer, letting his eyes drift closed as he spoke gruffly against the hollow of her throat. "I'm sorry if I'm too direct, but I want you to know…whatever you choose is what we'll do, as much or as little as you want. I'd be a damned liar if I said I wasn't thinking about making love to you ever since last January when I left you crying in that airport."

While he spoke, his body undulated against her palm, then she reluctantly slipped her hand up his shirtfront and pressed it against his chest. Beneath her palm his heart thudded crazily.

"Shh…Brian, don't say that."

He backed away, pinning her with a distracting, direct gaze. "Why? Because it's true of you, too?"

"Shh." She rested an index finger on his lips. He stared at her silently until at last the fires in his eyes seemed to subside. He clasped the back of the hand at his mouth, kissed its palm, then threaded its fingers through his own. "All right. Are you hungry?"

She smiled. "Ravenous."

"Should we go and find something to eat, then hit all the highlights of Fargo, North Dakota?"

"Let's."

With one lithe motion he was at the foot of the bed, one foot on the floor, the other knee on the mattress. He hauled her up against him and she landed on her knees with her arms around his neck, and his hands on her buttocks. He kissed her fleetingly, then rubbed the end of her nose with his own. "God, it's good to be with you again. Let's get out of here before I change my mind." With a squeeze and a pat he turned her loose.

They were walking hand in hand along the street in downtown Fargo when they suddenly stopped and stared each other up and down, then burst out laughing.

"You're wearing—"

"Do you realize—" they said in unison, then laughed again, standing back, assessing each other's clothing. They were both wearing white slacks, and the baby blue of her ruffle-necked blouse closely matched that of his knit pullover. She wore white tennis shoes on her feet and he white leather sport shoes with a Velcro-closed strap across the arch of his foot.

"If we dressed to please each other, I think we both did a good job," he said with a smile. "I like your blouse."

"And I like your shirt." Again they laughed, then caught hands as they moved on, exploring the entire length of the street from Main to Second Avenues.

The sun was warm on their backs, the sky overhead flawless cerulean. They had a sense of calm and an even greater one of delight in being together, swinging hands, watching their white-clad legs matching strides. The street was dotted with planters in which geraniums and petunias had been set out, and all along the street's length ash trees were beginning to break into first leaf. At the Old Broadway, they peered into the windows on the front doors and decided to give the old landmark a try. Inside, the decor echoed the charm of another era. The floor creaked and croaked as the waitress delivered their plate dinners of thick-slicked beef, potatoes and gravy and golden, buttered carrots.

"You haven't mentioned your mom and dad," Brian said, studying Theresa across the booth. "What did they say when you told them you were coming up here to meet me?"

She met his serious green eyes and decided to tell him the truth. "Mother assumed the worst. It wasn't a very pleasant scene." She dropped her eyes to her plate, drawing circles on it with a piece of beef.

Beneath the table his calf found hers and rubbed it reassuringly. He closed his ankles around one of hers and stopped the hand that had been pushing her fork in circles. She looked up at him.

"I'm sorry."

She laid her hand atop his. "Don't be. Something quite wonderful came about because of it." Wonder showed in her face. "Daddy. Would you believe he finally stood up to Mother?"

"Willard?" Brian asked in surprise.

"Willard," she confirmed, still with the amazed expression on her face. "He shouted 'Margaret, that's enough' and… and…" Theresa had great difficulty not smirking. "And hauled her off to the bedroom, slammed the door, and the next time I saw them she was calling him Will, and the two of them were cooing like mourning doves. That was the end of Mother's resistance."

Brian dropped his fork with a clatter, threw his hands in the air and praised, "Hallelujah!"

They were still chuckling about it when they returned to the street. They continued their stroll past the quaint shops and so to the far north end where they discovered the Fargo Theater with its vintage art deco marquee announcing a silent film special viewing and that Charlie Chaplin was playing tonight in *The Bank*.

"Do you like silent movies?" Brian asked hopefully.

"Love 'em." She grinned up at him.

"Whaddya say, should we give old Charlie a try tonight?"

"Oh, I'd love to."

"It's a date." He squeezed her hand, then led her across the street and they started back along the other side, peering in store windows. In one called Mr. T's, a bridal gown was displayed. Without realizing it, Theresa's feet stopped moving, and she stared at the mannequin. The sight of the white gown and veil, symbols of purity, brought to mind the coming night, the choice she had to make. She thought about other men she might meet in her life, the one she might possibly marry, and what he would think if she did not come to him as a virgin. But she found it impossible to imagine herself being intimate with any man but Brian.

While Theresa gazed at the bridal gown, two young men passed along the sidewalk. Brian watched their eyes assess her breasts—blatantly, neither of them trying to disguise their fascination. Their heads swiveled, gazes lingering as they drew alongside, then passed her. When they moved on, one of them must have made a lewd comment, for he did a little hip-swinging jive step while patting his thighs, then his companion laughed.

Brian was at first angry. Then he found himself assessing her breasts as a stranger would, and found, to his chagrin, that he was slightly embarrassed. Guilt followed immediately. He fought to submerge it, studying the back of Theresa's head as she gazed up innocently at the window display. But as they moved on up the street, he was conscious of the eyes of each man they met. Without exception, they all dropped to Theresa's breasts, and Brian's discomfort grew.

Scanlon, you're a hypocrite. The thought was distinctly nettlesome, so he hooked an arm around Theresa's neck, settled her against his hip as they ambled back to the car, and when they reached it, he gave her a tender kiss of apology. Her hands rested on his chest. When she opened her eyes they held a dreamy expression, and he felt small and unworthy for a moment, realizing how hurt she'd be if she suspected he'd been embarrassed over her generous endowment. He traced the outline of her lips with a single finger and said softly, "What do you say we get away from people for a while?"

"I thought you'd never ask."

He smiled, kissed her nose, settled her inside, then started

the engine. They crossed the river into Moorhead, drove out
onto the blacktop highway heading east, then left it behind to
wander the back roads between green woods, brown fields
and blue ponds where ducks and blackbirds nested. Spring was
burgeoning all around them. They felt it in the renewed warmth
of the sun, smelled it in the damp earth, heard it as the sound
of wildlife lifted through the air.

They discovered the lush wilds of the Buffalo River where
it surged under a culvert beneath their gravel road. Brian pulled
to the side, turned off the engine and invited, "Let's walk." She
slipped her hand into his with a glad heart, letting him lead her
down the steep bank to the dappled woods, where they picked
their way aimlessly along the surging spring-swelled waters
that rumbled southward. The river sang to them. The tangled
roots of a long-fallen tree stood silver in their path. Brian led
the way along the massive trunk to a spot where he could
mount it, then reached down and helped Theresa up beside him.
He walked the weathered trunk to its highest point, with her
right behind him. Now the river flowed at their feet. A fish
leaped. A trio of sparrows darted from the underbrush to the
tangled roots of their tree. From far away a crow scolded. Everything smelled fecund, growing, renewed. From behind,
Theresa lightly rested her hands on Brian's hips. He remained
as before, unmoving, imbibing, gathering sweet memories.
His hands covered hers, drew them firmly around his belt, and
his arms covered hers while she pressed her cheek and breasts
against his firm, warm back. A blue jay carped from a loblolly
pine, and the sun shimmered on the forest floor through the
partially sprouted leaves of the surrounding trees. Against
Brian's back Theresa's heart thrummed steadily. His palms
rubbed her arms, which were warm with gathered sunshine.

"Ahh…" he sighed, tilted his head back, said no more.

She kissed the center of his back. It was enough.

In time they moved on through the gold-and-green afternoon. As they ambled, they caught up on the past three months.
Brian had stories about Jeff and air-force rigors, the band, the
music they'd been working on. Theresa had anecdotes about

life with a teenage sister, incidents from school, plans for spring concerts.

But none of it mattered. Only being together had meaning for them.

They found a nest with three speckled eggs, built in the reeds where the river backwashed and bent. They turned back as the afternoon waned and hunger imposed its demands. They kissed in a basswood grove, then climbed the pebbled bank again and settled into the car for the ride back to town. At their doors in the motel Brian said, "I'll pick you up at your place in half an hour." A quick kiss and they parted.

Chapter 11

The knock at her door announced a freshly showered and shaved Brian dressed in tight jeans, an open-collared shirt of pale tan-blue-white plaid, and a lightweight sport coat the color of an almond shell. She took one look and felt her mouth watering.

"Wow," she breathed.

He smiled guilelessly, looking down at himself and said, "Oh, yeah?" Then he closed the door, eased his hips back against it, crossed his arms and grinned. "Come over here and say that, Brubaker."

She felt herself blushing, but swung away teasingly. "I'm not one of your groupies, Scanlon."

She was securing the latch of a trim gold bracelet when his strong hands closed over her wrists, dragging them around his neck. His eyes, ardent and determined, blazed into hers. "God, there are times when I wish you were." His mouth was warm, open and moist as it marauded hers. He swirled his tongue around her freshly applied lipstick, then delved brashly inside to stroke her teeth until they opened at his command. His tongue probed rhythmically in and out of her mouth, suggesting what was on his mind. He tasted of freshly brushed teeth and smelled like chrysanthemums and sage—not flowery, but spicy clean. He pulled back suddenly, leaving no question about the price he was paying for control. His stormy eyes sought and held hers. Then the storm cleared, he relaxed. His thumbs, still at her wrists, stroked lightly. Now it was his turn to declare breathily, "Wow."

Theresa's heart proved what a healthy, red-blooded twenty-five-year-old virgin she was. She was certain he could see it lifting the bodice of her blouse. She whispered thickly, "Let's go see what Charlie's up to."

At the Fargo Theater they were treated to a sensational performance by a local member of the American Theater Organ Society on an immense and wondrous pipe organ that rose out of the floor on a pneumatic lift. They sat in the balcony, because it was a dying species they'd have few more chances to experience. Theresa learned how readily Brian laughed at slapstick. While the organist tickled out an accompaniment, Charlie Chaplin duckwalked down a city street in his oversize shoes and baggy pants, went three times around a revolving door, then spent arduous moments whirling the dials of an imposing-looking vault. Brian snickered, slunk low in his seat. The vault door swung open and the lovable Charlie disappeared inside to return with his precious deposit: a scrub pail, mop and janitor's uniform. Brian rolled his head backward and hooted with full throat while Theresa's heart warmed more to the man beside her than to the one on the screen.

The organ created a musical echo of Charlie's misfortunes in leaving flowers for the black-eyed Edna Purviance, only to have the damsel believe they were a gift from the bank clerk named Charlie. When skulduggery started, the organ rumbled dramatically, creating vibrations through the theater seats. Beside her, Brian slumped low in his seat, trembling melodramatically, tossing his popcorn in the air when the heroine was tied and gagged, stamping and cheering when Chaplin came to her rescue, boo-hooing when the poor unfortunate bank custodian was left awakening from a dream, petting the rags of his floor mop instead of the waves of the damsel's head.

When the film ended and they returned to the street, Brian performed a superb imitation of Chaplin, knees crooked outward, shoulders rolling with his peculiar gait while he scratched his head with stiff fingers and made a vain attempt to open the door of the wrong car. He gave a Chaplinesque flap of the hands, looked around, dismayed, sad-eyed.

How easy it was for Theresa to gasp and clasp her hands before her, distraught at misfortune. She ran jerkily to her car, flung the door open, then stood on the pavement with eyes rolled heavenward in invitation.

Charlie Scanlon duckwalked to her, shyly studied his feet, swept into a clumsy bow, then waved her inside. She interlaced her fingers, simpered, then got in.

Brian made a swipe at the open door, missed, spun in a circle, missed again, spun another circle and finally connected with the difficult door and managed to slam it.

When he climbed in beside her and squeezed the invisible bulb of a horn and made a flatulent-sounding "T-o-o-t" out of the side of his mouth, they wilted with laughter. In time they grew too weak to continue. Then they looked at each other in silent discovery.

They ate an Italian supper at a place chosen at random, reminiscing about old movies, but always thinking about the end of the evening ahead. Would it bring *good night* or *good morning*?

Laughter was gone when they walked slowly, slowly down the hall to their doors. They stopped dead center between 106 and 108.

"Can I come in?" he asked quietly at last.

She met his searching eyes, feeling the awesome tugs of carnality and denial warping her heart. She remembered her mother's words, the bridal gown in the window. She touched his chest lightly. "Will you understand how hard it is for me that I have to answer no?"

His hands hung loosely at his sides. He sucked in a huge gulp of air, dropped his head down as his eyes closed, then braced both hands tiredly on his hips and studied the toes of his brown boots.

She felt childish and unworthy. Tears began to burn her eyelids. He saw and pulled her close, resting his chin against her hair. Though his body rested only lightly against hers, she was close enough to know that her nearness and this compulsion they both controlled so closely had aroused him. "I'm sorry, sweets," he whispered. "You're right and I'm wrong. But that doesn't make it any easier."

"Kiss me, Brian," she begged.

He took her head in both hands and tipped her face up for a deep, hungering kiss. But the pressure of his hands on her jaw and ears told of where he wanted those hands to be. And she clung to his wrists—the safest place—feeling beneath one thumb the surging rhythm of his pulse. They drew apart, troubled eyes clinging.

"Good night," he said raggedly.

"Good night," came her unsure reply.

Neither of them slept well, they confessed over breakfast. The day lolled before them; its hours would be too short, no matter how they were spent. Yet when considered in the light of their denial, those same hours seemed infinite. They browsed through West Acres Shopping Center, ate lunch in a McDonald's because their stomachs demanded filling, but neither of them cared the least about food. They roamed the green hills of Island Park and sat in its gazebo watching a group of children playing softball across the expanse of green grass. They had supper in the motel dining room, and afterward wandered into the casino. But while Brian sat at a table playing blackjack, a man with sleek black hair, wearing an expensive silk suit, sidled up to Theresa, gave her a blatant visual assessment, slipped his hands to her hips and whispered in her ear, "You alone, baby?"

It happened so fast Theresa hadn't time to react until the cloying scent of his aftershave seemed to plug her nostrils, and his wandering hands registered their insult.

Suddenly Brian interceded. "Get your hands off her, buddy," he growled, jerking the man's arm, spinning him away from Theresa, whose stunned eyes were wide and alarmed.

The man's eyes narrowed dangerously, then eased as lascivious speculation crossed his features. He pulled free of

Brian's hand, shrugged his shoulder to right the expensive suit jacket, and his eyes roved once over Theresa's breasts. "Can't say I blame you, fella. If those were mine for the night, I wouldn't be too quick to share 'em either."

Theresa saw the muscles bunch in Brian's jaw. His fists clenched.

"Don't, Brian!" She stepped between the two men, facing Brian, gripping his arm in an effort to turn him away. "He's not worth it," she pleaded. His arm remained steeled. "Please!" she whispered.

But Brian's livid face scarcely registered if he'd heard. He moved with mechanical deliberation, reaching down without looking to grasp Theresa's hand and remove it from his jacket. Then slowly, menacingly he clutched the man's lapels, lifting until his toes scarcely touched the carpet.

"You will apologize to the lady right now," Brian ground out, "or your teeth will be biting your own ass, from the inside out." Brian's voice was chilling as he held the stranger aloft, nose to nose.

"Okay, okay. Sorry, lady, I didn't know—"

Brian jerked him up another inch. Stitches popped on the expensive jacket. "You call that an apology, sucker? See if you can't do better."

The man's eyes were bugging. Sweat erupted on his sheeny forehead and beneath his lizardlike nose. "I...I'm really sorry, m-miss. I'd like to b-buy you both a drink if you'd let me."

Brian slammed him back down to the floor, released his lapels distastefully while shoving the unpalatable intruder back until he stumbled against a table. "Pour your goddamn drinks in your pants, buddy. Maybe it'll cool you off." He turned. "Let's get out of here, Theresa." His fingers were like brands as he led her by an arm to the casino door, then out into the carpeted hall. She felt his hand trembling on her elbow and had to run to keep up with him. Wordlessly he turned down the hall to their rooms and was fishing in his trousers pockets for the key even before they reached their destination. When he leaned to insert the key into 108, there was no question of where he expected her to go. The door swung back and he found her hand, leading her inside. There followed a solid thud, then they were ensconced in a world of unbroken black. His arms closed convulsively around her, his body pressed close, sheltering, rocking her as he spoke gruffly against her hair. "I'm sorry, sweets, God, I'm so sorry."

"Brian, it's all right." But she was still shaken and vulnerable and, now that it was over, felt like crying. But his protection eradicated the sudden need for tears. His arms had strength she'd never suspected. They clamped her so hard her back hurt as he bent it in a bow.

"God, I wanted to kill him!" Brian's fingers dug into her flesh, just below and behind her armpits, and she winced, lifting her hands instinctively to press against his chest.

"Brian, it doesn't matter…please, you're hurting me."

The pressure fell away. He jerked as if shot. "I'm sorry…I'm sorry…sorry…" The voice was pained in the darkness, then his hands were gentle on her, finding her face in the inkiness, fingertips caressing her temples, then sliding into her hair as his mouth sought hers. "Theresa…Theresa…" he muttered, then circled her again with his arms. "I'd never hurt you, but I want you, you know that. God, I'm no better than him," Brian finished miserably, then took her mouth with an abandon that sent tongues of fire licking down her stomach. His hands left her back and roamed up her sides, pressing hard, too hard, as if it were compulsion he was trying to fight. She clung, unwilling to stop him yet, blessing the darkness.

His caress trailed down over her small waist, took measure of her hipbones, then traveled with uniform pressure down her buttocks, cupping them, pulling her up and inward against his tormented body. Along her sides his warm hands moved, compressing the swelling sides of her breasts until all else ceased to matter but that she know more of the treasured warmth of his palms upon them.

In the dense blackness she felt herself swept off the floor. Her arms instinctively encircled Brian's neck. In four steps he reached the bed and set her upon it, then joined her.

"Brian, we should stop…" she whispered against his mouth.

His tongue drove deep once more, then he softly nipped her lips. "We'll stop whenever you say." His kiss made dissent impossible, and then so did his touch. He covered her breasts with both wide palms, pressing down hard and flat and firm, for she lay with her torso precisely aligned with his. He found her hand in the dark, clamped his fingers over the back of it, carried it to his mouth and bit the outer edge, then turned its palm against her own breast. "Feel," he whispered fiercely, rolling aside. The nipple was distended. Even through her bra and summer sweater she could feel it. "Let me touch it, too." Again he kissed her hand, then placed it on his ribs. "Let me teach you how good it can feel."

She could see nothing in the infinite darkness, but as she was devoid of sight, her other senses sharpened. His spicy smell, his brandy taste, the slight tremor in his voice were all magnified in their appeal. But above all, her body seemed finely honed to the sense of touch. His breath was like the whisk of a feather upon her face, the dampness his kiss had left felt cool on her lips, the hard contours of his masculinity took on nearly visible form, the seeking conviction of his hands moving toward the clasp of her bra was felt as if from another supremely sensitive dimension.

She whimpered softly, lifting a shoulder. The clasp parted and her breasts were free. But Brian's elbows remained at her sides, bracing him above her. Across her face he took soft, teasing nips with his teeth: chin, cheek, nostril, lip, jaw, even eyebrow—bone and all. The bites grew more evocative, tightening the coil of tension in her stomach. His hands splayed over her bare back. "Theresa…so soft," he murmured, knowing the full length and width of that vulnerably soft skin, then kneading it gently. "So innocent." In one smooth motion his hands skimmed her circumference while his hips pinned hers securely. Sweater and bra were eased up by his hands. Then the objects of her long despair became those of her awakening sexuality as they were enveloped in his palms—skin on skin, warm on warm, man on woman.

It was so good, so right, and made her yearn for the forbidden.

The callused fingers that knew a guitar's strings so intimately now plucked upon her, as one might surround and pluck the fragile seeds of a dandelion from its stalk, the span of his fingertips widening, narrowing, drawing upward, encouraging her nipples to follow and reach when his touch disappeared. And they did. Repeatedly her shoulders strained to follow, as if to say, please don't leave me yet.

His hips lay still upon hers, but his flesh was at its fullest, thick and solid between their bodies. At the moment she scarcely gave it a thought, so taken was she by the sweet swellings of these first caresses on her breasts. He turned his head aside and gently rubbed his hair across the naked nipples. "Ohh…" she sang softly, in delight, entwining her fingers in the hair at the crest of his skull, guiding his head, experiencing the silken texture upon her aroused flesh. A turn of that head, and now it was his cheek where his hair had been. Her hands neither commanded nor discouraged, but rested idly in his hair while she waited…waited….

And then it happened, the first wonder of his mouth upon her breast, a passing kiss of introduction—vague, soft—on her left nipple first, then upon her right. And she thought, *hello at last, my love.* Gradually, as he nuzzled, his lips parted until their sleek inner skin touched her. She felt the texture of teeth, closed yet, making her yearn for them to open, allowing entry. So still she lay, as still as a butterfly poised on a windless day—feeling, feeling, feeling. His silken tongue came to introduce her flesh into his mouth and lead her within where all was wet, warm and slippery soft.

"Ohhh…Bri…" His name drifted into silence, lost to the grander passion now building.

"Mmm…" he murmured, a sound of praise, while the warm breath from his nostrils dampened the swell of skin beyond reach of his mouth. "Mmm…" He was tugging now, sucking more powerfully until she twisted slightly in satisfaction. To each of her breasts he brought adulation, until it felt the threads of femininity seemed drawn from deeper within her…up, up, and into the man whose mouth taught her pleasure.

Combing his hair with limp fingers she charted the movements of his head. "Oh, Brian, it's so good…" she murmured. "All these years I've wasted…."

He lunged up, dragging his hips along her thighs, joining swollen lips to hers. "We'll make up for them," he promised into her open mouth. "Shh…just feel… feel…."

When his mouth took her breast again, it was with acute knowledge of her need, and just how far he could go to send her senses soaring without hurting her. He caressed with his palms while capturing a taut nipple between the sharp edges of his teeth, scissoring until a keen, welcome sting made her gasp. Then there came a point beyond which the arousal of her breasts alone would no longer suffice. It was painful in its yearning. It made her lift to him, made him press to her. He found her mouth in the dark; it had fallen slack in the throes of desire. His was hotter now, and as they kissed he undulated above her until her knees parted of their own accord, creating a lee into which his body arched, rocking against her.

No more difficult words had she ever spoken. "Brian, please…I can't do this."

"I know…I know," came his rough whisper, but his mouth covered hers as he continued the sinuous rhythm along her body, bringing desire knocking upon her heart's door, seeking entry, just as his body sought entry to hers.

"Brian, please don't…or soon I won't be able to stop you." Her hands clenched in his hair, pulling his head back. "But I must, don't you see?"

He stilled. Stiffened.

"Don't move," he ordered gruffly. "Not a muscle." They lay with their breathing falling hard against each other until with a soft curse he rolled from the bed and in the black void she heard him make his way into the bathroom. A line of light spilled, casting his shadow against the wall as he grasped the edge of the sink and leaned against it, his head hanging down.

She lay utterly still. Her pulse throbbed throughout her body. She closed her eyes until Brian returned and sank down on the foot of the bed, leaning his elbows on his knees while running both hands through his hair. Then, with a groan he fell backward, hands flopped palms up.

She laid a hand in his, and at her touch his fingers clasped hers tightly. He rolled toward her, pressing his face against her hip. When he spoke his words were muffled against her.

"I'm sorry."

"And I'm sorry if I led you on and made you expect more."

"You didn't lead me on. You told me from the start that you weren't coming here with sex on your mind. It was me who pushed the issue after promising not to. I thought I had enough control to settle for kisses." He gave a soft, rueful laugh and flung an arm over his eyes.

But she *had* come into his room with sex on her mind, with at least as much as she'd experienced. She had wanted those precious moments because if she decided to have the surgery she might forfeit them forever. She felt a pang of guilt, for it seemed she'd used Brian for her own ends, and now he lay beside her apologizing for his very natural desire. She considered explaining to him, telling him about the surgery. But now that she'd known the rapture to be found beneath his lips, she was doubly unsure about proceeding with it. And furthermore, it was difficult for her to believe that when June came and he was freed to the civilian world, there would not be countless other women he'd find more attractive than herself. June was a key word often mentioned in their letters, but Theresa realized how easy it was for a lonely man to make plans for the future, but when that future came, how easily those plans could be changed. The thought hurt, but it was best to be honest with herself.

There were no promises made between them. And until there were, she must avoid situations such as this.

"Brian, it's late. I should go back to my room."

He rolled onto his back again, but his fingers remained laced with hers. "You could stay if you want to, and all we'll do is sleep side by side."

"No, I don't think I have that much willpower." When she sat up to straighten her clothing she felt him watching and wished the bathroom light was off, dim though it was. Her hair was tousled, her hands shaky.

"Theresa…" He reached for her with the plaintive word.

Softly she begged, "Let me go now without persuasion…please. I'm only one step away from changing my mind, but if I did I think we'd both be unhappy with ourselves."

His hand fell. He eased off the bed, helped her up and they walked silently to the door. It yawned open, and they stood studying the carpet.

He looped an elbow around her neck and drew her temple to his lips. "I'm not disappointed in you." The words rattled quietly in his throat.

Relief flooded Theresa and left her weak. She sagged against him. "You're so honest, Brian. I love that in you."

His eyes met hers, earnest yet troubled, and still with a flicker of desire in their depths. "Tomorrow will be hard enough, saying goodbye after being together like this. It would only have been harder if we'd given in."

She raised up on tiptoe, brushed his lips with hers, then touched them fleetingly with her fingertips.

"I had begun to think I'd never find you in this big old world, Brian Scanlon…." But she could say no more without crying, so slipped into the loneliness of her own room and closed the door between them.

Chapter 12

Their last day together was bittersweet. They wasted precious hours silently pondering the lonesomeness they'd feel at parting. They suffered recriminations about the night before. They counted the weeks of separation ahead. Laughter was rare, and forced, and followed by long gazing silences that left them more unfulfilled than ever.

They checked out at eleven and drove aimlessly until 1:00 p.m. Brian was flying standby on his return flight, so she took him to the airport where they sat in the coffee shop at a table by the window, unable to be cheered or consoled.

"You have a long drive ahead of you. I think you should go."

She lifted startled eyes to his. "No. I'll wait with you."

"But I may not catch a plane until late afternoon."

"But…I…" Her lips started quivering, so she clamped them together tightly.

"I know," he said softly. "But will it be any easier if you stay to watch my plane take off?"

Dismally she shook her head and stared at her coffee cup through distorting tears. His hand covered the back of hers, squeezing it hurting-hard, his thumb stroking hers upon the handle of the cup. "I want you to go," he claimed, yet the unsteady words laced his request with depression. "And I want you to do it smiling." The tears swelled fuller. He tilted her chin up with a finger. "Promise?"

She nodded, and the motion jarred the tears loose and sent them spilling down her freckled cheeks. Frantically she wiped them away and pasted on the smile he'd requested. "You're right. It's a five-hour drive…." She reached for her purse, babbling inanities, making her hands look busy with important stuff, foolish words pouring from her lips while Brian sat across the table smiling sadly. She fell silent in midsentence, folded her lower lip between her teeth and swallowed an enormous lump in her throat.

"Walk me to the car?" she asked so low he could hardly hear.

Without a word he dropped some change on the table and rose. She moved a step ahead of him, but felt his hand at her elbow then sliding down to capture her fingers and hold them tighter. Then tighter.

At the car they stopped. Both of them stared at the metal strip around the driver's door. A truck pulled up beside them, someone got out and walked toward the terminal. Brian lifted Theresa's hand and studied its palm while scratching at it repeatedly with his thumbnail.

"Thank you for coming, Treece."

She felt as if she were suffocating. "I had a g-good…" But she couldn't finish, and when the sob broke, he jerked her roughly into his arms. A hand clamped the back of her head. Her fingers clenched the back of his shirt. His scent was thick and nostalgic where her nose was pushed flat against his chest.

"Drive safely." His voice rumbled a full octave lower than usual.

"Say h-hi to J-Jeff."

"June will be here before we know it." But she was afraid to think of June. What if he didn't come back to her after all? He was holding her so close all she could make out through her tears was the soft gray of his shirt. "Now I'm going to kiss you, then you get in that car and drive, do you understand?"

She nodded, her cheek rubbing a wide damp spot on the gray cloth.

"Don't think of today. Think of June."

"I…w-will."

He jerked her up. Their mouths joined for a salty goodbye. His hand clamped the back of her neck as he pressed his warm lips to her wet cheeks, as if to keep something of her—something—within his body.

He put her away from him with a sturdy push, opened the car door, then waited until the engine fired. Resolutely she put the car into Reverse, backed from her parking spot, then hung her arm out the window as she pulled forward. Their fingertips brushed as she drove away, and a moment later a turn of the wheel whisked his reflection from her rearview mirror.

Theresa had expected her mother to be inquisitive, but oddly, Margaret only asked the most impersonal questions. How is Brian? Did he mention Jeff? Was there a lot of traffic? Both Margaret and Willard seemed to sympathize with their twenty-five-year-old daughter who mooned around the house as if she were fifteen. Even Amy, sensing Theresa's despondency, steered clear.

On her calendar, Theresa numbered the days backward from June 24 and grew more and more irritable as she remained indecisive about the surgery.

May arrived, and with it hot weather and uncontrollable children at school. The kids were so antsy they could hardly be contained in the stuffy schoolroom.

Spring was concert season, and Theresa busily prepared for the last two weeks of school, when a combined evening performance of the choir, band and orchestra was scheduled. After-school meetings were necessary to coordinate the programs with the directors of the other two groups. It was a hectic time of year, but at the same time sad. She was sorry to have to say goodbye to some sixth graders as they moved into junior high and a new building and three of these managed to find out about Theresa's twenty-sixth birthday, presenting her with a birthday cake in class that day. The tenseness of the past days fled as she felt her heart brimming with special feelings for the three.

And the glow still lingered when she arrived home to find flowers and a note from Brian: "With love, until June 24th, when I can tell you in person." The flowers created a stir within the family. Amy was awed and perhaps a trifle envious. Margaret insisted the flowers be left in the center of the supper table, though it was impossible to see around the enormous long-stemmed red roses. Willard smiled more than usual, and patted Theresa's shoulder every time their paths crossed. "What's all this about June?" he asked. She gave him a kiss on the jaw, but had no reply, for she wasn't sure herself what June would bring. Especially if she decided to have the surgery.

At nine-thirty that night the phone rang. Amy answered it, as usual. "It's for you, Theresa!" Amy's eyes were bright with excitement. She anxiously shoved the receiver into Theresa's hand and mouthed, "It's him!"

Theresa's heart pattered. Only inadequate letters had passed between them since Fargo. This was the first phone call. Amy stood close, watching with keen interest while Theresa placed the phone to her ear and answered breathlessly, "Hello?"

"Hello, sweets. Happy birthday."

Theresa placed a hand over her heart and said not a word. It felt as if she'd been supping on sweet, sweet rose petals, and they'd all stuck in her throat.

"Are you there, Theresa?"

"Yes...yes! Oh, Brian, the flowers are just beautiful. Thank you." It was him! It was really him!

"God, it's good to hear your voice."

Amy was still three feet away. "Just a minute, Brian." Theresa shifted her weight to one hip, lowered the receiver and shot a piercing look of strained patience. Amy made a disgruntled face, shrugged, slipped her hands into her jeans pockets and grumbled all the way to her bedroom.

"Brian, I'm back. Had to get rid of a nuisance."

His laugh lilted across the wire, and she pictured him with chin raised, green eyes dancing in delight. "The kid, huh?"

"Exactly."

"I'm picturing you in the kitchen, standing beside the

cupboard, and Amy beside you, all ears. I've been living on memories just like those ever since I left you."

Love talk was foreign to Theresa. She reacted with a blush that seemed to heat her belly and burn its way up to her breasts and neck to her temples. Her heart raced, and her palms grew damp.

"Oh, Brian…" she said softly, and closed her eyes, picturing his face again.

"I've missed you," he said quietly.

"I've missed you, too."

"I wish I could be there. I'd take you to dinner and then out dancing."

The memory of being wrapped in his arms, with her breasts crushed against his corduroy jacket came back in vivid detail and made her body ache with renewed longing to see him again.

"Brian, nobody's ever sent me flowers before."

"That just goes to show the world is filled with fools."

She smiled, closed her eyes and leaned her forehead against the cool kitchen wall. "And nobody's ever plied me with flattery before either. Don't stop now."

"Your teeth are like stars…." He paused expectantly, and her smile grew broader.

"Yes, I know—they come out every night." She could hear his humor blossoming as he went on to the next line of the time-weary joke.

"And your eyes are like limpid pools."

"Yes, I know—cesspools."

"And your hair is like moonbeams."

"Oh-oh! I never heard that one." But by this time they were both laughing. Then his voice became serious once more.

"What were you doing when I called?"

She watched her fingertips absently smoothing the kitchen wall. "I was in my bedroom, writing a thank-you letter to you for the roses."

"Were you really?"

"Yes, really."

It was quiet for a long time. His voice was gruff and slightly pained when he spoke again. "God, I miss you. I wish I was there."

"I wish you were, too, but it won't be long now."

"It seems like six years instead of six weeks."

"I know, but school will be out by then, and we'll be able to spend lots of time together…if you want."

"If I want?" After a meaningful pause, he added, sexily, "Silly girl."

She thought her heart might very well erupt, for it seemed to fill her ears and head with a wild, sweet thrumming. To her amazement, his next words made it beat even harder.

"I wish you could feel what's happening to my heart right now."

"I think I know. The same thing is going on in mine."

"Put your hand on it."

Only a faraway musical bleep sounded across the telephone line as Theresa digested his order.

"Is it there?" he asked.

"N-no."

"Put it there, for me."

Timidly, slowly, she placed her hand upon her throbbing heart.

"Is it there now?"

"Yes," she whispered.

"Tell me what you feel."

"I feel like…like I've been running as hard as I can—it's like there's a piston driving in there. My hand seems to be lifting and falling with the force of it."

After a long moment of silence he said rather shakily, "That's where I want to be, in your heart."

"Oh, Brian, you are," she replied breathily.

"Theresa?" She waited, breathlessly. "Now slide your hand down."

Her lips dropped open. Her skin prickled.

"Slide it down," he repeated, more softly. The tremor was gone from his voice now. It was controlled and very certain.

Her hand dropped to her breast. "And that's where I want to kiss you…again. And do everything that follows. I'm sorry now that we didn't do it in Fargo. But when I get back, we will. I'm giving you fair warning, Theresa."

The line went positively silent. Theresa's eyes were closed, her breathing labored. Turning, she pressed her shoulder blades and the back of her head to the wall. His face came clearly to mind. She moved her hand back to her breast and riffled her fingers softly up and down. The tiny movements sent shudders of sensation down the backs of her thighs. The thought of the surgery sizzled through her mind, and she opened her mouth to ask him what he would think if he came back and found her with beautifully average breasts, but ones that might not be able to show response.

"Theresa," he almost whispered, again sounding pained. "I have to go. You finish your letter to me, and tell me all the things you're feeling right now, okay, sweets? And I'll see you in six weeks. Till then, here's a kiss. Put it wherever you want it." A pause followed, then his emotional, "Goodbye, Treece."

"Brian, wait!" She clutched the phone almost frantically.

"I'm still here."

"Brian, I…" Her throat worked, but not another sound came out.

"I know, Theresa. I feel the same."

She would have known he'd hang up without warning. He was a man who never said goodbye twice.

"I'm giving you fair warning, Theresa."

His words stayed with her during the following days while she continued weighing the possibility of undergoing breast surgery. She had a second talk with Dr. Schaum. He told her the time would be perfect, just when school ended for summer vacation, a time of low stress and less social contact—both desirable. She had learned that her insurance *would* cover the cost of the surgery because of the prognosis for late-life back troubles. She'd received a brochure from Dr. Schaum explaining the surgical procedure, what to expect beforehand and afterward. The discomforts could be expected to be minimal, but they were the least of Theresa's concerns. Neither was she especially bothered by the idea of possibly having to give up nursing—babies seemed so far in the future. But the possibility of losing an erogenous zone made her reluctant, and at times depressed, especially when remembering Brian's lips upon her, and the wonder of her own feminine response.

She grew short-tempered with her family and also with her students as the weather warmed. The children's temperaments grew feisty, too. Fights broke out on the playground, and tears were often in need of swabbing. While she performed the duty, Theresa often wished she had someone to swab her own tears, shed in secret at night, as the decision time came closer and closer. If she was going to have the surgery, the choice must be made and made soon. In two weeks summer vacation would start, and three weeks after that, Brian would come home.

She thought of greeting him in a cool, cotton T-shirt— green, maybe—with a new trim profile of her choosing. How amazing to think she could actually choose the contour of breast she preferred! When her nipples were replaced, they would be lifted to a new, perky, uptilted angle that would remain attractive for the rest of her life.

The idea beguiled.

The idea horrified.

I want to do it.

I can't do it. What would Brian say?

It's your body, not his.

But I want to share it with him. To the fullest.

You still can, even if the sensation doesn't come back.

I should at least discuss it with him.

On the basis of one weekend in Fargo that ended unfulfilled, a bouquet of roses and a seductive phone call?

But he said he wanted me to be exactly the same when he came back!

Supposing you're even better?

I'll have scars.

That will disappear almost completely.

But I loved being kissed there—suppose I lose the feeling?
Chances are you won't.
I'm scared.
You're a woman—the choice is yours.

A week before vacation she made her decision. When she told her parents, Margaret's face registered immediate shock and disapproval, her father's a gray disappointment that the body he'd bequeathed his daughter had turned out to be less than suitable.

As Theresa had expected, Margaret was the outspoken one. "I don't understand why you'd want to...to fool around with the body you've been given, as if it isn't good enough."

"Because it can be better, Mother."

"But it's so *unnecessary* and such an expense!"

"Unnecessary!" These were all the arguments she'd been expecting, yet Theresa was deeply disappointed in her mother's lack of understanding. "You think it's unnecessary?"

Margaret colored and pursed her lips slightly. "I should know. I've lived with a shape like yours all my life, and I've gotten along just fine."

Theresa wondered about all the hidden slights her mother had suffered and never disclosed. She knew for a fact there were backaches and shoulder aches. Very quietly the young woman asked, "Have you, Mother?"

Margaret discovered something important needing attention behind her and presented her back. "What a ridiculous question. Movie stars and playgirls tamper with their shapes, not nice girls like you." She swung around again. "What will people say?"

Theresa felt wounded that her mother, with typical lack of tact, could choose such a time to voice the fear uppermost in her mind—which was how it would affect herself. She cared so much about the opinion of outsiders that she let its importance overshadow the reason her daughter had come to this decision. With a sigh, Theresa sank to a chair. "Please, Mom, Dad, I want to explain...." She did. She went back to age

fourteen and described all her disenchantment with her ele-
phantine growth, and explained all that Dr. Schaum had pre-
dicted for her future. She omitted the details about her sexual
hang-ups, but explained why she'd worn the sweaters, hidden
beneath the violin, chosen to work with children and disliked
meeting strange men.

When she finished, Margaret's eyes moved to Willard's. She
mulled silently for a minute, sighed and shrugged. "I don't
know," she said to the tabletop. "I don't know."

But Theresa knew. She had gained confidence by confronting her parents about the trip to Fargo, and she was very certain
the surgery was the right thing for her. She sensed her mother
softening and realized her own self-assurance was changing
Margaret's opinion.

"There's just one more thing," Theresa went on. She met
Margaret's questioning eyes directly. "Could you get the day off
that Monday of the surgery and be there at the hospital,
Mother?"

Perhaps it was the realization that the young woman who was
slowly but surely snipping the apron strings still needed
Margaret's maternal understanding. Perhaps it was because
there'd been times in Margaret's life when she'd wished for the
courage her daughter now displayed. She squelched her misgivings, forced the squeamishness from her thoughts and answered,
"If you're bound to go through with it, yes, I'll be there."

But when she was alone, Margaret leaned weakly against
the bathroom door, compressing her own bulbous breasts with
her palms, overcome by pangs of empathetic transference. She
opened her eyes and dropped her hands, breathing deeply, admitting what courage it took for her daughter to make the
decision she had.

On Memorial Day, Theresa washed her hair by herself for
the last time, as she wouldn't be able to lift her arms for a while
after the surgery. She packed a suitcase with one very generously sized nightgown, and three brand-new pairs of pajamas,
size medium. She harnessed herself into her size 34DD utili-

tarian white bra, but packed several of size 34C—not blue, not pink, not even lacy; those would have to wait. She'd be wearing the smaller, sturdy white bra day and night for a month. She dressed in a size extra-large spring top, but packed a brand-new one, again size medium, that looked to Theresa as if it had been made for a doll instead of a woman.

The following morning, Margaret was there when they rolled Theresa into surgery on the gurney. She kissed her daughter's cheek, held her hand in both of her own, and said, "See you in a little while."

A couple of hours later, Theresa was taken to the recovery room, and an hour after that she opened her eyes and lifted a bleary smile to Margaret, who leaned close and brushed the thick, coppery hair back from Theresa's forehead.

"Mom…" The word was an airy whisper. Theresa's eyelids fluttered open twice, but her eyes remained unfocused.

"Baby, everything went just fine. Rest now. I'll be here."

But a limp, freckled hand lifted and dreamily explored the sheets across her breast. "Mom, am…I…beautiful?" came the sleepy question.

Gently restraining Theresa's hand, Margaret felt tears sting her eyes. "Yes, baby, you're beautiful. But you've always been. Shh…"

A drugged smile lifted the corner of Theresa's soft lips. "Brian…doesn't…know…yet…." The lethargic voice hushed into silence, and Theresa drifted away into the webbed world of sleep.

Later Theresa was lucid and alone in her hospital room for the first time. She'd been warned to limit all arm movement, but could not resist gingerly exploring the mysteries sheathed beneath the white sheets and contained within the new, stiff, confining bra. She stared at the ceiling while moving her hands hesitantly upward. As they came into contact with the greatly reduced mounds of flesh, Theresa's eyelids drifted closed. She explored as a sightless person reads braille. She knew the exact pattern of the incisions and found them covered with dressing inside the bra, thus she imagined more than felt their outline.

She felt no pain, for she was still under the influence of the anaesthetic. Instead, she knew only a soaring jubilation. There was so little there! She lightly grazed the upper hemispheres of both breasts, to find them unbelievably reduced in breadth. And from what she could tell, blind this way, it seemed her nipples were going to be as tip-tilted as the end of a water ski. She felt a surge of overwhelming impatience to see the revised, improved shape she'd been given.

I want to see. I want to see.

But beneath her armpits tiny tubes were inserted to drain the pleural cavity and prevent internal bleeding and pneumonia. For now, Theresa had to be content with imagination.

Amy came later that day, filled with smiles and flip teenage acceptance of the momentous move Theresa had made. She produced a letter bearing familiar handwriting, but teased her sister by holding it beyond reach. "Mmm…just a piece of junk mail, I think."

"Gimme!"

"Gimme?" Amy looked disgusted. "Is that the kind of manners you teach your students? *Gimme?*"

"Hand it over, snot. I'm incapacitated and can't indulge in mortal combat until these tubes are removed and the stitches dissolve."

Truthfully, as the day wore on, Theresa's discomfort had been growing, but the letter from Brian made her forget them temporarily.

Dear Theresa,
Less than four weeks and we're out. And guess how we'll be coming home? I bought a van! A class act, for sure. It's a Chevy, kind of the color of your eyes, not brown and not hazel, with smoked windows, white pin-striping and enough room to carry all the guitars, amps and speakers for an entire band. You're gonna love it! I'll

take you out for a spin the minute I get there, and maybe you can help me look for an apartment, huh? God, sweets, I can't wait. For any of it—civilian life, school, the new band, and you. Most of all *you*. (Theresa smiled at the three slashes underlining the last word.) Jeff and I leave here on the morning of the 24th. Should be pulling in there by suppertime. Jeff says to tell your mother he wants pigs-in-the-blanket for supper, whatever that is. And me? I want Theresa-in-the-blankets after supper. Just teasing, darlin'…or am I?

> Love,
> Brian

Theresa refolded the letter, but instead of putting it on her bedside table, tucked it beneath the covers by her hip. She looked up to find Amy sprawled, unladylike, in the visitor's chair.

"Brian bought a van. He and Jeff are going to be driving it home."

"A van!" Amy's eyes lit up like flashing strobes, and she sat up straighter in the chair. "All ri-i-ight."

"And Jeff says to tell mom he wants pigs-in-the-blanket for supper when they get here."

"Boy, I can't wait!"

"*You* can't wait? Every day seems like an eternity to me."

"Yeah." Amy glanced at the sheet beneath which the letter was concealed. "You and Brian, well…looks like you two got a thing goin', I mean, since you went up and met him and everything, you two must really be gettin' it on."

"Not exactly. But…" Theresa mused with a winsome smile. Beneath the covers she touched the envelope hopefully.

"But you've been writing to each other for five months, and he sent you the roses and called and everything. I guess things are startin' to torque between you two, huh?"

Theresa laughed unexpectedly. It hurt terribly, and she pressed a hand to her rib cage. "Oh, don't do that, Amy. It hurts like heck."

"Oh, gol…sorry. Didn't mean to blow your seams."

Theresa laughed again, but this time when she pressed the sheets against herself, she caught Amy's eyes assessing her new shape inquisitively.

"Have you…well, I mean…have you seen yourself yet?" Amy's eyes were wide, her voice hesitant.

"No, but I've felt."

"Well…how…" Amy shrugged, grinned sheepishly. "Oh, you know what I mean."

"They feel like I'm wearing somebody else's body. Somebody who's shaped like I always wished I could be shaped."

"They look a lot smaller, even under the blankets."

Theresa turned the top of the sheet down to her waist. "They are. I'll show you when we're both back home."

Amy jumped up suddenly, pushed her palms into her rear jeans pockets, flat against her backside. She looked ill at ease, but after taking a turn around the bed, stopped beside her older sister and asked directly, "Have you told him?"

"Brian?"

Amy nodded.

"No, I haven't."

"Gol, I probably shouldn't have asked." Amy colored to a becoming shade of pink.

"It's okay, Amy. Brian and I…really like each other, but I didn't feel our relationship had gone far enough for me to consult him about having the surgery. And I'm scared of facing him again because he doesn't know."

"Yeah…" Amy's voice trailed away uncertainly. She grew morose, then speculative and glanced at Theresa askance. "You could still tell him. I mean before he comes home."

"I know. I've been considering it, but I'm kind of dreading it. I…oh, I don't know what to do."

Amy suddenly brightened, putting on a jack-in-the-box smile and bubbling, "Well, one thing's for sure. As soon as we spring you from this joint, you and I are going shopping for all those sexy, cute, *tiny* size nines you've been dying to shimmy into, okay?"

"Okay. You've got a date. Soon as I can put my arms up over my head to get into them."

Dr. Schaum breezed around the corner into Theresa's room, the tails of his lab coat flaring out behind his knees. "So how is our miniaturized Theresa today? Have you seen yourself in a mirror yet?"

"No…" Theresa was taken by surprise at his abrupt, swooping entry and his first question.

"No! Well, why not? You haven't gone through all this to lie there wondering what the new Theresa Brubaker looks like. Come on, young lady, we'll change that right now."

And so Theresa saw her reshaped breasts for the first time, with Dr. Schaum holding a wide mirror against his belly, studying her over the top of it, awaiting her verdict.

The stitches were still red and raw looking, but the shape was delightful, the perky angle of the upturned nipples an utter surprise. Somehow, she was not prepared for the reality of it. She was…*normal*. And in time, when the stitches healed and the scars faded, there would undoubtedly be times when she'd wonder if she'd ever been shaped any differently.

But for now, a wide-eyed Theresa stared at herself in the mirror and beamed, speechless.

Dr. Schaum tipped his head to one side. "Do I take that charming smile to mean you approve?"

"Oh…" was all Theresa breathed while continuing to stare and beam at her reflection. But when she reached to touch, Dr. Schaum warned, "Uh-uh! Don't investigate just yet. Leave that until the tubes and sutures are removed."

Theresa returned home a couple of days later, the drainage tubes gone from beneath her arms, but the sutures still in place. Amy washed her sister's hair and waited on her hand and foot with a solicitude that warmed Theresa's heart. Forbidden to even reach above her to get a coffee cup from the kitchen shelf, Theresa found herself often in need of Amy's helping hand, and during the next few days the bond between the sisters grew.

They were given the go-ahead for the long-awaited

shopping spree at the end of the second week, when Theresa saw Dr. Schaum for a post-op checkup.

That golden day in mid-June was like a fairy tale come true for the woman who surveyed the realm of ladies' fashions with eyes as excited as those of a child who spies the lights of a carnival on the horizon. "T-shirts! T-shirts! T-shirts!" Theresa sang exuberantly. "I feel like I want to wear them for at least one solid year!"

Amy giggled and hauled Theresa to a Shirt Shack and picked out a hot-pink item that boasted the words, "Knockers Up!" across the chest. They laughed exuberantly and hung the ugly garment back with its mates and went off to get serious.

Standing before the full-length mirror in the first item she tried on—a darling sleeveless V-neck knit shirt of fresh summer green, held up by ties on each shoulder—Theresa wondered if she'd ever been this happy. The sporty top was nothing extraordinary, not expensive, not even sexy really, only feminine, tiny, attractive—and utterly flattering. It was the kind of garment she'd never been able to even consider before. Theresa couldn't resist preening just a little. "Oh, Amy, look!"

Amy did, standing back, smiling at her sister's happy expression in the mirror. Suddenly Amy's shoulders straightened as she made a remarkable discovery. "Hey, Theresa, you look taller!"

"I do?" Theresa turned to the left, appraised herself. "You know, that was something Diane DeFreize told me people would say afterward. And you're the second one who has." Theresa realized it was partly because her posture was straighter since her self-image had improved so heartily. Also, the absence of bulk up front carried the eyes upward rather than horizontally, creating the illusion of added height. She stood square to the mirror again, gave her reflection a self-satisfied look of approval and seconded, "Yes, I do."

"Wait'll Brian sees you in that."

Theresa's eyes widened and glittered at the thought. She ran a hand over her bustline, wondering what he'd say. She still hadn't told him.

"Do you think he'll like it?"

"You're a knockout in green."

"You can't see my strap marks, can you?" The wide, ugly indentations in Theresa's shoulders hadn't been erased yet, but Dr. Schaum said they would disappear in time. The shoulder ties of the top were fairly narrow, but wide enough to conceal the depressions in her skin.

"No, the ties cover them up. I think you should make it your first purchase. *And* be wearing it when Brian gets here."

The thought was so dizzying, Theresa pressed a hand to her tummy. *When Brian gets here. Only one more week.*

"I'll take it. And next I want to look for a dress—no, eight dresses! The last time I bought one that didn't need alteration was when I was younger than you are now. Dr. Schaum says I should be a perfect size nine."

And she was. A swirly-skirted summer sundress of pink was followed by another of navy, red-and-white flowers, then by a classic off-white sheath with jewelry neckline and belt of burnished brown leather. They bought tube tops and V-neck T-shirts (no crew necks for Theresa Brubaker this trip!) and even one blouse that tied just beneath the bustline and left her midriff bare. Jewelry, something Theresa had never wanted to hang around her neck before for fear it would draw attention to her breast size, was as exciting to buy as her first pair of panty hose had been, years ago. She chose a delicate gold chain with a tiny puffed heart, and it looked delectable, even against the red freckles on her chest. But somehow even those freckles seemed less brash to Theresa. Her choice of garment colors was no longer limited by available size, thus she could select hues that minimized her redness.

When the day ended, Theresa sat in her room among mountains of crackling sacks and marvelous clothes. She felt like a bride with a new trousseau. Holding up her favorite—the green shoulder-tie top—she fitted it against her front, danced a swirling pattern across the floor, then closed her eyes and breathed deeply.

Hurry, Brian, hurry. I'm ready for you at last.

Chapter 13

It was a stunning June day, with the temperature in the low eighties and Minnesota's faultless sky the perfect, clear blue of the delphiniums that bloomed in gardens along Johnnycake Lane. Across the street, a group of teenagers were waxing a four-year-old Trans Am. Next door, Ruth Reed was standing beside her garden, checking to see if there were blossoms on her green beans yet. Two houses down, the neighborhood four- and five-year-olds were churning their chubby legs on the pedals of low-slung plastic motorcycles, making engine noises with their lips. Up and down the street the smell of cooking suppers drifted out to mingle with that of fresh-cut grass as people just home from work tried to get a start on the mowing before mealtime. In the Brubakers' front yard, an oscillating sprinkler swayed and sprayed, twinkling in the sun like the sequined ostrich fan of a Busby Berkeley girl.

It was a scene of everyday Americana, a slice of ordinary life, on an ordinary street, at the end of an ordinary workday.

But in the Brubaker house, excitement pulsated. Cabbage rolls stuffed with hamburger-rice filling were cooking in a roaster. The bathroom fixtures gleamed and fresh towels hung on the racks. In the freshly cleaned room a bouquet of garden flowers sat on the piano—marigolds, cosmos, zinnias and snapdragons. The kitchen table was set for six, and centered upon it waited a slightly lopsided two-layer cake, rather ineptly decorated with some quite flat-looking pink frosting sweetpeas and the words, *Welcome home, Jeff and Brian*. Amy adjusted the cake plate one more time and turned it just a little in an effort to make it appear more balanced than it was, then stood back, shrugged and muttered, "Oh, horse poop. It's good enough."

"Amy, watch your mouth!" warned Margaret, then added, "There's not a thing wrong with that cake, so I want you to stop fussing about it."

Outside, Willard had a hedge trimmer in his hands as he moved along the precision-trimmed alpine current hedge, taking a nip here, a nip there, though not a leaf was out of place. Periodically, he shaded his eyes and scanned the street to the west, gazing into the spray of diamond droplets that lifted and fell, lifted and fell across the emerald carpet of lawn—his pride and joy. The kitchen windows were cranked open above his head, and he checked his wrist, then called inside, "What time is it, Margaret? I think my watch stopped."

"It's five forty-five, and there's not a thing wrong with your watch, Willard. It was working seven minutes ago when you asked."

In her bedroom at the end of the hall, Theresa put the final touches on the makeup that by now she was adept at applying. She buckled a pair of flat, strappy white sandals onto her feet, inspecting the coral polish on her toenails—they'd never been painted before this summer. Next, she slipped into a brand-new pair of sleek jeans, snapped and zipped them up, ran a smoothing palm down her thighs, and watched herself in the mirror as she worked the kelly-green top over her head, covering her white bra. She adjusted the knot upon her left shoulder, stood back and assessed her reflection. *You don't look like a Christmas tree, Theresa, but you look like*—she searched her mind for a simile Brian had used—*like a poppy blossom*. She smiled in satisfaction and flicked the lifter through her freshly cut and styled hair, fluffing it around her temples and forehead until it suited perfectly. Around her neck she fastened the new chain with the tiny puffed heart. At her wrist went a simple gold bangle bracelet. She inserted tiny gold studs in her ears and was reaching for the perfume when she heard her father's voice calling through the screened windows at the other end of the house.

"I think it's them. It's a van, but I can't tell what color it is."

Theresa pressed a hand to her heart. The hand wasn't yet used to feeling the diminished contour it encountered in making this gesture. Her wide eyes raked down her torso in the mirror, then back up. *What will he think?*

"Yup, it's them!" she heard in her father's voice, before Amy bellowed, "Theresa, come on, they're here!"

A nerve jittered in her stomach, and the buildup of anticipation that had been expanding as each day passed, thickened the thud of her heart and made her knees quake. She turned and ran through the house and slammed out the back door, then waited behind the others as the cinnamon-colored Chevy van purred up the street, with Jeff's arm and head dangling out the window as he waved and hollered hello. But Theresa's eyes were drawn to the opposite side of the van as she tried to make out the face of the driver. But the windshield caught and reflected the bowl of blue sky, and she saw only it and the branches of the elm trees flashing across the glass as the vehicle turned and eased up the drive, then stopped.

Jeff's door flew open, and he scooped up the first body he encountered—Amy—lifting her off her feet and swirling her around before doing likewise with Margaret, who whooped and demanded to be set on her feet, but meant not a word of it. Willard got a rough hug, and Theresa was next. She found herself swept up from the ground before she could issue the warning to her brother not to suspend her. But the slight twinge of discomfort was worth it.

Yet while all this happened, Theresa was primarily conscious of Brian slipping from the driver's seat, removing a pair of sunglasses, stretching with his elbows in the air and rounding the front of the van to watch the greetings, then be included in them himself. Theresa hung back, observing the faded blue jeans slung low on his lean hips, buckling at the knees from a long day of driving; the loose, off-white shirt with three buttons open; the naked V of skin at his throat; his dark, military-cut hair and eyes the color of summer grasses that smiled while Amy gave him a smack on the cheek, Margaret a motherly hug and Willard a handshake and affectionate pat on the shoulder.

Then there was nobody left but Theresa.

Her heart pounded in her chest, and she felt as if her feet were not on the blacktop driveway but levitated an inch above it. The sensuous shock of recognition sent the color sweeping to her face, but she didn't care. He was here. He was as good to look at as she remembered. And his presence made her feel impatient, and nervous, and exhilarated.

They faced each other with six feet of space between them.

"Hello," he greeted simply, and it might have been a verse from the great love poets of decades ago.

"Hello." Her voice was soft and uncertain and quavery.

They were the only two who hadn't hugged or touched. Her tremulous lips were softly opened. The corners of his mouth lifted in a slow crescent of a smile. He reached his hands out to her, calluses up, and as she extended her fingertips and rested them upon his palms, she watched the summer-green eyes that last December had so assiduously avoided dropping to her breasts. Those eyes dropped now, directly, unerringly, down to the freckled throat and the V-neck of her new knit shirt, and then lower, to the two gentle rises within. Brian's mouth went slightly lax as he stared in undisguised amazement.

His puzzled gaze darted back up to her eyes, while Theresa felt her face suffuse with brighter color.

"How are you?" she managed, the question sounding foolishly mundane, even in her own ears.

"Fine." He released her fingers and stepped back, replacing the sunglasses on his nose while she felt him studying her from behind the dark lenses. "And you?"

They were conversing like robots, both extremely self-conscious all of a sudden, both trying in vain to regain calm footing.

"Same as ever." They were scarcely out of Theresa's mouth before she regretted her choice of words. She wasn't the same at all. "How was your trip?"

"Good, but tiring. We drove straight through."

The others had preceded them up the back steps, and Theresa and Brian trailed along. Though he walked just behind her shoulder, she felt his eyes burning into her, questioning, wondering. But she couldn't tell his true reaction yet. Was he pleased? Shocked for sure, and taken aback, but beyond that, Theresa could only guess.

Inside, the Brubaker house was as noisy as ever. Jeff—exultant, roaring, fun loving—stood in the middle of the kitchen with his arms extended wide and gave a jungle call like Tarzan, while from somewhere at the far end of the house a popular new band sang rock, and at the near end a folk group crooned in three-part harmony. Margaret tended something on the stove, and Jeff surrounded her from behind with both arms, his chin digging into her shoulder, making her wriggle and giggle. "Dammit, Ma, but that smells rank! Must be my pigs-in-the-blanket."

"Listen to that boy, calling my cabbage rolls rank." She lifted a lid off a steaming roaster, and Jeff snitched a pinch of something from inside. "Didn't that Air Force teach you any manners?" his mother teased happily. "Wash your hands before you come snitching."

Jeff grinned over his shoulder at Brian. "I thought we were done with C.O.'s when we got our walking papers, but it looks like I was wrong." He patted his mother's bottom. "But this one's all bluff, I think."

Margaret whirled and whacked at his hand with a spoon, but missed. "Oh, get away with you and your teasing, you brat. You're not too old for me to take the yardstick to." But Jeff had leaped safely out of reach. He spied the cake, and gave an undulating whistle of appreciation, like that of a construction worker eyeing a passing woman in high heels. "Wow, would y' look at this, Brian. Somebody's been busy."

"Amy," put in Willard proudly.

Amy beamed, her braces flashing. "The dumb thing is listing to the starboard," Amy despaired, but Jeff wrapped an arm around her shoulders, squeezed and declared, "Well, it won't list for long cause it won't last for long. I'd say about twenty minutes at the outside." Then a thought seemed to occur to him. "Is it chocolate?"

"What else?"

"Then I'd say less than twenty minutes. Shh! Don't tell Ma." He picked up a knife from one of the place settings and whacked into the high side of the cake, took a slice out and lifted it to his mouth before anybody could stop him.

Everyone in the room was laughing as Margaret swooped toward the table with the steaming roaster clutched in a pair of pot holders. "Jeffrey Brubaker," she scolded, "put that cake down this minute or you'll ruin your appetite! And for heaven's sake, everybody sit down before that child forces me to get the yardstick out after all!"

Brian took it all in with a sense of homecoming almost as familial as if he were, indeed, part of the Brubaker clan. And it was easy to see Jeff was their mood-setter, the one who stirred them all and generated both gaiety and teasing. It was so easy being with them. Brian felt like a cog slipping into the notches of a gear. Until he sat across from Theresa and was forced to consider the change in her.

"Take your old place," Willard invited Brian, pulling a chair out while they all shuffled and scraped and settled down for the meal. During the next half hour while they gobbled cabbage rolls and crusty buns and whipped potatoes oozing with parsley butter, then during the hour following while they ate cake and leisurely sipped glasses of iced tea and caught up with news of each other, Brian covertly studied Theresa's breasts as often as he could.

Once she looked up unexpectedly while passing him the sugar bowl and caught his gaze on her green shirtfront. Their eyes met, then abruptly shifted apart.

How? Brian wondered. *And when? And why didn't she tell me? Did Jeff know? And if so, why didn't he warn me?*

The kitchen was hot, and Margaret suggested they all take glasses of iced tea and sit on the small concrete patio between the house and the garage. Immediately they all got to their feet and did a cursory scraping of plates but left the stacked dishes on the counter, then filed out to the side of the house where webbed lawn chairs waited.

While they relaxed and visited, Theresa was ever aware of Brian's perusal. He had slipped his sunglasses on again, even though the patio was in full shade now as the sun dipped behind the peak of the roof. But occasionally, as he lifted his sweating glass and drank, she felt his gaze riveted on her chest. But when she looked up and smiled at him, she could not be sure, for she saw only the suggestion of dark eyes behind the tinted aviator lenses, and though his lips returned the smile, she sensed it did not reach those inscrutable eyes.

"Oh, yeah!" Amy suddenly remembered. "Glue Eyes called and said you should be sure to call her as soon as you got home."

Jeff pointed an accusatory finger at his playful sibling. "Listen, brat, if you don't can it with that Glue Eyes business, I'll have Ma take the yardstick to *you*."

"Aw, Jeff, you know I don't mean it. Not anymore. She's really okay, I guess. I got to like her a lot last Christmas. But I've called her Glue Eyes for so long it kinda falls outa me, ya know?"

"Well, someday it's gonna fall out when you're standing right beside her, then what will you do?"

"Apologize and explain and tell her that when I was learning to wear makeup I tried to put it on exactly like she does."

Jeff gave her a mock punch on the chin, then bounded into the house to make the phone call, and returned a few minutes later, announcing, "I'm going to run over and pick up Patricia and bring her back here. Anybody want to ride along with me?"

Theresa was torn, recalling the ardent reunion embraces she and Brian had witnessed last time, yet not wanting to stay behind if Brian said yes. He seemed to be waiting for her to answer, so she had to make a choice.

"I'll help Amy and mother with the dishes while you're gone," she decided.

"I'll drive you, Jeff," Brian offered, stretching to his feet, adjusting his glasses and turning to follow Jeff to the van. Theresa watched him walk away, studying the back of his too-short hair, the places where the shirt stuck to his back in a tic-tac-toe design from the webs of the lawn chair, his hands moving to his hips to give an unconscious tug at the waistband of his jeans. His back pockets had worn white patches where he carried his billfold, and his backside was so streamlined the sight of it created a hollow longing in the pit of Theresa's stomach.

He's upset. I should have told him.

No, you had no obligation to confide in him. It was your choice.

In the van, the two men rode down the street where evening shadows stretched long tendrils across green lawns. Brian drove deliberately slow. He pondered, wondering how to introduce the subject, and finally attacked it head-on.

"Okay, Brubaker, why didn't you tell me?"

Jeff gave a crooked smile. "She looks great, huh?"

"Damn right she looks great, but my eyeballs nearly dropped onto the goddamn driveway when I saw her standing there with her...without her...aw hell, *they're gone.*"

"Yup," Jeff slouched low in the seat and grinned out the windshield. "I always knew there lurked a proud beauty inside my Treat."

"Quit beatin' around the bush, Brubaker. You knew, didn't you?"

"Yeah, I knew."

"Did she write and tell you and ask you not to tell me?"

"No, Amy did. Amy thought I should know, so I could warn you if I thought that was best."

"Well, why the hell didn't you?"

"Because I didn't think it was any of my business. Your relationship with Theresa's got nothing to do with me, beyond the fact that I'm lucky enough to be her brother. If she'd wanted you to know beforehand, she'd have told you herself. I figured, what business was it of mine to go stickin' my two cents worth in?"

"But…" Brian gripped the steering wheel. "But…*how?*"

"Breast-reduction surgery."

Brian's shaded brown lenses flashed toward Jeff. "Breast re—" He sounded flabbergasted. "I never heard of such a thing."

"To tell you the truth, neither had I, but Amy told me all about it in her letter. She had it done three weeks ago, right after school got out for summer vacation. Listen, man—" Jeff turned to watch his friend guide the van onto a broader double-lane avenue "—she's…I don't want to see her get hurt, okay?"

"Hurt?" Brian turned sharply toward Jeff, then back to his driving. "You think I'd hurt her?"

"Well, I don't know. You're kind of…well, you act kind of pissed off or something. I don't know and I'm not asking what went on between you and Theresa, but go easy on her, huh? If you're thinking she should have confided in you for some reason, just understand that she's a pretty timid creature. It'd be pretty damn hard for a girl like Theresa to even have the surgery, much less write and discuss it with a man—I don't care *how* close you'd been."

"All right, I'll remember that. And I'll cool it around her. I guess I backed off pretty suddenlike when we said hello, but Christ, it was a shock."

"Yeah, I imagine it was." They rode in silence for some minutes, then just as they approached Patricia's house, Jeff turned to Brian and asked in a concerned voice, "Could I ask just one question, Bry?"

"Yeah, shoot."

"Just exactly what *do* you think of Theresa?"

Brian pulled the van up at the curb before Patricia's house, killed the engine, removed his sunglasses and half turned toward Jeff, draping his left elbow over the steering wheel. "I love her," he answered point-blank.

Jeff let his smile seep up the muscles of his face, made a fist and socked the air. "Hot damn!" he exclaimed, then opened his door and jumped down to cross the yard on the run.

Brian watched Jeff and Patricia meet in the center of the

open stretch of lawn. Jeff flung his arms around the young
woman, who lifted her arms around his shoulders, and they
kissed, pressed tightly against each other. It was just the way
he'd been planning to greet Theresa.

Patricia's parents stepped out the front door and called, "Hi,
Jeff. Welcome home. Are you gonna stay this time?"

"Damn right, I am. And I'm gonna steal your daughter!"

"Somehow, I don't think she minds one bit," Mrs. Gluek
called back.

Patricia clambered up into the high van, scooted over and
gave Brian a peck on the cheek. "Hiya, bud. Long time, no see."

Jeff was right behind Patricia. "Come here, woman, and put
your little butt where it belongs, right on my lap." There were
only two bucket seats up front. Jeff pulled Patricia down on his
lap, and she laughed happily, flung her arms around his neck
and kissed him while the van started rolling.

The dishes were done when the van lumbered up the street a
second time, pulled into the driveway and began disgorging its
passengers. They meandered to the patio, where Margaret,
Willard and Amy joined them. When Theresa came out of the
kitchen onto the back step, she found Brian standing below her,
waiting.

Her heart did a flip-flop, and everything inside her went
warm and springing. He reached up a hand to take hers, and
she felt a wash of relief that he was touching her at last.

"Come here, I want to talk to you." He pulled her down the
steps to his side, and asked softly, "Do you think your folks
would mind if we went for a walk?"

"Not at all."

"Tell them, then. I want to be alone with you, even if it's in
the middle of a city street where people are sitting on their
doorsteps watching us pass by."

Her heart swelled with joy, and she stepped to the edge of
the patio, made their excuses and returned to Brian. He
captured her hand, and their joined knuckles brushed between
their hips as they ambled down the driveway and onto the

blacktop street that was still warm beneath Theresa's sandals after the heat of the summer day. The shadows were falling as evening settled in. The sun rested on the rim of the horizon like a golden, liquid ball. They passed between yards where other sprinklers played the hushed vespers of water droplets spraying greenery.

"Is there someplace we can go?" he asked.

"There's a park about two blocks away."

"Good."

Nothing more was said as they sauntered hand in hand down the center of the street.

"Hi, Theresa," called a woman who was sitting on her front steps.

"Hi, Mrs. Anderson." Theresa raised a hand in greeting, then explained quietly, "I used to babysit for the Andersons when I was Amy's age."

Brian made no reply, lifting a hand in silent greeting, too, then continuing on at Theresa's side, stealing glances at her breasts when she dropped her chin and watched the toes of her white sandals. He wondered what secrets her clothing concealed, what she'd been through, if she hurt, if she was healed. But mostly, he wondered why she hadn't trusted him enough to tell him.

The eastern sky turned a rich periwinkle blue as the sun slipped and plunged into oblivion, leaving the western horizon a blaze of orange that faded to yellow, then violet as they approached a small neighborhood park where a silent baseball diamond was surrounded by a grove of trees. Deserted playground equipment hovered in the stillness of dusk. Great, aged oaks were scattered across the expanse of open recreation area, creating blots of darker shadows beneath their widespread arms, while picnic tables made smaller dots between the trees. Brian led the way from the street onto a crunchy gravel footpath, taking Theresa beneath the shadow of an oak before he finally stopped, squeezed her fingers almost painfully, then turned her to face him.

She looked up into the twin black dots of his sunglasses. "You've still got your glasses on."

Without a word he removed them, and slipped a bow inside the waist of his blue jeans so the glasses hung on his right hip.

"I guess you're a little upset with me, aren't you?" she ventured in a perilously shaky voice.

"Yes, I am," he admitted, "but could we deal with that later?" His long fingers closed over both of her shoulders, drawing her close to his wide-spraddled feet, close to the length of his faded Levi's, close to the naked V of skin above his shirt where dark hair sprigged. Her heart was hammering under her newly reshaped breasts. Her body moved willingly against his, then their arms sought to hold, to reaffirm, to answer the question, Is this person all that I remembered?

Brian's lips opened slightly as he lowered them to hers, which waited with warm, breathless expectancy. Tears bit the back of Theresa's eyes, and she was swept with a feeling of relief so overwhelming her body seemed to wilt as the apprehension eased away into the twilight. Then the waiting ended. They clung with the newly revived reassurance that what they'd found in each other twice before was still as appealing and had been magnified by their time apart.

His mouth was June warm. Indeed, he even seemed to taste of summer, of all things she loved—flowers, music, lazy sprinklers and somewhere, the remembered scent of something he put on his hair. But he had ridden nine hours in a warm van, had crossed miles of rolling prairie in the wrinkled clothing he wore now, and from that clothing emanated a scent she had never quite known before—the scent of Brian Scanlon, male, inviting, a little dusty, a little soiled, but all man.

The kiss was as lusty as some of the rock songs she'd heard him sing, a swift succession of strokes, tugs and head movements that seemed to elicit the threads of feelings from the very tips of her toes and send them sizzling up her body. She poured her feelings into the kiss, meeting his mouth with an equal ardor. With his feet widespread, his midsection was flush against hers, and it felt good, hard, sexy. Theresa was vaguely aware of a difference in the feeling of her breasts pressed against his chest—the smallness, the new tightness, the ability to be closer as his forearm slipped down across her spine and reeled her even more securely against his hips.

"Theresa…" His lips were at her ear, kissing her temple while his beautiful voice lost its mild note and took on a foreign huskiness. "I had to do that first. I just had to."

"First?"

He released a rather shaky breath and backed away from her, searching her upturned face in the deep shadow of the oaks. "It occurs to me we've got some talking to do, wouldn't you say?"

"Yes." She dropped her eyes, blushing already.

"Come on." Capturing her hand, he led her to the nearby area where the swings hung as still as the silence over the park that in daytime rang with children's voices. A steel slide angled down, casting its shadow on the grass as the moon slipped up into the eastern sky and the first stars came out. Brian tugged her along to the side of a large steel merry-go-round and sat down, pulling her to sit beside him, then dropping her hand.

"So…" he began, following the word with a sigh, then leaned his elbows on his thighs. "There've been some changes."

"Yes."

He pondered silently, made an impatient, breathy sound, then burst out, "God, I don't know where to begin, what to say."

"Neither do I."

"Theresa, why didn't you tell me?"

She shrugged very childishly for a twenty-six-year-old woman. "I was afraid to. And…and I didn't know what…well, I mean, we're not…"

"What you're trying to say is that you didn't know my intentions, is that it?"

"Yes, I guess so."

"After what we shared in Fargo, and our letters, you doubted my intentions?"

"No, not *doubted*. I just didn't think we'd had enough time together to get our relationship on its feet." *I wasn't even sure you would come….*

"With me, Theresa, it's not the *amount* of time, but the *quality* of it, and our weekend in Fargo was quality for me. I thought it was for you, too."

"It was, but…but, Brian, we hadn't done much more than just…well, you know what I'm saying. What we did together didn't really mean a commitment or…" Her voice trailed away. This was the most difficult conversation she'd ever had.

Brian suddenly sprang to his feet, walked three paces away from the merry-go-around and swung to face her. "Couldn't you trust me enough to tell me, Theresa?" he accused.

"I wanted to, but I was scared."

"Of what?"

"I don't know."

"Maybe you thought I was some lecher who was only after you because you had big knockers, is that it? Did you think if you told me you didn't have them anymore, I'd brush you off? Is that what you thought?"

She was horrified. It had never entered her mind that he might consider such a thing. Tears blurred her eyes. "No, Brian, I never thought that…never!"

"Then why the hell couldn't you have trusted me enough to confide in me and tell me what you were planning, give me time to get accustomed to it before I walked into your yard totally unsuspecting? Christ, do you know what a shock it was?"

"I knew you'd be surprised, but I thought you'd be pleasantly surprised."

"I am, I was…." He threw his hands into the air exasperatedly and whirled, presenting his rigid back. "But, God, Theresa, do you know what I've been thinking about for six months? Do you know how many nights I've lain awake thinking about your…*problem* and figuring out ways to finesse you into losing your inhibitions, telling myself I had to be the world's most patient lover when I took you to bed for the first time, so I didn't put some irreversible phobia into you or make your hang-up worse than it already was?" Again he spun on her. "We may not have had time to share much, but what we did share was a pretty damn intimate baring of souls, and I think it gave me the right to be in on your decision with you, to share it. But you didn't even give me the chance."

"Now just a minute!" She leaped to her feet and faced him in the flood of moonlight that was growing brighter by the minute. "You've got no claim on me, no right to—"

"The hell I don't!"

"The hell you do!" Theresa had never fought or sworn in her life and was surprised at herself.

"The hell I don't! I love you, dammit!" he shouted.

"Well, that's some way to tell me, shouting at the top of your lungs! How was I supposed to know?"

"I signed all my letters that way, didn't I?"

"Well yes, but that's just a...a formal closing on a letter."

"Is that all you took it for?"

"No!"

"Well, if you knew I loved you, why couldn't you trust me? Had you ever stopped to think it might have been something I'd have welcomed sharing? Something that might have brought us even closer? Something I would have felt *honored* to share? But you didn't give me a chance, going ahead without a word like you did."

"I resent your attitude, Brian. It's...it's possessive and uninformed."

"Uninformed?" He stood belligerently now, his hands on his hips. "Whose fault is that, mine or yours? If you'd bothered to *inform* me, I wouldn't be so damn mad right now."

"I discussed it with people who didn't lose their tempers, like you're doing. A counselor at school, a woman who'd had the surgery before and a cosmetic surgeon who eventually performed the operation. I got the emotional support I needed from them."

He felt shut out and hurt. During the past six months he'd felt a growing affinity with Theresa. He'd felt they were slowly becoming intimates, and he'd returned here thinking she was ready to pursue not only an emotional relationship but a physical one as well. He found himself intimidated by the

changes in her body more than he'd been intimidated by her
abundant breasts—they'd been only flesh, after all, and that he
could approach and touch the same as he had other women's.
The psychological preparations he'd made for approaching
her again had been made at no little cost in both sleep and
worry. Now that he found it all for naught, he felt cheated. Now
that he knew she'd turned to others and implied they'd been
more help than he could have been, he felt misunderstood. And
now that he wasn't sure how long he'd have to wait to pursue
her sexually, he felt angry—dammit, he'd wanted to make love
to her, and soon!

"Brian," she said softly, sadly, "I didn't mean that the way
it sounded. It wasn't that I didn't think you'd support my
decision. But it seemed…presumptuous of me to involve you
in something so personal without any commitments made
between us." She touched his arm, but he remained stiff and
scowling, so she returned to sit on the merry-go-round.

He was very upset. And hurt. And wondering if he had the
right to be. He swung back to the merry-go-round, flopped
down several feet away from her and fell back, draping his
shoulders and outflung arms over the mound-shaped steel heart
of the vehicle. As he flopped backward he gave a single nudge
with his foot, setting the steel framework into motion. He lay
brooding, looking up at the stars that circled slowly above
him, getting a grip on his feelings.

Theresa sat with her shoulders slumped despondently,
feeling the slight rumbling vibrations rising up through the
tubular steel bars.

Oh, misery! She had thought this night of Brian's homecoming would see them close, loving, reveling in being
together once again. She felt drained and depleted and unsure
of how to deal with his anger. Perhaps he had a right to it;
perhaps he didn't. She was no psychologist. She should have
discussed it with Catherine McDonald and sought her advice
regarding whether or not to tell Brian her intentions.

The merry-go-round was set off-kilter, so centrifugal force
kept it moving in what seemed a perpetual, lazy twirl. The tears

gathered in Theresa's throat and then in her eyes. She brushed them away with the back of her wrist, turning away so he couldn't tell what she was doing.

But somehow he sensed it. A hand closed around her bare elbow and pulled her back and to one side. "Hey..." he cajoled softly. "Come here."

She draped backward across the domed center of the merry-go-round. The steel was icy beneath her bare arms as she angled toward him until only their shoulders touched, and the backs of their heads were pressed against the hard, hard metal as they studied the stars. Around and around. Dots of light on the blue-black sky twinkled like reflections of a revolving mirrored ball above a ballroom floor. Crickets had set up their endless chirping, and the night was growing damp, but it felt good against Theresa's hot face. The incandescent moon lit their draped bodies, the bars of the swing set and the crowns of the oak trees that passed slowly as Brian's foot kept nudging the beaten earth.

"I'm sorry, Theresa. I shouldn't have shouted."

"I am, too." She sobbed once, and in an instant, he'd pulled her close.

"Listen, sweets, could I have a couple days to get used to it? Hell, I don't know whether I'm allowed to look at them or not. I do, and I feel guilty. I don't, and I feel guiltier. And your family, all avoiding the issue as if you'd never had any other shape. Anyway, I guess I built my hopes up too high, thinking about tonight and what it was going to be like, seeing you again."

"Me, too. I certainly didn't want us to fight this way."

"Then let's not, not anymore. Let's go back and see if everybody else is as tired as I am. I've been awake since 2:00 a.m. I was too excited to sleep."

"You, too?" She offered a shaky smile.

He smiled down at her in return, brushed a knuckle over the end of her nose and kissed her lightly.

He'd meant to give her only that single light kiss, but in the end, he couldn't let her go with just that. Slowly, deliberately, he returned his mouth to hers, dipping his tongue into the secret warmth of her lips, which opened in welcome. His body spurted to life, and his shoulders quivered as he pressed his elbows to the metal surface on either side of her head. God, the things he wanted to do to her, to feel with her, to have her do to him. How long would he have to wait? The kiss lingered and lengthened, growing more dizzying than the slow circling of their perch. The way Theresa lay, sprawled backward over the curved metal, the outline of her breasts was lined by moonlight as they jutted forward. It was as sexy a pose as he'd ever seen her in, and he knew it would take no more than a quick shift of his palm, and he'd feel the relief of touching her intimately. He needn't touch her breast about which he was so unsure—her stomach looked hollow and inviting, and her slacks were very taut and alluring. He thought about running his hand down her ribs, exploring the warm inviting length of her zipper, and the sheltered spot between her legs as he'd done once before. But one thing might lead to another, and he had no idea if she was allowed to move, twist, thrust, if she had stitches, and where, and how many....

And once he started something, he had no intention of drawing back.

In the end, Brian pacified himself with the kiss alone. When it ended, he regretfully lurched to his feet, dragging Theresa with him, crossing the shadowy park toward the house where they could mingle with people and wouldn't have to confront the remaining issue...at least for a while.

Chapter 14

The others had gone inside where they were visiting and having second pieces of cake when Brian and Theresa walked up the driveway. The kitchen lights slanted out across the darkened yard and back step in oblique slashes of creamy brightness. Mosquitoes hummed and buzzed against the back screen door, and a June bug threw its crusty shell at the light time and again. Frogs and crickets competed for first chair in the nighttime orchestra. The moon was a pristine ball of white.

From inside came the voices of the group Theresa and Brian could see as they walked up the driveway. They were clustered around the kitchen table, but outside it was peaceful and private. Just short of the back step, Brian stopped Theresa with a hand on her arm.

"Listen, there were a lot of things I wanted to talk about tonight but..." The thought remained unfinished.

"I know." Theresa recalled the many subjects she had stored up and was eager to share with him.

"And just because I didn't get into any of them doesn't mean I'm still mad, okay?"

She was studying the middle button on his shirt, which faced her and the moon. By its light the gauze appeared brilliant white while her own face was cast in shadow. He touched her beneath the chin with a single finger, forcing her to tilt her head up. "Okay?" he asked softly.

"Okay."

"And I probably won't see you for a while after tonight, because Jeff and I have a lot of running around to do. I have to find an apartment and buy some furniture, and we want to start working on getting a band together right away. We have to renew our union cards and try to find a decent agent and audition the new drummer and bass guitarist and maybe a keyboard man, too. Anyway, I'm going to be jumping for a while. I just wanted you to know."

"Thanks for telling me." But her heart felt heavy with disappointment. Now that he was back, she wanted to be with him as much as possible. In his letters he'd suggested she could come along with him and help pick out furniture, but now he was eliminating her from that excursion. She could understand that he had a lot of mundane arrangements to make, just to get settled into an apartment, and that she'd only be in the way when they were auditioning new players, but somehow she'd thought they'd find time each day to see each other. But she smiled and hid the fact that she was crushed by his advance warning. Was this how fellows turned girls down gently? *No, she reprimanded herself, you're being unfair to Brian. He's not like that. He's honest and honorable. That's why he's warning you in the first place.*

The finger beneath her chin curled, and he brushed her jaw with his knuckles. "I'll call as soon as I've got my feet planted."

"Fine." She began turning toward the back step, but his hand detained her a second time.

"Wait a minute. You're not getting away without one more kiss."

She was swung around and encircled in warm, hard arms and pulled against his moonlit shirt. While his lips closed over hers, the picture of the naked V of skin at his neck came into Theresa's mind, and she suddenly wanted to touch it. Hesitantly, she slipped her hand to find it, resting her palm on the sleek hair and warm flesh, then sliding it upward to rest at the side of his neck while her thumb touched the hollow of his throat. The thudding of his pulse there surprised her. Lightly,

lightly, she stroked the warm, pliant depression. He made a soft, throaty sound, and his mouth moved over hers more hungrily. He clasped the back of her head and swept the interior of her mouth with lusty, intimate strokes of his tongue that sent liquid fire racing across her skin.

Some queer surge of latent feminine knowledge pulsed through Theresa. In her entire life, she'd never actively provoked a sexual response from a man. Instead, she'd always been too busy fighting off the bombardment of unwanted physical advances her partners seemed always too eager to display. Now, for the first time, *she* touched—a hesitant touch at best. But the response it kindled in Brian was at once surprising and telling. All she had done was stroke the hollow of his throat with her thumb, yet he reacted as if she'd done far more. The tenor of his kiss changed with a swift, swirling suddenness, and became totally sexual, not the insipid good-night gesture that it had begun to be.

It came as a surprise to think she, Theresa Brubaker, elementary music teacher, freckled redhead, inexperienced paramour, could generate such an immediate and passionate response by only the briefest of encouragements. Especially when she considered that he was a guitar man, a performer who had, admittedly, enjoyed all the adulation that went with his career. He must have known a great many very experienced women, far more experienced than her. Yet, he thrilled to her very inexperienced touch, and this in turn thrilled Theresa.

Realizing the power she possessed to stimulate this man, she suddenly grew impatient to test it further.

But she hadn't the chance, for as quickly as his ardor grew, he controlled it, lifting his head to suck in a great gulp of damp night air and push her gently away. "Lord, woman, do you know how good you are at that?"

"Me?" she asked, surprised.

"You."

"I'm not good at that at all. I've barely had any practice."

"Well, we'll remedy that when the time is right. But if practice makes perfect, I think you'll end up being more than I can handle."

She smiled and in the dark felt herself flush with pleasure at his words. "Hasn't anybody ever told you it's not nice to start things like that when you don't intend to finish them?" came Brian's husky teasing.

"I didn't start it. You did. I was heading into the house when you stopped me. But if you're done now, let's go in." Smiling, she turned toward the step again.

"Not so fast." Once more she was brought up short. "I can't go in just now."

"You can't?" She turned back to face him.

"Uh-uh. I'll need a couple of minutes."

"Oh!" Suddenly she understood and whirled around, presenting her shoulder blades. As she pressed her palms to embarrassed cheeks, he chuckled softly behind her shoulder, audaciously kissed the side of her neck and captured her hand. "Come on, let's go for a little walk through the backyard. That should cool me down. You can talk about school, and I'll talk about the Air Force. Those are two nice, safe, deflating subjects."

Brian treated sexuality with such frankness. Theresa wondered if she'd ever be as open about it as he was. Her body felt flushed with awareness, equally as charged as his. Thank heavens it didn't show on women!

They entered the kitchen five minutes later and pulled up chairs to join the others around the table, while Margaret sliced cake for them, and the conversation continued. When ten-thirty arrived, Jeff pushed his chair back, lifted his elbows toward the ceiling and gave a broad, shivering stretch while twisting at the waist.

"Well, I guess it's time I get Patricia home."

"Want to take the van?"

"Thanks, I'd love to."

Brian tossed Jeff the keys. "We'd better unload our suitcases first, 'cause I'm ready for the sack. I'll need my stuff."

While the unloading was being done, Theresa escaped to the lower level of the house to put out clean sheets and blankets for Brian's bed. She experienced a feeling of déjà vu, recalling the intimacies she and Brian had exchanged on this davenport, both on New Year's Eve and the following morning. Somehow, she realized it would be best not to have Brian encounter her here, with the mattress opened up and the bed between them, ready for use. So she left the bedding and the light on and said her good-night to him along with the rest of her family in the kitchen, before they each retired to their respective beds.

In the morning, Theresa was disappointed to discover both Brian and Jeff gone when she woke up. It was only a little before nine, so they must have been up early. The day stretched before her with an emptiness she hadn't anticipated. Many times she paused to wonder at how the absence of a single person could create a void this distracting. But it was true: knowing Brian was in town made it all the harder to be apart from him. It seemed he was never absent from her thoughts for more than an hour before his image popped up again, speaking, gesturing, sharing intimate caresses and kisses. And, too, angry.

It was the first time she'd seen his anger, and in the way of most lovers, Theresa found it now stimulating to remember how he'd looked and sounded when he was upset. Knowing this new facet of him seemed almost a relief. Everybody has his angry moments, and the way she was feeling about Brian, she thought it imperative to see both his best and worst sides, and the sooner the better. She had fallen totally in love with the man. If he asked her to make a commitment today, she'd do it without hesitation.

But the first day passed, and a second, and a third, and still she hadn't seen Brian again. Jeff reported he'd found a one-bedroom apartment in the nearby suburb of Bloomington. It was vacant, so Brian had paid his money and taken immediate occupancy. The two men had wasted no time going off to a furniture store to buy the single item that was essential: a bed. The news brought Theresa's glance sharply up to her brother, but Jeff rambled on, relating the story of how the two of them had hauled the bed to Brian's apartment in the van.

Theresa pictured him there, alone, while she lay in her bed alone, wondering if he thought of her as strongly as she thought of him each time she slipped between the sheets for the night. It was late June, the nights hot and muggy, and she blamed her restlessness on that. It seemed she never managed to sleep straight through a night anymore, but awakened several times and spent long, sleepless hours staring at the streetlight outside her window, thinking of Brian, and wondering when she'd see him again.

He called on the fourth day. Theresa could tell who it was by Amy's part of the conversation.

"Hello?... Oh, *hiiiii*... I hear you found an apartment... Must be kind of creepy without any furniture... Oh, a pool!... All riiiiight!... Can I really!... Can I bring a friend?... Sure she does... Sure she can... Yeah, she's right here, just a sec." Amy handed the receiver to Theresa who'd been listening and waiting in agony.

The smile on Theresa's face put the June sun to shame. Her heart was rapping out an I-missed-you tattoo that made her voice come out rather breathily and unnaturally high.

"Hello?"

"Hiya, sweets," he greeted, as if they'd never had a cross word between them. How absolutely absurd to blush when he was ten miles away, but the way he could pronounce that word always sent shafts of delight through her.

"Who's this?" she asked cheekily.

His laugh vibrated along the wires and made her smile all the more broadly and feel exceedingly clever for one of the first times in her life.

"This is the guitar man, you little redheaded tease. I just got my new phone installed and wanted to give you the number here."

"Oh." Disappointment deflated Theresa with a heavy *whump.* She'd thought he was calling to ask if he could see her. "Just a minute—let me get a pencil."

"It's 555-8732," he dictated. She wrote it down, then found herself tracing it repeatedly while the conversation went on. "I've got a nice apartment, but it's a little empty yet. I did get a bed, though." Had he gone on, she might not have become so flustered. But he didn't. He let the silence ooze over her skin suggestively, lifting tiny goose bumps of arousal at the imagery that popped into her mind at the thought of his bed and him in it. Theresa glanced at Amy who stood by listening, and hoped she'd had the receiver plastered hard enough against her ear that Amy hadn't gotten a drift of what Brian said.

"Oh, that's nice!" Theresa replied brightly.

Like a dolt, she went on speaking the most idiotic inanities.

"Very nice, indeed. But it needs breaking in. Have you ever broken in a bed?"

"No," she attempted, but the word was a croak, hardly discernible. She cleared her throat and repeated, "No."

"Maybe you can help me with this one."

Theresa was so red by this time that Amy's expression had grown puzzled. Theresa covered the mouthpiece, flapped an exasperated hand at her younger sister and hissed, "Will you go find something to do?"

Amy left, throwing a last inquisitive glance over her shoulder.

"I've got a pool, too," Brian was saying.

"Oh, I love to swim." It was one of the few sports in which she'd ever been able to participate fully.

"Can you?"

For a moment she was puzzled. "Can I?"

"Yes, I mean…are you allowed to…yet?"

"Oh." The light dawned. Was she healed enough to swim. "Oh, yes, I'm back to full activities."

"Why didn't you tell me that the other night?"

His question and the tone of his voice told her the reason for his pause. He'd been waiting for the go-ahead! The idea threw her into a semipanic, yet she was anxious to pursue her relationship with him, though she knew beyond a doubt there would be few days of total innocence once they began seeing each other regularly. Considering her old-fashioned sense of propriety, it naturally put Theresa in a vulnerable position, one in which she would soon be forced to make some very critical decisions.

"I…I didn't think about it."

"I did."

She realized it now—how lightly he'd held her when they caressed, as if she were breakable. Even when they'd kissed in the driveway near the back door, he'd pulled her head hard against him, but hadn't forced her body in any way.

Neither of them said anything for a full forty-five seconds. They were coming to grips with something unspoken. During that silence he told her his intentions as clearly as if he'd illustrated them by renting a highway billboard with a two-foot-high caption. He was ready for a physical relationship. Was she?

When the silence was broken, it was Brian who spoke. His voice was slightly deeper than usual, but quiet. "Theresa, I'd like us to spend next Saturday together…here. Bring your bathing suit, and I'll pick up some corned beef at the deli, and we'll make a day of it. We'll swim and catch some sun and talk, okay?"

"Yes," she agreed quietly.

"Okay, what time should I come and get you?"

She had missed him terribly. There was only one answer she could give. "Early."

"Ten in the morning?"

No, six in the morning, she thought, but answered, "Fine. I'll be ready."

"See you then. And, honey?"

Being called *honey* by Brian was something so precious it made her chest ache.

"Yes?"

"I miss you."

"I miss you, too."

It was Friday. Theresa had spent a restless night, considering the possibilities that lay ahead for her with Brian. She thought not only of the sexual tension between them, but of the responsibilities it brought. She had thought herself totally opposed to sex beyond the framework of marriage, but her brief experience in Fargo warned that when bodies are aroused, moral attitudes tend to dissolve and disappear in the expanding joy of the moment.

Would I let him? Would I let myself?

The answer to both questions, Theresa found, was an un-qualified *yes*.

The following day she went to the drugstore to buy sun-screen, knowing she'd suffer if she didn't apply an effective barrier to her pale, freckled skin that seemed to get hot and prickly at the mere mention of the word *sun.* She chose the one whose label said it had UVA and UVB protection, then ambled to a revolving rack of sunglasses and spent an enjoyable twenty minutes trying on every pair at least twice before choosing a rather upbeat pair with graduated shading and large round lenses that seemed to make her mouth appear feminine and vul-nerable when the oversize frames rested on her nose.

She wandered along the shelves, picking up odd items she needed: emery boards, deodorant, hair conditioner. Suddenly she came up short and stared at the array of products on an eye-level shelf. *Contraceptives.*

Brian's face seemed to emblazon itself across her subcon-scious as if projected on a movie screen. It seemed inevitable that he would become her lover. Yet why did it seem prurient to consider buying a contraceptive in advance? It somehow took the warm glow of love to a cooler temperature and made her feel cunning and deliberate.

Without realizing she'd done it, she slipped the dark glasses on, hiding behind them, though the price tag still dangled from the bow.

Theresa Brubaker, you're twenty-six years old! You're living in twenty-first-century America, where most women face this decision in their midteens. What are you so afraid of?

Commitment? Not at all. Not commitment to Brian, only to the undeniable tug of sexuality, for once she surrendered to it, there was no turning back. It was such an irreversible decision.

Don't be stupid, Theresa. He may keep you out by the pool all afternoon and all this gnashing will have been for nothing.
Fat chance! With my skin! If he keeps me out there all after-

noon I'll look like a brick somebody forgot in the kiln. He's already hinted he's going to take me into his bedroom to try out his bed.

So, buy something! At least you'll have it if you need it.

Buy what? I've never paid any attention to the articles about products like these.

So, pick one up and read the label.

But she checked the aisle in both directions first. Even the label instructions made her blush. How on earth could she ever confront the fact that she'd have to use this stuff while she was with a man? She'd die of embarrassment!

It's either that or end up pregnant, her unwanted-companion voice persecuted.

But I'm not that kind of girl. I've always said so.

Everybody's that kind of girl when the right man comes along.

Yes, things have changed so much since Brian came into my life.

She studied the products and finally decided on one. But on her way to the checkout stand, she bought a *Cosmopolitan* magazine and dropped it nonchalantly over her other selections when setting them on the counter. *Cosmopolitan,* she thought, how appropriate. But Helen Gurley Brown would scold me for not placing the contraceptive on top of the magazine instead of vice versa.

On her next stop at the Burnsville Shopping Center, she found it necessary to buy a new purse, one large enough to conceal her new purchase. She chuckled inwardly that it turned out to be her first purchase of a contraceptive that should lead the way to her buying something she'd wanted all her life: a shoulder bag. Her shoulders had carried more than their share of strain in years gone by. She'd never felt willing to hang a purse on them as well, though she'd often wanted to own one. Well, she did now.

But the chief reason she'd come to the clothing store was to shop for a bathing suit, another item that was expanding her clothing horizon, for the suits she'd worn in the past had had to be one-pieces, altered to fit.

Now, however, she tried everything from string bikinis to skirted one-piece jobs in the Hedy Lamarr tradition. She chose a very middle-of-the-road two-piece design that wasn't exactly tawdry, but fell just short of being totally modest. The fabric was the color of her father's well-kept lawn and looked like shiny wet leather when the light caught and reflected from it. The bright kelly green was a hue that in days of old she'd have said contrasted with her coloring too sharply—the old stop-and-go-light look. But somehow, since her surgery, Theresa's confidence had grown. And since the advent of Brian in her sphere, she had felt far less plain than she used to. This gift he'd given her was something Theresa meant to repay in some way someday.

The following morning she awakened shortly after five o'clock. The sun was peeking over the eastern horizon, turning the sky to a lustrous, pearly coral, sending streaks of brighter melon and pink radiating above the rim of the world. Closing her eyes and stretching, Theresa felt as if those shafts of hot pink were penetrating her body. She felt giddy, elated and as if she were on the brink of the most momentous day of her life.

The Maestro grinned down at her from the shelf, and it seemed as if he fiddled a gay, lilting love song to awaken her. She smiled at him, slithered lower in the bed, raised both arms above her head and rolled to her belly, savoring the keen satisfaction a simple act like that now brought into her life. It made her feel diminutive and catlike. Beneath her, the bulk was gone, in its place a body proportioned by a hand that had, in this case, improved upon Nature.

There were times when she still had difficulty realizing the change had happened and was permanent. Sometimes she found herself affecting mannerisms no longer necessary: crossing one arm and resting the opposite elbow on it to give momentary relief by boosting up her breasts, yet at the same time hiding behind her arms. Walking. Ah, but there simply hadn't been a chance to run yet. But she would, someday soon. Just to feel the ebullience and freedom of the act.

She threw herself onto her back, studied the ceiling and checked the clock. Was it broken? Or had only five minutes passed since she'd awakened? Would the rest of the morning go this slowly until Brian came to her?

It did.

In spite of the fact that she performed every grooming ritual with the pomp and time-consuming attention of a ceremony. She shaved her legs...all the way up. She filed her toenails into delicate rounded peaks and polished them with Chocolate Mocha polish. She gave herself a careful and complete manicure, painting her fingernails with three coats. She washed her hair and arranged it with care that was positively silly, considering she was going to leap into a swimming pool within minutes after she got there. But she spared no less care on her makeup. She took a bath and put an astringent after-bath splash up her legs and down her arms, and finally, when only a half hour remained, she put her bedroom in order, then hung up her housecoat and picked up the green bathing suit. She slipped into the brief panties, easing them up her legs and turning to present her derriere to the mirror, checking the reflection to find it firm, shapely and nothing she would change, even if she could. The elasticized brief rode across the crest of each hip bone, and just below her navel, exposing both it and the tender hollow of her spine.

As she turned to face the mirror again, with the strappy suit top in her hand, she assessed her reflected breasts. Dr. Schaum had told her to expect the scars to take a good six months to fade completely, but had assured her they would. Theresa opened the jar of cocoa butter and gently massaged a dollop of the soothing balm along the length of each scar. But as she finished, her fingertips remained on her left breast. But it was not the scar she saw. She saw a woman changed. A woman whose horizons had expanded in thousands of definable and indefinable ways since her surgery. She saw a woman who no longer cared that her freckles ran down her chest and up her legs, a woman who no longer considered her hair carrot-colored, but merely "bright," a woman whose medium, orange-sized breasts appeared almost beautiful to her own eyes. The nipples seemed to have shrunk from the surgery, and their perky position, pointed upward instead of down, never ceased to be a source of amazement.

She raised her arms above her head experimentally. When she did this, her breasts lifted with her arms, as they'd never done before. She pirouetted swiftly to the left, watching, to be rewarded by the sight of her breasts coming right along with her instead of swaying pendulously several inches behind the movement of her trunk.

A marvelous, appreciative smile burst across her face.

I am female. I am as beautiful as I feel. And today I feel utterly beautiful.

She hooked the bathing suit top behind her back, then lifted her arms to tie the strings behind her neck, examining the way the concealing triangles of sheeny green covered her breasts. She ran her fingertips along the deep V, down the freckled skin to the spot where the two triangles met. The wonder of the change was almost enough to make her high!

She hated to cover herself up. Oh, glorious, glorious liberation! How wonderful you feel!

She packed a drawstring bag with sunscreen, towels, hair lifter, makeup, cocoa butter, shampoo, a pair of jeans and a brand-new bra made of scalloped blue lace. Her thirty days of wearing the firm support bra were over. This little wisp of femininity was what she'd long craved. While stuffing her belongings in the bag, she realized even this was a new experience to be savored, for she'd never gone skipping off with boys to the beach when she was a girl. There was so much catching up to do!

By the time ten o'clock arrived, Theresa was not only ready, she was a totally self-satisfied ready.

The van turned into the driveway, and she stepped out onto the back step to await him. Through the windshield she saw him smile and raise a palm, then shut off the ignition, open the door and walk toward her.

He was wearing his aviator sunglasses, white swimming

trunks beneath an unbuttoned navy blue shirt with three zippered patch pockets, white buttons and epaulettes. The shirt's long sleeves were rolled up, exposing his arms from the elbow down, and its tails flapped in the light breeze as he approached. He moved around the front of the van in a loose-jointed amble, keeping his eyes on her face until he stood on the apron of the step below her, looking up. Lazily, he reached up to remove the glasses while every cell in her body became energized by his presence.

"Hello, sweets."

"Hello, Brian." She wanted very badly to call him an endearment, but the expressive way she spoke his name actually became an endearment in itself.

Was it she who reached first, or he? All Theresa knew later was that one moment she stood two steps above him, and the next, she was in his arms, sharing a hello kiss beneath the bright June sun at ten o'clock on a Saturday morning. She, the timid introvert who'd often wondered why some women were blessed with lives in which scenes like this were taken for granted, while others could only lie in their lonely beds at night and dream of such bliss.

It wasn't a passionate kiss. It wasn't even very intimate. But it swept her off the step and against his partially exposed chest while she circled his neck with both arms, captured in such a fashion that she was looking down at him. He lifted his lips, brushed them caressingly over hers, then dipped his head to bestow another such accolade to the triangle of freckles that showed above the coverup she'd put on. "Mmm... you smell good." He released her enough to allow her breasts and belly to go sliding down his body until she stood before him, smiling up at his admiring, stunning, summer eyes.

"Mmm...you do, too."

His hands rested on her hipbones. She was piercingly aware of it, even as they gazed, unmoving, into each other's faces and stood in broad daylight, for any of the neighbors to see.

"Are you ready?"

"I've been ready since 6:00 a.m."

He laughed, rode his hands up her ribs and turned her toward the door. "Then get your stuff and let's not waste a minute."

Chapter 15

The Village Green Apartments were tudor-trimmed stucco buildings arranged in a horseshoe shape around a dazzling aqua-and-white swimming pool. The grounds were wooded with old elms whose leafy branches drooped in the still summer morning. Theresa caught a glimpse of the pool as Brian passed it, then pulled around the far side of the second building. Glancing up, she saw small decks flanking the length of the stucco walls, and an occasional splash of crimson from a potted geranium in a redwood tub.

Inside, the halls were carpeted, papered and silent. Padding along with Brian at her shoulder, Theresa found herself unable to keep from watching his bare toes curl into each step as he walked. There was something undeniably intimate about being with a barefoot man. Brian's feet were medium sized, shaded with hair on his big toes, and it struck her how much more angular a man's foot was than a woman's. His legs were muscular and sprinkled with a modicum of hair on all but the fronts and backs of his knees. He stopped before number 122, unlocked the door and stepped back.

"It's not much yet, but it will be."

She entered a living room with plush, bone-colored carpeting. Directly across from the door by which they'd entered was an eight-foot-wide sliding glass door decorated with an open-weave drapery that was drawn aside to give a view of the pool and surrounding grassy area. The room held one chocolate-brown director's chair, a cork-based lamp sitting beside it on the floor and nothing else except musical equipment: guitars, amplifiers, speakers as tall as Theresa's shoulders and microphones.

Forming an L in juxtaposition with the living room was a tiny galley kitchen with a Formica-topped peninsula counter dividing it from the rest of the open area. A short hall presumably led to the bathroom and bedroom beyond.

Theresa stopped in the middle of the carpeted expanse. It seemed very lonely and barren, and it made Theresa somehow sad to walk into the quiet emptiness and think about Brian here all alone, with no furniture, none of the comforts of home, nobody to talk to or to share music with. But she turned and smiled brightly.

"Home is where the heart is, they say."

He, too, smiled. "So I've heard. Still, you can see why I invited you over to swim. It's about all I'm equipped to offer."

Oh, I wouldn't say that, came the sudden impulsive thought. She shrugged, one thumb hooking the drawstring of the carryall bag that was slung over her shoulder. She glanced around his living room again. "Swimming is one of the few active pastimes I've enjoyed ever since I was little. I love it. Is all this equipment *yours?*" She ventured across to the impressive array of sound equipment.

"Yup."

"Wow."

He watched her move from piece to piece, touching nothing until her eye was caught by a three-ring notebook lying open on the floor beside an old, beat-up-looking flat-top guitar. She knelt, examined the handwritten words, and looked up. "Your songbook?"

He nodded.

She turned the pages, riffling through them slowly, stopping here and there to hum a few bars. "It must have taken you years to collect all these."

She found herself drawn to the sheets simply because they

contained his handwriting, with which she'd grown so familiar during the past half year. The songs were arranged alphabetically, so she couldn't resist turning to the *S*s. *S-A, S-E, S-L, S-O*…and there it was: "Sweet Memories." Without realizing she'd done it, her fingers grazed the sheets feeling the slight indentation made by his ballpoint pen years ago.

Sweet memories of her own came flooding back. And for Brian, standing near, watching her, the same thing happened. He was transported back to New Year's Eve, dancing with her in his arms, then curling her against his chest before a slow, golden fire. But it was shortly after ten o'clock on a June morning, and he'd invited her here to swim. He brought himself back from his concentrated study of the woman kneeling before him to ask, "Would you like to change into your suit?"

Reluctantly she left her musings. "Oh, I have it on. All I have to do is jump out of this." She pinched the cover-up and pulled it away from both thighs, while grinning up at him.

"Well, I'm ready if you are."

"Just a minute. I think I'll leave my sandals in here." She rolled to a sitting position with one knee updrawn and began unbuckling the ankle strap. While she tugged at it, he moved closer to stand beside her and study the top of her head. She was terribly conscious of his chestnut-colored legs, sprinkled with hair, just at her elbow, and of his bare toes close to her hip.

"I wouldn't have taken you for a woman who'd wear toenail polish." Her hands fell still for a second, then tugged again and the first sandal came free. As she reached for the second one, she raised her eyes to find him standing with arms akimbo, looking down at her, the front panels of his shirt held aside by his wrists. His bare chest drew her eyes almost magnetically.

"I'm trying a lot of new things these days that I've never had the nerve to try before. Why? Don't you like it?"

He suddenly hunkered down, captured her foot and began removing her sandal. "I love it. You have the prettiest toes of any violin player I've ever gone swimming with." The sandal dropped to the floor, and to Theresa's astonishment, he carried the bare foot to his lips and kissed the underside of her big toe, then the soft, vulnerable skin of her instep. Her eyes flew open, and the blush began creeping up. Brian grinned and unconcernedly retained possession of her foot, lazily stroking its arch with a thumb. "Well, you said you were trying new things you'd never tried before, and I thought this might be one to add to your list." This time, when his teeth gently nipped at the sensitive instep, her lips fell open and her eyes widened.

Theresa stared at him. Her throat had gone dry, and she was unable to move. When he'd lifted her foot, she'd lost her balance and teetered back, so sat now with elbows locked and both hands braced on the carpet behind her. Suddenly she realized her fingers were clutching the fibers. Though her eyes were riveted on Brian's face, she was arousingly aware of his pose. Balancing on the balls of his feet, his knees were widespread, but pointed at her so that it was all she could do to keep her eyes from dropping to the insides of his thighs. She knew by some magical telepathy, though she hadn't looked, that his inner thighs were smoothed of hair, just as his knees were. The muscles of his legs were bulged and taut, his insteps curved like those of Achilles running. His unbuttoned shirt fell loose and wide at his hips. The elasticized fabric of his white bathing trunks was molded to his thighs and conformed to the masculine rises and ridges between his legs.

Swallowing the lump in her throat, Theresa carefully withdrew her foot.

"I think we'd better go out," she advised shakily.

"Right. Grab your bag." Straightening those alarmingly close knees, he reached a hand down and tugged her to her feet. He rolled the sliding screen back and she moved out into the sun ahead of him, her senses so fully awakened by his nearness that even the sound of the vinyl rollers gliding in the track made her feel as if they'd just wheeled smoothly up her spinal column. How odd to be stepping into the intense heat of the late June sun, yet be shivering and experiencing the titillating effect of goose bumps rising up her arms and thighs.

There was nobody else in the pool area this early in the day.

Yellow and white striped umbrellas were still closed, and the tubular plastic chairs and recliners were all pushed neatly under the tables. The concrete rectangle was surrounded by a broad stretch of thick green grass on all sides, and as Theresa crossed it, the cool blades tickled her bare toes.

The pool was stunningly clear, its surface shimmering slightly. In the aqua depths an automatic cleaning device snaked back and forth, back and forth, sweeping the pool floor.

Brian dipped one knee and stuck his toe in the water.

"It's warm. Should we go in right away and work off our breakfasts?"

"I was too excited to eat breakfast." Realizing what she'd said, she sucked on her lower lip and chanced a quick peek at the man beside her to find him gazing down benignly at her pink cheeks.

"Oh, really?"

"I'll never succeed as a femme fatale, will I? I don't think I was supposed to admit that."

"A femme fatale would keep a man guessing. But one of the first things I liked about you was that you didn't. I could read you as easily as you just read the words to 'Sweet Memories' in there. That *is* what you were reading, isn't it?"

"Yes."

"I wonder how many times I played it and thought of you during the past six months."

He stood so near, Theresa thought she could feel nothing more than the auburn hairs on his arms entwined with the strawberry blond ones on her own. His eyes held a sincerity mixed with controlled desire, and she met it with an expression much the same. On the cool ceramic coping upon which they stood, his right foot eased over an inch until his toes covered hers, and Theresa wondered if a touch that innocent could release such a wellspring of response within her body, what must the carnal act inspire? His voice was deep and held a note of self-teasing. "There. Now we're even. Whatever the male equivalent of the femme fatale is, I'm not it. I don't want to hold any of my feelings back from you. I never wanted to, not since the first day I met you."

"Brian, let's go swimming. I'm dying of the heat...whatever's causing it."

"Good idea. Especially since we have the place to ourselves for now."

He moved to the end of the pool and cranked open one of the umbrellas, then angled its top toward the sun. She flung her tote bag on the tabletop, then shrugged off her cover-up and tossed it over the back of a patio chair, her back to Brian.

She heard the buttons and zippers of his shirt hit the metal tabletop with a ping, and assumed he was standing behind her, studying her back. This was the moment about which she'd dreamed and fantasized for years. She, Theresa Brubaker, clad in a bathing suit that left just enough to the imagination, was about to turn and face the man she loved. And she didn't have to cross her arms over her chest, nor keep her towel draped around her neck, or hunch her shoulders to disguise the thrust of her feminine attributes.

She turned to find him staring, as she'd known he'd be. Neither of them moved for a long, silent stretch of time. His chest was bare, and the white trunks dipped just below his navel, leaving it surrounded by a thin line of hair leading from the wider dark mat above. His nipples looked like copper pennies in the shade of the umbrella. His ribs were lean. His lips were partially open. His eyes unabashedly scanned her from face to knees, then lingeringly moved back up again with the slow deliberation of an art critic.

"Wow," Brian breathed. And incredible as it seemed, even to herself, Theresa believed him. The airy word was all she needed to reaffirm her desirability. But she could imagine her damn freckles zinging to life on her blushing neck and cheeks, so she turned to open her bag and rummage through it for the sunscreen.

"You'll probably eat your word within an hour. You've never seen what happens to me when the sun hits my skin. I'm a living demonstration of why physicians refer to freckles as heat spots. And I burn to a brilliant neon pink." From the depths of her bag she retrieved the lotion and uncapped it, then squirted a generous curl into her palm. "Want some?"

"Thanks." He took the bottle, and they busied themselves applying the sweet-scented lotion to their arms, necks, faces and legs. When Theresa rubbed it along the edge of the V-neck on her suit, she felt his eyes following the movements of her palm and glanced up to find him putting lotion on his chest. Her eyes dropped to his long fingers that massaged the firm musculature, delving through crisp hair, leaving it glistening with oils. He took another squirt, handed the bottle to her, and they stared at each other's hands—his running across his hard belly and along the elastic waist of his trunks; hers traversing delicate ribs, and the horizontal line along the bottom of her bikini top before curving into the depression of her navel, then around her exposed hipbones.

The lotion was slick and fragrant. It smelled of coconut, citrus and a hint of berry, filling the air around them like ambrosia. Watching his hands gliding over his skin, Theresa conjured up the thought of them gliding over hers. She dropped to the chair and began doing her legs, stretching first one, then the other out before her, sensing his eyes following again as she stroked the tender flesh of her inner thighs. She kept her eyes averted but saw peripherally how he lifted one leg to hook his toes over the edge of a lawn chair and massage fruit-scented magic along the length of his leg. He'd turned to the side, and she had a chance to study him without being studied herself.

Her eyes traversed his curving back, the buttock, the raised thigh and the junction of his legs where secrets waited. It suddenly flashed across Theresa's mind why in Victorian times men and women were never allowed to go ocean bathing together. It was a decidedly sensual thing, studying a man in swim trunks.

She dragged her eyes away, wondering if she was supposed to feel guilty at this new and unexpected curiosity she harbored. She didn't. Not at all. She was twenty-six years old—it occurred to her it was high time this curiosity surfaced and was appeased.

"Will you put some on my back?" he asked.

"Sure, turn around," she answered jauntily. But when she

was squeezing the bottle, her outstretched palm trembled. His back was smooth and he had wide shoulders that tapered to trim hips, the skin taut and healthy. When her hand touched his shoulder he twitched, as if he, too, were keyed up with awareness, and had been awaiting that first touch with as great a sense of anticipation as she. When her fingers curved around his ribs to his sides, he lifted his arms slightly away from his body to allow her access. For a moment, she was tempted to run both hands all the way around his trunks and press her face to the hollow between his shoulder blades. Instead she squirted a coil of white into her palm and worked both hands unilaterally across the crests of his hard shoulders and up the sides and back of his neck, even into the hair at its nape. Already the hair was longer, which pleased her. She had never been crazy about his Air Force haircuts, for she'd imagined that if allowed to grow to collar length, his would curve gently in thick, free swoops. As her fingers massaged his neck, he tipped his head backward and a guttural sound escaped his throat. Her palms, as well as the nerve endings along the rest of her body, felt as if they were instantly on fire.

It grew worse—or better—when he turned and took the bottle from her slippery fingers, ordering quietly, "Turn around."

She spun from the ardor in his eyes, then felt his long palms pressing a cold mound of lotion against her bare flesh, then beginning to turn it warm with the friction and contact of skin upon skin. His touch made it extremely difficult to breathe, and impossible to control the tempo of her heart, which seemed to rise up and search out the spots his hand grazed, pounding right through the walls of her back. His fingers curved over her shoulder, up beneath her hair, forcing her chin to drop forward, spreading the essence of wondrous exotic delicacies all about her. He massaged the breadth of her shoulder blades, skipped over the elasticized back strip of her suit, and after taking another liberal amount of sunscreen, his fingertips eased up beneath the strap, running left to right beneath it, from just beneath her left armpit to the same spot under her right. Lower they went, down the delicate hollow of her back, and along the elastic of her emerald-green briefs, curving upon the sculptured hipbone, teasing at the taut rubberized waistband that cinched tightly against her flesh. The oils made his hands glide sensuously across her skin, and she shuddered beneath them.

His touch disappeared. She heard the faint sound of the cap being replaced on the bottle, then of the bottle meeting the aluminum tabletop. But she didn't move. She couldn't. She felt as if she'd never move again as long as she lived, not unless this fire in her veins was cooled and put out. If it wasn't, she'd stand there and burn into a cinder.

"Last one in's a moldy worm," came the heavy, aroused voice from behind her. Then she was sprinting to the end of the pool—running at last!—hitting the water stretched out full length, just at the instant Brian hit it. The shock was breathtaking. From the heat of a second ago her body dropped what seemed a full fifty degrees. She swam furiously, a powerful, controlled crawl to the far end of the pool, her body temperature stabilizing by the time she reached her goal.

Side by side they swam eight laps, and in the middle of the ninth, Theresa spluttered, waved limply and declared, "Goodbye, I think I'm drowning," then went under. When her head surfaced, he was treading water, waiting.

"Woman, I'm not through with you yet. Sorry, no drowning till I am." And unceremoniously he disappeared, came up in the perfect position to command her body in an exemplary demonstration of a Senior Lifesaving hold, with his left arm angled across her chest while he hauled her to the far end of the pool beneath the overhanging diving board.

She let herself go limp and he pulled along in an unresisting state of breathlessness and sensuality. His elbow clamped down on her left breast, and it felt wonderful.

At the pool wall he released her, and they both crossed their arms on the sleek concrete, resting their cheeks on their wrists while facing each other, both panting, feet flapping lazily on the surface of the blue water behind them.

"You're melting," he announced with a grin, reaching out a fingertip and running it beneath her right eye.

"Oh, my makeup!" She slipped under the water again and scrubbed at her eyelids before emerging sparkly lashed, and asking if she was still discolored.

"Yes, but leave it. It's very Greta Garbo."

"You're a very good swimmer."

"So are you."

"As I said before, it was about the only physical exercise that was easy for me when I was growing up. But I kind of gave it up, too, when I was in my late teens, because I was afraid it would...well, build up the muscles all the more, if you know what I mean."

He was studying her wet face carefully. "It seems like there are a lot of things you had to give up that I'd never have suspected."

"Yes, well that's all over now. I'm a new person."

"Theresa, is it...well, are you sure you aren't overdoing it, swimming so hard? It worries me, even though you said you're a hundred percent again."

As if to reaffirm her full recovery, she caught the edge of the pool and boosted herself up, twisting to a sitting position above him with her feet dangling in the water. "One hundred percent, Brian."

He joined her on the edge of the pool. She flung her hair back, feeling his eyes following each movement as she wrung her hair out and sent rivulets running down her back and over her shoulder. Beneath them the concrete was sun-warmed, and the water soon joined their flesh to the sleek surface with a tepid slipperiness.

He ran his hands over his cheeks to clear them of excess water, then wove his fingers through his hair, running them toward the back of his head, and studying the umbrella at the far end of the pool as he asked quietly, "Theresa, would you feel self-conscious answering some questions about your operation?"

"Probably. But ask them anyway. I've been working very hard on my self-image and on trying to overcome self-consciousness. But if you don't mind, I'd better have a little lotion on my face and back. I feel like most of it washed off."

They got to their feet, leaving dark gray footprints along the concrete as they made their way toward the opposite end of the pool. Theresa dried her hair, then spread her towel out on the soft grass and sat down on it while applying lotion to her face once more. When she was done, she flipped over and stretched out full length on her stomach, thinking it would be infinitely easier to answer his questions if she wasn't looking at him.

His hands eased over her skin, spreading it with lotion once more while he asked quietly, "When did you decide to have it done?"

"Remember when I wrote and told you I slipped in the parking lot and fell down?"

"I remember."

"It was right after that. When the doctor examined my back he told me I should look into having the problem solved permanently."

"Your back?"

"There's a lot of back and shoulder discomfort that goes along with it. People don't know that. The shoulders are especially vulnerable. I thought probably you'd noticed the grooves—they still show a little bit."

"These?" His fingertips massaged one of her shoulders, and she felt a heavenly thrill ripple through her body before he went on, "I wasn't exactly looking at your shoulders before, but I see the marks now. What else? Tell me everything about it. Was it hard for you, psychologically, I mean?"

Belly down, on a beach towel, with her cheek on the back of her hand, with her eyes closed, she told Brian everything. All about her misgivings, her mother's and father's initial reactions to her decision, her fears and uncertainties. She couldn't force herself to share that intimacy with him yet. If and when the time came, she'd be honest, but for now she glossed over that and the part about possibly being unable to nurse a baby.

When her recital was finished, he was still sitting beside her with his arm circling one updrawn knee. His voice was soft and disarming.

"Theresa, I'm sorry for getting mad at you my first night back. I never understood about a lot of it."

"I know. And I'm sorry I didn't at least write and tell Jeff, and let him tell you what my plans were."

"No, you were right. You didn't owe me anything. That first night when we went for a walk, I'll admit part of my problem was I was scared. I thought maybe now that you'd taken the big step you'd be out for bigger fish than this underage guitar man whose past isn't quite as pure as you deserve."

His words brought her head up. Bracing on one elbow she twisted to look back over her shoulder at him. "I long ago stopped placing any importance on the differences in our ages. You're more mature than most of the thirty-year-old men I work with at school. Maybe that's why you were so... I don't know. Understanding, I guess. Right from the first, I sensed that you were different from all the others I'd ever met, that you really did look into me, the person, and judge me by my inner qualities or shortcomings."

"Shortcomings?" He flopped down on his back almost underneath her partially lifted chest and touched the tangled locks above her left ear. "You don't have any shortcomings, sweets."

"Oh, yes I do. Everybody does."

"Where they been hidin'?"

She smiled at his playfulness, glanced down at her forearm, and answered, "Several thousand of them have been lurking just below the surface of my skin and are just now coming out to introduce themselves."

Indeed, her "heat spots" were heating up. The freckles on her arms had already grown so fat their perimeters were dissolving into one another.

He rolled his cheek against the towel, pulled her soft inner arm to his lips, and declared quietly, "Angel kisses." He kissed her again, higher, almost at the bend of elbow. "Have you been kissing any angels lately, Miss Brubaker?"

She studied his green eyes, and let her feelings show in her own. "Not as often as I want to." She smiled and added impulsively, "Gabriel."

"Then what do you say we remedy that?" With a swift flexing of muscle, he was on his feet, reaching out a hand to tug her up. He gathered towels, togs and lotion and handed her the bag. She followed willingly, walking at his side while one light hand guided her shoulders as she crossed the grass toward the sliding door of his apartment.

She stepped inside where it was cool and shaded. She heard him snap the lock on the screen door, then step to the drapery cord and draw the curtain closed until the midday light was even more subdued through the open weave of the fabric. It threw gentle checkers across the thick carpet and her bare toes. She had the fleeting thought that her hair was probably plastered to her head in some places and flying at odd angles in others, and that her makeup was all washed away. She was frantically scrambling to find her comb in the bottom of the tote bag when she heard him put on music and a guitar introduction softly filled the room. An insistent hand captured the drawstring bag and pulled it from her nervous fingers, as if Brian would brook no delays, no repairs, no excuses.

My world is like a river
As dark as it is deep....

As the poignant words met her ears, she was turned around by lean, hard fingers that closed over the sensitive spot where her neck met her shoulders. When his eyes delved into hers, he wordlessly searched out her palms and carried them up around his neck. His body was moving in rhythm to the music but so very slightly she scarcely felt the evocative sway of his shoulders beneath the soft flesh of her inner arms. But some magical force made her body answer the almost imperceptible beckoning as he swayed, drawing nearer and nearer until the fabric of her suit brushed the hair upon his chest. The invitation was wordless at first, as his warm palms found her naked back and pressed her lightly against him. Then he began humming softly, drawing away only far enough to continue searching her uplifted face while his palm gently caressed the hollow between her shoulder blades, then traced the depression down her spine. With only the slightest force he urged her hips closer, closer, until her bare stomach touched his—sleek to rough. He undulated slowly as if bidding her to join him. She responded with a first hesitant movement until she felt his hips and loins, confined by the taut piece of clothing that covered him, pressed firmly against her.

His breath was warm upon her mouth as he touched it first with the tip of his tongue, then lightly with the outermost surfaces of his lips. He was still humming. As her lips dropped open she felt the soft intonation tickling the crests of them. The sound, the feeling and his careful doling out of contact served only to tantalize, then he lifted his head and began singing the refrain that had been in her heart since she'd heard him sing the words with the battered old fifteen-dollar Stella in his lap.

Sweet memories,
Sweet memories...

When the voice on the record hummed the final notes and took the song home, she was settled securely against the full, hard length of Brian's body, feeling all its surfaces, ridges and textures as if she were on an elevated plane of sensory awareness.

In the thundering silence between songs, his hard body and soft voice combined in a message of latent passion. "Theresa, I love you, girl...so much...so much." It seemed too sweeping to take in. Their bodies no longer moved, but were pressed together until the naked skin of his thighs and belly seemed bonded to hers by the slightly oily, very fragrant suntan lotion whose aroma evoked images of tropical islands, warm sunlit shores and the calls of cockatoos. Her senses were filled with the smell of him, his warmth and firmness, but mostly with the sleek texture of his skin.

"Brian...my guitar man, I think I started loving you when you stepped off that plane and looked me square in the eye."

Another song had begun, but its rhythm went unheeded, for they were entwined in each other's arms, hearing only the beats of their hearts pressed together with nothing but two triangles of thin green material between them. The kiss lost all tentativeness and blossomed into a full complementary exchange of sleek tongues and throaty murmurs. His head moved sensuously above hers, wooing and winning her slow, sure acquiescences. Her inhibitions began dissolving until he felt her hips reaching toward a closer communion with his as she raised up on tiptoe to mold her curves more securely against his, all the while clinging to his sleek shoulders.

His palms moved down to learn the shape of her firm hipbones once more, then the solid flesh of her rounded buttocks, cupping them in both hands as he drew close.

He tore his mouth from hers, his eyes glowing with the fire of a passion too long denied. "Sweets, I promised I wouldn't come back here and force this issue. I said I'd take it slow, and give you time to—"

"I've had twenty-six years, Brian. That's long enough."

When he lifted his head she felt deprived at the loss of his warm lips and reached with her own, as if she suddenly couldn't get her fill of these long-delayed joys.

"Do you mean it, Theresa? Are you sure?"

"I'm sure. Oh, Brian, I'm so sure it hurts…right here." She took her palm and pressed it against her heart. "I thought I'd be afraid and uncertain when this moment came, but I'm not. Not at all. Somehow, when you love, you know." She gazed up at him in wonder, touching his lips with her fingertips. "You just know," she breathed.

"Yes, you know, darling."

Slowly he covered her shoulders with his hands and pressed her away from him to gaze into her ardent eyes while he spoke. "I want you to look around at this room." She felt herself turned until her bare back was pressed against his rough-textured chest. From behind he circled her ribs, his forearms resting just below her breasts, touching their undersides. "This room has no furniture because I wanted us to pick it out together. I thought about waiting to ask you until afterward, but I find I want to know first. Will you marry me, Theresa?

Just as soon as it can be arranged? And we can fill this place with furniture and your piano and music and maybe a couple of kids, and make sweet memories for the rest of—"

"Yes!" She spun and looped her arms around his neck, cutting off his words with the kiss and muffled word before lifting her mouth from his and singing, "Yes, yes, yes! I didn't know whether I wanted you to ask me before or after but it's probably best before, 'cause I probably won't do so well…." His eyebrows drew into a puzzled frown. "I'm not experienced at this part," she explained diffidently.

The next minute she was scooped up into his arms and felt his hard belly against her hip while he carried her down the hall to his bedroom.

"Trust me. You will be, as soon as it can be arranged."

From the bedroom doorway where he paused, she saw her marriage bed for the first time. It looked like any other bed, covered with a quilted spread of brown and blue that matched the two sheets haphazardly thrown over the curtain rods to lend the room privacy.

With her arms looped around his neck she drew his head down until his mouth joined hers.

Chapter 16

The trip to the bed in Brian's arms was like crossing the bridge of a rainbow connecting the earth to heaven. When she was a girl, Theresa had wondered, as all girls do from the time they feel the first stirrings of maturity, what the man would be like when the moment came? And the setting—would it be dark? Winter or summer? Day or night? Inside or outside? And our first intimate encounter—would it be rushed or slow? Silent or vocal? Reckless or poignant? Would it leave me feeling more— or less?

The sheets rippled at the windows. The sun brought the blue- and-brown pattern alive, backlighting it until the entwined colors danced upon the shimmering fabric, while from outside came the faraway voices of children who clanged the gate to the pool area, then whooped gleefully as they took their first plunge.

From the living room came the strains of love songs, distant now, unintrusive, but mellow and wooing. Brian's bare feet moved soundlessly across the carpet. His lips wore a faint smile, and his steady eyes rested upon Theresa's while he sat on the edge of the bed with her legs across his lap. Twisting at the hip he placed her the wrong way across the bed, across its width, lying on his side next to her with his knees slightly updrawn.

He braced up on one elbow, smiling down into her face, running the tip of an index finger along the rim of her lower lip. The smile had drifted from her face, and her lingering apprehensions were reflected in the wide brown eyes and the slightly parted lips.

"Are you scared?" he asked softly.

She swallowed and nodded. "A little."

"About anything in particular?"

"My lack of experience, among other things."

"Experience will take care of itself. What are the other things?" His fingers trailed along her jaw and began gently freeing the strands of hair from about her temples, absently arranging them in a bright corona about her head.

Already she felt the telltale blush climbing her chest. "I…" The words stuck, creating a tight knot in the center of her chest. "I don't…" His eyes left the hair he'd been toying with and met hers, but his fingers were still threaded through the red strands, resting upon the warm skull just above the left ear. "Oh, Brian." She covered her face with both hands. "This is so hard, and I know I'm blushing terribly, and there's nothing less becoming to a redhead than blushing, and I've never—"

"Theresa!" His gentle reprimand cut her off as he circled her wrists and forced her hands away from her face. She stared up at him in silence. The reprimand left his voice, and it became compelling. "I love you. Did you forget that? There's nothing you can't tell me. Whatever it is, we'll work it out together, all right? And, just to set the record straight, redheads look darling when they blush. Now, would you like to start again?"

The muscles in her stomach were jumping. Her fists were clenched, the tendons tight beneath his grasp. She sucked in a huge, fortifying gulp of air and ran the words out so fast she wouldn't have a chance to change her mind. "I don't want to get pregnant and I went to the drugstore yesterday and bought something to make sure I wouldn't but the instructions said I had to use it half an hour before and I don't know before *what* or how long anything takes because I've never done this before and oh please, Brian, let my hands go so I can hide behind them!"

To Theresa's amazement, he laughed lovingly and wrapped her in both of his arms, falling to his side and taking her along until they lay almost nose to nose. "Is that all? Ah, sweet Theresa, what a joy you are." He kissed the tip of her very red nose, then lay back, running a finger along the crest of her cheek. His voice was quiet and calm. "I had the same thought myself, so I came prepared, too. That means you have a choice, sweetheart. You or me."

She tried to say *me*, but the word refused to come out, so she only nodded.

"Well, now's the time." He sat up and tugged her along after him, and she padded to the living room for her purse, then back down the hall toward the bathroom.

When she returned to the bedroom he was lying on his back across the bed, still in his swim trunks, with his arm folded behind his head.

Through the open doorway he had watched the green bathing suit appear as she opened the bathroom door, crossed the hall and approached the bed. Long before she reached it, he'd extended a palm in invitation.

"Come here, little one."

She lifted one knee to the edge of the bed, placing her palm in his, and let him tug her down until she fell into the hollow of his arm, partially across his chest. His right arm remained beneath his head, but even one-handed he eased her closer, tighter, until she hovered above him, and his eyes conveyed the remainder of the message. She bent her head to touch his lips with her own, and the kiss began with a meeting no heavier than the morning mist settling upon a lily. It expanded into the first brief touch of tongue tips—tentative, introductory, promising. He tasted slightly sweet, as if some of the tropical sunscreen still lingered on his lips. His tongue sought the deeper secrets of her mouth, and hers his. Seek, touch, stroke, chase, devour—they shared each advancing step of the intimate kiss. Longing sang through her veins, enlivening each of her senses until she perceived each touch, sound, taste, sight and smell with that new, exultant keenness she'd discovered for the first time today. His relaxed pose lifted the firm muscles of his chest and exposed them in a way that invited exploration.

She let her hand seek out his neck first, recalling the throaty sound he'd uttered when she'd stroked that soft hollow once before. She allowed her thumb to explore the hard knot of his Adam's apple, and beneath the soft pad, the masculine point jumped as he swallowed. When her thumb slid down to the shallow well at its base, she felt his pulse racing there, pressing against her finger like a knocking engine.

It had happened again, that response she could kindle so effortlessly in this man. She sensed it and experimented, a little bit more. Her hand left his neck and flattened upon the firm rise of his chest, experiencing the rough texture of hair, then the tiny point of his nipple, which she first fanned, then scissored between her fingers, while bracing over him, moving her lips downward to touch the warm skin on his chest. She tasted him. Sweet oil and salt and sun and chlorine and coconut and papaya. She had not dreamed he would have taste, yet he did, and it was heady and sensual. Beneath her tongue the rough hairs of his body felt magnified, yet silky. Upon her lips she felt the faint oily residue left behind by the sunscreen. He was warm and resilient and utterly male.

Lifting her head, she felt drugged by senses that had sprung to life from the shield behind which they'd been protected for so many years. Suddenly she was eager to know all, feel all, to glut herself on every texture, hue and scent his body possessed. Her eyes met his, then dropped to travel across the shadowed throat, his ear, his nipples, his jaw where a tiny, tiny scab remained from some incidental nick of razor, perhaps. She touched it with a single fingertip, then pressed the length of her palm along the underside of the biceps of the arm bent beneath his head. She ran the hand down to his armpit, awed that even the wiry hair there could be something she craved to know, simply because it was part of his physical makeup.

"Brian," she breathed, looking into his eyes. "I'm like a child tasting candy for the first time. I never knew all these things before. I have so much to catch up on!"

"Catch then. We have a good seventy years."

A flickering smile passed her features, but was gone again, wiped away by this new rapt interest in his body. He closed his eyes, and like an eager child she twisted onto one hip, bracing a palm on the bed to get a better overview of this delicacy called Brian Scanlon. Still it wasn't enough. Finally, she pulled both legs up beneath her and sat on her haunches at his hip—looking, touching, familiarizing.

"You're…exquisite!" she marveled. "I never thought a man could be exquisite, but you are." His belly was hard, his ribs tapering to the indentation of his waist, just above the spot where his trunks sliced his abdomen. Within the white trunks she saw the mysterious raised contours of his arousal and wondered if it hurt him to be bound up so tightly.

She lifted her eyes to his and found he'd been watching her. A charming, lopsided grin bent the corner of his mouth.

"Darling girl." He lazily lifted his hand and ran a finger along the path of one string of her tie top, starting at the side of her neck, traveling beside it to the point where it met the band beneath her breasts. She shuddered with delight. "I don't think I'm the one who's exquisite." The finger idled up the opposite strap. Her eyelids felt weighted and a coil of anticipation wound through her stomach. His four fingertips traced the line of her collarbone, then moved downward, drawing a quartet of invisible Ss along the freckled mound of her breast. The faint tickle lifted the fine hairs on her bare stomach. He gave the other breast equal attention, fingering her skin with the brush of a dragonfly's wings. Her eyelids slid closed, and her head drooped slightly backward, listing to one side while his callused fingertips followed the first strap again, but this time also moved over the shimmery green triangle of fabric to graze the hidden, uptilted nipple that gave an unexpected spurt of sensation down her arms, stomach and straight to the seat of her femininity.

Her eyelids flew open. "Brian!"

A troubled look crossed his features as he misread her exclamation and withdrew his hand.

"Brian! There's feeling there!"

"What?" His fingers poised in midair.

"There's feeling there! It happened, when you touched me just then, something slithery and fiery went…went whooshing down my body, and…oh, Brian, don't you see? The doctor said sometimes the sensation never returns, and I've been scared to death thinking it hadn't come back to me."

He braced up on one elbow and cupped her jaw. "You never told me before."

"I am now, but oh Brian, it doesn't matter anymore, oh please, do it again!" she begged excitedly. "I want to make sure I wasn't just imagining it."

He toppled her over beside him, his lips joining hers to press her onto her back as his hand roamed across her ribs, and up, but stopped just short of her breast.

He lifted his head and she opened her eyes to find him gazing down intently into her eyes, his brows lowered in concern. "I won't hurt you, will I?"

"No," she whispered.

His mouth and hand moved simultaneously, the one to bestow a kiss, the other a caress. He contoured the warm globe of flesh with his palm, gently at first, then with growing pressure, squeezing, fondling, finally seeking out the nipple, which he tenderly explored through the slip of sheeny, damp material.

Her lips went slack and she dropped her shoulders flat to the bed, lolling in the new feelings of arousal. It was slighter than before, but there just the same. She concentrated hard on grasping it, blindly guiding his hand to the exact spot she thought would revive the strong spurt of sensation as before.

Braced above her, he watched the feelings parade across her face, and at last he reached for the bow at the nape of her neck. Her eyes opened as she felt it slipping free, but just before he could lower the green triangle, she stopped his hand.

"Brian, I have scars, but please don't let them stop you. They'll be there for several months yet, but then they'll fade. And they don't hurt, they only itch sometimes."

Some softening expression around his eyes told her he understood, and accepted. Then he peeled the first green tidbit of fabric down and laid it over her ribs, while she watched his eyes. They dropped to the vertical red scar, then flew back to her brown gaze. Wordlessly he stripped down the other half of the bathing suit top.

Where was the shame she had once known? Absent. Evaporated beneath the far greater impact of the loving concern that emanated from Brian's face.

He slipped his hands behind her back and came away with the suit top, then tossed it onto the pillows and rolled to give her his full attention again.

"How can it not hurt?" Gently he cupped her right breast, riding his thumb up the scar, then lightly, lightly circling the nipple. "Did they make an incision here?"

"Yes, but that scar is all healed."

"And here, too." He traced the faded crescent beneath, to its inception just below her armpit. "Oh God, it hurts me to think of them doing that to you." He lowered his head, trailing his lips along the lower contour scar.

"Brian, it's all over, and it wasn't nearly as bad as you'd think. If I hadn't done it, I might not have been able to overcome all my hang-ups and be here with you. I feel so different. So…"

He lifted his head and searched her with tortured eyes. "What do you feel? So…what?"

"Beautiful," she admitted, with a lingering note of shyness. "Feature that, would you?" She smiled and her voice became soft and accepting. "Theresa Brubaker with her red hair and freckles, feeling beautiful. But it's partly because of you. Because of how you treated me last Christmas. You made me believe I had the right to feel this way. You were all the things I'd ever hoped to find in a man."

"I love you." His voice was strange, throaty and deep, and not wholly steady. He dipped his head and touched his lips to the cinnamon-colored dots between her breasts. "Every freckle of you." He moved his mouth to the gentle swelling mound.

"Every red hair of you." And finally to the crest. "Every square inch of you."

He adored her with the gentle strokes of his tongue, and she lay in a blaze of emotions that sprang more from her consummate love for him than from the part of her he tenderly kissed.

"What's happening?" he queried, running his tongue down along the underside of her breast.

She sucked in a breath as a sensual response shuddered down her backbone. "I'm falling in love with my body, and your body, and what they can do to each other. I'm plunging through space…free-falling. Only it's so strange…I'm falling up."

He ran his tongue up to her nipple again, and closed his lips and tongue around it, murmuring some wordless accolade deep in his throat, while both of his arms reached behind her and his hands slid down to cup her buttocks and roll her firmly against him, both of them now on their sides.

"Mmm…you taste like summer…."

"Tell me," she whispered, threading her fingers through his hair, knowing an insatiable appetite for his words, as well as for his arousing touches.

"Sandy beaches and suntan oil that tastes like Popsicles and the sweetest fruit in the jungle…" He lightly nipped the top of a breast with his teeth. "Berries and coconut…" He slipped lower, licking the sensitive skin on the rib. "Mangos and kiwi… Mmm…" His mouth pressed moistly upon the softest part of her abdomen, just above the navel. "There's something else here…wait, let me see…." He dipped his tongue into her navel and made several seductive circles around and within it. "Mmm…I think it's passion fruit."

She felt him smile against her belly and smiled in return.

His mouth was arousingly warm, and his breath heated the silky triangle of fabric still covering her. His chest weighted her legs, then he lightly bit her through the bathing suit— fabric, hair and a little skin. Her ribs lifted off the bedspread, and she gasped while desire welled and bubbled over in her feminine depths. His fingers found the sensitive skin at the back of her knee, then his mouth warmed the flesh that she'd thought could not possibly know a heat any greater than it had already experienced. She trembled and lifted her hips from the bed, offering herself as fully as he cared to partake. He kissed her through the silky bikini and worked his chin firmly against the throbbing flesh within until she found herself moving against the hardness, seeking something...something....

And when her desire had grown to its fullest, he moved back up to join his mouth to hers, running his palms along the elastic waist of her briefs, then down inside to cup her firm backside while rolling his weight fully on top of hers, his hips undulating against hers while their mouths locked in a bond of mutual desire.

His weight lifted. She felt the wisp of fabric leave the juncture of her legs and inch downward along her thighs, then pass lower still until his mouth was forced to leave hers, and he eased the garment down and off, then tossed it over his shoulder to join its mate on the pillows.

He pressed her back, back, against the bed and caressed her bare stomach with his musician's fingers that were capable, she learned, of much more than adroitly strumming love songs. They raised a kind of music in her flesh as he explored the soft skin of her inner thighs, then the most intimate part of her body.

She was eager, and open, and not in the least abashed by his touch that sought and entered her virgin flesh. Love, that gift of the gods, took away all insecurities, all timidity, all shame, and allowed her the freedom to express her newfound femininity in the way she had so long dreamed.

A soft, passionate sound issued from her throat. She stretched and allowed him total access to explore her as he would, trembling at times, smiling at others, her heart a wild thing in her breast.

But just short of taking her over the edge of bliss, he lay back. And then it was her turn to explore. "Experience will take care of itself," Brian had said. And she believed it as she embarked upon her half of this maiden voyage toward mutuality.

She found the tight waist of his trunks and slipped her palms inside, against the skin of his lower spine, finding it cool from the slightly damp fabric.

Her caresses were restricted by the taut garment, yet she thrilled at the firmness beneath her palms and the inviting rhythm her touch had set off in his hips. He reached behind his back, found her arm and carried it up out of the elastic and around to his front, pressing it against the flattened, hidden hills between his legs, moving against her palm to initiate it into the ways of sexual contact.

To Theresa's amazement, her own voice begged throatily, "Take it off, Brian, please."

The words were partially muffled by his lips, but when the request had been made, he lifted his head and smiled into her beseeching eyes, his breath beating warmly upon her face.

"Anything you say, love."

He slipped to the edge of the bed, and she rolled onto her side and curled her body up like a lazy caterpillar, watching as he reached inside the garment and found a hidden string against his belly, tugged it, then stood and skinned the trunks down, down, down, before dropping to sit on the edge of the bed again and kicking the suit away across the carpet as he rolled toward her, reaching.

He was beautiful, and somehow it seemed the most natural thing in the world to reach out and caress him.

"Oh, Brian, you're silky...and so hot."

"So are you. But I think that's how we're supposed to be." He reached again for the entrance to her womanhood, touching it with a sleek, knowing rhythm until sensation dazzled her nerve endings. She closed her eyes and undulated with the protracted and relentless stroking.

"Brian, something's happening!"

"Let it. Shh..."

"But...but..." It was too late to wonder if it was torture or treasure, for in the next instant the question was answered for Theresa. A burst of sensation lifted her limbs and sent liquid explosions rocketing outward. Then she was shuddering, feeling spasms from the deepest reaches of her body, until she fell back sated, exhausted, gasping.

"Oh, sweet, sweet woman. The first time," he said against her neck after a minute, still holding her tightly. "Do you know how rare that is?"

"No...I thought from the movies that it happens to everyone."

"Not women, not all the time. Usually just men. You must have been storing it all these years, waiting for the right one to come along and set it free."

"And he did."

He smiled lovingly into her eyes, then kissed each lid, then her nose, then her swollen lips. And while he strung the kisses upon her face, he raised his body over hers and pressed it firmly to her entire length.

"I love you, darling—keep remembering that in case it hurts."

"I love you, Br—"

She never finished the word, for in that instant he entered her and she knew the sleek ligature of their two joined bodies, but no pain, only texture and heightened sensations building once again as his hips moved above hers. She felt only pleasure as he began moving, reaching back to teach her how to lift her knees and create a nesting place of warm, firm flesh that buttressed his hips as he shared the consummation of their love.

When he clenched his fists and quivered, she opened her eyes to find his closed in ecstasy. He rode the crest of his climax while she watched the reaction expressed on his beloved features—the closed, trembling eyelids, the flaring nostrils and the lips that pulled back in a near grimace as sweat broke out on his back and the muscles rippled for an exhausted moment. Then he shivered a last interminable time, called out at the final peak, and relaxed.

So this is why I was born a woman and Brian Scanlon was born a man, why we were meant to seek and find each other in this world of strangers. She caressed his shoulder blades, coveting the dead weight of him pressing her into the mattress beneath her.

"Oh, Brian it was so good…so good."

He rolled to his side and opened his eyes, lifting one hand that appeared too tired to quite succeed in the effort of caressing her face. It fell upon her cheek.

He chuckled—a rich, resonant sound from deep in his chest and closed his eyes and sighed, then lay unmoving.

She studied him in repose, smoothed the tousled hair above his temple. His eyes didn't open, and his palm didn't move. She knew an abiding sense of completion.

The noon sun lit the ceiling of the room by some magical twist of physics. The sheets at the window riffled lightly, and the sounds of the pool activity were constant now. From the living room came the repeated songs of the same playlist—she smiled, wondering how many times it had played.

"Do you know when I first became intrigued with you?"

She turned to find his eyes open, watching her. "When?"

They were still entwined, and he pulled her closer to keep possession of her while he went on. "It started when Jeff let me read a letter from you. In it you said you'd gone out on a date with somebody named Lyle, and he turned out to be Jack the Gripper."

She chuckled, recalling both the letter and the disastrous date. "That long ago?"

"Uh-huh. Two years or more. Anyway, after we laughed about it, and I wondered what kind of woman had written it, I began asking questions about you. Little by little I learned everything. About your red hair." He threaded his fingers into it just where her widow's peak would have been, had she one. "And your freckles." He trailed a finger down her nose. "And your endowment." He passed a palm down her breast. "And about the time Jeff defended you and punched out that kid, and about how you taught music in an elementary school and played violin, and how Jeff thought the sun rose and set in you, and how much he wanted you to be happy, to find some man who'd treat you honorably and wouldn't ogle and grope and grip."

"Two years ago?" she repeated, stunned.

"Longer than that. Closer to three now. Since Jeff and I were in Germany together. Anyway, when I saw your picture. It was one of your school pictures, and you were wearing a gray sweater buttoned around your shoulders, with a little white blouse collar showing from beneath. I asked Jeff a lot of questions then, and pieced together a picture of you and your hang-up even before I knew you. There have been times when I even suspected that Jeff filled me in on all the details about you in hopes that when I met you I'd be the first man to treat you right."

"Jeff?" she exclaimed, surprised.

"Jeff. Didn't you ever suspect that he engineered this whole thing from the start, feeding me tidbits about his marvelous, straight sister, who'd never had boyfriends, but who had so much to offer a man—the right man."

She braced up on one elbow and looked thoughtful. "Jeff! You really think so?"

"Yes, I do. As a matter of fact, he all but admitted it when we were on the plane back after Christmas. He suspected things had fired up between us and came right out and said it'd been on his mind a while that he wouldn't mind me as a brother-in-law."

She smirked and lifted a delicate jaw. "Remind me to give old Jeff a gigantic thank-you kiss next time I see him, huh?"

"And what about you? When did you start thinking of me as a potential lover?"

"The truth?" She peered up at him coquettishly.

"The truth."

"That night in the theater, when the love scene was on the screen. Your elbow was sharing the armrest with mine, and when the woman climaxed, your bones were almost cutting off my blood supply. Then when the man's face came on, showing him in the throes of rapture, your elbow nearly broke mine, and when it was over, *you* wilted."

"Me?" he yelped disbelievingly. "I did not!"

"You did, too. I was practically dying of embarrassment, and then you dropped your hands down to cover your lap, and I wanted to crawl underneath the seats."

"Are you serious? Did I really do that?"

"Of course I'm serious. Would I lie about a thing like that? I was so turned on myself I hardly knew what to do about it. Part of it was the movie, but part of it was you and your arm. After that I couldn't help wondering what it would be like with you. Somehow I knew you'd be good…and gentle…and just what a freckled redhead needed to make her feel like Cinderella."

"Do I make you feel like Cinderella?"

She studied him for a long moment, traced his lips with an index finger and nodded.

He captured the finger, bit it, then as his eyes closed, he lay very still, pressing her four fingertips against his lips.

"What are you thinking?" she whispered.

His eyes opened, but for a moment he didn't answer. Instead he pressed his palm to hers and threaded their fingers together with slow deliberation. His fingers squeezed possessively. Hers answered. "About tomorrow. And the day after that and the day after that, and how we'll never have to be alone again. There'll always be each other…and babies." His fingers gripped more tightly. His eyes probed hers. "Do you want babies, Theresa?"

He felt her grip relax, then tug away. His stomach went light with warning, and he gripped her hand to keep it from escaping. "Theresa?"

She gazed at his face, wide-eyed, and when he saw the color begin to heighten between her freckles, he leaned above her on an elbow, frowning. "Theresa, what is it?"

She brushed his chest with her fingertips, dropping her eyes to follow the movement instead of meeting his frown. "Brian, there's something I haven't told you about my surgery."

In a split second a dozen fledgling fears spiraled through him, all dire: the surgery had somehow taken away more than met the eye, and they'd never have the babies he was dreaming of.

"Oh, no, Brian, not that." She read his trepidation, soothingly bracketed his jaws. "I can have babies—all I want. And I *do* want them. But…" Again she dropped her eyes while her fingers rested against his chest. "But it's possible the surgery might affect my ability to nurse them."

For a moment he was still, waiting for the worst. Suddenly he crushed her tightly. "Is that all?" he sighed, relieved. She hadn't known he was holding his breath until it rushed out heavily upon her temple. Her lips were on his warm collarbone as he secured her fast and rocked her in his arms.

"It doesn't matter to me, but I thought you should know. I thought in case you had any feelings about it we should talk about it now. Some men might consider me only...well, half a woman or something."

He pulled back sharply. "Half a woman?" He sounded gruff as he squeezed her shoulders. "Never think it." Their eyes locked, and she read in his total love and approval. "Think about this." He drew her into the warm curve of his body as he rolled aside and snuggled her so near, his heartbeat was like a drum beneath her ear. "Think about everything we'll have some day—a house where there'll always be music and a gang of little redheaded rascals whose—"

"Brown-haired," she interrupted, smiling against his chest.

He went on with scarcely a missed beat. "Redheaded rascals whose freckles dance when—"

"Oh, no! No freckles! If you give me freckled, redheaded babies, Brian Scanlon, I'll—"

The rest was smothered by his kiss before he grinned at her, continuing. "Redheaded rascals whose freckles dance when they play their violins—"

"Guitars. I won't have anybody hiding under any violins!"

"Mrs. Scanlon, will you kindly stop complaining about this family of ours? I said they'll be redheads and I meant it. And they'll play violin in the orchestra and—"

"Guitars," she insisted. "In a band. And their hair will be deep brown like their daddy's."

She threaded her fingers through it and their eyes met, heavy-lidded again with resurgent desire. Their bodies stirred against each other, their lips met, tongues sipped and hearts clamored.

"Let's compromise," she suggested, scarcely aware of what she was saying, for already his hips were moving against hers.

He began speaking, but his voice was gruff and distracted. "Some redheads, some brown, some with freckles, some with guitars, some with vio—"

Her sweet seeking mouth interrupted. "Mmm-hmm…" she murmured against his lips. "But it'll take lots of practice to make all those babies." Her breasts pressed provocatively against his chest. She writhed once, experimentally, glorying in her newly discovered freedom. "Show me how we'll do it."

Their open mouths clung. His strong arm curved beneath her and rolled her atop him, then he settled her hips upon his, found the soft hollows behind her knees and drew them down until she straddled him in soft, feminine flesh. He pressed her hips away, and ordered thickly against her forehead, "Love me."

Her heart surged with shyness. Then love moved her hand. Hesitantly she reached, found, then surrounded.

Their smiles met, faltered, dissolved. Eyelids lowered as she settled firmly upon him. A guttural sound of satisfaction rumbled from his throat, answered by her softer, wordless reply. Experimentally she lifted, dropped, warming to his encouraging hands on her hips.

Drawing back, she found his eyes still shuttered, the lids trembling.

"Oh, Brian…Brian…I love you so much," she vowed with tears beginning to sting.

His eyes opened. For a moment his hands calmed the movement of her hips, then they reached to draw her face down as he kissed the outer corner of each eye. "And I love you, sweets…always," he whispered, drawing her mouth to his to complete the promise within it. "Always…always."

In the living room a new song started playing, sending soft music down the hall. To its lazy rhythm their bodies moved. They would build a repertoire of sweet memories throughout their years as man and wife, but as they moved now, reaffirming their love, it seemed none would be so sweet as this moment that bound them in promise.

When their bodies were gifted with the manifest of that promise, when the sweet swelling peaked and the shudders ceased, they reaffirmed it once again.

"I love you," spoke the man.

"I love you," answered the woman.

It was enough. Together, they moved on toward forever.

* * * * *

HER SISTER'S BABY

Janice Kay Johnson

JANICE KAY JOHNSON

The author of more than sixty books for children and adults, Janice Kay Johnson writes Harlequin Superromance novels about love and family—about the way generations connect and the power our earliest experiences have on us throughout life. Her 2007 novel *Snowbound* won a RITA® Award from Romance Writers of America for Best Contemporary Series Romance. A former librarian, Janice raised two daughters in a small rural town north of Seattle, Washington. She loves to read and is an active volunteer and board member for Purrfect Pals, a no-kill cat shelter.

Prologue

The cemetery was old, with the graves of each generation sprawling beyond the last. Ancient maples, leafless now, followed the lane that curved through the green sward. Even older were the first headstones, gray, sometimes tilting, their carved letters silent testament to long-past tragedies.

But the tragedy that had brought the mourners here today was as raw as the empty stretch of sloping land ready to receive the next generation. Beneath a tarp, dark earth was heaped beside the newly dug grave, where Sheila Elizabeth Delaney was being laid to rest.

In agony, Colleen Deering wrenched her gaze from the braced casket and stared unseeing at the small crowd huddled beyond it.

Oh, God. The pain cramped inside her chest, stealing her breath. She didn't know if she could bear it. Her sister had been only thirty two, happy in her marriage, looking forward to raising a family. *Why Sheila?* Colleen cried silently. *Why now?*

The minister was talking, his voice soothing, his utterances age-old and perhaps even true. Was everyone else listening? Colleen looked from face to face, struggling to find some link with another soul among this crowd of mourners.

Not unexpectedly she found it in the eyes of the man who faced her across her sister's grave. He truly was a stranger, this tall, broad-shouldered man who had remained dry-eyed throughout the ordeal, a silent, rigid presence. She supposed

some of the mourners were his friends, though he stood apart
from the others, staring at the gleaming, flower-draped casket
atop its supports. His expression was set, unrevealing. Only his
hands, curled into fists, gave away the anguish he otherwise disguised.

And then he lifted his head. His blue eyes, shockingly vivid
here, where even the sky wore the colors of mourning, met
Colleen's. In them she saw everything she felt and more.

She wished suddenly she knew him better, this man her
sister had loved. Instead of staring at each other across a rift,
they ought to have been able to offer each other comfort. After
all, Michael Delaney was—no, *had been*—Sheila's husband.

He was also the father of the unborn child Colleen carried.

Chapter 1

"Kim likes her teacher at least," Colleen said, turning on the faucet to rinse the breakfast dishes. "Mrs. Peters. Do you know her?"

"I don't think so." Sheila's tone was distracted.

She sat at Colleen's kitchen table sipping coffee, at first glance looking perfectly at home. She was a beautiful woman, but today she seemed brittle, edgy. She had lost weight, Colleen thought.

Chattering to cover her unease, Colleen said, "Well, Mrs. Peters is one brave woman. Last year she taught kindergarten. This year she's switched to sixth grade. Can you believe it?" She shook her head. "From five-year-olds jumping on desks to a roomful of preadolescent hormones."

Sheila gave an odd, twisted smile. "Don't parents make the same transition?"

Colleen grabbed the kitchen sponge. "Yes, but gradually, thank God."

Sheila neither laughed nor remarked, odd in itself since she had stopped by just to visit. Instead, as she idly stirred her coffee, there was unexplained tension in the way she held herself. She was too pale, with dark circles beneath her eyes. Without her usual smile, the lines beside her mouth were unhappy ones.

Colleen occupied herself scrubbing on the countertop while she tried to think of a tactful way to ask what was wrong.

Out of the blue Sheila said, "Do you know how much I envy you?"

Colleen turned, the sponge still in her hand. Her first instinct was to make some teasing remark despite her sister's strange tone. But when she saw the way Sheila's mouth twisted, the cloud in her huge brown eyes, Colleen said carefully, "What do you mean?"

"Isn't it obvious?"

"Given the fact that my small store of savings is almost gone and my business is barely breaking even, that Drew refuses to talk to his father when he calls while Kim cries herself to sleep…" Her laugh revealed more frustration than she'd known she felt. "No, it's not obvious."

"At least you have them." There it was again, the anger, the hurt, the envy.

"That's true." Colleen tossed the sponge into the sink and went to sit at the table. She touched Sheila's elegant, long-fingered hand. "Have you given up?"

Sheila's face contorted and then she bent her head to hide the tears Colleen had already seen in her eyes. "I can't go on like this," she said, on a hiccuping sob. "I've tried and tried, but I'm just pretending. I don't even tell Michael anymore when I'm ovulating. What's the point? We both know what'll happen. Do you know what he said the last time? 'Why are you doing this to yourself?'" Her hands curled into fists. "God."

"Doesn't he want children?"

"Oh." Her tone was suddenly lifeless. "I don't know." More than the tears, it was the emptiness in her eyes that scared Colleen. "No, that's not true. He always claimed he wanted a family. But of course, it's *my* body that's the issue. We both know that, even though he never blames me. But how can I give up? What would we have left?"

The idea of not having Drew and Kim was unthinkable, but Colleen tried to remember how she'd felt before they came into her life.

"A happy marriage, a beautiful home, a job you enjoy…"

Sheila hadn't even heard her. *"Nothing,"* she said fiercely.

"That's what. All I ever wanted is a family. I feel betrayed, as though somebody promised—" She broke off.

When Colleen came to her, Sheila buried her face in her sister's stomach and wrapped her arms around her waist with the intensity of a child who needs to hold on for dear life. Tears wet Colleen's cheeks. She murmured the kind of reassurances that satisfy a child. Sheila was beyond that, but what else could Colleen offer?

Maybe it was enough. At least she was *here*. Until three months ago, when Colleen had moved with her children to this small town in eastern Washington, all she'd been able to do was listen to her sister long-distance and sympathize. Of course she'd known that Sheila wanted children, and that she and Michael were disappointed because of how hard they'd tried without being able to conceive. But preoccupied by her own divorce, she hadn't fully understood how devastated her sister was by what she saw as her failure.

Well, things were different now. Colleen had moved to Clayton to be close to her sister. Obviously Sheila had needed Colleen just as much.

Finally Sheila let go of her and lifted her head. Mascara tracked down her cheeks and her peaches-and-cream complexion was blotched. "I want to hate somebody," she said with devastating simplicity. "But the only person I can hate is myself."

"That's ridiculous!" Colleen protested. "It's not as though you can help it. I can't imagine that Michael holds it against you."

"No," her sister said drearily. "Of course he doesn't. But I do."

Grasping for straws, Colleen asked, "What about the adoption agency?"

Sheila gave a mirthless laugh. "They've never even done a home study. We've been on their list for four *years*. And it could be many, many more years before we get a baby. I don't think they're going to give us one. There are never enough babies. Who knows, maybe they didn't like something about us. It would be so easy to trip up and never even know it."

"There must be other agencies...."

"I'm afraid they'd drop us from the list if they found out we'd gone somewhere else. Anyway, we'd be starting all over and I hear it's just as bad no matter what agency you're with." She mopped at her tears with a napkin. "I'm sorry, Col. I didn't mean to dump on you. I'm just...I'm at the end of my tether."

"Cry to your heart's content," Colleen declared. "That's what sisters are for."

Sheila's smile trembled and fresh tears washed away the old. "I'm so glad you're here. I've missed you. Since Mom died, I've felt so alone."

"Well, you're not." With a sting of anger, Colleen wondered what was wrong with Michael that his wife was so lonely. But this wasn't the time to ask. Instead, Colleen hugged her sister, brushing her curls back from her wet face. Sheila's hard veneer was gone; she might have been the fifteen-year-old who had cried when her older sister left for college.

"I'd do anything for you," Colleen said passionately. "You know that, don't you?"

"Yeah." Sheila gave another shaky smile. "It's ironic that the one thing I need is something you can't give me."

That was when the notion came to Colleen, simple, almost ridiculously obvious, breathtaking. Slowly, examining it from each side, she said, "Why not?"

"If you mean that you'll share Drew and Kim—" Sheila stopped dead, her eyes widening. "You're not thinking...?"

"Why not?" Colleen said again, recklessly.

Her sister jumped to her feet. "You're crazy."

"What makes you say that?" Instead of regretting her impulsive suggestion, Colleen liked it better the more she considered it. Pregnancy and childbirth had been embarrassingly easy for her.

Sheila shook her head. "Col, we're talking about nine months of your life! Morning sickness, stretch marks, getting as big as a cow! It's one thing to have your own children, but you'll have to give the baby up. And we'll have to use your eggs...."

"Yeah, but I actually *like* being pregnant," Colleen told her. "I can't claim to enjoy childbirth, but I was only in labor with Drew for three hours. No big deal."

She would have willingly embarked on forty-eight hours of labor, even a C-section, if only for the look in Sheila's eyes—the incredulous hope, the dawning wonder.

"You really mean it, don't you? You'd do this for me?"

"Of course I mean it." But Colleen felt obligated to warn, "Michael may not like the idea."

Sheila gave a quick shake of her head. "He won't mind. Why should he? It'd be his baby. And almost mine. At least you and I share the same genes. We even look alike."

Colleen wrinkled her nose. "Well…almost. You've always been prettier."

"Don't be silly." Sheila jumped to her feet. Her cheeks were pink and her eyes glowed. "You'd really do this for me?"

"In a second," Colleen told her. Then she smiled. "Well, not quite. We'll have to wait until the right time of the month."

Sheila made a face. "I'm an expert on that! I swear not an hour has passed in five years or more when I didn't think about what time of month it was, whether tonight we ought to try again, whether *this* time we'd get lucky.…" She let out a long, shuddering breath. "Part of me had given up and part of me never stopped hoping."

Tentatively Colleen introduced a note of practicality. "Do you know…well, how to go about it? I mean—" she was blushing now, too "—getting me pregnant?"

Sheila didn't seem to notice. "I'll bet our doctor would do it. After I talk to Michael, I'll call and find out." She suddenly laughed and snatched Colleen into a hug. "I can't believe this is happening! I've dreamed about it for so long!" In her mercurial way, Sheila suddenly sobered. "Oh, Col, I don't know if I can do this to you. Wouldn't it break your heart to give the baby away?"

"It won't be mine to give away. Consider it babysitting." Colleen gripped both of her sister's hands and gazed solemnly into her eyes. "I swear," she vowed, as much for herself as for her sister, "that I will never, even for a minute, think of the baby as mine. It's yours—and Michael's."

Sheila stared at her for a long moment, then sank onto a chair as though her legs had suddenly turned to jelly. "You do mean it."

Colleen's own legs felt a little weak, and she, too, sat down abruptly. Half in amazement at herself, Colleen said, "I really, really do. The only thing is…well, maybe you'd better not talk to Michael yet."

"What do you mean?" Sheila asked in quick alarm.

"I need to talk to Kim and Drew. I can't do something this drastic without giving them some voice in my decision." Colleen bit her lip. "I'm sorry. I should have talked to them before I got your hopes up."

"Don't be silly." Sheila bounced to her feet again, moving nervously, her voice deliberately light. "Of course they should come first. And promise me, if they don't like the idea, you won't put pressure on them. I don't want them feeling guilty. Okay?"

"Okay," Colleen agreed. "I'll call you the second I talk to them."

"And I'd better get to work." Sheila's gleaming auburn hair, worn in a stylish bob, shimmered as she bent to grab her purse. Then she gave Colleen a quick kiss on the cheek. When she straightened, she was unexpectedly blinking away new tears. "Col… I just want to say…" She tried to smile. "Look at me, not able to get out a simple thank-you. But I want to say it now. Even if nothing comes of this, thank you. Just…talking about it made me realize how much we mean to each other. We're lucky, aren't we?"

Colleen didn't even have a chance to answer. Sheila was already slamming the bottom half of the Dutch door and waving before she vanished down the walk. A moment later Colleen heard the throaty engine of her sister's bright red sports car.

Colleen wanted to talk to Drew and Kim *now,* but they were in school and she had to open the store at ten. In fact, she remembered, with a panicky glance at the clock, she'd promised to be there early so that the instructor for the class on appliqué could set up in the back room. Sheila would have to wait.

At dinner Colleen had to hear all about her kids' day at school before she could get a word in edgewise. It wasn't until afterward, when Kim and Drew were both helping her clean up, that Colleen realized the right moment had come. Hands in the soapy dishwater, she was suddenly struck by how many of life's decisions she'd made in the kitchen, how many crises had found her there. She just been drying the last pan the night when Ben had announced he wanted a divorce.

Shaking that particular recollection off, Colleen took a deep breath and said very casually, "I have something I want to discuss with you guys."

Drew had just come back from taking the garbage out to the can. Ignoring her, he complained, "This is a gross job. Why can't Kim do it? I'd rather dry dishes."

"That's not what I heard two weeks ago," Colleen reminded him. At the time he had whined that taking out the garbage only took a minute, while drying took forever.

"Yeah, but I didn't know then how garbage stinks."

Colleen smiled at him. "That probably means we should wash out the trash can. Saturday."

"But—"

Kim elbowed him. "Why don't you put a cork in it. Mom has something to say."

"Don't tell me what to do." Drew's square jaw jutted out just like his father's often had. "You're not my mother!"

Colleen sighed. "Kim, you might have phrased that a little more tactfully. Drew, I *am* your mother, and I do want to talk about something."

He subsided, mumbling, "Yeah, well, she always thinks *she* can give orders...."

Forging on, Colleen said, "You guys know how much your aunt Sheila and uncle Michael would like to have a baby."

Kim shot her brother a dirty look. "Why don't you give 'em Drew? *I* wouldn't miss him. And he's a baby, all right."

Drew had gotten as far as storming, "Talk about babies! You

should have seen *her* yesterday—" when Colleen covered his mouth with a soapy hand.

Giving her daughter a minatory look, she said, "Tempting though the idea occasionally is, I would never give either of you away. I'm actually kind of fond of you both."

Kim wrinkled her nose. *"Fond?"*

Colleen smiled and removed her hand from Drew's mouth. "Well, okay, maybe a little more than fond."

Drew scrubbed at his mouth with his T-shirt. "Gross. You didn't have to wash my mouth out with soap."

"If you'd shut it a little quicker, you wouldn't have gotten soap in there." Colleen was getting a headache. "Can you two just listen to me for a minute?" Reassured by their reluctant nods, she explained, "The problem is, your aunt Sheila can't get pregnant. There's something wrong with her eggs." Drew was beginning to squirm—he didn't want to hear any more about girls and sex than he absolutely had to—but she ignored him. "They've tried to adopt a baby, but they've been waiting forever. There just aren't very many babies available for adoption. So I got to thinking…well, that I could have one for her."

Her children stared at her with identical expressions of horror. Drew was the first to speak. "But who would be the *father?*"

This was the tricky part. The part, in fact, that she didn't like thinking about herself. "Your uncle Michael."

"But he's married to Aunt Sheila already."

Colleen tried to remember how much she had told Drew about sex and procreation. Hoping it was enough, she gave an upbeat explanation of how artificial insemination was done and how the pregnancy wouldn't really affect them that much. "I'd go to the hospital and have the baby, and then come home. Only instead of bringing it with me, like I did you guys, Aunt Sheila would take the baby. He—or she—would be both your cousin and your half brother."

She fielded a barrage of questions. Why *half* brother? What would Dad think? Would anybody *tell* the baby that his mom wasn't really his mom? At last the stream slowed, and Colleen said, "Some people might not approve of my doing this. I would have worried more about that if we were still back in Pacifica, but here hardly anybody would have to know."

"What about our friends?" Drew asked.

"What friends?" Kim muttered.

"You'll make some," Colleen said. "It just takes time. Especially in a new town where everybody else has known each other forever. And, Drew, I don't think the boys you've had over would even notice if I was pregnant. The only reason they ever come into the house is to look for something to eat."

He appeared to contemplate that briefly. "I guess I wouldn't care if one of *their* mothers was having a baby." His curled lip conveyed his opinion of the whole business.

"What do you think, Kim?" Colleen asked quietly. Her daughter was the one who hadn't wanted to move, who clung ferociously to her belief in her father however many times he failed her. Drew wasn't old enough to be traumatized by the snubs that might come his way if the community found out and disapproved of this pregnancy. But Kim was, and not even for Sheila would Colleen hurt her daughter.

After a minute, the eleven-year-old shrugged awkwardly. "It's okay with me, I guess. I think it's cool that you want to do it for her."

Colleen gave each of her children an impulsive hug. "Believe it or not," she informed them, "the time will come when you two are willing to admit how much you love each other, too."

Kim leveled a cool stare at her brother, who returned it in good measure. "Yeah, right," she said flatly.

"She's a *girl,*" Drew said.

Colleen laughed. So much for her only serious reservation about the step she contemplated taking. Now it was up to Sheila and Michael.

From that day on Colleen couldn't bring herself to face Michael. Suddenly he wasn't just Sheila's husband; he was a man. Even though the process of artificial insemination was completely impersonal, Colleen couldn't forget that Michael would be the father of the baby she'd carry. He might never touch her, but still some part of the two of them would be melded into one. They would have come together in the most intimate of ways.

What she should do was resolve her feelings, maybe even talk about them with Sheila. Coward that she was, Colleen avoided him altogether. Whenever Sheila suggested dinner, Colleen pretended she had to be at the shop but offered to meet her for lunch, instead. Drew's soccer game saved her from a Sunday barbecue at her sister and brother-in-law's house; the meeting of the local quilt guild happened to be the evening Sheila and Michael were having friends in for drinks. She could only pray that neither of them had put two and two together and realized why she was making excuses.

Once she narrowly escaped running into him at, of all disastrous places, the doctor's office. She'd just arrived for her second attempt at being inseminated and was dropping her chart into the in-basket at the nurse's station. She turned when she heard footsteps approaching and the nurse saying, "Right this way, Mr. Delaney. I'll just get you a cup...." Behind the nurse was Michael, his dark head bent as he listened to her, his face inscrutable.

Colleen had never moved faster in her life. She whisked out of sight through the nearest open door, her heart pounding and her knees weak. Thank heavens he hadn't been looking her way! What if they had come face-to-face? What would she have *said* to the man who was here to produce sperm to impregnate her, thanks to the doctor who insisted it had to be fresh for the optimum success rate?

Her heartbeat took another dizzying leap when the nurse spoke again, sounding so close that she had to be standing with Michael right on the other side of the door Colleen was hiding behind.

"Why don't I put you in this room?"

With a horrified glance over her shoulder, Colleen discovered she had taken refuge in an examining room. What if the nurse brought Michael in here? A wave of heat washed over Colleen's face.

But the footsteps receded, and a moment later she peeked out to see that he was gone. The nurse was hurrying toward her.

She looked startled to see Colleen emerging from a room. "Oh, Mrs. Deering, I didn't see you arrive. I'm afraid it will be a few minutes. You're welcome to stay in that room if you'd prefer, or I can call you back in when we're ready for you."

Colleen chose the privacy of the room to avoid any chance of meeting Michael as he was leaving, having handed over the precious cup.

For the first time it occurred to her to wonder, if she was embarrassed, what Michael must feel. She'd assumed that Sheila was accompanying him to these appointments, but he had undeniably been alone. How on earth did he get aroused, alone in the sterile surroundings of the clinic, knowing that the nurse waited just outside? Think how dreadful it would be to a man's ego if he had to admit that he just couldn't do it!

But apparently he could, because not fifteen minutes later the doctor was ready to do his part in the procedure that would magically produce life inside her even without the warmth and closeness of lovemaking.

She knew in a matter of weeks that she was pregnant, but Colleen wasn't about to raise her sister's hopes. Not yet. She waited another week, then closed her shop early one day and went by the clinic. A pregnancy test confirmed her hopes.

On her way out Colleen almost stopped in the waiting room to phone Sheila. But somehow a phone call didn't seem adequate for news so momentous. And surely it was too early in the afternoon for Michael to be home. She could stop by to exchange mutual congratulations with Sheila and then run.

Sheila confounded her.

"Don't be silly, the kids will be fine without you. You have to be here when I tell Michael. We're in this together, aren't we?"

"But it's your baby," Colleen protested weakly. "Wouldn't you like to be alone—"

They both heard the sound of the garage door opening.

"Oh, here's Michael now." Sheila jumped to her feet, face glowing. "I can hardly wait to tell him!" She danced several steps toward the kitchen, then stopped theatrically. "Or should I open some champagne and spring the news on him when I hand him the glass? I wonder if we have any…. Oh, I can't bear it." She spun toward the kitchen. "I've got to tell him. You don't mind, do you, Col?"

Sheila vanished into the kitchen and Colleen braced herself. For heaven's sake, Michael was her sister's husband! Colleen had known him, if distantly, for years, since she had been Sheila's matron of honor. He hadn't changed just because his sperm had impregnated the wrong sister. And besides, she had volunteered for this, hadn't she?

He was tugging absentmindedly at his tie and undoing the top button of his dress shirt when Sheila drew him through the kitchen doorway. His gaze went directly to Colleen and she saw a muscle twitch in his jaw. But his stillness gave nothing away; he only waited for the news he must surely have guessed.

Sheila's eyes were sparkling when she stopped, still holding her husband's hand, and cleared her throat. "Colleen has something she wants to tell us."

They faced Colleen and waited, Sheila expectantly, Michael with brows raised. Colleen made a face at her sister, but surrendered with as much grace as possible. "I'm pregnant," she said baldly. "Six weeks along. Your baby is due July 20."

The last thing she expected from Sheila, who already knew, was tears, but suddenly she was blinking them away as she smiled tremulously at Colleen. "I guess I still can't believe it. We're really going to have a baby." Her tone was filled with awe.

But what Colleen was waiting for was Michael's reaction. Sheila had talked about her hurt and disappointment at remaining childless as though it was hers alone. Colleen wondered now whether Michael didn't care as much whether they ever had children, or was only a typical male who didn't like to talk about how he really felt.

He was still staring at her, his blue eyes unnerving in their intensity. Just as the silence became uncomfortable, just as Sheila was turning in puzzlement to look up at him, he smiled.

Michael's smiles were rare, but worth waiting for. The first time she had met him, during a prewedding party, Colleen had watched him unobserved for several minutes before Sheila drew him over. Her first reaction hadn't been positive. He was so handsome she had felt intimidated and—unfair though it was—mildly irked at him for having that effect on her.

She'd just been brooding over whether she *wanted* to dislike her sister's intended when Sheila had pointed her out to him and Michael turned his head. Colleen felt first the shock of his blue eyes. But not until he smiled, with warmth, self-deprecation and real charm, had she understood why Sheila had fallen so hard for this man that she was planning a wedding within weeks of their meeting.

But today's smile, so slow in coming, crooked, a little shaky and completely genuine, reached Colleen in a way his more deliberate ones never had.

"Damn," he said softly. "It worked."

Colleen knew exactly how he felt. What had taken place in the doctor's office couldn't possibly have anything to do with this moment, with the life that would soon be fluttering in her womb. How could it have happened without the sweat and pleasure of two bodies meeting? But happen it had, and the proof was within her.

Colleen flushed, realizing that her hand was instinctively spread over her abdomen. Michael's gaze flicked down to her hand, then back to meet hers. His smile faded, and she felt that odd tension again, that self-consciousness. She was the fifth wheel here, an intruder on her sister's marriage.

She managed another smile. "I really need to get home. But I wanted to tell you… Well, that's obvious, isn't it? Anyway, congratulations again."

Michael took a few steps forward, blocking her way. Before

she could react, he bent to kiss her cheek. "The words are inadequate," he said roughly. "But I'll say them, anyway. Thank you."

Sheila was right behind him, giving Colleen a swift hug. "Didn't I tell you she was a sister in a million?" she asked her husband.

He shook his head, his blue eyes lingering on Colleen's face. "I never doubted it for a minute, but you've got to admit, this is above and beyond the call."

Colleen made a face. "You're going to have me blushing, for Pete's sake! Like I told Sheila, I loved being pregnant. I have every intention of enjoying this time just as much, only I can hand over the 2:00 a.m. feedings to you guys. That'll give you something to look forward to."

Michael's grin was wry, while his wife had a faraway look in her eyes. Very softly Sheila said, "You have no idea how much I do."

Chapter 2

Colleen was just peeling off her bra and reaching for her nightgown when the telephone rang. She might have felt a thrill of alarm had she not known Drew and Kim were both safely tucked into bed just down the hall. Still, who would call her at nearly ten o'clock at night?

She reached for the receiver with one hand and her hairbrush with the other. "Hello?"

"Colleen?" She almost didn't recognize Michael's voice. With no preamble he said, "Sheila's been in a car accident."

The hairbrush fell out of Colleen's hand, thumping on the carpet. "Oh, my God." She sagged onto the edge of the bed. "Are you at the hospital? Is she…?"

"The state patrol just called. I'm on my way. I thought you'd want to be there, too."

Already she was on her feet, reaching for her jeans. Action of any kind staved off the terror. "Did they say how she is?"

"Colleen—" his voice roughened "—I don't think it's good."

"Oh, no, please no," she whispered.

"If you can't leave the kids…"

"They'll be all right." *Please, please, let Sheila be, too.* "I'm on my way."

She awakened Kim and then drove through the rainy night to the hospital, running a red light once at a deserted intersection. Inside the hospital she was directed to a small waiting room. Michael was there, and the moment she saw him, she knew. His face was wet with tears.

Colleen's fingernails bit into her palms. "No. Not Sheila…"

"Oh, God." He bowed his head. His voice was thick. "She was speeding. You saw how wet the roads are. She, uh, she couldn't make a curve."

"No." Grief rose with shocking force, and Colleen, shaking her head vehemently, backed up until she came against a wall. "No!"

He kept talking, as though he had to say it. "She slammed on the brakes and skidded off the road straight into a telephone pole. They say…" Michael took a shuddering breath. "They say she died instantly."

Not Sheila. Oh, God, please…

He came to her then, her sister's husband, and held her. She held him as tightly and cried.

Sometime that night Colleen went mercifully numb. She stayed that way, going through the motions of life, until the funeral. And there, faced with Sheila's casket, Colleen couldn't hide anymore.

Across Sheila's grave, Colleen met Michael's eyes. His agony mingled with her own, and she remembered for the first time in days that she was pregnant. That she carried her sister's baby.

But her sister was gone.

She wouldn't think about it, Colleen told herself on a wave of fresh pain. She didn't dare. Not now. She could only deal with so much at a time. Her pregnancy could wait. Thank God that so few people knew and that she didn't show yet.

Colleen kept her promise to herself for hours on end that day. She just didn't have time to indulge her shock and grief. Instead, she acted as hostess at the reception, accepting condolences, checking in the kitchen with the volunteers from the church who were providing the food, keeping a sharp eye out for Kim and Drew. She had turned into an automaton, a grimace that masqueraded as a smile frozen on her face.

"Thank you for coming," she repeated over and over. "Yes, we'll miss her dreadfully." "No, it doesn't seem quite real." "How kind of you to offer, but I think we're fine."

Her hand stung from being patted so many times; her voice came to her own ears from a distance, as though it belonged to somebody else.

The first time the crowd parted and she came face-to-face with Michael, he merely nodded. The movement was jerky, as though his neck was stiff. Their eyes met, conveyed weariness and wariness in equal measure, and then Colleen turned away.

The next time, his large hand closed on her arm and he bent his head. "Are you all right?" he asked in an undertone.

Colleen looked down at his hand where it lay, brown and strong, on her forearm. She knew, without understanding why, that she was avoiding his gaze.

"I'm…managing," she said. "What about you?"

Michael withdrew his hand. "I'm fine," he said shortly. "How are your kids?"

But somebody was already claiming her attention, and she was vaguely aware that Michael had been engulfed in a bear hug. As aloof as he was, he must detest the necessity of accepting such physical intimacies from well-meaning people he hardly knew.

Of all the things that were said to her that afternoon, only one really penetrated—the words of a woman who had worked with Sheila.

Very kindly she said, "Poor Sheila longed so for children, but you must be grateful now that she didn't have any. It's so dreadful when young children lose their mother."

Colleen's hand spread protectively over her stomach and she took an involuntary step back. Nausea rose in her throat and she was momentarily unable to speak.

Something must have showed on her face, because the woman said hastily, "Of course, they would have been a consolation to their father. And to you."

Somehow Colleen escaped without disgracing herself. And endured more gentle pats, more well-meant comfort. All the while, she wept inside. *Oh, Sheila…*

* * *

Real panic didn't hit Colleen until several days after the funeral, when she awakened at five in the morning only to have to run for the bathroom with her stomach heaving.

Afterward, she wasn't sure she had the strength to stand. Still kneeling in front of the toilet, she reached up to flush it, her forehead resting on her arms.

When had she last eaten? Really eaten? Over the past few days, she'd fed the kids of course and made a pretense of eating herself, but that's all it was. At best, food was unappetizing; at worst, the idea of putting a bite in her mouth was enough to make her stomach quiver in protest.

But her stomach obviously didn't like total neglect, either.

She had to think about the baby, for its sake if not her own. She'd taken such care when she was pregnant with Kim and Drew, making sure she had so many dark green vegetables a day, so many citrus fruits. Not a drop of alcohol had crossed her lips, and she had avoided anyplace where people might be smoking. This baby, her gift to her sister, deserved as much.

And that was when fear began to trickle through her veins like a drug administered intravenously. Weak at first, then stronger and stronger, until she was panting for breath and blinking away the sweat that beaded her brow.

Dear God, what was she going to do?

She was pregnant. Inescapably, inarguably pregnant. Stuck, a victim by her own choice, trapped in an inexorable process that would carry her along willy-nilly.

And then what?

That was the really scary part. This wasn't her baby, was never *supposed* to be her baby. She was a long-term sitter, that was all. This child she carried was Sheila's.

The baby's not mine! she screamed inside, where only she could quail from the terror. *It's Sheila's! Sheila's, do you hear me? Bring her back!*

The grief tore at Colleen until she could no longer suppress the fear and sadness and sense of aloneness that had swamped her all week. Her hurt came out in huge, wrenching sobs, in the hot, salty taste of tears. Sheila was all she'd had, except for Kim and Drew, and they were children, for God's sake! Children, who needed her to be strong. What about *her?*

Just this once, she let herself be selfish, grieving not so much for her sister as for herself. She cried for her aloneness, for the burden she had taken on so joyfully and now could not lay down. She cried for her divorce, for her children, for the uncertain future.

"Mom?" The small, scared voice came from just behind her.

Colleen jerked around to see her daughter standing in the open bathroom door. Her eyes were wide and she clutched the faded baby quilt she had loved and now used as a throw on her bed, nothing important but always near.

"Mommy, are you okay?"

"Oh, sweetheart." Colleen squeezed her eyes shut and scrubbed at her wet face before she held out her arms. "If you don't mind getting soaked," she said as lightly as her tear-clogged throat would allow, "come here."

At eleven, Kim was too tall to sit on her lap, had been for several years, but somehow they still scrunched together on the bathroom floor.

Her cheek against her daughter's soft brown hair, Colleen said, "I'm just…letting it all out. Mostly none of this has seemed real. I'd lie there at night and part of me didn't believe Aunt Sheila was gone. I've been in shock, I guess. Suddenly this morning it hit me."

Kim turned brown eyes on her. "In the bathroom?" she said doubtfully.

"I was already here." It was on the tip of her tongue to add that she was having morning sickness. After all, Kim knew she was pregnant and why. But something stopped her. It apparently hadn't occurred to her daughter yet to think about what was going to happen with the baby, and Colleen didn't want to start her worrying. Until she herself talked to Michael and they made some decisions, she would just as soon not remind the kids of the inescapable fact of her pregnancy.

It developed that Kim was already worrying, but about something else, because she asked suddenly, "Will we move again? I mean, the only reason we came here is Aunt Sheila."

"Do you wish we would?"

Kim went still. "Not really."

"Even if it meant going back to Pacifica?"

There was a long pause before Kim muttered, "It's okay here." Not an answer, but an answer all the same.

"Well—" Colleen pressed a kiss to the top of her daughter's head, inhaling the scent that was still little girl "—I won't promise we'll never move again, but I'm sure not planning on it. For one thing we can't afford to. You know I sank everything we had into starting the business."

There was silence for a moment. Colleen's back had begun to ache because of her awkward position on the floor. But she didn't move a muscle.

"What if…well, if not enough people around here want to quilt?"

They had talked about this in some detail. After all, the risk was one they shared as a family. But if there was ever a time when even adults needed reassurance, it was right after a sudden death, when the uncertainty of life was brought shockingly home. So she said patiently, "Then I'll get a job. A regular, working-for-somebody-else, nine-to-five job. You know the kind."

"But you'd hate it."

"Hey." Colleen gave her daughter a small shake. "Most people have one, you know. I like owning my own business. But the world isn't going to end if it doesn't work out."

Kim nodded. After a minute she said, "Uh, Mom?"

"Yeah?"

"This is kind of uncomfortable."

Colleen groaned and collapsed, ending up on her back with Kim sprawled on top of her. Kim was giggling, the pinched look her face had worn this last week easing for the first time. Colleen knew she must look as wonderful as the leftovers she had a habit of forgetting in the back of the refrigerator, but she, too, felt a welcome easing inside.

Unfortunately it didn't last long. She tucked her daughter back in bed for a last hour or two of sleep before the alarm sounded. She'd no sooner kissed her softly when she saw, in her mind's eye, Sheila, sitting at the kitchen table.

At least you have them.

And the anguish roared back. It wasn't fair. Why had Sheila been cheated yet again, and finally, of the chance to hold her own child?

Colleen used the simple mechanism of denial to survive the next two weeks. The waistbands of her jeans and skirts were getting a little tight, but nothing she couldn't ignore. The kids were absorbed in their own concerns, and she had plenty to occupy her at the quilt shop.

Should she cancel classes that didn't completely fill or run them at a loss to build her customer base? What about a "fabric of the month" club, as many quilt shops had, in hopes of bringing in a little more money? But each new project took time, leaving her less for the kids, more weary.

Her increasing tiredness was something else she wouldn't let herself think about. Because if she did, she would also be forced to think about the pregnancy.

Which Michael was trying to make her do.

Except for Sheila's blithe communications, scarcely a message had been left on Colleen's answering machine since the move. Ben knew the kids weren't home during the day or after school; he called—when he bothered—in the evening. Kim hadn't made any friends yet, and Drew's skidded their bikes up the driveway on their way to the playing field, instead of picking up the phone. So when Colleen came home to the blinking red light for the third time that week, she looked at it as distrustfully as she would have a tarantula on her kitchen counter. She was in no hurry to push the play button.

Michael's last two messages had been increasingly peremptory, both with the same theme: they had to talk. If this was him again, she didn't want the kids to hear what he had to say.

But Drew, coming into the house behind her, had already

thudded up the stairs, and Kim hadn't followed her mother in at all. The fourteen-year-old boy next-door was shooting baskets in his driveway, which might have something to do with it. Kim insisted that all boys were jerks, but she thought of plenty of excuses to hang around the yard casually when Jerry was outside.

Maybe the talent at making excuses was hereditary, Colleen thought wryly. She'd made more than a few herself these past two weeks.

Reluctantly she pushed the flashing button. Michael's voice, deep but somehow remote, had unnerving immediacy, despite the fact it was recorded.

"Colleen, is there some reason you're not returning my calls? I know that this isn't the best time to think about the future, but we'll both feel more settled once we have it over with. Call me."

Colleen sank into one of the kitchen chairs. Well, she supposed that was reasonable enough. All Michael was doing was making it clear he was a decent man who was aware of his responsibility. She'd have more reason to be anxious if he *wasn't* calling her.

"So why don't you want to talk to him?" Colleen asked herself aloud. Then she made a face. "Dumb question. You know perfectly well why you don't want to. So put the groceries away, okay?"

As she nudged the refrigerator open and tried to find room for the gallon of milk, her memory popped up with something her ex-husband used to say.

You can run, but you can't hide.

In this case it was all too true. She wanted very badly to hide, at least for a while. She wasn't ready to make the kind of decisions that had to be made.

But hiding wasn't going to work. She was beginning to show, would have to wear maternity clothes soon. People would ask about her pregnancy. What would she say?

"Oh, the baby's not mine. Really, it belongs to this man who used to be married to my sister. I don't know him very well, but I'm sure he'll be a good father."

Impatiently she blinked away the moisture in her eyes. Damn it, the baby *was* his. And she had promised, hadn't she? Right here in this very kitchen, she had sworn she would never, even for a minute, think of the baby as hers.

But that was before Sheila died. Now Colleen was the only mother this baby would have. So what was more important? Michael's rights and her promise? Or the infant she carried within her?

Colleen accepted the bolt of cotton fabric from the customer. When she saw the tiny stylized flower on the deep rose background, she said, "Oh, I love this one. I couldn't resist buying a couple of yards myself. How much do you need?"

The woman tilted her head, considering. "Oh, Lord, why don't I ever write these things down? This is supposed to be the backing and binding for a crib quilt. I'm making it for my granddaughter."

"What pattern?" Colleen asked with interest.

"Tumbling Blocks. I've always wanted to try it, even though those set-in pieces can be tricky. Does three and a half yards sound like enough to you?"

"That should be plenty," Colleen assured her, and began measuring the rose calico. "What other colors are you including?"

She continued to chat with the woman, a regular customer, meanwhile using her rotary cutter to slice smoothly through the fabric. Folding the piece, she rang up the purchase.

"Why don't you bring it in when you're done? I'd love to see the finished product," she said. "In fact, I was thinking of having one of my monthly miniquilt shows just for crib quilts. What do you think?"

"That's a wonderful idea," the customer exclaimed. "At the rate my kids are producing grandchildren for me, crib size is about all I have time to make anymore."

Colleen already regretted the subject. Crib quilts made her think of cribs—and babies. She had a sudden picture of Kim as an infant, just tucked in. She lay on her tummy, knees pulled up, thumb buried in her rosebud of a mouth. Over her was the quilt Colleen had lovingly pieced and quilted, the one that was now faded and worn and loved.

This baby should have her—or his—own quilt. The idea was bittersweet, as would be the task.

Colleen was accepting the woman's check when the bell over the front door tinkled. With an automatic smile of welcome, she glanced up. But at the sight of the tall, dark-haired man closing the door behind him, her pulse took an uncomfortable jump and her smile faded.

Michael. He had run out of patience.

His gaze found and moved swiftly over her, as palpable as a touch, before he inclined his head and then glanced around the front room. Sheer masculinity made him out of place here among the row upon row of shelves that held bolts of cotton fabric in colors that flowed from one to the next, from lavender to deep violet to purple-blues, from the palest of creams to rusts and earthy browns. It was a feminine place, celebrating an art form that was woman's own, a way she'd had to express her creativity in a man's world that denied her other outlets.

This place was both challenge and refuge to Colleen, who saw all the colors and textures and patterns as possibilities— incomplete alone, but ready to play roles in the quilts that were as unique as the women who would make them.

But Michael's interest was cursory, not appreciative. He was here to pin her down, to limit her possibilities. She couldn't blame him—and yet a knot of resentment clogged her throat.

She was briefly rescued by a young woman, who had been browsing for the past half hour. Now she appeared from one of the inner rooms and asked, "Can I possibly get some advice?"

"You bet," Colleen assured her. She glanced at Michael as though he were only another customer. "If you don't mind waiting?"

"Not at all," he said imperturbably, and strolled over to a table spread with a display of quilting books. He picked one up as Colleen left the room.

All the while she discussed which shade of teal would work best next to a warm brown, inside she was panicking. Why was he so determined to corner her now? The baby wasn't due for six months. What was it that he wanted "settled"?

If only she knew him better, Colleen thought futilely; if only he didn't have that air of rigid control that had always struck her as cold.

If only she knew what was right: for him, for her and for the baby.

Why hadn't he let her hide just for a little longer? Why did he force her to remember?

Eventually Colleen had said everything there was to say about shading and contrast and why she thought one teal fabric, with a swirling design, was the most effective. The customer continued to stand there, staring indecisively at the several bolts of fabric fanned out on a table.

At last the young woman made an exasperated sound. "Fiddlesticks. I just can't make up my mind. I don't know what's wrong with me today. Listen, I think I'll just come back tomorrow. Maybe I'll bring my thirteen-year-old, if she's willing to risk being seen with me. Her taste in everything but boys is dependable."

Colleen laughed as expected, but refrained from mentioning, as she might otherwise have, that she had an eleven-year-old daughter who was already showing signs of the rebellion to come. Instead, she assured the woman that tomorrow was fine, and no, she didn't need to put the bolts away, Colleen would take care of it later. She followed her customer out to the front room and with the tinkle of the bell over the door, was left alone with Sheila's husband.

Only, of course, he wasn't anymore, which was another of those things Colleen didn't like to think about.

She curled her fingers so tightly into fists that her nails bit into her palms.

She was dimly aware that Michael had said something, but he had to repeat it. "We need to talk. Can I take you out to lunch?"

She retreated behind the cutting table. "The lunch hour is one of my busiest times."

He raised a dark brow and glanced around. "Then what about right now?"

"We might be interrupted."

"Tonight?"

"I don't want Kim and Drew…" She flushed at his expression and closed her eyes for a moment. Opening them, she gave him a twisted smile. "I'm sorry. Now is fine, as long as you don't mind if we're interrupted."

He looked at her for a moment, half frowning, then shoved his hands in his pockets and hunched his shoulders. He spoke in an oddly gruff tone. "It won't take long. I just wanted to make sure you knew that, as far as I'm concerned, Sheila's death doesn't change any of the arrangements about the baby. I still expect to pay your medical expenses and to take him after the birth."

He sounded so businesslike, talking about "arrangements" and "expenses." But what popped out of her mouth surprised even Colleen. "What if it's a her?"

Michael looked at her in bafflement. "What?"

"What if the baby's a girl?"

His dark brows drew together. "Did I say I didn't want a girl?"

She sounded truculent and didn't care. "You said 'him.'"

"Good God." He rubbed the back of his neck and spoke tersely. "You know what I meant. I won't deny that the English language is sexist. 'Him' was merely convenient shorthand. I don't give a damn whether the baby is a girl or a boy."

The fight abruptly left her. She knew she'd been petty, and she didn't even altogether know why. Michael was the baby's father, and his intention today presumably had been to reassure her she wasn't to be left holding the bag.

Colleen looked down at her hands, which all on their own had taken to lining up and squaring the objects beside the cash register: a pincushion, a book with the enrollments for quilting classes, some notes to herself and receipts on a spindle. There was undoubtedly something Freudian about this sudden need for tidiness, for order.

She looked up to see that Michael, too, was watching her hands in their obsessive task. With difficulty Colleen said, "I'm sorry. I…I'm not usually so combative. This has been a difficult few weeks."

"Granted."

Either she hadn't looked hard enough or he had just let his veneer crack, because she saw suddenly that his eyes were bloodshot, the lines carving his cheeks and between his brows so deep, he was no longer handsome. The hands he took out of his pockets had a tremor that explained why he had hidden them.

His chest rose and fell with a long breath. "I suppose I'm handling this badly," he said stiffly. "Somehow we never got to know each other very well. Considering the circumstances, I regret that. My intention today wasn't to upset you. I just thought we should…discuss it."

There he went again, being so reasonable that in comparison she felt even pettier. Worse yet, she knew herself for a coward.

"I'm sorry," Colleen said again, knowing he deserved at least that much. "You're right of course."

"I didn't intend—" Michael broke off. After an instant he grimaced. "Hell. We could apologize forever. Let me just say it again—as the bills come in, save them for me. You are seeing the doctor, aren't you?"

"Yes, of course." It was her turn to sound stiff. "But I think for the moment that I'd prefer to take care of the bills myself. I haven't said anything to my insurance company, and they do cover pregnancy.…"

"We've talked about that. They shouldn't have to." He was frowning again. "This pregnancy is on my behalf.…"

"It was for Sheila," she whispered, then more loudly, "I did it for Sheila!"

A spasm of pain twisted his face, and his voice was hoarse. "Do you think I don't know that?"

"I'm sorry." She whispered the words again, uselessly, but he didn't even acknowledge her regret.

"You're not thinking you'll keep the baby?"

"I'm not…thinking at all."

"Good." His words were clipped. "Don't."

The bell tinkled and the door swung open to let in two women who were laughing, but it was a moment before Colleen could wrench her gaze from the anger and pain riveting her. When she did at last, he left without another word, pulling the door shut behind him so hard the glass shivered.

She was shaking as she stared after him. In her heart Colleen knew she had behaved irrationally, but what had he expected? The baby was his only by the accident of fate that had made him Sheila's husband. It wasn't fair that he was here to claim it when she wasn't! *Sheila* was the one who had wanted and needed this child, who would have given anything for it. *Sheila,* not him!

You're not thinking you'll keep the baby?

Seeming not to notice Michael's abrupt departure, the two women had latched avidly onto a class list and were twittering as they pointed to one offering or another. They wavered in front of Colleen's eyes, not quite coming clear. They could have been new customers or her oldest. She wished they would go away.

But she smiled, anyway, and said in a voice that sounded only a little odd to her ears, "May I help you?"

Michael had driven half a mile before he realized that he was heading home, instead of back to work. Home, he thought grimly. What a joke. It was an emotional minefield, that place, every room, every piece of furniture, every small collectible, holding memories. And every damn one of them was painful right now.

Some nights he was tempted to move out, just check into a hotel. Maybe six months from now he could go home again, if such a thing was ever possible, decide what he wanted to keep, what he had to get rid of to get on with his life.

But something drew him back day after day, made him wander through the house, running a hand along the cool surface of the tile countertop in the kitchen, fingering the rough-soft texture of the quilt that had been Colleen's wedding gift to her sister, picking up one by one the tiny thimbles Sheila had collected, God knew why. At last he would pull out photograph albums and thumb through them until his eyes blurred and he couldn't see the pictures anymore.

The something that drew him was guilt. He was here and Sheila wasn't.

And six months from now, he would be doing a hell of a lot more than stumbling through the front door of a house that had been packed in mothballs to preserve it until he was ready. He would be a father, bringing home his newborn baby. A baby who would need to understand someday why he had a mother, but didn't really.

The wave of pain was expected, even obligatory, giving Michael time to pull off State Avenue onto a tree-lined residential street. He steered the car to the curb, set the hand brake and leaned his forehead against the steering wheel.

He couldn't afford to cry, had to go back to work, and he looked bad enough already, gaunt, hollow-eyed, shambling. He didn't want to subject the people he knew to any more of his grief. It was his, not theirs. He didn't like talking about any emotion that ran deep, had always been private.

Right now he was taking in air with great gasps, sweating as though he'd run three miles. Deliberately he wrenched his thoughts from the empty house to his wife's sister.

In pictures she looked so much like Sheila he'd been uncomfortable with the very idea that there existed such an almost perfect copy of his wife-to-be. Auburn hair, pale creamy skin, eyes a green-brown that made him think of forest pools and moss growing on tree trunks. Both women were medium height and slender.

But that first time he hadn't recognized Colleen across the crowded room, despite the uncanny resemblance. In life it didn't exist, or it was only the trappings, not the substance.

Sheila was like a butterfly: beautiful, dainty, quick-moving, somehow elusive. He'd always felt the need to touch her to be sure she was there.

But Colleen Deering was nothing like Sheila. She moved gracefully, but without the fluttering effect his wife had given. Her eyes were more direct, and yet she was grave, even reserved. She was the steady one, the patient one, the one you knew, just knew, would never lie or evade. Colleen wouldn't necessarily turn men's heads the way Sheila had, and yet she had some indefinable quality that would reward the looking, a stillness, a serenity, which he thought would be more peaceful than Sheila's restless fluttering.

Those early years of his marriage, he had been halfway jealous of Colleen, because she and Sheila were so close. The phone calls, the letters, never fully shared with him, the joy in their brief visits, the sadness in their partings, had made him conscious of his own fumbling attempts at intimacy, his silence when Sheila needed words, his dry eyes when she wanted tears. He could not be what her sister was to her, and he eventually gave up trying. Nor did he have that kind of closeness with his own parents or much older brother.

Yet the jealousy had died, envy become resignation and finally indifference. Much between him and Sheila had been killed by their failure to have children, the one thing she wanted most from him. How ironic that in the end it was her sister who gave her what he could not. His own role seemed minor, a mere bit part; he'd given seed for the sowing, but even the sowing was taken from him.

And yet he *knew,* on some visceral level, that this baby was his. He'd agreed to do this for Sheila, but from the moment Colleen had announced her pregnancy, his feelings for the baby had never had anything to do with Sheila. He was a man who had made a woman pregnant. The knowledge was uncomfortably sexual. He hadn't been able to look at his wife's sister, the mother of his baby, the same way again.

He'd been glad that she stayed away, so that he could pretend it wasn't so. She was a caretaker, a means to an end, a foster mother, a surrogate for his wife. The act of procreation that had taken place between him and her meant nothing, was a feat of modern medicine. The sperm could have come from any man; the womb belonged to any woman.

But it didn't. The seed was his. The body that cradled his unborn baby was hers. And the knowledge tormented him.

Chapter 3

It was for Sheila. I did it for Sheila! Colleen's voice was raw, her eyes blazed accusation, even hatred.

With a ragged cry, Michael lurched to a sitting position, fighting the covers tangled around him. "The baby's mine, damn you, mine!" he shouted.

When he looked around and saw only darkness and patterns of moonlight, Michael buried his face in his hands.

Sleep had become a time of nightmares.

Sometimes it was Sheila's death he saw. He was sitting in the passenger seat of her sports car, telling her to slow down, his foot convulsively pressing the floor where he wanted the brake to be. But she didn't seem to see him, didn't hear him; he was invisible to her. The tires skidded in a turn, but Sheila accelerated out of it. She had the radio on and was singing along. She was so happy she was snapping her fingers and be-bopping to the music, only a minimal amount of her attention on the road.

Michael knew the curve where she would die, saw it coming. She quit singing when she had to slam on the brakes, when the long skid began. In his nightmare, it wasn't the tele-phone pole he saw, but her face; it wasn't the crash he heard, but the music, which the police had told him was still playing when the next motorist came upon the scene.

Other times he dreamed that Sheila was still with him and

that she was pregnant. He kept asking where Colleen was, but Sheila never answered. She would look at him in puzzlement, as though she didn't know who he was talking about. And then he would wonder if this wasn't really Colleen, not Sheila at all. Of course she would be perplexed by his asking where she was. And so he would look closely, but he couldn't tell which sister he was with. He always woke up before he knew, and sometimes he would lie awake and strain to remember the woman in his dream so that he could decide once and for all. But in the frustrating way dreams had, the clear images would slip away.

And now he had a new nightmare designed to make the dark hours hell. Michael groaned and kicked off the covers, swinging his legs off the bed. This dream wasn't slipping away as conveniently, perhaps because he had been reliving something that had really happened. His mind had warped it, of course; he didn't think Colleen had looked at him with hatred. What he remembered seeing on her face was pain, but would she have said what she had unless she wanted to hurt him? Did she blame him somehow? Resent him because he was alive and Sheila wasn't? Or had Colleen always disliked him, and hidden it for her sister's sake? If so, how must she feel to be pregnant by him?

He swore under his breath and headed to the bathroom for a shower. The blast of hot water washed away the last ghostly images of his nightmare, but left his thoughts grim.

Colleen Deering wasn't just grieving; she sounded like a woman who was getting cold feet. If she hadn't yet considered changing her mind about their arrangement, he greatly feared she was working her way around to it.

He and Sheila and Colleen had sat down together and tried to think of every consequence, every misstep that could be taken on this unusual road to parenthood, but one possibility they hadn't anticipated: that Sheila would die before the baby had been handed over. Because the sisters were so close, because this pregnancy was a gift of love and not a cold-blooded contract, nothing had been put in writing. Colleen was pregnant with his baby, and he had no way of proving she had promised to hand the child over.

He didn't think she was a liar, but how well did he really know her?

Michael was thinking coldly now as he toweled himself dry. If she would let him pay even one of her bills for a prenatal visit to the doctor, that would be evidence an agreement existed. And she *had* agreed that he should pay them. So now was the time to continue some gentle pressure before her intentions solidified—if they were going to. God only knew she couldn't *want* to be pregnant on her own.

In the meantime he would continue to behave as though nothing had changed—even though his world had become an unfamiliar place.

"Mo-om!" Drew bellowed from the front room. "Uncle Michael's here!"

Colleen groaned and closed her eyes momentarily, leaning her forehead against the refrigerator. Just what she needed. It was five-thirty, she had just walked in the door, exhausted and starved, to discover she had forgotten to defrost the chicken she'd planned for dinner. And now Michael, apparently not satisfied with their talk, had to drop in unannounced. Wonderful.

But she straightened, blew her bangs off her forehead and headed for the front door. Before she got there, she pinned a pleasant smile in place, as much for Drew's sake as for her brother-in-law's.

"Michael. What a surprise."

Damn. Those blue eyes did it every time, leaving her feeling she'd been stripped—though not in a sexual sense. Instead, she was pretty sure he saw every ache, every moment of discouragement she'd suffered today, every bout of nausea or tears.

In the past his face would have given away nothing comparable, but that was no longer true. The lines were even deeper today, the skin stretched more tightly across cheekbones that were almost gaunt. He couldn't be sleeping any better than she was.

Colleen felt a pang of guilt. Maybe Michael wasn't trying to put pressure on her. Maybe he was looking for some comfort himself, from the one person he knew shared his grief.

"I'm sorry," he said with restraint, his gaze still on her face. "Is this a bad time?"

Why was it so hard for her to be casually friendly to him? "No, it's fine," she said, trying to convince herself, as well. "Really. Today was just one of those days. Come on in."

He didn't move over the threshold. "Actually, I stopped by to see if I could take you all out for a pizza. I didn't want to go home—" He stopped abruptly and hunched his shoulders in what she now recognized as a symptom of discomfiture. "It was just an impulse. If you already have dinner on…"

Colleen made a decision without conscious thought. "No, that sounds wonderful," she admitted. "I was just staring hopelessly into the cupboards. I think the can of chili was beating out the box of macaroni and cheese."

"Gross," Drew exclaimed.

"So my son, at least, will be eternally grateful." Colleen smiled at Michael. "Why don't you come on in while I try to round up Kim."

Which wasn't hard, since Colleen knew exactly where her daughter was. Kim was sulking out on the back-porch swing because some girl at school, who had been casually friendly, mentioned that she took horseback riding lessons at a stable outside town. Kim had immediately decided that if she had something in common with the other girl—namely, riding lessons—they would become bosom buddies. Coldhearted Mom hadn't even called the stable for prices before informing her daughter there was no way the budget would stretch that far.

What Kim didn't realize was how much it hurt Colleen to have to say no. For the hundredth time she wondered if she was being selfish in sinking everything they had into a business designed to give *her* satisfaction.

At least the prospect of going out for pizza cheered Kim up slightly, since right now Colleen couldn't afford even that very often. Better yet, at the pizza parlor Michael produced several dollars' worth of quarters so that Kim and Drew could play video games. For once the best of friends, they took off for the game room, leaving a peaceful oasis behind.

"Thank you," Colleen said quietly.

"They are my niece and nephew."

"True. It's just that I don't think of you…" Colleen stumbled to a halt, flushing. Oh, Lord. She must be tired to let something like that slip.

A glint of humor in his eyes, Michael lifted a dark brow. "What is it you don't think of me as?"

Resigned, Colleen admitted, "An uncle. A brother-in-law." She let out a breath. Would it help to put into words her unease with him, or would it add to the unspoken tension between them? "I'm not sure why, but I've just never felt like I knew you very well. Relatives are supposed to be…comfortable. Familiar."

The smile faded from his eyes, leaving something nameless in its wake. "Yeah, I know. It's been mutual."

So she hadn't imagined his stiffness toward her.

He was still talking. "Strange, too, when you look so much like—" he paused, the muscles along his jaw clenching "—her."

Colleen ignored the burning feeling in her nose that usually presaged tears. "Do you know, Sheila always said how much we looked alike, but I never thought we did. Even clothes didn't look the same on us." Colleen had a flash of remembrance, in which her fifteen-year-old sister paraded in front of the mirror in Colleen's sweater with a panache she herself would never have. The image faded just as the first tear fell. Starkly Colleen said, "Sheila sparkled."

Michael handed her a napkin. After Colleen had blown her nose he said abruptly, "Yes, she did. You know how I used to think of her? A stream running over rocks. The way sunlight glints off it, and the little trills it makes…" He swallowed and bowed his head. His eyes had a damp sheen when he lifted them to Colleen, and there was something almost angry in his voice. "When you were together, you and Sheila, I thought about that stream. She was the rapids and you were the deep pool below."

Colleen stared at him. Idiotically she said, "You mean, the one with the trout?"

His gaze was locked on her face. Only after a long, taut moment did he blink and give his head a small shake. "Yeah," he said, sounding oddly far-off. "The one with the trout and all the shades of green. Cold and clear, but somehow shadowy, too."

What an extraordinary conversation, Colleen thought. She couldn't quite decide whether she ought to feel flattered or insulted. What was most astonishing was how apt the analogy was, considering he didn't know her well.

From the time Sheila was born, she'd been in motion, chattering, dancing, at the playground swinging higher than everyone else, at parties the center of an admiring crowd. People had always been drawn to her glittering orbit, as though life could be lived more intensely in her presence.

Colleen had often been grateful she was the older of the two, because if their birth order had been reversed, she would have been fated to live in her sister's shadow. As it was, teachers and swim instructors and even her mother's friends had known her first, so there was no disappointment.

Colleen was well aware that she was different: quieter, slower to commit herself, more thoughtful. She had never laughed as easily, never effortlessly charmed anyone, didn't *feel* as passionately. Yet she was content enough with who she was, had her own strengths. Sheila might have chosen vivid, memorable colors and fabrics had she been making a quilt, but she lacked the patience to set the thousands of tiny stitches to create a masterpiece. As sisters and friends, they had balanced each other well. Perhaps that was why Colleen felt now as if Sheila had leapt off the other end of a seesaw, dropping her with a painful thud to the ground.

"I miss her," Colleen said, and balled the napkin in one hand.

Michael's mouth twisted. "She always drove too fast." A

mere observation, it was also an epitaph, symbolic of her entire life—and of its end.

They might have been in a bubble, she and Michael, separated from the noisy families and teenagers by its fragile, transparent walls. Colleen had never felt closer to him than she did now. Perhaps that was why she blurted out her single greatest regret. "Why couldn't Sheila have lived long enough to hold the baby?"

Michael sucked in a breath as though she had struck him, or perhaps she had only surprised him. He opened his mouth as though to say something, swallowed and managed to say huskily, "At least she knew you were pregnant."

Colleen had to blow her nose again. "I'm sorry. I'm not helping matters, am I?"

He seemed not to hear her. He was staring down into his mug of beer. "She's not the only one who wanted a child, you know."

Startled, Colleen met his gaze when he lifted it to look almost fiercely at her. Slowly she said, "I wondered sometimes."

"I always wanted one, even though I learned to accept that children wouldn't be part of our lives. Sheila couldn't. It was an obsession with her. Sometimes I thought... Oh, hell." His voice had thickened and he closed his eyes for a moment to regain control. "I thought she was so full of life herself it was an especially cruel irony that her body wouldn't let her create life."

Before Colleen could answer, she saw her kids wending their way through the tables toward her. Michael must have seen them, too, because he handed her another napkin.

She quickly swiped at her wet cheeks. "Oh, Lord, all I do is cry these days."

Michael shoved back the bench and stood. "That's our number being called." He set a course to intercept Drew and Kim, and when he spoke briefly to them, they turned to follow him.

Colleen was grateful for the couple of minutes he'd given her to compose herself. She hated to cry so much in front of her children. As many changes and upsets as they'd had in their lives the past few years, it was important that they had at least one parent who gave them a sense of safety, of certainty. She had to mourn, of course, but she knew they'd be frightened if they had any idea how scared and alone she really felt.

Her eyes were probably still red, but she hoped the dimness of the pizza parlor disguised that when she smiled at her daughter, who arrived with a tray of drinks. "So, did you set any new records on the video games?"

Kim gave her a searching look, but only shrugged. "I'm not very good."

"There are more important things in life to be good at."

The eleven-year-old rolled her eyes. "You don't have to tell me again. I know, I know. School's more important."

"It's boring," Drew said, handing out the plates.

Michael's gaze met Colleen's over her son's head. His mouth twitched. "School gets better as you go along. You can't say that about many things."

Kim's lip curled just enough to express her opinion. "I'm in fifth grade, and it hasn't gotten any better."

"Well, now, that's not quite true," Colleen reminded her. She reached out to break the string of cheese that stretched from her plate to the pizza. "Think back to Miss Fisher in kinder-garten."

"I remember her yelling all the time."

"Do you also remember how you pretended you were sick so you could stay home?"

"Not really, but…"

"First grade was no picnic, either. You cried every Monday morning."

"Well, yeah, but…"

"Come on, be honest." Colleen raised her eyebrows. "Fifth grade's not really so bad, is it?"

Kim wrinkled her nose in an expression that made her look unsettlingly like Sheila at that age. "Okay," Kim conceded. "I guess it's getting better."

"It can't get any worse," Drew muttered, shoving the last bite of his pizza in his mouth. "Can I have some more?"

Michael gave him another piece. "Come on," he said, "you must like some subject."

"Well…" Drew screwed his face up as if the question required painful thought. "Science is cool," he finally said. "Miss Cole has a black widow spider in an aquarium. She's gonna have babies."

"Miss Cole?" Michael asked with a straight face.

"No! The spider. Thousands and thousands of them."

Colleen set down her pizza. "Dare I ask what Miss Cole is going to do with them?"

Her son shrugged. "I don't know. Some of the kids are scared to sit on that side of the room, but I don't mind. Friday I pretended I was going to knock over the aquarium. Nicole screamed."

"Gee, I wonder why," Colleen murmured.

Surprisingly Michael grinned. "You know what I did when I was your age? Caught a rattlesnake in the apple orchard by the school and chased girls with it."

"Cool," Drew breathed. "You didn't get bit?"

Kim was gazing, horror-struck, at her uncle. Colleen shook her head. "Give him ideas, why don't you?"

"Actually, it was dumb as hell," Michael admitted. "I wore leather gloves, but I could easily have gotten bitten on my arms. I knew better, but I seem to recall that Timothy Chandler had called me a chicken."

"How come?" Drew asked.

"Don't remember that part." Michael shook his head. "All I do remember is spending the rest of the school year on detention. Not to mention being grounded at home."

"Wow." Drew chewed in silence for a minute, an unnervingly thoughtful expression on his face. At last he asked, "Did you go to my school?"

"Uh-huh. Doubt if you'd still find a rattlesnake in town anymore, though. It's a wonder the orchard is still there. School was on the outskirts in my day."

"You've lived here your whole life?" Kim asked.

"Not quite. I went away to college and worked in a bank in Seattle for a few years. That's when I met your aunt Sheila. After we married I decided to take a job here in Clayton."

"How come we haven't met your parents, then?" Drew demanded.

He smiled easily at the boy. "Because they've retired to Florida. They got tired of our winters, I guess. My brother took over the wheat farm. You've met him, I think."

"Is he our cousin or something?"

Colleen forgot to eat as she listened to Michael explaining that technically his brother wasn't related to Drew or Kim at all. The conversation progressed to first cousins and second cousins once removed, Michael quizzing them until Kim giggled. Nobody seemed to notice Colleen's silence; Michael continued to banter with the kids, and both of them, Drew especially, responded in a way that made her wonder whether they didn't miss their father more than she had guessed.

If she was suspicious, she'd think that Michael was making a special effort with her children in an attempt to demonstrate to her that he really was cut out to be a father. She certainly didn't recall him ever doing more than nodding hello or goodbye before.

And yet he related to them so easily. Didn't his brother have two girls? But Colleen didn't remember Sheila mentioning the nieces often, which surely she would have if she and Michael were a big part of their lives.

Colleen wished she knew what Michael was thinking. Under other circumstances it wouldn't have mattered why he was teasing Kim or listening to Drew's account of his escapades. But as things stood, it did. It mattered so much she couldn't trust her instincts. If she was to give up the baby, she had to be very sure that Michael would love him or her as much as Sheila would have. As much as she herself would.

Under the table, Colleen touched her stomach in an absurd need for reassurance that the gentle swell was still there, that she really was pregnant, that the baby was safe.

She had five and a half months to decide, she reminded herself; until then, nobody could make her give up her child.

Her doubts hadn't been erased by the time Michael dropped the kids and her off, but her general feelings toward him were positive.

Even so, she didn't leave an opening for him to insinuate himself into her home. When he reached for his door handle, she said quickly, "I'd better say good-night now. The kids have homework, and I usually try to put in an hour or two of quilting."

"Mom," Drew whined. "I don't have that much to do...."

Colleen silenced him a look. "Did you thank Uncle Michael for the pizza and all those quarters?"

Both children did so, then raced each other for the front door. Colleen was instantly aware of Michael in a way she hadn't been when Drew and Kim were bickering in the back seat. Her days were spent with women in the feminine world of her quilt shop. Since her divorce, she had become unused to men. In the close confines of the car, Michael seemed very large, his gaze disturbingly perceptive if guarded.

"Do you make quilts for sale?"

"On occasion." Colleen hoped he couldn't see through her outward composure. "In this case, a woman came to me with a quilt top that was a family heirloom, but it had never been quilted. It's very old and lovely, and I'm excited to have a chance to finish such beautiful work."

"I'll bet you're not charging enough."

In surprise Colleen asked, "What makes you think that?"

His smile was a little wry. "Sheila talked about your generous impulses. Was this one of them?"

Flustered, Colleen said, "I figured a job like this was good advertising. Mrs. Neely—do you know the family?—seems to be involved in everything going on in the community. If she's pleased and shows the quilt off..."

"Everyone else will figure they can take advantage of you, too."

"What a pessimistic outlook!"

"An occupational hazard." Michael nodded at her stomach. "How are you feeling?"

"Just fine," she said. "Michael, thanks for dinner. You were a lifesaver tonight."

Her evasion didn't work.

"Are you seeing the doctor regularly?"

"You asked me that already," Colleen said a little tartly. "I've done this before, you know."

"What does he say?"

"*She* tells me that everything is going exactly as it should be. There's not a whole lot a doctor can offer at this point. I'm not old enough to need amniocentesis, and the initial ultrasound doesn't show that much."

"Then what does she do?"

"Are you afraid I'm not getting my money's worth?"

He chose that moment to turn his head away and gaze out the windshield. "It ought to be *my* money's worth, but let's not make that the issue."

"Then what is?" she snapped.

He didn't answer immediately. When he did Michael still wasn't looking at her. "I'm…curious," he said, his tone stiff. "Unlike you, I haven't done this before. If Sheila and I'd had a baby in the usual way, I might have been going with her to appointments."

Shame washed over Colleen. Why was she so determined to think the worst of him? Of course he was interested; the baby was his, too. She kept forgetting that. This wasn't—yet—a competition between them.

"I'm sorry," she said past the lump in her throat. "I wasn't thinking. I take for granted stuff that seemed pretty amazing the first time around. Like the fact that the doctor will probably be listening to the baby's heartbeat by the next visit."

His eyes, so very blue, swung back to her and held her pinned. "She can hear the heartbeat? So soon?"

Colleen nodded. "Somehow that makes it seem real, doesn't it? To think that there's already another heart beating inside of me…." Just saying it brought back the awe she felt at the wondrous, mysterious business of creating life. There were no words powerful enough to describe it. "Well," she finally said, and cleared her throat. "If you wanted to come sometime… I'm sure you could listen."

He looked at her for a long moment. "You'd let me do that?"

Colleen floundered. "I...if you wouldn't feel embarrassed...."

"Does this doctor know why you're having the baby?"

Colleen bowed her head, staring down at her fingers, which twined nervously together. "There hasn't been any reason to tell her."

Michael's voice was hard now. "The plan was that you'd hand the baby over to us immediately in the hospital. I think it's fair to expect that the nurses and the doctor should know that ahead of time."

Anger flared. "I've only been to see the doctor once since the initial appointment. My sister had died the week before. The *plan* was the last thing on my mind."

Answering anger flickered in his eyes, then died. He turned again to stare ahead through the windshield, his hands wrapped so tightly around the steering wheel his knuckles were white. "You're right. It's my turn to apologize."

"Accepted," Colleen said very crisply. Opening her car door, she added, "Now, if you don't mind, I'll say good-night."

She slammed the door without allowing him a chance to respond. Hurrying up the walk, Colleen began to feel a little guilty for not thanking him again for dinner. On the other hand, he'd given her even more reason to suspect that this evening had been an investment on his part. He was obviously afraid she had changed her mind about giving the baby to him and figured he should remind her of his rights.

Was that so bad? Colleen wondered. Why didn't she just reassure him? A single parent already struggling financially, she wasn't really thinking she would keep this baby and raise it alone.

Was she?

Yes, but did he have rights, Colleen reminded herself, taking one side of the dialogue—or was it an argument?—she'd been silently conducting for the past week. She had implied—okay, *said*—that he would be welcome to come to her next appointment.

She remembered again the leap of interest, hope, in his eyes. This baby was his; he would be the one to carry the swaddled bundle out of the hospital, to buckle it gently into a car seat. The one to stumble out of bed in the dark hours, to sleepily stand by the microwave waiting for the formula to heat, the one to kiss the soft, fuzzy top of her child's head, breathing in the scent of baby and knowing the joy of cradling this tiny person.

She should have felt better because she could so easily picture him doing all that. Instead, her heart was squeezed in the grip of a sense of loss so profound she couldn't face it. Her mind yanked a curtain in front of the hurtful images, letting her deal rationally with the irrational.

His baby, she reminded herself. Never hers. He had a right to be part of the excitement and the choices made while the infant was still part of her.

Her hand reached for the telephone, hesitating yet again before lifting the receiver.

Maybe he was the father, but he wasn't in a relationship with her. She didn't *want* him there when the doctor lifted her shirt and gently palpated her abdomen. She didn't want Michael bending down with a stethoscope to hear the tiny thud, thud, of the baby's heartbeat.

But she had promised. *His baby,* that internal voice whispered.

On a long sigh, Colleen picked up the phone and dialed. Once she had identified herself, his secretary assured her that Mr. Delaney was in. A few clicks later, Michael said, "Hello, Colleen."

"Hello. I, um, called to let you know that my next doctor appointment is tomorrow. If you're really interested in coming—"

"What time?"

"Two o'clock. At the women's clinic on Second."

"I'll look forward to it."

Colleen hung up and took a deep breath. Her heart was racing as hard as if she had just committed herself to going up in the next space shuttle. Really, this was no big deal. If she'd still been alive, Sheila would have been going with her. Colleen ignored the sudden knot of pain and told herself she would think of Michael as a stand-in.

That was harder to do when the time actually came. Michael was already there when she arrived five minutes early at the clinic. She had the same sense of unreality she always did when she first saw him. In a dark, well-cut suit, he was formidably handsome, so effortlessly magnetic she felt both drawn and repelled. He was not the kind of man she'd been used to.

Her hesitation was brief. Feeling his eyes on her, she checked in at the front desk. When she went over to Michael, he set down the *Time* magazine he'd been thumbing through.

"You're here," she said. Brilliant. She could almost hear her son's favorite response. *Duh.*

She half expected some slightly more sophisticated sarcasm from Michael, but he only inclined his head. Before Colleen could take a seat or make some other intelligent remark, the nurse called her name.

Colleen felt unusually self-conscious during the familiar ritual, especially the weighing-in. She couldn't see Michael behind her, and she could only hope he had the good manners not to watch. Fortunately she hadn't gained an excessive amount. All she needed was to be chided in front of him.

In the examining room the nurse checked her blood pressure and pulse, then said cheerily, "The doctor will be with you shortly," and exited, closing the door behind her.

Colleen hadn't realized until now how tiny the examining room was. In trying to think of something to say, she became very conscious of her social inadequacies. They were made worse by the fact that Michael clearly wasn't in a chatty mood. He answered her feeble conversational forays with monosyllables. The wait seemed interminable, although it couldn't have been more than five minutes.

Just as the silence was becoming unendurable—and as Colleen was wondering whether Michael might actually be nervous—the doctor breezed in. A no-nonsense, middle-aged woman with a faint Scandinavian accent, she didn't look surprised to see Michael. "Ah, the father."

Colleen hadn't figured out what she would do if the doctor had said, "Ah, your husband." Fortunately she was saved. Of course maybe Michael would feel compelled to explain the situation. But their eyes met, very briefly, and then he stood and held out his hand. "Michael Delaney."

Dr. Kjorsvik shook it, then turned to Colleen. "How are you feeling?"

"Just fine." Not for anything would she have admitted it if she *wasn't* fine, not in front of him.

"Well, let's take a look." Colleen lay back when she was told to. Dr. Kjorsvik's deft fingers lifted her blouse, exposing the pale swell of stomach. She felt her way around for a moment, her gaze unfocused. Then she lifted the stethoscope to her ears and bent forward, pressing the cold diaphragm to Colleen's abdomen. "Hm," she murmured, and moved it. "Um-hm…ah." She lifted her head to smile at Colleen. "Clear as a bell."

No matter that she had been through this twice before, Colleen still felt the thrill. "Really?"

"You sound surprised," Dr. Kjorsvik said indulgently, then turned to Michael. "Would Dad care to listen?"

It should have been hugely embarrassing, but somehow wasn't. The wonder in his eyes erased any awkwardness. For nearly the first time, Colleen felt a connection between them, stripped to its essentials. He stayed very still and listened for the longest time. "Amazing," he murmured, and his reluctance was obvious when he gave the stethoscope back to the doctor.

She stuffed it in the pocket of her white coat. "Indeed it is. Tiny as the fetus is right now, he or she is already growing hair, even eyelashes. And fingernails and toenails. We're getting somewhere."

And then she breezed out, tossing over her shoulder a few instructions for Colleen.

Colleen didn't hear them. She had just discovered that her cheeks were wet with tears. Hurriedly she pulled her blouse down and rolled to one side to sit up, an operation she wouldn't be able to accomplish with much dignity in just a few more months. Her back to Michael, she surreptitiously wiped her cheeks.

The weird thing was that she had no idea why she was crying. Something had happened just now, deep inside her, as disorienting as the shifting of a fault in the earth's crust, but she couldn't yet describe the movement, even to herself. All she knew was that it had to do with this baby, this tiny being who would be laid in her arms, who would be born knowing how to root for her breast, who would recognize her voice and turn instinctively to her, the mother. It had to do with Michael, who had let her see how badly he wanted this baby and how much it would hurt him never to hold it. But there was more; there was her own father, whom she'd barely known, the husband who had walked out. There was the close circle of her mother and sister and her, and the aching loneliness she felt now without its warm embrace. Like a jigsaw puzzle, all the pieces had been jumbled, but not yet fitted together into a whole.

She breathed in slowly, deeply, and decided she wouldn't think about it right now. Later, she promised herself.

Cheeks dry, a lump in her throat, Colleen slid off the examining table. It took courage to face Michael and to accept her purse from him. Even her voice sounded odd to her. "Ready?"

He opened the door, but still blocked it. "Are you taking the vitamins she recommended?"

The question was so mundane, so far from her disorganized thoughts, she stared at him blankly before she took it in. Then she said, "Yes, of course."

"You're not worrying about your weight too much, are you?"

"I'm gaining enough weight," Colleen admitted, her cheeks warming.

"Good." He hesitated, then stepped aside.

She hurried past, holding herself stiffly to avoid brushing against him. In the waiting room, the receptionist looked up and smiled. "Would you like to make your next appointment?"

"Yes, thank you." To Michael, who had paused, too, Colleen said, "You go ahead. There's no reason for you to wait."

"All right." Those blue eyes met hers squarely. "Thank you," he said in a low voice.

Colleen gave a jerky nod and turned away, although she was preternaturally conscious of the door opening and closing behind him. It took only a minute to make the appointment for the following month.

Colleen was closing her purse when she remembered something. "Oh, shoot, I meant to bring you a claims form. Can I stick it in the mail?"

The receptionist waved an elegantly manicured hand. "Oh, we don't need it. Your husband already took care of the bill."

For a shocked instant, Colleen stared at the young woman. No wonder Michael had gotten here early. And left so willingly.

She managed to nod. "Thank you."

His BMW was easy to spot. He was just backing out. Colleen cut across the parking lot, telling herself she had a right to be angry. It felt good, healthy. In some part of her mind, she knew she *wanted* to dislike him. Had wanted to all along.

He saw her coming in the rearview mirror and braked. Just as she reached the car, his window glided down. "Is something wrong?" he asked.

"How dare you?" she said in a voice that shook.

His dark brows drew together. "What the hell...?"

"You knew perfectly well I'd resent your going behind my back to pay the doctor."

Michael's mouth thinned. "We have an agreement."

She was almost blind with her anger and her need to lash out at him. Very distinctly Colleen said, "You mean, my sister and I had an agreement. You and I never did."

Chapter 4

Even through her haze of anger, Colleen was chilled by the icy set of Michael's expression. But she was driven by a force too powerful, too instinctive, to allow reason to govern her behavior. She was a mother protecting her young, unable to convince herself this man was not the enemy.

His voice was dangerously soft. "Are you trying to tell me something?"

"You're darn right I am. Quit pressuring me!"

Pure rage flickered in his eyes. "I'll quit pressuring you the day you sign a contract confirming *our* verbal agreement. I know you were doing this for Sheila and not me. But she's gone, and I'm still here. And this baby is as much—no, damn it!—*more* mine than hers. By God, you're not stealing it from me."

His window glided up with the force of a door slamming, and the BMW shot away, tires squealing. Colleen jumped back. She was left standing in the parking lot, shaking, nauseated, angry.

And scared. Had she really threatened to keep the baby?

"Oh, Lord," she whispered. Startled by the honk of a horn, she collected herself enough to get out of the way of an oncoming minivan and go to her own car. She waited there until her hands quit shaking before she even attempted to start the engine.

Colleen managed—almost—to block the ugly scene from her mind. How else could she get through the day? In between waiting on customers, she spent the afternoon hanging a display of 1920s- and 1930s-era quilts borrowed from the local historical society, which didn't have the space to show them all.

Handling them would have been undiluted pleasure had her emotions not been in such turmoil. Most of these quilts had been treasured, probably seldom used, and the colors were as fresh as the day they'd been stitched together. They were bright and cheerful, with the gaiety of a flower garden full of annuals. Here was none of the subtlety of contemporary quilts, or the faded tints of nineteenth-century fabrics. The patterns were traditional: two Wedding Ring quilts, a Log Cabin, a Fence Rail and a Grandmother's Flower Garden. The stitching was fine, reflecting a skill nearly forgotten until the revival of the past decade.

And the texture… She would have loved quilts even if she'd been blind, Colleen thought, savoring the close-quilted layers between her fingers. There was comfort in the feel of a quilt, somehow stiff and soft at the same time, warmth that embraced a baby even as it had the strength to endure the centuries.

It was time she began a quilt for the baby. *Her* baby. The doing would comfort her, and if she started soon, her labor of love might not be tainted by knowledge of the future. Right now, for this brief time, the baby was a possibility, not a reality. Boy or girl, redhead or brunette, blue-eyed or brown, this oddly conceived child could be anything. Although the ache of loss played in the back of her mind, Colleen didn't yet have to face handing over her baby to the near stranger who was the father. Whatever the future held, the quilt would be her gift of love.

She knew without second thoughts what pattern she would use. Carousel Horses, intricately pieced in jewel colors, would chase each other among the clouds, puffy and white and layered. No border, she thought, nothing to confine them.

In quiet moments before closing, Colleen chose several fabrics, including a cloud print in a bluish white, knowing even as she concentrated on the details that it was a form of self-protection. This process was natural for her, and as long as she immersed herself in it, she could pretend that this pregnancy was just like her others.

At home she cooked dinner, helped Kim with homework on fractions and did flash cards with Drew. After they were in bed, Colleen cleaned up the kitchen and worked on Mrs. Neely's quilt, stretched in her quilt frame. Keeping her hands busy, however mindless the task, prevented her from thinking. She was safe.

Until she showered and, while rubbing her hair dry, glanced up to see herself reflected in the long mirror on the door. The sight was familiar and yet not; her skin was pale and she was still slender, but there were changes, subtle but unmistakable. Her breasts were fuller and her belly gently swelling. With the symmetrical oval of her face, she might have been a Renaissance madonna, the embodiment of the mysteries of womanhood.

Colleen gave her head a firm shake and looked again, more realistically. Botticelli wouldn't have liked the tiny lines traced beside her eyes, the freckles sprinkled on her nose, the sags here and there. His madonna was young and innocent, not the mother of an almost teenager.

"I must have been crazy," Colleen said aloud. But in her heart she knew she would do it all over again. For Sheila.

Curled in bed, staring at the faint light coming in the window from streetlamps, Colleen relived the scene in the parking lot.

My sister and I had an agreement. You and I never did.

She was still a little shocked at her own defiance. She was already the single mother of two children; she was already cutting every corner that could be cut just to scrape by financially from month to month. How could she add a baby to her burdens? Never mind the fact that he or she would be another mouth to feed, another child entitled to swimming lessons and Little League and band, all of which had to be paid for. No, it was the cost of day care that made the whole idea ludicrous, impossible.

Michael, a banker, could afford the best of everything for this baby. He could hire a nanny, buy a piano and a show horse and lessons to go with each, add a red Corvette for his child's sixteenth birthday. He could pay for an expensive private college. All of which would have sounded meaningless, except that she also knew he'd give something more important yet— love. She had seen it on his face today when he'd listened to those miraculous heartbeats, the beginning of his child's life.

And hadn't she promised her sister she would never, even for a minute, think of this baby as hers? Hadn't she said the baby is yours—and Michael's? How could she go back on her word now?

Colleen knew what she was doing. With all the precision of a quilt-maker, she was piecing a relentless, painful pattern excluding herself and her own hunger to hold this baby and never let go. She was employing cold reason to dam the flood of emotion.

Her bitter regret told her she'd succeeded, at least for now.

Michael was wrestling with the coffee machine when Colleen called the next morning. He wasn't a gourmet-coffee drinker; caffeine came more conveniently in a spoonful of dark granules. But Sheila had to have this damned, elaborate, high-tech coffee-maker, so he'd bought it for her for Christmas. The Christmas barely past, the one full of shining promise, thanks to Colleen.

The stupid machine sat on the gleaming tile countertop, too big to shove into hiding, reproaching him day after day. Just a week before, cursing, he had finally used it. Now, frowning, he was stabbing buttons when the phone rang.

Absently he reached for the receiver and grunted, "Yeah?"

"Michael? This is Colleen."

He forgot the coffeemaker and braced his hands on the countertop, hunching one shoulder to hold the receiver to his ear. "Colleen," he said neutrally.

Her voice was constrained. "I, um, lost my temper yesterday. I want to apologize."

He waited, knowing he should say something about losing his own temper, too, maybe express regret for driving away as he had, but his vocal cords seemed paralyzed.

After a moment she went on, sounding still more repressed, even lifeless. "I want you to know I wasn't implying I intend to keep the baby. I just…resent being coerced. Maybe more than I should, because I understand your worries. But I'm a little…raw emotionally right now."

His voice came out hoarse. "I'm the one who should apologize. Sheila had complete faith in you. I guess I'm showing a character flaw by being a suspicious bastard."

There was a small silence. Then, "I haven't given you very many reasons to trust me."

"God!" he said explosively, squeezing his eyes shut. "Your pregnancy is a gift. A decent man wouldn't demand a receipt along with it."

"Is that what you want? A bill of sale?"

"Apparently," he admitted. "An occupational hazard." Either that, or the insecurity of a man never very sure of his parents' love, or even his wife's.

"Well, I can't give you that, not yet." He thought he heard a sniff, and her next words were choked. "I won't promise, but I do know the baby is yours. I know you have…rights."

"I won't ask for anything else now," Michael said quickly. What she'd offered wasn't enough—he wanted promises signed in blood—but he recognized a concession when he heard it. Whatever else happened, Colleen was the mother of his baby, and he was increasingly certain she would continue to be. That he wouldn't be able to walk away, the sole possessor of his son or daughter. That he wouldn't be able to pretend the woman who had borne his child didn't exist.

He didn't even know if he wanted to.

"Well—" she definitely sniffled "—that's all I had to say. I'm sure I'll be talking to you."

"Colleen."

"Yes?" She sounded wary.

"Thank you."

She didn't ask what he was thanking her for, didn't say, "You're welcome." Instead, he heard the quiet click of the connection being cut.

It was a moment before he restored the receiver to its cradle, a moment during which he wondered where he now stood. Was he supposed to wait, doing nothing, while she made up her mind? Had Colleen meant only that she acknowledged his paternity, or that she knew she would have to hand over the baby? Would calls or visits be welcome or at least tolerated, or would both qualify as coercion?

Michael settled for a quick bowl of cereal and took his mug of strong, dark coffee with him in the car. It was getting harder, instead of easier, to live in that house, permeated with Sheila's personality. With more time and interest than he had, she'd chosen the furniture, papered the walls, curled her toes into the thick carpet. The colors were hers, the dishes, the brands he bought from habit at the grocery store.

He always had the feeling she'd walk back in any minute. No, not walk; she hardly ever moved so sedately. Danced, twirled, hurried. She'd been restless, tending to choose colors and furnishings that were stunning but unsettling, as though she hated being soothed.

Would the baby have changed her, brought her long-lasting contentment? She could be so fickle, her interests intense but short-lived. Even her friendships seemed transitory. Only her closeness to her sister and her desperate need for a baby had endured.

He recognized his thoughts for the criticism they were. They brought familiar, sharp-edged guilt that he didn't analyze. He was in no mood to contemplate his own lacks, which undoubtedly were responsible for the emptiness Sheila had sought so hungrily to fill.

He didn't know how good a mother she would have been; what counted now was how good a father he would be. Whether he liked it or not, he might well be in competition with Colleen, should their battle reach the courts.

Mrs. Neely ran her fingers over the soft folds of the magnificent Basket of Tulips quilt. When she'd brought the top to the store, she'd told Colleen how it had been appliquéd by her grandmother, then folded away in a trunk and never layered and quilted. Colleen had finished quilting and binding it only yesterday; the moment she called, the woman had hurried over.

Mrs. Neely was blinking back tears when she lifted her head. She groped in her purse for a tissue. "Oh, dear. I'm being silly. It's just that I can't help thinking how happy my grandmother would be to know her quilt has been finished. And so beautifully."

"Maybe she does know," Colleen suggested. From the beginning she felt an odd connection to the quilt's maker. She had never even seen a picture of her, yet she knew so much about her, this woman who had cut and appliquéd hundreds of tiny pieces with such care, and chosen colors so exuberant. Colleen had almost felt herself being watched as she worked, filling the background with a crosshatched design that gave the quilt texture and emphasized the beauty of the appliqué.

At her comment, Mrs. Neely had an arrested expression. "What a lovely thought. Do you know, I have the funniest feeling she does know. Oh, my dear, thank you so much. The money is totally inadequate—"

"Nonsense," Colleen interrupted with a smile. "The pay was not only generous, I'm grateful for the chance to finish such an exquisite quilt."

"Your own are just as beautiful," the older woman said. "Have you started a crib quilt yet?"

"A crib quilt?" Stupidly, she didn't understand.

"You are expecting, aren't you?"

Colleen felt the heat rush over her cheeks and the anguish tighten her throat. "I…yes, I…"

"Oh, dear. Was I prying?"

Somehow Colleen produced a smile of sorts. "No, no. I just didn't realize I showed yet. And…well, I'm planning a mini-show of crib quilts, and I thought for a second you were referring to it."

Even to herself, her explanation sounded weak. But Mrs. Neely was kind enough to say only, "When you reached up to the shelf for the quilt, I saw you in profile and felt sure you were pregnant." She smiled mischievously. "But I'll keep it quiet. Tell me, is your husband pleased?"

Like a projector clicking to the next picture, Colleen saw with her mind's eye Michael, bending over to listen to the baby's heartbeat, so close to her bare stomach she'd been able to feel the warmth of his breath. Colleen was disconcerted to have thought so automatically of him. Why hadn't the idea of a husband conjured up Ben?

She was flustered enough to blush again, but she returned some answer that wasn't quite a lie. Whatever it was satisfied Mrs. Neely, who caressed her quilt one more time before stuffing it back in the bag and taking her departure, leaving the much-needed check on the counter.

Alone for a precious few minutes, Colleen splashed cold water on her face in the tiny bathroom and gazed blankly at her image in the mirror. She should have anticipated this, planned what she would say. Of course people would start noticing soon! And while men in an office might not comment, her women customers surely would.

In the back of her mind, Colleen had intended to tell the truth. Sheila had popped into the shop often enough so that regular customers had met her. The community was so small, some had already known her.

But it was different now; everything was different. Colleen didn't even understand her own chaotic feelings. How could she tell people she was giving this baby away to a man she scarcely knew just because he could afford it and she couldn't, and because of a promise to her sister who was now laid to rest in the cemetery?

Would these women sympathize with her? Or condemn her?

She took care in the next few weeks to make sure nobody else noticed. It was easy to wear clothing that disguised her shape, baggy cotton sweaters, a loose, drop-waisted jumper over a turtleneck. She would need maternity clothes soon, and of course she hadn't kept hers from her previous pregnancies. Ben hadn't wanted more children—hadn't really wanted the ones they had. And once the divorce was final, she had firmly closed the door on her vague longing for another baby. So the maternity clothes had been sold at a garage sale, along with the other detritus of her married life.

She would make some, she decided, and as she looked at patterns at the local fabric store, she thought ironically about how domestic she suddenly was. She might be any other woman anticipating a baby.

But the pain that squeezed her chest reminded her that she wasn't. What she intended to do—and must do—would hurt for the rest of her life.

Michael was silent for these short weeks, allowing her to block from her mind as much as possible the threat he represented. And yet she felt guilty, remembering his ravaged face that day in her shop. Was he grieving alone without the comfort that reminders of his unborn child would bring him?

Ridiculous! He must have friends, and he had family of his own, a brother here in Clayton. He knew her as little as she knew him, he had admitted as much. She was the last person he would come to for comfort.

And yet she was curiously unsurprised when after dinner one evening she heard a knock on the door and opened it to find Michael on her front porch. He had changed after work to well-worn jeans and a blue shirt with the sleeves rolled up. He was too handsome, really, to be standing here. He stole her breath for an instant, before she thought practically, *Well, at least the baby ought to be beautiful.*

"Hello, Michael," she said. "Come in."

That was when she noticed that his hands were shoved in his jeans pockets and that his shoulders were hunched just enough to give away his diffidence.

"If this is a bad time…"

Colleen stepped back. "No, the kids are doing homework and I was thinking about paying bills. I'd rather talk to you."

His mouth twitched. "The devil and the deep blue sea?"

She made a face. "Oh, dear. I didn't mean that quite the way it sounded." Although the analogy was all too apt, she thought ruefully.

Kim called from the kitchen, "Mom, is somebody here?"

"Uncle Michael," Colleen called back before asking him, "Would you like a cup of coffee? Or tea?"

"If you don't go to a lot of trouble."

"I never do," Colleen admitted. "I can't taste the difference. But Sheila was such a connoisseur, I know she spoiled you. Maybe I should offer you a glass of apple juice, instead."

His grin was startling and completely disarming. "To tell you the truth, I could never tell the difference, either. I lied to her."

"Coffee it is," she said, smiling back despite herself. "Have a seat in the living room."

In the kitchen she filled the kettle and turned on the burner.

"What's he want?" Kim asked.

"I suppose he's checking up on me," Colleen said dryly. She turned from the stove to find that Michael had followed her and now stood in the kitchen doorway. His eyes met hers; a muscle jumped along his jaw, and then he disappeared.

Kim lifted her head. The chair scraped as she swiveled toward the doorway.

"Did he hear you?" she whispered.

"Yup." Colleen grimaced. "That'll teach me."

Michael was now in the living room, standing with his back to her, studying a collage of photographs—herself when she graduated from college, her mother with Sheila and her as children, Ben with five-year-old Kim on his shoulders, Drew riding a two-wheeled bike for the first time. Those pictures were the story of Colleen's life, symbolic moments preserved forever.

He must have sensed her presence, because he spoke without even glancing over his shoulder. "You and Sheila looked less alike as children."

"Perhaps because of the years between us. If you compare baby or school pictures, you'd have a hard time guessing who was who."

He made a sound of acknowledgment, only then turning to face her. Bluntly he asked, "Would you prefer I stay away?"

She flushed, lifting her hands in an apologetic gesture. "What I said in the kitchen was terribly rude. I'm sorry."

His mouth twisted. "Is it so hard to believe my motives aren't completely selfish?"

"No." Colleen bit her lip. "I meant it when I said I feel raw emotionally. I'm…not at my most reasonable. I just…" She groped for words. "I'm confused. I guess I need to think all this through on my own. But as long as you don't pressure me, I'm glad to see you. Sheila would have wanted us to be friends."

Friends. It was not a word she could connect with him. She could imagine a woman lusting for him, even loving him as her sister had, but friendship? Never. He was too remote, too distrusting, too reserved emotionally.

And yet, she suddenly remembered him at the pizza parlor. *You know how I used to think of her? A stream running over rocks. The way sunlight glints off it, and the little trills it makes…* And his peculiar addendum: *You were the deep pool below…the one with the trout and all the shades of green.*

She'd been startled to find him so poetic. But the comparisons he'd drawn were more; they were revealing and unexpectedly introspective. They were the words of a man she didn't really know, a man she shouldn't jump to conclusions about.

If he agreed that Sheila would have wanted them to be friends, he didn't say so, although it seemed to her his shoulders lost their rigid set. He nodded toward the window. "Is that your quilting frame?"

Grateful that her frame didn't hold the Carousel Horses, Colleen crossed the room. "Yes. I just started this quilt. I finished the commissioned one—I mentioned Mrs. Neely, didn't I? This one I'm planning to sell."

He was suddenly uncomfortably near, although he was looking down at her work. "Did you design the pattern?"

"No. This is a traditional one called Burgoyne Surrounded. See?" She touched the small white squares that were in sharp contrast to the rich blue background. "This is the Revolutionary army surrounding General Burgoyne's forces at Saratoga.

Or so the story goes. Actually, I've never heard of an example of the pattern any earlier than the 1850s or '60s, so heaven knows how it got its name."

Michael lifted his head to look at her, and she was lost, inescapably trapped by the vivid blue of his eyes. They were so penetrating she felt stripped of the pretense that had made her chatter. Curiously, she was able to note quite clinically in another part of her brain that his eyes were the precise shade of the quilt. Had she been thinking of him when she chose that fabric?

Like an idiot, she blurted, "I wonder if the baby will have your eyes."

Michael blinked, and some emotion flickered across his face. "Or your hair." He sounded gruff and cleared his throat. "You have beautiful hair."

When he lifted his hand to touch it, carefully winding a tendril around his finger, Colleen quit breathing. She was shockingly conscious that his hand was inches from her breast, and she was humiliated by her own awareness.

As much for herself as him, she whispered, "Sheila's was exactly the same color."

The hair slipped off his finger and his hands curled into fists as he withdrew them and shoved them into his pockets. She saw his face twist as he turned away.

"Yes," he said hoarsely.

Colleen touched his arm. "I didn't mean to remind you."

What she prayed was that he would never guess she had needed to remind *herself* that it was her sister he was thinking about. Not her.

"I don't need reminding." His voice was like skin scraped over gravel. When he turned to look at her, his face was still contorted. "I never forget."

"Mom!" Kim yelled from the kitchen. "The water's all going to boil away!"

"Oh, no," Colleen said guiltily. "I forgot about the coffee. If you'll excuse me a minute…"

"Let's skip it." His tone was distant now, his rigid control back in place. "Maybe this wasn't such a good idea."

"This?"

"Coming here." Michael rotated his shoulders as though to relieve tension. "Visiting." There was something ironic in the way he said the last.

Puzzled by his withdrawal, Colleen studied him. "Would you rather we don't talk about Sheila?"

Muscles bunched in his jaw. "It's not…easy for me."

"Do you have anyone else you can talk to?" She stopped. "I'm sorry. That's none of my business."

They both ignored another yell from Kim. Michael frowned as he looked at Colleen. "Why are you afraid of me?"

"Afraid?" she echoed. "Don't be silly." But he only waited, and she was edgy enough to give an unconvincing laugh. "I told you I've never felt really…comfortable with you, but that's a long ways from fear."

"Maybe 'afraid' is too strong a word." He gave his head a shake. "Never mind. I seem to have that effect on people."

"You're just…hard to get to know." Though his expression had closed, Colleen felt a need to soften his harsh analysis of himself. She pressed her lips together and tried again. "Maybe I never really tried. It would've been different if I hadn't been divorced. But three's such an awkward number…."

"Yeah. But we're not three anymore." He didn't even wait to see the expression on her face. "Hell. I'm sorry."

She tried to smile. "You don't need to be."

Michael swore under his breath. "I was right. This wasn't a good idea. One memorial service was enough."

"I'm not so sure about that," Colleen said. "I was numb during the funeral. I'm more ready to mourn now than I was then. If you want to talk about Sheila…"

"I don't."

Colleen was taken aback. "Well, if you change your mind…"

"I didn't come here to cry on your shoulder." Abrupt, unemotional, he was the stranger again. "Colleen, if you need anything, including money, call."

It would have been easy to be hurt by his withdrawal. But

why should she be? Everyone dealt with grief in individual ways. And it wasn't as though she'd ever expected to feel close to her sister's husband.

"I'll remember that," Colleen said. "And if you ever want to talk, you know where I am."

Michael gave a nod and was gone, leaving her dry-eyed and emotionally wrung out. Refusing to analyze her feelings, she went to the kitchen.

Her daughter looked up from her math book and said self-righteously, "I turned the burner off. I didn't want the house to burn down."

With a certain amount of restraint, Colleen said, "Thank you."

"Did Uncle Michael leave?"

"Uh-huh. I'm going to work upstairs. Yell if you need me."

On the way, she stuck her head into her son's room. He leapt out of hiding to deal her a mortal wound with his plastic sword.

A practiced mother, Colleen staggered and clung to the door molding. "Have mercy!"

"You die better than Evan does," Drew told her cheerfully.

She straightened. "Thanks. Time for your bath."

"Mo-om."

"Pretend I bled all over you," she suggested. "Warriors need to clean up after battles, you know."

Drew considered her point. "Oh, all right."

Her quilting frame took up so much of the living room Colleen had been forced to squeeze a good-size sewing table into her bedroom. Inching past her bed, she remembered the real-estate agent throwing open the door.

"This is the master suite," she had announced breezily.

It was neither a suite, nor contained room for a master, but Colleen managed in its limited space, which was all she could ask for. She and Ben had sold their house in California, but the equity divided two ways had left her with just enough to open the shop. Buying a house was out of the question. She'd been grateful rents were so much lower here in eastern Washington and glad to find a house that let the kids have separate bedrooms.

Colleen plugged in her iron and sat in front of her sewing machine, automatically reaching for two triangles. The pieces for the crib quilt were all cut out and neatly arranged to remind her of what went where. She lined up the edges and fed the first two triangles into her machine, then the next and the next, never lifting the feeder foot. When she had sewed everything that could be, she began snipping the thread between pieces and gently pressing seams to one side.

As Colleen half stood to lay the newly formed rectangles and squares out on the table so that she knew which seams to sew next, she felt an odd quiver deep inside her, a muscle protesting her position or a murmur of hunger or—

She froze, even quit breathing. There it was again, the tiniest of flutters, but unmistakable. She laid a hand on her belly and gently rubbed, as though this loving touch could be communicated through her skin and muscle and womb. A wondering smile trembled on her mouth even as she had to blink away tears.

There, again... It was as if a small fish were leaping inside her, as if a butterfly was breaking free of its cocoon, spreading its wings, tickling her. There was life inside her. Not even the heartbeat had convinced her, not in the way these first minute movements did.

Her womb was a cradle now, sheltering this tiny being. Soon, soon she would feel fists and toes, and this baby, amazingly growing inside her, would hear her voice and Kim's laughter and Drew's mock roars.

She wouldn't think about the time beyond that, the time when her womb became walls surrounding a space that was too small, when the baby fought to enter the new world outside.

The time when she could no longer protect her baby.

Chapter 5

Kim set a pile of dirty dishes by the kitchen sink. "Can I call Dad?"

Damn. Why now? Colleen asked silently, unanswerably.

If she—and Kim—were lucky, tonight Ben would succeed in sounding glad to hear from his daughter, interested in her life, reasonably regretful at the distance separating them.

Unfortunately those occasions were rare. Most often Kim's father was mildly annoyed at her interrupting his work or a favorite TV program or an intimate dinner with a "friend." Almost worse was when he wasn't home at all, because then Kim left a message on his answering machine. After that, for days she would leap up eagerly every time the phone rang. But the eagerness would fade, the brightness dim, because he usually forgot to return her calls.

"Of course you can," Colleen said matter-of-factly, turning on the water to rinse off a plate. "He's your father. You don't have to ask my permission."

Although she pretended not to listen, Colleen eavesdropped as she cleaned up the kitchen.

Ben was obviously there, because Kim said, "Hi, Dad. It's me." She hopped up on a bar stool at the counter. After a brief pause, she told him, "Nothing special. I just…wondered how you are."

Colleen ran water into the sink and missed the next exchange. She turned it off in time to hear Kim say, "I don't have any friends here. Well, maybe one. Our teacher moved us around in class Monday, and I'm sitting next to this girl. She's really cool, smart and popular and everything. But she acted like she doesn't mind sitting with me, and she said maybe I could come to her birthday party."

Colleen quit worrying about Ben and started worrying about this "really cool" girl. If she raised Kim's hopes of finding a friend and then smashed them, Colleen was going to…well, do something dire. Steal the black widow spider from the science room and drop it on the girl's desk.

Her instinct was so instantly protective, so fierce, that she made a face. Her kids had to fight their own battles, hard as it sometimes was to stand back. No matter how much Colleen wished she could help, Kim had to adjust to this new school alone and make her own friends. If only it was as easy for her as it was for Drew!

"Nothing's ever new," Kim was saying gloomily. "Well, except for Mom being pregnant."

Colleen's fingers tightened on the sponge. Oh, Lord. Why had she put off telling Ben herself?

"You didn't know she was pregnant?"

Colleen turned slowly to meet her daughter's eyes. Kim scrunched her face up in a look of contrition. "I'm sorry," she mouthed to her mother.

"Don't worry," Colleen said softly.

Through the receiver she could hear Ben saying something when Kim interrupted, "Um, do you want to talk to Drew?"

Colleen didn't quite have time to plug her ears before her eleven-year-old bellowed, "Drew! Dad wants to talk to you!"

His answering bellow was almost as loud. "I don't want to talk to him!"

Kim put the receiver back to her mouth and said quickly, "I guess he's doing homework or something. Well, I guess I'll talk to you later." She listened. "Oh. You want Mom?" She held out the phone. "Dad wants to talk to you."

"I wonder why," Colleen muttered. She watched her daughter beat a cowardly retreat, then took a fortifying breath and said, "Hi, Ben."

"What's this about a pregnancy?" Things could have been worse. He sounded more curious than accusatory.

Colleen sighed. "You want to know the truth? It's a mess."

"Messy affairs aren't your style."

Perversely, she half wished she could unfold a sordid tale of illicit love. If he hadn't been her children's father, she might have been tempted to manufacture one.

"I was acting as surrogate mother for Sheila. You know how she had trouble conceiving." He would know, that is, if he'd ever listened when Colleen passed on her sister's news. "Michael is the father, but it was my egg."

There was a long silence. At last Ben said, "Good God."

"That pretty much says it all."

"So, has Michael left you holding the bag?"

Just once she had to say it. "No, but I wish he had."

Another silence. Ben knew her too well. "You're the mother. You can fight him for custody."

"But I promised…"

"You could lie. Say we reconciled and it's mine."

Occasionally she remembered why she'd married Ben. The ethics of his suggestion were a little shaky, but his intentions were good.

"Thank you for the offer." Colleen smiled crookedly, even though he couldn't see her. "But they can do tests these days that establish paternity."

"Oh. Yeah. Well, hell, you *are* the mother. Why wouldn't the court award you custody?"

"Money, for one thing. He's a banker. I just started a business that isn't breaking even yet."

Her ex-husband said, "I won't offer to pay child support for this one."

Colleen was able to laugh. "I won't ask you, I promise. Although if we'd pretended we had that reconciliation…"

"Dumb idea."

Her second laugh was more genuine. "Well, I'll let you know how it goes."

"You do that." He was silent for a moment. "I take it Drew doesn't want to talk to me."

Kim had become good at making excuses. Colleen hadn't needed to, because Ben had never directly asked her. Now she didn't even hesitate.

"You take it right. He's feeling betrayed by you."

A pause. "I guess I'm not the world's greatest father."

"It wouldn't take a lot of effort to change that," she pointed out. "If you just called more often, the kids would feel like you're interested in them."

"Yeah. You're right. I'll do that."

Sure, Colleen thought cynically.

"Listen," Ben said, "if you get really hard up for money, I could probably help out."

Just like that, she felt like crying. "Thank you." She blinked hard. "That's nice of you. But I'm okay right now."

"Good, good." His agreement was a little too quick and hearty. "Say hi to Drew."

"Sure." Not that their son would be interested.

Colleen thought about Ben as she finished cleaning up the kitchen. His announcement that he wanted a divorce had been a shock. During the struggle since to manage on her own, she had surrendered to the temptation to alter her memories of Ben. She wanted to dislike him; a kernel of anger gave her strength where sadness would only have weakened her.

But once in a while she remembered the man she married, handsome in an engaging, boyish way. She thought about how he'd made her laugh, the fun they'd had dancing and going to the theater, trying out new restaurants in San Francisco, walking on the beach. Colleen had a sudden picture of Ben jumping onto a moving cable car, holding out a hand to her, grinning in a way that dared her to take chances. It was all so vivid: the crowded sidewalk, the Victorian row houses along the steep street that plunged toward the bay, the breeze ruffling his light brown hair, the sparkle in his hazel eyes and the creases in his cheeks.

Colleen dried her hands on the dish towel and hung it up, then wandered into the dark living room. She ran her fingers over the quilt stretched taut in the frame, but didn't turn on the lamp or reach for her thimble or needle.

She and Ben *had* been happy once upon a time. Their marriage had been a good one until Kim was born. No, that wasn't true. The pregnancy itself had changed everything.

It was an accident, but a welcome one as far as Colleen was concerned. They'd had several wonderful years of marriage, but gradually she had come to feel something was missing. She convinced herself most of the time that what she really needed was a new job, but other times she would see a display of baby clothes, so tiny, the fabrics so soft, or a mother jiggling a newborn against her shoulder, cooing gently, and Colleen would be stabbed by a primitive need to have a baby of her own to hold.

When she tentatively raised the subject with Ben, he dismissed it. Their condo was too small; they couldn't afford a house big enough for a family; day-care cost the world and she would get bored stuck at home. He always had an array of practical reasons why now wasn't the time. In retrospect she doubted that any time would ever have been right.

Once she was pregnant, Ben resigned himself to fatherhood. In his own way, she supposed he even loved Kim and Drew; after all, he'd agreed to the second pregnancy. But he didn't like the changes children brought, the nights he and Colleen couldn't afford to go out, her preoccupation with diapers and Kim's playgroup, the bright plastic toys that littered the living room, and even her friendships with other young mothers.

She had taken the class that started her new career when she was pregnant, with the vague idea of making a crib quilt. In the piecing and stitching of that first small project, Colleen learned a new passion, one that in some mysterious fashion gave her a sense of connection to past and future. She had never made something that would outlive her; she had never realized what a legacy had been left by women who had otherwise made little imprint on their world.

Ben resented her quilting, of course, along with her intense involvement in motherhood. Now she could understand his feelings. Suddenly he wasn't the center of her life; he must have felt as if he barely clung to the edges of it.

Well, her story was an old one, long ago concluded. Ben was what he was; somehow Kim and Drew would have to come to terms with that and realize it had nothing to do with them. But they would adjust; after all, she and Sheila had never known their father, either, and Colleen didn't remember feeling any lack. She had been mildly curious about him, that was all. Her mother had drawn a loving circle around her daughters that had made them feel safe. They hadn't needed a father.

Colleen laid her hands over her belly and felt the familiar stirring inside. This one, at least, had a father who cared. But was that enough? How would a child feel to know that his mother had given him away, not out of desperation or for his own welfare, but because he had been conceived for someone else?

"I don't know if I can do this," she whispered. "I don't know."

Michael intended to stay away, both for his sake and for Colleen's. They were grieving enough without egging each other on. Mostly he was numb now, done with the worst of it. He was empty inside, feeling almost nothing, which he knew was unnatural, but better than what had come before.

It still hurt like hell when some reminder of Sheila slipped past his guard. Like this morning, when he'd opened a drawer and there was her hairbrush with a few curling auburn hairs still clinging to the bristles. Part of her. His hand was shaking, but he hadn't been able to stop himself from touching that hair. As in his nightmare, however, he was seeing double: Sheila, shaking her short, stylish hair as she laughed, and Colleen, who had stared at him with huge, unreadable brown eyes as he fingered a lock of her hair. Alike, yet not alike.

He'd meant to stay away. So why was he sitting in his car right outside her rental house, trying to work up the guts to go knock on her door? Did he imagine that if he ingratiated himself with her, she'd willingly hand over his baby when the time came?

But he knew his reasons were more complicated than that. He felt…not protective, though that was the word that came to mind. Obligated, maybe. Colleen was carrying his baby. It was a physical and financial burden she shouldn't have to handle by herself.

He kept thinking of how alone she must feel. Colleen had moved to Clayton because of Sheila, and now Sheila was gone. Their mother had died a few years back; the father was out of the picture. Colleen was divorced, and from what Michael had seen, her husband had been damned worthless, anyway. Did Colleen have a single other friend in town? What if she got sick? Needed a loan? Just needed to talk?

"Yeah," he muttered, "and what makes you think she'd choose you to talk to?"

God knows, Sheila hadn't talked to him, not really, not the way she'd talked to her sister. He hadn't noticed at first. They'd had passion and good times and laughter. But later Michael could remember how often he passed the open bedroom door and saw Sheila sprawled on the bed, talking on the phone to Colleen. He would stand unnoticed in the hall for a moment, listening as she said things to her sister she never said to him, things he hadn't known she felt.

He still looked at other men sometimes, the ones who seemed to have happy marriages, and wondered if they lay in bed at night and talked to their wives. Could they say things in the darkness they couldn't in the daylight? Did other wives rub their cheeks against their husband's chests and murmur confidences?

Michael sometimes suspected Sheila had tried early on. He remembered times they'd made love, and she wanted to talk afterward. Her voice had poured over him, the topics all so ephemeral, so *feminine*—how she felt about something minor that had happened at work, or whether this friend seemed secretive and that one unhappy—that he had no clue how to answer.

He hadn't known—how could he have?—that she was testing him, dipping her toes into the water, and finding it too cold.

God. On a burst of frustrated energy, Michael jumped out of the car and slammed his door, striding up the walk before he changed his mind.

Colleen answered the doorbell. Surprise showed openly on her face. "Michael."

For a moment he was speechless at the sight of her. She hadn't been obviously pregnant the last time he saw her. Even at the doctor's office, her stomach had been nearly flat. But now…now her breasts were fuller and the gentle curve of her stomach pulled at the T-shirt she wore.

At the direction of his gaze, she flushed and tugged at her shirt. "I'm sorry, if I'd known you were coming…"

He shook his head abruptly. "No. I shouldn't stare. It's just…" He cleared his throat.

"I know, I know. I'm pregnant." She made a face. "In another month or two I'll look like a horse. Come on in. Can I get you—"

"I haven't had a cup of coffee here yet."

Her grin made her look younger, a pretty girl who couldn't be carrying her third child. "There's always a first time."

"Yeah." His hands felt awkward dangling at his sides, and he shoved them into his pockets. "Listen, I, uh, just wondered how you are."

Their eyes met, hers shadowed, more brown than green in this light. Her lashes fluttered and pink stained her cheeks.

"I'm…fine," Colleen said so softly he had to strain to hear. "Come on in."

He followed her to the kitchen, where Kim was hanging up the telephone. The girl's face glowed and she said wonderingly, "Lisa wants me to come to her birthday party. It's at the stables. We're going riding."

"Is that the really cool girl?" Colleen asked.

"Yes!" Kim jumped up and down, then flung herself into her mother's arms. "Oh, I can hardly wait!"

Laughing, Colleen hugged her daughter, then said pointedly, "Did you notice that Uncle Michael's here?"

"Yes, yes, yes!" Kim sang. Her feet barely touching ground, she danced to him, curtsied, said, "How do you do, sir?" and twirled out of the room.

Bemused, Michael watched her go. She flew up the stairs, singing in an uncertain soprano, her voice trailing away until it was cut off by the slam of a door.

Behind him Colleen said dryly, "I can hardly wait until she's a teenager."

"She's—" he did some quick mental calculations "—eleven?"

"Mm." She leaned a hip against the kitchen counter and shook her head. "Going on sixteen."

"Were you that skinny at her age?"

A secret smile played about Colleen's mouth as she gazed into the past. "Both of us were." She didn't seem to realize what she'd said. "I was so skinny my knees were knobby. All the other girls started getting figures, and I was still flat as a board. I was this height by the time I turned twelve. I hated P.E. The other girls looked like women. I looked like a flagpole without the flag."

Michael crossed his arms and leaned against the kitchen doorjamb. God, she was beautiful right now, her face soft, her reminiscent smile reminding him of how generous her mouth was. Even in the flat kitchen light, even pulled back in a severe ponytail, Colleen's hair shone with a rich fire. She had extraordinary eyes, too, the same color as Sheila's, but different somehow, not sparkling, more…serene. And right now her body was damned womanly. Ripe. Mysterious. Sexy.

God, she was beautiful.

Hell. How could he be attracted to her? His wife's sister. Michael swore viciously to himself and half turned away, leaning his head back against the door frame and closing his eyes.

"I'm sorry," Colleen said contritely. "I don't know why I was babbling on. Here, I'm putting water on to boil right now. See?"

He opened his eyes to find that her slender back was to him as she suited action to words.

His voice sounded a little scratchy as he said, "I, um, didn't mind your babbling."

Colleen went still for a moment, then turned slowly. Her eyes were huge in the pale oval of her face. "You didn't?"

"No." Michael moved his shoulders uneasily. This was the kind of thing that was hard for him to express. "It made me see you— And Sheila."

"She was always prettier."

"Humbug." It came out more forcefully than he'd intended, and Colleen looked surprised. Michael tried to smile. "You know, it's funny. Sheila always said the same thing. That *you* were prettier. She said she was always the little sister, skipping to catch up. But never—" he had to swallow. "Never as though she minded."

Colleen bowed her head. Her voice was next to inaudible. "I think she minded that I had children and she couldn't."

"Damn it, Colleen!"

Her head came up sharply, like a startled doe.

"You did the most incredible thing for her that any sister could. So don't start torturing yourself."

She pressed her lips together, blinked several times. Then she gave a tremulous smile. "You're right." The kettle behind her hissed softly. She didn't seem to notice. "Somehow we always end up back on the same subject, don't we? But I suppose that's inevitable. Sheila's the only thing we have in common."

"Not anymore."

She cast a quick look down at her stomach, then said in a stifled voice, "You're right. Of course."

"The pregnancy's going okay?" Put like that, it sounded impersonal, somehow outside her, like a special project he'd assigned at the bank.

"Yes." Letting the bald answer stand alone, Colleen turned away and busied herself spooning instant coffee into cups, pouring the boiling water, reaching into the refrigerator for milk.

"It's not getting in the way of work?"

With the milk carton in her hand, Colleen stopped dead. "Am I *that* huge?"

"No, I didn't mean to imply… Hell." Thank God, she looked amused by his stumblings. "It's just that I don't know that much about pregnancy," Michael tried to explain. "How uncomfortable you are."

"Well, I'm not going to take up ballet.…" She rose on her toes in a surprisingly graceful imitation of her daughter's performance. Colleen dropped back to her heels and shrugged. "But otherwise, it's business as usual. Do you want milk or sugar?"

"Black's fine." Michael accepted the mug from her, careful that his fingers didn't touch hers. "When does a woman get…"

"Enormous?" she suggested. "Grotesque?"

"I wouldn't put it that way." A little uncomfortably he said, "You look…beautiful pregnant."

Her eyes shied from his and pink touched her cheeks again. "Thank you. I wish…"

"That Sheila were here?" Strangely, he was able to say it without pain.

"That she could've been pregnant like this."

"She wouldn't have been like you," Michael said ruefully. "She'd have chafed at being slowed down, worried about her figure…"

"And gloried at the attention a pregnant woman attracts."

"Do you attract any yet?"

Another flutter of those thick lashes, calculated, he guessed, to hide her reaction. "Attract attention? I'm…starting to."

He took a deliberate swallow of coffee. "How do you handle it?"

"If you mean, do I tell them the circumstances, no, I don't."

Her tone warned that the subject was not a welcome one. Michael figured that he'd pushed it about as far as he dared. He said conversationally, "I'll bet men don't ask if you're pregnant."

"Sit down." She brought her coffee and sat at the round oak table, waiting until Michael did the same. "It's funny, I was thinking the same thing the other day. Women get personal quicker, anyway, and pregnancy is one of those shared experiences that gives us instant intimacy. But I find it a little peculiar to be comparing labors with some strange woman in line behind me at the grocery store."

"Is it—labor—very bad?" That wasn't what he'd meant to say.

Colleen looked down at her coffee mug, which she was cradling in her hands. She spoke quietly. "Not for me. Not really. There's a purpose to it all, you see. It's…different than pain from an injury."

He nodded, not knowing what to say.

"Don't worry."

"Is that what I was doing?"

She smiled. "Yes. And thank you."

The way her eyes met his, the sweetness in that smile, tugged sharply at something in his chest. Michael didn't like the feeling, didn't want to acknowledge the reason for it. So he changed the subject.

"Tell me how your business is going."

Later he wondered whether she had been as relieved as he was to discuss something relatively impersonal, or whether his earlier guess that she had nobody to talk to was right. Whatever the reason, Colleen poured out her worries, helped along by a few pointed questions from him.

They might have talked longer if they hadn't been interrupted by her son, who needed help with a homework assignment. Guessing that she would be involved with the kids until bedtime, Michael bowed out.

When Colleen repeated, as he opened the front door, "You know, you really don't have to run off," he shook his head.

"I've overstayed my welcome already." He hesitated, his hand on the doorknob. "Don't forget, if you need anything…"

"Thank you."

Michael turned to look at her. Her expression was still friendly, but also more reserved than a moment ago. He felt a sudden, fierce, almost angry longing for another smile of such sweetness, for her to mean it when she told him not to run off. He wanted…

Damn. He didn't know what he wanted. His own house not to be so empty, so cold compared to hers? Sheila to be waiting for him there? Some warmth somewhere in his life?

A moment later he started the car, ignoring his confusion, pushing it down where he'd pushed all his other emotions lately. He would have the warmth he craved once the baby was born. He'd have the kind of love he saw in Colleen's eyes when she looked at her children, and in theirs when they looked at her.

Seeing her so unmistakably, honest-to-God pregnant had done what even hearing the heartbeat hadn't—it had made the crazy business of fatherhood real for him. It had gotten him thinking.

He and Sheila had talked a little about names, but come to no conclusions. He tried to remember her favorites: Catherine for a girl, or Rachel, and for a boy...Cam. Cameron. Yeah, that was it.

Michael tried it out loud. "Cameron Joseph Delaney." Not bad.

Instead of looking for a day-care center, he'd hire a woman to come to his house days to take care of the baby, Michael decided, pulling away from the curb. That way some semblance of a real home would be waiting for him after work. Maybe he could find somebody who would also take over the housework and put dinner on. He'd like to open his front door and smell pot roast.

It was a little early to advertise, but soon, he told himself as Colleen's house diminished in his rearview mirror. He wouldn't want to wait too long.

"Catherine Delaney," he murmured. "Or is it Cam?"

Colleen was pinning the last blocks of the Carousel Horse quilt together when the baby started hiccuping. Her stomach bounced and she glanced down, startled. Then it bounced again and she laughed. This was one of the aspects of pregnancy she'd forgotten. Kim had had hiccups all the time, often just as Colleen was falling asleep.

"Not again," she said aloud, a smile curving her mouth.

"Who are you talking to?" Drew asked from the doorway.

Colleen carefully set down the quilt top, bristling with pins. "Myself. Who else?"

He advanced into the room, looking unusually serious. His short, dark blond hair was damp from his bath, and he wore red-striped flannel pajamas. Surprisingly, he was carrying his baby quilt, made from an old pattern with many names. The funny thing about the pattern was that, created in the mid-nineteenth century, it looked like beach balls. So that was how Colleen had made it: red and green and blue beach balls bouncing on a pale yellow background. Drew still slept with it—except when he had a friend over—but he'd never clung to his baby quilt as Kim had to hers.

"Feel this," she said, and laid his hand on her stomach. When it jolted, Drew jumped back.

"Hiccups," she told him.

He wrinkled his nose. "Hiccups? *Inside* you?"

"Yup."

"Cool."

"So what's up?" she asked.

He moved thin shoulders. "I'm ready to be tucked in."

"Is it bedtime?" As she stood, Colleen glanced at the clock. "Oh, no! I'm glad you came in. Where's Kim?"

"Reading. Does she ever do anything else?" He nodded past her toward the sewing table. "Is that the baby's quilt?"

"Yeah. What do you think?" She held it up.

The carousel horses were done in jewel tones, vibrant turquoise and teal and gold, with white flowing manes and black saddles. Under their feet flowed the clouds. The horses looked as though they might gallop right off the edges any moment.

He studied it with his head tilted, then nodded judiciously. "I like it."

"Good." Colleen laid the top over the back of the chair and gave Drew a quick hug. "Bed."

They went through their usual ritual: she lifted the covers of his bed, waited while he climbed in and tucked them around him, spreading his quilt over the top. Then she bent down, framed his face with her hands and kissed him.

"Sleep tight. Don't let the bedbugs bite."

"Mom."

She paused on her way to the door. "Yes?"

"Do we get to help name the baby?"

A blade of pure pain pierced Colleen's chest. "I don't know," she managed levelly. "Let's worry about it later, okay?"

"Do you worry now?"

She tried to smile. "Yeah. I worry about everything, you know that. Hey, that's what moms and dads are for."

"Dad never worries."

"That's not true. Sometimes parents worry the most when we know we haven't done the right thing."

"Well, I don't care about him, anyway." Drew's voice was flat. "Just don't name the baby after him, okay?"

If she hadn't felt so sad, Colleen might have laughed. "I can promise that much. The baby won't be named Ben."

"Good," he murmured drowsily.

Colleen had told Kim to get ready for bed, and a moment later she tucked her in, too. Then she went back to her sewing station. She picked up the quilt top, but let it fall onto her lap.

Memories washed over her and she closed her eyes. She saw the moment when the nurse first handed Kim to her, the small face red and scrunched up, tiny fingers curled into fists and big dark eyes looking so blindly at this new world. And oh, how it had felt, having her baby latch eagerly onto her breast, the small body curving so instinctively to Colleen's it was as though Kim had been created for no other purpose.

A few weeks later, Kim had smiled for the first time. Colleen had been up feeding her in the middle of the night, and suddenly Kim drew back from Colleen's breast, gazed up at her mother's face and smiled with unreserved love and delight.

And Drew, different from the moment he was born. He would smile at strangers when Kim would have frowned suspiciously. As soon as he learned to walk, he was toddling off to explore whenever his mother turned her back. He had nursed with the same intensity he brought to every task. When he was about a year old, the day came quite abruptly when he lost interest. He could carry a bottle with him on his explorations. At his mother's breast he had to be still, so why bother?

Colleen remembered her sharp regret. She knew that there wouldn't be another baby, that she would never again know this incredible closeness with another human being.

But now she could. Part of her desperate need to hold on to this baby was selfish, because she loved being a mother. But part of it was instinct that ran as deep as a baby's ability and drive to suckle at its mother's breast. Colleen had always known she would unhesitatingly die in place of one of her children. She discovered now that no promise on earth could supplant that fierce need to protect them.

Whether the decision was right or wrong, she knew suddenly she could not betray the baby she carried, the baby who was a part of her. Intellectually Colleen knew that Michael would be a good parent, but emotionally she knew only that *she* was the mother.

Colleen opened her eyes and felt the tears that soaked her cheeks. But she was at peace for the first time in months.

Whatever sacrifices had to be made, she would keep this baby. *Her* baby.

Chapter 6

Michael had a bad feeling from the moment his secretary's voice came through the intercom. "Mr. Delaney, Colleen Deering is here to see you."

He punched the button. "Send her in." By the time he rose to his feet and circled his desk, Roberta had ushered Colleen into his office. His first, assessing glance took in her rounded belly; she hadn't had a miscarriage, then, his instant and worst fear.

But her expression wasn't reassuring. It was strained, her face pale, and she clutched her purse tightly, holding it in front of her like a shield.

Michael nodded at his secretary to close the door before his gaze went back to Colleen. "Come and have a seat," he said, touching her arm lightly.

"Thank you."

He saw her settled before returning to his own leather swivel chair behind the mahogany desk. "What's up?" Michael asked.

"Thank you for seeing me." She was perched stiffly on the edge of the chair, her back straight. "I should have called, but I knew if I did you'd ask what I wanted to talk about, and I thought this was something I should say in person."

Muscles all over his body tightened, and he had to force himself to stay seated. "What is it? Are you okay?"

Her usually direct gaze shied from him. "I…" Colleen drew

a deep breath. "Yes. I'm fine. It's not that." With seeming effort she met his eyes again. "Michael…"

He wouldn't listen, was already shaking his head. "Colleen, don't do this. Damn it—"

"I have to!" she cried, her eyes huge and beseeching. "It's not you. I know you'd be a good parent. It's me. I just couldn't live with myself if I give away my baby."

"You were going to give him to your sister."

She squeezed her eyes shut and said in a low voice, "That was different."

Anger filled the great, searing hole in his gut. He stood and planted his hands on his desk, leaning forward. "You agreed," he said harshly. "A promise doesn't have to be in writing to stand as a legal contract. Or are you going to try to deny the baby is mine?"

She flinched, but held her chin up and met his gaze. "No, of course not. I know how much this baby means to you. The decision wasn't easy…."

"You've been making it since the day Sheila died."

"Maybe that's so, I don't know, but I didn't want to hurt you. I never wanted that."

He refused to acknowledge the pain in her voice. His own was gritty. "Don't think it's this simple. Morally, legally and biologically, that's my child you're carrying. By God, I couldn't stop Sheila from dying, but I can stop you from taking our baby!"

Colleen sucked in a long, quavery breath and stood. "You're right, Michael. Sheila's gone. Now *I'm* this baby's mother. That doesn't mean you can't be its father. We can talk about…about visitation or some kind of joint custody. Surely there's a way we can compromise…."

"Would you *compromise* with Drew and Kim?" He spat out the word. Her expression gave him his answer. "I didn't think so. Well, I don't want every other weekend, either. I've waited a long time to be a parent. You had no damned right to hold out hope and then snatch it back again because you don't feel like keeping your word!" He was shouting and didn't care. "I'll see you in court, and I'll fight with every weapon I have."

Michael was as sickened by himself as he was by her breach of faith. But there was no way back without losing the one thing that had kept him going—the certainty of taking his baby home with him.

Colleen was colorless, her freckles standing out in sharp relief. Her cheekbones were too prominent and she had her lips pressed together in a pale line.

"Very well," she said quietly. "I hoped we could keep it from that, but if there's no other way, I'll see you there."

"*Hell.* Colleen, think this through," he said urgently.

"I have. Believe me." Every word ached. "That's all I've done, night and day." With that she marched out. The whisper of his office door shutting behind her held devastating finality.

Michael's head dropped and he swore, long, obscenely, bitterly. He'd liked her, even trusted her.

I didn't want to hurt you. I never wanted that.

Maybe not, but she'd done it, anyway. Right now he felt as if his chest had been ripped open. Every breath was a fresh laceration.

He slumped down in his chair and buried his head in his hands. His fingernails bit into his scalp as he clawed for purchase in a world slipping out from under him.

God, oh God, oh God. How could he survive this? What if he lost in court, lost the one tiny promise of love and warmth and closeness? Would he spend the rest of his life watching other people from somewhere outside, always shut out, wondering how it would feel to have his son's first step be toward him, or hear his daughter's first giggle as he swung her in the air, terrifying her and thrilling her in equal measure. Or to have his toddler run to him when he hurt, because in Dad's arms was security.

After Sheila's death, Michael's brother had reminded him that he was young, he would get married again, there would be another chance to have children. But his brother didn't know how alienated Michael had already felt from Sheila, how aware that he had failed her and himself. Michael couldn't imagine trying again, knowing his own shortcomings.

But he had fathered a child. That baby, *his* baby, was his one chance at happiness. He would not, could not, give that up so that Colleen could satisfy her maternal urges. Damn it, she *had* children; he didn't!

Swearing again, Michael straightened, ran his fingers through his hair. He had himself under control again.

You usually do. He could hear Sheila's acid comment so clearly it was as though she were standing there. He grimaced. If she could see him right now, what would she feel? Betrayed by her sister? Or glad that someone had finally found a way to get to him?

The last time their hopes had been crushed, Sheila had flung her pain at him in bitter words. "Doesn't it ever hurt? Do you feel anything? Did you ever feel anything, or was I just a suitable choice for a wife?" Her laugh had scalded him. "Not so suitable, as it turns out. Barren wasn't what you had in mind, was it?"

Dear God. Even then, in the face of her agony, he hadn't been able to tell her how much he did feel. No, he'd said something despicable, something like, "Why are you putting yourself through this?" when actually he understood. God, he understood. They needed something to fill the emptiness.

And then Colleen had offered it, a gift of such magnitude, such unselfishness, he'd been stunned. His first reaction had been painfully mixed, gratitude swamped by the little boy inside crying, *Why hasn't anybody ever loved* me *this much?*

But somewhere in there he had accepted that he, too, was the lucky recipient of her generosity, if not her love. He'd never forgotten that the love wasn't for him, but he had cautiously begun to believe that the gift was.

Now she'd slapped his hand and snatched back her gift. But the little boy was still rebelling. You couldn't give something away and then take it back.

Michael, the man, flipped through his Rolodex, found his lawyer's number and picked up the phone.

The lawyer Colleen consulted was optimistic. "We're old-fashioned on this side of the mountains," he told her. "You'll still find that judges here believe in motherhood. The unusual conception might complicate things, but because your motive was your deep affection for your sister rather than profit, I think we can present it in a favorable light. Now, you say you're divorced?"

They went over her background one more time, with him nodding at last in satisfaction. "No skeletons in the closet. That's good."

Colleen had hoped for somebody a little older, even grandfatherly, but Joe Warren had come highly recommended. The fact that he'd stayed in eastern Washington for college and law school was approved of around here. One of her quilt-shop customers had told her, "If you just want to make a will or something, you can go to anyone, but if you need an attorney to represent you in court, he's the best in Clayton."

Colleen was made a little uneasy by the lawyer's enthusiasm. She had a feeling he *wanted* to go to court, that he wouldn't mind making headlines with this unconventional custody battle. A settlement didn't interest him. But when she hesitated, all she had to do was remember Michael's shouted *I'll see you in court, and I'll fight with every weapon I have!*

"Thank you," Colleen said at last, rising. She was reaching a point where getting out of chairs required some effort. "I was afraid you'd tell me my cause was hopeless. I feel better."

"I can't make any promises." He stood, too, a tanned, blond man, sleek in an expensive suit. But his grin reminded her a little of Ben's; it was almost boyish, exuberant. He was a man who loved what he did. "But I'll be surprised," he continued, "if any judge in our town can look you in the eye and order you to hand your baby over to this man, just because he happened to have been married to your sister."

Colleen had a twinge of guilt at the description of Michael. He was more, much more. Sheila had loved him. And he had loved her as much, or he would never have agreed to father this child Colleen carried. But she couldn't let guilt stop her from doing what she knew in her heart was right.

If only there was a way they could compromise! Even though Michael had rejected any such possibility, she might have suggested it again, if she could have thought of a solution that would satisfy both. But what?

She'd never thought true shared custody was ideal, where a child spent half his time with one parent and half with the other. She'd thought it would affect his sense of security and trust when his life was so fragmented. And, even if Colleen had custody, the more conventional ways of allowing a father to see his children daunted her. What if Ben had insisted on having Drew and Kim every summer, for example? How could she kiss them goodbye and put them on a plane to see their father, knowing how much they would miss her? And Drew wouldn't want to go; how could she make him?

Right now, if he had custody, Michael would probably be scrupulous—even generous—in allowing her visitation rights. Weekend visits sounded reasonable enough, but the future could hold almost anything. He might move to Seattle or Denver or New York City. He would surely remarry. A man changed when he had a new wife. What if they had a baby together and she resented the child who reminded him of his first wife? How much power would Colleen really have to fight him if he chose at some point to exclude her from their child's life?

Besides, Michael had made it plain that he wouldn't settle for visitation rights any more than she would. He wanted custody, and so did she. He wanted to raise their child as his; she wanted to raise it as hers. Unlike a divorcing couple, they had no past to bind them, no once-upon-a-time commitment to love and raise their baby together.

Colleen sighed. Back to work. She couldn't afford to leave the shop closed any longer than necessary. Especially since she now had a lawyer's fees to pay.

That evening she put off, yet again, explaining the situation to Kim and Drew. Eventually she would have to, but right now they were remarkably incurious about her pregnancy. Neither had asked whether the baby would still go to Uncle Michael. The closest either had come was Drew's question about naming the baby. The whole subject was a box of pins she didn't want to spill yet if she could possibly avoid it.

Unfortunately she discovered only a few days later that, in not telling them, she'd been asking for trouble.

It started innocuously enough. A crew of ladies swept into the shop at just after four-thirty, excitedly planning to pick out fabric for a class two evenings later. No way was less than half an hour enough time for them to make their selections, her to cut the fabric from the bolts and each to individually pay. There was also no way she was going to tell them, sorry, she was closing, and they could go to House of Fabrics down at the mall to do their buying.

As soon as they were all momentarily out of earshot, Colleen picked up the phone. Sounding breathless, her son answered.

"How are things going?" Colleen asked.

"Neat!" Drew said. "I was shooting hoops with—"

Colleen had to cover the receiver and smile at one of the women. "Yes, all the brown fabric is twenty-five percent off today. It's a good chance to stock up." Into the phone, she said, "Listen, I'm going to be late. You tell Kim, okay?"

"Yeah, but, Mom—"

"Can it wait until I get home?"

"I guess so, but—"

She rolled her eyes. "No buts. I'll see you in about forty-five minutes."

It was a full hour before she pulled into the driveway. She didn't pay much attention to the pickup parked in front of her house. Three young guys shared the house next door, and they had a constant stream of friends visiting.

So Colleen was completely unprepared when she walked into the kitchen from the garage. Drew was sitting on the counter, bumping his heels into the oak-veneer cupboard door below him, telling some story. She heard the rumble of a man's laugh and only then saw, with shock, a man sitting at her kitchen table.

The door swung shut behind her. "Drew?"

He turned his head, then hopped guiltily off the counter. "Oh, Mom. Cool. See who's here?"

She saw. "Michael."

He stood to face her, the amusement wiped from his face. "Hello, Colleen," he said quietly.

She looked back at her son. "You know you're not supposed to let anyone in when I'm not home."

Her son stuttered, "B-but, Mom, this is Uncle Michael!"

She drew in a breath to tell him sharply that when she said anyone, she *meant* anyone, but stopped herself in time. This was her fault for keeping secrets. "Yes, of course," she made herself say. "Where's Kim?"

"She went to find our Monopoly game. Uncle Michael said he'd play with us."

"Only until your mother came home," he said, sounding stiff. "She and I have something to talk about, and then I'd better be going."

"Scoot," Colleen said, nodding toward the door. Drew made a face but went. Crossing her arms, Colleen looked back at Michael. "What do you want?"

If he hadn't pushed his hands into the pockets of his slacks, she wouldn't have guessed that he felt her hostility. His expression remained impassive, and he spoke formally. "Only to find out how you are."

"You mean, how your baby is."

"No, that isn't what I meant. Believe it or not, I do care about your well-being. You're Sheila's sister."

"Excuse me," Colleen snapped, "if I find it hard to believe it was out of deep affection for me that you coerced my kids into letting you in."

So much for impassivity. He scowled at her. "I didn't coerce anybody into doing anything. They invited me in. I stayed because Drew told me he didn't like being home alone."

Colleen gritted her teeth. "He wasn't alone. He has a sister. And I don't appreciate being condemned for my parenting practices by somebody who doesn't know the first thing about children!"

Just as coldly Michael said, "I know that's my child you're carrying, and I wouldn't want him left alone with an eleven-year-old girl."

Colleen dropped her purse with a thump on the counter, mainly to remove the temptation of swinging it at him. "For your information, she'll be twelve by then. But as it happens, I wouldn't dream of leaving the baby with her. That's a little different from leaving kids the ages of Drew and Kim alone for an hour. Now, are you satisfied?"

"No, damn it, I'm not!" He swung away to pace the narrow width of her kitchen, then back to face her. He was still frowning, dark brows meeting, the creases in his cheeks deeper. "I understand that your kids are home alone because you can't afford to pay someone to be here with them. Colleen, you have to know that you can't take care of this baby, too."

She couldn't help flinching, but she lifted her chin and said with quiet dignity, "Money is nice. Fortunately for the vast majority of families, it's not essential for good parenting. You may convince some judge that it is, but I hope and trust that you'll eventually find out differently."

His jaw muscles bunched, and he looked away. "Money's not the issue."

"You've certainly tried to make it the issue," she fired back. Inside, she was shaking, but she was determined not to let him see that. "Do you imagine that you can buy this baby?"

"Is that what you think of me?"

"What should I think?" she asked uncompromisingly.

His mouth twisted. "I didn't want to be enemies."

"That's what happens when you take somebody to court."

She saw the spasm his hands made tightening into fists, buried though they were in his pockets. In a low voice he said, "We both think we know what's best for this baby. Does that mean we have to hate each other?"

Meeting his eyes across the kitchen, she felt the sudden burn of tears. "I want to hate you!" Colleen cried, shocking herself with the passion of her words. She scrubbed at the tears. "Don't you understand?"

Suddenly he was right in front of her, handing her a paper towel she hadn't seen him reach for. "Yeah," he said huskily. "I understand. I've tried to hate you, too."

Colleen blew her nose on the coarse paper towel, then wadded it up. Keeping her gaze fixed on the ball of paper in her hand, she said almost inaudibly, "This wasn't an easy decision for me, you know."

"Has anything between us ever been easy?"

Colleen gave her head a small shake.

Roughly he said, "I wonder if anything ever will be."

"I...I don't know," she whispered.

He reached out and with devastating gentleness wiped a tear from her cheek. "However this comes out, we're stuck with each other."

She nodded.

"I just...wanted to be able to visit you sometimes." He sounded awkward, nothing like the assured, handsome man she remembered at her sister's side. "I seem to, uh, be drawn here. You've probably noticed."

Another nod. She couldn't make herself lift her head and meet his gaze.

"I knew it would upset you, but I hoped—" Michael stopped abruptly. "Never mind. I shouldn't have come. I'm sorry, Colleen."

In that moment, she felt incredibly selfish. She had so much. He had so little. She'd lost her sister, but she still had her children. Who did Michael have?

The baby chose that moment to stretch, wriggling restlessly. Sheila, more of a believer in such things than Colleen, would have said it was a sign.

Colleen took a deep breath and said hurriedly before she could change her mind, "Would you like to feel the baby move?"

Lifting her head, she saw the blaze of some incredible emotion in his blue eyes. "Do you mean...touch you?"

Her throat tight, she nodded.

He slowly lifted a hand toward her stomach, but stopped with it an inch or so away. She stared down at it, large, dark and blunt-fingered, scarred in a few places, such a contrast to her own hand, which was much smaller, paler, softer but for the calluses on her fingertips from the quilting needle. It took more courage than she'd thought she possessed to lift her shirt and take his hand in her own, placing it carefully over the swell their baby made.

Her skin shivered in reaction to his touch, and something heated and frightening, almost sexual but not quite, tightened inside of her. And at such a small thing—his hand spread over her belly.

For a moment they stood there, so still she wasn't breathing, and then the baby wriggled again, poking at Colleen hard enough to make her jump, before somersaulting into a new position.

She looked up to see incredulity on Michael's face and the same wonder he'd displayed at the doctor's that day. But something else was in his eyes, something unsettling. It matched her own shocking awareness.

Then his expression closed as completely as if a shutter had dropped; very carefully, Michael lifted his hand from her belly and stepped back. His fingers flexed before he shoved his hands in his pockets.

He cleared his throat. "That's…pretty amazing. It must feel strange."

"Even a little exasperating sometimes." She didn't sound any more natural than he had. "The baby sleeps when I'm active during the day. I guess it must feel like…well, like I'm rocking him." In some part of her mind, Colleen noted her use of the masculine pronoun. For no discernible reason she had started thinking of the baby as a boy. Even as she pondered the oddness of that, she continued, "So at night when I'm trying to sleep, the baby wakes up. He, or she—" this last took conscious effort "—figures it's playtime. I think he's going to be a gymnast. But being so active always gives him the hiccups. All of which makes it hard to sleep."

"You must have really loved Sheila."

His unthinking comment should have reintroduced tension between them, brought Colleen's grief to the forefront of her mind. But maybe, just maybe, her sister had been gone long enough now that Colleen didn't have to mourn every time she heard Sheila's name. When she could think and feel about Michael in ways that had nothing to do with her sister.

So instead, Colleen smiled, if ruefully. "Well, pregnancy is an adventure."

He looked away from her. "Right now, you probably wish it didn't have to end."

There was no need to add, *Because when it ends you'll lose your baby.* The sadness that clutched at her chest reminded her. And it reminded her that he was the one who wanted to take her baby. *He* was the threat, the enemy.

Her expression must have given away her thoughts, because Michael retreated, emotionally and physically.

"I'd better go, let you get on with dinner. Thank you, Colleen." He inclined his head.

"You're welcome." The traditional response sounded silly, but what else could she say?

She heard a scuttling in the hall, but the kids had made their getaway before she and Michael emerged from the kitchen. At the front door, he said in that same formal tone, "I won't bother you again."

Colleen felt suddenly very tired. It would have been better, easier, if she could have hated him. But as he'd pointed out, when had anything between them ever been easy?

"If you want, you can come again," she said, her tone matter-of-fact, as though she offered nothing meaningful.

Light flared in his eyes, momentarily mesmerizing her. Then he managed to shield his reaction, giving it away only by the rough timbre of his voice. "That's...generous of you."

"Even if I'm not generous in the one way that counts?"

His cheek twitched. "I told you, I tried to hate you. It didn't work."

He didn't wait for a response. As she watched him cross the small front lawn with his long strides, heading for the pickup truck, Colleen was crowded with a chaotic mix of emotions. Foremost, and most confusing, was the way her body reacted to him. Why now? She'd never even been altogether sure she *liked* her sister's husband. She'd certainly never been attracted to him.

"Damn it, Sheila," Colleen said under her breath, "why didn't you just marry some jerk who'd be happy to have me raise his kid?"

Sighing, she eased the front door closed and turned to face the music. "Okay, guys," she said resignedly, "you can come out now."

First Kim, then Drew, appeared in the living room doorway. Kim's dark eyes were big. "Mom, what did you mean, 'that's what happens when someone takes you to court'?"

Colleen made a face. "I guess it's time I tell you what's going on."

They didn't really understand of course. How could they? But Colleen thought perhaps Drew and Kim had been worrying about the future more than she'd realized, because she had the impression they were reassured to know she intended to fight for the baby.

"How come you're so...so polite to him?" Kim asked, nose wrinkled.

"Maybe," Colleen suggested wryly, "you should wonder how come *he's* so polite to me! After all, I'm the one who is breaking my word."

"Yeah, but Aunt Sheila's dead. The baby was for her."

"This baby is your uncle Michael's, too. I think he cares as much about it as I do."

"He's just a father," Drew said, shrugging. "It's not the same thing."

Colleen looked at her son in dismay. He'd made similar remarks before, but she'd attributed them to unresolved anger aimed at Ben. This time he sounded only puzzled, even indifferent. How dreadful that a boy who would grow up to be a man, perhaps a father, really believed men didn't love their own children.

And she had convinced herself that his failed relationship with his dad didn't matter.

Colleen reached out and tilted his chin up so he had to look at her. Gently she said, "Sweetie, all men aren't like your father."

"How do you know?" He jerked away. "You said you didn't have a father, either."

"Well, you do." She sounded sharper than she'd intended. "Lately he's been trying harder than you have."

"Yeah," Kim chimed in. "I keep telling you he misses us. Dad wants us to visit."

Colleen seriously doubted it. Or did she *want* not to believe it?

"Sweetie—"

"Don't keep calling me that." Her son averted his face.

"All right. Drew." Colleen bit her lip, then continued reasonably, "I know you've had friends who have fathers who care a lot. Remember how Andy's dad coached your soccer team? And Colin lived with his father. He used to take you fishing. Have you forgotten that?"

Drew gave a sulky shrug, still not looking at her.

"Anyway," Colleen went on, too briskly, "we'll still be seeing your uncle Michael sometimes. Talking to lawyers is part of the way we're trying to figure out how we can both be good parents once the baby is born. Right now we don't agree, but that doesn't mean we're enemies."

"I heard you say you *wanted* to hate him," Kim said. "So how come you're telling us now that you don't?"

"That was a private conversation," Colleen said. "You guys had no business listening."

She might as well not have wasted her breath. The discussion degenerated into an argument about whether the fact that she hadn't told them what was going on justified their eavesdropping.

Drew lost interest first, and Kim was eventually distracted by a reminder that tomorrow was the birthday party at the horse stable. Lisa's mother was picking up all four girls at school and taking them directly there. Colleen was to come for Kim at five-thirty on her way home after closing the quilt shop. She'd arranged for Drew to go home with another boy.

She had no trouble finding the place the next day; it was hard to miss miles of crisp, white, board fencing and long green barns, trimmed with white. A discreet sign announced Whispering Winds Arabians.

Colleen could have sworn she smelled money, instead of manure, when she got out of the car. This, of course, was where Kim had wanted to take riding lessons. She hadn't mentioned them lately, but today's outing would no doubt change that, Colleen thought ruefully.

Inside huge sliding doors, she found a long aisle lined with stalls. Dainty gray and brown muzzles poked between the bars as she went in search of the party. She couldn't resist stopping to stroke a few; searching lips told her she should have brought some carrots.

Eventually she came to a central intersection; ahead was a tack room and showers where two teenagers were soaping up young horses even her uneducated eye recognized as gorgeous. To the left was a huge, covered arena.

Her timing was perfect; Kim was just slipping off a pretty bay, helped by a man in boots and cowboy hat. She saw her mother and hurried over, without a word passing the other girls who were dismounting.

No hello. "I'm ready to go home."

Puzzled, Colleen asked, "Did you have a good time?"

"It was okay," Kim said shortly.

Hiding her perturbation, Colleen nodded back at the arena. "You'd better go thank Lisa for inviting you."

Kim's facade cracked. "Do I have to?" she whispered.

Colleen managed a smile at the woman who handed the reins of one of the horses to a girl and came toward them. "Yes, you have to," she whispered back. "Is that Lisa's mother?"

Kim's head bobbed. Colleen gave her a firm push in the small of her back. Out of the corner of her eye, she watched her daughter cross the arena, scuffing her feet in the sawdust. One of the girls was a miniature version of her mother, down to the dark curls she flipped nonchalantly over her shoulder as she waited for Kim.

Kim said woodenly, "Thanks for inviting me, Lisa."

Colleen didn't hear any reply, because the girl's mother had reached her, saying brightly, "I'm so glad Kim could come. She seemed excited about the horses."

"She'd love to take lessons," Colleen said, smiling. She wouldn't have admitted at gunpoint that she couldn't afford them. "It was nice of you to have her."

She was excruciatingly aware of the way the other girls bunched together and whispered when Kim started back toward her. She wanted to kill them. Instead, she smiled again, thanked Lisa's mother and steered Kim down the aisle.

Kim held up until she got in the car. The second she slammed the door, she burst into tears.

Colleen gathered her daughter in her arms. Cheek against her straight, brown hair, she said, "Tell me about it."

The eleven-year-old wailed, "Her mother made her invite me because I'm new! One of the other girls told me. Lisa just *ignored* me. It was horrible!"

"But I thought she was friendly at school."

Kim's voice was muffled. "Sometimes she is. Sometimes she pretends I'm not there."

"Why do you want to be friends with her, then?"

Her answer was a fresh sob. "She's the most popular girl at school!"

Colleen held her away. "There have to be nicer girls you could make friends with."

"You don't understand!"

Oh, she understood, all right. Colleen remembered a girl who'd moved to her own hometown in seventh grade, immediately becoming the object of adoration for both girls and boys, including the boy Colleen had a crush on. How she'd hated her! But she'd have forgotten all her envy in a second if only the girl had drawn her into that magical circle of the most popular kids.

Now she contented herself with, "I'm sorry. Here, blow your nose. We have to pick Drew up on the way home, and you don't want him to see you crying."

That was enough to galvanize Kim, who wasn't about to give her brother a weapon in their ongoing battles. But just as Colleen was getting out of the car to go and collect Drew, Kim said passionately, "I wish we'd never left Pacifica! I had *friends* there!"

She was quiet all evening. When Colleen kissed her goodnight, Kim said, "I want to go home, Mom. There's no reason we have to stay here, is there? I mean, Aunt Sheila's dead. And I hate it here! I really hate it!"

The mattress gave as Colleen sat on the edge of the bed. "Oh, honey," she said regretfully, "there are all sorts of reasons we can't go. You know that. We've talked about it. There's the shop, and Drew's made friends now, and Uncle Michael will want to see the baby often once it's born."

Her daughter flared back, "You mean, I can't see *my* father just so this…this *baby* can see his? Well, it's not fair!" She turned her face away.

Colleen touched Kim's shoulder, but her hand was shaken off. "Honey, you know there are other reasons."

Kim didn't say anything. Colleen sighed. "I understand that you miss your dad, but the move's been good for all of us. You'll make friends here, I know you will. But I am sorry about today. Now, good night. I love you."

She sounded more sure than she felt. Colleen lay awake herself, going over and over again the decisions she'd made and the few options left. Had she been foolish to pull up roots so ruthlessly out of some vague need for family? Would the kids have been happier if they'd stayed in Pacifica?

But she knew in her heart that neither had been all that content there. Kim was forgetting how often her father had canceled visits at the last minute, how hard on all of them it had been to have Colleen commuting to San Francisco, working long hours. Kim had detested the before- and after-school care, and her closest friend had moved away last year, anyway.

Sleepless, Colleen told herself that Kim would get over this. Something like this could have happened just as easily back in Pacifica. Kim *would* make friends. She was a nice girl. If only summer vacation wasn't looming so close! The hills around town were green with the new shoots of wheat, and in town daffodils and tulips bloomed in every garden. As a child, Colleen had loved summer vacation, but it was different for her kids. They would have to go to day camp, which would make it harder yet for Kim to meet other girls her age since the kids at camp tended to be younger.

Kim was still subdued the next morning. Colleen dropped both kids off at school and watched as Drew raced off to join a group of boys wrestling on the playground. In contrast, Kim trudged up the front steps, looking terribly alone in the middle of a crowd.

Colleen was depressed and weary all day. Closing time had never been more welcome. But she walked in the door at home to the sight of her two kids glaring at each other.

"Don't tell me what to do!" Kim yelled.

Colleen groaned inwardly. What now?

"Okay," she interrupted. "What's going on?"

Drew answered, but she didn't hear him. All her attention was on Kim, whose eyes glittered and whose mouth was set in defiant lines.

"I talked to Dad," she said, tossing her head. "And he says I can come and live with him."

Chapter 7

Colleen's purse slipped out of her fingers. She felt peculiarly distant, detached, but still aware of a knife blade of pain. Both the kids were staring at her, but she couldn't seem to think of anything to say.

She'd worried sometimes, when first divorced, that one of them might someday choose to live with Ben, but in her heart she hadn't believed it. Drew wanted nothing to do with his father, and Kim and she were so close. So now her first thought was that her decision to keep the baby was the cause of this. Had she chosen one child at the cost of another?

"Mom, are you all right?" Drew asked.

"Yes, just—" Colleen gave her head a shake "—let me sit down."

Kim stood aside, still defiant, but looking scared, too.

Colleen sat heavily at the kitchen table. She closed her eyes, took a deep breath and said, "Okay, tell me again."

"Dad says I can go live with him."

"You're crazy!" her brother told her. "He doesn't want us. Anyway, remember what weekends with him were like?"

Colleen saw only her daughter. "Your father actually said, in so many words, that you could come and live with him?"

"Well, he said…" Kim bit her lip. "I don't know what he said! But Dad meant I could come."

"Yeah, sure," Drew muttered.

His sister spun to face him. "Are you calling me a liar?"

"Yeah, I'm calling you a—"

Colleen covered her ears. "Stop!" She so seldom yelled they both looked at her in shock.

"Drew." She tried to speak calmly. "This is something Kim and I need to discuss privately. Why don't you go up to your room and do your homework?"

"I don't have any."

"Then you can turn on the TV."

"Can I watch *Guts?*"

"I don't care what you watch."

"Wow." He shot out of the kitchen, leaving thick silence in his wake.

Colleen nodded toward the table. "Sit down."

Kim silently obeyed. Her chin was thrust out, but Colleen saw her lower lip tremble.

"I'm sorry you're so unhappy here."

"I'll *never* make friends!" Kim burst out.

Colleen stood and swiftly circled the table. She crouched by her daughter and enveloped her in a hug. "Oh, honey, I know it's hard. I haven't been much help, have I?"

Kim was crying now in huge gasps. "Why won't you let us move home?"

Colleen pressed her cheek against Kim's soft hair. Holding back the tears, she said, "Because I can't. And because I'm not so sure Pacifica *is* home anymore."

"We all had friends…"

Colleen held Kim at arm's length so she could see her daughter's tearstained, red-splotched face. "Do you remember what loose ends you were at after Theresa moved?"

"At least I *knew* other kids."

"But you didn't have a good friend any more than you do here."

Kim ducked her head. "Dad was there."

"So he was." Colleen brushed the fine brown bangs back from Kim's eyes. "I'm sorry you can't see him more often. That's the one bad part about moving. But—" she had to force the words past the lump in her throat "—has it occurred to you that if you lived with him, you wouldn't be able to see Drew and me very often, either?"

Kim's face contorted with another sob. "But I'm so unhappy!" she wailed.

Somewhere in the middle of holding her daughter, Colleen remembered that Kim was still a little girl. She remembered how impulsive an eleven-year-old was, how unthinking. And her own hurt receded.

"Honey, I can't let you go live with your father. If you were sixteen years old and positive that was what you wanted to do, I might agree once I'd talked to him. But you're not sixteen, you're eleven. I promise to help you adjust here as much as I can. Maybe this summer you could visit your dad for a couple of weeks if he agrees. But," she concluded firmly, "you're not going to live with him."

"Oh, Mom!" With a new torrent of tears, Kim flung herself back into her mother's arms and wailed, "I was afraid you'd say yes!"

Patting her daughter's back, Colleen thought it would have been funny if it didn't hurt so much.

Once the tears subsided she sat back on her heels. "Goodness, look at you. Here, let me get you a tissue." She carried some in her purse, and in a moment she'd grabbed several and handed them to Kim, who mopped her cheeks and blew her nose.

"All right," Colleen said, "let's get down to brass tacks. Why did you announce you were going to live with your father if you didn't really want to?"

Kim sniffed. "I thought I wanted to until I told you. And then suddenly I was really scared."

Colleen sighed. "Is he waiting to hear from me?"

"Well—" Kim nibbled uncertainly on her lower lip "—I'm not really sure...." She drew the last word out.

Colleen fixed a stern expression on her face. "Does your dad know you were planning to move in with him?"

Kim hunched her shoulders and spoke in a rush. "Well, I

said I hated it here and he said it was too bad we'd moved and why didn't I visit this summer. So I said I didn't want to wait that long, that I wished I lived with him, and he said we could talk about it. So I thought…well, that he was saying okay." She looked beseechingly up at her mother.

Colleen knew damn well that Ben didn't have the slightest desire to have a preadolescent girl living with him. But he had never liked to say no. He'd always foisted the unpleasant task off on her. Just as he had this time.

But nothing on earth could have made her tell their daughter that her father didn't really want her. So Colleen said only, "I'll call him later. Maybe we can set the date for a visit with him this summer if he can get some time off."

Kim gave a jerky nod.

Colleen kissed her and then picked up her purse to plop it on the table. With forced good cheer she asked, "How does French toast sound for dinner?"

"Drew doesn't like it."

"Drew doesn't like anything. I'll open him a can of chili."

Kim waited until her mother was wearily contemplating the contents of the can cupboard. "Mom?"

"Uh-huh?"

"Are you mad at me?" Kim asked in a small voice.

"Mad?" Colleen turned quickly. Her heart almost broke at the sight of the apprehension on Kim's face, and she hurried to hug her close again. "Sweetheart, of course not! I want you to be able to talk to me about anything, anything at all. Don't hide stuff that's bothering you just because you think you might hurt my feelings. Will you promise me that?"

After a second Kim's head bobbed against Colleen. Then she heaved a huge sigh. "I guess I didn't like Lisa that much, anyway."

Colleen squeezed her shoulders. "That's the spirit, kiddo."

Despite Colleen's invitation, Michael had no intention of abusing the privilege of being able to visit. He made himself wait for two long weeks before he picked up the phone.

"Can I take you all out for pizza again?" he asked.

"Do you like spaghetti?" Colleen countered. "I owe you a dinner. Why don't you join us, instead?"

"I don't want to barge in on you," he said gruffly. "Why don't I just stop by later in the evening?"

She was polite enough not to ask why he wanted to come at all. Instead, she challenged, "Afraid my cooking will be as bad as my coffee?"

He was cornered. "Name a time."

Michael arrived at her place at five-thirty on the nose, just as Drew popped a wheelie on his bike and slid to a stop in the driveway. Blocking Michael's way, the boy stuck his chin out and asked almost belligerently, "Does Mom know you're coming?"

Last time he was here, they'd been best friends. Why the change? Michael wondered, afraid he knew. He said only, "She invited me."

"Oh." Drew scuffed his feet on the pavement and thought about it. "Well, I guess you can come in, then."

Michael would have been amused if he wasn't already so conscious of being an intruder. "Thank you," he said gravely.

Drew dropped his bike on the lawn and led the way in. They followed the aroma of Italian cooking to find Colleen in the kitchen.

Michael's instant response to the sight of her was sexual, which dismayed the hell out of him. Her vibrant hair was bundled in a loose knot from which tendrils curled on her long, slender neck. She was slim, fine-boned, her creamy redhead's complexion flushed from the heat of the stove. But it was her pregnancy that jolted him like a fist in the stomach. The swell of her belly was visible evidence of her fertility, her femininity. God help him, Michael was reminded on a physical level that his seed was in her, that their bodies together had created the baby she carried, though he had never touched her. Her pregnancy gave her a softness, a mystery, the more potent for his part in it.

The realization shot to hell the excuse he'd fabricated to let himself off the hook: if he reacted sexually to Colleen, it was only because she looked like Sheila. But right this minute Colleen didn't. And he wanted her, anyway.

Oh, God. What if she ever guesses?

Think about it later, he told himself.

"Uncle Michael's here," Drew announced. "He says you invited him."

Colleen's head turned and her startled gaze flew directly to Michael's.

"Yes, I did," she said, sounding just a little breathless. "He's having dinner with us. Hello, Michael."

"You mean, we're not having macaroni and cheese again?" Drew asked.

Michael pretended not to notice the look she gave her son. "You'll have your uncle thinking we never eat anything else."

"Yeah, well, sometimes it seems like…" The kid subsided under her stare.

"Go wash your hands and then come set the table," she told him before smiling at Michael as prettily as if he was a truly welcome guest. "I'm sorry I'm running behind. Although I don't suppose you're used to eating this early, anyway. But with children you find yourself making changes…" Colleen puffed her bangs off her forehead and threw up her hands. "I can't seem to say the right thing to save my life! Let me try again. Would you care for a glass of wine? I'm afraid it's not very good wine, but—"

He interrupted. "If I can't tell exotic brewed coffee from instant, what makes you think my taste in wine is any better?"

This time Colleen's smile was grateful. "Coming right up."

Michael was careful to keep the conversation light, leaning one hip against a counter and sipping a mediocre burgundy while Colleen dropped the spaghetti in boiling water and checked the garlic bread in the oven.

"Business is picking up," she was saying as she carried the food to the table. "But not as much as I'd like. The fabric store at the mall is part of a chain. They can undercut me on prices, and I know even some of my regular customers only come to me for the kind of fabrics they can't get there."

"So you need a bigger customer base. Play on your selection, the fact that you carry unusual fabrics. An easy way of getting at a large audience is those coupons that are distributed in the mail," Michael suggested. "I hear they're effective."

"I assumed they were expensive."

"I don't believe they are, and the return can be very high." Kim appeared in the doorway, and Michael smiled. "Hello."

"Hi," she mumbled with one of those shrugs kids do so well. She wandered over to her chair and slumped dejectedly into it.

Michael glanced with raised brows at Colleen, and she rolled her eyes. "Later," she mouthed, and he nodded.

She called Drew to the table, where they all bowed their heads and said a brief grace before passing around bowls. Kim brightened a little at the sight of the spaghetti.

"Cool. I thought we were having hot dogs tonight."

Colleen's cheeks turned pink again. "Obviously," she said lightly, "I need to vary the menu."

Before Michael could say anything, Drew turned to him and asked in a conversational way, "Uncle Michael, are you taking my mother to court?"

"Drew!" Colleen exclaimed, dropping one of the bowls with a clunk. "For heaven's sake! This is something Uncle Michael and I need to figure out. It's none of your business." To him, she said, "I'm sorry. I…well, I had to explain."

The boy ducked his head. "I just wanted to know what court *is*."

Kim's lip curled. "Gol, don't they teach you little kids anything?"

In measured tones Colleen said, "Kim, you don't talk to your brother that way. Drew, we'll discuss it later."

The coward in Michael wanted him to take the out she'd offered. But he was suffering enough guilt where she was concerned. So he shook his head.

"No, that's okay. Drew, one kind of court is when somebody is arrested by the police for a crime, like stealing." He explained about trials and juries as simply as he could manage.

When Drew nodded, Michael continued, "In a case like your mother's and mine, there's no jury. But somebody has to decide who our baby will live with once he—" Michael glanced at Colleen "—or she is born. If we can't, we'll go to court and both tell our stories to a judge, who will then decide for us."

Drew's forehead crinkled. "But what if you don't like what he decides?"

Michael's eyes met Colleen's. The one look was enough to tie a knot in his gut. Then her gaze shied away and she said very steadily, "One of us probably won't like what the judge decides, but we'll both have to accept it. Unfortunately I can't always have my way, any more than Uncle Michael can."

"I wish you wouldn't talk about it!" Kim burst out. "I don't want to think about the baby!"

Drew stuck his tongue out at her, but Colleen reached over and squeezed her hand. "I'm sorry, honey. We'll change the subject now."

Michael couldn't seem to tear his gaze away from her slender hand, wrapped around her daughter's. He was torn between two powerful forces: terrible hunger for a touch that tender—God help him, for *her* touch—and bitter envy. If just once in his life he'd been able to reach out that readily, he might not be so alone now.

Colleen gently disentangled her fingers, breaking the spell, but when Michael lifted his gaze he found her watching him. Some knowledge of what he felt was in her eyes, and for a shattering moment their gazes held. At last, by sheer force of will, Michael looked away.

Neither of the kids seemed to have noticed anything, although how they could have missed the tension between their mother and him, he couldn't imagine. He was damned careful not to look at Colleen again for a few minutes, until Drew had told them enthusiastically and at great length about soccer sign-ups.

"I brought home a paper about it, Mom," he told her eagerly, at the same time stuffing garlic bread into his mouth. "It's only twenty dollars: I can play, can't I? Ian's gonna. He says his dad might coach, except he coached his sister's team last year and he might again. I don't know why he'd want to coach *girl's* soccer."

Kim snapped, "What makes you think *boys* are so much better?"

"Guys!" Colleen exclaimed. "Can't we have peace until we finish eating?"

Kim subsided into unhappy sullenness, and, once assured by his mother that, yes, he could play soccer, Drew began to gobble his spaghetti. Michael watched him out of the corner of his eye. Did all boys his age eat that much? Or was their usual diet so depressing, he was grabbing what he could while the chance was there?

Colleen managed to make the rest of the meal more pleasant than the beginning, although she couldn't possibly be as relaxed as she seemed. She probably wished he'd go to Timbuktu, Michael thought ruefully.

If so, she was too good a hostess to show it. After dinner, she set the kids to clearing the table and made coffee for Michael and herself. They carried it into the living room.

The living room was cramped. Colleen's quilting frame took up a large space in front of the picture window, while a handsome sectional overfilled the rest of the room. Michael assumed it was from her more prosperous married life, like the maple coffee table and end tables. They didn't fit with the slightly shabby, builder's-grade tan carpet, or the outdated, avocado green drapes.

Once he'd sat down, Colleen settled about as far from him as possible.

With her legs curled under her and her long hair slipping out of its knot, Colleen had no resemblance to Sheila. That should have let him relax. Oddly enough, the fact that he wasn't having to deal with his unresolved feelings for his wife made him more conscious of Colleen, not less.

He didn't want to be so aware of her every breath that he waited for the faint rise and fall of her chest. He didn't want to find his gaze wandering from her face down the length of her throat to the hollow at the base, where he imagined her pulse beating.

Michael looked away. He hoped to God she hadn't noticed his reaction to her. Of course, he found that she was watching him over the rim of her coffee cup.

She said abruptly, "It seems as if we always talk about me. How are things going for you, Michael?"

He couldn't decide whether she really wanted to know or was grabbing for the first topic that occurred to her.

"Fine," he said, hoping she didn't push it. "How are you feeling, Colleen?"

"Back to me, huh?" Her extraordinary eyes were steady and unsettlingly perceptive, her tone tart. "Amazingly enough, I'm fine, too. Now we've shot two subjects. What do *you* want to talk about?"

"How about Kim for starters?"

His choice was a smart one, because Colleen grimaced and looked down at her coffee. Away from him, thank God. She said, "It's tough at her age. She hasn't made a single friend yet, and she's feeling awfully lonely."

Michael frowned. "What about Drew?"

"Oh, he's fine, which doesn't help matters. We have a little jealousy working here, too. The trouble is, it's easier for a kid Drew's age, especially—at the risk of sounding sexist—for a boy. They seem to do things in crowds, and they're perfectly happy to add one more. On the other hand, the fifth-grade girls go in pairs. As Kim puts it, they all have best friends already."

"And it's almost summer vacation. What are you going to do with them once school's out?"

Colleen sighed. "Probably the YMCA day camp. Kim's really too old for it, but she's not old enough to stay by herself all day. What else can I do?"

If the last was a plea, he couldn't answer it. Instead, he studied her, for the first time in weeks, months, shedding his own preoccupations to wonder about her motives. He'd thought about her plenty, but mostly in relation to himself. Realizing that, Michael felt selfish as hell.

"Why did you move?" he asked. "Was it just to be near Sheila?"

Colleen set down her coffee cup and smiled a little sadly. "We came to Clayton because of Sheila. I had lots of reasons for moving."

"What were they?" he asked quietly.

Layers of complex emotions shadowed her eyes, reminding him that she had depths he had never seen. Her response wasn't quite what he'd expected, any more than most of what she did was.

"Let's make a deal," Colleen said, lifting her chin in an unmistakable challenge. "I'll tell you why I moved if you'll tell me how you really are."

Not by a twitch did he show her how little he wanted to open the door she was knocking on.

"Why?"

"Because I don't know you." She shrugged gracefully. "Because I never will if we don't get past 'fine.'"

Michael wanted to tell her to forget it. He had no desire to talk about sleepless nights and emptiness so vast it echoed. He didn't want to talk about guilt, or why he was hanging around her house like a hopeful stray.

But she was the one person he couldn't keep evading. They shared something too basic: their unborn baby. She had a right to learn enough about him so she could trust him with their child.

He let out a long breath. "All right."

"Well." Suddenly she wasn't so anxious to meet his eyes. "There were lots of reasons. The kids and I kept the house after my divorce, but I got so I didn't want to live with memories. And it didn't really suit us on our own."

"Too big?"

"Too expensive," Colleen said. "Plus, I slowly realized it wasn't the kind of house I'd have chosen on my own. Sort of like this couch." She ran a hand over the plush surface. "After a while, you start thinking about things like that."

He already had. But Michael wasn't ready to admit that, even if he'd wanted to take the chance of interrupting her musings.

"Originally I figured I should stay where the kids could see Ben often, but…oh, it didn't work out all that well." She pushed her hair back from her face. "Ben had a habit of forgetting he'd made plans with them. Or they'd spend the weekend with him, and he'd either be absorbed in paperwork the whole time or he'd hire a babysitter so he could go out. It was one disappointment after another. I thought it might be good for them to be far enough away that they didn't have any expectations of him anymore. I thought it would be easier if they *couldn't* visit him than to have him not bother."

When she lapsed into silence, Michael nodded his head toward her. "What about you?"

"Me?" Looking surprised, Colleen returned from wherever her thoughts had taken her.

"Do you miss anything you left behind?" Michael asked. He didn't usually get that personal, but he found he was very curious to know how she felt about her ex-husband.

Like a bird studying something intriguing, Colleen tilted her head to one side. "You mean Ben, don't you?"

He shrugged, pretending disinterest. "Your job, city life, friends."

"Not city life. Not Ben." Her wrinkled nose gave her ex-husband the same status as something moldy in the back of the refrigerator. Michael was oddly gratified. Colleen went on, "Friends, of course. But Sheila was here," she added simply.

As she'd observed once, all roads led to Sheila. Michael chose not to follow this one. "I should let you get back to the kids."

She saw right through him. "Not on your life. It's your turn."

"I meant it when I said I was fine. What do you want me to say?"

All the humor was suddenly gone from her eyes; instead, they held compassion. "You don't look fine."

"I don't sleep very well," he said on a surge of anger. "So what? There's nothing unusual about that."

Still she wouldn't let it go, though her voice was soft. "Do you miss her?"

Janice Kay Johnson   *401*

"No!" he snapped. "Yes! Hell, I don't know."

Crinkles formed between her brows. "Are you mad at her for dying?"

"Damn, you don't know when to stop, do you?" He hadn't even been aware of rising to his feet. All he knew was that he was standing now, glowering down at her.

Colleen tilted back her head to look at him. Other than that, she didn't move at all. She sure as hell wasn't scared of him. He'd have felt like the lowest crud on earth if she had been.

"Well, are you?" she asked again.

His voice was raw. "No. I feel guilty. Here I am, left with everything she ever wanted on earth. Why didn't I die, instead? Hell, I drive over the speed limit sometimes, too. So why her? Why?" He was shouting, but still Colleen didn't quail.

"Sheila wanted *you,*" she said, uncoiling to stand in front of him. He was shocked to feel her hand laid gently on his cheek, even more shocked to realize he was crying. "If you'd died, she wouldn't have had you anymore."

"She didn't want me." Michael shook his head blindly. "Not anymore. Maybe not ever. She wanted to be married. She wanted children. I just happened to be there."

Colleen's hand stilled; she slowly pulled back. Looking perturbed, she searched his face, her eyes huge, pools he could drown in if he didn't get a grip on himself.

"That's not the way Sheila talked about you."

He cursed and shoved his fingers into his hair, backing up until he bumped into the coffee table. "Don't listen to me. All I do every night is lie in bed and think. I've thought fifty times about every moment of our lives. If you do that, after a while you start imagining things."

"I did wonder sometimes from the way she talked..." Colleen began slowly.

Michael tasted acid in his throat. "Forget it. I'm tired, that's all. There's a reason I didn't want to go past 'fine.'"

"You should talk about how you feel."

"No." He shook his head. "I'd say things I didn't even mean. Listen, I'd better go. Tell Kim and Drew—" Michael stopped.

One second she was with him, the next Colleen's attention had turned elsewhere. Inward. When she focused on him again, she smiled. "Come here," she said, her voice velvet. "Talk to your son."

He couldn't resist. A minute ago she'd been Pandora opening the forbidden box, but now she was holding open the gates to heaven. He crouched in front of where she'd sank back down on the couch. She took his hand again, just as she had the night in the kitchen, and set it on her belly under her shirt.

Her skin was smooth, warm, the nicest thing he'd ever touched. His entire being was focused on that one point of contact. But it wasn't enough. The moment in the kitchen when he'd realized he was attracted to *her,* not to the memory of his wife, had changed everything. He wanted to move his hand, caress her. He wanted...

Something poked at his hand. Michael looked at her in shock. "What the hell was that?"

Her lips still had that tender curve, and her eyes were soft. "A foot or a knee. Maybe he just elbowed you."

"He?"

Colleen made a face at him, but her eyes still had that dreamy quality. "For some reason I think it's a boy."

"Yeah. Me, too."

"Really?"

"Uh-huh." Michael moved his hand over the tight, silken surface of her stomach, felt the baby shifting within her. It was the damnedest thing. Only reluctantly did he finally remove his hand and stand up. "Amazing."

"It is, isn't it?" Her gaze touched his and skittered away. Somewhere in there, she, too, had become self-conscious.

Michael escaped as quickly as he could after that, knowing he'd been a fool to come at all, but unable to regret the evening.

And knowing damned well that by tomorrow he'd be counting the days until he could visit again.

Michael ran the sandpaper back and forth again and again over the wide plank of oak. At this stage, he could have used his belt sander, but some no doubt primitive instinct insisted he use his bare hands as much as possible to build this toy chest. The pull on his shoulder muscles, the gritty texture under his fingers, were satisfying.

So was the feel of the wood when he ran his fingers over it. Different woods had different textures. From long practice, he could tell with his eyes closed whether he was working with cherry or oak or maple.

This shop was the one part of the house that was entirely Michael's. His stamp showed: racks and pegboards provided a place for every tool; screws and nails were sorted and labeled in tiny, plastic drawers; the room was spotlessly clean.

Sheila had called him obsessive. He could never convince her that he organized tools so that he could put his hand on what he needed when he needed it. Every tool was rust-free, well oiled and in its place.

He hadn't decided yet whether to paint the toy chest or just finish it with linseed oil. Little kids liked bright colors, but then the beautiful grain of these slabs of oak was wasted. Maybe he'd paint part of it—say, the sides—and use a clear finish on the top. Or just paint the letters of his son or daughter's name. They were going to be carved out of the solid oak lid, not tacked on. Cameron. Or maybe Catherine. He wouldn't finish the chest until he knew.

It wasn't as if he wouldn't have time after the baby was born. He hadn't memorized a developmental timetable yet, but even he knew that babies couldn't roll over for a few months, much less dig a stuffed animal out of a toy chest.

Michael's hand slowed as his thoughts drifted. As ignorant as he was, the idea of bringing the baby home and having sole responsibility was a little scary. He didn't even know how to change a diaper.

"To hell with the environment," he muttered. "I'll buy paper diapers." How wrong could you go with them? All he had to do was watch a few Pampers or Huggies commercials on TV. Free lessons.

Anyway, he wouldn't be the first parent who'd had to learn

on the go. Probably most had to. For all her hunger for parent-hood, Sheila hadn't even babysat as a teenager.

"I tried it once," he remembered her saying, her nose wrin-kling in the same expression of distaste he'd seen on Colleen's face when she talked about her ex-husband. "This little monster wanted to run after his parents when they left. Every time I turned my back, he unlocked the front door and took off. I spent the entire evening with one hand braced on the door. That was it for babysitting. I told Colleen she could have it. *I* worked at Joe's Burgers, instead."

Of course, as a new mother she would have had a sister to call at every minor alarm. Colleen would have coached her through any crisis. Michael tried to imagine himself picking up the phone at midnight to ask Colleen what to do with a baby who wouldn't quit screaming. It would be all but admitting he wasn't capable.

Michael supposed his brother's wife would give him advice. They'd never been close, partly because she and Sheila hadn't hit it off, but Jennifer was a nice enough woman, with two kids of her own. But she wouldn't drop everything to come running over, either.

His hand stopped altogether. He grimaced, looking down at the plank without really seeing it. Once in a while he wondered if he was crazy, thinking he could raise a child by himself, thinking he could do anywhere near as good a job as Colleen. He'd seen the way she hugged her children and smiled at them and gave them quick kisses in passing, all so naturally. He pictured himself trying to do the same, as awkward as she was comfortable with physical affection.

Was he going to let his dream go that easily? he wondered. If he compromised now, he might as well say goodbye to it. On his own, he would *have* to learn how to parent. As a weekend father, he'd never get over being awkward. He would never know what it felt like to come first in a little boy's eyes.

Hell. Michael tossed down the sandpaper. There he went again, adding up reasons to justify what he was doing to Colleen. How many times had he gone over the same basic facts, counting them off like a clerk taking inventory?

Janice Kay Johnson   405

Michael knew instinctively that nothing cut deeper to the
bone than the loss of a child. If he hurt at the idea, what must
Colleen feel? Bringing a baby home from the hospital was a pipe
dream for him; for her, it was real. To go through labor and then
walk out of the hospital with empty arms would tear her apart.

He rose to his feet with sudden violence and threw the first
thing that came to hand—a rasp. It clattered off the potbellied
woodstove at the other side of the room and fell to the floor.
"Damn it," he said explosively, "she should have thought of
that before she agreed to have my baby!"

Why in God's name hadn't he stayed away from her? But
no, he'd had to go knocking on her door, driven by some
bizarre need to know her better, this woman who was the
mother of his baby. Well, look where it had gotten him. He'd
discovered his wife's sister was everything Sheila hadn't been.
He'd discovered that his body responded sexually to Colleen
in a way it hadn't to Sheila in a long time. He'd discovered that
he didn't want to hurt this woman who should have stayed a
stranger.

But that was exactly what he was doing. Every day that
passed, he was hurting her. And her kids.

For starters, she couldn't afford that lawyer she'd had to hire
to fight him. Thanks to Sheila, he knew damn near to the penny
what Colleen had sunk into the shop and what she was living
on. One of the things that was keeping Michael awake nights
was wondering what she'd cut back on to pay Joseph Warren's
ninety bucks an hour. How many nights lately had Colleen
served her kids macaroni and cheese or canned chili for dinner
because she couldn't afford anything else?

"Hell," he said again, and gave the rasp a frustrated kick
before he picked it up and put it in its place.

He might as well face it, Michael thought in anguish. He
wasn't going to be able to seize his own happiness at Colleen's
expense.

So what was the answer?

Chapter 8

"Ah, yes. Mr. Delaney." The hostess picked up two menus from a rack. "This way, please."

Michael stood back courteously for Colleen to go ahead of him. She would just as soon have trailed behind. She'd reached the point in her pregnancy where she felt herself waddle. It didn't help that her maternity wardrobe hadn't included a dress even remotely suitable for a restaurant this elegant. But then, in silk she would only have looked like a maharajah's elephant instead of a working one.

Some consolation.

The hostess seated them in a private alcove. The table was covered with a heavy white cloth; twin flames flickered atop tall white tapers set in silver candlesticks. Colleen accepted a leather-covered menu and opened it, making a pretense of scrutinizing the choices. But the truth was that she was too nervous to care what she ate.

What did Michael want to talk to her about? What was it that couldn't be discussed on the phone, or in her living room during one of his occasional visits?

"The London broil is good," Michael said suddenly. "Or the filet mignon."

"London broil sounds fine." Colleen closed the menu. The moment she set it down on the table, she was sorry. She could have hidden behind it for several more minutes.

"Wine?" he asked with lifted brow.

"I'd better stick to milk," she said.

"Milk?" His gaze dropped from her face to her stomach. "Oh. I'm sorry."

"That's okay."

Silence. The candlelight, intended to be romantic, cast shadows on his face, emphasizing the starkness of his cheekbones and his deep-set eyes. He'd lost weight, Colleen thought. She wished she could see him better, guess what he was thinking.

The waiter appeared just when the silence was becoming unbearably thick. "May I take your orders?"

But he left too soon, leaving them in their small circle of golden candlelight, alone as they had never been before.

Well, she'd been a coward long enough. Whatever he had to say couldn't be worse than worrying about it.

"Why are we here, Michael?"

She could feel the increased tension, though he didn't move a muscle. "You wouldn't rather wait until we've eaten?"

Colleen shook her head.

"All right." In a dark suit and white shirt, he was a stranger again, handsome, remote. "I've been thinking. You suggested once that we share custody. I'm prepared to consider the idea now."

On some level, she had guessed this was coming. "Why?" she asked.

"Because I made the mistake of getting to know you. You were…an abstraction originally. Selfish as it sounds, I didn't take your feelings into account. Once I add them to the equation, I have to admit it makes more sense for us to work something out."

His speech was smooth, businesslike. *The equation?* How many points had represented her emotions, how many his? Colleen didn't make the mistake of thinking him unemotional; she had seen too much pain in his eyes, seen his desperate need for his child. But even now he couldn't admit what he felt.

Carefully Colleen asked, "What did you have in mind?

His impassivity cracked. "I don't know. Alternate weeks. Or you have him Monday through Thursday, me Friday through Sunday. Something like that."

Tears stung at her eyes and she bowed her head, blinking hard. Ridiculous to cry, but she couldn't seem to stop herself. She felt as if somebody were wringing out her heart, twisting it to squeeze out every last drop of hurt and pity.

His chair scraped as he leaned forward. "Did I say something wrong?"

"No." Colleen shook her head blindly. "No, it's nothing. Pregnant women get emotional."

He didn't buy it, but he sat back. Out of the corner of her eye, she saw the waiter approaching. Grabbing the stiff, elaborately folded napkin, Colleen surreptitiously mopped her tears.

The salads and drinks placed in front of them interested Michael no more than they did her. Even after the waiter left, he made no move to pick up his fork.

As though they hadn't been interrupted, he challenged, "Can you think of a better alternative?"

"For us?" she said bitterly. "No. For the baby, almost anything would be better."

His shoulders had a rigid set. "What the hell does that mean?"

She knew how hard it must have been for him to reach a point where he was willing to compromise. He'd probably expected gratitude from her. She couldn't blame him if he was angry.

"Can you imagine what it would be like?" Colleen begged for his understanding. "To go home from school three days a week to one place, and then have to go somewhere else the other days? To want to tell Mom something, but today 'home' is with Dad? To wake up nights and not remember where you are?"

"Yes, I can imagine!" The suppressed violence in Michael's voice shocked her more than his offer had. "But what the hell do you suggest? That we slice the kid down the middle so we can each keep half?"

"No. I think maybe…" This was hard to say. In a rush, to get it over with, she said, "Maybe there's no way all three of us *can* be happy. And I don't want a defenseless child to be the unhappy one just so you and I can get what we want."

"Damn it!" He pushed back from the table and half stood, then forced himself to sit again, his entire body radiating tension. "You're the one who suggested this in the first place. Now you throw it back in my face!"

Colleen spoke past the lump in her throat. "I'm sorry. I hadn't thought then. But I have now. Endlessly. And I don't want to raise our little boy or girl that way. I'd almost rather give him up."

A caustic laugh escaped him. "But you're not willing to give him up, are you?"

Wordlessly Colleen shook her head. She felt him glaring at her, but she didn't look up. Meeting his gaze now would be a form of challenge; it would acknowledge that they were enemies. And perhaps she was a coward, too; she didn't want to see the contempt that must be in his eyes, the dislike.

"Then I guess we'll be seeing each other four weeks from now in court." His voice was flat; he reached for his silverware. "Let's have dinner."

Colleen had never sat through a longer meal. The food was tasteless, the candlelight and china and fine linen a mockery. She and Michael were trapped in a bubble of silence, isolated from the murmur of voices around them, the click of silverware on china, a throaty laugh, the efficient waiters. She tried not to look at him; the few times their gazes glanced off each other, he was as quick to return his attention to his food as she was.

She wondered how they appeared to the other diners, the waiter. A handsome man, a pregnant woman, candlelight… Would anybody else notice that they weren't speaking, didn't meet each other's eyes?

Afterward Michael took care of the bill and escorted her out, careful not to touch her. Outside, the warmth of the day still lingered though the sun had long since set. A canopy of stars glittered in the velvet darkness of the sky.

And still that terrible silence held. Michael opened the car door for her, circled around the front and got in himself. Colleen fastened her seat belt, then knotted her hands together on her lap and stole a glance at him. In the indirect light from the dashboard, his face was harsh, frowning, wiped clean of any soft emotions. Though the engine purred, he shoved the gearshift roughly into First, accelerating hard enough that the car leapt forward.

Colleen stared sightlessly out the window. Inside she was a mass of anguish and guilt and searing regret. She wanted to reach out and touch Michael, not drive him away! In her mind's eye she saw him the last time she had laid his hand on her belly. In that touch she had felt warmth and strength and yearning. She had wanted to sway toward him, to lay her head on his shoulder, to feel his arms around her. All impossible now.

Was she wrong, horribly wrong, to go back on her word?

The five-minute trip across town took an eternity, but at last the BMW swung into her driveway. Michael turned off the ignition and reached for his door handle.

"No!" In the well of silence, the one word was shockingly loud. Colleen struggled to moderate her voice. "Please. You don't need to walk me in."

Michael went still for a moment, then sat back, wrapping both hands around the steering wheel. Without looking at her he said, "You won't change your mind?"

"If I knew what was right—"

He interrupted her coldly. "I didn't ask you what was right. I asked if you've made up your mind once and for all."

Colleen desperately fumbled for the door handle. "I don't know!"

For an instant his control disintegrated. His voice was a painful rasp. "Good God, how did we get into this?"

Colleen succeeded in opening her side door. "Sheila," she said, scarcely recognizing her own voice. "We both loved Sheila."

For the first time Michael turned to look fully at her. Voice raw, he asked, "What do you think she'd tell us to do?"

Colleen had no answer. If Michael was right about their

marriage, perhaps Sheila would prefer Colleen to raise the child who had been a gift between sisters. But Colleen couldn't help remembering how eager Sheila had been to tell Michael about the pregnancy. She'd held nothing back then; there'd been no suggestion that the baby was only for her, that she thought he didn't want it or wouldn't love it. No, she'd expected him to share her joy, and he had.

And so Colleen cried, "I don't know, damn you!" Her voice cracked. "If I knew, I'd do it!"

That night as she lay in bed, her window open so that moonlight and the scent of the roses she'd planted drifted in, she relived that last brief conversation.

What do you think she'd tell us to do?

Why hadn't she lied and said, "I think Sheila would want me to raise her baby"?

Colleen knew the answer. Because whatever else she had done to Michael, she'd never lied to him. And although she'd known her sister better than anybody else in the world, Colleen hadn't the slightest idea what Sheila would have wanted for this baby.

Now, in the night when ghosts were supposed to walk, Colleen begged, *Sheila! Come back! Tell me what you want!*

But she felt nothing; no comforting presence, no sisterly touch. She tried to picture Sheila and saw only the teenager, laughing, twirling, dancing away from some responsibility or another. For the life of her, Colleen couldn't seem to dredge up the woman her sister had become, the woman who yearned so for a child of her own.

That woman, Colleen remembered bleakly, had died because she was careless, certain despite everything of her own invulnerability. And if the baby had been of her body, it would have died, too, that day.

No, there would be no help from Sheila. She lay silent now, her restlessness forever quieted. And Colleen was alone, as she had never been before.

Colleen hadn't been this scared since the dreadful day word came that her mother had had a heart attack. The flight to

Seattle and taxi trip to the hospital had passed in a blur, but her wait for the doctor was all too clear in Colleen's memory. The hard, plastic seats, the coffee machine and paper cups, the magazines she picked up and put down when she couldn't seem to make sense of the words. And then the footsteps in the hall, the door opening. She had slowly risen to her feet, her heart hammering, her throat thick with unshed tears, knowing when she saw the doctor's face, before he spoke a word, that she had come too late. That the loving circle had been broken.

This waiting room wasn't so different, though the seats were upholstered. She'd opened a *People* magazine to an article on the latest sensational murder, but even the lurid details couldn't draw her out of her cycle of worries.

Where was her lawyer? What if he didn't show up? Would they postpone? What if this particular judge regarded the role of surrogacy with such distaste that he was biased from the start? Would having turned down Michael's offer of joint custody go against Colleen?

A footstep outside brought her head up. Joe Warren appeared in the doorway of the small waiting room, and Colleen's heart jumped, then resumed a hasty rhythm that made her dizzy. She felt a dreadful mix of terror and relief.

"It's time," he said, then raised a brow when he saw her face. "Hey, don't worry. Piece of cake."

Of course *he* looked completely relaxed; his hair was damp, as though he'd come straight from the health club. She could picture him playing a hard game of racquetball, maybe lying afterward in the sauna, dressing leisurely, taking his time getting to the courthouse. Half of her fiercely resented his casual attitude; the rest of her was comforted that he apparently regarded this as routine.

She struggled to her feet, feeling the baby lurch as her motion startled it, then followed Joe Warren past the reception area in the small courthouse to an unmarked door. To her surprise, inside was a conference room, not the anticipated courtroom. Her heart skipped another beat when she saw that Michael was already there, seated on the far side of the long table beside another man. His dark head was bent as he listened to something his lawyer was saying, but he looked up when she entered.

For just an instant their eyes met, Michael's bloodshot, some flicker of emotion showing in them before a betraying muscle in his cheek jerked and he turned away.

Colleen wanted to cry out. But, painfully conscious of his lawyer watching her, she kept her head bent as she sat. If only her pregnancy weren't so conspicuous! She could no longer secretly touch her stomach under the table and tell herself her baby was safe. The birth was so close, and yet her child's fate was out of her hands. All she could do was plead her case today. But a complete stranger, the judge who would walk through the door, could condemn her with a few strokes of his pen.

Joe Warren had described Judge Garner as innovative but unpredictable with custody cases. What if he decided that, in agreeing to the contract with Michael and Sheila, Colleen had given up all parental rights? What if she couldn't even visit?

By now her heart was slamming against the wall of her chest; she was sweating, and the hands she pressed against her stomach were shaking. *Calm down,* she told herself. *Breathe slowly.*

Joe Warren didn't seem to notice her panic. He exchanged a few friendly remarks with Michael's attorney, then opened his briefcase and pulled out legal forms and a yellow lined pad covered with notes, arranging them neatly before him.

Almost immediately the bailiff appeared and they stood for the judge's entrance. Colleen had imagined a dignified, white-haired gentleman, but it was a woman who swept in, her black robe settling around her when she stopped abruptly at the head of the table. Middle-aged, with graying dark hair fastened in a bun, she had shrewd brown eyes and a pursed mouth. She seemed to assess Michael and Colleen as she sat down, arranging her robes around her.

She laid her gavel on the table, produced a pair of half glasses and perched them on her nose, then peered at the paperwork in front of her. After a moment she looked up over the rims of her glasses. "Well, gentlemen, Mrs. Deering, shall we get started? As you can see, I prefer an informal atmosphere. I find it helps prevent an adversarial approach. Mr. Warren, why don't you explain the situation."

Colleen's lawyer smiled persuasively. "Thank you, Your Honor. As you can see, Mrs. Deering is expecting a baby in just a few weeks...."

Colleen listened in silence as he described her move to Clayton, her contract with her sister and her sister's death.

So much emotion, such drastic decisions, reduced to so little!

The judge leaned back in her chair, folded her hands and steepled her fingers under her chin. "So," she said after a moment. "I gather Mrs. Deering is less inclined to give her baby up to her sister's husband."

Her baby. With painful hope, Colleen wondered if the pronoun indicated that the judge sympathized. Or was it a casual reference?

"Exactly," Joe Warren said. "She was willing to go to extraordinary lengths for her beloved sister, but her acquaintance with Mr. Delaney isn't close. What Mrs. Deering could do for her sister, she doesn't feel able to do for a near stranger who was related to her only by marriage. A mother already, she can't face the agony of giving up her baby under these drastically changed circumstances."

Judge Garner's incisive gaze cut through Colleen's veneer of calm before being leveled at Michael's side of the table. "Mr. McDermott, have you any argument with the facts as Mr. Warren has presented them?"

Michael's lawyer, an older man, shook his head. "I don't believe Mr. Delaney and Mrs. Deering have any dispute over past history. The question is who will have custody. Mr. Delaney understands Mrs. Deering's qualms. He sympathizes with her pain at losing her sister, and shares it. But the fact remains that he and his wife had a verbal agreement with Mrs. Deering—she was to carry his child to term, then hand it over. I feel sure that even Mrs. Deering is aware that a contract doesn't have to be written to be binding. Mr. Delaney lost his wife. He does not want to lose his son or daughter, too."

Throughout the attorney's plea, the judge had scrutinized Michael. Despite herself, Colleen did the same. He held his head up and unflinchingly met the judge's gaze. His expression was almost detached, the emotion beneath betrayed only by clenched jaw muscles and his very stillness.

Colleen wondered what that rigid control cost him. Did he ever go home and slam his fists into the wall, scream at the fates? Or was he never able to let go?

The judge pursed her lips. "Mr. Delaney, Mrs. Deering, have you two attempted to reach a resolution on your own, or is compromise out of the question?"

For the first time since they'd begun, Michael looked directly at Colleen. His expression was implacable; he was passing the buck to her and daring her to lie.

Her attorney said smoothly, "Custody is difficult to compromise over. I believe Mrs. Deering is reasonable—"

"Yes," Colleen interrupted. "Yes. We have discussed it, without coming to a conclusion. Michael—Mr. Delaney—feels it's his right to raise his child. But this is my baby." She knew she was begging and didn't care. "I know I can provide a loving home. We discussed—he suggested—joint custody, with alternate weeks or something like that. I refused. I believe with all my heart that children need routine and security and stability. I don't think those can be provided with alternating homes. We reached a stalemate."

Judge Garner directed a look of inquiry at Michael. "Mr. Delaney, is that a fair description of your negotiations?"

"Yes. I, uh…" His face twisted, and Michael shoved his fingers through his hair. "Yes," he repeated, his voice hoarse.

"Hm." The judge leaned back in her chair and appeared to contemplate them for what must have been a full minute. She drummed her fingers on the table, and Colleen was riveted to them. The tap-tap-tap might have been her heart, drumming in her ears. She sat frozen, enduring the wait, terrified of its end. She didn't look at Michael, couldn't bear to see his expression in case the decision went for her.

Finally the fingers stopped drumming and the judge said

abruptly, "Mr. Delaney, Mrs. Deering, I have the impression that you're both well-meaning people, that you want the best for your baby. Now, I can make a decision. That's my job. But wouldn't you really rather make your own?"

Colleen's attorney leaned forward. "Your Honor…"

Judge Garner's glance silenced him. "Let's set a new date two weeks from now. In the meantime, I recommend that you attempt again to arrive yourselves at a parenting plan. Should you fail to, I'll do it for you." She picked up the gavel, whacked it on the table, then tucked her glasses into a pocket of her robe and swept out of the room, the court clerk and bailiff behind her.

In her wake, Colleen felt numb. She looked across the table at Michael and his attorney, but they appeared peculiarly far away and slightly distorted, as though thick glass separated her from them. Even Mr. Warren's voice sounded distant.

"…set up a meeting. Would Thursday…?"

Apparently they set a time and place; she nodded, though she didn't really hear. Her attorney solicitously helped her to her feet and escorted her out of the conference room. Colleen didn't look back to see if Michael was following. She tried to concentrate on what Joe Warren was telling her. He talked all the way out to her car, assuring her that the postponed hearing was a good sign, indicating that the judge was sympathetic.

"If she was hostile to the idea of surrogacy, we wouldn't have gotten this response. I'm confident that, at worst, she'll settle on joint custody, and she may go all the way for us. Now, we can meet with Mr. Delaney and McDermott, but if you'd rather hold firm…"

"No." Colleen stopped at her car. She tried to smile. "The judge is right. We should decide ourselves. Will you call me with the time?"

"Hey." He lightly cuffed her on the arm. "Cheer up. Things will work out."

"Thank you," she said tearfully, and hurried to get in, hoping he hadn't seen that she was crying.

Afterward, she didn't even remember the drive home. Thank God, she hadn't had to go back to work. Melissa Anderson, a woman of about Colleen's age who'd taught several classes in machine quilting at her shop, had offered to fill in anytime. Colleen had an hour before the kids got home from school.

She lay down on her bed and fell asleep almost instantly. She woke up, disoriented, when the front door burst open and Drew bellowed, "Hi, Mom! How come you're home?"

She got up and wandered to the top of the stairs. "Hi, guys. I had a headache and came home to lie down. But I'm feeling a little better. How was your day?"

Drew dropped his pack on the hall floor. "Soccer sign-ups end this week. Can we go to the library and sign up tonight?"

Right this second, Colleen didn't care if the check bounced. "I suppose," she said. "How was your day, Kim?"

She shrugged. "We got moved again in class. Now I'm sitting next to a *boy*. He's a jerk."

Drew had already disappeared into the kitchen. Colleen heard the refrigerator door open.

"Is he really a jerk," she asked as she came down the stairs, "or just your average eleven-year-old boy?"

Kim shrugged. "I don't know, they're all jerks. How do you tell the difference?"

"Good question."

Colleen had the weird feeling that she was outside herself watching as she maintained a perfectly normal conversation with her daughter. She was tired, bone deep, but Kim didn't seem to notice that anything was wrong.

As Colleen made dinner and then took Drew to the library to sign him up for soccer, she kept blocking any thoughts at all about the hearing. *Later,* she told herself. *Tomorrow. Just don't think about it right now.*

She tucked the kids in bed at their normal nine o'clock, then went into the living room, turned on the lamp beside the quilting frame and sat down. Her thimble protecting the finger that pushed the needle through the layers of quilt, she popped the knot at the end of the thread through the top. From long practice, Colleen began a line of tiny, even stitches.

She saw Judge Garner's face, but shoved the image back

into hiding. *Not now.* Michael's face twisting. *Tomorrow,* she told herself. Heard the judge saying, "I can make a decision. But wouldn't you really rather make your own?" *I won't think about it.*

Colleen's hand rocked faster and faster, until she blinked and saw that the stitches were getting bigger, uneven.

"Damn," she whispered, and stopped, closing her eyes.

A knock on the front door brought her head up. Who would come by at nine-thirty? Colleen dropped her thimble onto the stretched quilt and hurried to answer.

She flicked on the porch light and opened the door a crack with the chain on. Michael stood on the front step.

Her heart lurched uncomfortably. He was large and solid, the kind of man who could make a woman feel safe for the rest of her life.

My enemy, she thought, but the part of her that so inexplicably responded to him didn't believe it.

"Can I come in?"

Colleen gave herself a shake. "Yes, of course. I'm sorry." She unhooked the chain and opened the door. "Come on into the living room."

He followed her. "Are the kids in bed?"

She turned to face him. "Yes."

"Good. I, uh, waited in hopes we could talk alone."

Michael wasn't doing anything to change her sense of unreality. Was she supposed to offer him coffee? Discuss whether their attorneys had earned their fees?

"I don't mean to be unfriendly, but what do you want to talk about?" Colleen asked.

He just stood there, hands at his sides, somehow filling the room with his presence. Perhaps it was the dark house or the silence from upstairs that made her so painfully aware of the hour and the fact that he was a man and she was a woman. Or perhaps she had the power of prescience.

For what he said was, "Will you marry me, Colleen?"

Chapter 9

Stunned, Colleen stared at Michael. Without taking her eyes off him, she backed up until her legs bumped the sofa, then sank onto it. Marry him?

"Don't say anything yet," he urged swiftly. "Will you just listen for a minute?"

She bobbed her head, still too shocked to speak or even know what she felt.

Now he pushed his hands into his pockets and began to pace. "I've been thinking. It's not like this baby—our baby—was an accident. He was created out of love. Maybe not in the usual way, but that doesn't matter now. What does is that he deserves two parents." He paused and looked at her.

Colleen nodded again, automatically.

Michael took a deep breath. "I was remembering what you said about how all three of us couldn't be happy. And then it occurred to me that there's one way we could be. There are other advantages to marriage for both of us. I know you're struggling financially. I can change that. I know you worry about your kids not seeing their father very often. I… They might not accept me, but if they did…" His shoulders hunched. "I'm willing to try."

"But—" her voice was a croak "—what about you?"

For the first time Michael looked away from her. Roughly he said, "I hate going home. It's so damned empty. I've thought about selling the house, but a condo doesn't hold a lot of appeal. When I'm over here, I see what I'm missing. That makes it even harder to go home."

"But…marriage?"

He stopped his pacing right in front of her. Michael's eyes, never bluer, met hers. His expression was unguarded, leaving him vulnerable. "I won't say I'm in love with you," he said very directly, "but I'll do my damnedest to make ours a decent marriage. I think we have that potential. Unless the whole idea is repugnant to you."

Colleen's heart squeezed. "No, I…no. I'm just…you took me by surprise." A half-hysterical giggle escaped her. "Oh, Lord. I sound like some Victorian young lady. Except I'm not young. Michael, are you *sure?*"

"Yeah. I'm sure."

Colleen sat, staring up at him, this man she had trouble remembering had ever been her sister's husband. She studied him as though she had never seen his face before. He had movie-star looks: a high forehead and Slavic cheekbones, a straight, patrician nose and a mouth that gave little away. Only the lines from nose to mouth and beside his eyes showed his age and kept him from being too handsome. And those eyes of his, clear and blue as a high mountain lake, unexpected with his tan and his straight, dark hair.

Repugnant? Hardly, Colleen thought, a little stunned at what she'd just discovered about herself. Why had she never acknowledged how attracted she was to this man? Why had she told herself so many lies to explain her physical reaction to him?

Dumb question—there was something almost biblical in the prohibition: *Thou shalt not covet thy sister's husband.* It was natural that she had walled away the knowledge, hiding it even from herself. But Sheila was gone now, and it was Michael's baby Colleen carried. Nothing had to stop them now.

But…did she *like* him? Colleen wondered a little wildly. She supposed she must, she realized with near surprise, or she would have succeeded in hating him, as hard as she'd tried.

Michael wasn't an easy man to know, but what woman really did know the man she was going to marry? Some things had to be taken on faith. Instinct was all she could trust.

Michael shifted uneasily, and she realized how long she'd been staring at him. She gave her head a shake to clear it and looked down at her hands, which rested protectively over the mound of her stomach and the child within.

"Is that a no?" Michael asked, sounding strained.

"No," Colleen said, in a sort of wonder. "It's a yes."

He crouched in front of her, and a part of her noticed how the denim strained over the muscles of his thighs. Urgently he asked, "Do you mean that? You'll marry me?"

It was the best she could do for her baby, Colleen told herself. And Michael would be a good father to her children if they let him.

"Yes." She felt very peculiar, light-headed, like a helium balloon. It was unsettling, this feeling, but exhilarating, too. "Yes," she repeated. "I'll marry you."

His expression didn't change, he didn't smile, but the invisible tension charging the air vanished. Michael's shoulders relaxed, his voice was still deep, but less gruff. "Good."

"How do we…well, go about it?" Colleen had a sense of déjà vu. She'd said that once before, to her sister.

The reminder was jolting. Colleen sent out a silent plea, as she had the other night. *Sheila? Are you there? Do you mind?*

She expected silence, the vacuum she'd felt that other night, but this time her call was answered differently. A sensation of warmth enfolded her, of comfort and closeness, as though somebody had just hugged her.

But not Michael. He had stood up and retreated a few steps, as if the practicalities allowed him to restore his guard. "I thought—" he cleared his throat "—we'd talk to the pastor of the church Sheila and I attended."

Sheila. Feeling grief and joy in equal parts, Colleen mused about connections. The same minister who had buried her sister would marry Colleen and baptize her child when the time came. The choice seemed right, if also painful.

"Okay," she said steadily. "I suppose we'd better make it soon."

His gaze flicked to her stomach, then met hers again. "I'll call him tomorrow and let you know what he says."

"All right." That familiar sense of unreality was overtaking her. Had she really just agreed to marry a man about whom she had never consciously thought in romantic terms? A man who had never kissed her?

"Well," Michael said, sounding as awkward as she suddenly felt, "I'll get out of here and let you go to bed. I'm, uh, sorry I didn't buy a ring."

"That's okay." Colleen struggled up from the soft cushions. "I'm not a diamond-solitaire kind of woman."

"I wouldn't have chosen diamonds for you," he said surprisingly. "An emerald would suit you better."

You were the deep pool below. The one with the trout and all the shades of green. Cold and clear, but somehow shadowy, too.

He had a talent for saying the unexpected, for leaving her at a loss as to how to respond. Well, she'd have to learn how, Colleen thought tartly, or this marriage would be very short.

"Thank you," she said, trying for dignity, "but don't feel you have to buy a ring. It's not like ours will be that kind of marriage."

Michael's brows had drawn together during her stiff little speech, but his voice was mild. "I take the 'until death do us part' stuff seriously. I wouldn't have asked you to marry me otherwise."

She flushed. "Well, of course not, but we shouldn't pretend... I mean, I should be honest with the kids, don't you think?"

He was suddenly remote. "That's up to you of course. They're your children."

Colleen could only nod.

Michael took a step toward her. With one hand, he raised her chin. Before she could do more than feel a shiver deep inside, he bent his head and kissed her. His mouth was warm, but the kiss was frustratingly brief. As he lifted his head, she tried to read his expression, but without success.

"Good night," he said, and turned away.

By the time she reached the door, Michael was halfway down the walk. "Good night," she called, but he apparently didn't hear her. He got into his pickup without looking back.

Slowly, Colleen shut the door and turned the dead bolt. Then she closed her eyes and rested her forehead against the door frame.

What on earth had she agreed to?

Colleen at his side, Michael stood stiffly before the altar, facing the minister. Michael's brother, Stephen, waited a few steps away, as did a friend of Colleen's from the quilt shop. Behind them only the first pews were occupied, on one side with Drew and Kim, and on the other with Stephen's wife and two children.

Every cough, every shuffle of feet, was magnified in the almost empty church, with its polished, wood floor and high, arched ceiling. Late-afternoon sunlight poured in brilliant, jeweled colors through the stained-glass window.

He should be listening to Pastor Norman, who was lecturing them about the duties and joys of the marital state, perhaps in lieu of the counseling he normally would have required but had forgiven this time for the sake of the baby. But his words, however wise, didn't seem to be penetrating. Other occasions were overlaid on this one, like a double-exposed photograph. Michael's first wedding. Sheila in traditional white satin and lace, radiantly beautiful, her face perfectly made-up, a star attracting all eyes in the midst of solemnity. He remembered the funeral, this same man talking about death and rebirth and eternity. And now Colleen, quietly dignified in the soft drape of a peach-colored dress that let her pregnancy be what it was: the supremely feminine moment.

"Marriage is a promise," Pastor Norman declared, "a sacred trust. You must have trust that this man, of all others, that this woman, of all others, will hold in cupped hands your pain, your fears, your dreams, and never let them slip away."

Why did he believe in this ceremony, in binding a woman

to him, Michael wondered, when he knew perfectly well how often cupped hands could open and let pain and fears and dreams slip away? Why did he feel so sure that he was safe in Colleen's hands, that she gave only promises she would keep?

As though in logical succession, he wondered how her children felt about his marrying their mother. They had arrived with her, Kim in a green dress with ruffles, her brown hair French braided, Drew tugging at his necktie; both were unnaturally solemn and still. Even without looking at them, Michael could feel the intensity of their gazes.

His attention snapped back to the ceremony when at last the white-haired minister turned to Colleen, the open Bible in his hands.

"Do you, Colleen, take this man, Michael, to have and to hold from this day forward, for better or for worse, for richer or for poorer, in sickness and in health, to love and to cherish, till death do you part?"

She was pale, her skin almost translucent against the rich fire of auburn hair drawn back into a loose French roll. Her voice was a thin thread. "I do."

The minister's earnest gaze turned to Michael and he repeated his question. "I do," Michael responded, without hesitation, without glancing at Colleen. He would rather have walked barefoot up a rattlesnake-infested gully than show any of the emotions that twisted his gut.

"The ring?"

Michael reached into his pocket and produced the antique gold band encrusted with tiny emeralds that he had known was meant for Colleen the moment he saw it. The emeralds were leaves on a wandering vine etched in the gold. The ring was quietly pretty, as she was, and had the old-fashioned air of dignity that was so much a part of her.

Michael turned to her and held out the ring. Her lips parted when she saw it, but whatever protest she had meant to make, she swallowed. She must have realized, just as he had, that it was too late now for any kind of argument, too late for regrets. Touching her hand as little as possible, he slipped the ring onto her slender finger. It fit perfectly and looked right there, as he'd known it would.

In sonorous tones the minister proclaimed, "I now pronounce you husband and wife. Those whom God hath joined together, let no man put asunder." He paused for effect, then smiled faintly. "You may kiss the bride."

For the first time, a little color showed on Colleen's cheeks. Her lashes fluttered, and then she looked up at Michael with wide eyes in which he read apprehension.

She was more than pretty, he thought, his heart squeezing. Even pale, even with shadows beneath her eyes, Colleen had the gentle beauty of a tiny, fragrant violet, the subtle grace of fine-grained wood, the warmth of a crackling fire. In the instant before he bent his head, Michael imagined her as an old woman and knew she would still be pretty, her fine bones more prominent, her skin crinkly and soft, her smile as warm.

She lifted a hand and rested it tentatively on his shoulder as their lips touched, lingered. He had to force himself to lift his head.

God, forgive me, Michael begged, *for wanting this woman. Sheila, forgive me.*

Their gazes met and held for a second too long, his gaze betraying all his torment. The emotions he saw in hers were just as complicated, defying him to understand them. He seldom prayed, but now he did: *Dear God, let us have done the right thing.*

If it was the wrong thing, they would suffer; they would punish themselves for the rest of their lives. This minute he felt enormous guilt. He had selfishly seized what he wanted when he saw the chance, even though he didn't deserve it—he didn't deserve *her;* even though Sheila, whom he had also promised to love and cherish, was only a few months cold.

He automatically went through the motions, turning Colleen to face their families. He saw her teeth close on her full lower lip as Drew and Kim rose to their feet but waited, instead of coming forward, too grave and self-contained for their ages. Michael's sister-in-law, Jennifer, hurried to hug each in turn, smiling with the forced gaiety of a good hostess.

"What a lovely ceremony! You look beautiful, Colleen."

Colleen gave a soft sigh and glanced down at her stomach. "How nice of you to say so. This isn't exactly how a woman imagines looking on her wedding day."

"You're beautiful," Michael said roughly. "Pregnancy suits you."

Jennifer glanced at him with surprise and faint speculation, which he ignored. Behind him, Stephen said, "Well, do I get to kiss the bride?"

Michael's brother, although about the same height, looked almost nothing like him. Stephen had sandy, sun-streaked hair and a grin that still reminded Michael of Dennis the Menace. Their personalities were different, too; instead of retreating in the face of their parents' remoteness, as Michael had, Stephen had sought affection and approval elsewhere. They were closer as adults than they'd been as children, though that still meant no more than a phone call every week or so.

Colleen smiled and tilted her face up for the obligatory kiss on her cheek, then said, "Drew, Kim, come here. Have you met Michael's brother and sister-in-law? Mr. and Mrs. Delaney…"

"Actually, it's Uncle Stephen and Aunt Jennifer now," Stephen pointed out.

Again Michael noticed the betraying flutter of lashes. It was probably no surprise that Colleen hadn't considered all the consequences of marriage, given the hurried arrangements they'd made. But seeing the emotions flit across her face, he wondered, Did she not like the idea of her children acquiring new relatives?

Jennifer said brightly, "And here are Stacey and Crystal." Michael's nieces stepped forward with a reluctance to match Drew and Kim's. Jennifer went on, "Stacey is eleven, Crystal fourteen. I hope you'll all be friends."

The younger kids gave each other sidelong glances and mumbled greetings. Only Crystal had the poise to smile and say, "Hi."

Colleen introduced her matron of honor. "Melissa teaches machine-quilting classes at my shop. She's been nice enough to offer to take over temporarily when the baby comes."

Melissa Anderson was petite and dark-haired, the posses-sor of a quick smile and a tendency to chatter. Michael didn't have the impression that she and Colleen were especially close. He was bothered that Colleen hadn't invited any old friends. Maybe she had, and they hadn't been able to make it. But maybe not; maybe she hadn't wanted any of them here because she didn't regard this marriage as meaningful or permanent. She had claimed not to find him repugnant, but that didn't mean she felt any attraction. If that was so, he couldn't blame her if she didn't want to make much of the ceremony.

His brooding was interrupted by Jennifer, who looked around expectantly. "Shall we go on to the restaurant?"

A poor excuse for a wedding reception, the dinner couldn't be called a success. The kids sat at one table, and despite Jennifer's effort to get them talking, Michael heard little but whispers between siblings.

Stephen offered an obligatory toast. After it was drunk, an awkward pause followed. Then Colleen said stiffly, "I want to thank all of you for coming. Our marriage is a little unconven-tional, and you've been nice about it."

"Don't be silly!" Jennifer said after a silent moment of communication with her husband. "We're all for it. I don't see how you two could have come up with a better solution."

Michael thought she was even telling the truth. Jennifer was a nice woman who, like Colleen, believed family came first.

Stephen and Melissa tripped over each other hastening to agree.

Colleen gave a wobbly smile. "Thank you. I only hope Michael's parents don't mind."

"They sent their best wishes," Michael said, hearing the flatness in his own voice.

Little crinkles appeared on Colleen's smooth brow. "You said they retired to Florida?"

Stephen said, "Yeah, on a nice little lake. I imagine they figured they could only make one trip, and they'd save it to see their new grandchild."

"I suppose that makes sense."

But Michael could tell that it didn't really, not to her. When Kim got married someday, Colleen would be there no matter what.

"We're not close," he said brusquely, and was sorry when she gave a tiny nod and looked away.

Eventually Melissa asked about their plans.

"To tell you the truth," Colleen admitted, "we haven't gotten very far in discussing the future. It's not as though we've planned a honeymoon or anything like that. This was all kind of sudden."

Her friend sounded surprised. "But what are you going to do for the immediate future?" She stopped, looking flustered. "Not that it's any of my business."

Colleen's cheeks flushed, and she studiously avoided meeting Michael's eyes. She gave a laugh that didn't sound natural. "We did get that far. Michael's coming home with me. That way…well, we don't have to uproot the kids while we consider our next step."

"I'll sell my house." He hadn't consciously decided; the words just seemed to come of their own volition, but they sounded right. "I don't see how we could live in it."

She looked at him as though no one else was in the room. He wished it were true, that his sister-in-law hadn't steamrolled him into this dinner. Colleen sounded tentative. "I've been thinking about it since we talked. If you're just worried that I'd be uncomfortable…"

"It's Sheila's house," he said gruffly. "Let's make a new start."

She searched his face. "Michael, if this is for me…"

"For both of us. Let's buy a big house, one where all the kids can have their own rooms. And I need an office, and you a sewing room." His voice had quickened. Funny he could see it so clearly. An old house, with a huge kitchen and a wide front porch and gnarled apple trees. And lilacs, and maybe an acre or two with a barn. And a rope swing. He'd always wanted one himself.

But he abruptly remembered the other people around the

table. "We can talk about it," he said neutrally. "See what Drew and Kim think."

The party broke up shortly thereafter, probably to the relief of everyone. Unfortunately that left Michael to trail Colleen up to her front porch, toothbrush and pajamas in hand. He had followed her home in his own car, wishing he could hear the conversation taking place ahead of him in her old Honda. After parking behind her in the driveway, he was now waiting patiently for her to unlock her front door. Beside him her two kids were shifting from foot to foot.

"Jeez, Mom," the nine-year-old finally whined.

"It's just stuck." She blew out a puff of air, and her voice vibrated with tension. "Michael…?"

It seemed symbolic that he had to let himself into her house, rather than sweeping her across his own threshold. The lock gave immediately, and Michael thought he heard her mutter something about hating helpless women.

Brushing past Michael, Drew thundered up the stairs, flinging his tie over the banister as he went. Kim wasn't far behind.

"Can I change, Mom?" she called as she went.

"I suppose…" Colleen's voice trailed off at the slam of a bedroom door. She offered Michael an apologetic grimace. "I'm sorry. Drew hates what he calls 'stiff' clothes, and Kim was sure she looked like a five-year-old in that dress. Of course she loved it back when I bought it last fall."

"That's okay. This is their house."

They were still standing in the front hall. Colleen bit her lip and looked around. "I guess it's yours now, too."

Was she trying to see it through his eyes? If so, she didn't need to worry. Maybe this house was just a rental, but she had made it a home. A quilt in shades of blue and green in a kaleidoscopic pattern hung on the wall. Below it, on an antique cherry side table with turned legs, was a stoneware pitcher filled with bright yellow roses. The table needed refinishing, the pitcher had probably cost a dime at a garage sale, but the effect was charming and cozy. It reminded him of Colleen and why he was so drawn to her.

He had to clear his throat. "I'll try not to get in your way. You don't have to change anything because of me."

"Don't be silly!" She frowned, but she also crossed her arms over her swollen belly, as though to hunch in on herself. "I don't want you feeling like a guest."

Which was exactly what he did feel like—an unwelcome guest, at that. Colleen would probably give anything right this minute for him to disappear, go home to his own house. He'd even thought of suggesting he do just that, but, damn it, he should start as he meant to go on! And he meant this to be a real marriage.

"We, um, haven't talked about sleeping arrangements," she began, her cheeks pinkening, and he interrupted.

"I'd figured on the couch for now."

"Oh, dear." She nibbled on her lower lip. "That's not fair to you. But I...I don't know what else to suggest...."

"It'll be fine," he said quietly. He wanted badly to touch her, if only in reassurance, but instinct told him he would alarm her if he did. Maybe he was wrong—she was comfortable with physical affection in a way he'd never been—but he didn't want to take the chance. "Why don't you just do whatever you normally would? Unless you want to talk."

"I suppose we should." She gave an unconvincing laugh. "But if you don't mind, I think I'd rather wait. I guess getting married is enough for one day."

On the surface, the evening was pleasantly domestic. Colleen quilted, Michael pretended to read first the newspaper, then a book. The kids appeared on and off, mostly to request snacks. About the third time, Colleen sighed. "I suppose this means neither of you ate your dinner."

Underneath the surface flowed powerful undercurrents. Except for stolen glances, Drew and Kim ignored Michael. He himself read sentences over and over, and still they made no sense. His nerves prickled with his awareness of Colleen. He felt every breath she took, every time she looked at him. The silence was worse than the conversation they weren't having.

He couldn't relax, couldn't think of any excuse to get out

of the room for more than a minute. Gritting his teeth, Michael wondered what had made him think he had a place here. This marriage had about as much chance of succeeding as a chronic check bouncer did of getting a loan.

The only reason Colleen had married him was to hold on to her child. Maybe the thought of financial security had influenced her, too, he didn't know. But she didn't want him, she didn't love him, and chances were she didn't even like him. Things hadn't changed much; what still counted was his ability to father a child.

Without thinking, he swore under his breath, which earned him an anxious glance. Unable to stand the tension for another minute, Michael shot to his feet.

He said the first thing that came into his head. "I'm going to go shave."

"Shave?" She looked alarmed.

Hell. A normal groom probably did shave before his wedding night so his whiskers wouldn't scrape his bride's face. Michael seemed to remember doing so on his honeymoon with Sheila. He couldn't think of any subtle way now of denying that he had designs on Colleen, so all he did was add, "And brush my teeth."

"Oh." Blushing, she jumped up with unflattering alacrity. "I'd better get the kids tucked into bed. Then I'll find you some blankets."

"No hurry," he said.

Whisking out of the room, she said hastily, "No, no, I'm tired, too. It's been a long day."

His sardonic eye took in the clock on the end table. Eight forty-five, and they were going to bed. Separately.

What a wedding night.

Would she and Michael laugh someday, looking back at their wedding night? Colleen punched her pillow and turned again, trying to find a comfortable position. The baby kicked her right in the pelvic bone, as though to remind her of his presence. Colleen made a face into the darkness. Why kid herself about

Michael's reasons for marrying her? He was a decent man who would do his best, but it wasn't her he wanted. It was his son or daughter. Theirs was a marriage of convenience, plain and simple.

Surely it would get easier, Colleen thought plaintively. Of course tonight had been awkward! Even her wedding night with Ben had been. Marriage was a big step. Who knew what to expect? The thing to do, she decided, was to be practical about this, try not to read all sorts of emotion into it. In just a few days, she and Drew and Kim would become used to having Michael here; they would settle on a routine, and tonight's awkwardness would be forgotten.

Although maybe he was right that they should look for a new house. Originally Colleen had been surprised when he suggested moving in with her, instead of her and the kids moving in with him.

"Just temporarily," he'd said, in that calm voice she sensed he was using to lull her fears. "That way you don't have to worry about packing yet, and things won't change too suddenly for Drew and Kim."

Now, Colleen could admit to how relieved she had been. Part of her was convinced that her sister would have approved her decision to marry Michael. But telling herself that was one thing; moving into Sheila's house, hanging her clothes in Sheila's closet, eventually sleeping in Sheila's bed, was another. If their marriage was to have any chance at all, they couldn't live with Sheila's ghost.

Colleen laboriously shifted again, feeling as if she had a bowling ball plopped on her bladder. "Kiddo," she said under her breath, "you're a load."

Michael had been nice about sleeping on the couch. She'd just *assumed* they wouldn't sleep together, at least until after the baby was born. Not until they'd walked in the door tonight did she realized they hadn't talked about it. Of course he couldn't possibly *want* a woman who was eight months pregnant, but probably they should have discussed it. There were lots of things they should have talked about, but especially that one. Sex.

Did he want her at all? Did he assume they would make love as soon as it was practical, or was it something that would come when—if—they were both ready? When Michael kissed and touched her, would he be thinking about Sheila?

This was the first time Colleen could remember wishing she and Sheila hadn't so resembled each other. Every time Michael looked at her, he must be reminded of Sheila. Would he ever quit seeing Sheila and see *her?*

Sighing, she rolled over for the tenth time or so. *Her wedding night.* It was almost funny.

Colleen found herself remembering Ben, the way he touched her, the feel of his body fitting to hers. Mostly their sex life had been comfortable, familiar. Any magic had faded away long before Kim was born. She couldn't remember caring very much. She'd vaguely thought that sex was a small part of marriage, and she was otherwise content. Obviously, Ben hadn't been. She didn't even blame him.

Contentment didn't seem like the kind of emotion a woman would feel with Michael. From things Sheila and he had said, Colleen guessed that all had not been well with their marriage. But Sheila hadn't descended to feeling anything as dull as contentment or irritation. She'd sometimes been angry, perhaps lonely or hurt. But Colleen had never doubted that Sheila still longed for her husband—for the man Colleen had just married—with all her being.

But she was gone, and Colleen now had everything that had been hers. Except Michael's love.

Did she even want it? Colleen was far from sure. Marriage was one thing; it meant an extra paycheck, somebody to talk over problems with, run Drew to soccer on occasion, mow the lawn, check the oil in her car.

But love—that was something else. Michael Delaney was an intense man. He wouldn't give his love lightly, and he would expect as much in return. Thanks to her upbringing, the only real relationship she'd ever had with a man was her marriage to Ben, and with him she'd been able to hold something back. That reserve had prevented her from being devastated by the divorce. It had allowed her to make her children the center of her life.

Colleen didn't know that she wanted to change that. Of course, Michael hadn't asked her to—might never ask her to. So why worry?

No, what they needed to do was have a nice, sensible discussion and lay everything out on the table. She would tell him that sex would be fine eventually—when they knew each other well enough. Which they didn't yet.

A children's ditty floated through her mind. *First comes love, then comes marriage, then comes the baby in the baby carriage.*

Talk about backward, she thought sleepily. In their case, first came the baby, then the marriage. Love was optional.

Chapter 10

"This place has 3500 square feet, and it's loaded with amenities. You'll love the kitchen," the Realtor enthused, as she climbed out of the car.

Colleen accepted Michael's hand and eased herself out of the backseat. "How do you feel?" he murmured.

"I'm fine," she said, although she pressed a hand to her lower back, which seemed to have a perpetual ache these days.

The Realtor, a pleasant woman named Evelyn Coats, was talking about the landscaping, the three-car garage and the rec room *plus* a family room. Colleen scarcely listened. Instead, she gazed up at the pretentious English Tudor facade. She couldn't imagine living in a place like this. Maybe in the normal course of events, a person would gradually get used to wealth. She, on the other hand, had been struggling to pay for groceries just a few weeks ago.

Reluctantly Colleen followed the Realtor and her husband inside. How odd it still felt to think of him that way!

Inside, the coolness was a relief after the June heat of eastern Washington, but she hated on sight the black-and-white marble foyer and the cream carpet in the living room off to one side.

She hadn't liked any of the houses they'd seen today. The price range Michael had given Evelyn still staggered Colleen. She kept feeling as if somebody would slap her hand and tell her she didn't belong here.

"Michael..." she said tentatively.

But he was disappearing after Evelyn toward the kitchen and didn't hear her. Instead of following them, Colleen drifted into the living room and looked out the bay window. The house stood halfway up a dry hillside, the winding road lined with equally ostentatious houses in this new, upscale development. Below, Clayton was a green oasis; mature elms and maples lined the streets of pleasant old houses. In the apple orchards on the outskirts, trees marched in disciplined lines, heavy branches propped up with sticks. Beyond town were the hills, gold-green waves of wheat fields beside purple stripes of fallow earth that swept in curves over the crests.

"You don't like it."

The carpet was so thick she hadn't heard him coming. She tried to hide her start. She didn't want Michael to know how unsettlingly aware she was of him when he stood this close. Her nerves prickled, and even without turning she knew how lean and broad-shouldered he was in his dark business suit, how silent and contained the way he moved. She even knew that his face would be impassive, that he would be taking care not to give away his own feelings.

"Do you?" she asked.

The pause probably only lasted a few seconds, but to her it stretched out painfully. Still gazing out the window, she noticed Evelyn hurrying down the driveway to the car and leaning in as she hunted for something.

"No."

Damn him for being so uncommunicative, Colleen thought in frustration. It wasn't as though she hadn't tried; several times they had sat down to talk. Michael had suggested again that they put his house on the market and look for a new one. Colleen had agreed. If it was all right with her, he would call the Realtor. Fine. She had groped to remember all the other things she'd meant to discuss with him and could think of only one. Sex. As distant, as coolly polite as the conversation had been, there was no way on God's green earth she could ask, "Do you want to have sex with me? Or do you not care?"

And somehow, with that one subject lingering unresolved, with the constant wondering on her part, if not his, any openness between them had been barred. They had stayed strangers coexisting in the same house. When he cleaned up the kitchen after dinner, Colleen thanked him. When she cooked breakfast, he thanked her. They conducted polite conversations. Instead of getting used to his presence, she was more aware of it by the day. More aware of *him*.

But some things had to be said.

Colleen took a deep breath. "Michael, I don't know if this is such a good idea. Somehow when we talked about it, I wasn't picturing houses on this scale. Buying a place like this would be such an expensive commitment. And under the circumstances..."

She felt his sudden tension. "The circumstances?"

Why pretend? Colleen lifted her chin. "What if our marriage doesn't last?"

A flash of raw emotion crossed his face before he snapped, "Is that the attitude you went into this with?"

Colleen pressed a hand to her throat. "I didn't say—"

"Is our marriage so bad?"

She had a sudden memory of two days before, when she'd come home from work exhausted to find that Michael had already started dinner. He'd sat her down, made her a cup of herb tea and helped Kim with her math homework. Right this minute, it wasn't what Michael had done that she remembered; it was the tenderness she'd imagined she saw in his eyes.

"No," she said huskily, shaking her head. "No, it's not bad."

As simply as that, the atmosphere changed. He was still looking at her, but his eyes held a light that quickened her pulse, made her swallow hard. The air shimmered with unspoken emotions—all those things they should have said and hadn't. She was suddenly quite sure that he wanted to kiss her, that he was going to kiss her, and she forgot everything else in a rush of yearning for something she hadn't even known she wanted.

But they both heard the front door slam, and as quickly

as a slide projector clicks to the next frame, Michael was stepping back.

His voice was hoarse, however, letting her know she hadn't imagined the stark hunger in his eyes. "We've made the commitment. Let's not worry about the money side of it. I think we'll be happier when we move."

Before she could respond, Evelyn appeared in the arched entry to the living room. She carried the multiple-listing book. "Why don't we sit down and take a look. Obviously I'm not clear on what you want."

In the kitchen they all sat at the built-in booth and thumbed through the dog-eared pages showing houses for sale. Colleen was surprised when Michael zeroed in on a couple of old houses, both of which had acreage. Daily, it seemed, she had to readjust her image of him. Sheila's taste had apparently predominated more in her marriage than Colleen had realized.

"We'd better save looking at them for another day," he said at last, glancing at his watch.

Evelyn promised to make appointments with the owners for Saturday morning, and they headed back to the realty office.

Over dinner that evening, Michael suggested that Drew and Kim come with them on Saturday. So far, they still seemed to think of him as Uncle Michael, a favored visitor. His approach to them was diffident. On the couple of occasions he'd asked for help, there had been no suggestion he was issuing an order. Colleen wasn't quite sure what would happen when that changed.

She'd told them about her decision to marry him in the same, upbeat way she'd presented her foray into surrogacy. They had asked a few questions. Would Uncle Michael live with them? Would their last name change? Had he kissed her? She had been left uneasily wondering how they really felt about it, but knowing she couldn't change her mind. Drew and Kim would adjust. They *had* to.

Now, he reminded the kids, "It'll be your house, too."

"Sure, I don't mind going," Kim said, shrugging.

"What kind of house do you wish we'd buy?" Michael

asked. He nodded at Drew. "Would you pass the broccoli, please?"

"I want my own bedroom," Kim said.

"You have your own bedroom now," Colleen said pointedly.

"Yeah, but if the baby's a girl, I'll bet you'd stick her in with me."

Drew scrunched up his face. "Or with me if he's a boy."

"Uh…" Colleen met Michael's amused eyes. "Probably," she admitted.

"And a family room would be cool, so we could have two TVs. Then we wouldn't have to fight about what to watch."

"Yeah!" Drew agreed. "And a hill for sledding."

Michael grinned, more relaxed than Colleen remembered seeing him with the kids. "I won't promise that. But we'll take it into consideration."

"I want a sunken bathtub," Kim chimed in. "Remember how Lorelei had one, Mom?"

"Uh-huh. It always sounded like the height of decadence," Colleen said.

"What's decadence?" Drew asked.

"Luxury," Michael said. When Drew still looked puzzled, he added, "Steak, instead of hamburger."

Kim, who had just taken a bite of her hamburger, said around the full mouthful, "Now that we have all of Uncle Michael's money, can we be decadent and eat steak, instead of hamburger?"

Colleen winced. Maybe, in her explanations, she had leaned a little too heavily on the practical reasons for her marriage to Michael. As sharply as she ever spoke to the kids, she said, "That was rude. Please apologize to your uncle—" She stopped, realizing she hadn't improved matters.

"Why don't we just make it Michael," he suggested, sounding unperturbed, not looking at her. "If you two are comfortable with that."

Drew frowned. "Aren't you our uncle anymore?"

"I don't think so. Here, do you want the catsup?"

Her son ignored the distraction. "What are you, then?"

Colleen touched his hand, half in warning. "Your stepfather. Do you remember our talking about it?"

Loudly Kim said, "I won't call him Dad."

Colleen glanced quickly at Michael, but if he was hurt by this first, small rebellion, he didn't show it.

"You have a father," he said, his tone mild. "That's why I suggested you just use my name. Unless you have a better idea."

Kim bent her head so that a curtain of brown hair hid her face. She pushed her baked beans around with her fork. "No, I guess that's all right."

"Sure," Drew said.

Colleen used the lull in the conversation to change the subject. "Drew, after dinner I want you to clear the table. Kim, you load the dishwasher, please. Then both of you be sure to finish your homework."

"Are you going somewhere?"

"A Lamaze class." Colleen picked up her dishes and took them to the sink. "You learn about childbirth in them. Your…Michael is going with me. The sitter should be here any minute."

"You already had *us*," Kim said. "How come you're taking a class?"

When Colleen came back to the table, she planted a kiss on the top of her daughter's head. "You know what, kiddo? I haven't had a baby in nine years. Just like I have to read your math book sometimes before I can help you, I figured it wouldn't hurt to brush up on the breathing techniques."

Michael stood, too, and smiled at Colleen over Kim's head. The rare smile transformed his lean face and reminded her of the simple joy and wonder there the day she'd announced her pregnancy. She felt an uncomfortable tug in her chest when he said, "Your mom may know everything, but I don't. I need a class. Otherwise, while your mom's in labor I'll be standing around wringing my hands."

Colleen's sense of humor had deserted her these past weeks, but now she felt a bubble of amusement at the picture. "Maybe you should pace and tear at your hair, instead," she suggested.

His smile widened into a grin, crooked and sexy. "You never know, I might even faint."

But at the class that evening, Colleen could see that he was taking his part in the business of childbirth far too seriously to opt out by keeling over. It was a very strange hour. There they were, the two of them, a couple just like all the others. The participants ranged from the absurdly young, a frightened-looking girl who couldn't have been more than eighteen with a long-haired boy no older, to several couples in their thirties. Most held hands as the instructor talked about the stages of labor.

Colleen looked down at her own enormous belly a little ruefully. She was obviously the closest to the end; under other circumstances, she would have started the four-week course at least a month ago. But Sheila was to have been her partner in labor, the one who sat beside her tonight, and since her sister's death, Colleen had blocked out thoughts of everything they'd intended to do together.

Asking Michael had been an impulse. Even as the words came out of her mouth the previous week, she'd half hoped he'd make an excuse. But in her heart she'd known he wouldn't. He'd glanced up from the newspaper and said with what sounded like deliberate casualness, "Sure, if you'll be comfortable having me there." But his expression had told her more. For that moment, Michael wasn't a stranger staying with her; he was her husband.

In the classroom, the lights went out and a film began to roll. Colleen sneaked a glance at Michael and saw that he was watching with obvious fascination. She made herself look back at the screen, where a woman, cheerfully smiling through the early stages of labor, was having a fetal monitor hooked up.

Ben had attended Lamaze classes with her, though reluctantly. He'd felt like an idiot puffing and panting, he said, and made her feel foolish, too. But during labor itself, he was a rock, encouraging, supportive, occasionally funny. It had been one of his better moments, Colleen reflected.

She had a flash of remembering herself alternately whimpering and swearing, and Ben holding her hands throughout.

"You tell 'em!" he'd said, his face inches from hers. Then, "Breathe, damn it!"

As she remembered it, her nightgown had been hiked up around her waist, her feet were in the stirrups, and she'd been sweating and gasping and pushing. Not a pretty sight.

What a horrifying thought. Did she really want *Michael* to see her like that? Worse yet, for that to be his first sight of her naked?

Some introduction to marriage.

The woman on the screen wasn't smiling anymore, but she wasn't screaming or swearing, either. No, she was dutifully doing her breathing while her unruffled husband rubbed her back. No sweat there.

Colleen sneaked another look at Michael, only to find that now he was watching her. She gave a weak smile and firmly fixed her eyes on the screen, though she remained so conscious of him beside her that she didn't even notice the triumphant conclusion to the film. Before she knew it, the lights were back on.

The instructor beamed at them. "Now, husbands, help your wives get comfortable on these mats. On your side, ladies."

Husbands got a lesson in giving back rubs, which had the saving grace that Michael was behind Colleen when he lifted her shirt and laid his large, warm hands on her back. Her reaction was shockingly intense, considering how essentially impersonal the contact was. Heat rushed over her in a tide, leaving goose bumps in its wake. He could hardly fail to notice them, but she was grateful that at least he couldn't see her expression.

Colleen closed her eyes when Michael began to gently knead her shoulders, then the long muscles on each side of her spine. It was natural for her to be starved for physical affection, she told herself briskly—except, she couldn't help remembering, that the couple of times she'd dated since her divorce, she hadn't felt any desire at all to get physical, much less be affectionate.

Never mind, she told herself. *Quit analyzing everything. Just enjoy.*

Michael seemed to know all the places that ached, and his

deft touch untied knots that fussing about him had probably tied in the first place. But he also seemed to have a second sense about all the spots where she was most responsive. His fingers lingered on her neck and then traveled slowly, sensuously, down her spine to the small of her back. She imagined his hand traveling lower yet and gave a small groan, arching her back before she snapped her eyes open.

Good Lord, she was about to start rubbing against him like a cat in heat!

"Excellent!" the instructor proclaimed, standing just above Colleen. "See how you've relaxed her? A good massage is invaluable during labor." She proceeded to the front of the room and clapped her hands. "All right, class, let's work on the first stage of breathing now."

Colleen felt like an idiot all over again as she panted rhythmically to Michael's coaching. She could feel the heat in her cheeks, and her skin still tingled everywhere he'd touched. His deep voice was calm as he counted for her and then said, "Now, a deep breath. That's right," but she couldn't help noticing he was looking at her mouth and not meeting her eyes.

No wonder. She had forgotten how, well, *intimate* this was. What on earth had possessed her to ask him to come? He'd probably imagined the joys of seeing his son born without realizing he was going to have to hold her hand for hours first. But unless he chickened out, there was no way she could uninvite him.

In the BMW on the way home she asked, "Well, what did you think?"

"Does that breathing stuff really do any good?"

"Believe it or not, it does. Probably anything that distracted a person would work."

They traveled several blocks in silence, the interior of the car dark. Abruptly Michael asked, "Are you scared?"

"Scared?" She glanced at him in surprise. "Heavens, no! To tell you the truth, I'm looking forward to getting it over with. It'll be nice to be able to get out of bed again without it being a major production. I must look like a beached whale."

"You don't."

"Really?" she said hopefully.

"No. You look—" He stopped.

"I look?" Colleen prompted, in a near whisper.

"I told you." Michael spoke gruffly. "Beautiful."

"Thank you." What else could the poor man have said? Colleen studied his profile. "Michael, you don't have to do this if you don't want to."

"Do this—?" Frowning, he glanced at her. "What do you mean?"

The edge to his question made her feel defensive. "Stay with me when I'm in labor. If you'd rather not…"

"Don't be ridiculous," he said dauntingly, ending the discussion.

As soon as they got home, while he was still closing the garage door, Colleen paid the babysitter, a teenager who lived down the street. The head start gave her a chance to escape upstairs to kiss the kids good-night and go straight to bed herself, even if it was absurdly early. She had done that a lot lately, sometimes quilting on the baby's Carousel Horses, using her hoop, but also discovering somewhat to her surprise that she could fall asleep at eight-thirty. She only hoped that Michael attributed her early bedtimes to pregnancy, not cowardice.

The next three days were long. Colleen sat as much as possible at work, but even so, by closing time her ankles were swollen and she was exhausted. Melissa had started out by taking over for an hour or so, when Colleen was desperate, but now she was working Saturdays and Sundays, and she'd insisted she could manage by herself for three or four weeks after the baby was born.

"I'll turn all your hand quilters into machine quilters," she'd promised impishly. "Just think how much faster they'll be able to churn out quilts, and how much more fabric they'll need!"

Business was steadily increasing, thank goodness, enough to pay Melissa's salary. Colleen kept reminding herself that she didn't have to worry so much about money anymore, but deep inside she didn't quite believe it—or wouldn't let herself believe it. Anyway, she had no intention of becoming dependent on Michael. Her shop was more than her joy; it was her safety net.

Saturday morning Michael insisted on taking the whole family out for breakfast before they met the Realtor at the first house. The kids were so excited about the prospect of having waffles at a restaurant, it made Colleen realize how few treats they'd had this past year.

"Can we order *anything?*" Drew asked, wide-eyed as he looked at the glossy menu.

"Why not?" Michael said, with a grin that made him look almost as young as her son.

Kim asked daringly, "Can I have a side of smoked ham *and* waffles?"

"You bet."

Colleen opened her mouth to ask if Kim really thought she could eat that much, then closed it. Michael was having fun indulging them. Did it matter if they didn't eat every bite? Thrift had become so ingrained in her she had trouble accepting that she didn't have to be so careful anymore. Maybe that was typical of someone in her circumstances who was newly married. Or maybe it was because she didn't *feel* married.

Evelyn Coats was waiting for them at the first house, a Victorian that would have had more charm if housing developments hadn't sprung up all around it. When Evelyn asked if they wanted to see inside, Michael glanced at Colleen with a lifted brow.

"It's up to you," she said, and wondered at his frown.

"Let's go on to the next place," he said.

On the way, they briefly discussed whether they ought to lower the asking price on his house. At the moment, his cleaner was coming in twice a week, but otherwise the house sat empty.

Colleen wondered how Michael felt about the prospect of going through Sheila's things and deciding what to save and what to get rid of. Everything that Sheila had touched or used or worn would hold memories. Even with everyday stuff—

kitchen utensils or linen—some had been wedding presents, or the object of one of Sheila's passing obsessions. How many times had Colleen heard her sister say, "Col, you should see it! I've absolutely got to have one."

Perhaps cleaning out his house would be cathartic for Michael. Obviously he didn't want to live with those memories, but closing the door and walking away hadn't resolved anything. The memories were waiting, preserved, as though the house he'd shared with Sheila had been frozen in time.

Colleen shook herself out of her brooding when the car slowed to turn into a driveway. This place looked more promising even from the quiet road. The turn-of-the-century house was on the outskirts of the old part of town within bike-riding distance of the elementary school. The houses here were all well cared for in a comfortable way. Many still had an acre or more, and behind them stretched a young orchard of apple trees knee-deep in grass.

"Looks like it might be possible to keep a horse here," Michael said casually.

Colleen would have liked to clap her hand over his mouth. It wasn't fair to raise Kim's hopes like that when so much was up in the air.

But it was too late.

"Cool," Kim breathed as Michael drew the car to a stop behind Evelyn's. Both kids were out in a flash, heading for a small barn, painted gray-blue to match the house, with double doors standing open.

Despite her disquiet about their expectations, Colleen didn't even watch them go. She was pierced by an achingly sweet feeling of homecoming. The tall, straight house with gingerbread trim, a wide porch and a bay window reminded her of the one she'd grown up in, though it had been on a smaller scale. Perhaps it was the smells of freshly mown grass, the heady scent of the white, old-fashioned roses climbing the porch, that brought a sudden rush of memories: herself playing dress-up on the porch in her mother's clothes, tucking a rose behind her ear; her mother twirling her until they were both so dizzy they fell down laughing on the grass; hiding under the porch, peering out through the latticework, determined to stay there despite the cobwebs and the damp earth, watching as Sheila—maybe five or six at the time—ran from shrub to shrub in the yard hunting for her with cries of, "I know you're there!" and getting increasingly anxious.

Colleen gave her head a shake. Evelyn was talking about the new roof and remodeled kitchen, but Michael, although seeming to listen attentively, was watching Colleen. She crossed her arms self-consciously and said, at the first pause, "Well, shall we go in?"

The kids, chattering about the two stalls and the pasture, joined them as they wandered through the ground floor of the old house. The small front parlor had a window seat, as she'd somehow known it would; when she'd been about Kim's age, Colleen had spent hours reading and dreaming on the window seat. The kitchen was huge, with a brick floor, glass-fronted maple cabinets and tile countertop, the modern appliances discreetly hidden behind false fronts. Ceilings were high, the twelve-inch molding refinished to a warm glow. After following Michael and Evelyn through the library, dining room and back parlor, Colleen emerged into the hall just in time to look up and see her son swinging his leg over the stair banister preparatory to sliding down.

One look from Colleen had him innocently waiting at the top of the staircase. From there he and Kim ran ahead, calling, "I claim this bedroom!"

"I understand a third bathroom has been added here in the master suite…." Evelyn pushed open a door. "Oh, look at the claw-footed tub!"

Colleen stood in the middle of the large bedroom with sash windows that overlooked the lawn and the orchard, and thought, *This house is perfect. If only…*

At last she identified the source of the ache that gripped her heart. *If only we really were a family.* Instead, she had to wonder, Would Michael take another of the bedrooms? How long could they live together as strangers?

Beside her, he said quietly, "The small room next door would make a good nursery."

"Yes."

He must have expected more, because his gaze stayed on her face. At last he gestured around them. "What do you think?"

"Do *you* like it?"

"Why do you keep doing that?" The edge she seldom heard was in his voice.

"Doing what?"

"Deferring to me. As if you don't have an opinion."

"I…" If she'd had time to think, she would have been more careful, but as it was, the truth just slipped out. "It's your money."

"*Our* money." His voice was still quiet, but real anger glittered in his blue eyes. "I don't remember signing a prenuptial agreement that labeled yours and mine. This is a community-property state, you know."

Evelyn was down the hall somewhere now; Colleen heard her talking to one of the kids. She and Michael were alone in the bedroom that would be theirs if they bought the house, the room in which they might someday share a bed like the four-poster here now.

"Do you *feel* married?" Colleen asked, surprising herself.

He blinked, silent for a moment. "Yes," he said finally in an odd tone. "I took the vows seriously."

Even the promise to love and cherish? she wondered. "I'm sorry," she said, pushing her hair back from her forehead. "There have just been so many changes lately. I guess I'm overwhelmed. Sometimes I have this feeling of…unreality. Do you understand?"

"Yeah." Michael let out a long breath. "You're right. I've been pushing you. Shall we forget moving for now?"

She should have felt relieved. She realized she'd been disgruntled from the start of their house hunting. The rental was *hers*, and on some level she hadn't wanted to surrender it, even if it was too small, even if they could afford a nicer place. However irrational, she would have said, "Yes, let's forget it," had Michael asked her yesterday. Or even this morning. But now…

Colleen looked around at the bedroom, with its pale yellow wallpaper and lacy window valances, the gleaming oak floor and the black claw-foot of the deep porcelain bathtub with shiny brass fittings she could just see through the open door. Over the windowsill peeked one of those roses, elegantly packed with white petals that swirled around a green button eye. She could hear Drew's excited voice as he discovered the entrance to an attic, and the tap-tap-tap that could only be Kim twirling in one of the spacious bedrooms down the long hall.

Feeling as though she were stepping out of an airplane, trusting the parachute someone else had packed, Colleen admitted in a rush, "To tell you the truth, I love this house."

It wasn't what he'd expected. Michael's face was blank for an instant as though he'd braced himself for disappointment. When her admission at last sank in, his grin dawned slowly. "Yeah? Me, too. Shall we buy it?"

She blinked. "Just like that?"

"Why not?"

"Can you…can *we* afford it?"

His smile took her breath away. "Hell, yes."

"All right." Colleen gave a little nod, then a firmer one. "Let's do it."

Michael grabbed her hands, swung her in a circle, then planted a kiss on her cheek before vanishing out the bedroom door. Astonished, she stared after him. Then she smiled, feeling a funny little fizz of excitement mixed with her terror.

"Well, baby," she said, patting her stomach. "Shall we go look at your room?"

They'd made one more childbirth class. It was a good thing she'd already been through this twice, Colleen reflected, sitting on the edge of the bed now and waiting for the contraction to pass. If she'd needed more than a refresher, she would have been out of luck. When her muscles relaxed their grip, she hurriedly slipped into her robe and opened the bedroom door.

"Michael?" she called. "Hey, kids!"

"Do I have to get up?" Kim groaned from her bedroom.

"Yes, and hurry," Colleen said. "Wake your brother."

Could Michael have left for work already? she worried. But she'd have sworn she'd heard the kettle whistling in the kitchen only a few minutes ago. Colleen raised her voice and tried again. "Michael?"

He came out of the kitchen to stand at the foot of the stairs, a cup of coffee in his hand, his white shirt unbuttoned and a tie dangling around his neck. Even with another contraction coming on, Colleen noticed the expanse of brown chest and lean stomach, with only a dusting of dark hair.

"Yeah?" His expression altered and he set his cup down on the hall table. "Are you all right?"

"Um." She tried to smile, closed her eyes and leaned against the door frame. A small gasp escaped her. By the time the pain receded and she opened her eyes, Michael was at her side. She licked dry lips. "It's showtime."

Michael's hands closed on her upper arms. "Now? Good God, I don't know if I'm ready. Are *you* ready?"

Colleen gave a weak laugh. "I don't think that matters."

He was suddenly all business. "Can you get dressed while I rouse the kids?"

"Sure."

His hands slid down her arms, lingering, caressing. "Then I'll get them in gear." She'd have sworn he released her reluctantly. But the moment she turned away, he was moving. His bellow would have roused the dead. "Kim! Drew! Up and at 'em!"

Colleen eased herself back down on the bed to wait out the next contraction. They were coming closer and closer together. "Well, Sheila," she said softly, "our baby is impatient. I think that's a good sign. So wish me luck, okay?"

A moment later, smiling, she reached for her bra.

Chapter 11

Colleen concentrated with all her being on Michael as the wave of pain lifted her and flung her forward. She gripped his hand so hard it must have hurt, focused desperately on his face. His blue eyes glittered and he wiped sweat from his forehead with his forearm, bared below the rolled-up sleeves of his shirt.

"One, two, three," he said steadily, "push!"

Groaning, sweating, Colleen gritted her teeth and squeezed her muscles tight.

"I see the head," her doctor reported. "That's it, keep pushing!"

Gasping, Colleen complied, though she wanted to scream and quit. The world had narrowed to this room, to the graph that showed the rise and fall of her contractions, to Michael's calm voice and clever hands and vivid blue eyes.

When the contraction washed away, Colleen seized the brief respite to close her eyes. She felt Michael's hand smooth her hair away from her sweaty face, and she tilted her head to prolong the caress.

This labor was longer than her others, more intense. She'd been at the hospital seven hours now, most of it in the grip of powerful contractions. Her baby was big, the doctor thought, and none too eager to come out. Colleen didn't know what she would have done without Michael, who'd been at her side from the beginning, encouraging, nagging, comforting, letting her feed off his strength.

"Here we go again," he said, the tension in his voice telling her that he hurt and hoped with her. "Breathe. That's it. One, two, three, *push!*"

Through the haze of her narrowed focus, she was only dimly aware of Dr. Kjorsvik declaring, "The baby's head is out! Keep pushing, keep pushing."

With an exultant cry, Colleen felt the baby slip out. She fell back against the pillows, sobbing for breath.

Now Michael's hand was the one to squeeze hers almost painfully. "You did it!"

A thin cry brought Colleen back up on her elbows. Dr. Kjorsvik stood, holding up a kicking, squalling, red baby. "You have a son," she announced.

At the sight, Michael looked as stunned as if somebody had punched him. It was as though he hadn't believed in his heart that a real baby would come out of all this. Colleen remembered feeling a little like that herself the first time.

Michael's white shirt was wrinkled, his dark hair standing in tufts, his exhaustion showing in bloodshot eyes and the deepened grooves between nose and mouth. But apparently he at last believed, for he turned an unfettered grin on Colleen, his exhilaration and astonishment almost childlike.

"Incredible," he murmured.

She was vaguely aware that she was smiling as foolishly. "We did it."

"You did."

She swallowed hard and reached out to take his hand, which closed warmly around hers. Her emotions felt raw. She suddenly wanted even more from him; she wanted to burrow her face into his shoulder, maybe even shed a few tears in the strong circle of his arms. But her inhibitions were flooding back, and the strength of her own feelings confused her.

"Nine pounds, three ounces," the nurse told them from Colleen's other side. "Who wants this cutie?"

However anxious she was to hold her son, Colleen deliberately held back. Let Michael have this moment.

"I guess I do," he said, sounding less than sure. The nurse

gently laid in his outstretched arms the now cleaned and bundled infant whose tiny face was screwed up in a look of utter misery. The uncertain but wondering expression on Michael's face as he gazed down at his son would have been comical, had it not unexpectedly brought tears to Colleen's eyes. "He's so…little," he said, looking at her. "He hardly weighs anything."

The nurse smiled. "Believe it or not, that's hefty for a newborn. Does he have a name yet?"

Obviously afraid he would drop his son, Michael passed him to Colleen. For the first time, she cuddled her new baby close. She gently stroked a finger down his wrinkled cheek.

At the same moment, she and Michael both spoke. "Well, I thought…"

"What do you think of…"

They stopped. "You first," she said.

"I thought, if you didn't object, that maybe we could name him Cameron."

"For Sheila," Colleen said softly, her smile tremulous. She remembered talking about names with her sister. Perhaps it wasn't surprising that Michael, too, wanted the son who would have been Sheila's to bear a name she had chosen. Sheila must be on both their minds at this moment, which would have meant so much to her.

Michael nodded, his eyes on his son.

"Cameron," she murmured, rubbing her cheek against the dark fuzz on the baby's head. "Cameron Delaney. I like it."

In the unfathomable way of babies, Cameron had recognized the soft pillow of her breasts, because he turned his face against her and began rooting for a nipple. Colleen laughed and started to open her gown. Then on a sudden surge of shyness, she hesitated. Michael had seen just about everything else today, but not her breasts. On the other hand, if she was planning to nurse, she was going to have to get used to him watching.

Heavens, she was blushing! Well, no wonder. How many women had had a baby fathered by a man who had never seen her breasts?

Cameron was beginning to make unhappy squeaks. Colleen took a deep breath and parted her hospital gown, trying to leave the fold so that it partially shielded her from Michael's gaze. Gently she guided Cameron's seeking mouth to her nipple, where he immediately got the idea and latched on.

Only then, horribly conscious of her hot cheeks, did Colleen let herself look up. Michael still stood beside the bed, his fascinated gaze on his son. Or was it on her breast?

Blushing even more fiercely now, Colleen concentrated on her newborn son, whose tiny fingers were curled into fists as he suckled. Dark hair like his daddy's, she thought, and blue eyes—at least for now. His nose looked like Kim's, but then with baby noses it was hard to tell. He was long and skinnier than Drew or Kim at birth.

"Cameron," she whispered, savoring the feel of his name, the tug on her nipple, the incredible closeness. Would Michael feel that bond, too? she wondered. She had never thought Ben felt the same way about their children as she did. Was that true for all men, or would Michael be different?

He was still watching his son, she discovered, and seemed unaware that she was studying him. Lean, dark and sexy, this man was her husband, the father of her baby, and yet so many of his thoughts and dreams were still mysteries to her. Colleen had one of those moments of disorientation, even disbelief. Nearly a year ago, she had agreed to carry his child, a momentous enough decision, but since then her world had turned upside down, and sometimes she didn't recognize it.

My husband, she thought, disbelievingly. *Sheila, where are you?* But she couldn't seem to summon a memory of her sister at this moment. Colleen tried to imagine the day as it had been intended to be: herself cradling the baby, her son, kissing the silky top of his head, and with regret and love handing him to her sister.

The thought was unimaginable now, but then, Sheila was gone, and nothing could bring her back or change the way things had come to pass.

My husband.

Colleen blinked and realized he was gazing at her.

His voice was deep. "Well?"

Time for another blush. "Well, what?"

"Any conclusions?"

"I was trying to decide if he looks like you," she lied.

She'd said the right thing. He stared down at his son. "God, I hope not," he said fervently.

Colleen was surprised into a giggle. "Well, you don't have quite so many wrinkles."

"Yet."

"And, um, you have a little more hair."

Darkly, Michael said, "For a few more years. Did I tell you my father's losing his?"

This time when she laughed, her nipple slipped out of Cameron's mouth. He had fallen sound asleep. Colleen hurriedly covered herself with her gown.

The nurse appeared as though summoned. "Let me take him off to the nursery so he can be checked over," she said briskly, "and you can get cleaned up and we'll find you a room."

"I'll go call the kids," Michael said. "Do you want to see them?"

His sister-in-law was to have picked them up from the day camp several hours ago. "Could I?" she asked hopefully.

His eyes were tender, his smile lopsided. "I'm on my way."

A moment later he was gone, and her son was whisked off to the nursery. Only then did her tiredness sink in. She felt teary, and had never been so grateful for anything as she was for the warmed blanket the nurse tucked around her.

Later she vaguely remembered being transferred to a room, but she must have slept, because suddenly she became aware of Drew bouncing on her bed and Kim hovering shyly in the doorway, Michael behind her with his hand on her shoulder.

Colleen reached out one arm to Drew to give him a hug, then her other to Kim. "Come here, sweetie."

"Are you okay, Mom?" Kim asked, circling the bed to perch on its edge.

"You bet." Colleen smiled at Michael. "Do you want to go get Cameron?"

"One Cam, coming up," he agreed, and disappeared.

"We saw him through the glass," Drew said.

"What did you think?"

"To tell you the truth—" he wrinkled his nose "—well, he was kind of ugly."

"That's not true! He's cute," Kim said indignantly.

"He'll be a lot cuter in a few days," Colleen told them. "It's been a rough day for him, you know. All babies look funny for a while. Even you two did."

"Yeah, well, Kim still looks funny," Drew said, laughing uproariously at his joke. He gave a few more bounces and dodged the arm she flung out.

They were distracted by Michael's arrival with a bassinet. Inside it, the bundled baby was astonishingly small, only his face showing below a knitted cap. The motion had awakened him and he was trying to lift his head.

The frustration of failing brought a few grunts and snorts that escalated into a cry. Michael gingerly picked up his son and handed him to Colleen. Drew and Kim watched unblinkingly as Colleen eased open her gown and helped Cam find her breast. She knew darn well she was blushing again. It was a long moment before she sneaked a peek at Michael, to find him staring at the precise place their son was latched on to her breast.

She felt a tingling, and then a warmth that settled between her legs. Mildly shocked, she tried to convince herself that her response wasn't sexual. Her uterus was supposed to contract when her newborn nursed. That was all she was feeling.

Except she couldn't quite bring herself to look at Michael again.

When Cam had given up struggling for the milk that hadn't come in yet, Colleen let the kids take turns holding him, instructing them in how to support his head and how to pat him gently on the back until he burped. Out of the corner of her eye, she was aware of Michael listening intently, and realized he probably knew no more about babies than they did. Cam gazed fuzzily at them and seemed to have no objection to their efforts. Eventually she let Kim change his damp diaper and then he snuggled sleepily into the curve of Colleen's body.

She'd half expected jealousy—surely that would come—but right now even Drew was more fascinated than resentful.

"His belly button's gross." Drew made the same face he did when she put corn chowder on the dinner table. "It's going to fall off?"

"Uh-huh."

"Can I keep it when it does?"

Michael covered his laugh with a cough.

"See how little his fingernails are," Kim whispered.

Over her head, Colleen looked at Michael, who had pulled a chair up to the bed. He smiled at her, and she found herself smiling back, as though there was no tension between them, no doubts or fears or hesitation.

She felt tired, contented, accepting. *My husband.* No, better yet, *my family.* She had made the right decision, she thought. There might be a few rough spots ahead, but it was all going to work out fine. She knew it.

Things were going well. Too well, Michael thought. Nothing worth having was as easy as these two weeks since Cam's birth had been.

He stopped in the living room doorway, taking in the cozy scene. Colleen was curled on a corner of the sofa, nursing Cam, who was patting her pale breast. Michael almost groaned at the sight. He could easily become jealous of his own son.

Drew was off at a friend's house, but Kim sat on the other end of the sofa working a crossword puzzle in a desultory way.

Michael leaned one shoulder against the door frame. "Kim, any chance you'd empty the dishwasher?"

The eleven-year-old dropped her pencil and jumped up. "Sure," she said cheerfully.

Michael realized he wasn't the only one who was waiting for the other shoe to drop. Small creases furrowed Colleen's brow as she watched her daughter willingly depart for the kitchen.

"This is unnatural. I'm starting to get worried about her."

"It'll wear off," he said, wandering into the living room. Despite himself, his gaze locked on his wife's open shirt. At that precise moment, Cam pulled back, exposing a damp, pink nipple. *Hell,* Michael thought savagely, wrenching his gaze away. He dropped onto the sofa, aware out of the corner of his eye that Colleen had flushed and covered herself. He'd no idea how much of what he felt she was sensing, but clearly it was enough to make her uncomfortable.

"Evelyn called," he said, with no particular inflection. "We have an offer on my house. She thinks it'll be in the ball park."

Colleen lifted Cam to her shoulder and patted his back. "Oh, good."

He waited, sensing she wasn't done.

"Michael, have you thought about cleaning the house out?"

"God, yes." He leaned his head back against the couch. "Sometimes I'm tempted just to hire movers and have them throw everything in boxes and put 'em away in storage. But I suppose we'll want some of the furniture, at least."

"Will it be so painful?" Colleen asked softly.

"Not painful." He wondered if he was lying. "Overwhelming. One decision after another. I'm not sure I'm ready to be ruthless yet. Getting rid of her stuff seems…" Michael hesitated, tapping his fingers on his knee. What a bizarre conversation to have with a new wife. In with the new, out with the old. Even more bizarre, given the relationship of his two wives. And yet, he knew that historically it had been common for men to marry their dead wives' sisters. Maybe the reasons hadn't been that different than his and Colleen's.

Colleen finished his thought for him. "A betrayal." He heard her take a deep breath. "If you want help…"

"Thanks." His smile felt more like a grimace. "I haven't opened Sheila's closet since before the funeral. I had to pick something out…" Hell. He wouldn't think about that. "I didn't know she had so many clothes. Dresses, blouses, sweaters. She must have owned thirty pairs of shoes. We could just give it all away, I suppose. Or keep things you or Kim would use. I don't know. You can do whatever you think's best, if you're willing to deal with it."

She managed a nod before they were interrupted by Kim, who stood in the doorway.

"Can I call Dad?"

"Honey, you don't have to ask my permission."

When Kim made no move to leave, Michael glanced up to see a peculiar expression on her face, a mix of defiance and trepidation. Abruptly she asked, "You know how I'm supposed to go to Dad's in a few weeks?"

Colleen put a hand to her head. "Oh, Lord, I haven't gotten the airline reservation yet. I'm sorry, sweetie, I'll—"

"No. The thing is, I don't want to go."

"You don't want—" Colleen stopped, obviously flabber-gasted. "But you were so anxious…"

"That was before." Kim shrugged with elaborate noncha-lance. "I want to be here when we move and stuff. And Cam would probably forget me if I was gone even for a couple of weeks."

"But you've been complaining about being bored from the minute school let out!"

Michael rarely intervened. What did he know about kids? But Kim was flushing and he could tell that Colleen just didn't get it. Casually he asked, "Do you want to think about it for Christmas vacation?"

"Yeah, sure. Maybe. Anyway, I'll call Dad." She vanished from the doorway.

Colleen shook her head dazedly. "Maybe I should have stayed in the hospital."

"Or we could check Kim in for the next four or five years."

"Aargh!" She managed to scream in a whisper, if such a thing were possible. It didn't take much to wake Cam, asleep on her shoulder. "Do you know, not that long ago we had a crisis because Kim decided she was going to live with her dad. And now she doesn't even want to visit him?"

"Jealous?" Michael suggested.

"Of what? Who?"

"Cam, probably. Me, maybe."

One minute, they were talking. The next, Colleen gave an artificial-sounding laugh. "Oh, I can't imagine. I suppose she thinks Cam'll be crawling any minute and doesn't want to miss it. And Lord knows, her relationship with her father warms and cools on any given day depending on whether or not he's returned one of her phone calls."

Did she not want to admit Kim might be suffering from any real confusion? Or did she view his comment as criticism and didn't want to hear it from him?

"You know her best," he said mildly. "You've never said how the kids felt about our marrying."

She raised her eyebrows. "They took it fine. They haven't said anything to you about it, have they?"

"No."

"I'll talk to Kim. If she's jealous of anybody, it's probably Cam. Don't worry about it." Colleen carefully straightened and put her bare feet to the floor. "Do you suppose I can get Cam into the crib without waking him?"

"Why don't I try?" he offered, starting to stand.

But Colleen shook her head. "We'd probably wake him up handing him off. Wish me well. If I fail you'll hear an almighty scream."

Michael waited until after she'd left the room to snatch up the nearest object, a magazine, and slam it to the floor. Really mature, he thought in disgust, bending to pick it up and smooth the pages. But what the hell other outlet did he have for his frustration?

If he'd thought he was marrying Colleen for a home, he might as well admit now he'd been dreaming. They'd been married a month now, and he was still a guest. Maybe more than ever a guest. A couple of conversations like this one had left no question who the parent around here was. How many times had she told him not to worry about the kids? It was as if she held up a sign that said Not Your Problem.

Hell. He was probably overreacting, expecting too much too quickly. He wanted to be an instant father, but Colleen and the kids didn't see him that way. Maybe never would.

Patience, he told himself.

The front door slammed just as the phone rang. Feet thundered through the front hall to the kitchen at the same time Kim raced down the stairs yelling, "I'll get it! Drew! I'm expecting a call!"

The phone was cut off on the third ring and a moment later Drew bellowed, "Mom!"

Right behind him was Kim, yelling, "Mother, tell him it's rude to race somebody for the phone! What a jerk!"

Michael was mighty tempted just to put his feet up on the coffee table and let Colleen handle all three kids and the telephone, too. But he knew exactly how many times she'd been up during the night. Surely even Superwoman occasionally admitted she could use a hand.

By the time he got out there, Colleen was storming down the stairs. Cam's wail from the open bedroom door trailed her. "How many times do I have to tell you to be quiet!" she snapped. "I was just getting Cam down for a nap, and now listen!"

"I can't help it," Kim said furiously. "He's such a brat! He just *had* to beat me to the phone."

Drew gave her a push. "I was there first!"

Kim lunged for her brother just as Michael collared both kids. "Let's have a little talk. Colleen—" he nodded toward the kitchen "—the phone is apparently for you."

Without waiting for her reaction, he steered Drew and Kim into the living room. "All right. Sit down."

They sat.

"Is it unreasonable for your mother to ask you to keep your voices down?"

Kim stuck out her tongue at her brother. "If he wasn't such a little jerk—"

"Was he the one who yelled in the hall right outside the bedroom?"

"I wouldn't have yelled if he—"

"I was the closest one to the phone," Drew said, smirking.

Michael held up a hand. "Enough. Your mom was up off and on all night with the baby, and she needs a nap she's not going to get now. She was intending to let you stay home tomorrow from the day camp, but you guys have blown it. We'd better have cooperation from you, or you won't be staying home Tuesday, either."

The boy jumped to his feet. "That's not fair! Just 'cuz *she's* got a big mouth—"

His sister's sullenness became outright anger. "I'm going to talk to Mom!"

"What about?" None of them had heard Colleen enter the room.

"You promised we could stay home tomorrow," the eleven-year-old said. "*He* says we have to go."

Colleen looked at him. "You told them they had to go to day camp?"

Michael crossed his arms. By God, she'd better back him up. "I told them," he said levelly, "that we'd agreed they could stay home these next couple of weeks only if they gave you a hand when you need it and didn't get in the way of your getting your rest. This is the third time they've woken up Cameron this weekend. I'd say they're not taking us very seriously."

Her hesitation was brief, but long enough to make him mad as hell. When she turned to the kids, Colleen shook her head. "Michael's right. Tomorrow will give you time to think about whether you can try a little harder."

"Mo-om!" Kim wailed.

"Sweetie, I know you hate it, and maybe making you go is a little harsh—"

Harsh! Gritting his teeth, Michael said, "Kim, why don't you go see if you can rock Cam back to sleep. Drew, you didn't take out the garbage this morning. Please do it."

"You're not my father!" Kim screeched, and ran from the room.

"I just came home to get a snack—" Drew stopped. "Gol,

it wasn't even full." His gaze dropped from Michael's and he muttered, "Oh, all right."

The slam of a bedroom door upstairs raised the pitch of Cam's screams. Michael waited until Drew slouched out.

"I take it you don't like the way I handled this," he said.

"I didn't say that," Colleen protested. She tiredly pushed back the heavy mass of hair from her face. "It's just that Kim doesn't have any friends at all—"

"And therefore she should get away with anything at home?"

Colleen's chin came up. "I didn't say that, either! But maybe we should have talked about this—"

Michael swore and turned his back. "Hell, I knew I should have stayed out of it."

"Now wait a minute! I agreed with you, didn't I?"

"Reluctantly." He faced her again, distantly aware that he was overreacting, but too frustrated to shut up. "Sends quite a message to the kids, doesn't it?"

Colleen was so pale he reached out a hand to her, but she stepped aside. "Damn it, Michael, I'm doing my best. If it isn't good enough, you can…you can stuff it!" Back straight, she stalked out.

Michael swore again, feeling like a heel. He should be upstairs rocking their son, instead of sulking down here because Colleen hadn't provided a ready-made place for him in the household. What the hell had gotten into him?

He knew the answer, and he didn't like it.

"Rock-a-bye, baby, in the treetop. When the wind blows…"

Colleen faltered when she heard the front door close quietly and a moment later the sound of the pickup backing out of the driveway. But Cam stirred against her shoulder and she resumed the hypnotic rhythm of the lullaby.

"…the cradle will rock," she murmured. "When the bough breaks, the cradle will fall, and down will come baby, cradle and all."

She held her breath for a moment in hope, but Cam's wobbly

head bobbed and he began to scream. On a sigh Colleen lifted her shirt and guided him to one breast, but he wouldn't nurse. She checked his diaper. Dry. And still his legs churned and he sobbed as though she was hanging him upside down by his heels.

"Cameron Delaney, what are we going to do with you?" Colleen asked. "Where do you suppose your daddy went?"

Cam didn't know and didn't care. He kept kicking and screaming and pummeling her with tiny fists. He quit crying only as long as she walked with him.

"Was your father as disagreeable at your age?" she asked the red-faced baby. "Probably."

Her every attempt to ease him into the crib failed. She desperately needed some sleep, but obviously she wasn't going to get it. Finding some slip-on tennis shoes, she carried Cam out to the hall. "Kim," she called, "I'm going to take Cam for a drive."

After the air-conditioned house, the garage was warm and the car even more so. She rolled down her window and buckled Cam in his seat, then put on her sunglasses. As usual, the baby liked riding in the car. Within a couple of blocks he'd settled down, shoving the two middle fingers of his left hand into his mouth.

Colleen drove with no particular destination in mind, hardly even noticing the summer heat, her thoughts completely given to this afternoon's scene. Was Michael justified in being angry with her? But what could she have done differently? Maybe she was too soft on the kids, but immediately following two major upsets in their lives—her marriage and Cam's birth, not to mention the earlier move—didn't seem like the moment to crack down. And she was used to being the only parent. If she didn't always know instantly how to react when Michael stepped in, why couldn't he understand that?

Her mind returned to the sound of his pickup backing out of the driveway. How upset was he? Where would he have gone? Surely not to his house; she knew he'd hardly set foot in it since their wedding day. Maybe the office, or maybe he was driving aimlessly around, too, wondering just as she was if they'd made a mistake.

But the alternatives were no more acceptable today than they'd been when she'd made her decision. Less acceptable, now that Cam was an individual, instead of an abstraction. No, marriage had been the only way. It was just requiring more adjustment than either she or Michael had anticipated. Surrendering her autonomy was hard for her, but trying to fit in when he didn't have a defined role must not be any picnic for Michael, either. And meantime they were trapped together in a small house, constantly playing on each other's nerves.

Trouble was, Colleen thought grumpily, she hadn't really *needed* a husband, and she didn't know what to do with one now that she had him. She'd done fine on her own. She wasn't even sure she wanted a man in her bed, though her body kept trying to tell her it did.

But that was just proximity, she told herself. Living with a man, it was hard *not* to start wondering what it would be like with him—not to catch herself studying his hands, long-fingered and strong, or remembering that glimpse of smoothly muscled chest and fine, curling, dark hair. Or reliving their two brief kisses, one accompanied by a proposal, one a wedding ring, and extrapolating therefrom—if she had lifted her hands and laid them on his shoulders, would he have taken her into his arms? Had she imagined the instant when his mouth firmed, before he stepped back? Did he *feel* anything, or had his kisses been perfunctory, obligatory?

Frowning fiercely at the direction of her thoughts, Colleen looked around and discovered she'd had a destination, after all. She'd driven straight to the cemetery.

Deciding not to argue with her subconscious, she turned her small car into the lane that curved between the maples. To each side, sprinklers flung glistening arcs of water over the velvety grass between gravestones, keeping it green even in the midst of a dry, hot summer.

Another turn and she was in the new part of the cemetery. With a sense of inevitability, she saw Michael's pickup ahead, parked on the verge. Across the grass, he stood with his back to the road, looking very alone. At Sheila's grave.

Colleen pulled in behind his truck, set the emergency brake and turned off the ignition. Cam had finally, blessedly, fallen asleep, but she wasn't going to leave him in the car, even if taking him out woke him.

With no shade here, the heat struck her like a wall when she stepped out of her car. It must be ninety-five degrees today; the air was completely still. She could hear the shush, shush, shush of a sprinkler, the distant sound of cars. A backhoe stood deserted beside rawly turned earth. Colleen gently lifted Cam out of his seat and snuggled him, half-awake, against her shoulder as she started across the plush grass.

Michael had turned and was waiting for her. He still wore jeans and a chambray work shirt, the rolled-up sleeves and ratty canvas shoes with no socks his concession to the heat. Here away from the house, when she hadn't had a chance to brace herself to see him, the impact of his presence was even stronger. Living with him, she sometimes forgot how handsome he was—her feelings toward him were so complicated, so messy, they filtered the way she saw him.

But beyond broad shoulders and those startling blue eyes was something amorphous. She could feel tension radiating from him, yet it was always so contained she wondered if she was imagining things. He shuttered his thoughts easily, leaving her guessing what he felt by the slight huskiness in his deep voice, the unconscious hunching of his shoulders. His remoteness made her want to goad him, make him *feel* something. It made her want, with eternal female idiocy, to shatter his self-control.

Not smart, she told herself, stopping a few feet from him. His eyes were hidden by dark glasses, his expression was enigmatic. She was suddenly conscious of the patches of sweat between her shoulder blades and under her arms, that her hair clung to her neck, and that her face, untanned and incapable of tanning, was flushed from the heat.

Michael nodded and reached for Cam. Colleen gratefully surrendered their son.

Anxious that Michael not think she was following him, she said, "I didn't know you were here. I was just driving around."

"I've been meaning to come for a while."

"Me, too," she admitted.

Almost reluctantly Colleen looked down at the polished gravestone, flush with the grass. The inscription was bald: Sheila's name, the thiry-two year span of her life, *May she rest in peace.*

Are you? Colleen cried inside. Or was Sheila too restless a spirit to find peace?

"It sounds dumb," Colleen said aloud, "but I brought Cam to meet her." She hadn't even known that herself.

"It's not dumb." Michael spoke roughly. "I had thought… some Sunday, we could all come."

"We still could."

He didn't answer directly. Instead, his voice softened. "Are you hot, big boy? No? Just sleepy. Mom was such a brute she wouldn't let you nap, would she?" Michael's large hands dwarfed their son, but they were gentle, secure.

Colleen felt a peculiar pang she couldn't quite identify. It wasn't envy, but something close. If their marriage had been different, she would have heard that tone of voice from Michael before, known the security of being held by him. She might have been standing close enough to him now to be brushed by his shoulder, to reach out and tickle Cam, instead of stiffly keeping her distance.

Colleen stared down at the stone, at the lawn that grew over her sister's grave as though the ground had never been disturbed, and begged for an answer. Was it selfish to covet something that was never meant to be hers, something that death had snatched from her beloved sister? Even from the grave, would Sheila want to hold her husband?

Beside Colleen, Michael asked suddenly, "Could you really have given him—Cameron—to Sheila, if she'd lived?"

Colleen looked at her son, so small, so vulnerable, cradled in his father's strong arms, and felt a terrible constriction of her heart. Dear Lord, could she have? Or had she deceived herself all along?

But then she remembered Sheila looking up at her as she

had that day in Colleen's kitchen, her eyes so desperate. She saw the little sister she'd fought with, comforted, encouraged and loved. She saw her best friend. And she nodded slowly.

"I think…I would have thought of him as hers from the beginning. She would have loved him."

"Yeah." He cleared his throat. "She would have."

Oh, Sheila, Colleen thought sadly, but she was past tears now. Too much had been set in motion that day when one sister offered a gift to another. Whatever bitterness Sheila might have felt about all she'd lost, she wouldn't want her memory to take anything from Cameron. She'd want her husband and sister to do the best they could for the son she had named.

"Ah, well." Michael looked over Cam's head at her, regret in his voice, but not unbearable grief. "Cam's going to get sunburned. What do you say? Shall we go home?"

There was that pang again, that longing for something indefinable. *Home.*

And Colleen nodded.

Chapter 12

"Smells good."

Colleen jumped. The paring knife slipped and she came close to adding some blood to the strawberries she was slicing for dessert. Michael had a gift for appearing unheard; he was always just *there,* with no warning.

To hide her start, she offered a smile that was probably unconvincing. "Thanks. It'll be ready in a minute."

Instead of leaving, Michael leaned against the counter and crossed his arms. Apparently he was settling in comfortably to watch.

For no good reason, Colleen felt crowded. She realized ruefully that she felt that way most of the time these days. Cam was a month old now, and this house was too small for a family of five, especially when the two adults were trying very hard not to touch each other.

It had taken a while for her to realize that was what they were doing. She would rush to get through a doorway before he reached it; he would step well back to let her go by in the hall; at the dinner table she'd pass a serving dish to Drew at her right, rather than giving it directly to Michael. Ridiculous, but somehow necessary.

It was as though touching might actually be dangerous. What an absurd notion, she thought again, but uneasily. She wasn't afraid of Michael. And it wasn't as though they could barely keep their hands off each other. It was true that occasionally she surprised an expression on his face that was somehow raw, frustrated. Desperate. But of course she might be imagining things. She might be imagining even the tension, so thick it could be used as quilt batting.

A moment like this was more typical. Michael's eyes were cool, guarded.

"Did you want to talk about something?" she asked.

"Not really." He hunched his shoulders. "No, that's not true. I'm going to take Friday off work and tackle the house. Any chance you'd come? Or are you sick of packing?"

"Don't be silly. Of course I'll come." She hesitated. "Would you mind if Kim helps? She seems to be feeling left out these days."

Just yesterday, Kim had told Colleen glumly that this was the worst summer of her life. Colleen couldn't argue. Kim's twelfth birthday had come and gone with only a family party. She didn't have a single friend to invite even to go to a movie with her.

"Why not?" Michael sounded relieved. "Thanks. Which reminds me. Are you still planning to go back to work next week?"

"Yes, I think so." Colleen spooned strawberries onto the shortcake in each bowl, concentrating on the task, trying not to be so aware of his every breath, his every expression. "Why?"

"Have you thought of taking Kim with you? Couldn't she learn to help?"

Of course she could. So why, Colleen wondered, troubled, hadn't she thought of it herself? Kim's self-esteem was at an all-time low; it would be good for her to feel she was really helping out at the shop.

But Colleen also discovered how petty she was capable of being. She hated it that Michael had had to suggest something so obvious concerning *her* daughter.

"I'll think about it," she said. "Did Kim suggest it?"

"No. I noticed how disgruntled she looked when you said you were taking Cam with you. My first thought was that she

could just hang out. Read or something. My niece—Stacey—
is a heck of a good cook." He shrugged. "She's the same age.
No reason Kim couldn't measure yardage and use scissors…"

"A rotary cutter. It's awfully sharp." So was her tone.

Despising herself, Colleen was careful not to look up,
although she felt Michael's gaze on her.

After a moment he said flatly, "Okay, it's a lousy idea.
Forget it."

"I didn't say that."

"No?"

"No, it's a good idea." Colleen closed her eyes for a heartbeat before she admitted, "I wish I'd thought of it myself."

"What the hell difference does it make?"

"I don't know!" she cried. "I just feel…" *Threatened.* But
she didn't understand why and couldn't have begun to explain
herself. She shook her head. "Nothing. Never mind. I'll ask
Kim if she wants to go."

Michael chose to back off, for which Colleen was grateful.
She knew she'd behaved badly. She seemed to be at her worst
when he was being the nicest. Was she *trying* to drive him off?

The worrisome thought stayed with her over the next few
days. She watched the way she had of insinuating herself in
Michael's conversations with the kids, gradually taking over.
She did it so subtly she wasn't sure anyone else noticed, but
she began to remember times with Ben when she had done the
same. Had she resented his letting the kids down one minute,
then being best buddies with them the next? Or had she ever
given him a chance in the first place?

She'd always known that her marriage to Ben had been fine
until she had Kim. She'd blamed the failure on him; *he* didn't
really want children; *he* didn't want to change their lives to ac-
commodate Kim and later Drew; *he* resented her putting the
kids first.

But it was becoming painfully obvious that *she* didn't want
Michael to be a real, honest-to-God parent to Kim and Drew.
Or even Cam? she wondered guiltily. She was breast-feeding,
which meant that logically she took the lion's share of baby

care, but it wouldn't hurt Cam to have a few more bottles. Maybe even a regular bottle or two a day that Michael gave him.

Colleen started listening to the voice in her head, the one that wasn't quite conscience but might as well have been. If she considered taking a nap, instead of picking up the living room, her inner voice would demand, *What if somebody dropped by and saw the house looking like this? What would they think of you?* Kim would beg to skip her bath one night and Colleen would hear a mental chide: *Kim can't possibly put off washing her hair until another night; the teacher might think you don't care if your children are clean!*

But there were other refrains, familiar from her childhood, that she hadn't even realized were still playing in her memory. *Women are perfectly capable,* the voice—her mother's voice, Colleen finally realized—said briskly. *We don't need your father. You've never missed your father, have you? We're just fine on our own.* How often had she heard her mother say with disdain, *Her* father *is bringing her? Where's her mother?*

Men were second-best. Possibly useful in their own way, but not as parents. Women were family, a loving circle.

Colleen remembered how Drew had sneered at the idea of a father meaning much of anything to his friend. Was he echoing her? Was she echoing her own mother, who'd tried to make up for a loss she'd never let Colleen and Sheila realize they had suffered?

Had Colleen made certain that Ben was kept outside the loving circle? Was she now pushing Michael out, too?

Would Sheila have done the same?

Colleen found it fatally easy to brood on such subjects the next day when she tackled Sheila's closets and drawers. Michael carried in Cam's bassinet and heaps of cardboard boxes, picked up at the grocery store. The room, carpeted in plush burgundy, was dominated by the king-size bed covered by the Rose of Sharon quilt that had been Colleen's wedding gift to her sister and Michael.

Sheila had loved the glorious "Song of Solomon" in the

Bible: "Let him kiss me with the kisses of his mouth: for thy love is better than wine. I am the Rose of Sharon, and the lily of the valleys." The appliqué pattern was an old one and had been Sheila's choice, rather than the traditional Wedding Ring.

Now Colleen went to the bed and touched the quilt, with its rose-colored flowers and green leaves and stems against a muslin background, quilted in a crosshatch with a feather border.

"I'd forgotten the quilt," she said, feeling a lump in her throat.

Behind her, Michael said quietly, "I thought, if you don't object, that we'd put it away for Cameron. When he marries."

"What a good idea." She blinked and gave herself a shake. "I'll fold it when we're done here."

"Then I'll get to work. Do whatever you want with her stuff."

He added something about his workshop, but Colleen scarcely heard him. She'd turned away from the bed and now stood frozen in front of her sister's dresser, caught by a silver-framed picture in the midst of the clutter. In the photograph, their mother sat in the middle, her arms around Colleen and Sheila. She and her sister had been perhaps thirteen and sixteen, Colleen guessed, pretty in the way of the young, but still gawky, unfinished. They looked happy, mother and daughters, their smiles and closeness genuine. As if she were that age again, Colleen could close her eyes and remember the warmth and security she'd thought was forever.

She had never really rebelled; she had always been good friends with her mother. Sadness brought an immediate lump to her throat, but she ignored it, studying the photograph with new eyes. How odd she'd never much thought about the fact that she and Sheila didn't look at all like their mother. Irene Muir had been dark-haired and dark-eyed, with white skin she took care to protect. Her cheekbones and nose were Slavic; there was pride in her carriage and the tilt of her chin. In contrast her daughters were softer, with auburn hair and freckles and faces that were rounder, less decided.

Their coloring and bone structure must have come from

their father. But Colleen would never know for sure, because her mother hadn't kept a single picture of him. Colleen had half expected to discover some photos tucked away somewhere when she and Sheila cleaned out their mother's house after her death. But they hadn't found one. No letters, either, nothing personal. The day he left, he'd ceased to exist; their mother must have thrown away anything that would remind her of him.

Colleen had a few vague memories of her father, the kind that might have been real or made-up. If she'd asked questions, her mother had deflected them. He wasn't important; if his daughters had meant anything to him, he wouldn't have walked away. Colleen felt almost traitorous when she wondered if he might have tried to see them, to write or call. Could the woman who had thrown away every picture of him also have torn up letters?

Well, Colleen would never know. But she had an unsettling awareness that she would never think about her mother and her own childhood in quite the same way again.

She picked up the photograph and laid it carefully, facedown, in a box labeled To Keep.

"What do you want me to do, Mom?" Kim was patting her baby brother's back. "I think he's asleep."

"Oh, bless you! Let's try not to be too noisy." Colleen glanced around. "Why don't you tackle the drawers? It'll be easier to decide about that stuff than her nicer clothes in the closet."

In the end they put most of Sheila's clothes in the boxes that would go to a charity. Colleen could have worn some of the dresses, but didn't think she wanted to. And she was just enough taller so that nothing else fit—even Sheila's shoes were a hair too small for her. She packed a couple of boxes with things Kim thought she might wear—sweaters, jeans, jackets and sweatshirts. Colleen might be bothered the first time she saw Kim in them, but was too practical to get rid of everything.

At first Colleen was uncomfortable even at being in the bedroom Michael had shared with Sheila; when she laid the first few garments out on the huge bed, the Song of Solomon ran through her head: "His left hand is under my head, and his right hand doth embrace me." She imagined Michael in the bed. Michael and Sheila. "My beloved is mine and I am his: he feedeth among the lilies." The two of them laughing, him smiling down at her, bending his head to kiss her, his shoulders sleek and bare…. Flinching, Colleen drew a mental curtain. She felt as though she were violating his privacy. No, it was worse than that, more disturbing. She didn't *want* to think about him and her sister together. With determination she blocked out awareness of where she was; the room was a storehouse of Sheila's possessions. It had nothing to do with Michael.

Behind her, Kim said, "I wonder why Aunt Sheila kept this ratty old sweatshirt."

Colleen let the silk dress she was folding fall unheeded. She went over to plop down on the bed by her daughter. "Oh, I remember that. The Kittens were a high school sorority. How unfeminist!"

"Did you belong?"

Smiling reminiscently, Colleen shook her head. "They were the in-crowd, the cheerleaders, the girls who dated the jocks. I was too quiet and studious for them, though of course I envied them dreadfully. That's funny." She touched the shirt. "I'd forgotten she joined. I was off at college by then, but Sheila wrote me about some of the activities."

"Then you weren't superpopular?" Kim asked casually, as if her answer didn't really matter. Colleen wasn't deceived.

"Nope. If your aunt Sheila had been older, I probably would have been painfully jealous of her."

"And look. I found this ring in her underwear drawer." Kim dropped a chunky boy's ring with a high school emblem on it into Colleen's hand.

She held it up. "Why, this was our high school ring. We were the Tigers."

"Is that how come the sorority was the Kittens?"

"Uh-huh. I suppose Steve Galvin gave it to her. He was her boyfriend in high school. The quarterback, wouldn't you know." Her voice was dry. "Actually," she admitted, "along with being a hunk he was a pretty decent guy."

Kim listened raptly. "But they broke up."

"Yeah, but it wasn't anything dramatic. I think he went off to Cal State Davis and your aunt Sheila to the University of Washington. I didn't hear much about him after that." Colleen thoughtfully bounced the ring in her palm. "I suppose she couldn't bring herself to toss it. The dumbest things bring back memories."

"But what should we do with it?"

Colleen didn't even hesitate. "Keep it. I had a box here somewhere...." She looked helplessly around at the disorder.

"There's the one with the stuff for me," Kim said.

"Yeah, but I had one just for keepsakes."

"A remembering box." Kim stood up. "I know where it is."

A remembering box. Colleen felt a wrench of the sadness she hadn't been letting herself feel. Softly she said, "That's a nice way to put it."

As the morning wore on, they added a few other items to the box: some photographs, a packet of letters from Colleen when she was in college, a Breyer horse statue left from the herd Sheila had collected as a child. Any jewelry of obvious value Colleen set aside to ask Michael about; the clothes were all in labeled boxes by noon. Just when she was about to send Kim to look for him, Michael appeared in the bedroom doorway.

His gaze went straight to the empty closet, then back to Colleen, sitting on the stripped bed nursing Cam. As it always did, his gaze dropped briefly to his son—or to her open blouse. She felt a familiar stirring inside, a warmth unrelated to her joy at holding Cam.

"You're done already?" Michael sounded surprised, but a rough timbre in his voice made her think again about that fleeting glance at her breast.

"Thanks to Kim." Hoping her own voice didn't sound unnatural, Colleen smiled at her daughter. "She's been a big help."

He grinned at Kim. "I'll let her finish my workshop, then. The way I've been tossing stuff in boxes, I'm afraid I'll never be able to find anything again."

Kim was actually blushing, which made Colleen realize how hungry for compliments she was. "I don't mind," she said shyly.

"How about some lunch first?" Colleen suggested.

"I ordered a pizza. I hope that's all right. Should be here any minute."

"Cool," Kim pronounced.

Michael glanced around the bedroom, then looked directly at Colleen. "Thank you. I feel like a coward. This can't have been easy for you, either."

"You know," Colleen said, surprising even herself, "it really wasn't too bad. A lot of her clothes I'd never seen before. And some things triggered happy memories. Kim and I held a sort of wake. I think it was good for me."

His blue eyes searched hers with unsettling intensity, as though he sought some deeper meaning. "I'm glad," he said gruffly.

"Do you want us to tackle the kitchen this afternoon?" Colleen asked.

"You bet." The doorbell chimed and Michael said, "Ladies, I do believe lunch has arrived."

In the kitchen they all pulled up stools to the curved eating space at the end of the counter. "Drew'll be jealous," Kim said with satisfaction as she watched her stepfather dish up the pizza.

"Well, you worked for it," Colleen said. "He could've helped, too."

"He would've been in the way," Kim said with older sibling superiority. "He would have asked you about every single thing."

"Don't you know that women are the ones who are naturally indecisive?" Michael said with a straight face. He handed over a plate of pizza with everything on it.

Kim sank her teeth into the first piece and protested around the bite, "Well, it's not true!"

"I'd be insulted," Colleen told him, "if I hadn't seen too many women staring at bolts and bolts of fabric, totally unable to make up their minds."

"That's because the fabrics are all so pretty," Kim said, chewing. "I bet men couldn't decide which one they liked the best, either."

"I can vouch for that," Michael agreed. "You ought to see men at the lumberyard. You ought to see *me* at the lumberyard."

"What's to like there?" Kim asked doubtfully.

"I'll show you." He stood up. "Come on. Bring your pizza."

Colleen didn't know if the invitation included her, but not even a door slammed in her face could have stopped her. Something in his expression told her that what he was going to show them was special to him, might even be a key to the puzzle of his personality. Holding Cam against her shoulder, she trailed her husband and daughter.

His workroom off the garage was in the same state as the bedroom; half of it was taken up by tall stacks of cardboard boxes, all labeled in black marker. She wished she'd seen it before he'd started packing. Sheila had offhandedly mentioned Michael's workshop, but Colleen realized she hadn't asked what he *did* in it. She had vaguely assumed it was the kind of place men had so that they could fix things around the house. The place he'd keep his drill and plumbing snake. Despite the fact that most of his tools were packed, she could see that wasn't the kind of workshop he had.

For one thing, the table saw—or radial arm saw, or whatever it was—was world's away from any household tool she'd ever seen. What's more, it was cleaner than her kitchen stove. Along one wall, built-in bins still held lumber, but not the average, rough two-by-fours; instead, each section corraled planks and rounds and big chunks of wood distinctive from that in any other section. Cherry and bird's-eye maple and oak and others she didn't recognize. She picked up a chunk that was dark and unexpectedly heavy.

"Ebony," Michael said.

Colleen set it down and looked around. "You made the

cherry secretary in the living room," she said in astonishment. "And the hall table. They're exquisite! I had no idea—"

"Uh-huh." He was clearly uncomfortable with the praise. "Right now I'm making a toy chest. I'll finish it once we're moved." He showed them the box, the corners smoothly fitted and rounded, the lid not yet hinged. "I'll carve 'Cameron' here on top. Maybe paint the letters."

"It's absolutely gorgeous," Colleen said, still in a state of shock. She held Cam up and said softly, "What do you think, sweetie? Look what your daddy made for you." Smiling at Michael, she said, "Why don't you throw over that bank work and open a cabinet shop?"

"I've thought about it, believe me." He seemed unaware that his hand was sliding lovingly over the richly grained wood. "But I don't know if you can make a living at it. I'm a perfectionist. I spend forever on one piece. Besides, I'm not sure both of us should be in high-risk, low-profit businesses."

Kim was visibly torn between passionate jealousy and admiration. Shyly she reached out and stroked the side of the toy box.

With one perceptive glance, Michael took in her struggle. Sounding diffident, he said, "Would you like me to build you something next, Kim? You could even help, if you'd like."

Her lashes lifted to reveal brown eyes filled with hope. "Really? You'd make me something? And...and show me how to do it?"

"You bet." Michael's smile, slow and warm and maybe a little relieved that she hadn't thrown his offer back in his face, was just for Kim. It showed a side of him Colleen hadn't seen before. "Think about what you'd like. I could build a bookcase or a jewelry box." He shrugged. "Even a desk, if you'd like."

Eagerly Kim said, "With little places to put stuff? You know, all those nooks and tiny drawers?"

"You mean, like a rolltop?" Michael reached for a pencil and tablet of paper out on the workbench. "But smaller. Like this?"

"Neat." Kim edged up to him and pointed as he sketched. "Maybe put little drawers there. In the middle."

With peculiar, mixed feelings, Colleen realized she'd been forgotten. Kim was now hanging over his shoulder, abandoning both shyness and her stiff rejection of him.

Damn it, Colleen thought, here she went again! Jealous of her own daughter. Jealous because Michael never relaxed like that with her. He'd never even told her about his woodworking. Why hadn't he when they were talking about her quilt-making?

Stranger yet, Colleen thought, was why Sheila had never mentioned it, beyond snippets— "Oh, Michael's hiding in the workshop. I don't dare try to drag him out." Or an amused, "Michael feels about lumberyards the way I feel about Nordstrom's."

The truth was, Sheila hadn't talked about Michael much at all. Until this minute, Colleen hadn't realized how little. No wonder he seemed like a stranger to her.

Her mind jumped to the obvious corollary. Had *she* talked about Ben much in those endless conversations with her sister? The kids, of course; Sheila had always been hungry for news about them. But Ben—Colleen genuinely couldn't remember, which alarmed her.

She could see the pattern now, a legacy from their mother. The men in their lives didn't really matter. Couldn't be allowed to matter. After all, men upped and left when they felt like it. They didn't feel the same about their children as women did.

Why had she never seen it before? She was ashamed to realize how much of her behavior had been formed unconsciously, how destructive, as well as comforting, that loving circle had been.

These past months she'd been lost without her mother's and sister's love and support, but she knew suddenly that, on her own, she was freer than she'd ever been in her life. Their loving grip had brought comfort, but had also held her back. She was almost light-headed with an odd kind of relief. She didn't understand the strength of her reaction until her gaze, unbidden, went straight to Michael, who was still explaining something to Kim.

That inner voice, recorded in childhood, would not have let her have the marriage she desperately wanted. It would not have let her unreservedly love any man, far less Michael, who would demand much more of her than Ben ever had.

She had no idea what her expression gave away, but Michael turned his head just then, and whatever he'd been saying trailed off. They looked at each other, only each other, with rare intensity. Colleen's dizziness increased. She suddenly existed in two dimensions: in the one, she felt Cam's wet diaper and his feet kicking her, knew Kim was turning in puzzlement to see why she'd lost Michael's attention—while in the other, she was falling down a tunnel like Alice into Wonderland, with Michael at the bottom. His eyes burned into hers, melting the icy core of resistance she had guarded so carefully.

He took a step toward her. Irresistibly drawn, she took a step toward him. And then, predictably, reality intruded. Cam started crying, and Kim said loudly, as though she sensed she was being excluded from something, "Remember, our pizza's getting cold."

Just like that, it was over, whatever had happened between them. Michael answered Kim, said he'd change Cam's diaper, why didn't Colleen and Kim go eat. Colleen nodded and handed over the baby, now squalling lustily. Shaken, she wondered, Had she imagined the searing heat in Michael's eyes?

Well, maybe she had, maybe she hadn't. But she needed to acknowledge, if only to herself, what she felt. What she had fought so hard against admitting. She wanted Michael. She wanted, as she had never wanted anything in her life, to know what it felt like to have his hands on her body, his mouth on hers, his control shattered by her. Only her.

If that was a betrayal of her sister's memory, then so be it.

What in hell had she seen or understood to bring that look to her face? Yesterday in his workshop something had changed. Colleen had reached a conclusion. But what?

Michael turned restlessly on the couch, either bumping the

back of it or hanging off the edge. He'd had more comfortable places to sleep. But it wasn't comfort that made him wish he were upstairs in Colleen's bed.

Staring into the darkness, he wondered what she looked like sleeping. Did she curl in on herself like a cat, or sprawl extravagantly over the width of her bed? What if her husband reached for her and kissed her awake? Would she be grumpy or softly accepting?

Okay, admit it, Michael thought in disgust. What he really wanted to know was how passionate she could be. Would her eyes be dreamy? Did she whimper or cry out or whisper her love? Did she grab for what she wanted or wait passively for it to come to her?

Michael groaned and flipped onto his back. He was an idiot to torture himself. He wasn't going to find out what kind of lover Colleen was until they trusted each other in a hundred other ways. He had a feeling that wouldn't be any easier for her than it would be for him.

Like yesterday. In the months that came before, he had been tempted a dozen times to show her the chest he was making for Cam, but his woodworking had always been for him alone. It was his escape, his release. Private. Not that Sheila had ever resented the time he spent in his shop or given a damn either way. She liked the pieces he'd made for the house, but they were just furniture to her. She'd never seemed to realize how much of himself went into them. He'd always thought he preferred it that way. In the predictability of wood, in the precision of working it, in the beauty he could release when his skill was great enough, he found analogies to his inner self. When he stepped into his shop and shut the door behind him, he was himself in a way he couldn't be anywhere else.

From the beginning, he had seen a parallel in Colleen's quilt-making. Her craft demanded the same precision, and she was equally a perfectionist. Yet he'd seen the pleasure the simple combination of colors gave her; he'd seen her finger her quilts, absentmindedly but joyfully. Clearly she did it for herself, though the quilts themselves were sometimes made for other people. But the process itself satisfied her.

Because she understood her own motivations, he'd known she would look below the surface. He hadn't been sure he wanted that. But he had doomed himself the day he married her. Yesterday he'd thought, why not now?

But that dazed look on her face—what could that possibly have had to do with his hobby? He'd have sworn she was in shock, as though he'd changed in some radical way right before her eyes. Either that, or she had.

He hadn't overlooked the battles Colleen was waging with herself. Something about the fact that they were now married had made her retreat. Generous enough to let him lay his hands on her bare stomach so he could feel his son move, Colleen was now going to ridiculous extremes to avoid his touch. And she'd become fiercely possessive of her children.

Most telling of all was that she had not even started to piece a wedding quilt. She was a woman who marked all of life's landmarks with quilts—quilts that celebrated and stored memories. He'd been stunned by the work and the love that had gone into the quilt she'd made for her sister's wedding to a man Colleen had never met. But thus far her own marriage did not, in her eyes, deserve a quilt. That scared him, as nothing else did.

But he couldn't blame her for everything. She couldn't trust somebody she didn't know, and he hadn't let her know him. Not deep down inside, where he felt unlovable. Not the Michael who had been an outsider in his own house and who felt like one all over again now.

But he had another chance. Colleen was as different from Sheila as maple was from alder. She was a woman who loved easily, who touched easily, who might take his hand if only he reached out first. He couldn't live with himself if the failure this time was because of his own cowardice.

He had to take the chance that Colleen just plain wouldn't like him once she discovered who he really was.

Chapter 13

The long telephone cord allowed Colleen to carry food to the table as she listened with half her attention to the man on the other end.

"I have to tell you, you're the seventh parent I've called, and none of the other six are willing to consider coaching the boys' soccer team. I have only two more to call, so the odds aren't good. Unfortunately the kids can't play without a coach. We hate to disappoint them, but we won't have any choice but to cancel."

He had all her attention now. "Drew would be so disappointed," she said unhappily. "But there's just no way I can volunteer. I just had a baby. Five weeks old."

The man from the soccer club sounded philosophical. "Well, that's a heck of an excuse. I don't suppose you can think of anyone else? An aunt or uncle, grandparent...?"

Colleen made a slow half turn to face the dinner table, where her family was already seated. Drew and Kim were listening, her son with alarm. But it was to Michael that she looked. Michael, who wanted to be a parent to her children. He met her gaze and raised an eyebrow.

"Just a moment, Mr. Lloyd." Colleen covered the receiver. "Drew, they can't find a soccer coach for your age level."

"Will you coach, Mom?" He fixed her with pleading eyes. "Please?"

"Drew—" she shook her head "—I can't. I'm sorry."

"You mean, I won't be able to play?"

Colleen looked back at Michael. His expression was ironic. He knew darned well she was setting him up. But he'd asked for it, hadn't he?

"I'll coach," he said.

"Mom," Drew begged. "I really want—" He stopped, then said incredulously, "*You'll* coach?"

"If you want me to."

Colleen couldn't help but notice how expressionless Michael's face was, how unemphatic his voice. He was braced for rejection, and no wonder. Neither Kim nor Drew had welcomed him with open arms. She held her breath herself, waiting for Drew's response.

"You'd really do that?" Drew asked doubtfully.

"I said I would, didn't I?"

"Do you know how to play?" His tone was still grudging.

"Uh-huh." Michael took a roll and passed the basket to Kim. "I played in college."

Drew's eyes got big. "Hey, that's cool! Ian's dad never played. Sometimes he has to look up rules in this little book he carries around. That's what Ian says, anyhow."

Growing impatient, Colleen prodded him. "Is that a yes?"

Her son glanced at her as though she were an idiot. "Well, sure." He turned back eagerly to Michael. "Will you let me be striker since I'm your kid? Well, sort of your kid? The striker gets to score all the points, you know."

Michael laughed and stood, pushing back his chair. "At your age, everybody should get turns to play all the positions. You don't really want me to treat you differently from the others, do you?"

Her son scrunched up his nose. "I guess not."

"Yes, he does," Kim said, rolling her eyes.

"What do *you* know?" her little brother snapped. "Don't tell *me*—"

Colleen squelched them both with a look. When Michael smiled ruefully down at her and took the phone, she mouthed, "Thank you."

He inclined his head, his eyes amused. Into the phone he said, "Mr. Lloyd? My name's Michael Delaney. I'm Drew's stepfather. I've just been talked into coaching soccer."

As they discussed times and places, Colleen put the last bowl on the table and sat down. "Let's start," she said. "Kim, will you pass the peas?"

When Michael came to the dinner table at last he said, "Well, the coaching clinic is next week. We'll start practice the week after that."

Through dinner he and Drew dominated talk with a discussion of what boys were on the team and what drills they would run in practices. Colleen had no sooner finished eating than she heard Cam crying. She sighed. "Kim, can you start cleaning up?"

"Drew and I'll do it," Michael offered.

Colleen waited for a rebellion that didn't come.

"Sure," Drew said. "Can I call Ian first to tell him you're coaching?"

"I don't see why not," Michael conceded.

"Then I'll make good my escape." Colleen smiled at Michael. "I don't know what I'd do without you." She tried to say it lightly so that he wouldn't necessarily think she meant anything special. But she'd been trying to find small ways to let him know her attitude toward their marriage had changed. She was discovering how hard that was. She was ridiculously shy, feeling like a thirteen-year-old girl working up the nerve to flirt with a boy she liked. A boy who might not be the slightest bit interested in her.

But Michael gave her a look that was half thoughtful, half something that set her heart to pounding. In a voice that didn't slow her pulse any he said, "Good."

Blushing, Colleen hurried upstairs. Cam had kicked all his covers off and his diaper had leaked enough that she was going to have to change his crib sheet. At the sight of her, he quit crying.

Colleen reached for him. "What a messy boy," she said in the same voice she would have used to tell him how incredibly handsome he was. "Are you hungry? I think you need a dry bottom first. What do you say?"

He didn't *say* anything. He smiled. Really smiled, his whole body wriggling with delight because Mommy was here.

Grinning foolishly back, she said, "Oh, pumpkin. If I call Daddy, will you smile again?"

His short legs kicked happily, and she carried him to the bedroom door. "Michael!" she called. "Michael, can you come here?"

"Is something wrong?" He took the stairs two at a time.

"Nope." Her own smile was so huge she couldn't hide it. "I want you to see something." Her voice gentled. "Hey, big boy, look who's here." She turned Cameron so that he could see his daddy.

Thank goodness, he obliged. He gave Dad a happy, toothless grin. Michael cooed and tickled him, then looked up at Colleen with as much wonder and pride as any father had ever felt. "Isn't this a little early?"

"Well, reasonably." Secretly amused, she said, "But he's a big, strong boy. He'll be toddling along after you before you know it."

"He will be, won't he?" Michael gazed at his son with an expression of bemusement that tugged at Colleen's heart. "It's funny," he said. "I could have lived without having a child. Sometimes I was impatient with Sheila because she couldn't resign herself the way I had. But now…" He shook his head, as though he'd run out of the right words. But then he said them. "Already I can't imagine life without Cam."

"I know," Colleen said softly. Not once—not once!—had Ben ever shared her joy so explicitly. Moved by instinct greater than her inhibitions, she touched Michael's hard jaw, bristly with a Saturday's growth of beard. She whispered, "You don't expect to feel so strongly."

His hand caught hers and held it against his cheek; his eyes had darkened to navy when they met hers. For a wordless moment they looked at each other, even Cam forgotten, before Michael let her hand go. His voice had a rich, dark texture.

"No," he said. "You don't expect it." Something told her he wasn't talking anymore about being a parent.

Behind him, Kim said, "Mom, what are you— Oh. I didn't know Michael— Forget it." The last sounded almost sullen.

"She's all yours," Michael said so easily Colleen was left wondering if she'd imagined the way he'd just spoken to her.

You don't expect it. No, she decided, half terrified, half exhilarated. She hadn't imagined anything.

"I've got to change Cam," Colleen told her daughter. A little regretfully she watched Michael head down the stairs without a backward glance. "And nurse him. Did you have a question?"

Kim hung her head. "I just wanted to talk."

"This is the perfect time." Hoping her cheeks weren't bright pink, Colleen smiled at Kim. "Come on."

Kim sat on one side of the queen-size bed while Colleen changed Cam's diaper at the foot. "Is something bothering you?" she asked gently.

"Not really." Kim watched Cam kicking and waving his hands.

Colleen let the silence grow, waiting her daughter out.

"When are we going to move?" Kim asked suddenly.

"We think the weekend after next. Thank heavens. I'm going to be glad to have Cam in his own room. This one's a squeeze." Which was putting it mildly. The crib blocked her approach to her chest of drawers. Now she had to climb over the bed to get a clean pair of underwear. "We'll barely be moved before you start school. Just think, you'll be able to walk. No bus."

"Is Michael going to sleep with you after we move?"

Question of the year. But not one she wanted to discuss with a twelve-year-old. "Probably," she said. "Although maybe not at first. We'll see." She straightened, lifting Cam high into the air and then bringing him down for a big kiss. "Mealtime," she announced.

Kim scooted over and Colleen sat on the bed, leaning against the headboard and unbuttoning her shirt enough to free the flap on her bra.

Out of the blue Kim said, "I called Dad last week."

"I remember. But he wasn't home, was he?"

Kim shook her head. A curtain of hair shielded her face and she tried to sound careless. "He never called me back."

Damn him, Colleen thought, with easily aroused fury. But she didn't let it sound in her voice. "Have you called again?" she asked gently. "You know how absentminded he can be."

Still hiding behind her shiny brown hair, Kim didn't answer for a moment. Then she burst out, "It's not fair! How come Michael has to coach Drew's soccer?"

Colleen turned her head to stare at her daughter. "What on earth does Drew's soccer have to do with your dad? What does it have to do with *anything?*"

Kim mumbled, "I'll bet if I played, he wouldn't coach my team."

Naively Colleen tried logic. "Honey, you didn't *like* soccer the time you tried it. You hated getting kicked, remember?"

"I *know* I didn't like soccer!" Kim flared. "But I'll bet if I did some other sport, he wouldn't coach that, either."

Oh, boy. Colleen shifted Cam to her other breast. Then, carefully choosing her words, she said, "In the first place, I'll bet he would. Michael's trying to be friends with you guys. In the second place… I thought you didn't *want* him doing things for you as if he were your father."

"Yeah, well, Drew's a traitor. *He* said that, too, but look at him now." She heaved a huge sigh. "Once the kitchen is clean, they're going to go out in the backyard and kick the soccer ball around."

"Didn't they invite you?"

"I didn't want to go."

This time the silence was a long one. Colleen contemplated her daughter, noticing subtle changes. She was definitely getting breasts. And though her legs were still long and skinny, her hips weren't boyishly narrow anymore. Even her face had filled out a little. Colleen had once thought Kim looked like Ben, but now she wasn't so sure. Kim's cheekbones had more in common with Colleen's mother, as did her beautiful brown eyes. She'd been acting almost like a teenager; Colleen now had to face the fact that her daughter almost looked like one, too.

"Mom?" Kim said.

Cam drew back from Colleen's breast and smiled up at her. Tickling his toes, she laid him on the bed and then buttoned up. "Yes?"

In a rush Kim asked, "Do you think Michael's cute?"

Shocked despite herself, Colleen hesitated. *Don't blow it,* she warned herself. *Or she may never talk to you again.* Taking a deep breath, she admitted, "Yeah. I think he's cute."

Kim went back into hiding behind her hair. Colleen had to strain to hear her next words. "I, um, well, I kind of think so, too."

Oh, boy, Colleen thought. She didn't know how to deal with this. She hadn't *had* a father or a stepfather! But almost immediately she remembered spending the night at a friend's house what seemed like a century ago. Had they been about Kim's age? Colleen couldn't even recall the girl's name, but she did remember the crush her friend had had on her stepfather. Hard to forget, when she had gone on and on about him, stopping herself every couple of minutes to exclaim, "I'd *die* if he knew! Or if *my mother* knew. That would be even worse!"

Funny the way things came back to you. The memory was enough to let her reach for Kim's hand and give it a squeeze. "You know what? That's perfectly normal. He's a very attractive man, and here he is living with us. And stepdads are safe."

Kim looked up, her expression shy and painfully hopeful. "The boys my age are all such *nerds.*"

Colleen realized that Kim must really have been worrying about her feelings toward Michael. So she wrinkled her nose. "I know what you mean. At your age, they're all shrimps, too." More seriously she added, "I think maybe for a girl her father—or a stepfather—sets a standard for her. Something boys and eventually men she dates have to measure up to. You know what I mean?"

Kim was frowning in concentration. "Do you think Dad's a better standard, or Michael?"

Colleen opened her mouth, closed it, opened it again—and then had to laugh at herself. Giving Kim a quick hug, she said, "I've got to tell you the truth. There's no way I can fairly answer that. Mostly I'm not mad at your father anymore, but I can't look at him objectively, either. It makes me angry when he doesn't call you back, or on visits when he didn't pay any attention to you. It's too easy for me to see the bad things about him and not the good. But here I've just married Michael, so I'm still noticing the good, instead of the bad. I guess you've got to think this one out for yourself, kiddo."

"Even though I really love Dad—" Kim's face twisted, belying her exaggeratedly casual tone "—I think, well, that maybe Michael's a better husband. I mean, he's always here helping and stuff. He doesn't make excuses. So, even though I don't know whether he'll be a good father yet, I guess maybe I'll sort of think of him as what I want. Someday."

Colleen hadn't cried in weeks, but right this minute she had to bite her lip hard to keep tears from falling. She waited a moment for the stinging in her eyes and the tightness in her throat to go away before she answered.

"Well," she said, not quite lightly enough to fool her daughter, "you'll change your mind about fifty times before you really and truly fall in love and get married, but it sure wouldn't hurt to keep an eye out for somebody like Michael."

Kim had quit listening. At a yell of triumph coming through the open bedroom window, she bounced up and went to look out. "Drew can't kick worth beans," she announced. "And he thinks he's good enough to be striker! Maybe I will go out and play."

"Have fun," Colleen called after her daughter, who was already dancing out of the room. Smiling, Colleen held her hands for Cam to grab her thumbs. Softly she sang, "The itsy, bitsy spider went up a water spout." She lifted and lowered his arms in time with the tune. "And down came the rain and washed the spider out."

At Cam's round-eyed wonder and slowly dawning smile,

she leaned down and kissed him, savoring his baby scent. "You know what, little spider?" Colleen whispered. "I think I love your daddy."

It was getting easier to smile at Michael, even to touch him. Especially to touch him. Easier, at least, when other people were around, when the casual hand she laid on her husband's arm looked perfectly natural. She hadn't quite worked up the nerve yet to do the same when they were alone.

But, oh, how tempted she was. Lots of evenings, of course, she quilted at her frame once the kids were in bed, or packed what little wasn't already in boxes. She hadn't made as much progress on the Burgoyne Surrounded quilt as she would have liked, but then she wasn't as desperate for money, either. Michael was busy packing, too, or working at the computer he'd set up in the living room.

But other times, like now, they would both sit on the couch, each reading or Colleen quilting a smaller piece in a hoop, a safe distance between them, but not so safe that she couldn't have reached across it. Tonight she was working on a wall-size Fan quilt, embellished with bits of lace, which would be an entry into a regional show. She packed five stitches onto the tiny needle, then sneaked a peek at Michael.

His feet were on the coffee table and the newspaper was spread out on his lap. The pages rustled as he shifted slightly, and he frowned at something he was reading. His left hand lay on the couch not far from her. Colleen studied it sidelong, guiltily enjoying the perilous and therefore exhilarating experience of watching Michael unobserved. In the suits he wore to work, he was sleek and sophisticated, all except his strong, brown hands, with the scars and rough fingertips she had noticed and wondered about before. Now she'd seen those same fingertips stroking the wood in his shop, and she knew.

So she wondered something else. What would happen if she just slipped her fingers into the curve of his? Would they tighten? Might he even lift her hand to his mouth, or maybe tug until she scooted across the distance separating them? She hadn't moved the needle in a full minute; she scarcely breathed, watching her husband out of the corner of her eye and wondering.

He caught her that way, looking up so swiftly she couldn't evade the disturbing intensity in his blue eyes. Just like that, the very air was charged with nameless tension. Colleen was paralyzed, pinned by his piercing gaze.

She swallowed, moistened dry lips. His fingers uncurled and he slowly lifted his hand as though he was going to touch her, cup her cheek in his palm, run a rough fingertip over her lips… Oh, Lord, how she wanted him to!

But like an idiot, she leapt to her feet and babbled, "Oh, dear! I think I hear Cam," before bolting. Upstairs she hid in the bathroom and stared at her flushed face in the mirror, disgusted with herself. How could she want something so badly and yet be afraid for it to happen?

Or was she afraid it *wouldn't* happen?

Well, the moment of truth would soon be at hand, Colleen realized the next day. She lay on her back on the examining table at her doctor's office, contemplating the poster on the ceiling that depicted a hippopotamus lovingly nuzzling her stout offspring. Colleen liked the poster better now than she had when she'd been shaped like the hippo. To one side the nurse was cuddling Cam and telling him what a sweetheart he was, while Dr. Kjorsvik did an exam.

At last the doctor straightened, peeling off her plastic gloves. With her usual briskness, she said, "Everything looks good. No more restrictions on sexual intercourse. There may be a little soreness at first, but you know that. You have two other children, don't you?"

It wasn't really a question, but Colleen was glad to have something to talk about as she sat up, meanwhile trying to cover herself with that ridiculous hospital gown. "Yes, in another year my daughter will be able to babysit. Sometimes I think I'm too old for this." She couldn't help smiling at Cam, who was keeping an anxious eye on her as the nurse cooed to him. "But only in the middle of the night."

A glimmer of humor showed in Dr. Kjorsvik's slate-blue eyes. "He'll be sleeping through the night soon. Then you'll be freer to enjoy—" she paused ever so slightly "—your own night's sleep."

On that note a flustered Colleen departed, collecting Kim from the waiting room. As she strapped Cam into his car seat, she wondered whether Michael knew that a woman usually was discouraged from having sex for the six weeks after birth. Would *he* be thinking about the fact that his son was, as of today, six weeks old?

"Let's go see how soccer practice is going," she suggested to Kim.

Her daughter sighed and let out a puff of air that fluttered her bangs. "It's *hot*."

Colleen didn't even bother to agree. After leaving the air-conditioned building, she already felt sweat trickling down her temples. Her legs, bare in shorts, stuck to the car seat. Early summer here had been gorgeous, with the vast blue sky and the streets shady with huge old maples. But now the broad leaves hung limply and the wheat had been harvested to leave stubble. The only saving grace was the dryness, which made the heat more endurable than it would have been in a humid climate.

The soccer fields, donated by a local wheat farmer, bordered an apple orchard. Painted white goalposts and lines on the grass delineated the several playing fields. The gravel parking lot was half-full, and she spotted five separate practices going on.

Michael was down at the far end, surrounded by a herd of little boys. She parked as close as possible, and Kim followed reluctantly when she tied Cam's sun hat on and headed across the close-mown grass toward the sideline.

Colleen smiled at Michael, who grinned a little ruefully at her over the boys' heads. "Hey, Kim," he called. "How would you like to be the goalie so we can have even sides?"

"Sure," she said, looking happier immediately. She loped toward the goal and leapt up to touch the crosspiece.

Colleen found a shady spot under a maple and settled down on the grass to watch. It was oddly peaceful here, the shouts of the players and coaches muted in the still air, the buzz of a passing bee a pleasant counterpoint. She spread out a small quilt and Cam fell asleep immediately. Colleen blinked a little sleepily herself and watched as the boys, divided into two teams, swarmed the ball the moment Michael tossed it into play. He let them go for a few minutes, then blew his whistle, freezing them.

"Okay, don't move! Take a look around. Ian, what's your position?"

"Um…" Wide-eyed, Ian pointed off toward one side.

"That's right. Wing. Jacob, you're a wing, too. What are you doing in the middle?"

The boys grinned sheepishly and retreated to their places. Michael went down the roster, sorting them out again. "Remember, sometimes you've got to help out, but most of the time you trust your teammates to play their positions and to pass. They can't pass to you if you're not where you're supposed to be. If you're all clumped up in the middle, you trip over each other. Okay." He gave another blast on the whistle. "Let's go!"

Colleen could see improvement over a week ago, when they'd either been stepping back to politely let someone else have the ball, or kicking it without paying any attention to where the goal or a teammate was. Drew seemed to be having the time of his life, charging into the fray and kicking wildly without any of Kim's timidity. That set her to thinking about differences between the sexes, and before she knew it she was watching Michael.

Which, if she were honest with herself, was what she'd come for. He had changed after work into athletic shorts, and she admired his muscular, tanned legs dusted with dark hair. Even better, he wore a tank top that left bare sleek, powerful shoulders. Damp with sweat, the fabric clung to his chest and back. He kept wiping his face on his forearm or the hem of his shirt, and his hair was tousled. He moved lightly on the balls of his feet, staying just ahead of the boys, his attention always on them. He was quick to stop them and point out mistakes, but just as quick to grin, with a flash of white teeth, and clap a boy on the back for a good pass or great defense.

It made Colleen's heart ache to watch him. How close she had come to robbing Cam, and Drew and Kim, too, of Michael. But the intensity of her own feelings scared her. She was finding it so easy to forget that theirs was a marriage of convenience; that Michael might still be grieving for Sheila to the point where he wasn't ready to love again.

Colleen heaved a deep sigh and touched Cam's flushed cheek. Time to quit dreaming and go home to start dinner.

The rest of her family showed up just as she finished slicing vegetables for a stir-fry. At the table, Drew chattered happily about soccer practice and the goal he'd almost scored on his sister. Kim was obviously feeling pretty good about having stopped the ball. Michael listened and commented without correcting any of Drew's more extravagant claims.

Leaving the kids to clean up the kitchen, Michael and Colleen moved into the living room. He sat on the couch and began unlacing his athletic shoes. "How was your day?"

Here was her big chance. Colleen's heart began to drum, but she picked up her sewing basket and opened it, answering casually, "Oh, fine. I had a doctor's appointment today."

Michael dropped his shoes and looked up. "What for?"

"Just a six-week checkup." Colleen automatically measured out a strand of thread and snipped it off.

"And?" he probed. Being the subject of his complete attention made her sympathize with microbes in a lab. Except, of course, that she *wanted* him to be interested. Very interested.

"Dr. Kjorsvik says I'm fine."

"Did you think you weren't fine?"

It took every bit of acting ability she possessed to glance up at him with an expression of vague surprise. "No, it's just routine. Before you go back to..." *Sex.* Colleen frantically sought for an alternative. "Um, normal life."

"Normal life," he echoed. His eyes were unreadable.

By this time, her cheeks no doubt glowed. She might as well have lit neon signs that said, *Yes, that's right. Sex.*

"I…well, I guess I have a few more pounds to lose, but that's normal." She shouldn't have used that word again. "I mean, after all, it's only been six weeks. And when you're nursing, you lose quickly, thank goodness. All those calories going into Cam, you know."

Michael just sat there looking at her. Probably in disbelief that she was rattling on this way.

Even so, she'd have kept going if she could have thought of a single more thing to say. But unless she planned to give him her hip and bust measurements, she wound down.

"Well, anyway, other than that the day was…" Not normal. Anything but normal. "…pretty much like always."

He was still contemplating her, his eyes a dark blue, which usually meant he was doing some concentrated thinking. "Good," he said at last.

Good? What did that mean? Was he talking about her day or her body? Had he even received her clumsily sent message?

Kim stuck her head in the living room. "I'm done, Mom."

"Thanks, hon," Colleen said absently. Where the heck had she put her needle?

"I'm bored. Can I go ride my bike?"

Michael turned his head. "I have a suggestion. How about if we all go to a movie? We're all packed, and once we've moved it'll take us weeks to unpack. I thought this might be a good night."

"Wow! Can we? Please, Mom?"

Colleen was a little ashamed that they'd done so few things this summer that were fun. Kim didn't have much to look forward to these days. With the move tomorrow, probably they should stay home and get a good night's sleep. And, of course…

"What about Cam?"

"I'll bet Jennifer would watch him," Michael suggested. "Maybe Stacey could come with us."

Colleen hadn't left Cam yet. It was always hard the first

time. Even so, the hopeful look in her daughter's eyes decided her. "Let's give her a call."

His sister-in-law agreed, and half an hour later they dropped off Cam, two bottles and his playpen. The ranch house was a handsome one, separated from the fields, golden with wheat not yet harvested, by a windbreak of poplars. The hill was crowned by long irrigation pipes on huge wheels that allowed them to be moved around.

Colleen had been here only once, when Stephen and Jennifer had invited them for dinner. Kim hadn't had a chance that time to get to know Stacey, who had been at a friend's that evening.

Now Michael didn't give Colleen more than a brief chance to chat with Jennifer. "We'd better get this show on the road if we're going to have time to buy popcorn first." He was already herding the kids back to the car. Stacey went, but shyly.

"Thanks for taking Stace," Jennifer said. "They always want summer to come, and then they're so bored. Thank goodness school's starting Tuesday." She accepted Cam with a smile. "And don't worry. I'll take good care of this gorgeous boy."

"I know you will." Even so, Colleen had to tear herself away.

The movie was the latest sci-fi epic, with enough laser guns to make Drew happy and enough adventure and romance for the two girls. Colleen and Michael shared a popcorn, and in the dark they kept reaching for a handful at the same time. Each touch sent a brief thrill through her. She was as self-conscious as a girl on her first date, painfully aware of Michael's every shift in his seat.

She jumped when he nudged her and held out the popcorn bucket. "More?" he asked in a low voice.

Colleen shook her head, and he leaned forward to set it on the floor. When he sat back, he laid his arm on the back of her seat, so that her neck brushed it. Her heart stepped up its pace, and she sneaked a glance at his profile. His whole attention appeared to be on the screen.

Colleen's tiny sigh of disappointment must have been

audible, because Michael wrapped his hand around her shoulder and squeezed. "Don't worry," he whispered. "Cam's fine."

"I know," she whispered back.

It figured, she thought morosely. She was having romantic fantasies, and *he* was looking at her as the mother of his son.

On the other hand, she realized an instant later, he hadn't removed his hand. It rested loosely on her shoulder, not all that many inches away from her breast. He was definitely cuddling her, if in an absentminded way. Surely he couldn't be unaware that his arm was around her.

No, because his hand tightened again and gently massaged her shoulder and upper arm. Colleen totally lost track of what was happening on the screen. She was awash in a sea of pleasurable sensation. For the first time in her life, she passionately wished her children were elsewhere. She hadn't necked at the movies since... She couldn't remember. High school, anyway. She very much wished she could tonight.

But no, Drew sat right next to her, and Stacey and Kim were on the other side of Michael. If Drew even noticed that Michael's arm was around her, he'd probably pretend he was gagging.

Just before the lights came up, Michael casually removed his arm. She glanced at him as they stood, but he was listening to Stacey on his other side. The talk on the way out was about the movie, which the kids all thought was the greatest. By the time they reached the car, Colleen gave up expecting some significant look from Michael. He was treating her just as he always did. In the car, Stacey and Kim got far enough to discover they would have the same homeroom teacher this year, Mr. Griggs.

They returned Stacey and picked up Cam, who Jennifer claimed had been a sweetheart for her. At the sight of his mother, he began to sob as though his heart was broken.

"He's already laying a guilt trip on you," Jennifer said cheerfully.

Colleen had to laugh. At home she carried Cam upstairs, where he latched eagerly on to her breast. The bottle he'd emptied just wasn't the same, he seemed to be telling her. She tenderly rubbed his back and whispered, "You sleepy, pumpkin?"

He pulled back from her breast and patted it before making a happy, gurgling sound. Definitely wide-eyed. Colleen burped him and felt his head wavering only a little as he looked around. Just when she would have liked him to go down early. She could hear Michael supervising teeth-brushing and apparently even braiding Kim's hair. Dared she hope he was hurrying them to bed for a reason?

Colleen boosted Cam into the air and then eased him close enough for them to rub noses. "Are you sure you're not sleepy?" she asked hopefully.

He grinned. Despite everything, she grinned back.

So much for true romance.

So much, anyway, she discovered when she went back downstairs after kissing Drew and Kim good-night. Michael was in front of his computer, frowning at the numbers on the screen. When she ventured a hello, he barely glanced at her.

Unnoticed, she stood there behind him, stunned at the change from charming date to indifferent stranger. She felt like a child who had just had somebody pop her first helium balloon. She wanted to cry, scream, plead. But she wasn't a child, and she had her pride. Her pride, and a husband who wasn't interested.

Quietly she turned and went back upstairs.

Morning brought no time for self-consciousness. It was the beginning of Labor Day weekend—and moving day. Thanks to their excitement, the kids were amazingly cooperative, and the whole thing went reasonably smoothly. Even so, Colleen barely had the kitchen in working order by Tuesday, the first day of school.

Drew liked his teachers "okay," he announced, bursting in the door at the end of the day. If Kim found middle school—with six different classrooms and teachers—confusing, she wasn't about to let on. "They treat us like grown-ups," she told her family at dinner. "It's cool."

Colleen went back to work full-time that week, taking Cam with her. She'd set up his playpen right beside the counter. She was still letting him nap whenever it suited him, even though he wasn't sleeping through the night.

The first two weeks in the new house were exhausting. Colleen would hustle the kids out the door mornings, lunches packed, then get Cam and herself ready. At five-thirty in the afternoon, she walked back in. Some evenings, Michael made dinner; others, he and Drew had soccer practice and she had to manage. Then, in addition to helping the kids with their homework, she and Michael unpacked and rearranged furniture. Cam usually went down for the night at around nine, and even at eight weeks was still insisting on a feeding at two or three in the morning.

Usually the first thin cries were enough to penetrate Colleen's sleep. One night Cam had worked up to a full-fledged temper tantrum by the time she struggled to wake up enough to understand who wanted her.

She opened one eyelid and saw the fuzzy green numbers on her clock: 2:15. He'd only been asleep an hour. Colleen groaned and longingly closed her eyes again. But of course Cam went right on, sounding like a fire engine parked in the hall.

Putting him in his own bedroom was supposed to have made it easier for him to sleep. For *her* to sleep. So far, no cigar. Maybe before he'd been comforted by the small sounds of his mother sleeping only a few feet away. Whatever. He hated his bedroom in this new house.

Colleen was just bleary enough to stop in confusion when she found the hall light already on. As she stood there swaying, the high-pitched screaming abruptly ended.

She stumbled to the door of the nursery. Light from the hall let her see Michael sitting in the rocking chair with Cam nestled against his bare shoulder. They were rocking back and forth rhythmically, Michael murmuring a song of which she caught only a whisper. His eyes were closed and his cheek rested against Cam's fuzzy head. Even as tired as she was, the picture her husband and son made brought a painful, joyous lump to her throat.

Cam was so tiny with his knees drawn up, dwarfed by the breadth of his daddy's shoulders. Oh, God, she thought, Michael was beautiful, a lock of dark hair falling over his forehead, the golden light from the hall casting shadows beneath high cheekbones, muscles supple under his skin, another shadow where hair formed a V on his chest. And his tenderness, his patience…

The vicious knife blade of pain was deep inside her, stealing her breath, before she even saw it coming. Why can't he love *me?* she asked in silent agony.

Colleen was still frozen there in the doorway when Michael opened his eyes. They stared at each other, though his rocking didn't change rhythm. Nor did he look away from her when, still cradling Cam, still murmuring, "Rock-a-bye, baby," Michael eased to his feet. Cam never lifted his head and stirred only slightly when Michael laid him in the crib and gently covered him with the soft weight of his Carousel Horses quilt.

Her husband came silently toward her on bare feet. Colleen retreated into the hall until her back was against the wall. Michael paused to pull the nursery door almost closed behind him, leaving just a crack for light to spill in. Then he faced her, wearing only pajama bottoms, his body lean and very male.

Colleen was suddenly aware of how quiet the house was, of the darkness in her bedroom and down the stairwell. She couldn't tear her eyes away from Michael's bare chest and knew in the same instant how little her thin, cotton nightgown covered. Goose bumps rippled over her skin and she hugged herself, trying absurdly to cover as much as possible.

His voice was low and just a little rough, as she imagined his fingertips would be. "You could have stayed in bed."

Or had he said, "You *should* have stayed in bed"?

"I—" she moistened dry lips "—didn't realize…"

His mouth twisted and he looked at her—really looked, openly, hungrily. And when his eyes met hers again, the molten glow in them came close to shocking her. Did shock her.

"I guess—" her lips formed the words, but they were soundless "—I'll go back to bed." She took a step sideways, bumped the molding on Kim's closed door. Colleen's bare foot was feeling for another step when Michael took one stride and swung her up into his arms. She caught a glimpse of his face, skin stretched taut across strong bones, eyes smoldering and teeth clenched, before he nudged off the hall light with his elbow and swept her across the threshold into her bedroom, a bride to her belated wedding night.

Chapter 14

Colleen regretted the darkness even while she was grateful for it. She wanted to see Michael, but was glad he couldn't see her. What if he was disappointed?

He hadn't said a word yet, just carried her into her bedroom. Beside the bed, he lowered her to her feet without releasing her. Knowing she couldn't be seen let Colleen be bold. Leaning forward, she pressed her parted lips to his chest, moved her hands tentatively on his bare, smooth shoulders and felt a ripple of reaction, heard a swift intake of breath. Then his mouth captured hers in a way nothing like those dutiful kisses that had been part of becoming Michael's wife.

This one was almost savage. His formidable control was shattered. He devoured her mouth, demanded entrance until his tongue found hers in long, erotic strokes. Already her bones were dissolving. She answered him in kind, kissing him as frantically as he kissed her. She had waited so long, dreamed so many nights of this, of Michael's lean, tough body pressing her back against the bed until her knees began to buckle. But he held her up, too, one hand moving restlessly over the small of her back, the curve of her hip, exploring, kneading. The other he'd plunged into her loose hair, gripping it to angle her head for his mouth to ravish hers.

Colleen needed to breathe, didn't care if she ever did again. But she sucked in air greedily when Michael's mouth left hers to travel, hot and damp, along her jaw, down her neck, to nip at her shoulder. Was she the one whimpering, making tiny sounds of need? She was shaking, he was shaking. Now he'd gripped her nightgown and was gathering it, pausing long enough to cup her breasts and squeeze, before he pulled the gown over her head and tossed it over his shoulder. He kicked off his pajama bottoms in one move. And then he lifted her again, sliding her body along his in an exquisite, slow caress until she wrapped her legs around his waist and he let them both fall onto the bed.

Every sensation was heightened. She no longer knew where she ended and he began, which texture was covers beneath her naked back and which the feel of his leg between hers. The heated need inside her was a tightening thread that might snap if he thrummed it with a careless hand. But he was never careless; he touched her, stroked her, as he had stroked the wood he loved, creating the satin finish that showed the richness beneath.

And, oh, Lord, she touched him, found the contours of muscles and the tendons that were tight, wrenched rough groans from him and used fingernails to tell him what she needed.

The darkness wrapped them like a quilt, muffling the small, frantic sounds of lovemaking. The urgency had snatched her so quickly, driven by touch and the one glimpse of his face, that all of this must have been happening fast, yet it might have taken forever. He entered her with a thrust that brought a shudder of pleasure in its wake. Michael was trying to slow down, she could feel the strain in the quivering muscles of his arms and back, but she didn't want slow, not this time.

With distant astonishment Colleen heard herself whispering, crying, "Please, please, please," and Michael drove into her faster and faster. The bed shook, the covers tangled beneath her, he rolled onto his back so that she could sink onto him as the convulsions started and multiplied, sending out ripples of feelings so intense she couldn't name them.

His own release was as violent; he gave a ragged cry against her neck, his body arching into one last spasm before he sagged back into the covers. Collapsing, Colleen lay sprawled atop him, pleasurably weak, momentarily at peace, her thoughts unfocused.

Only slowly did bits of awareness surface—the sandpaper texture of his jaw against her cheek, the hard, swift beat of his heart beneath her breast, his hand moving almost idly up and down her spine, the way their legs were tangled together and her undignified position.

She hesitated, lifted her head. Although her eyes had adjusted to the dark, she still couldn't make out Michael's features. If only he would say something, pull her mouth down to his for another kiss, one of tenderness, instead of passion.

As swiftly as passion had risen, icy doubt was chilling her. If only just once he had called her name. How could she know in the darkness what Michael thought or felt? What if he had never wanted *her?* Tiredness lowered inhibitions; night brought dreams hard to separate from reality. The possibility lodged in Colleen's throat: *I look like Sheila.*

Which sister had Michael made love to?

On the thought of Sheila, shame washed over Colleen. "Oh, Col!" her sister had exulted not so many years ago. "I've met the most incredible man." And another time, "When he touches me, I just become a mass of little shivery atoms. It's so amazing." Her voice had had a funny little catch, perplexity and wonder and delight. "I never knew I had it in me. Or that some man could find it in me."

Colleen had always believed that she and Sheila were very different beneath the surface. But maybe not. Maybe they had been genetically programmed to be attracted to the same man. A man who could substitute one sister for the other? she wondered.

Trying not to overreact, she disentangled herself. Michael let her go. Too easily? *Say my name,* she begged silently. *Tell me what you feel.*

But instead, he swore.

Colleen turned her head. "What?"

"Cam."

And she heard it, too, the first snuffling whimpers that presaged another storm.

She moaned, but Michael was already rolling away from her. "He can't be hungry. I'll take care of him. You go back to sleep."

Her mouth silently framed the words *come back*. But he couldn't hear what she didn't say. She felt his weight leave the bed, heard the rustles as he searched for and put on his pajama bottoms, the creak of a floorboard under bare feet. When he turned on the hall light, she blinked against the brightness, her eyes registering only his dark silhouette.

Wide-awake, Colleen lay there, torn between a terrible feeling that she had just betrayed her beloved sister and a yearning equally as powerful for Michael to return, to whisper her name, to kiss her again. To want *her,* not Sheila.

And she lay there awake long after the hall light went out, long after she heard his door down the hall close.

Heaven and hell, wrapped up in one night.

Everything Michael had ever wanted except a few small words had been his—the weight of Colleen's breasts in his hands, her breathless, throaty cries, her shivers and her legs opening to receive him, her arms holding him tight.

But afterward she'd scrambled away as if she'd discovered herself in bed with the wrong man. He'd felt her flood of realization and the subtle tension in the body so intimately in contact with his.

What did he do so terribly wrong that the women he loved wanted passion but nothing that cut deeper? He and Sheila had called what they felt love, but the gut-wrenching vulnerability he'd imagined between husband and wife, the baring of secret fears and hopes, had never materialized.

His fault, Michael thought, as he stared at his own face in the bathroom mirror and adjusted his tie. Last night, why hadn't he said, *I've never touched anything as soft as your skin?* Or, *I need you?* Or even, *I thought I might die if I didn't have you soon?* Why were simple words—the ones that really meant something—so hard for him to say?

But they hadn't flowed out of her, either, he reminded himself grimly, giving his tie a last tug. She'd been straight-forward enough about her motives in marrying him: her children. And last night's passion…well, she hadn't had a man in her bed for a long time; years, probably. She'd needed him last night, but he wondered if she had blocked out who he was.

But at some point she had remembered.

He turned away from the mirror. He didn't want to think about Sheila, didn't want to acknowledge that, although he had claimed to love her, he had never felt for her a fraction of last night's desperate hunger and intense satisfaction.

Downstairs he found Colleen already in the kitchen and Cam in the playpen. She gave Michael a quick, almost shy glance from where she was unloading the dishwasher.

"Good morning."

"Good morning," he said gruffly. He stopped at the playpen. Cam lay on his back, staring wide-eyed at his own hands, which he was slowly bringing together and then separating. Michael shook his head. "How come he doesn't have bags under his eyes?"

He'd surprised a chuckle out of her. "Are you kidding? With all the naps he takes?"

"I wonder how well it would go over if the bank closed for a siesta?"

"Oh, dear." She straightened, looking the way she would if Drew had announced he had an earache. "I'm sorry. You must be dreadfully tired."

The truth came more easily than he'd expected. "Some things are worth it."

Her lashes fluttered and her cheeks pinkened. "Well, Cam—"

"I'm not talking about Cam."

Her face was always expressive. Anxiety and pleasure and feminine vanity warred briefly. But at last she offered a small, tentative smile. "Oh, good."

Michael crossed the kitchen and threaded the fingers of one hand into her vibrant hair. He closed his eyes and kissed her, savoring her soft mouth, her morning taste of mint and tea, the way her lips parted and she leaned toward him.

Lifting his head and releasing her, stepping back, was agonizing. Michael flexed his fingers and curled them into fists before shoving them in his pockets.

Colleen looked as shell-shocked as he felt. The tremble in her soft, lower lip and the cloudiness in her moss-green eyes made him wish he'd been able to see her face last night as he made love to her. Right as he entered her, and then at the end. Next time…

But he tamped down on the thought. Last night it had just happened, too quickly for reflection or guilt, taking them both by surprise. But if he deliberately went to Colleen's bed….

Her thoughts had obviously paralleled his, because Colleen said quietly, "Last night…it was wonderful. And now I feel so guilty, as though I've done something wrong." She drew a shaky breath. "Tell me…"

"That I feel the same?" His voice was raw.

She quivered as though he'd struck her. "I was going to say, tell me what an idiot I'm being."

His own guilt was magnified tenfold by hers. Michael felt as though his chest had been scalded. "Who am I to tell you that?" To his own ears, he sounded as though he was speaking from a great distance away. "I promised Sheila eternity. I didn't even stay in mourning for ten months."

He didn't wait for a response, didn't want to see any more pain in Colleen's eyes. He left without breakfast, without finding out whether he was supposed to take Drew or Kim somewhere. Right this second, he couldn't deal with anybody else's expectations.

How could he when he knew how selfish he really was? The taste of heaven last night had been too sweet. Whether Colleen was ready or not, Michael wasn't going to be able to stay away from her for long.

By the time he got home from work, Michael had pulled himself together enough to draw Colleen aside. "I'm sorry," he said roughly. "Talking about Sheila this morning, it just got to me. I, uh, I don't know…"

Colleen laid a hand over his mouth and shook her head. "No, don't say anything. I wanted reassurance, and I didn't stop to think that I might make you feel as bad."

A muscle in his jaw jerked. "Don't worry. I felt guilty as hell all on my own."

Colleen pressed her lips together and turned quickly away. "Dinner's almost ready."

Dinner. Kids. An evening meeting of the soccer coaches to set a game schedule. The mundane in the midst of melodrama.

Michael came home from the meeting inexpressibly weary. He felt a little better the minute he parked in front of the barn. The old house was lit and welcoming; in seeing generations come and go, it fit perfectly his idea of a real home.

He let himself in quietly, locking the front door behind him, then paused to glance into the living room. Colleen was there, quilting at the large frame they'd decided to set up there so she could be with the family while she worked.

Lamplight cast a warm glow over her; her reflection in the small panes of the bay window was timeless. How many women had quilted in this house, making bedcovers to keep their families warm?

Colleen wore a loose cotton dress that exposed a delicate collarbone and a long, graceful neck. Her heavy, auburn hair was bundled at her nape, and her arms were slender and pale in what should have been an awkward pose, but was utterly natural for her. She seemed absorbed in her work, and patient beyond his understanding.

Would she be as patient with him?

"Hello," he said.

She started and lifted her head. "Oh, Michael. How was the meeting?"

"Eight Saturday games, two Sunday. Most of the boys' coaches wanted to stick the girls' teams with the Sunday games."

She made a face. "Figures."

Michael leaned against the arched opening. "A few of us

thought the inconvenience should be spread around equally. We won."

"A small victory for the rights of women."

He let himself smile back. "You bet."

Her face was soft, her eyes enigmatic. "Can you sit down?"

Go slowly, give her time to think, Michael told himself. He shook his head. "I have work to do."

"Oh. Fine."

He wanted to believe she was disappointed, but she could just as well be relieved. "Kids in bed?"

"Yes, but reading. Although to tell you the truth—" her nose crinkled "—I think Drew has that wretched hand-held electronic game he borrowed from Ian under the bed covers. I could swear I heard a beep before I stuck my head in."

"I don't think it'll warp him for life," Michael said mildly.

Colleen made a face. "No, of course not. But as a mother, I have a duty to make him feel guilty for…" Her voice died, and they stared at each other.

God, he wanted her. Wanted to put his lips to her throat, his hands on her lush breasts. He wanted to rip that dress over her head and see her milky, pale skin and the pink-brown areolae of her nipples, the silky hair that must be as richly colored as that on her head. He'd dreamed a million times…

But when had the dreams started? Had he wanted Colleen even when Sheila was alive?

That was the question he couldn't afford to ask. Even now, he flinched away from it.

"I'll say good night to the kids." He sounded hoarse. "And see you in the morning."

Colleen gave a tiny nod. Her stricken expression stayed with him even after he booted the computer in his office. Could she possibly be hurt that he'd made clear he wasn't coming to her bed? Had he misunderstood her completely?

She was so reserved the next day he had to wonder again. For the first time in weeks she was prickly when he asked Kim to do a chore and a minor scene erupted. He was just ticked off enough to decide that if Colleen couldn't take steps to do something about Kim's unhappiness, he would, and why the hell should he consult her, anyway?

At dinnertime even the kids picked up on the tension. He caught a few speculative looks, but Kim apparently was old enough to keep her thoughts to herself—or to wait and talk to her mother, rather than him. Actually, Michael was surprised when Drew trailed him outside.

"What are you doing?"

"Trying to decide where we should have the garage built. I don't want my car outside when winter comes."

"Oh." Drew hoisted himself onto the porch railing. "Are you and Mom mad at each other?"

Michael's first instinct was to lie. He ignored it. "Yeah, I guess we are. Grown-ups get mad, too, you know."

"Are you going to get divorced?" The boy was trying hard to sound untroubled. He didn't quite succeed.

"Afraid you'll lose your soccer coach?"

"Well, yeah." Drew swung his legs, and his eyes wouldn't meet Michael's. "But, um, it's been kind of cool having, well, almost a dad. You know?"

The kid might as well have reached right into Michael's chest and given his heart a little twist. "Yeah." He cleared his throat. "It's been cool having almost a son, too."

Drew looked up anxiously. "But you have a real son."

Michael gave him a crooked grin. "He's no fun yet."

The boy's face cleared. "Mom says he won't even be able to *walk* for a year! Walking's easy!"

"So will pitching be for you when you're a foot taller."

"I guess," Drew conceded. He kept swinging his legs. "*Are* you getting divorced?"

"No divorce."

"Well, then, I've been thinking. Could we get a puppy?"

Michael coughed to hide his smile. "Uh…have you talked to your mom about this?"

Drew's brown eyes were wide and innocent. "No. I thought I'd ask you first."

"Ah. Well, why don't you see what she says?"

"Right now?" He jumped down from the railing. "Cool!"

Michael opened his mouth to suggest he wait until his mother was in a better mood, but he was too late. The screen door was already slamming shut and Drew was bellowing, "Mom!"

Five minutes later, Colleen stalked out onto the porch. "You said he could have a dog."

Michael crossed his arms. "Actually, no, I didn't. But is there any reason he can't?"

Her mouth opened and then she snapped it shut. "He lied."

Michael was momentarily able to see the humor in all this. "Would you put it that strongly?"

"Yes!" Colleen gave an exasperated sigh. "No. I'm just not used to them going behind my back."

He gave her a minute before suggesting calmly, "You know, I suspect kids in any family play one parent off against the other. Didn't they try that with Ben?"

She frowned. "Drew wasn't old enough. Kim…maybe." It was grudging. "But Ben didn't do a heck of a lot of parenting." Some emotion Michael wished he could decipher flickered across her face. "You're right," she said shortly, and went back into the house.

"Damn it to hell," Michael muttered, and turned to stare out at the yard. Dusk was slipping over the eastern hills, purple and gray and cool. The leaves were turning brilliant shades of scarlet and yellow.

Were he and Colleen getting anywhere? he wondered. Or were they being pulled back by the undertow?

On the positive side: she was being honest with herself, even though her insight was obviously unwelcome some of the time. Positive: the kids seemed to be learning to accept him. Positive: he and Colleen had made love and been compatible—a pallid word for what they had actually felt.

Negative: they were both ridden with guilt. Negative: he didn't know whether she wanted him back in her bed or not. Negative: he didn't know what she felt, and she didn't know what he felt.

To both the last two points, there was only one way to find out. And to hell with Sheila's ghost.

For a change Cam went down for the night at about the same time as Drew and Kim. Michael hung around downstairs, pretending to read the paper, while Colleen quilted. When she finally announced she was going to bed, he promptly rose to his feet.

"I think I will, too."

Her eyes rolled like those of a spooked horse, but she sounded only a little breathless when she said, "Do you want to lock up?"

"Sure."

Upstairs he brushed his teeth, shaved for a second time in the day and, in the office where he was also sleeping, stripped down to his jeans. Then, as nervous and excited as a sixteen-year-old kid his first time, Michael went down the hall to Colleen's bedroom.

Her door stood half-open, as it always did so she could hear Cam in the night; the lamp beside her bed was still on. Under his hand, her door opened silently, but she was waiting for him, sitting up in bed, ramrod straight, her eyes huge and dark.

Just as silently, Michael closed the door behind him. She watched wordlessly as he went around to the other side of the bed, but she flushed and looked away when he reached for the snap on his jeans. He stepped out of them and tossed them onto a chair, then slipped quickly into bed. Lying on his side, braced on one elbow, he looked at her.

Colleen's silken, heavy mass of hair was confined in a fat braid. Her nightgown was different from the other night's, but the white smocked fabric was as thin, and this one, too, was sleeveless and scoop-necked.

Michael reached out and cupped her cheek in one hand, turning her head to face him. Her lips were compressed, her lashes lowered. But she was no coward; after a bare moment they lifted to reveal eyes as deep and mysterious as that deep, green pool to which he had once compared her.

He knew he should say something; he knew he shouldn't have walked in here and climbed into her bed without asking tacitly or otherwise for permission. But words never had been his strong suit.

With his thumb he traced the line of her lips, felt them soften, part, her breathing quicken. Suddenly she sucked in a breath and turned to reach for her lamp switch.

"No," he said quickly. She hesitated, but didn't turn back to him. His voice was scratchy. "I want to see you."

"But I'm—" She clamped down on whatever she'd been going to say, but she still wasn't looking at him.

"Beautiful." He didn't sound like himself.

"Thirty-five years old. I've had three children."

"You're a woman, not a teenage girl. I don't want a girl."

"But Sheila—" Colleen stopped again.

He didn't want to think about Sheila, but this was one time he was going to have to. "Sheila?"

"She was younger. And slimmer. And she'd never had a baby."

Michael had her flat under him before she could think twice. He bent his head and kissed her until she began to shiver. When he lifted his head he said grittily, "You are not Sheila, and I never thought you were. Your faces looked a little alike to people who didn't know you well. The rest of you doesn't."

"But…you've never seen…"

"I've touched you." He raised himself on his elbows. "Your breasts are bigger…."

"Because I'm nursing."

"All the time." Her nipples were tight and hard. Michael rubbed his mouth against them through the fine cotton of her gown and felt another little quiver in the body waiting quiescently under him. "You only have freckles on your nose." He scooted her nightgown up and rejoiced in the way her hips rose to help him take it off. Her skin was just as pale and creamy as he'd imagined, her curves as gentle. Her belly was a little soft under his hand, but to each side were the peaks of pelvic bone. And her hair… Michael sat up. "It's like licks of flame," he said, tangling his fingers in the curls, feeling the heat and damp beneath.

Now her eyes were so dark he couldn't have seen their

color. She was breathing in tiny gasps, her hands clutching the covers. Shyly she said, "You have a nice body yourself."

"But not a boy's."

Her gaze dropped to the forceful evidence of his arousal. "No, thank goodness," she said, that little bit of huskiness in her voice an aphrodisiac. As if he needed one.

"I want *you*," he said straight out, and braced himself for her answer.

"I don't suppose you'd believe me if I said I didn't want you." She was trying to tease him, and he knew she was thinking about that unmistakable dampness his fingers had discovered.

But he said, almost grimly, "I'd believe you," and hoped she knew what he was trying to tell her.

Apparently she did, because her lashes lifted and she studied him inscrutably for a moment long enough to scare the hell out of him. And then she smiled, still shyly, and held her arms out to him. A simple gesture, and a powerful one. One a man could wait his whole life for.

He went into her arms and closed his mind to anything outside the circle of her embrace. They would have to talk soon; passion couldn't vanquish guilt. But tonight he was going to take what she offered, and not wish he deserved more.

One minute Michael's eyes were molten with hunger for her, and he made her feel sexy and womanly and maybe even loved. And the next he damn near shut her fingers in the doors he used to guard himself, he slammed them shut with so little warning.

One *minute* wasn't quite right, though; one *night* he made love to her until she had no more identity or resistance than a little pool of amoebas, happy in their simplicity. But come morning he was back to his silent, frowning self. Which he'd been ever since. Polite, helpful—and distant. Two nights now she had waited for him to come to her bed. But no, he'd apparently felt strong and able to resist her feeble lures. And she didn't have the guts to stalk down the hall and climb into *his* bed.

Maybe she should be flattered that he regarded her as a

forbidden fruit. No man had ever found her that exotic before. But she had always valued calm, a life of security and confidence and tranquillity.

Tranquillity. Colleen almost snorted, which startled a customer who turned from the bolts of solid-color cotton. "Pardon me?"

"Just mumbling to myself," Colleen admitted.

The older woman smiled. "I do it all the time."

"Do you need any help?"

"Um—" she tilted her head "—well, I like this pale green with the sunflower print, but then the brown doesn't look right. What do you think?"

"Are you determined to have the green?"

"Heavens, no."

"Well, then, how about a pale yellow or cream?" She reached unerringly for the bolt she wanted. "Like this."

The woman blinked. "Perfect! Bless you. Cut them before I change my mind."

Colleen was still brooding about her marriage on the way home at five-thirty. Maybe that was why she suddenly found herself headed for the rental that had been home the past year. In the absence of conscious direction, habit had taken over. On impulse, instead of turning at the next intersection, she decided to drive by the house.

New renters had already moved in. A tricycle sat on the sidewalk, a teenage boy was dribbling a basketball in the driveway and eyeing the hoop above the neighbor's garage. Colleen stopped on the other side of the street and just sat looking for a minute, trying to find inside herself the woman who had lived contentedly here.

All she discovered was that she wouldn't go back even if she could. Back before Cam, back when Michael was her sister's husband, a remote man she'd always felt a little uncomfortable around....

Back before Sheila had died.

But the reminder didn't have the impact it once had.

"We have to go on," she said softly. This time she didn't

expect an answer. Sheila was gone, alive only in their memories. Which was as it ought to be.

Ten minutes later, Colleen turned into her own driveway. She had parked and was getting out when two girls came tearing around the corner of the house.

"Hey, Mom!" Kim called. "Stacey's here."

"So I see," Colleen said, smiling at the other girl. "Is your mom or dad here, Stacey?"

"No, I just came over to hang out with Kim." She shrugged nonchalantly. "What a neat house. And barn."

Kim was fairly dancing with excitement. "Mom, Stacey's parents say she can take horseback-riding lessons. Can I take them, too? Michael says it's up to you."

"Honey, they're expensive."

Her daughter's joy dimmed. "But you said maybe I could get a horse. I mean, why else did you buy a place with a barn and pasture?"

"Because we liked the house." Colleen closed her eyes. "Kim, I'll think about it. Do you suppose I can take Cam out of his car seat and have something cold to drink before we make any decisions?"

"Sure." Kim's voice went flat and her shoulders had sagged. "You'll say no, anyway."

"I haven't yet." Aware of Stacey's presence, Colleen didn't add, "But I will if you go on this way."

Inside, Colleen deposited Cam in the playpen and went to the refrigerator. Behind her, Michael said, "Hi. How was your day?"

"Fine." She grabbed a can of soda pop and flipped open the top, bumping the refrigerator door shut with her hip. "Yours?"

Damn, just the sight of him, arms crossed, shoulders filling the doorway, was enough to make her weak. Where was her pride?

"Did you see Kim?" His voice was slow and deep.

"I gather she's acquired a bosom buddy."

His dark brows went up. "Is that bad?"

"Don't be silly. I like Stacey. If their friendship amounts to anything, I'll go down on bended knee." Colleen tried to ignore the tension creeping up her neck, tightening around her forehead. "Was this your idea?"

"Um-huh." He was using that calm, neutral tone he had undoubtedly perfected for business negotiations. The one designed to smooth feathers, to keep emotion out of the discussion. "I figured if they were stuck with each other for the day, something might come of it."

He expected her to be jealous, she realized; jealous because he'd been able to do something for Kim that she hadn't. And she'd asked for it, after the way she'd acted the first few times he took some initiative with the kids.

Colleen took care to keep her own tone as deliberately calm. "She said something about riding lessons."

He just watched her with those vivid eyes. "Seems like a good idea to me."

"Michael...do you know what they cost?"

He shrugged. "We can afford them."

Now, when she least needed it, was when her pride reared its ugly head. She'd gladly have accepted everything he could do her children if only he had married her for love, which she could return in equal measure. But theirs had been a bargain—and an unequal one. At moments like this, she felt like a kept woman.

Her hesitation was brief, but even that was too long.

Just like that, his teeth clenched. "You'd rather live on what you make, wouldn't you?"

She felt she owed him honesty. "Michael, being able to support myself was important to me. These days I feel a little like the beggar maid. Anyway, you shouldn't have to fork over money for everything my kids want."

"I gather," he said, his tone remote, "that you don't exactly feel married. At least, not 'for richer or for poorer.'"

"Michael—"

His eyes glittered. "Or are you in this marriage at all?"

Chapter 15

Anger rushed through Colleen. It came easily, a wave breaking over her head. "Maybe that's a question you should ask yourself," she snapped.

Michael loomed over her like a thunderhead. "What's that supposed to mean?"

It means, do you love me or don't you? She couldn't say that. But she could come close.

"One night you're in my bed telling me I'm beautiful, and the next night you can't go into hiding fast enough!"

His voice rose. "You haven't exactly been handing me an invitation!"

"Well, I won't be tonight, either!"

Michael leaned toward her, his teeth set. "According to you," he said silkily, "it's *my* money that bought your bedroom. That makes it mine."

Colleen inhaled sharply. "Do you think you've bought me?"

They stared at each other. Suddenly Michael bowed his head. He was breathing as though he'd been running. "You know I don't," he said quietly. "Colleen—"

"No." She shook her head and backed away. "I don't want to talk about it right now."

"Uncle Michael…" Stacey stopped in the doorway and looked wide-eyed from one to the other. "I'm sorry." She started to retreat, stopped, bit her lip. "Um, my mom's here to get me."

"I'll go out," Colleen said quickly. She made a distinct circle around Michael. She hoped the smile she gave her niece by marriage didn't look as faked as it was. "So, Stacey, do you like middle school?"

"Yeah, it's okay. I'm glad Kim and I have classes together."

They found Kim outside talking to Jennifer, who smiled at Colleen. "Sounds like the girls had a good time today."

"Looks like it," Colleen agreed. "We'll have to do this again."

"Mom, can Kim come over after school Monday?" Stacey asked. She gave Kim a shy glance. "If she wants to."

Kim turned pleading eyes on Colleen. "Can I, Mom?"

The two mothers agreed that, yes, that would be fine, and Colleen promised to pick Kim up at six.

When the station wagon backed out, Colleen glanced at her daughter to find her face averted. "Honey…" Colleen sighed. "I'm sorry. I was cranky today."

"I know we don't have the money," Kim said unexpectedly. "I shouldn't have asked you. I just thought…well, that maybe we did now, since you're married."

"I guess we do," Colleen admitted. "I'm just so used to thinking one way, I'm having trouble readjusting. But Michael and I talked about it, and lessons would be fine."

"Really?" Kim breathed, instantly up from the depths. "With Stacey?"

"Sure. I'll talk to her mom."

"Oh, thank you, thank you, thank you!" Kim gave her a quick squeeze. "Where's Michael?"

"In the house…" Kim was already on her way. Colleen stood in the middle of the yard, reluctant to go back in herself. Michael was right; they did have to talk. But she didn't look forward to it. She didn't want to hear him admit how he really felt about her and the marriage.

They succeeded in getting through the evening without the kids noticing anything wrong. Colleen was very careful not to give signals Michael might have taken as an invitation—not because she didn't want him to come to her bed, she admitted rather unhappily to herself, but because of her pride.

Michael came, anyway, silently in the dark. This time she didn't know he was there until she felt the bed give under his weight. To her shame, she didn't protest. Instead, at the first touch of his hand, need clenched inside her and she went willingly, even eagerly, into his arms. Neither spoke, though they sighed and moaned and sobbed for breath. The time might come when their lovemaking could be sweet and lingering, when they could laugh or tease or tantalize. But not yet; stark hunger drove them to snatch desperately at these rare moments, at the sensual stroke of rough fingertips on her breasts, at the shiver of muscles under her palms, at the shudder of pleasure when they came together. In the dark they had to admit nothing; passion was enough.

It held Michael there when Colleen got up once in the middle of the night to nurse Cam; it brought them together again in another feverish coupling. But when she awakened in the morning to find herself alone, the emptiness that clutched at her was greater than this bed or this room.

She needed more than the coming together of their bodies, more than physical release. And she was terribly afraid that that was all either had sought or found in each other's arms. She wasn't even sure how to name what they'd done last night. Was it lovemaking? Colleen wondered with self-loathing, or just plain sex?

Michael had just discovered the difference between having sex and making love. He had made love to a woman for only the fourth time in his life last night. The knowledge was like an ulcer, eating away at him from the inside out.

Michael dipped the sponge into the bucket of warm, soapy water and sloshed it over the hood of Colleen's car. The activity was just about right for his state of mind today. The kids were washing his car at the same time so he could supervise, though as attentive as he was, they could have been using it as a water slide.

No, his mind was mired in the past, trying to understand how he could have made such a mistake in his first marriage and wondering whether, if Sheila hadn't died, he would ever have recognized quite how fundamental that mistake had been.

Because the truth was, he had married the wrong sister. Lifting the wiper blades to get at the windshield, Michael had a flash of remembering the dreams he'd had shortly after Sheila died, the ones in which he hadn't been able to tell which sister he was with. He hadn't had the dreams in a long time. And for a good reason. He doubted he would even see a resemblance between the two now if they were standing side by side.

If he'd met Colleen first, he would never have looked twice at Sheila. It was the ways in which they were similar that had attracted him to Sheila; but it was the ways in which Colleen was different that reached him most powerfully.

He didn't feel guilty anymore because Sheila was dead and he wasn't; he didn't even feel guilty because he had married Colleen. No, what got to him was the fact that on some gut level he couldn't help rejoicing, because only Sheila's death would have let him find and have the woman he loved.

But he was going to lose her if he didn't soon come to terms with his self-knowledge.

He made a sound of disgust and reached for the hose. Maybe he already had come to terms and just hadn't yet figured out a way to make it palatable for Colleen.

On Monday, as much to corner himself as to corner her, Michael left the bank early and drove over to her shop. Here they couldn't be interrupted by the kids. If she had customers, he'd just wait until closing time. But the only car in the gravel parking lot out front was Colleen's.

She was perched on a stool behind the tall front counter, her head bent, contemplating a fan of fabric swatches. When the bell over the door rang, she looked up, smiling automatically. "Hello…oh, hi, Michael." With a mother's quick alarm, she added, "Something wrong?"

"Nope." He let the door close behind him and the bell tinkled again. "Busy?"

"Heavens, no. Cam's sleeping." She nodded at the playpen,

then made a face. "Actually, the place was dead today. House of Fabrics is having a forty percent off sale this week."

"Your customers will all show up Monday to buy more fabric to go with whatever they bought there."

This time her smile was grateful. "I hope so. What's up?"

"I thought this might be a good chance for us to talk."

Colleen studied him gravely. After a moment she nodded.

Michael paced the length of the small room and stopped in front of the window. He turned to face her and pushed his hands into his pockets.

"I should start," he said abruptly. "I always figured that Sheila told you everything. That she talked about our marriage and our problems."

Her voice was whisper soft. "I suppose that didn't make you feel any too happy. I never realized... I guess Sheila didn't, either."

"No." He moved his shoulders to loosen tight muscles. "And, yeah, it bothered me. I, uh... Hell, this sounds petty." He made himself say it, anyway. "I was jealous of you before I ever met you. A couple of times I overheard the tail end of one of Sheila's conversations with you. She didn't talk like that to me. She claimed to love me, but I don't think she ever trusted me. She didn't have to, because she had you."

He caught a glimpse of the odd expression on Colleen's face before she bowed her head. Her voice was strained. "There's something I should tell you."

"Wait. Let me finish." Michael swung away again and gazed, unseeing, out the window. "Our marriage was in trouble years ago." He made a rough sound in his throat. "No, that's not right. It wasn't that we fought or either of us took up with someone else. I just...felt empty, and I think Sheila did, too. Or maybe she didn't, God, I don't know. She had you to talk to. She didn't need me."

The compassion in Colleen's eyes was too close to pity. "Sheila never said a word of this to me. I'd have sworn she was in love with you. Only once..."

"What?"

"I told you about it. That once, she sounded angry because

you didn't seem to understand why she kept trying to get pregnant despite her miscarriages."

"No, I didn't understand. It was crazy. She might as well have been rubbing sandpaper over raw skin. I figured…" He let out a long breath. "I figured she was desperate to fill the emptiness we both felt. I wasn't enough for her. Never had been enough. I used to wonder…" God, it was hard to bare himself. He felt Colleen's gaze even though his face was averted. "I wondered why she didn't leave me, why she didn't find a man who could love her the way she wanted to be loved. But I don't think she ever even looked. All she wanted was a baby. For that, she needed me. I used to think that was all she kept me for."

"I…really don't think it was that simple," Colleen said with seeming difficulty. "I've been doing a lot of thinking lately myself."

Now he did look at her, expecting to see open pity. Instead, her luminous eyes held distress and weariness and even guilt.

"You know that our own father walked out on us when we were young."

Michael nodded.

"Even though I still have a few memories of him, I've always told everybody I didn't really miss him. Now I think that Mom was so determined to make sure we didn't, she overdid it. Probably it wasn't on purpose, but I can still hear her voice, telling me we didn't need him. I thought she was brave and strong." Colleen gave a funny, twisted smile. Her eyes had a far-off look. "Maybe she was. For sure, Mom was just doing the best she could. But I think Sheila and I heard it so many times, neither of us were left with the ability to trust any man, much less admit to ourselves we needed him."

She kept talking, and Michael listened without interrupting. He wasn't the only one who had dammed up his emotions. But it developed that not all her guilt had to do with Sheila. Colleen had decided that she'd pushed Ben away, and though Michael never had thought all that highly of her ex-husband, he hadn't known the two of them together well enough to tell if there was any merit in her conclusion. The rest of it—her belief that

Sheila had done the same to him—he didn't dare allow himself to buy one hundred percent. It would have let him off the hook, given him an excuse when he didn't deserve one.

But maybe there was something to her theory. Maybe it explained why Sheila never seemed to mind how shallow their relationship was. And maybe it explained why she hadn't looked for another man. According to Colleen, she wasn't programmed to need a man. She was programmed to have babies and raise them and be strong, to trust her mother and her sister, but never her husband.

But Michael knew damn well that the kind of man he was hadn't helped matters. Sheila had to have been hungry for love and tenderness and attention—all things he hadn't known how to give her. All needs she'd thought a child would fill.

On the heels of his sadness that she had never had that child was relief. Because the child was no longer an abstraction. It was Cam, small and vulnerable, who would have had to carry the burden of his mother's needs.

It was her husband who should have carried them.

And so he'd failed in his marriage, whatever his excuse. What scared him was that he'd fail again. He couldn't lose Colleen now that he'd found her. But he had no idea what she needed from him.

And he wasn't sure he was capable of letting her see how badly *he* needed her.

She had lapsed into silence, staring down at the fan of fabric samples on the counter in front of him. He moved his shoulders uncomfortably inside his suit jacket and looked away himself, scrutinizing bolts of calicos shading from navy to ice blue as though they could tell him something.

His voice sounded gravelly, and he made himself look back at Colleen. His wife. "I don't know if this got us anywhere, but I thought you should know. I won't say I haven't mourned Sheila, because I have. But…not the way you probably thought."

Colleen nodded. Her gaze touched his, shied away, came nervously back. "Then why—" She stopped.

"Why the guilt?" *Because I love you, and I didn't love her.* He might have had the nerve to say it if he'd had any reason to think Colleen loved him. Any reason except the way she responded to him sexually. He cleared his throat. "It just felt sometimes as though I picked up and moved on so quickly. One minute everything we did was for her. The next, she was gone, and you and I were haggling over the baby. Now here we are married, making the kind of family Sheila wanted, but we're doing it for us, not her." He rubbed a hand over his face. "And she hasn't been dead a year."

In a few stark sentences he'd destroyed any chance of saying, *I love you.* But Colleen surprised him.

"Not just for us," she said spiritedly. "For Cam, too. And Drew and Kim."

"True."

Her back was very straight, her cheeks pink. "You know, it would be easy to feel guilty forever because we're alive and Sheila's dead. But what's the point? We aren't doing her any good."

"True."

Colleen eyed him suspiciously. "Are you agreeing just so you don't hurt my feelings?"

"No." Was he smiling? "I do agree. Everything you say makes sense. I didn't say I was always rational."

"Emotions never are," Colleen told him with childlike solemnity. She made the conversion to being thoroughly adult when she added, "Thank heavens."

"Why thank heavens?"

She scrunched up her face. "Because I'm a gutless wonder. If I didn't follow my feelings sometimes, instead of thinking everything out, I'd be paralyzed by indecision."

The difference between them was he never followed his feelings. Or at least, Michael amended in faint surprise, he never used to. Asking Colleen to marry him had been an impulse. Not entirely, though; he'd buttressed his decision with all sorts of rational reasons why it was the thing to do. But that wasn't why he'd asked her; he'd asked her because it had felt right.

And God knows he hadn't hauled her off to bed because calm reason had told him the time had come. Calm reason had been screaming, *Stop!* He'd told it to go to hell.

The idea amused him. It also made him wonder if there wasn't hope for him. If he could be swept away by passion, surely he could manage a few simple words. *I love you. I need you.*

"Well." Colleen stood up behind her barricade. "If I don't get going, I'll be late picking up Kim."

"I'll do that," Michael offered. "Do you want me to grab something for dinner on the way home? Chinese, maybe?"

"I put a roast out to defrost this morning. Besides—" she was lifting Cam from the playpen and making silly faces at him "—cooking dinner is about the only thing I do that makes me feel useful."

Michael stiffened. Why was money such a sticking point for her?

But she surprised him yet again with a pert smile. "Not that I mind having a cleaning woman. I can't say I want to go back to dusting and vacuuming. Or cleaning bathrooms, heaven forbid."

Generous to the end. He was a lucky man, even if Colleen never came to love him.

The thought was infinitely depressing.

Now here we are married making the kind of family Sheila wanted, but we're doing it for us, not her.

Colleen went home feeling more optimistic than she had since the day Michael asked her to marry him. He hadn't just sought her out to talk to her, he'd sought her out to send a message.

He'd wanted her to know that he hadn't been madly in love with Sheila, that his heart hadn't been broken by her death. Was there any chance at all, Colleen wondered, that he'd been trying to say that he was free to love again? Free to love her?

Well, then, her argumentative inner voice demanded, why didn't he just *tell* you he loves you?

Maybe because he didn't have a clue how she felt? After all, as far as he knew, she'd married him only to keep Cam—and, of course, she thought ruefully, for his money.

Well, he'd taken the first step. She should be grateful for that much, and patient. Besides, they had a lifetime together.

Michael came to her bed that night. As he made love to her, he told her how beautiful she was, and he quivered at her touch. But he said not a word about how he felt, and as a result, neither did she. When she was dragged out of a deep sleep by Cam's cries and Michael mumbled, "I'll get him," before rolling away, Colleen reached after him.

"You know," she said sleepily, "you could come back."

He went still. "Do you want me to?"

"Uh-huh," she murmured.

His hand smoothed her hair off her face, and she brushed her lips against his wrist. "You could sleep here every night," she said a little less sleepily. She held her breath waiting for his answer.

"Is that what you want?" he asked again, his voice deep.

"I wouldn't have said it if I didn't." Her heart was pounding hard now at her boldness. "But if you're more comfortable having your own bedroom, that's okay."

"No." He bent down and kissed her, his mouth lingering even as Cam's cries escalated. "Oh, hell," Michael muttered. "Don't go anywhere."

"I won't," Colleen said breathlessly.

The very next day, he moved in, taking over the second closet. Colleen felt more secure in her marriage and less like someone who has an illicit lover slipping into her bedroom in the wee hours of the night.

But she still had to face the fact that Michael hadn't said a word about his feelings. His silence was unsettling. Would the kind of explosive passion they had endure if love wasn't part of it, sending down deep roots to anchor their marriage?

Her uneasiness came to a head that night when they went into their bedroom. Michael dropped his shirt on a ladder-back chair and sprawled on the bed wearing jeans and nothing else. Colleen grabbed her nightgown and headed for the bathroom.

"Why are you going in there to undress?" he asked her.

Colleen stopped with her back to him. "To protect you?" she ventured.

"I'm a big boy." His voice was husky. "I like to take risks."

"Michael..." As she turned to face him, excitement shivered in her, but also some primal terror. She didn't want him to see her body's every flaw, all exposed at once. If she stood before him naked, she would be painfully vulnerable.

"Come here."

"No, I... No." She shook her head hard. "I'd rather not."

He studied her from the bed, where he lay with the pillows bunched behind him. Lines were etched between his dark brows. Colleen held his gaze defiantly.

"What are you afraid of?"

She hardly knew the answer herself, except that she had to protect herself.

"I don't know." It wasn't as though he hadn't seen her, but somehow this was different. She clutched the nightgown in a death grip. "I just..."

"Never mind." His expression had closed. "I don't want you to do anything that makes you uncomfortable."

Yes, but why had it? Colleen spent the next day brooding about her own reaction. She hadn't been especially modest around Ben, and her third pregnancy hadn't wreaked such havoc with her body that she had to be ashamed of it. No, there was another explanation.

Probably she was afraid of losing Michael if he was disappointed; maybe more afraid of losing him because of the very strength of her feelings. And, after all, her first husband had walked out on her.

But Colleen knew in her heart that Michael wasn't the kind of man who would leave a woman because her body wasn't flawless. Still, it took such trust to stand naked, with nothing to hide behind, in front of a man. A woman had to be secure in her beauty or secure in his love. And she wasn't either.

She had begun to believe that he liked her. She knew he wanted her. But neither fact meant that this wasn't still a marriage of convenience as far as he was concerned. Neither fact meant that he would have chosen her out of all the women in the world.

The scary part was that she was driven to know one way or the other. The uncertainty was killing her. She had to ask. But it wasn't fair to expect him to reveal his innermost emotions without her doing so, as well. And if she did—if she told Michael she loved him and then he hesitated, or fumbled for an answer, or even admitted he didn't love her... Her heart squeezed at the thought. Oh, Lord, what would it do to them? Could they maintain even the kind of marriage they had if one was in love and the other wasn't?

She'd told him she was a coward, and now she discovered how much of one. After the kids went to bed, he sat down on the couch with the newspaper. Colleen sneaked a glance at him just as she had when she wondered what it would be like to have his hands touching her.

Suddenly she realized he was looking straight at her, one eyebrow lifted in faint surprise at whatever he saw in her expression.

"Is something wrong?" he asked.

Now, Colleen told herself, and opened her mouth. Incredulous, she felt herself shaking her head. "I was just thinking. I'm sorry. Was I staring blankly at you?"

His eyes narrowed for a heartbeat, but he didn't comment.

And in bed that night, under the antique nine-patch quilt that covered them, she tried to whisper, "I love you." But it stuck in her throat, and Colleen told herself she wanted to see the expression on his face when she made her declaration.

Three little words. Easy to say to the kids. Wrenchingly difficult to say to Michael.

Drew came tearing into the kitchen, chanting, "Kim has boobies, Kim has boobies!"

His sister was in hot pursuit. "You're a brat, Andrew Deering!"

Colleen turned from the hot stove to find that Michael had just walked in the back door, suit jacket slung over his shoulder. He reached out a long arm and effortlessly snagged his stepson. "Let's have a little talk," he suggested. Only Colleen heard the suppressed amusement in his voice.

"Mo-om!" Kim wailed, stopping in the middle of the kitchen. "I'm so humiliated!"

Michael held Drew in a hammerlock. "You know," he said conversationally to Kim, "you'll have plenty of chances to get him back. I don't think it's occurred to him yet how humiliated *he'll* be when his voice starts cracking or when his friends are shaving and he's not, or when he's still a little shrimp and they're nudging six feet."

"Who says I'll be a little shrimp?" Drew protested.

Michael set him on his feet. "You may not be," he agreed. "But, hey, who knows? If you tease her about something she can't help, like her body, you're asking for it back."

Kim's cheeks were still bright pink, but her voice had moderated when she said, "Yeah, you ought to think about it."

Drew thought. For about five seconds. He gave a big grin. "Who cares if I can shave or not? That won't embarrass me. Not like *boobies* embarrass Kim."

"Aargh!" She lunged for him, he dodged, and they were off again, out of the kitchen.

Michael called after them, "Guys, keep it down," but the sounds of battle had moved into the living room. He shook his head, but he was laughing when he kissed Colleen on the cheek. "Sorry. I gave it my best."

What a peculiar moment to realize afresh how much she loved him. It had happened while he was holding Drew in the only way a nine-year-old boy would accept and talking to Kim as though she were an adult. Patiently. Kindly. He was the father her kids needed so desperately, and her heart suddenly felt as though it were being squeezed in a giant fist.

There she stood, wooden spoon dripping spaghetti sauce unheeded onto the stove top, wearing an apron and a sweatshirt that said The One Who Dies with the Most Fabric...Wins!

And just like that, Colleen blurted, "I love you."

Michael's smile slowly died. He stared at her for so long she began to feel aghast at what she'd set in motion. Her heart pounded in her ears and she was on the verge of apologizing, of trying somehow to retreat, when he suddenly closed his eyes.

When he opened them again, they blazed with a fire so hot she was seared. He took a step toward her. "Say that again."

"Make him shut up, Mom!"

Her children exploded back into the kitchen, and behind them came Cam's thin cry. Michael backed away and gave his head a shake. By the time he looked at her again, the fire was banked. Colleen wanted to follow Cam's example and weep.

Michael said huskily, just for her ears, "You know how to pick your moment."

Colleen half laughed, half groaned. All those ideal times she could have chosen, and she had to declare her love right in the middle of Drew and Kim quarreling.

"Kim flushed my slime down the toilet! Just for that I'm going to—"

"Set the dinner table," Michael said. He grasped both kids by the upper arms and turned them toward the dining room. Over their heads, he gave Colleen one last look of near desperation before he marched them out. "Drew, do you believe every word your sister says? I seriously doubt she really flushed—" The swinging door cut off his voice.

Colleen sagged against the stove. Dear God. She'd done it. For better or worse. But which? He had to love her! How would she survive if he didn't? If what she had seen in his eyes had been pity and regret, not need that cut to the bone. Could she have deluded herself?

Her mind jumped like a grasshopper in dry grass. Cam. Was Michael taking care of him? Michael...

Something burned her hand and she yanked it back, straightening. The spaghetti sauce was bubbling furiously, spattering the stove and her.

"Damn," she muttered, and stuck her hand under cold water. It was shaking, she saw, and no wonder.

That evening was the single, longest of her life. Neither of the kids, still bickering, seemed to notice how quiet the two adults were. Michael answered Drew's questions, Colleen heard about the horseback-riding lesson to which Jennifer had chauffeured the two girls today. Every once in a while Michael's gaze met Colleen's, and though his expression didn't change, awareness flared in his eyes and her heart skipped a beat.

Ridiculous to be married and unable to find a moment to themselves, but it was as though even Cam had joined a conspiracy to keep Mom and Dad busy. When Drew and Kim settled down at the table with homework, the phone rang and the father of one of Michael's soccer players wanted to discuss—at length—the amount of playing time his boy was getting. And then, of course, Cam insisted on nursing, which Michael watched with a grimness that secretly pleased Colleen.

The kitchen had to be cleaned, Drew persuaded to take a bath, Cam's diaper changed. Colleen rocked him to sleep and laid him in his crib with the care she gave a soufflé. He stiffened, she held her breath—and then he relaxed and sucked noisily on his fist. Colleen tiptoed out.

Michael was waiting at the foot of the stairs. When he saw her, he straightened from where he leaned against the banister. His eyes didn't leave hers from the moment she started down.

All the way she looked at him: the shadow beneath his cheekbones, a mouth that could be astonishingly sexy, his straight, dark hair and dark brows that made his vivid blue eyes even more startling. He was large and solid and devastatingly handsome. And hers. For better or worse.

He didn't touch her when she reached the foot of the stairs, just stood there with his hands at his sides.

Colleen moistened dry lips. "Michael—"

"Did you mean it?"

Beyond pretense, she gave a small nod.

His voice was uneven. "Say it again."

"I love you," she whispered.

"God." He closed his eyes and blindly reached for her.

She stumbled into his arms and laid her head against his chest, where she could feel the slam of his heartbeat. He held her so tightly she knew he needed to be held just as much.

Against her hair Michael said roughly, "I never thought I'd hear you say that."

"I love you so much it scares me," she said, and waited for him to tell her the same.

Instead, she felt him take a long, shuddering breath, and then he held her away from him. A muscle jumped in his cheek, and his eyes searched hers. When he finally spoke, it was hoarsely. "Why?"

Her heart skipped a beat. "*Why?* Why what?"

His hands actually dropped from her arms; his face was set in lines of harsh restraint. "I know I'm not an easy man to love. Not even my own parents loved me." He said it almost indifferently, as a matter of fact. "I'm not taking the blame. They're the kind of people who should never have had kids. God knows why they did. I know it wasn't my fault, they were just as distant with Stephen, but somehow I never learned…" At last a spasm of pain twisted his face and he broke off. Colleen lifted one hand to his cheek, and he turned his mouth against her palm. His voice was muffled. "I didn't know how to make Sheila love me. I don't know how to make you."

Colleen's throat was thick with tears. "I already love you," she said in a voice that shook. "Michael, listen to me." She lifted her other hand and cradled his face, holding it so that he had to look at her. "Sheila did love you, as much as she could. And me…I spend every day wondering how I could have been so lucky. You're the father my kids deserved. You're patient and kind and gentle and sexy. Every time I look at you, my heart jumps and my stomach does a flip-flop and my knees get weak. I love you," she said again. "I'll spend the rest of my life convincing you, if…if you want me to."

He crushed her convulsively in his arms. "I need you," he whispered into her hair. "I love you. God, I love you."

And finally his mouth found hers in a kiss so achingly

tender, so wondering, her cheeks were wet with tears by the time he lifted his head.

Michael wiped her cheeks gently with his thumb. "I've loved you since long before Cam was born. I think maybe I knew it the first time you lifted your shirt and let me put my hand on you. I never expected..." His voice had become ragged. "Never dreamed..."

One confession deserved another. "Do you want to know something really awful?" Colleen asked. She didn't wait for an answer. "I think maybe I was always attracted to you. I never liked being around you. It made me uncomfortable. I didn't let myself know why."

Huskily Michael said, "The first time I ever saw you, I felt as if somebody had punched me. I told myself it was surprise, because I'd expected you to look more like Sheila. I think even then I knew better." He was silent for a moment. Somehow Colleen knew what he was going to say even before he said it. "How do you think she would feel about us?"

Colleen thought of Cam, with his plump cheeks and downy hair, and she thought of her sister, whose joy for life had never been selfish. She had wanted a baby, but never at anybody else's expense. Her hand had held Colleen's through every hurt in both their lives, never slackening until the day she died. Maybe she hadn't learned to open their loving circle to others, but she would rejoice because Colleen had.

With sudden, unshakable certainty, Colleen said softly, "She'd be rooting for us all the way."

"I think she would be, too."

This kiss was sweet and passionate and mysterious, everything life with Michael would be. When he swung her into his arms and started up the stairs, she whispered against his throat, "I do believe I'm in the mood to undress in front of you. Slowly."

His laugh was husky. "I do believe I'm in the mood to enjoy that." And for the second time he carried her across the threshold of their bedroom door, a husband impatient to celebrate his marriage in the best of all possible ways.

Afterward Colleen snuggled up to Michael, reveling in his warmth and the strong beat of his heart and the idle way his fingers played with the curls at the nape of her neck.

Sleepily, contentedly, she said, "Did I tell you that some boy wants Kim to be his girlfriend?"

Michael's hand stopped. Colleen lifted her head. "I'm sorry. You were trying to sleep. I'll shut up."

"No!" She felt the bob of his Adam's apple, and then he said more moderately, "No, I'd like to hear about it. I'd like to hear anything you want to tell me."

Still she hesitated, but he pulled her head back down on his shoulder. "The kid must be some quick worker."

Reassured, Colleen gave him a quick kiss. "No kidding. He sent her a note the third day of school. Well, actually his friend sent Stacey a note in school. You know how it works. Kim says she thinks he's cute, but he's only the third-cutest boy in her class, so she isn't sure."

How she had missed having someone to talk to! Really talk to. She wasn't sure which she valued most—the desperate hunger in his eyes that only she could appease or the intimacy of this kind of talking.

But it hardly mattered, did it? In Michael, her husband, lover and friend, she had both.

Not two days later Colleen started piecing a traditional Wedding Ring quilt. She told Michael that it was the circles overlapping that held meaning for her.

"Loving circles," she said.

Looking at the tiny pieces she would stitch so patiently together to make a whole, symbolizing what her marriage meant to her, Michael believed at last that this woman would hold him and love him and, at night under this quilt, share her hopes and deepest heartaches with him. For a lifetime.

* * * * *

THE HARLEQUIN BESTSELLING AUTHOR COLLECTION

CLASSIC ROMANCES IN COLLECTIBLE VOLUMES FROM OUR BESTSELLING AUTHORS

Available September 2010

SHERRYL WOODS

DREAM MENDER

and

LINDA LAEL MILLER

PART OF THE BARGAIN

Available wherever books are sold.

www.eHarlequin.com

BSC0910

THE HARLEQUIN BESTSELLING AUTHOR COLLECTION

CLASSIC ROMANCES IN COLLECTIBLE VOLUMES FROM OUR BESTSELLING AUTHORS

On sale September 2010.

SAVE $1.⁰⁰

on the purchase of 1 or more books from the HARLEQUIN® BESTSELLING AUTHOR COLLECTION

Coupon expires March 31, 2011.
Redeemable at participating retail outlets. Limit one coupon per customer.
Valid in the U.S.A. and Canada only.

52609204

5 65373 00076 2   (0100)0 11670

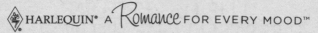

PASSION

For a spicier, decidedly hotter read—
these are your destinations for romance!

Silhouette Desire®
Passionate and provocative stories
featuring rich, powerful heroes and
scandalous family sagas.

Harlequin® Blaze™
Fun, flirtatious and steamy books
that tell it like it is, inside and outside
the bedroom.

Kimani™ Romance
Sexy and entertaining love stories
with true-to-life African-American
characters who heat up the pages
with romance and passion.

HARLEQUIN® A *Romance* FOR EVERY MOOD™

SUSPENSE & PARANORMAL

Heartstopping stories of intrigue and mystery—
where true love always triumphs.

Harlequin Intrigue®
Breathtaking romantic suspense. Crime
stories that will keep you on the edge of
your seat.

Silhouette® Romantic Suspense
Heart-racing sensuality and the promise
of a sweeping romance set against the
backdrop of suspense.

Harlequin® Nocturne™
Dark and sensual paranormal
romance reads that stretch the
boundaries of conflict and desire,
life and death.

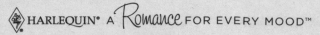